CHUNG KUO

BOOK THREE

THE WHITE MOUNTAIN

"The way never acts yet nothing is left undone.
Should lords and princes be able to hold fast to it,
The myriad creatures will be transformed of their
   own accord.
After they are transformed, should desire raise its
   head,
I shall press it down with the weight of the nameless
   uncarved block.
The nameless uncarved block
Is but freedom from desire,
And if I cease to desire and remain still,
The empire will be at peace of its own accord."

– Lao Tzu, *Tao Te Ching*, Book One, xxxvii
(Sixth Century BC)

DAVID WINGROVE

CHUNG KUO

BOOK THREE

— 中国 —

THE WHITE MOUNTAIN

NEW ENGLISH LIBRARY
Hodder and Stoughton

Copyright © David Wingrove 1991

First published in Great Britain in 1991 by New English Library hardbacks

New English Library paperback Edition 1992

British Library C.I.P.

Wingrove, David
 The white mountain. –
 (Chung Kuo)
 I. Title II. Series
 823 [F]

 ISBN 0-450-56847-4

Printed and bound in Great Britain for Hodder and Stoughton Paperbacks, a division of Hodder and Stoughton Ltd, Mill Road, Dunton Green, Sevenoaks, Kent TN13 2YA. (Editorial Office: 47 Bedford Square, London WC1B 3DP) by Clays Ltd, St Ives plc. Photoset by Rowland Phototypesetting Ltd, Bury St Edmunds, Suffolk.

To Lily Jackson
from your grandson David on the occasion of
your ninety-fifth birthday
with a lifetime's love

INTRODUCTION

Chung Kuo. The words mean "Middle Kingdom" and since 221 BC, when the First Emperor, Ch'in Shih Huang Ti, unified the seven Warring States, it is what the "black-haired people", the Han, or Chinese, have called their great country. The Middle Kingdom – for them it was the whole world; a world bounded by great mountain chains to the north and west, by the sea to east and south. Beyond was only desert and barbarism. So it was for two thousand years.

By the turn of the twenty-second century, however, Chung Kuo had come to mean much more. For more than a century, the Empire of the Han had encompassed the world, the Earth's bloated population of forty billion contained in vast, hive-like cities that spanned whole continents. The Council of Seven – Han lords, *T'ang*, each more powerful than the greatest of the ancient emperors – ruled Chung Kuo with an iron authority, their boast that they had ended Change and stopped the Great Wheel turning. But Change was coming.

It had begun twelve years before, when a new generation of powerful young merchants – Dispersionists, formed mainly of *Hung Mao*, or Westerners – had challenged the authority of the Seven, demanding an end to the Edict of Technological Control, the cornerstone of Han stability, and a return to the Western ideal of unfettered progress. In the spate of assassination and counter-assassination that followed, something had to give, and the destruction of the Dispersionist starship, *The New Hope*, signalled the beginning of the "War-that-wasn't-a-War", an incestuous power struggle fought within the City's levels. The Seven won that War, but at a price they could ill afford. Suddenly they were weak – weaker than they had been in their entire history. The new T'ang were young and inexperienced. Worse than that, they were divided against themselves.

But the War was only the first small sign of greater disturbances to come, for down in the lowest levels of the City, in the lawless regions "below the Net" and in the overcrowded decks just above, new currents of unrest have awoken. In the years since the War, *Ko Ming* – revolutionary – groups have proliferated, and none more powerful or deadly than the *Ping Tiao*, or Levellers. The War was no longer a struggle for power, but for survival . . .

CONTENTS

MAJOR CHARACTERS

Ascher, Emily – Trained as an economist, she joined the *Ping Tiao* revolutionary party at the turn of the century, becoming one of its policy-formulating Council of Five. A passionate fighter for social justice, she was also once the lover of the *Ping Tiao*'s leader, Bent Gesell.

DeVore, Howard – A one-time Major in the T'ang's Security forces, he has become the leading figure in the struggle against the Seven. A highly intelligent and coldly logical man, he is the puppet master behind the scenes as the great "War of the Two Directions" takes a new turn.

Ebert, Hans – Son of Klaus Ebert and heir to the vast GenSyn Corporation, he has been promoted to Major in the T'ang's Security forces, and is admired and trusted by his superiors. Ebert is a complex young man; a brave and intelligent officer, he also has a selfish, dissolute and cruel streak. Allying himself to DeVore's cause, he has ambitions to become not merely a prince among men but a ruler.

Fei Yen – "Flying Swallow", daughter of Yin Tsu, one of the heads of the "Twenty-Nine", the minor aristocratic families of Chung Kuo. Once married to Han Ch'in, the murdered son of Li Shai Tung, she has subsequently married his brother, Li Yuan, nine years her junior. This classically beautiful woman is fragile in appearance but strong-willed and fiery, as proved in her secret affair with Tsu Ma, T'ang of West Asia.

Haavikko, Axel – Smeared by the false accusations of his fellow officers, Lieutenant Haavikko has spent the best part of ten years in debauchery and self-negation. A good, honest man at heart, he has joined with his friend Kao Chen in a determination to expose the man who besmirched his reputation years before – Hans Ebert.

Kao Chen – Once a *kwai*, a hired knife from the Net, the lowest level of the great City, Chen has raised himself from those humble beginnings and is now a Captain in the T'ang's Security forces. As friend and helper to Karr and a close associate of Haavikko, Chen is one of the foot-soldiers in the War against DeVore.

Karr, Gregor – Major in the T'ang's Security forces, Karr was recruited by Marshal Tolonen from the Net. In his youth he was a "blood" – a to-the-death combat fighter. A huge giant of a man, he is the "hawk" Li Shai Tung plans to fly against his adversary, DeVore.

Lehmann, Stefan – Albino son of the former Dispersionist leader, Pietr Lehmann, he has become a lieutenant to DeVore. A cold, unnaturally dispassionate man, he seems to be the very archetype of nihilism, his only aim to bring down the Seven and their great City.

Li Shai Tung – T'ang of Europe and one of the Seven, the ruling Council of Chung Kuo, Li Shai Tung is now in his seventies. For years he has been the fulcrum of the Council and unofficial spokesman for the Seven, but the murder of his heir, Han Ch'in, weakened him, undermining his once-strong determination to prevent Change at all costs.

Li Yuan – Second son of Li Shai Tung, he has become heir to City Europe after the assassination of his elder brother. Thought old before his time, his cold, thoughtful manner conceals a passionate nature, as expressed in his marriage to the fiery Fei Yen, his dead brother's wife.

Mach, Jan – A maintenance official in the Ministry of Waste Recycling and a part-time member of Li Shai Tung's Reserve Security force, Mach has a second identity, as one of the Council of Five, the policy-formulators of the *Ping Tiao* revolutionary movement. But his dissatisfaction with their activities has led him to form his own faction, the *Yu*, who are destined to become a new and yet darker force within the depths of City Europe.

Tolonen, Jelka – Daughter of Marshal Tolonen, Jelka has been brought up in a very masculine environment, lacking a mother's influence. However, her genuine interest in martial arts and in weaponry and strategy masks a very different, more feminine side to her nature; a side brought out after the unsuccessful attack on her by *Ping Tiao* terrorists.

Tolonen, Knut – Marshal of the Council of Generals and one-time General to Li Shai Tung, Tolonen is a big, granite-jawed man and the staunchest supporter of the values and ideals of the Seven. Possessed of a fiery, fearless nature, he will stop at nothing to protect his masters, yet after long years of War even his belief in the necessity of stasis has been shaken.

Tsu Ma – T'ang of West Asia and one of the Seven, the ruling Council of Chung Kuo, Tsu Ma has thrown off a dissolute past to become one of Li Shai Tung's strongest supporters in Council. A strong, handsome man in his mid-thirties, he has recently extricated himself from a secret affair with Fei Yen which – had it become public – might easily have destroyed the Seven.

Wang Sau-leyan – Young T'ang of Africa. Since his father's murder he has thrown off his former ways and become a sharp and cunning adversary to Li Shai Tung and the old guard among the Seven. An abrasive, calculating figure with sybaritic tastes, he is the harbinger of Change within the Council of the Seven.

Ward, Kim – Born in the Clay, that dark wasteland beneath the great City's foundations, Kim has a quick and unusual bent of mind that has marked him out as potentially the greatest scientist in Chung Kuo. His vision of a giant star-spanning web, formulated in the darkness, has driven him up into the light of the Above. Now, after a long period of personality reconstruction, he has been placed on the staff of Li Yuan's Wiring Project.

Ywe Hao – Born into the lowest levels of City Europe, Ywe Hao – "Fine Moon" – joined the *Yu*, a terrorist organisation, after the murder of her elder brother. A strong, idealistic woman, she represents the new tide of indignant rebellion that is stirring in the depths of the great City.

* * *

THE SEVEN AND THE FAMILIES

* * *

An Liang-chou – Minor-Family Prince.

An Sheng – Head of the An family (one of the "Twenty-Nine" Minor-Families).

Chi Hsing – T'ang of the Australias.

Chun Wu-chi – Head of the Chun family (one of the "Twenty-Nine" Minor Families).

Fan Ming-yu – Minor-Family courtesan.

Fu Ti Chang – Minor-Family Princess.

Hou Tung-po – T'ang of South America.

Hsiang K'ai Fan – Minor-Family Prince; heir to the Hsiang Family (one of the "Twenty-Nine" Minor Families).

Hsiang Shao-erh – Head of the Hsiang Family (one of the

"Twenty-Nine" Minor Families) and father of Hsiang K'ai Fan, Hsiang Te-shang and Hsiang Wang.

Hsiang Te-shang – Minor-Family Prince and youngest son of Hsiang Shao-erh.

Hsiang Wang – Minor-Family Prince and second son of Hsiang Shao-erh.

Lai Shi – Minor-Family Princess.

Li Feng Chuang – half-brother of and adviser to Li Shai Tung.

Li Shai Tung – T'ang of Europe.

Li Yuan – second son of Li Shai Tung and heir to City Europe.

Mien Shan – Minor-Family Princess.

Pei Ro-hen – Head of the Pei Family (one of the "Twenty-Nine" Minor Families).

Tsu Ma – T'ang of West Asia.

Tsu Tao Chu – nephew to Tsu Ma.

Wang Sau-leyan – T'ang of Africa.

Wei Feng – T'ang of East Asia.

Wu Shih – T'ang of North America.

Yin Chan – Minor-Family Prince; son of Yin Tsu.

Yin Fei Yen – "Flying Swallow"; Minor-Family Princess and wife of Li Yuan.

Yin Han Ch'in – son of Yin Fei Yen.

Yin Sung – Minor-Family Prince; son of Yin Tsu.

Yin Tsu – Head of the Yin Family (one of the "Twenty-Nine" Minor Families) and father of Fei Yen.

★ ★ ★

FRIENDS AND RETAINERS OF THE SEVEN

★ ★ ★

Auden, William – Captain in Security.

Chan Teng – Master of the Inner Chambers at Tongjiang.

Chang Li – Chief Surgeon of City Europe.

Chang Shih-sen – personal secretary to Li Yuan.

Ch'in Tao Fan – Chancellor of East Asia.

Chung Hu-yan – Chancellor of Europe.

Ebert, Berta – wife of Klaus Ebert.

Ebert, Hans – Major in Security and heir to GenSyn.

Ebert, Klaus Stefan – Head of GenSyn (Genetic Synthetics) and adviser to Li Shai Tung.

Fen Cho-hsien – Chancellor of North America.

Haavikko, Axel – Lieutenant in Security.

Haavikko, Vesa – sister of Axel Haavikko.

Heng Yu – Minister of Transportation for City Europe.

Hua – personal surgeon to Li Shai Tung.

Hung Feng-chan – Chief Groom at Tongjiang.

Hung Mien-lo – Chancellor of Africa.

Kao Chen – Captain in Security.

Karr, Gregor – Major in Security.

Nan Ho – Master of the Inner Chambers to Li Yuan.

Nocenzi, Vittorio – General of Security, City Europe.

Peng Lu-hsing – Minister of the *T'ing Wei*, the Superintendancy of Trials for City Europe.

Scott, Anders – Captain in Security and friend of Hans Ebert.

Sheng Pao – Minister for Finance of East Asia.

Shepherd, Ben – son of Hal Shepherd.

Shepherd, Beth – wife of Hal Shepherd.

Shepherd, Hal – adviser to Li Shai Tung and Head of the Shepherd family.

Shou Chen-hai – *Hsien L'ing* or Chief Magistrate of Hannover *Hsien*.

Sun Li Hua – Master of the Royal Household at Alexandria.

Tolonen, Helga – wife of Jon Tolonen.

Tolonen, Jelka – daughter of Marshal Tolonen.

Tolonen, Jon – brother of Knut Tolonen.

Tolonen, Knut – Marshal of the Council of Generals and father of Jelka Tolonen.

Viljanen, Per – Lieutenant in Security; Assistant to Marshal Tolonen.

Wang Ta Chuan – Master of the Inner Palace to Li Shai Tung.

Wu Ye-lun – Security Surgeon at Bremen *Hsien*.

Yen Shih-fa – groom at Tongjiang.

Yen T'ung – Third Secretary to the Minister of the *T'ing Wei*.

Yu – surgeon to Li Yuan.

★ ★ ★
THE TRIADS
★ ★ ★

Feng Shang-pao – "General Feng"; Big Boss of the 14K.

Ho Chin – "Three-Finger Ho"; Big Boss of the Yellow Banners.

Hui Tsin – Red Pole (the 426, or Executioner) to the United Bamboo.

Li Ch'in – "Li the Lidless"; Big Boss of the Wo Shih Wo.

Lu Ming-shao – "Whiskers Lu"; Big Boss of the Kuei Chuan (Black Dog).

Mu Li – "Iron Mu"; Big Boss of the Big Circle.

Wong Yi-sun – "Fat Wong"; Big Boss of the United Bamboo.

Yao Tzu – "Glory to One's Ancestors"; a Red Pole (the 426, or Executioner) to the Big Circle.

Yun Yueh-hui – "Dead Man Yun"; Big Boss of the Red Gang.

★ ★ ★

PING TIAO

★ ★ ★

Ascher, Emily – economist and member of the Council of Five.

Gesell, Bent – unofficial leader of the *Ping Tiao* and member of the "Council of Five".

Mach, Jan – maintenance official for the Ministry of Waste Recycling and member of the Council of Five; founder of the split-off *Yu* faction.

Mao Liang – Minor-Family Princess and member of the Council of Five.

Quinn, Richard – member of the Council of Five.

★ ★ ★

YU

★ ★ ★

Chi Li – alias of Ywe Hao.

Edel, Klaus – brother of Vasska.

Erika – member of Ywe Hao's terrorist cell.

Vasska – member of Ywe Hao's terrorist cell.

Veda – member of the *Yu* Council of Five.

Ywe Hao – "Fine Moon"; female terrorist from the Mid-Levels.

OTHER CHARACTERS

★ ★ ★

Architect – theoretical psychologist in Department of Character Reconstruction.

Barycz, Jiri – Communications Officer on the Wiring Project.

Beattie, Douglas – alias of DeVore.

Cherkassky, Stefan – retired Security special-services officer and friend of DeVore.

Curval, Andrew – experimental geneticist, working for ImmVac.

Debrenceni, Laslo – Acting Administrator at Kibwezi Station.

DeVore, Howard – former Major in Li Shai Tung's Security forces.

Drake, Michael – supervisor at Kibwezi Station.

Ebert, Lutz – half-brother of Klaus Ebert.

Ellis, Michael – Assistant Director on the Wiring Project.

Enge, Marie – woman server at the Dragon Cloud teahouse.

Fan Tseng-li – private surgeon of Bremen *Hsien*.

Fang Shuo – underling to Shou Chen-hai.

Ganz, Joseph – alias of DeVore.

Golden Heart – young prostitute bought by Hans Ebert for his household.

Hammond, Joel – official on the Wiring Project.

Kao Ch'iang Hsin – daughter of Kao Chen and Wang Ti.

Kao Jyan – eldest son of Kao Chen and Wang Ti.

Kao Pang-che – private secretary to Minister Heng.

Kao Wu – second son of Kao Chen and Wang Ti.

Kung Lao – young boy; friend of Ywe Hao.

Kung Yi-lun – young boy; friend of Ywe Hao.

Kustow, Bryn – American; friend of Michael Lever.

Lehmann, Stefan – albino son of former Dispersionist leader Pietr Lehmann and lieutenant to DeVore.

Lever, Charles – "Old Man Lever", Head of the ImmVac pharmaceuticals company of North America; father of Michael Lever.

Lever, Michael – American; son of Charles Lever.

Leyden, Wolfgang – Security guard at Hannover *Hsien*.

Lo Wen – personal servant to Hans Ebert.

Loehr – alias of DeVore.

Mu Chua – Madam of the House of the Ninth Ecstasy, a singsong house or brothel.

Novacek, Lubos – merchant; confidant of Minister Heng.

Reid, Thomas – sergeant in DeVore's forces.

Reynolds – alias of DeVore.

Schwarz – lieutenant to DeVore.

Shou He – second wife to Shou Chen-hai.

Shou Wen-lo – first wife to Shou Chen-hai.

Spatz, Gustav – Director of the Wiring Project.

Stevens, Carl – American; friend of Michael Lever.

Su Chen – wife of Ywe Chang.

Sweet Flute – *mui tsai* (slave girl) to Hans Ebert.

T'ai Cho – friend of Kim Ward.

Tarrant – Company head.

Tong Chou – alias of Kao Chen.

Ts'ui Wei – citizen of Bremen *Hsien*.

Tuan Ti Fo – old Han mystic and master of *wei chi*.

Tuan Wen-ch'ang – trader from the Martian Colonies.

Turner – alias of DeVore.

Wang Ti – wife of Kao Chen.

Ward, Kim – "Clayborn" orphan and scientist.

Wiegand, Max – lieutenant to DeVore.

Wong Pao-yi – steward to Shou Chen-hai.

Ywe Chang – uncle to Ywe Hao.

Ywe Sha – mother of Ywe Hao.

★ ★ ★

THE DEAD

★ ★ ★

Berdichev, Soren – Head of SimFic and later leader of the Dispersionist faction.

Chung Hsin – "Loyalty"; bondservant to Li Shai Tung.

Feng Chung – Big Boss of the Kuei Chan (Black Dog) Triad.

Fest, Edgar – Captain in Security.

Hou Ti – T'ang of South America; father of Hou Tung-po.

Hwa – master "blood", or hand-to-hand fighter, below the Net.

Kao Jyan – assassin; friend of Kao Chen.

Lehmann, Pietr – Under-Secretary of the House of Representatives and first leader of the Dispersionist faction; father of Stefan Lehmann.

Li Ch'ing – T'ang of Europe; father of Li Shai Tung.

Li Han Ch'in – first son of Li Shai Tung and heir to City Europe; brother of Li Yuan.

Li Hang Ch'i – T'ang of Europe; great-grandfather of Li Shai Tung.

Li Kou-lung – T'ang of Europe; grandfather of Li Shai Tung.

Lin Yua – first wife of Li Shai Tung.

Shang – "Old Shang"; Master to Kao Chen when he was a child.

Tsao Ch'un – tyrannical founder of Chung Kuo.

Wang Ta-hung – third son of Wang Hsien; elder brother of Wang Sau-leyan.

Wen Ti – "First Ancestor" of City Earth/Chung Kuo, otherwise known as Liu Heng; ruled China 180–157 BC.

Wyatt, Edmund – Company head.

Ywe Kai-chang – father to Ywe Hao.

FALLEN PETALS

---·-·---

"The guests are gone from the pavilion high,
In the small garden flowers are whirling around.
Along the winding path the petals lie;
To greet the setting sun, they drift up from the ground.

Heartbroken, I cannot bear to sweep them away;
From my eager eyes, spring soon disappears.
I pine with passing, heart's desire lost for aye;
Nothing is left but a robe stained with tears."

– Li Shangyin, *Falling Flowers* (Ninth Century AD)

FALLEN PETALS

Li Yuan reined in his horse and looked up. On the far side of the valley, beyond the tall, narrow spire of Three Swallows Mount, a transporter was banking, heading for the palace, two *li* distant. As it turned he saw the crest of the *Ywe Lung* emblazoned on its fuselage and frowned, wondering who it was. As far as he knew his father was expecting no one.

He turned in his saddle, looking about him. The grassy slope led down to a dirt track that followed the stream for a short way then crossed a narrow wooden bridge and snaked south towards Tongjiang. He could follow that path back to the palace or he could finish the ride he had planned, up to the old monastery then south to the beacon. For a moment longer he hesitated, caught in two minds. It was a beautiful morning, the sky a perfect, cloudless blue; the kind of morning when one felt like riding on and on forever, but he had been out three hours already, so maybe it was best if he got back. Besides, maybe his father needed him. Things had been quiet recently. Too quiet. Maybe something had come up.

He tugged at the reins gently, turning the Arab's head, then spurred her on with his heels, leading her carefully down the slope and along the path, breaking into a canter as he crossed the bridge. He was crossing the long meadow, the palace just ahead of him, when a second transporter passed overhead, the insignia of the Marshal clearly displayed on the undersides of its stubby wings. Yuan slowed, watching as it turned and landed on the far

3

side of the palace, a cold certainty forming in his guts.

It had begun again.

At the stables he all but jumped from the saddle, leaving the groom to skitter about the horse, trying to catch hold of the reins, while he ran on, along the red-tiled path and into the eastern palace.

He stopped, breathless, at the door to his father's suite of rooms, taking the time to calm himself, to run his fingers quickly through his unruly hair, but even as he made to knock, Chung Hu-yan, his father's Chancellor, drew the door of the ante-room open and stepped out, as if expecting him.

"Forgive me, Prince Yuan," he began, without preamble, "but your father has asked me if you would excuse him for an hour or so. A small matter has arisen, inconsequential in itself, yet urgent."

He hesitated, wondering how far he could push Hu-yan on this, but again Hu-yan pre-empted him.

"It is nothing you can help him with, Prince Yuan. I assure you of that. It is a . . . *personal* matter, let us say. No one has died, nor is the peace of Chung Kuo threatened, yet the matter is of some delicacy. In view of special circumstances your father thought it best that he consult his cousin, Tsu Ma and the Marshal. You understand, I hope?"

Yuan stood there a moment longer, trying to read something in Chung Hu-yan's deeply-creased face, but the old man's expression was like a wall, shutting him out. He laughed, then nodded.

"I am relieved, Hu-yan. I had thought . . ."

But he had no need to say. It had been on all their minds these past few months. Where would their enemies strike next? Who would they kill? In many respects this peace was worse than the War that had preceded it; a tenuous, uncertain peace that stretched the nerves almost to breaking point.

He smiled tightly then turned away, hearing the door pulled closed behind him. But even as he walked back he was beginning to wonder what it was that might have

rought Tsu Ma so urgently to his father's summons. *A
ersonal matter* . . . He turned, looking back thoughtfully,
nen shrugged and turned back, making his way past bow-
ng servants and kneeling maids, hurrying now.

Maybe Fei Yen knew something. She was always hear-
ng snippets of rumour that his own ears hadn't caught, so
naybe she knew what this was. And even if she didn't,
he had ways of finding such things out. Women's ways.

He laughed and broke into a run. And then maybe he
vould take her out in the palanquin. One last time before
he was too far advanced in her pregnancy. Up to the
nonastery, perhaps. Or to the beacon.

Yes, they could make a picnic of it. And maybe, after-
vards, he would make love to her, gently, carefully, there
n the grassy hillside, beneath the big open sky of northern
China. One last, memorable time before the child came.

He stopped before her door, hammering at it and calling
er name, laughing, all of his earlier fears forgotten, his
ead filled with the thought of the afternoon ahead.

"What is it, Yuan?" she asked, opening the door to him
lmost timidly, her smile uncertain. "Are you drunk?"

In answer he drew her to him, more roughly than he
ad meant, and lifted her up, crushing her lips with his
wn. "Not drunk, my love. No. But happy . . ."

★ ★ ★

i Shai Tung had taken his guests through to the Summer
House. Servants had brought *ch'a* and sweetmeats and then
leparted, leaving the three men alone. Tolonen stood by
he window, looking down the steep slope towards the
rnamental lake, while Tsu Ma and Li Shai Tung sat, fac-
ng each other, on the far side of the room. So far they had
aid nothing of importance, but now Li Shai Tung looked
p at Tsu Ma and cleared his throat.

"Do you remember the first time you came here? That
lay you went riding with Yuan and the Lady Fei?"

Tsu Ma met his gaze unflinchingly. "That was a good
lay. And the evening that followed, out on the lake."

5

Li Shai Tung looked down. "Ah yes, Yuan told me that . . ."

He smiled; sourly, Tsu Ma thought, fearing the wor...

The old T'ang raised his head again, the smile fadi... altogether. "And you recall what we spoke of that day?

Tsu Ma nodded, his mouth dry, wishing the old m... would be more direct. If he knew, why didn't he say som... thing? Why this torment of indirectness? "We spoke ... Yuan's Project, if I remember accurately," he said, looki... across at Tolonen momentarily, recalling that they h... appointed the old man to oversee the whole business. B... what had this to do with him and Fei Yen? For surely th... was why he had been summoned here this morning at su... short notice. He looked down, filled with shame for wh... he had done. "I am sorry, Shai Tung, I . . ."

But Li Shai Tung seemed not to have heard. He carri... on, as if Tsu Ma had said nothing.

"We spoke afterwards, too, didn't we? A week or ... later, if I recall. At which time I made you a party to m... thoughts."

Tsu Ma looked up, frowning. He had heard of indire... tion, but this . . . Then he understood. This had nothi... to do with Fei Yen and him. Nothing at all. He laughe... relief washing through him.

Li Shai Tung stared at him, astonished. "I am afraid... find it no laughing matter, cousin." He half-turned, loo... ing at the Marshal. "Show him the file, Knut."

Tsu Ma felt himself go cold again. He took the file a... opened it, the faintest tremor in his hands. A moment lat... he looked up, his face a picture of incomprehension.

"What in Hell's name is all this?"

The old T'ang held his head stiffly, his anger bare... controlled. "Inventions. Machines. Devices that would ... the ruin of Chung Kuo. Every last one of them breaki... the Edict in a dozen, maybe twenty different ways."

Tsu Ma glanced through the file, amazed by what ... saw, then shook his head. "But where did they come fror... Who invented them? And why?"

Tolonen spoke up for the first time. "They're SimFic mainly. From the traitor Berdichev's papers. We saw them long ago – three, maybe even four years ago – but in different form from this. Li Shai Tung ordered them destroyed. But here they are again, the same things but better than before."

"Better?"

Li Shai Tung nodded. "You recall that we talked of a young boy. A clever one, by the name of Kim Ward. Well, this is his work. Somehow he got hold of these papers and worked on them. The improvements are his. In one sense it's quite amazing, in another quite horrifying. But the fault does not lie with the boy."

Tsu Ma shook his head, still not understanding how all of this connected, nor why Li Shai Tung should consult him on the matter. "But if not the boy, then who?"

"That's exactly what I asked the Marshal to find out. He came upon these files by accident, you understand. Six months had passed and I wanted to know what was happening with Yuan's Project. So, secretly, without the Project Director's knowledge, the Marshal trawled the Project's files."

Tsu Ma leaned back in his chair. "I see. And you didn't want Yuan to know that you were checking up on him?"

Li Shai Tung nodded. "It seemed best. It was not that I felt he would lie to me, just that he might act as a . . . as a filter, let's say. But this. This shocked me."

"Then Li Yuan is responsible for this file? It was he who gave the originals to the boy to work on?"

"Yes . . ." Bitterness and anger were etched starkly in the old man's face.

"I see . . ."

He understood. Li Shai Tung had asked for him because he alone could be trusted, for he alone among the Seven knew of the existence of the Project. Even Wu Shih was under the impression that Li Shai Tung was only considering matters. Yes, and he understood the necessity for that, for were it to become common knowledge it could only

7

do them harm. Wang Sau-leyan, certainly, could be counted on to use it to foment trouble in Council and try to break the power of the Li family.

But that was not really the issue at hand. No. The real problem was that Li Shai Tung felt himself affronted. His son had not acted as a son should act. He had lied and cheated, no matter the good intent that lay behind the act. Indeed, to the old man that was probably the worst of it. Not that these things existed, for they could be destroyed, as easily as if they had never been, but that Li Yuan had sought to conceal them from him. It was this part of it on which he sought Tsu Ma's advice. For who was closer to his son than Tsu Ma? As close, almost, as a brother. . .

Li Shai Tung leaned closer. "But what should I do, Tsu Ma? Should I confront him with these . . . *things*?"

"No . . ." Tsu Ma took a breath. "I would say nothing."

"Nothing?"

He nodded, holding the old man's eyes. "What good would it do? Yuan acted from your best interests. Or so he believes. So I'm sure he believes. There was no desire to harm you, only an . . . an eagerness, let us call it, an impatience in him, that can be set down to his youthfulness. Look upon these as folly. Arrange an accident and have all record of these things destroyed. The Marshal could arrange something for you, I'm certain. But say nothing. Do not damage what is between you and your son, Shai Tung."

The old man shook his head, momentarily in pain. "But he has lied to me. Deceived me."

"No . . . Your words are too strong."

"It is unfilial . . ."

Tsu Ma swallowed, thinking of his own far greater deceit, then shook his head again. "He loves you, Shai Tung. He works hard for you. Unstintingly hard. There is nothing he would not do for you. In that he is anything but unfilial. So let things be. After all, no real harm is done."

His words came strong and heartfelt, as if it were himself he was pleading for, and when Li Shai Tung looked up at him again there were tears in the old man's eyes.

"Maybe you're right. Maybe I am being too harsh." He sighed. "You are a good friend to him, Tsu Ma. I hope, for his sake, you are ever so." He turned, looking at the Marshal. "And you, Knut? What do you say?"

Tolonen hesitated, then lowered his head. "Tsu Ma is right. I had come here ready to argue otherwise, but having heard him I am inclined to agree. Say nothing. The rest I will arrange."

"And the boy?"

Tolonen looked briefly to Tsu Ma, then met his master's eyes again. "I would leave the boy for now, *Chieh Hsia*. Li Yuan will discover for himself how dangerous the boy is. And who knows, that may prove the most important thing to come from all of this, neh? To learn that knowledge is a two-edged sword?"

Li Shai Tung laughed; but it was an unhealthy, humourless sound. "Then it will be as you say, good friends. It will be as you say."

* * *

Fei Yen had been quiet for some while, staring out across the circular pool towards the distant mountains. Now she turned, looking back at him.

"Why did you bring me here?"

Li Yuan met her eyes, smiling vaguely, unconscious, it seemed, of the slight edge to her voice.

"Because it's beautiful. And . . ." He hesitated, a strange, fleeting expression crossing his features, then he looked down. "I haven't said before, but Han and I used to come here as boys. We would spend whole afternoons here, playing among the ruins. Long ago, it seems now. Long, long ago." He looked up at her again, searching her eyes, as if for understanding. "When I rode out this morning, I knew I had to come here. It was as if something called me."

9

She turned, shivering, wondering still if he was playing with her. If, despite everything, he *knew*. Behind him the ancient Buddhist stupa stood out against the blue of the sky, its squat base and ungainly spire something alien in that rugged landscape. To its left rested the yellow silk palanquin he had insisted she be carried in, its long poles hidden in the waist-length grass, the six runners squatting nearby, talking quietly among themselves, their eyes averted. Further up the hillside she could see the entrance to the ruined monastery where she had come so often with Tsu Ma.

It had all come flooding back to her; all the old feelings reawakened, as sharp as ever. *Why now?* she had asked herself, horrified. *Why, when I have finally found peace, does it return to torment me?* She had listened to Yuan abstractedly, knowing Tsu Ma was once more in the palace, and had found herself wanting to run to him and throw herself upon his mercy. But it could not be. She was this man's wife. This *boy's* wife. So she had chosen. And now it could not be undone. Unless that was why the old man had summoned Tsu Ma.

For one brief, dreadful moment she imagined it undone. Imagined herself cast off, free to marry Tsu Ma, and saw the tiny movement of denial he would make. As he had done that time, here, beside the pool. She caught her breath, the pain of that moment returned to her.

I should have been your wife, Tsu Ma. Your strength. Your second self.

Aiya, but it was not to be. It was not her fault that she had fallen for Tsu Ma. No. That had been her fate. But this too was her fate. To be denied him. To be kept from him forever. To be married to this child. She looked down, swallowing back the bitterness.

"What is it, my love?"

She looked at him, for the moment seeing nothing but his youth, his naïvety; those and that awful old-man certainty of his. Then she relented. It was not his fault. He had not chosen to fall in love with her. No, he had been nothing but kindness to her. Even so, her heart bled that it was he and not Tsu Ma who had brought her here today.

"It's nothing," she answered him. "Only the sickness."

He stared at her, concerned, real sympathy in his expression as he struggled to understand her. But he would never understand her.

"Should we go back?" he asked softly, but she shook her head.

"No. It's all right. It'll pass in a while."

She looked away again, staring out towards the south and the distant beacon, imagining him there, waiting for her, even now. But there were only ghosts now. Distant memories. Those and the pain.

She sighed. Was it always so? Did fate never grant a full measure? Was it the lot of everyone to have this lesser satisfaction – this pale shadow of passion?

And was she to cast that to the winds? To choose nothing rather than this sometimes-bitter compromise? She shook her head, anguished. Oh, she had often thought of telling him; had had the urge to let the words float free from her, like acids, eating into the soft dream of love he had built about him. And what had kept her from that? Was it pity for him? A desire not to be cruel? Or was it simple self-interest on her part?

She turned, looking at him again. Did she love him? *Did* she?

No. But neither did she hate him. It was as she'd said so often to herself. He was a good man. A good husband. But beyond that. . .

She closed her eyes, imagining herself in Tsu Ma's arms again, the sheer physical strength of him thrilling beyond words, the strange, mysterious power of him enfolding her until her mind went dark and her nerve ends sang with the sweetness of his touch.

And could Li Yuan do that for her? She shuddered. No. Never in ten thousand years.

* * *

11

"If you would wait here a brief moment, *Shih* Nan, I will let my master know you are here."

Nan Ho, Li Yuan's Master of the Inner Chambers, returned the First Steward's bow, then, when the man had left, turned, looking about him. It was not often that he found himself in one of the mansions of the Minor Families and he was not going to miss this opportunity of seeing how they lived. He had seen the balcony on his way in; now he crossed the room quickly and stood there just inside the window, looking out across the grounds. Down below the *chao tai hui* – the entertainment – was in full swing, more than a thousand guests filling the space between the old stone walls.

He took a step further, out on to the balcony itself, fascinated by the range of outlandish fashions on display, amused by the exaggerated gestures of some of the more garishly-dressed males, then froze, hearing voices in the gallery behind him. He drew in closer to the upright, drawing the long silk curtain across a fraction to conceal himself. It would not do to be seen to be so curious, even if he were here on the Prince's business.

At first he was unaware of the import of what was being said, then a single phrase made him jerk his head about, suddenly attending.

He listened, horrified, the laughter that followed the words chilling him. And as their footsteps went away down the stairs, he came out and, tiptoeing quietly across the tiled floor, leaned over the stairway to catch a sight of the men who had been talking, drawing his head back sharply as they turned on the landing below.

Gods! he thought, all consideration of the business he had come for gone from his mind. He must do something, and immediately, for this matter would not wait. He must nip it in the bud at once.

He was still standing there, his hands gripping the marble of the balustrade, when Pei Ro-han entered the gallery from the far end.

"Master Nan? Is that you?"

He turned, flustered, bowing twice, then hurried forward, kissing Pei's offered ring hand. He straightened up and, after the briefest pause to collect his thoughts, came directly to the point.

"Forgive me, my lord, but something has just happened that I must attend to at once. I was waiting here, just by the window there, when four men entered the gallery, talking among themselves. Not wishing to disturb them, I took a step outside, on to the balcony, yet what I overheard is of the gravest importance. Indeed I would go so far as to say that it threatens the security of our masters."

Pei Ro-han had gone very still. There was a small movement in his normally placid face, then he nodded. "I see. And what do you wish to do, Master Nan?"

In answer Nan Ho went to the balcony again, his head bowed, waiting for Pei to come across. When the old man stood beside him, he pointed out across the heads of the crowd to four men who were making their way to one of the refreshment tents on the far side of the walled garden.

"Those are the men. The two in red silks and the others in lilac and green. If you could detain them on some pretext for an hour or two, I will see if I can bring the Marshal here. He will know best how to deal with this matter."

"Are you sure that is wise, Master Nan? Should we not, perhaps, simply keep an eye on them and prevent them from leaving?"

Nan Ho shook his head vigorously. "Forgive me, but no, my lord. They must be isolated at the earliest opportunity, for what they know is dangerous. I cannot say more, but the safety of my masters is at stake here and I would be failing in my duty if I did not act."

Pei smiled, immensely pleased by this show of loyalty. "I understand, Nan Ho. Then go at once and bring Marshal Tolonen. I, meanwhile, will act my part in this."

★ ★ ★

Kim sat there in the semi-darkness, the room lights doused, the soft, pearled glow of the screen casting a faint, silvered radiance over his face and upper arms. He had worked through the night then slept, waking only an hour past, entranced, fearful, filled with the dream he'd had.

Her eyes. He had dreamed of Jelka Tolonen's eyes. Of eyes so blue that he could see the blackness beyond them; could see the stars winking through, each fastened on its silver, silken thread to where he stood, looking through her at the universe. He had woken, shivering, the intensity of the vision scaring him. What did it mean? Why was she there, suddenly, between him and the stars? Why could he not see them clearly, but through the startling blueness of her eyes?

He had lain there a while, open-mouthed with astonishment, then had come and sat here, toying with the comset's graphics, trying to recreate the vision he had had.

A spider. As so often he had been a spider in his dream; a tiny, silvered, dark-eyed creature, throwing out his web, letting the threads fly outward to the stars on tiny spinners that caught the distant sunlight and converted it to silk, flying onward, faster and ever faster to their various destinations. But this time it had been as if a great wind was blowing, gathering all of the threads into a single twisted trunk, drawing them up into the blueness of those eyes that floated like twin planets above where he crouched. Only on the far side of those eyes, where the blue shaded into black, did the trunk seem to blossom, like the branches of a tree, a million tiny threads spreading out like the fine capillaries of a root system, thrust deep into the earth of the universe.

Kim shivered, staring down at the thing he had made, first in his dreams and then here in the flatness of the screen. So it had always been for him: first he would see something and then he would act on what he'd seen. But this? How could he act on this? How could he pass his web through the young girl's eyes?

Or was that what it meant? Was he being too literal? Did this vision have another meaning than all those that had preceded it?

He shook his head then cleared the screen, only then realising how fast his heart was beating, how hard it seemed suddenly to breathe. Why was that? What did it mean?

He stood, angry with himself. It was only a dream, after all. It didn't *have* to mean anything, surely? No, he was better off concentrating on finishing off the work for Prince Yuan. Another two, maybe three days should see that done. Then he could send it through. He would ask Barycz for the favour.

He leaned forward, about to bring up the lights, when the screen came alive again. A message was coming through. He leaned back, waiting, one hand touching the keyboard lightly, killing the hardprint facility.

The words appeared in the official Project typescript, headed by the symbol of a skull surrounded by a tiny nimbus of broken lines. It was an instruction for him to go to the medical centre at once for his three-monthly check-up.

Kim sat back thoughtfully. It was too early. He wasn't due his next medical for another ten days. Still, that wasn't so unusual. Not everyone was as punctilious as he. Even so, he would make sure it wasn't one of Spatz's tricks.

He tapped out the locking combination, then put in the code, touching Cap A to scramble it. Cap L would unscramble when the time came to unlock, but until then Prince Yuan's files would be safe from prying eyes. Yes, they could take the comset apart, component by component, and never find it.

He looked up at the watching camera and smiled, then, going across to the corner, poured water from the jug into the bowl and began to wash.

★ ★ ★

Tolonen stood and came round his desk, greeting Prince Yuan's Master of the Inner Chambers.

"Master Nan, how pleasant to see you here. What can I do for you?"

15

Nan Ho bowed low. "Forgive me, Marshal. I realise how busy you are, but this is a matter of the most extreme urgency."

"So my equerry leads me to believe. But tell me, what has happened, Master Nan? Is the T'ang's life in danger?"

Nan Ho shook his head. "It is not the T'ang but young Prince Yuan who is threatened by this matter. Nor is it a matter of life but of reputation that is at stake."

The old man frowned at that. "I don't understand. You mean Prince Yuan's reputation is threatened?"

"I do indeed, Marshal. I was at Pei Ro-han's mansion on my master's business, when I overheard something. A rumour. A most vile rumour, which, if it were to become common knowledge, might do irreparable damage not only to my master but to the Seven. Such damage might well have political consequences."

Tolonen was watching him, his lips slightly parted. "Could you be more specific, Master Nan? I mean, what kind of rumour is this we're talking of?"

Nan Ho lowered his eyes. "Forgive me, Marshal, but I would rather not say. All I know is that there are no grounds whatsoever for such a rumour and that the perpetrators have but one purpose, to create a most vile nuisance for the Family that you and I deem it an honour to serve."

He glanced up, seeing that his words had done the trick. At the thought of the Li Clan being harmed in any way, Tolonen had bristled. There was a distinct colour at his neck, and his grey eyes bulged with anger.

"Then what are we to do, Master Nan? What steps might we take to eradicate this vileness?"

Nan Ho smiled inwardly, knowing he had been right to come direct to Tolonen. "Pei Ro-han has detained the men concerned before they could spread their wicked rumour. He is holding them until our return. If, through them, we can trace the source of these rumours, then we might yet stand a chance of crushing this abomination before it takes root."

16

Tolonen gave a terse nod, then went back to his desk, giving brief instructions into his desk-top comset before he turned back.

"The way is cleared for us. We can be at Lord Pei's mansion in half an hour. One of my crack teams will meet us there. Let us hope we are not too late, neh, Master Nan?"

Yes, thought Nan Ho, the tightness at the pit of his stomach returning. *For all our sakes, let us hope we can stop this thing before it spreads.*

* * *

The two men stood at the barrier, waiting while the Marshal's party passed through on the down transit. When it had gone they turned, their eyes meeting briefly, a strange look passing between them.

"Passes . . ." the guard seated beyond the barrier said, waving them on with one hand.

Mach flipped open the tiny warrant card he was carrying in his left hand and offered it to the guard. The guard took it without looking at him. "Face up to the camera," he said tonelessly.

Mach did as he was told, staring up into the artificial eye. Somewhere in central records it would be matching his retinal prints to his service record. A moment later a green light flashed on the board in front of the guard. He handed the card back, again without looking at Mach, then held out his hand again.

Lehmann came forward a pace and placed his card into the guard's hand. This time the guard's eyes came up lazily, then took a second look as he noted the pallor of the man.

"You sick or something?"

Mach laughed. "So would you be if you'd been posted to the Net for four years."

The guard eyed Lehmann with new respect. "That so, friend?"

Lehmann nodded, tilting his face up to stare at the camera.

"Four years?"

"Three years eight months," Lehmann corrected him, knowing what was in the false record DeVore had prepared for him.

The guard nodded, reading from the screen in front of him. "Says here you were decorated, too? What was that for?"

"Some bastard Triad runner got too nosy," Lehmann said, staring back at him menacingly. "I broke his jaw."

The guard laughed uncomfortably and handed back the card. "Okay. You can go through. And thanks . . ."

Out of earshot Mach leaned close. "Not so heavy, friend."

Lehmann simply looked at him.

Mach shrugged. "Okay. Let's get on with this. We'll start with the boxes at the top of the deck."

They took the deck-lift up, passing through a second check-point, then sought out the maintenance shaft that led to the first of the eighteen communications boxes that serviced this deck.

Crouched in the narrow tunnel above the floor-mounted box, Lehmann took a small cloth bag from the pocket of his tunic. Tilting his head forward, he tapped first one and then the other of the false lenses out into his hand, placing them into the bag.

Mach was already unscrewing the first of the four restraining bolts. He looked up at Lehmann, noting what he was doing. "Are you sure you ought to do that? There are cameras in these tunnels, too."

Lehmann tucked the bag away. "It'll be okay. Besides, I can't focus properly with those false retinas in place."

Mach laughed. "So DeVore doesn't think of everything."

Lehmann shook his head "Not at all. He's very thorough. Whose man do you think is manning the tunnel cameras?"

Mach slowed, then nodded thoughtfully. "Uhuh? And how do you think he does that? I mean, he's got a lot of riends, your man DeVore. It seems odd, don't you think? I mean, how long is it since he quit Security? Eight years now? Ten?"

"It's called loyalty," Lehmann said coldly. "I thought you understood that. Besides, there are many who feel as you and I. Many who'd like to see things change."

Mach shook his head slowly, as if he still didn't understand, then got to work on the second of the bolts.

"You think that's strange, don't you?" Lehmann said after a moment. "You think that only you low-level types should want to change how things are, but you're wrong. You don't have to be on the bottom of this shit-heap to see how fuck-awful things are. Take me. From birth I was set to inherit. Riches beyond your imagination. But it was never enough. I never wanted to be rich. I wanted to be free. Free of all the restraints this world of ours sets upon us. Chains they are. It's a prison, this world of ours, boxing us in, and I hate that. I've always hated it."

Mach stared up at him, surprised and, to a small degree, amused. He had never suspected that the albino had so much feeling in him. He had always thought him cold, like a dead thing. This hatred was unexpected. It hinted at a side to him that even DeVore knew nothing of.

The second bolt came free. He set to work on the third.

"I bet you hated your parents, too, didn't you?"

Lehmann knelt, watching Mach's hands as they turned the bolt. "I never knew them. My father never came to see me. My mother . . . well, I killed my mother."

"You . . ." Mach looked back at him, roaring with laughter, then fell silent. "You mean, you really did? You *killed* her?"

Lehmann nodded. "She was a rich Han's concubine. An rfidis addict too. She disgusted me. She was like the rest of them, soft, corrupt. Like this world. I set fire to her, in her rooms. I'd like to do the same to all of them. To burn the whole thing to a shell and pull it down."

Mach took a deep breath through his nose, then set to work again. "I see. And DeVore knows this, does he?"

19

"No. He thinks I'm someone else, some*thing* else."

"I see. But why tell me?"

"Because you're not what he thinks you are either."
Lehmann reached across him, beginning to unscrew the
final bolt. "DeVore sees only enemies or pale shadows of
himself. That's how he thinks. Black and white. As if this
were all one great big game of *wei chi*."

Mach laughed. "You surprise me. I'd have
thought . . ." Then he laughed again. "I'm sorry. I'm
doing what you said he does, aren't I? Assuming you're
something that you're not."

The last screw came loose. Between them they gently
lifted the plate from the connecting pins and set it to one
side. Beneath the plate was a panel, inset with tiny slip-in
instruction cards. At the base of the panel was a keyboard.
Lehmann tapped in the cut-out code he'd memorised then
leaned close, studying the panel. His pale, thin fingers
searched the board, then plucked five of the translucent
cards from different locations. He slipped them into the
pouch at his waist, then reached into his jacket and took
out the first of the eighteen tiny sealed packets. When a
certain signal was routed through this board, these five
would be triggered, forming a circuit that overrode the
standard instruction codes. To the back-up system it
would seem as if the panel were functioning normally, but
to all intents and purposes it would be dead. And with all
eighteen boxes triggered in this way, communications to
the deck would be effectively cut off.

He slotted the five wafer-thin cards into place, reset the
cut-out code, then, with Mach's help, lowered the plate
back on to the connecting pins.

"There," Mach said. "One down, seventeen to go.
Pretty easy, huh?"

"Easy enough," Lehmann said, taking one of the
restraining bolts and beginning to screw it down. "But
only if you've the nerve, the vision and the intelligence to
plan it properly."

Mach laughed. "And a few old friends, turning a blind eye."

Lehmann turned his head slightly, meeting Mach's eyes. "Maybe. And a reason for doing it, neh?"

★ ★ ★

Kim had heard the alarm from three decks down but made nothing of it, yet coming out of the transit he remembered it again. Pulse quickening, he began to run towards his room.

Even before he turned the corner into his corridor he saw signs of what had happened. A long snake of hose ran from the corner hydrant, flaccid now. On the far side of it, water had pooled. But that was not what had alerted him. It was the scent of burning plastics.

He leapt the hose, took three small, splashing steps, then stopped. The door to his room was open, the fire-hose curving inside. Even from where he stood he could see how charred the lintel was, could see the ashy residue of sludge littering the floor outside.

"What in the gods' names . . . ?"

T'ai Cho jerked his head around the door. "Kim!" he cried, coming out into the corridor, his face lit up. "Oh, thank the gods you're safe. I thought . . ."

He let himself be embraced, then went inside, facing the worst. It was gone. All of it. His comset was unrecognisable, fused into the worktop as if the whole were some strange, smooth sculpture of twisted black marble. The walls were black, as was the ceiling. The floor was awash with the same dark sludge that had oozed into the corridor.

"What happened?" he asked, looking about him, the extent of his loss – his books, his clothes, the tiny things he'd called his own – slowly sinking in. "I thought this kind of thing couldn't happen? There are sprinklers, aren't there? And air-seals."

T'ai Cho glanced at one of the maintenance men who were standing around, then looked back at Kim. "They failed, it seems. Faulty wiring it looks like."

Kim laughed sourly, the irony not lost on him. "Faulty wiring? But I thought the boxes used instruction cards."

One of the men spoke up. "That's right. But two of the cards were wrongly encoded. It happens sometimes. It's something we can't check up on. A mistake at the factory . . . You know how it is."

Only too well, Kim thought. *But who did this? Who ordered it done? Spatz? Or someone higher than him? Not Prince Yuan, anyway, because he wanted what was destroyed here today.*

He sighed, then shook his head. It would take weeks, months perhaps, to put it all together again. And if he did? Well, maybe it would be for nothing after all. Maybe they would strike again, just as he came to the end of his task, making sure nothing ever got to Li Yuan.

He turned, looking at his old friend. "You shouldn't have worried, T'ai Cho. But I'm glad you did. I was having my three-monthly medical. They say I'm fine. A slight vitamin C deficiency, but otherwise . . ." He laughed. "It was fortunate, neh? I could have been sleeping."

"Yes," T'ai Cho said, holding the boy to him again. "We should thank the gods, neh?"

Yes, thought Kim. *Or whoever it was decided I was not as disposable as my work.*

* * *

Nan Ho stood in the cool of the passageway outside the room, mopping his brow, the feeling of nausea passing slowly from him. Though ten minutes had passed, his hands still trembled and his clothes were soaked with his own sweat. In all his forty years he had seen nothing like it. The man's screams had been bad enough, but the look in his eyes, that expression of sheer terror and hopelessness, had been too much to bear.

If he closed his eyes he could still see it. Could see the echoing kitchen all about him, the prisoner tied naked to the table, his hands and feet bound tight with cords that bruised and cut the flesh. He bared his teeth, remembering the way the masked man had turned, the oiled muscles of his upper arms flexing effortlessly as he lifted the tongs from the red-hot brazier and turned them in the half-light. He could see the faint wisp of smoke that rose towards the ceiling, could hear the faint crackle as the coal was lifted into the cooler air, even before he saw the glowing coal itself. But most of all he could see the panic in the young man's eyes and recalled what he had thought.

Forgive me, Fan Ming-yu, but I had to do this. For my master.

The man had begun to babble, to refute all he had been saying only a moment before, but the torturer's movements seemed inexorable. The coal came down, slowly, ever so slowly it seemed, and the man's words melted into shrieks of fearful protest. His body lifted, squirming, desperate, but all of its attempts to escape only brought it closer to the implement of its suffering.

The torturer held back a moment. One leather-gloved hand pushed the man's hip down, gently, almost tenderly it seemed. Then, with the kind of care one might see from a craftsman, tracing fine patterns on to silver, he brought the coal down delicately, pressing it tightly against the man's left testicle.

Nan Ho had shuddered and stepped back, swallowing bile. He had glanced, horrified, at Tolonen, seeing how the old man looked on impassively, then had looked back at the man, unable to believe what he had seen, appalled and yet fascinated by the damage the coal had done. Then, turning away, he had staggered out, his legs almost giving way under him, the screams of the man filling his head, the smell of charred flesh making him want to retch.

He stood there a moment longer, calming himself, trying to fit what he had just witnessed into the tightly-ordered pattern of the world he knew, then shook his head. It was not his fault. He had had no choice in the matter. If his master had been any other man, or if the Lady Fei had chosen any other man but Tsu Ma to be her lover. But . . . well, as it was, this had to be. To let the truth be known, that was unthinkable.

Tolonen came outside. He stood there, staring at Nan

Ho a moment, then reached out and held his shoulder. "I am sorry, Master Nan. I didn't mean it to upset you. It's just that I felt you ought to be there, to hear the man's confession for yourself." He let his hand fall, then shrugged. "There are more efficient ways of inflicting pain, of course, but none as effective in loosening a tongue. The more barbaric the means of torture, we find, the quicker the man will talk."

Nan Ho swallowed, then found his voice again. "And what did you discover?"

"I have a list of all those he spoke to. Few, fortunately. And his source."

"His source?"

"It seems you acted not a moment too soon, Master Nan. Fan Ming-yu had just come from his lover. A young man named Yen Shih-fa."

Nan Ho's eyes widened. "I know the man. He is a groom at the stables."

"Yes," Tolonen smiled grimly. "I have contacted Tongjiang already and had the man arrested. With the very minimum of fuss, you understand. They are bringing him here even now."

Nan Ho nodded abstractedly. "And what will you do?"

The Marshal swallowed, a momentary bitterness clouding his features. "What can I do? It is as you said, Master Nan. This rumour cannot be allowed to spread. But how prevent that? Normally I would trust to the word of such *ch'un tzu*, but in a matter of this seriousness it would not be enough to trust to their silence. A man's word is one thing, but the security of the State is another. No, nor would it serve to demote them below the Net. These four are men of influence. Small influence, admittedly, but their absence would be noticed and commented upon. No, in the circumstances we must act boldly, I'm afraid."

Nan Ho shuddered. "You mean they must die."

Tolonen smiled. "Nothing quite so drastic, Master Nan. It is a matter of a small operation." He traced a tiny line across the side of his skull. "An incision here, another here . . ."

"And their families?"

"Their families will be told that they took an overdose of something illicit. Pei Ro-han's surgeons had to operate to save them, but unfortunately there was damage – serious damage – to those parts of the brain that control speech and memory. Most unfortunate, neh? But the T'ang, in his generosity, will offer compensation."

Nan Ho stared at the Marshal, surprised. "You know this?"

"I have already written the memorandum. It will be on Li Shai Tung's desk this evening."

"Ah, then the matter is concluded?"

"Yes. I think we can safely say that."

"And the groom? Yen Shih-fa?"

Tolonen looked down, clearly angry. "Yen Shih-fa will die. After we have made sure he has done no further mischief."

Nan Ho bowed his head. "I understand . . ." Yet he felt no satisfaction, only a sense of dread necessity; that and a slowly mounting anger at his young master's wife. This was her fault, the worthless bitch. This was the price of her selfishness, her wantonness.

Tolonen was watching him sympathetically. "You have served your master well, Nan Ho. You were right. If this rumour *had* taken root . . ."

Nan Ho gave the slightest nod. He had hoped to keep the details from Tolonen, but it had not proved possible. Even so, no harm had been done. Fan Ming-yu's insistence on the truth of what he had said – that Tsu Ma *had* slept with the Lady Fei – had shocked and outraged the old man. Nan Ho had seen for himself the fury in Tolonen's face as he leaned over the man, spittle flecking his lips as he called him a liar and a filthy scandal-monger. And thank the gods for that. No. Not for one moment had the Marshal believed it could be true. Tsu Ma and the Lady Fei. No. It was unthinkable!

And so it must remain. For a lifetime, if necessary. But how long would it be before another whispered the secret to one they trusted? How long before the rumour trickled out again, flowing from ear to ear like the tributaries of a great river? And then?

"I am pleased that it has all worked out so well, Marshal," he said, meeting the old man's eyes briefly. "But now, if you need me no longer, I must see Pei Ro-han. I have yet to complete the business I came here to transact."

"Of course," Tolonen said, smiling now. "You have done all that needs to be done here, Master Nan. For which I thank you. However, I can deal with the rest."

"Good. Then you'll excuse me."

He bowed and was beginning to turn away when Tolonen called him back.

"Forgive me, Master Nan, but one small thing. This morning, as I understand it, was the first time Tsu Ma had visited Tongjiang for three, almost four months. Now, without saying for a moment that I believe it to be true, such rumours have no credibility – even among such carrion as these – unless there are some few small circumstances to back them up. What crossed my mind, therefore, was that this was possibly some old tale, renewed, perhaps, by Tsu Ma's visit this morning? I wondered . . ." He hesitated, clearly embarrassed by what he was about to say. "Well, to be frank, I wondered if you had heard any whisper of this rumour before today, Master Nan. Whether . . ."

But Nan Ho was shaking his head. "Maybe you're right, but personally I think it more likely that the T'ang's visit put the idea into the young groom's head, neh? Dig a little and I'm sure you'll find a reason for his malice. It would not be the first time that such mischief has come from personal disappointment."

Tolonen considered that a moment, then nodded, satisfied. "Well, it was just a passing thought. Go now, Master Nan. And may the gods reward you for what you have done here today."

* * *

It had taken the best part of six hours to work their way down through the deck, but now they had only this last box to deal with and they were done. Both men had been quiet for some time, as if the stream of talk between them had dried up, but now Mach looked across at his pale companion and laughed.

"What is it?" Lehmann asked tonelessly, concentrating on unscrewing the last of the restraining bolts.

"I was just thinking . . ."

Again he laughed. This time Lehmann raised his eyes, searching his face. "Thinking what?"

"Just about what you might have become. With your father's money. I mean. You could have been a right bastard, neh? Beating them at their own game. Making deals. Controlling the markets. Under-cutting your competitors or stealing their patents. Did that never appeal to you?"

Lehmann looked down again. "I considered it. But then, I considered a lot of things. But to answer you, *Shih* Mach. No, it never appealed to me. But this . . ." He eased the bolt out and set it down. "This is what I've always wanted to do."

"Always?" Mach helped him remove the plate, then sat back on his haunches, watching.

"Since I can remember," Lehmann went on, tapping the cut-out code into the keyboard. "I've always fought against the system. Ever since I knew I could. In small ways at first. And later . . ."

Mach waited, but Lehmann seemed to have finished.

"Are you really as nihilistic as you seem, Stefan Lehmann? Is there nothing you believe in?"

Lehmann's pale, thin fingers hovered over the panel a moment, then quickly plucked the five tiny cards from their slots. Mach had watched Lehmann do this eighteen times now, noting how he took his time, double-checking, making absolutely sure he took the right ones. It was impressive in a way, this kind of obsessive care. And necessary in this case, because the configuration of each panel was different. But there was also something machine-like about the way Lehmann went about it.

He waited, knowing the albino would answer him when he was good and ready; watching him take out the tiny sealed packet and break it open then slip the replacement cards into their respective slots.

"There," Lehmann said. "That's all of them. Do you want to test the circuit out?"

Mach was about to answer when there was a banging on the tunnel wall beneath them.

"Shit!" Mach hissed between his teeth. "What the fuck is that?"

Lehmann had turned at the noise, now he waited, perfectly still, like a lizard about to take its prey. *Wait*, he mouthed. *It may be nothing.*

There was silence. Mach counted. He had got to eight when the banging came again, louder than before and closer, almost beneath their feet. Moments later a head appeared at the hatchway further along.

"Hey!" the guard said, turning to face them. "Are you authorised to be in there?"

Mach laughed. "Well, if we're not we're in trouble, aren't we?"

The guard was pulling himself up into the tunnel, hissing with the effort. Mach looked to Lehmann quickly, indicating that he should do nothing. With the barest nod Lehmann leaned back, resting his head against the tunnel wall, his eyes closed.

The guard scrambled up, then came closer, his body hunched up in the narrow space. He was a young, dark-haired officer with the kind of bearing that suggested he had come out of cadet-training only months before. "What are you doing here?" he asked officiously, one hand resting lightly on his sidearm.

Mach smiled, shaking his head. "Don't you read your sheets?"

The young guard bristled, offended by Mach's off-hand

28

manner. "That's precisely why I'm here. I've already checked. There's no mention of any maintenance work on the sheets."

Mach shrugged. "And that's our fault? You should get on to Admin and find out what arsehole fucked things up, but don't get on our backs. Here." He reached inside his tunic and pulled out the papers DeVore had had forged for them.

He watched the guard's face; saw how the sight of something official-looking mollified him.

"Well? Are you satisfied?" Mach asked, putting out his hand to take the papers back.

The guard drew back a step, his eyes taking in the open box, the exposed panel. "I still don't understand. What exactly are you doing there? It says here that you're supposed to be testing the ComNet, but you can do that without looking at the boxes, surely?"

Mach stared back at him, his lips parted, momentarily at a loss, but Lehmann came to the rescue. He leaned forward casually and plucked one of the tiny cards from the panel in front of him, handing it to the guard.

"Have you ever seen one of these?"

The guard studied the clear plastic of the card then looked back at Lehmann. "Yes, I . . ."

"And you know how they function?"

"Vaguely, yes, I . . ."

Lehmann laughed. A cold, scathing laughter. "You don't know a fucking thing, do you, soldier boy? For instance, did you know that if even a single one of these instruction cards gets put in the wrong slot then the whole net can be fucked up. Urgent information can be misrouted, emergency calls never get to their destinations. That's why we take such pains. That's why we look at every box. Carefully. Meticulously. To make sure it doesn't happen. Understand me?" He looked up the guard savagely. "Okay, you've been a good boy and done all your checking, now just piss off and let us get on with the

job, neh? Before we register a complaint to your superio
officer for harassment."

Mach saw the anger in the young guard's face, the swal
lowed retort. Then the papers were thrust back into hi
hand and the guard was backing away down the tunnel.

"That was good," Mach said quietly when he was gone
"He'll be no more trouble, that's for sure."

Lehmann looked at him, then shook his head. "Here,
he said, handing him the plate. "You finish this. I'm goin;
after our friend."

Mach narrowed his eyes. "Are you sure that's wise?
mean, he seemed satisfied with your explanation. And i
you were to kill him . . ."

Lehmann turned, his face for that brief moment ver
close to Mach's, his pink eyes searching the *Ping Tia*
leader's.

"You asked if I believed in anything, Mach. Well, there'
one thing I do believe in – I believe in making sure."

* * *

Li Yuan rode ahead, finding the path down the hillside
Behind him came the palanquin, swaying gently, the si
carriers finding their footholds on the gentle slope with
practised certainty, their low grunts carrying on the stil
evening air.

Li Yuan turned in his saddle, looking back. The sun wa
setting in the west, beyond the Ta Pa Shan. In its dyin;
light the pale yellow silks of the palanquin seemed dyed
bloody red. He laughed and turned back, spurring hi
horse on. It had been a wonderful day. A day he woul
remember for a long time. And Fei Yen? Despite her sick
ness, Fei had looked more beautiful than ever. And ever
if they had not made love, simply to be with her ha
somehow been enough.

He threw his head back, feeling the cool breeze on hi
neck and face. Yes, motherhood suited Fei Yen. The
would have many sons. A dozen, fifteen sons. Enough t
fill Tongjiang. And daughters too. Daughters who woul

ook like Fei Yen. And then, when he was old and silver-
haired, he would have a hundred grandchildren; would
gather his pretties about his throne and tell them of a summer day – *this* day – when he had gone up to the ruins
with their grandmother, the Lady Fei, and wished them
into being.

He laughed, enjoying the thought, then slowed, seeing
lights floating, dancing in the darkness up ahead. Looking
back he raised a hand, signalling for the carriers to stop,
then eased his mount forward a pace or two. No, he was
not mistaken, the lights were coming on towards them.
Then he understood. They were lanterns. Someone – Nan
Ho, most likely – had thought to send out lantern-bearers
to light their way home.

He turned, signalling the carriers to come on, then
spurred the Arab forward again, going down to meet the
party from the palace.

He met them halfway across the long meadow. There
were twenty bearers, their ancient oil-filled lanterns
mounted on ten *ch'i* wooden poles. Coming up behind
were a dozen guards and two of the young grooms from
the stables. Ahead of them all, marching along stiffly, like
a young boy playing at soldiers, was Nan Ho.

"Master Nan!" he hailed. "How good of you to think
of coming to greet us."

Nan Ho bowed low. Behind him the tiny procession
had stopped, their heads bowed. "It was but my duty, my
lord."

Li Yuan drew closer, leaning towards Nan Ho, his voice
lowered. "And the business I sent you on?"

"It is all arranged," Nan Ho answered quietly. "The
Lord Pei has taken on the matter as his personal responsibility. Your maids will have the very best of husbands."

"Good." Li Yuan straightened up in his saddle, then
clapped his hands, delighted that Pearl Heart and Sweet
Rose would finally have their reward. "Good. Then let us
go and escort the Lady Fei, neh, Master Nan?"

Li Yuan galloped ahead, meeting the palanquin at the

edge of the long meadow. "Stop!" he called. "Set the palanquin down. We shall wait for the bearers to come."

As the chair was lowered there was the soft rustle of silk from inside as Fei Yen stirred. "Yuan?" she called sleepily. "Yuan, what's happening?"

He signalled to one of the men to lift back the heavy silk at the front of the palanquin, then stepped forward, helping Fei Yen raise herself into a sitting position. Then he stepped back again, pointing out across the meadow.

"See what Master Nan has arranged for us, my love."

She laughed softly, delighted. The darkness of the great meadow seemed suddenly enchanted, the soft glow of the lanterns like giant fireflies floating at the end of their tall poles. Beyond them on the far side of the meadow, the walls of the great palace of Tongjiang were a burnished gold in the sun's last rays, the red, steeply-tiled roofs like flames.

"It's beautiful," she said. "Like something from a fairy-tale."

He laughed, seeing how the lamplight seemed to float in the liquid darkness of her eyes. "Yes. And you the fairy princess, my love. But come, let me sit with you. One should share such magic, neh?"

He climbed up next to his wife then turned, easing himself into the great cushioned seat next to her.

"All right, Master Nan. We're ready."

Nan Ho bowed, then set about arranging things, lining up the lantern-bearers to either side of the palanquin then assigning six of the guards to double-up as carriers. He looked about him. Without being told the two grooms had taken charge of the Arab and were petting her gently.

Good, thought Nan Ho, signalling for the remaining guards to form up behind the palanquin. But his satisfaction was tainted. He looked at his master and at his wife and felt sick at heart. How beautiful it all looked in the light of the lanterns, how perfect, and yet . . .

He looked down, remembering what he had done, what seen that day, and felt a bitter anger. *Things should be as*

32

they seem, he thought. *No*, he corrected himself: *things should seem as they truly are.*

He raised his hand. At the signal the carriers lifted the palanquin with a low grunt. Then, as he moved out ahead of them, the procession began, making its slow way across the great meadow, the darkness gathering all about them.

* * *

"Well, how did it go?"

Lehmann threw the pouch down on the desk in front of DeVore. "There was a slight hitch, but all the circuits are in place. I had to kill a man. A Security guard. But your man there, Hanssen, is seeing to that."

DeVore studied Lehmann a moment. "And nobody else saw you."

"Only the guards at the barriers."

"Good." DeVore looked down, fingering the pouch, knowing that it contained all the communication circuits they had replaced, then pushed it aside. "Then we're all set, neh? Ten days from now we can strike. There was no problem with Mach, I assume?"

Lehmann shook his head. "No. He seems as keen as us to get at them."

DeVore smiled. *As he ought to be.* "Okay. Get showered and changed. I'll see you at supper for debriefing."

When Lehmann was gone he got up and went across the room, looking at the detailed diagram of Security Central that he'd pinned on the wall. Bremen was the very heart of City Europe's Security forces; their "invulnerable" fortress. But it was that very assumption of invulnerability that made them weak. In ten days time they would find that out. Would taste the bitter fruit of their arrogance.

He laughed and went back to his desk, then reached across, drawing the folder towards him. He had been studying it all afternoon, ever since the messenger had brought it. It was a complete file of all the boy's work; a copy of the file Marshal Tolonen had taken with him to Tongjiang that very morning; a copy made in Tolonen's

33

own office by Tolonen's own equerry, a young man he had recruited to his cause five years earlier, when the boy was still a cadet.

He smiled, remembering how he had initiated the boy, how he had made him swear the secret oath. It was so easy. They were all so keen; so young and fresh and ripe for some new ideology – for some new thing they could believe in. And he, DeVore, was that new thing. He was the man whose time would come. That was what he told them, and they believed him. He could see it in their eyes; that urgency to serve some new and better cause – something finer and more abstract than this tedious world of levels. He called them his brotherhood and they responded with a fierceness born of hunger. The hunger to be free of this world ruled by the Han. To be free men again, self-governing and self-sustaining. And he fed that hunger in them, giving them a reason for their existence – to see a better world. However long it took.

He opened the file, flicking through the papers, stopping here and there to admire the beauty of a design, the simple elegance of a formula. He had underestimated the boy. Had thought him simply clever. Super-clever, perhaps, but nothing more. This file, however, proved him wrong. The boy was unique. A genius of the first order. What he had accomplished with these simple prototypes was astonishing. Why, there was enough here to keep several Companies busy for years. He smiled. As it was he would send them off to Mars, to his contacts there, and see what they could make of them.

He leaned back in his chair, stretching out his arms. It would be time, soon, to take the boy and use him. For now, however, other schemes prevailed. Bremen and the Plantations, they were his immediate targets – the first shots in this new stage of the War. And afterwards?

DeVore laughed, then leaned forward, closing the file. The wise man chose his plays carefully. As in *wei chi*, it did not do to play too rigidly. The master player kept a dozen subtle plays in his head at once, prepared to use whichever best suited the circumstances. And he had more than enough schemes to keep the Seven busy.

But first Bremen. First he would hit them where it hurt the most. Where they least expected him to strike.

Only then would he consider his next move. Only then would he know where to place the next stone on the board.

AT THE
BRIDGE OF CH'IN

"The white glare recedes to the Western hills,
High in the distance sapphire blossoms rise.
Where shall there be an end of old and new?
A thousand years have whirled away in the wind.
The sands of the ocean change to stone,
Fishes puff bubbles at the bridge of Ch'in.
The empty shine streams on into the distance,
The bronze pillars melt away with the years."

– Li Ho, *On And On For Ever*, Ninth Century AD

CHAPTER·1

Scorched Earth

Li Shai Tung stood beside the pool. Across from him, at the entrance to the arboretum, a single lamp had been lit, its light reflecting darkly in the smoked-glass panels of the walls; misting a pallid green through leaves of fern and palm. But where the great T'ang stood it was dark.

These days he courted darkness like a friend. At night, when sleep evaded him, he came here, staring down through layers of blackness at the dark, submerged forms of his carp. Their slow and peaceful movements lulled him, easing the pain in his eyes, the tenseness in his stomach. Often he would stand for hours, unmoving, his black silks pulled close about his thin and ancient body. Then, for a time, the tiredness would leave him, as if it had no place here in the cool, penumbral silence.

Then ghosts would come. Images imprinted on the blackness, filling the dark with the vivid shapes of memory. The face of Han Ch'in, smiling up at him, a half-eaten apple in his hand from the orchard at Tongjiang. Lin Yua, his first wife, bowing demurely before him on their wedding night, her small breasts cupped in her hands, like an offering. Or his father, Li Ch'ing, laughing, a bird perched on the index finger of each hand, two days before the accident that killed him. These and others crowded back, like guests at a death feast. But of this he told no one, not even his physician. These, strangely, were his comfort. Without them the darkness would have been oppressive: would have been blackness, pure and simple.

Sometimes he would call a name, softly, in a whisper,

and that one would come to him, eyes alight with laughter.
So he remembered them now, in joy and at their best.
Shades from a summer land.

He had been standing there more than two hours when
a servant came. He knew at once that it was serious; they
would not have disturbed him otherwise. He felt the tenseness return like bands of iron about his chest and brow;
felt the tiredness seep back into his bones.

"Who calls me?"

The servant bowed low. "It is the Marshal, *Chieh Hsia*."

He went out, shedding the darkness like a cloak. In his
study the viewing screen was bright, filled by Tolonen's
face. Li Shai Tung sat in the big chair, moving Minister
Heng's memorandum to one side. For a moment he sat
there, composing himself, then stretched forward and
touched the contact-pad.

"What is it, Knut? What evil keeps you from your bed?"

"Your servant never sleeps," Tolonen offered, but his
smile was half-hearted and his face was ashen. Seeing that,
Li Shai Tung went cold. *Who is it now?* he asked himself.
Wei Feng? Tsu Ma? Who have they killed this time?

The Marshal turned and the image on the screen turned
with him. He was sending from a mobile unit. Behind him
a wide corridor stretched away, its walls blackened by
smoke. Further down, men were working in emergency
lighting.

"Where are you, Knut? What has been happening?"

"I'm at the Bremen fortress, *Chieh Hsia*. In the barracks
of Security Central." Tolonen's face, to the right of the
screen, continued to stare back down the corridor for a
moment, then turned to face his T'ang again. "Things are
bad here, *Chieh Hsia*. I think you should come and see for
yourself. It seems like the work of the *Ping Tiao*, but . . ."
Tolonen hesitated, his old, familiar face etched with deep
concern. He gave a small shudder, then began again. "It's
just that this is different, *Chieh Hsia*. Totally different from
anything they've ever done before."

Li Shai Tung considered a moment, then nodded. The

skin of his face felt tight, almost painful. He took a shallow breath, then spoke. "Then I'll come, Knut. I'll be there as soon as I can."

★ ★ ★

It was hard to recognise the place. The whole deck was gutted. Over fifteen thousand people were dead. Damage had spread to nearby stacks and to the decks above and below, but that was minimal compared to what had happened here. Li Shai Tung walked beside his Marshal, turning his bloodless face from side to side as he walked, seeing the ugly mounds of congealed tar – all that was left of once-human bodies – that were piled up by the sealed exits, conscious of the all-pervading stench of burned flesh, sickly sweet and horrible. At the end of Main the two men stopped and looked back.

"Are you certain?" There were tears in the old T'ang's eyes as he looked at his Marshal. His face was creased with pain, his hands clasped tightly together.

Tolonen took a pouch from his tunic pocket and handed it across. "They left these. So that we would know."

The pouch contained five small, stylised fish. Two of the golden pendants had melted, the others shone like new. The fish was the symbol of the *Ping Tiao*.

Li Shai Tung spilled them into his palm. "Where were these found?"

"On the other side of the seals. There were more, we're certain, but the heat . . ."

Li Shai Tung shuddered, then let the fish fall from his fingers. They had turned the deck into a giant oven and cooked everyone inside; men, women and their children. Sudden anger twisted like a spear in his guts. "*Why?* What do they want, Knut? What do they want?" One hand jerked out nervously, then withdrew. "This is the worst of it. The killings. The senseless deaths. For what?"

Tolonen had said it once before, years ago, to his old friend, Klaus Ebert; now he said the words again, this

41

time to his T'ang. "They want to pull it down. All of it. Whatever it costs."

Li Shai Tung stared at him, then looked away. "No . . ." he began, as if to deny it; but for once denial was impossible. This was what he had feared; his darkest dream made real. A sign of things to come.

He had been ill of late. For the first time in a long, healthy life he had been confined to bed. That too seemed a sign. An indication that things were slipping from him. Control – it began with one's own body and spread outward.

He nodded to himself, seeing it now. This was personal. An attack upon his person. For he *was* the State. *Was* the City.

There was a sickness loose, a virus in the veins of the world. Corruption was rife. Dispersionism, Levelling, even this current obsession in the Above with longevity – all these were symptoms of it. The actions of such groups were subtle, invidious, not immediately evident, yet ultimately they proved fatal. Expectations had changed and that had undermined the stability of everything.

They want to pull it down.

"What did they do here, Knut? How did they do this?"

"We've had to make some assumptions, but some things are known for certain. Bremen Central Maintenance report that all communications to Deck Nine were cut at second bell."

"All?" Li Shai Tung shook his head, astonished. "Is that possible, Knut?"

"That was part of the problem. They didn't believe it, either, so they wasted an hour checking for faults in the system at their end. They didn't think to send anyone to make a physical check."

Li Shai Tung grimaced. "Would it have made a difference?"

"No. No difference, *Chieh Hsia*. There was no chance of doing anything after the first ten minutes. They set their fires on four different levels. Big, messy, chemical things.

Then they rigged the ventilators to pump oxygen-rich air through the system at increased capacity."

"And the seals?"

Tolonen swallowed. "There was no chance anyone could have got out. They'd blown the transit and derailed the bolt. All the inter-level lifts were jammed. That was part of the communications blackout. The whole deck must have been in darkness."

"And that's it?" Li Shai Tung felt sickened by the callousness of it all.

Tolonen hesitated, then spoke again. "This was done by experts, *Chieh Hsia*. Knowledgeable men, superbly trained, efficiently organised. Our own special services men could have done no better . . ."

Li Shai Tung looked back at him. "Say it, Knut," he said softly. "Don't keep it to yourself. Even if it proves wrong, say it."

Tolonen met his eyes, then nodded. "All of this speaks of money. Big money. The technology needed to cut off a deck's communications – it's all too much for normal *Ping Tiao* funding. Out of their range. There has to be a backer."

The T'ang considered a moment. "Then it's still going on. We didn't win the War after all. Not finally."

Tolonen looked down. Li Shai Tung's manner disturbed him. Since his illness he had been different. Off-balance and indecisive, withdrawn, almost melancholy. The sickness had robbed him of more than his strength; it had taken some of his sharpness, his quickness of mind. It fell upon the Marshal to lead him through this maze.

"Maybe. But more important is finding out who the traitor is in our midst."

"Ah . . ." Li Shai Tung's eyes searched his face, then looked away. "At what level have they infiltrated?"

"Staff."

He said it without hesitation, knowing that it had to be that high up the chain of command. No one else could have shaped things in this manner. To seal off a deck, that took clout. More than the *Ping Tiao* possessed.

Li Shai Tung turned away again, following his own thoughts. Maybe Yuan was right. Maybe they should act now. Wire them all. Control them like machines. But his instinct was against it. He had held back from acting on the Project's early findings. Even this – this outrage – could not change his mind so far.

"It's bad, Knut. It's as if you could not trust your own hands to shave your throat . . ."

Tolonen laughed; a short, bitter bark of laughter.

The old T'ang turned. "You have it in hand, though, Knut." He smiled. "You, at least, I trust."

The Marshal met his master's eyes, touched by what had been said, knowing that this was what shaped his life and gave it meaning. To have this man's respect, his total trust. Without thinking, he knelt at Li Shai Tung's feet.

"I shall find the man and deal with him, *Chieh Hsia*. Were it my own son, I'd deal with him."

★　★　★

At that moment, on the far side of the world, Li Yuan was walking down a path on the estate in Tongjiang. He could smell the blossom in the air, apple and plum, and beneath those the sharper, sweeter scent of cherry. It reminded him of how long it had been since he had been here; of how little had changed while he had been gone.

At the top of the terrace he stopped, looking out across the valley, down the wide sweep of marble steps towards the lake. He smiled, seeing her, there on the far side of the lake, walking between the trees. For a moment he simply looked, his heart quickened just to see her, then he went down, taking the steps in twos and threes.

He was only a few paces from her when she turned.

"Li Yuan! You didn't say . . ."

"I'm sorry, I . . ." But his words faltered as he noted the roundness of her, the fullness of her belly. He glanced up, meeting her eyes briefly, then looked down again. *My son*, he thought. *My son*.

"I'm well."

"You look wonderful," he said, taking her in his arms, conscious of the weeks that had passed since he had last held her. But he was careful now and released her quickly, taking her hands, surprised by how small they were, how delicate. He had forgotten.

No, not forgotten. Simply not remembered.

He laughed softly. "How far along are you?"

She looked away. "More than halfway now. Twenty-seven weeks."

He nodded, then reached down to touch the roundness, feeling how firm she was beneath the silks she wore, like the ripened fruit in the branches above their heads.

"I wondered . . ." she began, looking back at him, then fell silent, dropping her head.

"Wondered what?" he asked, staring at her, realising suddenly what had been bothering him. "Besides, what's this? Have you no smiles to welcome your husband home?"

He reached out, lifting her chin gently with his fingers, smiling, but his smile brought no response. She turned from him petulantly, looking down at her feet. Leaf shadow fell across the perfection of her face, patches of sunlight catching in the lustrous darkness of her hair, but her lips were pursed.

"I've brought you presents," he said softly. "Up in the house. Why don't you come and see?"

She glanced at him, then away. This time he saw the coldness in her eyes. "How long this time, Li Yuan? A day? Two days before you're gone again?"

He sighed and looked down at her hand. It lay limply in his own, palm upward, the fingers gently bent.

"I'm not just any man, Fei Yen. My responsibilities are great, especially at this time. My father needs me." He shook his head, trying to understand what she was feeling, but he could not help but feel angered by her lack of

45

welcome. It was not *his* fault, after all. He had thought she would be pleased to see him.

"If I'm away a lot, it can't be helped. Not just now. I would rather be here, believe me, my love. I really would . . ."

She seemed to relent a little; momentarily her hand returned the pressure of his own, but her face was still turned from his.

"I never see you," she said quietly. "You're never here."

A bird alighted from a branch nearby, distracting him. He looked up, following its flight. When he looked back it was to find her watching him, her dark eyes chiding him.

"It's odd," he said, ignoring what she had said. "This place . . . it's changed so little over the years. I used to play here as a child, ten, twelve years ago. And even then I imagined how it had been like this for centuries. Unchanged. Unchanging. Only the normal cycle of the seasons. I'd help the servants pick the apple crop, carrying empty baskets over to them. And then, later, I'd have quite insufferable belly-aches from all the fruit I'd gorged." He laughed, seeing how her eyes had softened as he spoke. "Like any child," he added, after a moment, conscious of the lie, yet thinking of a past where it had really been so. Back before the City, when such childish pleasures were commonplace.

For a moment longer he simply looked at her. Then, smiling, he squeezed her hand gently. "Come. Let's go back."

On the bridge he paused and stood there, looking out across the lake, watching the swans moving on the water, conscious of the warmth of her hand in his own.

"How long this time?" she asked, her voice softer, less insistent than before.

"A week," he said, turning to look at her. "Maybe longer. It depends on whether things keep quiet."

She smiled – the first smile she had given him in weeks.

"That's good, Yuan. I'm tired of being alone. I had too much of it before."

He gave a single nod. "I know. But things will change. I promise you, Fei. It will be better from now on."

She raised her chin, looking at him intently. "I hope so. It's so hard here on my own."

Hard? He looked across the placid lake towards the orchard, wondering what she meant. He saw only softness here. Only respite from the harsh realities of life. From deals and duties. Smelled only the healthy scents of growth.

He smiled and looked at her again. "I decided something, Fei. While I was away."

She looked back at him. "What's that?"

"The boy," he said, placing his hand on her swollen belly once more. "I've decided we'll call him Han."

★ ★ ★

Lehmann woke him, then stood there while he dressed, waiting.

DeVore turned, lacing his tunic. "When did the news break?"

"Ten minutes back. They've cleared all channels pending the announcement. Wei Feng is to speak."

DeVore raised an eyebrow. "Not Li Shai Tung?" He laughed. "Good. That shows how much we've rattled him." He turned, glancing across the room at the timer on the wall, then looked back at Lehmann. "Is that the time?"

Lehmann nodded.

DeVore looked down thoughtfully. It was almost four hours since the attacks. He had expected them to react quicker than this. But that was not what was worrying him.

"Has Wiegand reported back?"

"Not yet."

DeVore went into the adjoining room and sat in the chair, facing the big screen, his fingers brushing the controls on the chair's arm to activate it. Lehmann came and stood behind him.

The *Ywe Lung* – the wheel of dragons, symbol of the Seven – filled the screen. So it did before every official announcement, but this time the backdrop to the wheel was white, signifying death.

Throughout Chung Kuo, tens of billions would be sitting before their screens, waiting pensively, speculating about the meaning of this break in regular programming. It had been a common feature of the War-that-wasn't-a-War, but the screens had been empty of such announcements for some while. That would give it added flavour.

He looked back at Lehmann. "When Wiegand calls in, have him switched through. I want to know what's been going on. He should have reported back to me long before this."

"I've arranged it already."

"Good." He turned back, smiling, imagining the effect this was having on the Seven. They would be scurrying about like termites into whose nest a great stick had just been poked; firing off orders here, there and everywhere; readying themselves against further attacks; not knowing where the next blow might fall.

Things had been quiet these last few months. Deliberately so, for he had wanted to lull the Seven into a false sense of security before he struck. It was not the act itself but the context of the act that mattered. In time of war, people's imaginations were dulled by a surfeit of tragedy, but in peacetime such acts took on a dreadful significance. So it was here.

They would expect him to follow up – to strike again while they were in disarray – but this time he wouldn't. Not immediately. He would let things settle before he struck again, choosing his targets carefully, aiming always at maximising the impact of his actions, allowing the Seven to spend their strength fighting shadows while he gathered his. Until their nerves were raw and their will to fight crippled. Then – and only then – would he throw his full strength against them.

He let his head fall back against the thick leather cushioning, relaxing for the first time in days, a sense of well-being flooding through him. Victory would not come overnight, but then that was not his aim. His was a patient game and time was on his side. Each year brought greater problems for Chung Kuo – increased the weight of numbers that lay heavy on the back of government. He had only to wait, like a dog harrying a great stag, nipping at the heels of the beast, weakening it, until it fell.

Martial music played from the speakers on either side of the screen. Then, abruptly, the image changed. The face of Wei Feng, T'ang of East Asia, filled the screen, the old man's features lined with sorrow.

"People of Chung Kuo, I have sad news . . ." he began, the very informality of his words unexpected, the tears welling in the corners of the old man's eyes adding to the immense sense of wounded dignity that emanated from him.

DeVore sat forward, suddenly tense. What had gone wrong?

He listened as Wei Feng spoke of the tragedy that had befallen Bremen, watching the pictures dispassionately, waiting for the old man to add something more – some further piece of news. But there was nothing. Nothing at all. And then Wei Feng was done and the screen cleared, showing the *Ywe Lung* with its pure white backdrop.

DeVore sat there a moment longer, then pulled himself up out of the chair, turning to face Lehmann.

"They didn't do it . . . The bastards didn't do it!"

He was about to say something more, when the panel on his desk began to flash urgently. He switched the call through, then turned, resting on the edge of the desk, facing the screen.

He had expected Wiegand. But it wasn't Wiegand's face that filled the screen. It was Hans Ebert.

"What in hell's name has been happening, Howard? I've

49

just had to spend two hours with the Special Investigation boys being grilled! Bremen, for the gods' sakes! The stupid bastards attacked Bremen!"

DeVore looked down momentarily. He had deliberately not told Ebert anything about their designs on Bremen, knowing that Tolonen would screen all his highest ranking officers – even his future son-in-law – for knowledge of the attack. Caught out once that way, Tolonen's first thought would be that he had once again been infiltrated at staff level. It did not surprise him, therefore, to learn that Tolonen had acted so quickly.

"I know," he said simply, meeting Ebert's eyes.

"What do you mean, you *know*? Were you involved in that?"

Ignoring Ebert's anger, he nodded, speaking softly, quickly, giving his reasons. But Ebert wasn't to be placated so simply.

"I want a meeting," Ebert said, his eyes blazing. "*Today!* I want to know what else you've got planned."

DeVore hesitated, not for the first time finding Ebert's manner deeply offensive, then nodded his agreement. Ebert was too important to his plans just now. He needn't tell him everything, of course. Just enough to give him the illusion of being trusted.

"Okay. This afternoon," DeVore said, betraying nothing of his thoughts. "At Mu Chua's. I'll see you there, Hans. After fourth bell."

He broke contact, then sat back.

"Damn him!" he said, worried that he had still heard nothing. He turned. "Stefan! Find out where the hell Wiegand is. I want to know what's been happening."

He watched the albino go, then looked about the room, his sense of well-being replaced by a growing certainty.

Lehmann confirmed it moments later. "Wiegand's dead," he said, coming back into the room. "Along with another fifty of our men and more than a hundred and fifty *Ping Tiao*."

DeVore sat down heavily. "What happened?"

Lehmann shook his head. "That's all we know. We've intercepted Security reports from the Poznan and Krakov garrisons. It looks like they knew we were coming."

DeVore looked down. Gods! Then the harvest was untouched, City Europe's vast granaries still intact. He could not have had worse news.

He shuddered. This changed things dramatically. What had been designed to weaken the Seven had served only to make them more determined.

He had known all along what the probable effect of a single strike against Bremen would have. Had known how outraged people would be by the assault on the soldiers' living quarters – the killing of innocent women and children. That was why he had planned the two things to hit them at the same time. With the East European Plantations on fire and the safe haven of Bremen breached, he had expected to sow the seeds of fear in City Europe. But fear had turned to anger, and what ought to have been a devastating psychological blow for the Seven had been transformed into its opposite.

No wonder Wei Feng had spoken as he had. That sense of great moral indignation the old man had conveyed had been deeply felt. And there was no doubting that the watching billions would have shared it. So now the Seven had the support of the masses of Chung Kuo. Sanction, if they wanted it, to take whatever measures they wished against their enemies.

DeVore sighed and looked down at his hands. No. Things could not have turned out worse.

But how? How had they known? Despair turned to sudden anger in him. He stood abruptly. Wiegand! It had to be Wiegand! Which meant that the report of his death was false; a fabrication put out for them to overhear. Which meant . . .

For a moment he followed the chain of logic that led out from that thought, then sat again, shaking his head. No, not Wiegand. His instinct was against it. In any case,

Wiegand didn't have either the balls or the imagination for such a thing. And yet, if not Wiegand, then who?

Again he sighed, deciding to put the base on full alert. In case he was wrong. In case Wiegand had made a deal and was planning to lead Tolonen back here to the Wilds.

★ ★ ★

Emily Ascher was angry. Very angry. She trembled as she faced her four compatriots on the central committee of the *Ping Tiao*, her arm outstretched, her finger stabbing towards Gesell, the words spat out venomously.

"What you did was *vile*, Bent. You've tainted us all. Betrayed us."

Gesell glanced at Mach then looked back at his ex-lover, his whole manner defensive. The failure of the attack on the Plantations had shaken him badly and he was only now beginning to understand what effect the Bremen backlash would have on their organisation. Even so, he was not prepared to admit he had been wrong.

"I knew you'd react like this. It's exactly why we had to keep it from you. You would have vetoed it . . ."

She gave a high-pitched laugh, astonished by him. "Of *course* I would! And rightly so. This could destroy us . . ."

Gesell lifted his hand, as if to brush aside the accusation of her finger. "You don't understand. If our attack on the plantations had succeeded . . ."

She batted his hand away angrily. "No. I understand things perfectly. This was a major policy decision and I wasn't consulted." She turned her head, looking across at the other woman in the room. "And you, Mao Liang? Were *you* told?"

Mao Liang looked down, shaking her head, saying nothing. But that wasn't so surprising: since she had replaced Emily in Gesell's bed, it was as if she had lost her own identity.

She looked back at Gesell, shaking her head slowly. "I understand, all right. It's back to old patterns. Old men meeting in closed rooms, deciding things for others." She uffed; a sound of pure disgust. "You know, I really believed we were beyond all that. But it was all lip-service, wasn't it, Bent? All the time you were fucking me, you really despised me as a person . . . After all, I was only a woman. An inferior being. Not to be trusted with *serious* matters."

"You're wrong . . ." Gesell began, stung by her words, but she shook her head, denying him.

"I don't know how you've the face to tell me I'm wrong after what you've done." She turned slightly. "And you, Mach. I know this was all your idea."

Mach was watching her, his eyes narrowed slightly. "There was good reason not to involve you. You were doing so well at recruiting new members."

Again she laughed, not believing what she was hearing. "And what's that worth now? All that hard work, and now you've pissed it all away. My word. I gave them my word as to what we were, and you've shat on it."

"We're *Ko Ming*," Gesell began, a slight edge to his voice now. "Revolutionaries, not fucking hospital workers. You can't change things and have clean hands. It isn't possible!"

She stared back at him witheringly. "*Murderers*, that's what they're calling us. Heartless butchers. And who can blame them? We destroyed any credibility we had last night."

"I disagree."

She turned, looking at Mach. "You can disagree as much as you like, Jan Mach, but it's true. As of last night this organisation is dead. You killed it. You and this prick here. Didn't you see the trivee pictures of the children who died? Didn't you see the shots of those beautiful, blond-haired children playing with their mothers? Didn't something in you respond to that?"

"Propaganda . . ." began Quinn, the newest of them, but a look from Gesell silenced him.

Ascher looked from one to the other of them, seeing how they avoided her eyes. "No? Isn't there one of you with the guts to admit it? *We* did that. The *Ping Tiao*. And this time there's nothing we can do to repair the damage We're fucked."

"No," Mach said. "There is a way."

She snorted. "You're impossible! What way? What could we possibly do that could even begin to balance things in our favour?"

"Wait and see," Mach said, meeting her eyes coldly. "Just wait and see."

$$\star \quad \star \quad \star$$

DeVore sat back on the sofa, looking about him at the once opulently furnished room, noting how the fabrics had worn, the colours faded since he had last come here. He picked up one of the cushions beside him and studied it a moment, reading the Mandarin pictograms sewn into the velvet. *Here men forget their cares.* He smiled. So it was once. But now?

He looked up as Mu Chua entered, one of her girls following with a fully laden tray. She smiled at him, lines tightening about her eyes and at the corners of her mouth.

"I thought you might like some *ch'a* while you were waiting, *Shih* Reynolds."

He sat forward, giving the slightest bow of his head. "That's kind of you, Mother."

As the girl knelt and poured the *ch'a*, DeVore studied Mu Chua. She too was much older, much more worn than he remembered her. In her sixties now, she seemed drawn, the legendary ampleness of her figure a thing of the past. Death showed itself in her: in the sudden angularity of her limbs and the taut wiriness of her muscles; in the slackness of the flesh at neck and arm and breast. He had known her in better days, though it was unlikely she remembered him.

She was watching him, as if aware of how he looked at her. Even so, when she spoke again, her smile returned, as strong as ever. He smiled back at her. Though the body failed, the spirit lived on, in spite of all she'd suffered.

"Shall I let him know you're here?"

He shook his head, then took the offered bowl from the
rl. "No, Mu Chua. I'll wait."

She hesitated, her eyes flicking to the girl then back to
m. "In that case, is there anything you'd like?"

Again he smiled. "No. Though I thank you. Just let him
ow I'm here. When he's done, that is."

He watched her go, then looked about him, wondering.
u Chua's old protector, the Triad boss, Feng Chung,
d died three years back, leaving a power vacuum down
re below the Net. Rival Triads had fought a long and
oody war for the dead man's territory, culminating in
e victory of Lu Ming-Shao, or "Whiskers Lu" as he was
tter known. No respecter of fine detail, Lu had claimed
u Chua's House of the Ninth Ecstasy as his own, letting
u Chua stay on as Madam, nominally in charge of
ings. But the truth was that Lu ran things his way these
ys, using Mu Chua's as a clearing house for drugs and
her things, as well as for entertaining his Above clients.

Things had changed, and in the process Mu Chua's had
st its shine. The girls here were no longer quite so care-
e, and violence, once banned from the house, was now
regular feature of their lives.

So the world changes, thought DeVore, considering
hether he should make Whiskers Lu an offer for the place.

"Has something amused you?"

He turned sharply, surprised that he'd not heard Ebert
ter, then saw that the Major was bare-footed, a silk *pau*
awn loosely about his otherwise naked body.

DeVore set the *ch'a* bowl down beside him and stood,
cing Ebert.

"I thought you were in a hurry to see me?"

Ebert smiled and walked past him, pulling at the bell
pe to summon one of the girls. He turned back, the smile
ll on his lips. "I was. But I've had time to think things
rough." He laughed softly. "I ought to thank you,
oward. You knew that Tolonen would screen his staff
ficers, didn't you?"

DeVore nodded.

55

"I thought so."

There was a movement to their right, a rustling of the curtains, and then a girl entered, her head lowered. "You called, Masters?"

"Bring us a bottle of your best wine and two . . ." he looked at DeVore, then corrected himself, "no, make that just one glass."

When she was gone, DeVore looked down, for the first time letting his anger show.

"What the fuck are you up to, Hans?"

Ebert blinked, surprised by DeVore's sudden hostility. Then, bridling, he turned, facing him. "What do you mean?"

"I ought to kill you."

"Kill me? Why?"

"For what you did. It didn't take much to piece it together. There was really no other possibility. No one else knew enough about our plans to attack the Plantations. It had to be you who blew the whistle."

Ebert hesitated. "Ah . . . that." Then, unbelievably, he gave a little laugh. "I'm afraid I had to, Howard. One of our captains got a whiff of things. If it had been one of my own men I could have done something about it, but the man had already put in his report. I had to act quickly. If they'd taken them alive . . ."

DeVore was breathing strangely, as if preparing to launch himself at the bigger man.

"I'm sure you see it, Howard," Ebert continued, looking away from him. "It's like in *wei chi*. You have to sacrifice a group sometimes, for the sake of the game. Well, it was like that. It was either act or lose the whole game. I did it for the best."

You did it to save your own arse, thought DeVore, calming himself, trying to keep from killing Ebert there and then. It wouldn't do to be too hasty. And maybe Ebert was right, whatever his real motive. Maybe it had prevented a far worse calamity. At least the fortresses were safe. But it still left him with the problem of dealing with the *Ping Tiao*.

"So Wiegand's dead?"

Ebert nodded. "I made sure of that myself."

Yes, he thought. I bet you did. He forced himself to unclench his fists, then turned away. It was the closest he had come to losing control. Don't let it get to you, he told himself, but it did no good. There was something about Ebert that made him want to let fly, whatever the consequences. But no – that was Tolonen's way, not his. It was what made the old man so weak. And Ebert, too. But he was not like that. He used his anger; made it work *for* him, not against him.

The girl brought the wine, then left them. As Ebert turned to pour, DeVore studied him, wondering, not for the first time, what Hans Ebert would have been had he not been born heir to GenSyn. A low-level bully, perhaps. A hireling of some bigger, more capable man, but essentially the same callous, selfish type, full of braggadocio, his dick bigger than his brain.

Or was that fair? Wasn't there also something vaguely heroic about Ebert – something that circumstance might have moulded otherwise? Was it his fault that he had been allowed everything, denied nothing?

He watched Ebert turn, smiling, and nodded to himself. Yes, it *was* his fault. Ebert was a weak man, beneath it all, and his weakness had cost them dear. He would pay for it. Not now – he was needed now – but later, when he had served his purpose.

"*Kan pei!*" Ebert said, raising his glass. "Anyway, Howard. I've better news."

DeVore narrowed his eyes. What else had Ebert been up to?

Ebert drank heavily from his glass, then sat, facing DeVore. "You're always complaining about being underfunded. Well . . ." his smile broadened, as if at his own cleverness, "I've found us some new backers. Acquaintances of mine."

"Acquaintances?"

Ebert laughed. "Friends . . . People sympathetic to what we're doing."

DeVore felt the tension creep back into his limbs. "What have you said?"

Ebert's face cleared, became suddenly sharper. "Oh, nothing specific, don't worry. I'm not stupid. I sounded them first. Let them talk. Then, later on, I spoke to them in private. These are people I trust, you understand? People I've known a long time."

DeVore took a long breath. Maybe, but he would check them out himself. Thoroughly. Because, when it came down to it, he didn't trust Ebert's judgment.

"What sums are you talking about?"

"Enough to let you finish building your fortresses."

DeVore gave a small laugh. Did Ebert know how much that was, or was he just guessing? One thing was certain: he had never told Hans Ebert how much even one of the great underground fortresses cost.

"That's good, Hans. I'll have to meet these friends of yours."

* * *

Mu Chua closed the door behind her, furious with Ebert. She had seen the bruises on the girl's arms and back. The bastard! There'd been no need. The girl was only fourteen. If he'd wanted that he should have said. She'd have sent in one of the older girls. They, at least, were hardened to it.

She stood still, closing her eyes, calming down. He would be out to see her any moment and it wouldn't do to let him see how angry she was. Word could get back to Lu Ming-Shao, and then there'd be hell to pay.

She shuddered. Life here could still be sweet – some days – but too often it was like today: a brutish struggle simply to survive.

She went to her desk and busied herself, making out his bill, charging him for the two sessions and for the wine and *ch'a*. She paused, frowning, as she thought of his guest.

There was something strangely familiar about *Shih* Reynolds – as if they'd met some time in the past – but she couldn't place him. He seemed a nice enough man, but could that really be said of anyone who associated with that young bastard? For once she wished she had overheard what they were talking about. She could have – after all, Lu Ming-Shao had put in the surveillance equipment only four months back – but a lifetime's habits were hard to break. She had never spied on her clients and she didn't intend to start now; not unless Lu specifically ordered her to.

Mu Chua froze, hearing Ebert's voice outside, then turned in time to greet him as he came through the door into her office.

"Was it everything you wished for, Master?"

He laughed and reached out to touch her breast familiarly. "It was *good*, Mu Chua. Very good. I'd forgotten how good a house you run."

Her smile widened, though inside she felt something shrivel up at his touch. Few men touched her these days, preferring younger flesh than hers; even so there was something horrible about the thought of being used by him.

"I'm pleased," she said, bowing her head. "Here," she said, presenting her bill, the figures written in Mandarin on the bright red paper.

He smiled and, without looking at the bill, handed her a single credit chip. She looked down, then bowed her head again.

"Why, thank you, Master. You are too generous."

He laughed, freeing her breasts from her robe and studying them a moment. Then, as if satisfied, he turned to go.

"Forgive me, Major Ebert . . ." she began, taking a step towards him.

He stopped and turned. "Yes, Mother Chua?"

"I was wondering . . . about the girl."

Ebert frowned. "The girl?"

Mu Chua averted her eyes. "Golden Heart. You

remember, surely? The thirteen-year-old you bought here. That time you came with the other soldiers."

He laughed; a strangely cold laugh. "Ah, yes . . . I'd forgotten that I got her here."

"Well?"

He looked at her, then turned away, impatient now. "Look, I'm busy, Mu Chua. I'm Major now, I have my duties . . ."

She looked at him desperately, then bowed her head again, her lips formed into a smile. "Of course. Forgive me, Major." But inwardly she seethed. Busy! Not too busy, it seemed, to spend more than two hours fucking her girls!

As the door closed behind him she spat at the space where he had been standing, then stood there, tucking her breasts back inside her robe, watching her spittle dribble slowly down the red, lacquered surface of the door.

"You bastard," she said softly. "I only wanted a word. Just to know how she is – whether she's still alive."

She looked down at the credit in her hand. It was for a thousand *yuan* – more than four times what she had billed him for – but he had treated it as nothing.

Perhaps that's why, she thought, closing her hand tightly over it. *You have no values because you don't know what anything is really worth. You think you can buy anything.*

Well, maybe he could. Even so, there was something lost in being as he was. He lacked decency.

She went to the drawer of her desk and pulled out the strong box, opening it with the old-fashioned key that hung about her neck. Rummaging about amongst the credit chips she found two for two hundred and fifty *yuan* and removed them, replacing them with Ebert's thousand. Then, smiling to herself, she felt amongst her underclothes and, after wetting herself with her finger, placed the two chips firmly up her clout.

She had almost saved enough now. Almost. Another month – two at the most – and she could get out of here. Away from Whiskers Lu and bastards like Ebert. And maybe she would go into business on her own again. For, after all, men were always men. They might talk and dress differently up there, but beneath it all they were the same creatures.

She laughed, wondering suddenly how many *li* of First Level cock she'd had up her in the fifty years she had been in the business. No. In that respect, nothing ever changed. They might talk of purity, but their acts always betrayed them. It was why she had thrived over the years – because of that darkness they all carried about in them. Men. They might all say they were above it, but, try as they would, it was the one thing they could not climb the levels to escape.

★　★　★

Fei Yen stood there before him, her silk robes held open, revealing her nakedness.

"Please, Yuan . . . It won't hurt me."

His eyes went to her breasts, traced the swollen curve of her belly, then returned to her face. He wanted her so much that it hurt, but there was the child to think of.

"*Please* . . ."

The tone in her voice, the *need* expressed in it, made him shiver then reach out to touch her. "The doctors . . ." he began, but she was shaking her head, her eyes – those beautiful, liquid-dark eyes of hers – pleading with him.

"What do they know? Can they feel what I feel? No . . . So come, Yuan. Make love to me. Don't you know how much I've missed you?"

He shuddered, feeling her fingers on his neck, then nodded, letting her undress him, but he still felt wrong about it.

"I could have hurt you . . ." he said, lying beside her afterwards, his hand caressing her stomach tenderly.

She took his hand and held it still. "Don't be silly. I'd have told you if it hurt." She gave a little shudder, then looked down, smiling. "Besides, I want our child to be

61

lusty, don't you? I want him to know that his mother is loved."

Her eyes met his provocatively, then looked away.

* * *

Tolonen bowed deeply, then stepped forward, handing Li Shai Tung the report Hans Ebert had prepared on the planned attack on the Plantations.

"It's all here?" the T'ang asked, his eyes meeting Tolonen's briefly before they returned to the opening page of the report.

"Everything we discussed, *Chieh Hsia*."

"And copies have gone to all the generals?"

"And to their T'ang, no doubt."

Li Shai Tung smiled bleakly. "Good." He had been closeted with his Ministers since first light and had had no time to refresh his mind about the details. Now, in the few minutes that remained to him before the Council of the Seven met, he took the time to look through the file.

Halfway through he looked up. "You know, Knut, sometimes I wish I could direct input all this. It would make things so much easier."

Tolonen smiled, tracing the tiny slot behind his ear with his right index finger, then shook his head. "It would not be right to break with tradition, *Chieh Hsia*. Besides, you have servants and Ministers to assist you in such matters."

Yes, thought the T'ang, and as you've so often said, it would only be another way in which my enemies could get to me. I've heard they can do it now. Programmes that destroy the mind's ability to reason. Like the food I eat, it would need to be "tasted". No, perhaps you're right, Knut Tolonen. It would only build more walls between Chung Kuo and I, and the gods know there are enough already.

He finished the document quickly, then closed it, looking back at Tolonen. "Is there anything else?"

Tolonen paused, then lowered his voice slightly. "One thing, *Chieh Hsia*. In view of how things are developing, shouldn't we inform Prince Yuan?"

Li Shai Tung considered a moment, then shook his head. "No, Knut. Yuan has worked hard these last few weeks. He needs time with that wife of his." He smiled, his own tiredness showing at the corners of his mouth. "You know how Yuan is. If he knew, he would be back here instantly, and there's nothing he can really do to help. So let it be. If I need him, I'll instruct Master Nan to brief him fully. Until then, let him rest."

"*Chieh Hsia.*"

Li Shai Tung watched his old friend stride away, then turned, pulling at his beard thoughtfully. The session ahead was certain to be difficult and it might have helped to have had Yuan at his side, but he remembered the last time, when Wang Sau-leyan had insisted on the princes leaving. Well, he would give him no opportunity to pull such strokes this time. It was too important. For what he was about to suggest . . .

He shuddered. Twenty years too late, it was. He knew that now. Knew how vulnerable they had become in that time. But it had to be said, even if it split the Council. Because unless it was faced – and faced immediately – there could be no future for them.

He looked about him at the cold grandeur of the marble hallway, his eyes coming to rest on the great wheel of the *Ywe Lung* carved into the huge double doors, then shook his head. This was the turning point. Whatever they decided today, there was no turning back from this, no further chance to right things. The cusp was upon them. And beyond?

Li Shai Tung felt a small ripple of fear pass down his spine, then turned and went across to the great doorway, the four shaven-headed guards bowing low before they turned and pushed back the heavy doors.

* * *

Wei Feng, T'ang of East Asia, sat forward in his chair and looked about him at the informal circle of his fellow T'ang, his face stern, his whole manner immensely dignified. It

63

was he who had called this emergency meeting of the Council; he who, as the most senior of the Seven, hosted it now, at his palace of Chung Ning in Ning Hsia province. Seeing him lean forward, the other T'ang fell silent, waiting for him to speak.

"Well, cousins, we have all read the reports, and I think we would all agree that a major disaster was only narrowly averted, thanks to the quick action of Li Shai Tung's Security forces. A disaster which, whilst its immediate consequences would have befallen one of our number alone, would have damaged every one of us, for are not the seven One and the one Seven?"

There was nodding from all quarters, even from Wang Sau-leyan. Wei Feng looked about him, satisfied, then spoke again.

"It is, of course, why we are here today. The attack on Bremen and the planned attacks on the East European Plantations are significant enough in themselves, but they have far wider implications. It is to these wider implications – to the underlying causes and the long-term prospects for Chung Kuo – that we must address ourselves."

Wei Feng looked briefly to his old friend, Li Shai Tung, then lifted one hand from the arm of his chair, seventy-five years of command forming that tiny, almost effortless gesture. All of his long experience, the whole majesty of his power was gathered momentarily in his raised hand, while his seated form seemed to emanate an aura of solemn purpose and iron-willed determination. His eyes traced the circle of his fellow T'ang.

"These are special circumstances, my cousins. Very special. I can think of no occasion on which the threat to the stability of Chung Kuo has been greater than it is now."

There was a low murmur of agreement, a nodding of heads. To Li Shai Tung it felt suddenly like old times, with the Council as one not merely in its policy but in its sentiments. He looked across at Wang Sau-leyan and saw how the young T'ang of Africa was watching him, his

64

eyes filled with a sympathetic understanding. It was unexpected, but not, when he considered it, surprising, for this – as Wei Feng had said – threatened them all. If some good were to come of all that horror, let it be this – that it had served to unify the Seven.

He looked back at Wei Feng, listening.

"Not even in the darkest days of the War was there a time when we did not believe in the ultimate and inevitable triumph of the order which we represent. But can we say so with such confidence today? Bremen was more than a tragedy for all those who lost friends and family in the attack – it was a show of power. A statement of potentiality. What *we* must discover is this: who wields that power? What is that potentiality? The very fact that we cannot answer these questions immediately concerns me, for it indicates just how much we have lost control of things. For Bremen to have happened . . . it ought to have been unthinkable. But now we must face facts – must begin to think the unthinkable."

Wei Feng turned slightly, the fingers of his hand opening out, pointed towards Li Shai Tung.

"Cousins! It is time to say openly what has hitherto remained unexpressed. Li Shai Tung, will you begin?"

Their eyes turned to the T'ang of Europe expectantly.

"Cousins," Li Shai Tung began softly. "I wish I had come to you in better days and spoken of these things, rather than have had adversity push me to it. But you must understand that what I say here today is no hasty, ill-considered reaction to Bremen, but has matured in me over many years. Forgive me also if what I say seems at times to border on a lecture. It is not meant so, I assure you. Yet it seemed to me that I must set these things out clearly before you, if only to see whether my eyes, my brain deceived me in this matter, or whether my vision and my reason hold good."

"We are listening, cousin Li," Tsu Ma said, his expression willing Li Shai Tung to go on – to say what had to be said.

Li Shai Tung looked about him, seeing that same encouragement mirrored in the faces of the other T'ang, even in the pallid, moon-like face of Wang Sau-leyan. "Very well," he said, keeping his eyes on Wang Sau-leyan, "but you must hear me out."

"Of course," Wei Feng said quickly, wanting to smooth over any possibility of friction between the two T'ang. "There will be ample time afterwards to discuss these matters fully. So speak out, Shai Tung. We are all ears."

He looked down, searching inside himself for the right words, knowing there was no easy way to put it. Then, looking up, his face suddenly set, determined, he began.

"You have all read Major Ebert's report, so you understand just how close the *Ping Tiao* came to succeeding in their scheme to destroy large areas of the East European Plantations. What you haven't seen, however, is a second report I commissioned. A report to ascertain the probable economic and social consequences had the *Ping Tiao* succeeded."

He saw how they looked among themselves and knew that the matter had been in all their minds.

"It was, of necessity, a hastily compiled report, and I have since commissioned another to consider the matter in much greater detail. However, the results of that first report make fascinating and – without exaggerating the matter – frightening reading. Before I come to those results, however, let me undertake a brief résumé of the situation with regard to food production and population increase over the past fifteen-year period."

He saw how Wang Sau-leyan looked down and felt his stomach tighten, instinct telling him he would have to fight the younger T'ang on this. Well, so be it. It was too important a matter to back down over.

He cleared his throat. "Back in 2192 the official population figure for the whole of Chung Kuo was just short of thirty-four billion – a figure which excluded, of course, the populations of both Net and Clay. I mention this fact because, whilst the figure for the Clay might, with good reason, be overlooked, that for the Net cannot. The relationship of Net to City is an important one economically, particularly in terms of food production, for whilst we have no jurisdiction over the Net, we nonetheless produce all the food consumed there.

"Unofficial estimates for 2192 placed the population of the Net at just over three billion. However, the growing number of demotions over the period, added to an ever-increasing birth-rate down there have given rise to latest estimates of at least twice that number, with the highest estimate indicating a below-Net population of eight billion.

"Over the same period the population of the City has also climbed, though not with anything like the same rate of growth. The census of 2200 revealed a rounded-up figure of 37.8 billion – a growth rate of just under half a billion a year."

Li Shai Tung paused, recalling the reports his father had once shown him from more than two hundred years ago – World Population Reports compiled by an ancient body called the United Nations. They had contained an underlying assumption that, as Man's material condition improved, so his numbers would stabilise, but the truth was otherwise. One law alone governed the growth of numbers – the capacity of Humankind to feed itself. As health standards had improved, so infant mortality rates had plummeted. At the same time life expectancy had increased dramatically. With vast areas of the City being opened up yearly, the population of Chung Kuo had grown exponentially for the first century of the City's existence. It had doubled, from four to eight billion, from eight to sixteen, then from sixteen to thirty-two, each doubling a matter of only thirty years. Against such vast and unchecked growth the United Nations' estimate of the world's population stabilising at 10.2 billion was laughable. What had happened was more like the ancient tale of the Emperor and the *wei chi* board.

In the tale the Emperor had granted the peasant his wish

– for one grain of rice on the first square of the board,
twice as much on the second, twice as much again on the
third and so on – not realising how vast the final total was,
how far beyond his means to give. So it was with the
Seven. They had guaranteed the masses of Chung Kuo
unlimited food, shelter and medical care, with no check
upon their numbers. It was madness. A madness that could
be tolerated no longer.

He looked about him; saw how they were waiting for
him, as if they knew where his words led.

"That rate of growth has not, thankfully, maintained
itself over the last seven years. However, births are still
outstripping deaths by two to one, and the current figure
of thirty-nine and a half billion is still enough to cause us
major concern, particularly in view of the growing problems with food production."

So here he was, at last, speaking about it.

He looked across at Wu Shih, then back to Tsu Ma,
seeing how tense his fellow T'ang had grown. Even Wei
Feng was looking down, disturbed by the direction Li Shai
Tung's words had taken. He pressed on.

"As you know, for the past twenty years I have been
trying to anticipate these problems – to find solutions without taking what seems to me now the inevitable step. The
number of orbital farms, for instance, has been increased
eight hundred per cent in the past fifteen years, resulting
in fifty-five per cent of all Chung Kuo's food now being
grown off-planet. That success, however, has caused us
new problems. There is the danger of cluttering up the
skies; the problem of repairing and maintaining such vast
and complex machineries; the need to build at least four
and possibly as many as twelve new spaceports, capacity
at the present ports being strained to the limit. Added to
this, the cost of ferrying down the produce; of processing
it and distributing it has grown year by year. And then, as
we all know, there have been accidents."

He saw, once again, how they looked among themselves. This was the Great Unsaid. If the Seven could be

said to have a taboo it was this – the relationship of food production to population growth. It was Chung Kuo's oldest problem – as old as the First Emperor, Ch'in Shih Huang Ti himself – yet for a century or more they had refused to discuss it, even to mention it. And why? Because that relationship underpinned the one great freedom they had promised the people of Chung Kuo – the one freedom upon which the whole great edifice of Family and Seven depended, *the right to have an unlimited number of children.* Take that away and the belief in Family was undermined; a belief which was sacrosanct – which was the very foundation stone of their great State, for were they not themselves the *fathers* of their people?

Yes. But now that had to change. A new relationship had to be forged, less satisfactory than the old, yet necessary, because without it there would be nothing. No Seven, no State, nothing but anarchy.

"We know these things," he said softly, "yet we say nothing of them. But now it is time to do our sums: to balance the one against the other and see where such figures lead us. All of which brings me back to the report I commissioned and its central question – what would have happened if the *Ping Tiao* had succeeded in their attack on the Plantations?"

"Li Shai Tung . . . ?" It was Wei Feng.

"Yes, cousin?"

"Will we be given copies of this report of yours?"

"Of course."

Wei Feng met his eyes briefly, his expression deeply troubled. "Good. But let me say how . . . unorthodox I find this – to speak of a document none of us has seen. It is not how we normally transact our business."

Li Shai Tung lowered his head, respecting his old friend's feelings. "I understand, cousin, but these are not normal times, nor is this matter . . . orthodox, shall we say. It was simply that I did not feel I could submit such a document for the record. However, when the detailed report is ready I shall ensure each of you receives a copy at once."

Wei Feng nodded, but it was clear he was far from happy with the way things had developed, despite his words about "thinking the unthinkable". Li Shai Tung studied him a moment, trying to gauge how strongly he felt on the matter, then looked away, resuming his speech.

"However, from our first and admittedly hurried estimates, we believe that the *Ping Tiao* attack would have destroyed as much as thirty-five per cent of the East European growing areas. In terms of overall food production this equates with approximately ten per cent of City Europe's total."

He leaned forward slightly.

"Were this merely a matter of percentage reductions the problem would be a relatively minor one – and, indeed, short term, for the growing areas could be redeveloped within three months – but the fact is that we have developed a distribution network that is immensely fragile. If you will forgive the analogy, we are like an army encamped in enemy territory which has tried to keep its supply lines as short as possible. This has meant that food from the Plantations has traditionally been used to feed the eastern *Hsien* of City Europe, while the food brought down from the orbitals – landed in the six spaceports on the west and southern coasts – has been used to feed the west and south of the City. If the Plantations failed it would mean shipping vast amounts of grain, meat and other edibles across the continent. It is not impossible, but it would be difficult to organise and immensely costly."

He paused significantly. "That, however, would be the least of our problems. Because production has not kept pace with population growth, the physical amount of food consumed by our citizenry has dropped considerably over the past fifteen years. On average, people now eat ten per cent less than they did in 2192. To ask them to cut their consumption by a further ten per cent – as we would undoubtedly have to in the short term – would, I am told, return us to the situation we faced a year ago, with wide-spread rioting in the lower levels. The potential damage of that is, as you can imagine, inestimable.

"But let me come to my final point – the point at which my worries become your worries. For what we are really talking of here is not a question of logistics – of finding administrative solutions to large-scale problems – but an on-going situation of destabilisation. Such an attack, we could be certain, would be but the first, and each sub-sequent attack would find us more vulnerable, our resources stretched much further, our options fewer. What we are talking of is a downward spiral with the only end in sight our own. My counsellors estimate that it would need only a twenty-five per cent reduction in food supplies to make City Europe effectively ungovernable. And what can happen in Europe can, I am assured, be duplicated elsewhere. So you see, cousins, this matter has brought to our attention just how vulnerable we are in this, the most important and yet most neglected area of government."

He fell silent, noting the air of uneasiness that had fallen over the meeting. It was Wu Shih, T'ang of North America, who articulated what they were all thinking.

"And what is your answer, Shai Tung?"

Li Shai Tung took a small, shuddering breath then answered. "For too long we have been running hard to try to catch up with ourselves. The time has come when we can do that no longer. Our legs cannot hold us. We must have controls. Now, before it is too late."

"Controls?" Wang Sau-leyan asked, a faint puzzlement in his face.

Li Shai Tung looked back at him, nodding. But even now it was hard to say the words themselves. Hard to throw off the shroud of silence that surrounded this matter and speak of it direct. He raised himself slightly in his chair, then forced himself to say it.

"What I mean is this. We must limit the number of children a man might have."

The silence that greeted his words was worse than

anything Li Shai Tung had ever experienced in Council. He looked to Tsu Ma.

"You see the need, don't you, Tsu Ma?"

Tsu Ma met his eyes firmly, only the faintness of his smile suggesting his discomfort. "I understand your concern, dear friend. And what you said – there is undeniably a deal of truth in it. But is there no other way?"

Li Shai Tung shook his head. "Do you think I would even raise the matter if I thought there were another way? No. We must take this drastic action and take it soon. The only real question is how we go about it, how we can make this great change while maintaining the status quo."

Wei Feng pulled at his beard, disturbed by this talk. "Forgive me, Shai Tung, but I do not agree. You talk of these things as if they *must* come about, but I cannot see that. The attack on the Plantations would, I agree, have had serious repercussions, yet now we are forewarned. Surely we can take measures to prevent further attacks? When you said to me earlier that you wished to take decisive action, I thought you meant something else."

"What else could I have meant?"

Wei Feng's ancient features were suddenly unyielding. "It's obvious, surely, cousin? We must take measures to crush these revolutionaries. Enforce a curfew in the lower levels. Undertake level by level searches. Offer rewards for information on these bastards."

Li Shai Tung looked down. That was not what he meant. The solution was not so simple. The dragon of Change had many heads – cut off one and two more grew in its place. No, they had to be far more radical than that. They had to go to the source of the problem. Right down to the root.

"Forgive me, cousin Feng, but I have already taken such measures as you suggest. I have already authorised young Ebert to strike back at the *Ping Tiao*. But that will do nothing to assuage the problem I was talking of earlier. We must act, before this trickle of revolutionary activity becomes a flood."

Wu Shih was nodding. "I understand what you are say-ing, Shai Tung, but don't you think that your cure might prove more drastic than the disease? After all, there is noth-ing more sacred than a man's right to have children. Threaten that and you might alienate not just the revolu-tionary elements but the whole of Chung Kuo."

"And yet there are precedents."

Wei Feng snorted. "You mean the *Ko Ming* emperors? And where did that end? What did that achieve?"

It was true. Under Mao Tse-tung the *Ko Ming* had tried to solve this problem more than two hundred years before, but their attempt to create the one-child family had had only limited success. It had worked in the towns, but in the countryside the peasants had continued having six, often a dozen, children. And though the situations were far from parallel, the basic underlying attitude was unchanged. Chung Kuo was a society embedded in the concept of the Family, and in the right to have sons. Such a change would need to be enforced.

He looked back at Wu Shih. "There would be trouble, I agree. A great deal of trouble. But nothing like what must ultimately come about if we continue to ignore this problem." He looked about him, his voice raised momen-tarily, passionate in its belief. "Don't you *see* it, any of you? We *must* do this! We have no choice!"

"You wish to put this to a vote, Shai Tung?" Wei Feng asked, watching him through narrowed eyes.

A vote? He had not expected that. All he had wanted was for them to carry the idea forward – to agree to bring the concept into the realm of their discussions. To take the first step. A vote at this stage could prevent all that – could remove the idea from the agenda for good.

He began to shake his head, but Wang Sau-leyan spoke up, taking up Wei Feng's challenge.

"I think a vote would be a good idea, cousins. It would clarify how we feel on this matter. As Shai Tung says, the facts are clear, the problem real. We cannot simply ignore it. I for one support Shai Tung's proposal. Though we must think carefully how and when we introduce such measures, there is no denying the need for their introduction."

Li Shai Tung looked up, astonished. Wang Sau-leyan . . . *supporting* him! He looked across at Tsu Ma, then to Wu Shih. Then perhaps . . .

Wei Feng turned in his chair, facing him. "I take it you support your own proposal, Shai Tung?"

"I do."

"Then that is two for the proposal."

He looked at Wu Shih. The T'ang of North America looked across at Li Shai Tung, then slowly shook his head.

"And one against."

Tsu Ma was next. He hesitated, then nodded his agreement.

"Three for, one against."

Next was Chi Hsing, T'ang of the Australias. "No," he said, looking to Li Shai Tung apologetically. "Forgive me, Shai Tung, but I think Wu Shih is right."

Three for, two against.

On the other side of Wang Sau-leyan sat Hou Tung-po, T'ang of South America, his smooth, unbearded cheeks making him seem even younger than his friend, Wang. Li Shai Tung studied him, wondering if, in this as in most things, he would follow Wang's line.

"Well, Tung-po?" Wei Feng asked. "You have two children now. Two sons. Would you have one of them not exist?"

Li Shai Tung sat forward angrily. "That is unfair, Wei Feng!"

Wei Feng lifted his chin. "Is it? You mean that the Seven would be exceptions to the general rule?"

Li Shai Tung hesitated. He had not considered this. He had thought of it only in general terms.

"Don't you see where all this leads us, Shai Tung?" Wei Feng asked, his voice suddenly much softer, his whole manner conciliatory. "Can't you see the great depth of bitterness such a policy would bring in its wake? You talk of the end of Chung Kuo, of having no alternative, yet in this we truly have no alternative. The freedom to have children – that *must* be sacrosanct. And we must find other solutions, Shai Tung. As we always have. Isn't that the very reason for our existence? Isn't that the *purpose* of the Seven – to keep the balance?"

"And if the balance is already lost?"

Wei Feng looked back at him, a deep sadness in his eyes, then turned, looking back at Hou Tung-po. "Well, Tung-po?"

The young T'ang glanced at Li Shai Tung, then shook his head.

Three for. Three against. And there was no doubt which way Wei Feng would vote. Li Shai Tung shivered. Then the nightmare must come. As sure as he saw it in his dreams, the City falling beneath a great tidal wave of blood. And afterwards?

He thought of the dream his son, Li Yuan, had had, so long ago. The dream of a great white mountain of bones, filling the plain where the City had once stood. He thought of it and shuddered.

"And you, Wei Feng?" he asked, meeting his old friend's eyes, his own lacking all hope.

"I say no, Li Shai Tung. I say no."

* * *

Outside, in the great entrance hall, Tsu Ma drew Li Shai Tung aside, leaning close to whisper to him.

"I wish a word with you, Shai Tung. In private, where no one can overhear us."

Li Shai Tung frowned. This was unlike Tsu Ma. "What is it?"

"In private, please, cousin."

They went into one of the small adjoining rooms and closed the door behind them.

"Well, Tsu Ma? What is it?"

Tsu Ma came and stood very close, keeping his voice

low, the movements of his lips hidden from the view of any overseeing cameras.

"I must warn you, Shai Tung. There is a spy in your household. Someone very close to you."

"A spy?" He shook his head. "What do you mean?"

"I mean just that. A spy. How else do you think Wang Sau-leyan has been able to anticipate you? He knew what you were going to say to the Council. Why else do you think he supported you? Because he knew he could afford to. Because he had briefed those two puppets of his to vote with Wei Feng."

Li Shai Tung stared back at Tsu Ma, astonished not merely at this revelation, but by the clear disrespect he was showing to his fellow T'ang, Hou Tung-po and Chi Hsing.

"How do you know?" he asked, his own voice a hoarse whisper now. It was unheard of. Unthinkàble.

Tsu Ma laughed softly, and leaned even closer. "I have my own spies, Shai Tung. That's how I know."

Li Shai Tung nodded vaguely, but inside he felt a numbness, a real shock, at the implications of what Tsu Ma was saying. For it meant that the Seven could no longer trust each other. Were no longer, in effect, Seven, but merely seven men, pretending to act as one. He shuddered. This was an ill day. He shook his head. "And what . . . ?"

He stopped, turning, as the knocking on the door came again.

"Come in!" said Tsu Ma, stepping back from him.

It was Wei Feng's Chancellor, Ch'in Tao Fan. He bowed low.

"Forgive me, *Chieh Hsia*, but my master asks if you would kindly return. Urgent news has come in. Something he feels you both should see."

They followed Ch'in through, finding the other five T'ang gathered in Wei Feng's study before a huge wallscreen. The picture was frozen. It showed a shaven-headed Han, kneeling, a knife held before him.

"What is this?" Li Shai Tung asked, looking to Wei Feng.

"Watch," Wei Feng answered. "All of you, watch."

As the camera backed away, a large "big-character" poster was revealed behind the kneeling man, its crude message painted in bright red ink on the white in Mandarin, an English translation underneath in black.

PING TIAO INNOCENT
OF BREMEN TRAGEDY
WE OFFER OUR BODIES
IN SYMPATHY WITH
THOSE WHO DIED

The camera focused on the man once more. He was breathing slowly now, gathering himself about the point of his knife. Then, with a great contortion of his features, he cut deep into his belly, drawing the knife slowly, agonisingly across, disembowelling himself.

Li Shai Tung shuddered. *Our* bodies . . . did that mean? He turned to Wei Feng. "How many of them were there?"

"Two, maybe three hundred, scattered throughout the City. But the poster was the same everywhere. It was all very tightly co-ordinated. Their deaths were all within a minute of each other, timed to coincide with the very hour of the original attack."

"And were they all Han?" Tsu Ma asked, his features registering the shock they all felt.

Wei Feng shook his head. "No. They were evenly distributed, Han and *Hung Mao*. Whoever arranged this knew what he was doing. It was quite masterful."

"And a lie," said Wu Shih, angrily.

"Of course. But the masses will see it otherwise. If I had known I would have stopped the pictures going out."

"And the rumours?" Tsu Ma shook his head. "No, you could not have hushed this up, Wei Feng. It would have spread like wildfire. But you are right. Whoever organised this understood the power of the gesture. It has changed things totally. Before it we had a mandate to act as we wished against them. But now . . ."

Li Shai Tung laughed bitterly. "It changes nothing, cousin. I will crush them anyway."

"Is that wise?" Wei Feng asked, looking about him to gauge what the others felt.

"Wise or not, it is how I will act. Unless my cousins wish it otherwise?"

Li Shai Tung looked about him, challenging them, a strange defiance in his eyes, then turned and hurried from the room, his every movement expressive of a barely controlled anger.

"Follow him, Tsu Ma," Wei Feng said, reaching out to touch his arm. "Catch up with him and try to make him see sense. I understand his anger, but you are right – this changes things. You must make him see that."

Tsu Ma smiled, then looked away, as if following Li Shai Tung's progress through the walls. "I will try, Wei Feng. But I promise nothing. Bremen has woken something in our cousin. Something hard and fierce. I fear it will not sleep until he has assuaged it."

"Maybe so. But we must try. For all our sakes."

CHAPTER·2

GODS OF THE FLESH

"Kuan Yin preserve us! What *is* that?"

DeVore turned, looking at his new lieutenant. "Haven't you ever seen one of these, Schwarz?" He stroked the blind snout of the nearest head, the primitive nervous system of the beast responding to the gentleness of his touch. "It's a *jou tung wu*, my friend, a meat-animal."

The *jou tung wu* filled the whole of the left-hand side of the factory floor, its vast pink bulk contained within a rectangular mesh of ice. It was a huge mountain of flesh, a hundred *ch'i* to a side and almost twenty *ch'i* in height. Along one side of it, like the teats of a giant pig, three dozen heads jutted from the flesh: long, eyeless snouts with shovel jaws that snuffled and gobbled in the conveyor-belt trough that moved constantly before them.

The stench of it was overpowering. It had been present even in the lift coming up, permeating the whole of the stack; marking the men who tended it with its rich indelible scent.

The factory was dimly lit, the ceiling somewhere in the darkness high overhead. A group of technicians stood off to one side, talking softly, nervously amongst themselves.

Schwarz shuddered. "Why does it have to be so dark in here?"

DeVore glanced at him. "It's light-sensitive, that's why," he said, as if that were all there was to it, but he didn't like it either. Why had Gesell wanted to meet them here? Was the lighting a factor? Was the bastard planning something?

DeVore looked past Schwarz at Lehmann. "Stefan. Here."

Lehmann came across and stood there silently, like a machine waiting to be instructed.

"I want no trouble here," DeVore said, his voice loud enough to carry to the technicians. "Even if Gesell threatens me, I want you to hold off. Understand me? He'll be angry. Justifiably so. But I don't want to make things any more difficult than they are."

Lehmann nodded and moved back.

There was the sound of a door sliding back at the far end of the factory. A moment later five figures emerged from the shadows. Gesell, the woman, Ascher, and three others – big men they hadn't seen before. Looking at them, DeVore realised they were bodyguards and wondered why Gesell had suddenly found the need to have them.

The *Ping Tiao* leader wasted no time. He strode across and planted himself before DeVore, his legs set apart, his eyes blazing, the three men formed into a crescent at his back menacingly.

"You've got some talking to do this time, *Shih* Turner. And you'd better make it good!"

It was the second time Gesell had threatened DeVore. Schwarz made to take a step forward, but found Lehmann's hand on his arm, restraining him.

"You're upset," DeVore said calmly. "I understand that. It was a fuck-up and it cost us dear. Both of us."

Gesell gave a small laugh of astonishment. "*You*? What did it cost you? Nothing! You made sure you kept your hands clean, didn't you?"

"Are you suggesting that what happened was *my* fault? As I understand it, one of your squads moved into place too early. That tipped off a Security captain. He reported in to his senior commander. At that point the plug had to be pulled. The thing wouldn't have worked. If you calmed down a while and thought it through you'd see that. My man on staff *had* to do what he did. If he hadn't, they'd have been in place, waiting for your assault squads. They'd have taken some of them alive. And then where would you be? They may have been brave men, *Shih* Gesell, but the T'ang's servants have ways of getting information from even the stubbornest of men.

"As for what I lost. I lost a great deal. My fortunes are bound up with yours. Your failure hurt me badly. My backers are very angry."

DeVore fell silent, letting the truth of what he'd said sink in.

Gesell was very agitated, on the verge of striking DeVore, but he had been listening – thinking through what DeVore had been saying – and some part of him knew that it was true. Even so, his anger remained, unassuaged.

He drew his knife. "You unctuous bastard . . ."

DeVore pushed the blade aside. "That'll solve nothing."

Gesell turned away, leaning against the edge of the trough, the *jou tung wu* in front of him. For a moment he stood there, his whole body tensed. Then, in a frenzy of rage, he stabbed at the nearest head, sticking it again and again with his knife, the blood spurting with each angry thrust, the eyeless face lifting in torment, the long mouth shrieking with pain, a shriek that was taken up all along the line of heads, a great ripple running through the vast slab of red–pink flesh.

Gesell shuddered and stepped back, looking about him, his eyes blinking, then threw the knife down. He looked at DeVore blankly, then turned away, while, behind him, the blind snouts shrieked and shrieked, filling the foetid darkness with their distress.

The technicians had held back. Now one of them, appalled by what the *Ping Tiao* leader had done, hurried across, skirting Gesell. He jabbed a needle-gun against the wounded head, then began rubbing salve into the cuts, murmuring to the beast all the while as if it were a child. After a moment the head slumped. Slowly the noise subsided, the heads grew calm again, those nearest falling into a matching stupor.

"Still," DeVore said after a moment, "you've contained

the damage rather well. I couldn't have done better myself."

He saw how Gesell glanced uncertainly at Ascher and knew at once that he'd had nothing to do with the ritual suicides. He was about to make a comment when a voice came from the darkness to his left.

"You liked that? That was my idea."

DeVore turned slowly, recognising Mach's voice. He narrowed his eyes, not understanding. Mach was the last person he would have expected to have tried to save the reputation of the *Ping Tiao*. No. The collapse of the "Levellers" could only bolster the fortunes of his own secret movement-within-a-movement, the *Yu*.

Unless. . . He turned back, watching Gesell's face as Mach came towards him.

Of course! Gesell was out! Mach was now the *de facto* leader of the *Ping Tiao*. It was what he had sensed earlier; why Gesell had been so touchy. Why he had begun to surround himself with thugs. Gesell knew. Even if it hadn't been said, he knew. And was afraid.

Mach seemed taller, broader at the shoulder than before. Then DeVore understood. He was wearing uniform – the uniform of the Security Reserve Corps. His long dark hair was coiled tightly in a bun at the back of his head and he had shaved off the beard he usually wore. He strode across casually, smiling tightly at Gesell, then turned his back on his colleagues.

"You've balls, Turner, I'll grant you that. If I'd been in your shoes, this is the last place I'd have come."

DeVore smiled. "I gambled. Guessed that the surprise of seeing me here would make you listen to me. Even your friend, the hot-head over there."

Gesell glared back at him, but said nothing. It was as if Mach's presence neutralised him.

Mach was nodding. "I'm sorry about that. Bent lets things get on top of him at times. But he's a good man. He wants what I want."

DeVore looked from one to the other, trying to make

out exactly what their new relationship was. But one thing was clear: Mach was number one. He alone spoke for the *Ping Tiao* now. Overnight the illusion of equality – of committee – had dissipated, leaving a naked power struggle. A struggle which Mach had clearly won. But had he won anything of substance? Had he won it only to see the *Ping Tiao* destroyed? If so, he seemed remarkably calm about it.

"And what do you want?" he asked. "Something new, or the same old formula?"

Mach laughed. "Does it matter? Are you interested any longer?"

"I'm here, aren't I?"

Mach nodded, a slightly more thoughtful expression coming to his face. "Yes." Again he laughed. It was strange. He seemed more relaxed than DeVore had ever seen him. A man free of cares, not burdened by them.

"You know, I was genuinely surprised when you contacted us. I wondered what you could possibly want. After Bremen I thought you'd have nothing to do with us. I did what I could to repair the damage, *but* . . ." he shrugged, "well, we all know how it is. We are small fish in the great sea of the people, and if the sea turns against us . . ."

DeVore smiled inwardly. So Mach knew his Mao. But had he Mao's dour patience? Had he the steel in him to wait long years to see his vision made real? His creation of the *Yu* suggested that he had. And that was why he had come. To keep in touch with Mach. To cast off the *Ping Tiao* and take up with the *Yu*. But it seemed that Mach had not yet done with the *Ping Tiao*. Why? Were the *Yu* not ready yet? Did he need the *Ping Tiao* a while longer – as a mask, perhaps, to his other activities?

He looked down, deciding how to play it, then smiled, meeting Mach's eyes again.

"Let's just say that I believe in you, *Shih* Mach. What happened was unfortunate. Tragic, let's say. But not irreparable. We have patience, you and I. The patience to rebuild from the ashes, neh?"

Mach narrowed his eyes. "And you think you can help?"

DeVore reached into his tunic pocket and took out the ten slender chips, handing them across to Mach.

Mach looked at them then laughed. "Half a million *yuan*. And that'll solve all our problems?"

"That and four of my best propaganda men. They'll run a leaflet campaign in the lower levels. They'll reconstruct what happened at Bremen until even the most cynical unbeliever will have it on trust that the Seven butchered fifteen thousand of their own to justify a campaign against the *Ping Tiao*."

Mach laughed. "And you think that will work?"

DeVore shook his head. "No. I *know* it'll work. The Big Lie always does."

"And in return?"

"You attack the Plantations."

Mach's eyes widened. "You're mad. They'll be waiting for us now."

"Like they were at Bremen?"

Mach considered. "I take your point. But not now. We've lost too many men. It'll take time to heal our wounds, and even more to train others to take the place of those we lost."

"How long?"

"A year, perhaps. Six months at the very least."

DeVore shook his head. "Too long. Call it a month and I can promise twenty times the money I've just given you."

Mach's mouth opened slightly, surprised. Then he shook his head. "For once it's not a question of money. Or haven't you heard? The T'ang's men raided more than a dozen of our cells this afternoon. To all intents and purposes the *Ping Tiao* has ceased to exist in large parts of City Europe. Elsewhere we're down to a bare skeleton. That's where I've been, inspecting the damage. Touring the ruins, if you like."

DeVore looked past Mach at the others. No wonder the woman had been so quiet. They had known. Even so, his reasoning remained sound. Until the fortresses were ready, he needed an organisation like the *Ping Tiao* to burrow away at the foundations of the City and keep the Seven under pressure. The *Ping Tiao*, or maybe the *Yu*. When the *Yu* were ready.

He was silent a moment, then nodded. "I see. Then you had best use my men to bolster your numbers, *Shih* Mach. Five hundred should be enough, don't you think? I'll arrange for Schwarz here to report to you two days from now. You'll have command, naturally."

Mach narrowed his eyes. "I don't understand. Why don't you just attack them yourself? I don't see what you get out of doing it this way."

"You don't trust me, then?"

"Damn right, I don't!" Mach laughed and half turned away, then turned back, coming right up close to DeVore. "Okay. Let's have no more games between us, *Major*. I know who you are, and I know what you've done. I've known it some while now. It explains a lot. But this . . . this just doesn't fit together."

DeVore stared back at him, undaunted. Of course he knew. Who did he think let him know?

"Start thinking clearly, Mach. How could I get that many men into position without Security finding out about it? No. I need you, Mach. I need you to find false identities for these men. To find them places to live. To organise things for me. Beyond that we both need this. In my case to placate my backers; to let them see that something real, something tangible is being done against the Seven. You to bring new blood to your movement; to prove that the *Ping Tiao* isn't moribund."

Mach looked away thoughtfully, then nodded. "All right. We'll do as you say. But I want the funds up front, and I want them three days from now. As token of your good faith."

It would be difficult, but not impossible. In any case, Ebert would pay. He'd fucked things up, so he could foot the bill.

DeVore offered his hand. "Agreed."

Mach hesitated, then took his hand. "Good. Three days then. I'll let you know where we'll meet and when."

As he made his way back to the transporter, DeVore considered what had been said and done. Whatever happened now, Gesell was dead. After the raid on the Plantations if necessary, but before if it could be arranged. That was the last time he would put himself at risk with that fool.

He smiled. It had all seemed very bleak yesterday, when the news had first broken, but it was going to be all right. Maybe even better than before, in fact, because this gave him a chance to work much closer with Mach. To make him his tool.

In that Mach and the *jou tung wu* were alike. Neither was conscious of the role they served. Of how they were fattened only to be slaughtered. For that was their ultimate purpose in life. To eat shit and feed others. The *jou tung wu* to feed the *mei yu jen wen*, the "sub-humans" of the City, and Mach – a finer, tastier meat – to feed himself.

He laughed. *Yes, Mach, I mean to eat you. To make your skull my rice bowl and feast upon your brains. Because that's how it is in this little world of ours. It's man eat man, and always has been.*

He slowed as he came closer to the transporter, checking for signs that anything was wrong, then, satisfied, he ducked inside, leaving his lieutenants to follow in the second craft.

He sat down at once, strapping himself in, the craft rising steeply even before the door was fully closed, the pilot following his earlier instructions to the letter, making sure there was no possibility of pursuit, no chance of ambush.

As the ground fell away he smiled, thinking of the equation he had made in his head. Yes, they were all meat-animals, every last one of them, himself included. But he could dream. Ah yes, he could dream. And in his dreams he saw them – finer, cleaner beasts, all trace of grossness excised from their natures. Tall, slender creatures, sculpted like glass yet hard as steel. Creatures of ice, designed to survive the very worst the universe could throw at them. Survivors.

No . . . More than that. Inheritors.

He laughed. That was it – the name he had been looking for. *Inheritors*. He keyed the word into his wrist set, then closed his eyes and let his head fall back, relaxing.

Yes. Inheritors. But first he must destroy what stopped them from coming into being. In that, Tsao Ch'un had been right. The new could not come into being while the old remained. His inheritors could not stand tall and straight in that cramped little world of levels. So the old must go. The levels must be levelled, the walls torn down, the universe opened up again. In order that they might exist. In order that things could go forward again – onward to that ultimate of mind's total control of matter. Only then could they stop. Only then could there be surcease.

He shivered. That was the dream. The reason, no, the motivating force behind each action that he took – the dark wind blowing hard and cold at his back. To bring them into being. Creatures of ice. Creatures *better* than himself. What finer aim was there? What *finer* aim?

* * *

Hans Ebert stopped in the doorway, lowering his head in a bow of respect, then came on, the fully laden tray held out before him. As he came near, Nocenzi, Tolonen and the T'ang moved back slightly, letting him put it down in the space they had cleared. They had been closeted together three hours now, discussing the matter of reprisals and the new Security measures.

Li Shai Tung smiled, accepting a bowl of *ch'a* from the young Major. "You shouldn't have, Hans. I would have sent a servant."

Ebert's head remained lowered a moment longer. "You were in deep discussion, *Chieh Hsia*. I felt it best to see to things myself."

The old T'ang laughed softly. "Well, Hans, I'm glad

you did. I did not realise how much time had passed, nor how thirsty I had grown."

The T'ang made to sip from the bowl, but Ebert cleared his throat. "Forgive me, *Chieh Hsia*. But if you'd permit me?"

Li Shai Tung frowned, then saw what Ebert meant. He handed him the bowl, then watched as the young man sipped, then wiped where his lips had touched with a cloth before handing back the bowl.

The T'ang looked to Tolonen and Nocenzi and saw how his own pleasure was mirrored in their faces. Ebert was a splendid young man, and he had been right to insist on tasting the *ch'a* before he drank it.

"One cannot be too careful, *Chieh Hsia*."

Li Shai Tung nodded. "You are quite right, Hans. What would your father say, eh?"

"To you, nothing, *Chieh Hsia*. But he would most certainly have chastised me for failing in my duties as his son if I had let you sip the *ch'a* untasted."

Again the answer pleased the three older men greatly. With a last bow to his T'ang, Ebert turned and began to pour for the General and the Marshal.

"Well, Knut," continued the T'ang where he had left off, "do you think we got them all?"

Tolonen straightened slightly, taking the bowl from Ebert before he answered.

"Not all, *Chieh Hsia*, but I'd warrant it'll be a year or more before we have any more trouble from them, if then. Hans did a fine job. And it was good that we acted when we did. If we had left it even an hour later we wouldn't have got anyone to inform on the scum and we would never have got to those cells. As it was . . ."

As it was they had practically destroyed the *Ping Tiao*. After the awfulness of Bremen there had been smiles again. Grim smiles of satisfaction at a job well done.

"I wish I had known," the T'ang said, looking away. "I might have pushed things a little less hard in Council.

Might have waited a while and tried to convince my fellow T'ang rather than coerce them."

"Forgive me, *Chieh Hsia*, but you acted as you had to," Nocenzi said, his voice free of doubt. "Whether the threat be from the *Ping Tiao* or from another group, the problem remains. And as long as population outstrips food production it can only get worse."

"Yes, Vittorio, but what can I do? The Council will hear nothing of population measures and I have done all that can be done to increase productivity. What remains?"

Nocenzi looked to Tolonen, who gave the slightest nod, then turned to young Ebert. "Hans, you know the facts and figures. Would you like to spell it out for us?"

Ebert looked to his T'ang, then set his *ch'a* down. "*Chieh Hsia?*"

"Go ahead, Major."

Ebert hesitated, then bowed his head. "Forgive me, *Chieh Hsia*, but when I learned what had been planned against the Plantations, I decided, after consultation with Marshal Tolonen, to commission a report. One separate from those you had asked us to compile."

The T'ang looked briefly to Tolonen, then frowned. "I see. And what was in this report?"

"It was quite simple, *Chieh Hsia*. Indeed, it asked but one highly specific question. What would it cost in terms of manpower and finances to guard the Plantations adequately?"

"And the results of your report?"

Tolonen interrupted. "You must understand, *Chieh Hsia*, that Ebert acted only under my strict orders. Nor would I have mentioned this had you been successful in Council. It's just that I felt we should be prepared for the worst eventuality. For the failure of our action against the *Ping Tiao* and the . . . the hostility, let us say, of the Seven to your scheme."

The T'ang looked down, then laughed. "I am not angry, Knut. Gods, no. I'm glad to have such fine men as you three tending to my interests. If I seem angry, it is at the need for us to take such measures. At the wastefulness of it all. Surely there's no need for us to breed and breed until we choke on our own excess of flesh!"

He looked about him angrily, then calmed, nodding to himself. "Well, Hans? What would the cost be?"

Ebert bowed. "In men we're talking of a further half million, *Chieh Hsia*. Six hundred and fifty thousand to be absolutely safe. In money – for food, billeting, equipment, salaries and so forth – it works out to something like eighty-five thousand *yuan* per man, or a total somewhere between forty-two and fifty-five billion *yuan* per year.

"However, this scenario presumes that we *have* half a million trained Security guards ready for placement. The truth is, if we took this number of men from their present duties there would be a substantial increase in criminal activity throughout the levels, not to say a dramatic rise in civil disturbance at the very bottom of the City. It would reduce current strength by over twenty-five per cent, and that could well result in a complete breakdown of law and order in the lowest fifty levels."

"And the alternative?"

"To take a much smaller number, say fifty thousand, from present strength, then recruit to make up numbers. This, too, creates problems, primarily in training. To accommodate such an influx we would have to expand our training programme considerably. And the cost . . . forgive me, *Chieh Hsia*, but that alone would account for an estimated twenty billion, even before we equipped and trained the first recruit."

Li Shai Tung considered a moment, then shook his head. "I don't like it, *ch'un tzu*. To finance this would mean making cuts elsewhere, and who knows what troubles that would bring? But what choice do we have? Without enough food . . ."

He shrugged. It came back to the same thing every time. Population and food. Food and population. How fill the ever-growing ricebowl of Chung Kuo?

Tolonen hesitated, then bowed his head. "Might I suggest a solution, *Chieh Hsia?*"

"Of course."

"Then what of this? What if we were to adopt part of Hans's scheme? Aim for a force of, say, a quarter of a million, to be stationed on the Plantations, concentrated at key points to maximise their effectiveness. This to be phased in by degrees, at a rate of, say, fifty thousand every six months. That would take the strain off the training facilities while at the same time minimising the social effects."

"But that would take too long, surely?"

"Forgive me, *Chieh Hsia*, but the one thing Hans neglects to mention in his report is the effectiveness of his action against the *Ping Tiao*. If our problems of recruitment and training are great, imagine theirs. They've been routed. They won't easily recover from that. As I said earlier, it'll be a year at the very least before they're in any fit state to cause us problems, and there's no terrorist group of comparable size to take their place."

The T'ang considered a moment, then nodded. "All right. We shall do as you say, Knut. Draw up the orders and I'll sign them." He turned, looking at Ebert. "You have served me well today, Hans Ebert, and I shall not forget it. Nor shall my son. But come, let's drink this fine *ch'a* you brought before it cools."

The three men bowed as one. "*Chieh Hsia . . .*"

*   *   *

Li Yuan looked up from the document he was reading and yawned.

"You should take a break, my lord," Chang Shih-sen, his personal secretary said, looking across at him from his desk on the far side of the room. "I'll finish off. There are only a few things remaining."

Li Yuan smiled. They had been working since seven and it was almost midday. "A good idea, Shih-sen. But it's

91

strange that my father hasn't contacted me. Do you think he's all right?"

"I am certain of it, my lord. You would be the first to hear were your father ill."

"Yes . . ." He looked down at Minister Heng's memorandum again, then nodded. "It's interesting, this business with the Shepherd boy, don't you think?"

"My lord . . ." Chang Shih-sen was watching him, smiling.

Li Yuan laughed. "All right. I know when I'm being bullied for my own good. I'll go, Shih-sen. But make sure you get an acknowledgment off to Heng Yu this afternoon. I've kept him waiting two days as it is."

"Of course, my lord. Now go. Enjoy the sunshine while you can."

Li Yuan went out into the brightness of the Eastern Courtyard, standing there a moment at the top of the broad steps, his hand resting on the cool stone of the balustrade. He looked about him, feeling totally at peace with the world. There was such order here. Such balance. He stretched, easing the tiredness of sitting from his limbs, then went down, taking the steps two at a time before hurrying across the grass, his silk *pau* flapping about him.

There was no sign of Fei Yen and her maids in the gardens, nor in the long walk. The ancient, wall-enclosed space was still and silent. At the stone arch he turned, considering whether he should go to her rooms, then decided not to. She needed her rest. Now more than ever. For their son's sake.

As ever the thought of it made him feel strange. He looked across at the ancient, twisted shapes of the junipers that rested in the shade of the palace walls, then turned his head, tracing the curved shape of the pool with his eyes. He held himself still, listening, and was rewarded with the singing of a bird, the sound distant, from across the valley. He smiled, sniffing the cool, late morning air, finding a faint scent of herbs underlying it.

It was a good day to be alive.

He turned, looking at the great upright of the arch, then let his fingers trace the complex, interwoven patterns in the stone. All this had stood here a thousand years and yet the pattern seemed freshly cut into the stone. As if time had no power here.

He turned, making his way towards the stables. It had been some time since he had seen his horses. Too long. He would spend an hour and make a fuss of them. And later, perhaps, he would exercise Fei's horse, Tai Huo.

The great barn of the stables was warm and musty. The grooms looked up from their work as he entered, then hurried forward to form a line, bowing from the waist.

"Please . . ." he said. "Carry on. I'll not disturb you."

They backed away respectfully, then turned, returning to their chores. He watched them a while, some part of him envying the simplicity of their existence, then he looked upwards, drawing in the strong, heady scents of the barn – scents that seemed inseparable from the darkly golden shadows of the stalls.

Slowly he went down the line, greeting each of the horses in its stall. The dark-maned barb, Hei Jian – "Black Sword" – lifted her broad muzzle in greeting, letting him pat then smooth her flank. Mei Feng – "Honey Wind" – the elegant Akhal-teke, was more skittish, almost petulant, but after a moment he relented, letting Li Yuan smooth the honey-gold of his flank, his sharp ears pricked up. He was the youngest of the six horses, and the most recently acquired, a descendant of horses that had served the wild herdsmen of West Asia thousands of years earlier.

Next was his brother's horse, the black Arab he had renamed Chi Chu – "Sunrise". He spent some time with it, rubbing his cheek against its neck, feeling a kinship with the mare that he felt with none of the others. Beside it was the white Arab, the horse he had bought for Fei Yen, Tai Huo – "Great Fire". He smiled, seeing the creature, remembering the night he had brought Fei Yen blindfolded to the stables to see him for the first time. That time they had made love in the stall.

He turned, looking past the horse's rump, then frowned. The fifth stall was empty. The Andalusian – his father's present to him on his twelfth birthday – was not there. He went out and stood there at the head of the stall, looking into the empty space, then turned, summoning the nearest of the grooms.

"Where is the Andalusian?"

The groom bowed low, a distinct colour in his cheeks. "I . . . I . . ." he stammered.

Li Yuan turned, looking back at the stall, his sense of wrongness growing. From outside he heard a clamour of voices. A moment later a tall figure appeared in the great doorway. Hung Feng-chan, the Chief Groom.

"My lord . . ." he began hesitantly.

Li Yuan turned, facing him. "What is it, Hung?"

Hung Feng-chan bowed low. "The Andalusian is being . . . exercised, my lord."

Li Yuan frowned, his eyes returning to the empty stall. "Exercised, Hung? I thought they were only exercised first thing. Is something wrong with the animal?"

"My lord, I . . ."

"The gods help us, Hung! What is it? Are you keeping something from me?"

He looked about him, seeing how the grooms had stopped their work and were looking on, their flat Han faces frightened now.

"Is the horse *dead*, Hung? Is that it?"

Hung bowed his head lower. "No, my lord . . ."

"Then in the gods' names, what *is* it?"

"Nan Hsin is being ridden, my lord."

Li Yuan straightened up, suddenly angry. "Ridden? Who gave permission for anyone to ride the beast?"

Hung Feng-chan was silent, his head bowed so low that it almost touched his slightly bent knees.

Li Yuan's bark of anger was unexpected. "Well, Hung? Who is riding Nan Hsin? Or do I have to have it beaten from you?"

Hung raised his head, his eyes beseeching his young

master. "My lord, forgive me. I tried to talk her out of it . . ."

"Tried to . . ." He stopped, sudden understanding coming to him. Fei Yen. He was talking about Fei Yen. It couldn't be anyone else. No one else would have dared countermand his orders. But Fei was seven months pregnant. She couldn't go riding, not in her condition. The child . . .

He rushed past the Chief Groom and stood in the great doorway, looking out. The palace was to his left, the hills far off to the right. He looked, scanning the long slope for a sight of her, but there was nothing. Then he turned back, concern for her making him forget himself momentarily, all control gone from his voice, a naked fear shaping his words.

"Where is she, Hung? Where in the gods' names is she?"

"I . . . I don't know, my lord."

Li Yuan strode across to him and took his arms, shaking him. "Kuan Yin preserve us, Hung! You mean you let her go out, alone, unsupervised, in *her* condition?"

Hung shook his head miserably. "She forbade me, my lord. She said . . ."

"*Forbade* you?! What nonsense is this, Hung? Didn't you realise how dangerous, how *stupid* this is?"

"My lord, I . . ."

Li Yuan pushed him away. "Get out of my sight!" He looked about him, furious now. "Go! All of you! Now! I don't want to see any of you here again!"

There was a moment's hesitation, then they began to leave, bowing low as they moved about him. Hung was last.

"My lord . . . ?" he pleaded.

But Li Yuan had turned his back on the Chief Groom. "Just go, Hung Feng-chan. Go now, before I make you pay for your foolishness."

Hung Feng-chan hesitated a moment longer, then, bowing to the back of his prince, he turned and left dejectedly, leaving Li Yuan alone.

* * *

Hans Ebert ran up the steps of the Ebert Mansion, grinning, immensely pleased with his day's work. It had been easy to manipulate the old men. They had been off-balance, frightened by the sudden escalation of events, only too eager to believe the worst-case scenario he had spelled out for them. But the truth was otherwise. A good general could police the East European Plantations with a mere hundred thousand men, and at a cost only a tenth of what he had mentioned. As for the effect on the levels, that too had been exaggerated, though even he had to admit that it wasn't known precisely what effect such an attack would have at the lowest levels of the City.

He went through to his suite of rooms to shower and change. As he stripped off, he stood over his personal comset, scrolling through until he came upon a cryptic message from his uncle.

Beattie asks if you'll settle his bar bill for him. He says a thousand will cover it.
Love, your Uncle Lutz.

Beattie was DeVore. Now what did DeVore want ten million for? Ebert kicked off his shorts and went across to the shower, the water switching on as soon as he stepped beneath the spray. Whatever DeVore wanted, it was probably best to give him just now. To pacify him. It would be easy enough to reroute that much. He would get on to it later. Just now, however, he felt like making his regular sacrifice to the gods of the flesh. He closed his eyes, letting the lukewarm jets play on him invigoratingly. Yes, it would be good to have an hour with the *mui tsai*. To get rid of all the tensions that had built up over the last few days.

He laughed, feeling his sex stir at the thought of her.

"You were a bargain, my lovely," he said softly. "If I'd paid ten times as much, you'd have been a bargain."

The thought was not an idle one. For some time now

he had thought of duplicating her. Of transferring those qualities that made her such a good companion to a vat-made model. After all, what wouldn't the Supernal pay for such delicious talents? GenSyn could charge five times the price of their current models. Fifty times, if they handled the publicity properly.

Yes, he could see the campaign now. All the different, subtle ways of suggesting it without actually saying it: of hiding the true function of their latest model and yet letting it be known . . .

He laughed then stepped out, into the drying chamber, letting the warm air play across his body. Or maybe he would keep her for himself. After all, why should every jumped-up little merchant be able to buy such pleasures?

He threw on a light silk gown and went through, down a small flight of steps into the central space. The mansion was shaped irregularly, forming a giant G about the gardens. A small wooden bridge led across a narrow stream to a series of arbours. Underfoot was a design of plum blossom, picked out in small pale pink and grey pebbles, while on every side small red-painted wooden buildings, constructed in the Han style, lay half-hidden among the trees, their gently sloping roofs overhanging the narrow ribbon of water that threaded its way backwards and forwards across the gardens.

The gardens were much older than the house. Or at least, their design was, for his grandfather had had them modelled on an ancient Han original, naming them the Gardens of Peace and Prosperity. The Han character for longevity was carved everywhere, into stone and wood, and inlaid into mosaic at the bottom of the clear, fast-running stream. Translucent, paper-covered windows surrounded the garden on all sides, while here and there a moondoor opened on to new vistas – on to another tiny garden or a suite of rooms.

Hans stopped in the middle of the gardens, leaning on the carved wooden balustrade, looking down at his reflection in the still, green water of the central pond. Life was good. Life was very good. He laughed, then looked across at the three ancient pomegranate trees on the far side of the pool, noting how their trunks were shaped like flowing water; how they seemed to rest there, doubled in the stillness of the water. Then, as he watched, a fish surfaced, rippling the mirror, making the trees dance violently, their long, dark trunks undulating like snakes.

And then he heard it, unmistakable. The sound of a baby crying.

He turned, puzzled. A baby? Here? Impossible. There were no children here. He listened then heard it again, clearer now, from somewhere to his left. In the servants' quarters.

He made his way around the pool and across the high-arched stone bridge, then stood there, concentrating, all thoughts of the *mui tsai* gone.

A baby. It was unmistakably a baby. But who would dare bring a baby here? The servants knew the house rules. His mother's nerves were bad. They knew that, and they knew the rules . . .

He pulled the robe tighter about him, then climbed the steps, hauling himself up on to the terrace that ran the length of the servants' quarters. The sound came regularly now; a whining, mewling sound, more animal than human. An awful, irritating sound.

He went inside, finding the first room empty. But the noise was louder here, much louder, and he could hear a second sound beneath it – the sound of a woman trying to calm the child.

"Hush now . . ." the voice said softly. "Hush, my pretty one."

He frowned, recognising the voice. It was Golden Heart, the girl he had bought from Mu Chua's singsong house ten years back. The girl he had taunted Fest with before he'd killed him.

Yes, Golden Heart. But what was she doing with a baby?

He made his way through, slowly, silently, until he

stood there in the doorway of her room, looking in. The girl was crouched over a cot, her back to him, cooing softly to the child. The crying had stopped now and the baby seemed to be sleeping. But whose child was it? And who had given permission for it to be brought into the house? If his mother found out she would have them dismissed on the spot.

"Golden Heart?"

The girl started, then turned to face him, the blood drained from her face.

"Excellency . . ." she said breathlessly, bowing low, her body placed between him and the cot, as if to hide the child.

He stepped into the room, looking past her. "What's happening here?"

She half turned her head, clearly frightened, taking one small step backwards so that she bumped against the edge of the cot.

"Whose child is that?"

She looked up at him, her eyes wide with fear. "Excellency . . ." she repeated, her voice small, intimidated.

He saw and understood. He would get nothing out of her by frightening her, but it was important that he knew whose child it was and why it had been brought here. Whoever it was, they would have to go, because this was too serious a breach of house rules to be overlooked. He moved closer, then crouched down before the girl, taking her hands and looking up into her face.

"I'm not angry with you, Golden Heart," he said softly, "but you know the rules. The child shouldn't be here. If you'll tell me who the mother is, I'll arrange for her to take the child away, but you can't keep her here. You know you can't."

He saw doubt war with a strange, wild hope in her face and looked down, puzzled. What was happening here? He looked up at her again, his smile encouraging her.

"Come, Golden Heart. I'll not be angry. You were only

looking after it, after all. Just tell me who the mother is."

She looked away, swallowing almost painfully. Again there was that strange struggle in her face, then she looked back at him, her eyes burning wildly.

"The child is yours. Your son."

"Mine?" He laughed sourly, shaking his head. "How can it be mine?"

"And mine," she said softly, uncertainly. "Our child . . ."

He stood, a cold anger spreading through him. "What is this nonsense? How could *you* have a child? You were sterilised years ago."

She bowed her head, taken aback by the sudden sharpness of his voice. "I know . . ." she said. "But I had it reversed. There's a place . . ."

"Gods!" he said quietly, understanding what she had done. Of course. He saw it now. She must have stolen some jewellery or something to pay for it. But the child . . .

He pushed past her, looking down at the sleeping infant. It was a large baby, five or six months in age, with definite Eurasian features. But how had she kept him hidden? How kept her pregnancy from being noticed?

"No . . . I don't believe you."

She came and stood beside him, resting her hands against the rail of the cot, her chest rising and falling violently, a strange expectation in her face. Then she bent down and lifted the child from the cot, cradling him.

"It's true," she said, turning, offering the child to him. "He's yours, Hans. When I knew I'd fallen I had him removed and tended in a false uterus. After the birth I had him placed in a nursery. I'd visit him there. And sometimes I'd bring him back here. Like today."

"Secretly," he said, his voice calm, distant, a thousand *li* from his thoughts.

"Yes . . ." she said, lowering her head slightly, willing

now to be chastised. But still she held the child out to him, as if he should take it and acknowledge it.

"No," he said, after a moment. "No, Golden Heart. You had no child. Don't you understand that? That thing you hold doesn't exist. It can't be allowed to exist. GenSyn is a complex business and you had no right to meddle in it. That thing would be an impediment. A legal nightmare. It would . . . inconvenience things. Can't you see that?"

A muscle twitched beneath her left eye, otherwise she made no sign that she had understood the meaning of his words.

"It's all right," he said. "You won't be punished for your foolishness. But this . . ." he lifted his hand vaguely, indicating the sleeping child, "this can't be allowed. I'll have someone take it now and destroy it."

Her whimper of fear surprised him. He looked at her, saw the tears that were welling in her eyes, and shook his head. Didn't she understand? Had she no sense at all?

"You had no right, Golden Heart. You belong to me. You do what *I* say, not what you want. And this . . . this is ridiculous. Did you really think you could get away with it? Did you really believe for a moment . . . ?"

He laughed, but the laughter masked his anger. No. It was not on. And now his mood was broken. He had been looking forward to the *mui tsai*, but now even the thought of sex was suddenly repugnant to him. Damn her! Damn the stupid girl with her addle-brained broodiness! He should have known something was up. Should have sensed it. Well, she'd not have another chance, that was certain. He'd have the doctors make sure of it this time. Have them make it irreversible.

And the child? It was as he'd said. The child didn't exist. It could not be allowed to exist. Because GenSyn would be threatened by its existence: the very structure of the company undermined by the possibility of a long, protracted inheritance battle in the courts.

He looked at the girl again, at the pathetic bundle she held out before her, and shook his head. Then he turned away, calling out as he did so, summoning his servants to him.

* * *

Li Shai Tung's figure filled the tiny overhead screen, his face grave, the white robes of mourning he wore flowing loosely about him as he came slowly down the steps to make his offering before the memorial plaque. Beneath the screen, its polished surface illuminated by the flickering light from the monitor, another, smaller plaque had been set into the foot of the wall, listing all those who had died in this small section of the deck.

Axel Haavikko knelt before the plaque, his head bowed, his shoulders hunched forward. His face was gaunt, his eyes red from weeping. He had not slept since the news had come.

He had thought himself alive again, reborn after years of self-destruction – years spent in idle, worthless dissipation – that moment in Tolonen's office twelve years before, when Hans Ebert had betrayed him, put behind him finally, his life redeemed by his friendship with Karr and Chen, made sense of by their common determination to expose Ebert – to show him for the hollow, lying shit he was. But all that was as nothing now. The light that had burned in him anew had gone out. His sister was dead. Vesa, his beloved Vesa, was dead. And nothing – *nothing* – could redeem the waste of that.

He took a shivering breath then looked up again, seeing the image of the T'ang reflected in the plaque where Vesa's name lay. Vesa Haavikko. It was all that remained of her now. That and the relentless ghosts of memory.

On that morning he had gone walking with her. Had held her arm and shared her laughter. They had got up early and gone down to see the old men and their birds in the tree-lined Main at the bottom of Bremen stack. Had sat at a café and talked about their plans for the future. And afterwards he had kissed her cheek and left her to go on duty, never for a moment suspecting that it was the last time he would ever see her.

He moaned softly, pressing his hands against his thighs in anguish. Why her? She had done nothing. If anyone, it was he who deserved punishment. So why her?

He swallowed painfully, then shook his head, but the truth would not be denied. She was dead. His beloved Vesa was dead. Soul-mate and conscience, the best part of himself, she was no more.

He frowned then looked down, suddenly bitter, angry with himself. It was his fault. He had brought her here, after all. After long years of neglect he had finally brought her to him. And to what end?

A tear welled and trickled down his cheek.

He shuddered, then put his hand up to his face. His jaw ached from where he had been gritting his teeth, trying to fend off the images that came – those dreadful imaginings of her final moments that tore at him, leaving him broken, wishing only for an end to things.

An end . . . Yes, there would be an end to everything. But first he had a score to settle. One final duty to perform.

He took a deep breath, summoning the energy to rise, then grew still, hearing a noise behind him: a gentle sobbing. He half turned and saw her there, kneeling just behind him to his right, a young woman, a *Hung Mao*, dressed in mourning clothes. Beside her, his tiny hand clutching hers, stood a child, a Han, bemusement in his three-year-old face.

He looked down, swallowing. The sight of the boy clutching his mother's hand threw him back across the years; brought back the memory of himself, standing there before his mother's plaque; of looking down and seeing Vesa's hand, there in his own, her fingers laced into his, her face looking up at him, not understanding. Two she had been, he five. And yet so old he had felt that day; so brave, they'd said, to keep from crying.

No, he had never cried for his mother. But now he

would. For mother and sister and all. For the death of all that was good and decent in the world.

★　★　★

Li Yuan was standing in the stable doorway when she returned, his arms folded across his chest, his face closed to her. He helped her from the saddle, coldly silent, his manner over-careful, exaggeratedly polite.

She stared at him, amused by this rare display of anger, trying to make him acknowledge her presence, but he would not meet her eyes.

"There," she said, pressing one hand against the small of her back to ease the ache there. "No harm done."

She smiled and went to kiss him.

He drew back sharply, glaring at her, then took her hand roughly and led her into the dark warmth of the stable. She went reluctantly, annoyed with him now, thinking him childish.

Inside he settled the horse in its stall then came back to her, making her sit, standing over her, his hands on his hips, his eyes wide with anger.

"What in hell's name do you think you were doing?"

She looked away. "I was riding, that's all."

"Riding . . ." he murmured, then raised his voice. "I said you weren't to ride!"

She looked up, indignation rising in her. "I'm not a child, Li Yuan. I can decide for myself what's best for me!"

He laughed scornfully, then turned, taking three steps away from her. "*You* can decide, eh?" He stopped, looking directly at her, his expression openly contemptuous. "*You* . . ." He shook his head. "You're seven months pregnant and you think riding is *best* for you?"

"No harm was done," she repeated, tossing her head. She would *not* be lectured by him! Not in ten thousand years! She turned her face aside, shaking now with anger.

He came across and stood there, over her, for a moment the image of his father, his voice low but menacing. "You say that you're not a child, Fei Yen, yet you've acted like one. How could you be so stupid?"

Her eyes flared. Who was he to call her stupid? This . . . this . . . *boy*! He had gone too far. She pulled herself up awkwardly from the chair and pushed past him. "I shall ride when I like! You'll not prevent me!"

"Oh, won't I?" He laughed, but his mouth was shaped cruelly and his eyes were lit with a sudden determination. "Watch! I'll show you how . . ."

She was suddenly afraid. She watched him stride across the straw-strewn tiles, a coldness in her stomach. He wouldn't . . . But then the certainty of it hit her and she cried out – "*No-o-oh!*" – knowing what he meant to do. She screamed it at his back, then went after him, nausea mixing with her fear and anger.

At the far end of the stable he turned, abruptly, so that she almost ran into him. He seized her upper arms, his fingers gripping the flesh tightly, making her wince.

"You'll stand here and watch. You'll witness the price of your stupidity!"

There was so much anger, so much real venom in his words that she swayed, feeling faint, paralysed into inaction by this sudden change in him. As she watched, he took the power-gun from the rack and checked its charge, then went down the row of horses.

At the end stall he paused and turned to look at her, then went in, his hand smoothing the flank of the dark horse, caressing its long face, before he placed the stubby gun against its temple.

"Goodbye," he whispered, then squeezed the trigger, administering the high-voltage shock.

The horse gave a great snort, then collapsed on to the floor of the stall, dead. Fei Yen, watching, saw how he shuddered, then stepped back, looking at what he'd done, his face muscles twitching violently.

Appalled she watched him move down the stalls, her horror mounting as the seconds passed.

Five mounts lay dead on the straw. Only the last of them

remained, the horse in the third stall, the black Arab that had once been Han's. She stood there, her hands clenched into tight fists, looking in at it. She mouthed its secret name, a cold numbness gripping her, then turned, looking at Li Yuan.

Li Yuan was breathing deeply now. He stood there in the entrance to the stall, for a moment unaware of the woman at his side, looking in at the beautiful beast that stood so proudly before him, its head turned, its dark eyes watching him. His anger had drained from him, leaving only a bitter residue: a sickness gnawing at the marrow of his bones. He shook his head, wanting to cry out for all the pain and anger she had made him feel, then turned and looked at her, seeing now how ill her beauty sat on her.

Like a mask, hiding her selfishness.

He bit his lip, struggling with what he felt, trying to master it. There was the taste of blood in his mouth.

For a moment longer he stood there, trembling, the gun raised, pointed at her. Then he threw it down.

For a time afterwards he stood there, his hands empty, staring down at the red earth floor, at the golden spill of straw that covered it, a blankness at the very core of him. When he looked up again she was gone. Beyond the stable doors the sky was a vivid blue. In the distance the mountains showed green and grey and white, swathed in mist.

He went out and stood there, looking out into the beauty of the day, letting his numbness seep down out of him, into the earth. Then he turned back and went inside again, bending down to pick up the gun.

The child, that was all that mattered now; all that was important. To make the Seven strong again.

"I'm sorry, Han," he whispered gently, laying his face against the horse's neck. "The gods know I didn't wish for this." Then, tears blurring his vision, he stepped back and rested the gun against the horse's temple, easing back the trigger.

CHAPTER · 3

THE WAY OF DECEPTION

Fei Yen went back to her father's house. For a week Li Yuan did nothing, hoping she would return of her own free will, then, when there was no sign of her returning, he went to see her, taking time off from his duties.

The Yin house defences tracked him from twenty *li* out, checking and rechecking his codes before granting him permission to set down. He landed his private craft in the military complex at the back of the estate, in a shadowy hangar where the sharp sweet scents of pine and lemon mingled with the smell of machine oils.

Two of Yin Tsu's three sons, Sung and Chan, were waiting there to greet him, bowed low, keeping a respectful silence.

The palace was on an island at the centre of a lake; an elegant, two-storey building in the Ming style, its red, corbelled roof gently sloped, its broad, panelled windows reminiscent of older times. Seeing it, Li Yuan smiled, his past memories tinged with present sadness.

The two sons rowed him across the lake, careful not to embarrass him with their attentions. Fei's father, Yin Tsu, was waiting on the landing stage before the palace, standing beneath an ancient willow whose shadow dappled the sunlit water.

He bowed low as Li Yuan stepped from the boat.

"You are welcome, Li Yuan. To what do I owe this honour?"

Yin Tsu was a small, neat man. His pure white hair was cut short about his neck in an almost occidental style,

107

slicked back from his high forehead. He held himself stiffly now, yet despite his white hair and seventy-four years he was a sprightly man with a disposition towards smiles and laughter. Just now, however, his small, fine features seemed morose, the tiny webs of lines at the corners of his eyes and mouth drawn much deeper than before.

Li Yuan took his hands. Small hands, like a woman's, the skin smooth, almost silky, the fingernails grown long.

"I need to see my wife, Honoured Father-in-Law. I must talk with her."

A faint breeze was blowing off the water. Fallen leaves brushed against their feet then slowly drifted on.

Yin Tsu nodded his head. Looking at him, Li Yuan saw the original of his wife's finely featured face. There was something delicate about it; some quality that seemed closer to sculpture than genetic chance.

"Come through. I'll have her join us."

Li Yuan bowed and followed the old man. Inside, it was cool. Servants brought *ch'a* and sweetmeats while Yin Tsu went to speak to his daughter. Li Yuan sat there, waiting, rehearsing what he would say.

After a while Yin Tsu returned, taking a seat across from him.

"Fei Yen will not be long. She wants a moment to prepare herself. You understand?"

"Of course. I would have notified you, Yin Tsu, but I did not know when I could come."

The old man lifted his chin and looked down his tiny nose at his son-in-law. Unspoken words lay in the depth of his eyes. Then he nodded, his features settling into an expression of sadness and resignation.

"Talk to her, Yuan. But please, you must only talk. This is still my house. Agreed?"

Li Yuan bowed his head. Yin Tsu was one of his father's oldest friends. An affront to him would be as an affront to his father.

"If she will not listen, then that will be an end to it, Yin Tsu. But I must try. It is my duty as a husband to try."

His words, like his manner, were stilted and awkward. They hid how much he was feeling at that moment: how much this meant to him.

Yin Tsu went to the window, staring out across the lake. It was difficult for him too. There was a tenseness to each small movement of his that revealed how deeply he felt about all this. But then, that was hardly surprising. He had seen his hopes dashed once before, when Yuan's brother Han had been killed.

Li Yuan sipped at his *ch'a* then set it down. He tried to smile, but the muscles in his cheeks pulled the smile too tight. From time to time a nerve would jump beneath his eye, causing a faint twitch. He had not been sleeping well since she had left.

"How is she?" he asked, turning to face Yin Tsu.

"In good health. The child grows daily." The old man glanced across, then looked back at the lake. His tiny hands were folded together across his stomach.

"That's good."

On the far side of the room, beside a lacquered screen, stood a cage on a long, slender pole. In the cage was a nightingale. For now it rested silently on its perch, but once it had sung for him – on that day he had come here with his father to see Yin Tsu and ask him for his daughter's hand in marriage.

He sat there, feeling leaden. She had left him on the evening of the argument. Had gone without a word, taking nothing, leaving him to think on what he had done.

"And how is Li Shai Tung?"

Li Yuan looked up blankly. "I beg your pardon, Honoured Father?"

"Your father. How is he?"

"Ah," he breathed in deeply, returning to himself. "He is fine now, thank you. A little weak, but . . ."

"None of us are growing any younger." The old man shook his head, then came across and sat again, a faint smile on his lips. "Not that we would even if we could, eh, Yuan?"

Yin Tsu's remark was far from innocuous. He was referring to the new longevity process. Already, it was said, more than a thousand of the Above had had the operation and were taking the drugs regularly. And that without concrete evidence of the efficacy of the treatment – without knowing whether there were any traceable side-effects. Such men were desperate, it seemed. They would grasp at any promise of extended life.

"Only ill can come of it, Yuan. I guarantee." He leaned forward, lifting the lid to look into the *ch'a* kettle, then summoned the servant across. While the servant hurried to replenish it, Li Yuan considered what lay behind his father-in-law's words. This was more than small talk, he realised. Yin Tsu was talking to him not as a son but as a future colleague. It was his way of saying that, whatever transpired, they would remain friends and associates. The interests of the Families – both Major and Minor – superseded all else. As they had to.

When the servant had gone again, Yin Tsu leaned forward, his voice a whisper, as if he were afraid of being overheard.

"If it helps at all, Li Yuan, my sympathy's with you. She acted rashly. But she's a headstrong young woman, I warn you. You'll not alter that with bit and bridle."

Li Yuan sighed then sipped at his *ch'a*. It was true. But he had wanted her both as she was and as he wanted her; like caging fire. He glanced up at Yin Tsu and saw the concern there, the deep-rooted sympathy. And yet in this the old man would support his daughter. He had sheltered her; given her refuge against her husband. He could sympathise but he would not help.

There was a sound, movement, from the far end of the long room. Li Yuan looked up and saw her in the doorway. He stood up as Yin Tsu looked round.

"Fei Yen . . . Come through. Li Yuan is here to see you."

Li Yuan stepped forward, moving to greet her, but she walked past him, as though he were not there. He turned, pained by her action, watching her embrace her father gently.

She seemed paler than he remembered her, but her tiny form was well rounded now, seven and a half months into its term. He wanted to touch the roundness of the belly, feel the movements of the growing child within. For all her coldness to him, he felt as he had always felt toward her. All of it flooded back, stronger than ever: all the tenderness and pain; all of his unfathomable love for her.

"Fei Yen . . ." he began, but found he could say no more than that. What *could* he say? How might he persuade her to return? He looked pleadingly to Yin Tsu. The old man saw and, giving the slightest of nods, moved back, away from his daughter.

"Forgive me, Fei, but I must leave now. I have urgent business to attend to."

"Father . . ." she began, her hand going out to touch him, but he shook his head.

"This is between you two alone, Fei. You must settle it here and now. This indecision is unhealthy."

She bowed her head, then sat.

"Come . . ." Yin Tsu beckoned to him. He hesitated, seeing how she was sitting, her head down, her face closed to him, then went across and sat, facing her. Yin Tsu stood there a moment longer, looking from one to the other. Then, without another word, he went.

For a time neither spoke or looked at the other. It was as if an impenetrable screen lay between them. Then, unexpectedly, she spoke.

"My father talks as if there were something to decide. But I made my decision when I left you." She looked up at him, her bottom lip strangely curled, almost pinched. It gave her mouth a look of bitterness. Her eyes were cold, defiant. And yet beautiful. "I'm not coming back, Li Yuan. Not ever."

He looked at her, meeting her scorn and defiance, her anger and bitterness, and finding only his own love for

111

her. She was all he had ever wanted in a woman. All he would ever want.

He looked down, staring at his perfectly manicured nails as if they held some clue to things.

"I came to say that I'm sorry, Fei. That I was wrong."

When he looked up again he saw that she had turned her face aside. But her body was hunched and tensed; her neck braced, the muscles stretched and taut. She seemed to draw each breath with care, her hands pressed to her breasts as if to hold in all she was feeling.

"I was wrong, Fei. I . . . I overreacted."

"You *killed* them!" She spat the words out between her teeth.

You almost killed my child . . . But he bit back the retort that had come to mind, closing his eyes, calming himself. "I know . . ."

There was a second silence, longer, more awkward than the first. Fei Yen broke this one too. She stood, making to leave.

He went across and held her arm, keeping her there. She looked down at his hand where it gripped her arm, then up at his face. It was a harsh, unsparing look; a look of unfeigned dislike. There was defiance in her eyes, but she made no move to take her arm away.

"We have not resolved this, Fei."

"*Resolved* . . ." She poured all the scorn she could muster into the word. "I'll tell you how you could *resolve* this, Li Yuan." She turned to face him, glaring at him, the roundness of her stomach pressed up hard against him. "You could take *this* from my belly and keep it safe until its term was up! That's what you could do!" The words were hard, unfeeling. She laughed bitterly, sneering at him. "Then you could take your gun and . . ."

He put his hand over her mouth.

She stepped back, freeing herself from his grip. Then she looked at him, rubbing her arm where he had held it, her eyes watching him all the while, no trace of warmth in them.

"You never loved me," she said. "Never. I know that now. It was envy. Envy of your brother. You wanted everything he had. Yes, that was it, wasn't it?" She nodded, a look of triumph, a hideous smile of understanding on her lips.

It was cruel. Cruel and untrue. He had loved his brother dearly. Had loved her too. Still loved her, even now, for all she was saying. More than the world itself.

But he could not say it. His face had frozen to a mask. His mouth was dry, his tongue stilled by her anger and bitterness and scorn.

For a moment longer he watched her, knowing that it ended here; that all he had wanted was in ruins now. He had killed it in the stables that day. He turned and went to the door, determined to go, not to look back, but she called out to him.

"One thing you should know before you leave."

He turned, facing her across the room. "What is it?"

"The child." She smiled; an ugly movement of the mouth that was the imperfect copy of a smile. "It isn't yours." She shook her head, still smiling. "Do you hear me, Li Yuan? I said the child isn't yours."

In the cage at the far end of the room the bird was singing. Its sweet notes filled the silence.

He turned away, moving one leg at a time until he was gone from there, keeping his face a blank, his thoughts in check. But as he walked he could hear her voice, almost kind for once. *One thing*, it said, then laughed. *One thing*.

★ ★ ★

"Is this it?" DeVore asked, studying the statue of the horse minutely, trying to discern any difference in its appearance.

The man looked across at him and smiled. "Of course. What were you expecting? Something in an old lead bottle, marked with a skull and crossbones? No, that's it, all right. It'd make arsenic seem like honeydew, yet it's as untraceable as melted snow."

DeVore stood back, looking at the man again. He was

113

nothing like the archetypal scientist. Not in his dress, which was eccentrically Han, nor in his manner, which was that of a low level drug dealer. Even his speech – scattered, as it was, with tiny bits of arcane knowledge – seemed to smack of things illicit or alchemical. Yet he was good. Very good indeed, if Ebert could be trusted on the matter.

"Well? Are you happy with it, or would you like me to explain it once more?"

DeVore laughed. "There's no need. I have it by heart."

The toxicologist laughed. "That's good. And so will your friend, eh? Whoever he is."

DeVore smiled. *And if you knew exactly who that was, you would as soon sell me this as cut your own throat.*

He nodded. "Shall we settle, then? My friend told me you liked cash. Bearer credits. Shall we call it fifty thousand?"

He saw the light of greed in the man's eyes and smiled inwardly.

"I thought a hundred. After all, it was a difficult job. That genetic pattern . . . I've not seen its like before. I'd say that was someone special. Someone well bred. It was hard finding the chemical key to break those chains down. I . . . well, let's say I had to improvise. To work at the very limit of my talents. I'd say that deserved rewarding, wouldn't you?"

DeVore hesitated, going through the motions of considering the matter, then bowed his head. "As you say. But if it doesn't work . . ."

"Oh, it *will* work, my friend. I'd stake my life on it. The man's as good as dead, whoever he is. As I said, it's perfectly harmless to anyone else, but as soon as *he* handles it the bacteria will be activated. The rest . . ." he laughed ". . . is history."

"Good." DeVore felt in his jacket pocket and took out the ten bearer credits – the slender chips identical in almost every respect to those he had given Mach a week earlier. Only in one crucial respect were they different: these had been smeared with a special bacteria – one designed to match the toxicologist's DNA. A bacteria prepared only days earlier by the man's greatest rival from skin traces DeVore had taken on his first visit here.

DeVore watched the man handle, then pocket the chips. Dead, he thought, smiling, reaching out to pick up the statue the man had treated for him. Or as good as, give a week or two.

And himself? Well, he was the last person to take such chances. He had made sure he wore a false skin over both hands before handling the things. Just in case.

Because one never knew, did one? And a poisoner *was* a poisoner, after all.

He smiled, holding the ancient statue to his chest, then laughed; seeing how the man joined his laughter, as if sharing the cruel joke he was about to play.

"And there's no antidote? No possible way of stopping this thing once it's begun?"

The man shook his head, then gave another bark of laughter. "Not a chance in hell."

* * *

It was dark where Chen sat. Across from him a ceiling panel flickered intermittently, as if threatening to come brightly, vividly alive again, but never managing more than a brief, fitful glow. Chen had been nursing the same drink for more than an hour, waiting for Haavikko to come, his ill ease growing with every passing minute. More than ten years had passed since he had last sat in the Stone Dragon – years in which he had changed profoundly – yet the place remained unchanged.

Still the same shit-hole, he thought. A place you did well to escape from as quickly as you could. As he had.

But now he was back, if only briefly. Still, Haavikko could hardly have known, could he?

No. Even so, the coincidence made Chen's flesh crawl. He looked about him uncomfortably, as if the ghost of Kao Jyan, or the more substantial figure of Whiskers Lu, should manifest themselves from the darkness and the all-pervading fug to haunt him.

"You want wings?"

He glanced at the thin young girl who had approached him and shook his head, letting disgust and a genuine hostility shape his expression.

"You prefer I suck you? Here, at table?"

He leaned towards her slightly. "Vanish, scab, or I'll slit you throat to tail."

She made a vulgar hand sign and slipped back into the darkness, but she wasn't the first to have approached him. They were all out to sell something. Drugs or sex or worse. For a price you could do anything you liked down here. It hadn't been so in his day, but now it was. Now the Net was little different from the Clay.

He sat back. Even the smell of the place nauseated him. But that was hardly surprising: the air filters couldn't have been changed in thirty years. The air was recycled, yes, but that meant little here. He swallowed, keeping the bile from rising. How many times had each breath he took been breathed before? How many foul and cankered mouths had sighed their last, drug-soured breath into this putrid mix?

Too many, he thought. Far, far too many.

He looked across. There was someone in the doorway. Someone tall and straight and wholly out of place in this setting. Haavikko. He'd come at last.

He got up and went across, embracing his friend, then holding him off at arm's length, staring up into his face.

"Axel . . . how are you? It's been a long time since you came to us. Wang Ti and the boys . . . they've missed you. And I . . . well, I was worried. I'd heard . . ." he paused, then shook his head, unable to say.

Haavikko looked aside momentarily, then met his friend's eyes. "I'm sorry, Chen, but it's been hard. Some days I've felt . . ." He shrugged, then formed his face into a sad little smile. "Well . . . I've got what you asked for. I had to cheat a little, and lie rather a lot, not to mention a little bit of burglary, but then it's hard being an honest man when all about you are thieves and liars. One must pretend to take on their colouring a little simply to survive, neh?"

Chen stared at him a moment, surprised by the hardness in his voice. His sister's death had changed him. Chen squeezed his shoulder gently, turning him towards his table.

"Come. Let's sit down. You can tell me what you've been up to while I go through the file."

Axel sat. "You remember Mu Chua's?"

Chen took the seat across from him. "No. I don't think I do."

"The House of the Ninth Ecstasy?"

Chen laughed. "Ah . . . Is that still going?"

Haavikko stared down at his hands. "Yes, it's still going. And guess what? Our friend Ebert is still frequenting it. It seems he visited there no more than a week back."

Chen looked up, frowning. "Ebert? Here? Why would he bother?"

Haavikko looked back at him, a bitter resentment in his eyes. "He had a meeting, it seems. With a *Shih* Reynolds."

"How do you know this?"

"The Madame, Mu Chua, told me. It's funny . . . I didn't even raise the matter of Ebert, she just seemed to want to talk about him. She was telling me about this girl she'd sold to Ebert – a fourteen-year-old named Golden Heart. I remember it, strangely enough. It was more than ten years back, so the girl could well be dead now, but Mu Chua was anxious to find out about her, as if the girl were her daughter or something. Anyway, she told me about a dream this girl had had – about a tiger coming from the west and mating with her and about a pale grey snake which died. It seems this was a powerful dream – something she couldn't get out of her mind – and she wanted me to find out what became of the girl. I said I would and in return she promised to let me know if Ebert or his friend returned. It could be useful, don't you think?"

"This Reynolds – do we know who he is or what he was meeting Ebert about?"

"Nothing, I'm afraid. But Mu Chua thinks he's been there before. She said there was something familiar about him."

"*Ping Tiao*, perhaps?"

"Perhaps . . ."

Chen looked down at the file, touching his wrist band to make it glow, illuminating the page beneath his fingers. For a while he was silent, reading, then he looked up, frowning.

"Is this all?"

Haavikko looked back at him blankly a moment, his mind clearly elsewhere, then nodded. "That's it. Not much is it?"

Chen considered a moment, then grunted. Hans Ebert had supposedly instigated an investigation into the disappearance of his friend, Fest, but the investigation had never actually happened. No witnesses had been called, no leads followed up. All that existed was this slender file.

"And Fest? Is there any sign of him?"

Haavikko shook his head. "He's dead. That's what the file means. They did it. Ebert and Auden. Because we'd got to Fest, perhaps, or maybe for some other reason – I've heard since that Fest was getting a bit too talkative for Ebert's liking even before we approached him. But whatever, they did it. That file makes me certain of it."

Chen nodded. "So what now?"

Haavikko smiled tightly. "The girl, Golden Heart. I'm going to find out what happened to her."

"And then?"

Haavikko shrugged. "I'm not sure. Let's see where this leads."

"And Ebert?"

Haavikko looked away, the tightness in his face revealing the depth of what he felt.

"At first I thought of killing him. Of walking up to him in the Officers' Club and putting a bullet through his brain.

But it wouldn't have brought her back. Besides, I want everyone to know what he is. To see him as I see him."

Chen was quiet a moment, then reached out and touched Haavikko's arm, as if consoling a child. "Don't worry," he said softly. "We'll get him, Axel. I swear we will."

*　*　*

Klaus Ebert stood on the steps of his mansion, his hands extended to the Marshal. Jelka watched as he embraced her father, then stood back, one hand resting on Tolonen's shoulder. She could see how deep their friendship ran; how close they were. More like brothers than friends.

Ebert turned, offering his hands to her, his eyes lighting at the sight of her.

He held her close, whispering at her ear. "You really are quite beautiful, Jelka. Hans is very lucky." But his smile only made her feel guilty. Was it really so hard to do this for them?

"Come. We've prepared a feast," Ebert said, turning, putting his arm about her shoulders. He led her through, into the vast, high-ceilinged hallway.

She turned her head, looking back at her father and saw how he was smiling at her. A fierce, uncompromising smile of pride.

It all went well until she saw him. Until she looked across the room and met his eyes. Then it came back to her: her deep-rooted fear of him – something much greater than dislike. Dread, perhaps. Or the feeling she had in her dreams sometimes. That fear of drowning in darkness. Of a cold, sightless suffocation.

She looked down, afraid that her eyes would reveal what she was thinking. It was a gesture that, to a watching eye, seemed the very archetype of feminine modesty: the bride obedient, her husband's thing, to be done with as he willed. But it wasn't so.

Her thoughts disturbed her. They hung like a veil at the back of her eyes, darkening all she saw. Head bowed,

119

she sat beside her future mother-in-law, a sense of horror growing in her by the moment.

"Jelka?"

The voice was soft, almost tender, but it was Hans Ebert who stood before her, straight-backed and cruelly handsome. She looked up, past the silvered buttons of his dark blue dress uniform to his face. And met his eyes. Cold, selfish eyes, little different from how she had remembered them, but now alert to her. Alert and open to her womanhood. Surprised by what he saw.

She looked away, frightened by what she saw – by the sudden interest where before there had only been indifference. *Like a curse*, she thought. *My mother's curse, handed down to me. Her dying gift.* But her mouth said simply, "Hans," acknowledging his greeting.

"You're looking very nice," he said, his voice clear, resonant.

She looked up, the strength of his voice, its utter conviction, surprising her. Her beauty had somehow pierced the shell of his self-regard. He was looking down at her with something close to awe. He had expected a child, not a woman. And not a beautiful woman, at that. Yes, he was surprised by her, but there was also something else – something more predatory in that look.

She had changed in his eyes. Had become something he wanted.

His sisters stood behind him, no longer taller than her. They watched her enviously. She had eclipsed them overnight and now they hated her. Hated her beauty.

"Come! Drinks everyone!" Klaus Ebert called, smiling at her as he passed, oblivious of the dark, unseen currents of feeling that swirled all about him in the room. And all the while his son watched her. Her future husband, his eyes dark with the knowledge of possession.

She looked away, studying the palatial vastness of the room. It was a hundred *ch'i* across, high-ceilinged and six-sided, each wall divided into five by tall, red-painted pillars. The walls were a dark, almost primal green, double doors set into the centre of each wall. Those doors filled the space between floor and ceiling, pillar and pillar. Vast doors that made her feel as though she had shrunk in size. GenSyn giants stood before the pillars to either side of each door, the dark green uniforms of the half-men blending in with the studded leather of the door covering.

A border of black tiles, glassy black and bright with darkness, surrounded the central hexagonal space. Huge, claw-footed plinths rested on this polished darkness, each bearing a man-sized vase: brutal-lipped and heavy vases, decorated in violent swirls of red and green and black. Elongated animals coiled about the thick trunk of each vase, facing each other with bared fangs and flaring eyes. On the walls beyond hung huge, wall-sized canvases in thick gilt frames, so dark as to seem in permanent shadow; visions of some ancient forest hell, where huntsmen ran on foot, axe or bow in hand, after a wounded stag. Again there was the green of primal forest, the black of shadows, the red of blood; these three repeated in each frame, melting into one another as in a mist.

A dark red carpet lay lush, luxuriant beneath her feet, while the ceiling above was the black of a starless night.

A voice spoke to her, close by. She smelled a sickly sweetness, masking some deeper, stronger scent. Turning, she met a pink-eyed stare. A three-toed hand held out a glass. The voice was burred, deep, sounding in the creature's throat. She looked at it aghast, then took the offered glass.

The creature smiled and poured the blood red liquid into the slender crystal. Again she saw the lace at its cuffs, the neat whiteness of its collar. But now she saw the bright, red roughness of the sprouting hairs on its neck, the meat-pink colour of its flesh, and felt her skin crawl in aversion.

She stood and brushed past it, spilling her wine over the creature's jacket, the stain a vivid slash of colour on the ice-white velvet of its sleeve.

The creature's eyes flared briefly, following her figure as she crossed the room towards her father. Then it looked down at its sleeve, its brutal lips curled back with distaste at the spoiled perfection there.

★ ★ ★

Li Shai Tung sat at his desk, his hands resting lightly to either side of the tiny porcelain figure, his face a mask of pain and bitter disappointment. He had tried to deny it, but there was no doubting it now. Tsu Ma's last message made it clear. It was Wang Ta Chuan. Wang, his trusted Master of the Inner Palace, who was the traitor.

The old T'ang shuddered. First the boy, Chung Hsin, and now Wang Ta Chuan. Was there no end to this foulness? Was there *no one* he could trust?

He had done as Tsu Ma had suggested after the last meeting of the Council; had looked for the spy within his household and concluded that only four people had been privy to the information Wang Sau-leyan had used against him; four of his most senior and trusted men: Chung Hu-yan, his Chancellor; Nan Ho, Master of Yuan's chambers; Li Feng Chuang, his brother and adviser; and Wang Ta Chuan.

At first it had seemed unthinkable that any one of them could have betrayed him. But he had done as Tsu Ma said; had brought each to him separately and sown in them – casually, in confidence – a single tiny seed of information, different in each instance.

And then he had waited to hear what Tsu Ma's spies reported back, hoping beyond hope that there would be nothing. But this morning it had come. Word that the false seed had sprouted in Wang Sau-leyan's ear.

He groaned, then leaned forward, pressing the summons pad. At once Chung Hu-yan appeared at the door, his head bowed.

"*Chieh Hsia?*"

Li Shai Tung smiled, comforted by the sight of his Chancellor.

"Bring Wang Ta Chuan to me, Hu-yan. Bring him, then close the doors and leave me with him."

Li Shai Tung saw the slight query in his Chancellor's eyes. Chung Hu-yan had been with him too long for him not to sense his moods. Even so, he said nothing, merely bowed and turned away, doing his master's bidding without question.

"A good man . . ." he said softly, then sat back, closing his eyes, trying to compose himself.

Wang Ta Chuan was a traitor. There was no doubt about it. But he would have it from the man's lips. Would have him bow before him and admit it.

And then?

He banged the table angrily, making the tiny porcelain statue shudder.

The man would have to die. Yet his family might live. *If* he confessed. *If* he admitted of his own free will what he had done. Otherwise they too would have to die. His wives, his sons, and all his pretty grandchildren – all to the third generation as the law demanded. And all because of *his* foolishness, *his* foulness.

Why? he asked himself for the hundredth time since he had known. Why had Wang Ta Chuan betrayed him? Was it envy? Was it repayment for some slight he felt had been made to him? Or was it something darker, nastier than that? Did Wang Sau-leyan have some kind of hold on him? Or was it simply greed?

He shook his head, not understanding. Surely Wang had all he wanted? Status, riches, a fine, healthy family. What more did a man need?

Li Shai Tung reached out and drew the statue to him, studying it while he mulled over these thoughts, turning it in his hands, some part of him admiring the ancient craftsman's skill – the beauty of the soft blue glaze, the perfect, lifelike shape of the horse.

It was strange how this had returned to him. Young Ebert had brought it to him only that morning, having recovered it in a raid on one of the *Ping Tiao* cells. It was one of the three that had been taken from the safe in Helmstadt Armoury and its discovery in the hands of the

Ping Tiao had confirmed what he had always believed.

But now the *Ping Tiao* were broken, the horse returned. There would be no more trouble from that source.

There was a knocking on the outer doors. He looked up, then set the statue to one side. "Come!" he said imperiously, straightening in his chair.

Chung Hu-yan escorted the Master of the Inner Palace into the room, then backed away, closing the doors behind him.

"*Chieh Hsia?*" Wang Ta Chuan said, bowing low, his manner no less respectful, no less solicitous than it had always been.

"Come closer," Li Shai Tung ordered. "Come kneel before the desk."

Wang Ta Chuan lifted his head briefly, surprised by his T'ang's request, then did as he was told.

"Have I displeased you, *Chieh Hsia?*"

Li Shai Tung hesitated, then decided to broach the matter directly; but before he could open his mouth, the doors to his study burst open and Li Yuan stormed in.

"Yuan! What is the meaning of this?" he said, starting up from his chair.

"I am sorry, Father, but I *had* to see you. It's Fei . . . She . . ." Li Yuan hesitated, taking in the sight of the kneeling man, then went across and touched his shoulder. "Wang Ta Chuan, would you leave us? I must talk with my father."

"*Yuan!*" The violence of the word surprised both the Prince and the kneeling servant. "Be quiet, boy! Have you forgotten where you are?"

Li Yuan swallowed, then bowed low.

"Good!" Li Shai Tung said angrily. "Now hold your tongue and take a seat. I have urgent business with Master Wang. Business that cannot be put off."

He came from behind the desk and stood there over Wang Ta Chuan. "Have you something to tell me, Wang Ta Chuan?"

"*Chieh Hsia?*" The tone – of surprise and mild indig-

124

nation – was perfect, but Li Shai Tung was not fooled. To be a traitor – to be the perfect copy of a loyal man – one needed such tricks. Tricks of voice and gesture. Those and a stock of ready smiles.

"You would rather have it otherwise, then, Master Wang? You would rather I told you?"

He saw the mask slip. Saw the sudden calculation in the face and felt himself go cold. So it was true.

Li Yuan had stood. He took a step towards the T'ang. "What is this, Father?"

"Be quiet, Yuan!" he said again, taking a step towards him, the hem of his robes brushing against the kneeling man's hands.

"*Father!*"

He turned at Yuan's warning, but he was too slow. Wang Ta Chuan had grabbed the hem of the T'ang's ceremonial *pau*, twisting the silk about his wrist, while his other hand searched amongst his robes, emerging with a knife.

Li Shai Tung tried to draw back, but Wang Ta Chuan tugged at the cloth viciously, pulling him off balance. Yet even as the T'ang began to fall, Li Yuan was moving past him, high-kicking the knife from Wang's hands, then spinning on his hips to follow through with a second kick that broke the servant's nose.

Li Shai Tung edged back, watching as his son crouched over the fallen man.

"No, Yuan . . . *No!*"

But it was no use. Li Yuan was as if possessed. His breath hissed from him as he kicked and punched the fallen man. Then, as if coming to, he stepped back, swaying, his eyes glazed.

"Gods . . ." Li Shai Tung said, pulling himself up against the edge of the desk, getting his breath.

Li Yuan turned, looking at him, his eyes wide. "He tried to kill you, Father! Why? What had he done?"

The old T'ang swallowed drily, then looked away, shaking his head, trying to control himself; trying not to give voice to the pain he felt. For a moment he could say nothing; then he looked back at his son.

"He was a spy, Yuan. For Wang Sau-leyan. He passed on information to our *cousin*."

The last word was said with a venom, a bitterness that surprised them both.

Li Yuan stared at his father, astonished. "A traitor?" He turned, looking down at the dead man. "For a moment I thought it was one of those things. Those copies that came in from Mars. I thought . . ."

He stopped, swallowing, realising what he had done.

Li Shai Tung watched his son a moment longer, then went back round his desk and took his seat again. For a time he was silent, staring at his hands, then he looked up again. "I must thank you, Yuan. You saved my life just then. Even so, you should not have killed him. Now we will never know the reason for his treachery. Nor can I confront our cousin without the man's confession."

"Forgive me, Father. I was not myself."

"No . . . I could see that." He hesitated, then looked at his son more thoughtfully. "Tell me. When you came in just now – what did you want? What was so important that it made you forget yourself like that?"

For a moment it seemed that Yuan would answer; then he shook his head. "Forgive me, Father, it was nothing."

Li Shai Tung studied his son a moment longer, then nodded and reached out, holding the tiny statue to him as if to draw comfort from it.

★ ★ ★

Klaus Ebert and the Marshal stood there, face to face, their glasses raised to each other.

"To our grandchildren!"

Ebert nodded his satisfaction, then leaned closer. "I must say, Jelka is lovelier than ever, Knut. A real beauty she's become. She must remind you of Jenny."

"Very much . . ."

Tolonen turned, looking across. Jelka was sitting beside

Klaus's wife, Berta, her hands folded in her lap, her blonde hair set off perfectly by the flowing sky blue dress she was wearing. As he watched, Hans went across and stood there over her, handsome, dashingly elegant. It was the perfect match. Tolonen turned back, almost content, only the vaguest unease troubling him. She was still young, after all. It was only natural for her to have doubts.

"Hans will be good for her," he said, meeting his old friend's eyes. "She needs a steadying influence."

Klaus nodded, then moved closer. "Talking of which, Knut, I've been hearing things. Unsettling things." He lowered his voice, his words for the Marshal only. "I hear that some of the young bucks are up to old tricks. That some of them are in rather deep. And more than youthful pranks."

Tolonen stared at him a moment, then nodded curtly. He had heard something similar. "So it is, I'm sad to say. The times breed restlessness in our young men. They are good apples gone bad."

Ebert's face showed a momentary distaste. "Is it our fault, Knut? Were we too strict as fathers?"

"You and I?" Tolonen laughed softly. "Not we, Klaus. But others?" He considered. "No, there's a rottenness at the very core of things. Li Shai Tung has said as much himself. It is as if Mankind cannot live without being at its own throat constantly. Peace, that's at the root of it. We have been at peace too long, it seems."

It was almost dissent. Klaus Ebert stiffened, hearing this bitterness from his friend's lips. Things were bad indeed if the Marshal had such thoughts in his head.

"Ach, I have lived too long!" Tolonen added, and the sudden ironic tone in his voice brought back memories of their youth, so that both men smiled and touched each other's arms.

"All will be well, Klaus, I promise you. We'll come to the root of things soon enough. And then" – he made a movement of pulling up and then discarding a plant – "then we shall be done with it."

They looked at each other grimly, a look of understanding passing between them. They knew the world and its ways. Few illusions remained to them these days.

Tolonen turned to get a fresh drink, and caught sight of Jelka, getting up hastily, the contents of her glass splashing over the serving creature who stood beside her. He frowned as she came across.

"What is it, my love? You look like you've seen a ghost!"

She shook her head, but for the moment could not speak. There was a distinct colour in her cheeks.

Klaus Ebert looked at her, concerned. "Did my creature offend you, Jelka?" He looked at her tenderly, then glared at the creature across the room.

"No . . ." She held on to her father's arm, surprised by her reaction to the creature. "It's just . . ."

"Did it frighten you?" her father asked gently.

She laughed. "Yes. It did. It . . . surprised me, that's all. I'm not used to them."

Ebert relaxed. "It's my fault, Jelka. I forget. They're such gentle, sophisticated creatures, you see. Bred to be so."

She looked at him, curious now. "But why?" She was confused by this. "I mean, why are they like that? Like goats?"

Ebert shrugged. "I suppose it's what we're used to. My great-grandfather first had them as servants and they've been in the household ever since. But they really are the most gentle of creatures. Their manners are impeccable. And their dress sense is immaculate."

She thought of the fine silk of the creature's sleeves, then shuddered, recalling childhood tales of animals that talked.

That and the musk beneath the scent; the darkness at the back of those blood-pink eyes. Impeccable, immaculate, and yet still an animal at the back of all. A beast for all its breeding.

She turned to look but the serving creature had gone, as if it sensed it was no longer welcome. Good manners, she thought, but there was little amusement to be had from it. The thing had scared her.

"They breed true," Ebert added. "In fact, they're the first of our vat-bred creatures to attain that evolutionary step. We're justly proud of them."

Jelka looked back at her future father-in-law, wondering at his pride in the goat-thing he had made. But there was only human kindness in his face.

She looked away, confused. So maybe it was her. Maybe she was out of step.

But it was ugly, she thought. The thing was ugly. Then, relenting, she smiled and took the glass of wine Klaus Ebert was holding out to her.

* * *

An hour later the ritual began.

Overhead the lighting dimmed. At the far end of the room, the huge doors slowly opened.

It was dark in the hallway beyond, yet the machine glowed from within. Like a pearled and bloated egg, its outer skin as dark as smoked glass, it floated soundlessly above the tiled floor, a tightly focused circle of light directly beneath it. Two GenSyn giants guided it, easing it gently between the pillars of the door and out across the jet black marble of the tiles.

Jelka watched it come, her stomach tight with fear. This was her fate. Unavoidable, implacable, it came, gliding towards her as in a dream, its outer case shielding its inner brilliance; masking the stark simplicity of its purpose.

She held her father's arm tightly, conscious of him at her side; of how proudly he stood there. For him this moment held no threat. Today his family was joined to Klaus Ebert's by contract – something he had wished for since his youth. And how could that be wrong?

The machine stopped. The GenSyn servants backed away, closing the doors behind them. Slowly the machine sank into the lush carpeting: dark yet pregnant with its inner light.

Beyond it, in the shadows, a stranger stood at Klaus Ebert's side. The two were talking, their hushed tones drifting across to where she stood. The man was much smaller than Ebert; a tiny creature dressed entirely in red. The Consensor. He looked at her with a brief, almost dismissive glance, then turned back.

Dry-mouthed, she watched him turn to the machine and begin to ready it for the ceremony.

"*Nu shi* Tolonen?" He stood before her, one hand extended.

It was time.

She took his hand. A small, cool hand, dry to the touch. Looking down she saw that he wore gloves: fine sheaths of black, through which the intense pallor of his skin showed. Holding her hand, he led her to the machine.

The casing irised before her, spilling light. She hesitated then stepped up, into the brilliance.

He placed her hands on the touch-sensitive pads and clamped them there, then pushed her face gently but firmly against the moulded screen of transparent ice, reaching round her to attach the cap to her skull, the girdle about her waist. The movements of his hands were gentle, and for a time her fear receded, lost in the soothing comfort of his touch, but then, abruptly, he moved back and the door irised closed behind her, leaving her alone, facing the empty space beyond the partition.

There was a moment of doubt so great her stomach seemed to fall away. Then the wall facing her irised open and Hans Ebert stepped up into the machine.

Her heart began to hammer in her breast. She waited, exposed to him, her body held fast against the ice-clear partition.

He smiled at her, letting the Consensor do his work. In a moment he was secured, his face pressed close against her own, his hands to hers, only the thinnest sheet of ice between them.

She stared into his eyes, unable to look away, wanting to close her eyes and tear herself away, she felt so vulnerable, so hideously exposed to him. The feeling grew in her, until she stood there, cowed before his relentless stare, reduced to a frightened child. And then he spoke.

"Don't be afraid. I'd never hurt you, Jelka Tolonen."

The words seemed to come from a thousand *li* away, distant, disembodied; from the vast emptiness beyond the surface of his pale blue eyes. And yet, at the same time, it was as if the words had formed in her head, unmediated by tongue or lip.

And still he looked at her. Looked through her. Seeing all she was thinking. Understanding everything she was feeling. Emptying her. Until there was nothing there but her fear of him.

Then, in her mind, something happened. A wall blew in and three men in black stepped through. There was the smell of burning and something lay on the floor beside her, hideously disfigured, bright slivers of metal jutting from its bloodied flesh.

She saw this vividly. And in the eyes that faced hers something happened: the pupils widened, responding to something in her own. For a moment she looked outwards, recognising Hans Ebert, then the memory grabbed at her again and she looked back inwards, seeing the three men come towards her, their guns raised.

Strangely, the memory calmed her. *I survived*, she thought. *I danced my way to life.*

The partition between them darkened momentarily, leaving them isolated. Then it cleared, a circular pattern of pictograms forming in the ice; a tiny circle of coded information displayed before each of their pupils, duplicated so that each half of their brains could read and comprehend. Genotypings. Blood samplings. Brain scans. Fertility ratings. Jelka felt the girdle tighten, then a momentary pain as it probed her.

Figures changed. The ice glowed green. They were a perfect genetic match. The machine stored the figures dispassionately, noting them down on the contract.

The green tinge faded with the pictograms. Again she found herself staring into his eyes.

He was smiling. The skin surrounding his eyes was pulled tight in little creases, his eyes much brighter than before.

"You're beautiful," said the voice in her head. "We'll be good together. Strong, healthy sons, you'll give me. Sons we'll both be proud of."

She pictured the words forming in the darkness behind his eyes: saw them lift and float across, piercing the ice between them; entering her through her eyes.

Her fear had subsided. She was herself again. Now, when she looked at him, she saw only how cruel he was, how selfish. It was there, at the front of his eyes, like a coded pictogram.

As the machine began its litany she calmed herself, steeling herself to outface him: *No. You'll not defeat me, Hans Ebert. I'm stronger than you think. I'll survive you.*

She smiled, and her lips moved, saying "Yes", sealing the contract, putting her verbal mark to the retinal prints and ECG traces the machine had already registered as her identifying signature. But in her head the Yes remained conditional.

I'll dance my way to life, she thought. *See if I don't.*

* * *

DeVore looked down at the indicator at his wrist then peeled off the gas mask. Outside his men were mopping up, stripping the corpses before they set fire to the level.

Gesell was unconscious on the bed, the Han girl beside him.

He pulled back the sheet, looking down at them. The woman had small, firm breasts with large, dark nipples and a scar that ran from her left hip almost to her knee. DeVore smiled and leaned forward, running a finger slowly down the clean-shaven slit of her sex. *Too bad*, he thought. *Too bad.*

He looked across. Gesell lay on his side, one arm

cradling his head. A thick dark growth of hair covered his arms and legs; sprouted luxuriantly at his groin and beneath his arms. His penis lay there, like a newborn chick in a nest, folded softly into itself.

Looking at the man, DeVore felt a tight knot of anger constrict his throat. It would be easy to kill them now. Never to let them wake. But it wasn't enough. He wanted Gesell to know. Wanted to spit in his face before he died.

Yes. For all the threats he'd made. All the shit he'd made him eat.

He drew the needle-gun from his pocket and fitted a cartridge, then pushed it against Gesell's chest, just above the heart. Discarding the empty cartridge, he fitted another and did the same to the girl. Then he stepped back, waiting for the antidote to take effect.

The woman was the first to wake. She turned slightly, moving towards Gesell, then froze, sniffing the air.

"I'd keep very still if I were you, Mao Liang."

She turned her head, her eyes taking in his dark form, then gave a tiny nod.

"Good . . . Your boyfriend will be back with us in a moment. It's him I want. So behave yourself and you won't get hurt. Understand?"

Again she nodded, then shifted back slightly as Gesell stirred.

DeVore smiled, drawing the gun from inside his tunic. "Good morning, my friend. I'm sorry to have to disturb your sleep like this, but we've business."

Gesell sat up slowly, knuckling his eyes, then went very still, seeing the gun in DeVore's hand.

"How the fuck did you get in here?" he said softly, his eyes narrowed.

"I *bought* my way in. Your guards were only too happy to sell you to me."

"Sell . . ." Understanding came to his face. He glanced at the girl then looked back at DeVore, some eternal element of defiance in his nature making him stubborn to the last.

133

"Mach will get you for this, you fucker."

DeVore shrugged. "Maybe. But it won't help you, eh, Bent? Because you're dead. And all those things you believed in – they're dead too. I've wiped them out. There's only you left. You and the girl here."

He saw the movement almost peripherally; saw how her hand searched beneath the pillow and then drew back; heard the tiny click as she took off the safety.

He fired twice as she lifted the gun, the weighted bullets punching two neat holes in her chest, just below her heart. She fell back, dead.

Gesell moved forward sharply, then stopped, seeing how DeVore's gun was trained on him, pointed directly at his head.

"You were always a loudmouth, Gesell."

Gesell glared at him. "We should never have worked with you. Emily was right. You never cared for anyone but yourself."

"Did I ever say otherwise?"

Gesell sat back, his face tense. "So why don't you do it? Get it over with?"

"I will . . . don't worry, but not with this."

He threw the gun down. Gesell stared back at him a moment, then made his move, scrambling for the gun. DeVore stepped back, drawing the spray can from his pocket, watching as Gesell turned and pointed the gun at him.

"It's empty."

Gesell pulled the trigger. It clicked then clicked again.

DeVore smiled, then stepped closer, lifting the spray, his finger holding down the button as the fine particles hissed from the nozzle.

He watched Gesell tear at the thin film of opaque, almost translucent ice that had formed about his head and shoulders; saw how his fingers fought to free an air-hole in the soft, elastic stuff, but already it was growing hard. Desperation made Gesell throw himself about, bellowing;

but the sound was distant, muted. It came from behind a screen that cut him off from the air itself.

DeVore emptied the can then cast it aside, stepping back from the struggling figure. Gesell's arms and hands were stuck now – welded firmly to his face. For a moment longer he staggered about, then fell down, his legs kicking weakly. Then he lay still.

DeVore stood over Gesell a moment, studying his face; satisfied by the look of panic, of utter torment, he could see through the hard, glass-like mask, then looked up. Mach was watching him from the door.

"He's dead?"

DeVore nodded. "And the woman, too, I'm afraid. She drew a gun on me."

Mach shrugged. "It's all right. It would have been difficult. She was in love with him."

"And Ascher?"

Mach shook his head. "There's no trace of her."

DeVore considered that a moment, then nodded. "I'll find her for you."

"Thanks." Mach hesitated, then came in, looking down at Gesell. "I liked him, you know. I really did. But sooner or later he would have killed me. He was like that."

DeVore stood, then reached out, touching Mach's arm. "Okay. We've finished here. Let's be gone. Before the T'ang's men get here."

CHAPTER·4

CARP POOL AND TORTOISE SHELL

Kim turned in his seat, looking at Hammond. "Well? What do you think he wants?"

Hammond glanced at him, then looked away nervously, conscious of the overhead camera.

Kim looked down. So it was like that. Director Spatz was putting pressure on him. Well, it made sense. After all, it wasn't every day that Prince Yuan came to visit the Project.

He looked about him, noting how Spatz had had his suite of offices decorated specially for the occasion, the furnishings replaced. It was a common joke on the Project that Spatz's offices were larger – and cost more in upkeep – than the rest of the Project put together. But that was only to be expected. It was how arseholes like Spatz behaved.

Kim had been on the Wiring Project for almost a year now, though for most of that time he had been kept out of things by Spatz. Even so, he had learned a lot, keeping what he knew from Spatz and his cronies. From the outset he had been dismayed to learn how little they'd progressed. It was not that they didn't know about the brain. The basic information they needed had been discovered more than two centuries before. No, it was simply that they couldn't apply it. They had tried out various "templates" – all of them embellishments on what already existed – but none of them had shown the kind of delicacy required. In terms

136

of what they were doing, they were crude, heavy-handed models, more likely to destroy the brain than control it; systems of blocks and stimulae that set off whole chains of unwanted chemical and electrical responses. As it was, the wiring system they had was worthless. A frontal lobotomy was of more use. Unless one wanted a population of twitching, jerking puppets.

And now, in less than five hours, Prince Yuan would arrive for his first annual inspection. But Spatz was taking no chances. He remembered the last visit he had had – from Marshal Tolonen – and was determined to keep Kim away from things.

Well, let him try, Kim thought. Let him try.

As if on cue, Spatz arrived, Ellis, his assistant, trailing behind him, a thick stack of paper files under his arm. He had seen this aspect of officialdom before. Most of the time they shunned real paperwork, preferring to keep as much as possible on computer, yet whenever the big guns arrived out would come thick stacks of paper.

And maybe it worked. Maybe it *did* impress their superiors.

"Ward," Spatz said coldly, matter-of-factly, not even glancing at Kim as he sat behind his desk.

"Yes, *Shih* Spatz?"

He saw the tightening of the man's face at his refusal to use his full title. Spatz was a fool when it came to science, but he knew disrespect when he saw it. Spatz looked up at Ellis and took the files from him, sorting through them with a great show of self-importance, before finally setting them aside and looking across at Kim.

"I understand you've requested an interview with Prince Yuan."

Kim stared back at him, making no response, wanting to see how Spatz would deal with his intransigence; how he would cope with this direct assault on his authority.

"Well . . ." Spatz masked his anger with a smile. His face set, he raised a hand and clicked his fingers. At once Ellis went across and opened the door.

Kim heard footsteps behind him. It was the Communications Officer, Barycz. He marched up to the desk and handed over two slender files to add to the pile at Spatz's elbow.

Are you trying to build a wall against me, Spatz? Kim thought, smiling inwardly. Because it won't work. Not today, anyway. Because today Prince Yuan will be here. And I'll let him know exactly what you've been doing. You know that, and it scares you. Which is why I'm here. So that you can offer me some kind of deal. But it won't work. Because there's nothing you can offer me. Nothing at all.

Spatz studied the first of the files for a while, then held it out to Hammond.

Kim saw the movement in Hammond's face and knew, at once, that the file was to do with himself.

Hammond read through the file, the colour draining from his face, then looked up at Spatz again. "But this . . ."

Spatz looked away. "What is the matter, *Shih* Hammond?"

Hammond glanced at Kim fearfully.

"Is it a problem, *Shih* Hammond?" Spatz said, turning to look at his Senior Technician. "You only have to countersign. Or is there something you wish to query?"

Kim smiled sourly. He understood. They had constructed a new personnel file. A false one, smearing him.

"Sign it, Joel," he said. "It doesn't matter."

Spatz looked at him and smiled. The kind of smile a snake makes before it unhinges its jaws and swallows an egg.

Hammond hesitated, then signed.

"Good," Spatz said, taking the document back. Then, his smile broadening, he passed the second file to Ellis. "Give this to the boy."

Kim looked up as Ellis approached, conscious of the look of apology in the Assistant Director's eyes.

"What is this?"

Spatz laughed humourlessly. "Why don't you open it and see?"

Kim looked across. Hammond was looking down, his shoulders hunched forward, as if he knew already what was in the second file.

Kim opened the folder and caught his breath. Inside was a sheaf of paper. Hammond's poems and his own replies. A full record of the secret messages they had passed between them.

He looked at Spatz. "So you knew?" But he knew at once that neither Spatz nor Barycz was behind this. They were too dull-witted. There was no way either of them could have worked out what was going on. No, this was someone else. Someone much sharper than either of them. But who?

Spatz leaned forward, his sense of dignity struggling with his need to gloat.

"You thought you were being clever, didn't you, Ward? A regular little smart-arse. I bet you thought you were *so* superior, neh?" He laughed, then sat back, all humour draining from his face. "For your part in this, you're under report, Hammond, from this moment. But you, Ward – you're *out*."

"Out?" Kim laughed. "Forgive me, *Shih* Spatz, but you can't do that. I'm Prince Yuan's appointment. Surely only he can say whether I'm out or not."

Spatz glanced at him disdainfully. "A formality. He'll have my recommendation, backed by the personnel file and the complaints of disruption filed against you by several staff members."

Out of the corner of his eye he saw Hammond start forward. "But you promised . . ."

Spatz interrupted Hammond, his face hard. "I promised nothing, if you recall. Now for the gods' sakes, hold your tongue! Even better, leave the room. You've served your purpose."

Hammond rose slowly. "I've served my purpose, eh? Too fucking right I have." He leaned forward, setting his hands firmly on the edge of the desk, facing the Director. As if sensing what he intended, Spatz drew the file towards him, then handed it to Ellis at his side.

"If you say another word . . ."

Hammond laughed, but his face was filled with loathing for the man in front of him. "Oh, I've nothing more to say, Director Spatz. Just this . . ."

He drew his head back and spat; powerfully, cleanly, catching Spatz in the centre of his face.

Spatz cried out, rubbing at his face with the sleeve of his gown; then, realising what he had done, he swore.

"You bastard, Hammond! My silks . . ." Spatz stood, his face livid with anger, his hands trembling. "Get out! Get your things and be gone! As from this moment you're off the Project."

For a moment longer, Hammond stood there, glaring at him, then he moved back, a tiny shudder passing through him.

"Joel, I . . ." Kim began, reaching out to him, but Hammond stepped back, looking about him, as if coming to from a bad dream.

"No. It's fine, Kim. Really it is. I'll survive. The Net can't be worse than this. At least I won't have to pawn myself every day to *hsiao jen* like this pig-brained cretin here!"

Spatz trembled with rage. "Guards!" he yelled. "Get the guards here, now!"

Hammond laughed. "Don't bother. I'm going. But fuck you, Spatz. Fuck you to hell. I hope Prince Yuan has your arse for what you're trying to do here today." He turned, then bent down, embracing Kim. "Good luck, Kim," he whispered. "I'm sorry. Truly I am."

Kim held him out at arm's length. "It's all right. I understand. You're a good man, Joel Hammond. A good man."

He stood, watching him go, then turned back, facing Spatz.

"So what now?"

Spatz ignored him, leaning forward to talk into the intercom. "Send in the nurse. We're ready now."

Kim looked at Ellis; saw how the man refused to meet his eyes. Then at Barycz. Barycz was pretending to study the chart on the wall behind Spatz.

"Prince Yuan will ask about me," Kim said. "He's certain to."

Spatz smiled coldly. "Of course he will. But you won't be there, will you?"

He heard the door open, the nurse come in.

"And then he'll ask why I'm not there . . ." he began, but the words were choked off. He felt the hypodermic-gun pressed against his neck and tried to squirm away, struggling against the strong hand that held his shoulder, but it was too late.

The hand released him. Slumping down into the chair, he felt a fiery cold spreading through his veins, leaving him numb, his nerve-ends frozen.

"I-wb . . ." he said, his eyes glazing. "I-jibw . . ."

Then he fell forward, scattering the sheaf of poems across the floor beside him.

★　★　★

Li Yuan stepped down from his craft and sighed, looking about him. The roof of the City stretched away from him like a vast field of snow, empty but for the small group of officials who were gathered, heads bowed, beside the open hatchway.

He looked north to where the City ended abruptly on the shores of the icy Baltic, then turned to smile at his personal secretary, Chang Shih-sen.

"Have you ever seen it when the cloud is low, Chang? The cloud seems to spill from the City's edge like water over a fall. But slowly, very slowly, as in a dream."

"I have never seen that, my lord, but I should imagine it was beautiful."

Li Yuan nodded. "Very beautiful. I saw it once at sunset.

All the colours of the sky seemed captured in those endless folds of whiteness."

Chang Shih-sen nodded, then, softly, mindful of his place, added, "They are waiting, my lord."

Li Yuan looked back at him and smiled. "Let them wait. The day is beautiful. Besides, I wish a moment to myself before I join them."

"My lord . . ." Chang backed away, bowing.

Li Yuan turned, moving out from the shadow of the craft into the mid-afternoon sunlight. Chang was a good man. Kind, hard-working, thoughtful. But so his father's Master of the Inner Palace, Wang Ta Chuan had been. It made one think. When the fate of so many were in one's hands, who *could* one trust?

He took a deep breath, enjoying the freshness, the warmth of the sunlight on his arms and back. Last night, for the first time since he had married Fei Yen, he had summoned a woman to his bed – one of the serving girls from the kitchens – purging himself of the need that had raged in his blood like a poison. Now he was himself again.

Or almost himself. For he would never again be wholly as he was. Fei Yen had changed that.

Who was it? he wondered for the thousandth time. *Who slept with you while I was gone? Was it one of my servants? Or was it someone you knew before our time together?*

He huffed out his sudden irritation. It was no good dwelling on it. Madness lay that way. No, best set such thoughts aside, lest he find himself thinking of nothing else.

And what use would I then be to my father?

He shivered, then, calming himself, turned back, summoning Chang.

* * *

"Is this all?"

Spatz, stood before the seated Prince, bowed his head. "I am afraid so, my lord. But you must understand – I have been working under the most severe restraints."

Li Yuan looked up, his disappointment clear. "Just what do you mean, Director?"

Spatz kept his head lowered, not meeting the Prince's eyes. "To begin with, I have been effectively two short on my team throughout my time here."

Li Yuan leaned forward. "I do not understand you, Director. There is no mention in your report of such a thing."

"Forgive me, my lord, but the matter I am referring to is in the second file. I felt it best to keep the main report to matters of . . . of science, let us say."

The Prince sat back, irritated by the man's manner. If he'd had his way, Spatz would have been replaced as Director, but Spatz was his father's appointment, like Tolonen.

He set the top file aside, then opened the second one. It was a personnel report on the boy, Ward.

Li Yuan looked up, surprised. Could Spatz have known? No. He couldn't possibly have known about Kim and the special projects. But that too had been a disappointment. After the first report he had heard nothing from the boy. Nothing for ten months. At first he had assumed that it was taking much longer than the boy had estimated or that his work on the Project was taking up his time, but this explained it all.

He read it through then looked up again, shaking his head. The boy had been at best lethargic, uncooperative, at worst disruptive to the point of actual physical violence.

"Why was I not told of this before now?"

Spatz hesitated. "I . . . I wished to be charitable to the boy, my lord. To give him every chance to change his ways and prove himself. I was conscious of his importance to you. Of your special interest. So . . ."

Li Yuan raised his hand. "I understand. Can I see the boy?"

"Of course, my lord. But you must understand his condition. I am told it is a result of his 're-structuring' at the clinic. Occasionally he falls into a kind of torpor where he won't speak or even acknowledge that anyone is there."

"I see." Li Yuan kept the depth of his disappointment from his face. "And is he like that now?"

"I am afraid so, my lord."

"And his tutor, T'ai Cho?"

Spatz gave a small shrug of resignation. "A good man, but his loyalty to the boy is . . . shall we say, misguided. He is too involved, my lord. His only thought is to keep the boy from harm. I'm afraid you'll get little sense from him either."

Li Yuan studied Spatz a moment longer, then closed the file.

"You wish to see the boy, my lord?"

Li Yuan sighed, then shook his head. "No. I think I've seen enough." He stood. "I'm disappointed, Spatz. Hugely disappointed. I expected far greater progress than this. Still, things are on the right lines. I note that you've made some headway towards solving things on the technical front. That's good, but I want more. I want a working model twelve months from now."

"My lord . . ." The note of pure panic in the Director's voice was almost comical; yet Li Yuan had never felt less like laughing.

"Twelve months. Understand me? For my part, I'll make sure you have another dozen men – the best scientists I can recruit from the Companies. As for funding, you're quite correct, Director. It *is* inadequate. Which is why I'm tripling it from this moment."

For the first time Spatz's head came up and his eyes searched him out. "My lord, you are too generous."

Li Yuan laughed sourly. "Generosity has nothing to do with it, Director Spatz. I want a job done and I want it done properly. We under-funded. We didn't see the scale of the thing. Well, now we'll put that right. But I want results this time."

"And the boy?"

Li Yuan stood, handing the main copies of the files to Chang Shih-sen, then looked back at Spatz.

"The matter of the boy will be dealt with. You need worry yourself no further in that regard, Director."

* * *

Barycz locked the door of the communications room, then went to his desk and activated the screen. He tapped in the code, then waited, knowing the signal was being scrambled through as many as a dozen sub-routes before it got to its destination. The screen flickered wildly then cleared, DeVore's face staring out at him.

"Is it done?"

Barycz swallowed nervously, then nodded. "I've despatched copies of the files to your man. He should have them within the hour."

"Good. And the boy? He's out of it, I hope?"

Barycz bowed his head. "I've done everything as you ordered it, *Shih* Loehr. However, there is one small complication. The Director has ordered Hammond off the Project. With immediate effect."

DeVore looked away a moment, then nodded. "Fine. I'll see to that." He looked back at Barycz, smiling. "You've done well, Barycz. There'll be a bonus for you."

Barycz bowed his head again. "You are too kind . . ." When he looked up again the screen was dark.

He smiled, pleased with himself, then sat back, wondering how generous Loehr planned to be. Maybe he'd have enough to move up a deck – to buy a place in the Hundreds.

Barycz sniffed thoughtfully, then laughed, recalling how Hammond had spat in the Director's face.

"Served the bastard right . . ." he said quietly. Yes. He was not a spiteful man, but he had enjoyed the sight of Spatz getting his deserts. Enjoyed it greatly.

* * *

Lehmann stood in the doorway, looking in. "Ebert's here."

DeVore looked up from the *wei chi* board and smiled.

"Okay. I'll be up in a while. Take him through into the private suite and get one of the stewards to look after him. Tell him I won't be long."

DeVore watched his lieutenant go, then stood. He had been practising new openings. Experimenting. Seeing if he could break down old habits. That was the only trouble with *wei chi* – it was not a game to be played against oneself. One needed a steady supply of opponents; men as good as oneself – better if one really wished to improve one's game. But he had no one.

He stretched and looked about him, feeling good, noticing his furs where he had left them in the corner of the room. He had been out early, before sunrise; had gone out alone, hunting snow foxes. The pelts of five were hanging in the kitchens, drying out, the scant meat of the foxes gone into a stew – a special meal to celebrate.

Yes, things were going well. Only a few weeks ago things had seemed bleak, but now the board was filling nicely with his plays. In the north, the *Ping Tiao* were effectively destroyed and Mach's *Yu* were primed to step into the resultant power vacuum. In the east his men were in position, awaiting only his order to attack the Plantations, while to the west he was building up a new shape – seeking new allies among the élite of City North America. Added to these were two much subtler plays – the poisoned statue and his plans for the Wiring Project. All were coming to fruition. Soon the shapes on the board would change and a new phase of the game would begin – the middle game – in which his pieces would be in the ascendant.

And what was Ebert's role in all this? He had ambitions, that was clear now. Ambitions above being a puppet ruler. Well, let Ebert have them. When the time came, he would cut him down to size. Until then he would seem to trust him more.

DeVore laughed. In the meantime, maybe he would offer him the girl, the lookalike. She had been meant for Tolonen – as a "gift" to replace his murdered daughter – but Jelka's survival had meant a change of plans. He studied the board thoughtfully, then nodded. Yes, he would give Ebert the lookalike as an early wedding gift. To do with as he wished.

He smiled, then leaned across and placed a white stone on the board, breaching the space between two of the black masses, threatening to cut.

★ ★ ★

Hans Ebert stood by the open hatchway of the transporter, his left hand gripping the overhead strap tightly as the craft rose steeply from the mountainside.

DeVore's "gift" was crouched behind him against the far wall of the craft, as far from the open hatchway as she could. He could sense her there behind him and felt the hairs rise along his spine and at the back of his neck.

The bastard. The devious fucking bastard.

He smiled tightly and waved a hand at the slowly diminishing figure on the hillside far below. Then, as the craft began to bank away, he turned, looking at the girl, smiling at her reassuringly, keeping his true feelings from showing.

Games. It was all one big game to DeVore. He understood that now. And this – this "gift" of the girl – that was part of the play, too. To unsettle him, perhaps. Or mock him. Well . . . he'd not let him.

He moved past her brusquely and went through into the cockpit. Auden turned, looking at him.

"What is it, Hans?"

He took a breath then shook his head. "Nothing. But you'd best have this." He took the sealed letter DeVore had given him and handed it across. "It's to Lever. DeVore wants you to hand it to him when you meet the Americans at the spaceport. It's an invitation."

Auden tucked it away. "What else?"

Ebert smiled. Auden was a good man. He understood things without having to be told. "It's just that I don't trust him. Especially when he 'puts all his stones on the table'. He's up to something."

Auden laughed. "Like what?"

Ebert stared out through the frosted glass, noting the bleakness of their surroundings. "I don't know. It's just a feeling. And then there's his gift . . ."

Auden narrowed his eyes. "So what are you going to do with her?"

Ebert turned back, meeting his eyes briefly, then jerked away, pulling the cockpit door closed behind him.

* * *

The girl looked up as Ebert came back into the hold, her eyes wide, filled with fear. He stopped, staring at her, appalled by the likeness, then went across and stood by the open hatchway, looking outwards, his neat-cut hair barely moving in the icy wind.

"I'm sorry," he said, against the roar of the wind. "I didn't mean to frighten you." He glanced round, smiling. "Here . . . come across. I want to show you something."

She didn't move; only pressed tighter against the far wall of the cabin.

"Come . . ." he said, as softly as he could against the noise. "You've nothing to be afraid of. I just want to show you, that's all."

He watched her: saw how fear battled in her with a need to obey. *Yes*, he thought, DeVore would have instilled that in you, wouldn't he? She kept looking down, biting her lip, then glancing up at him again, in two minds.

Yes, and you're like her, he thought. Physically, anyway. But you aren't her. You're just a common peasant girl he's had changed in his labs. And the gods alone know what he's done to you. But the real Jelka wouldn't be cowering there. She would have come across of her own free will. To defy me. Just to prove to me that I didn't frighten her.

He smiled and looked down, remembering that moment in the machine when she had glared back at him. It had been then, perhaps, that he had first realised his true feelings for her. Then that he had first articulated it inside his head.

I'm in love with you, Jelka Tolonen, he had thought, surprised. *In love.*

So unexpected. So totally unexpected.

And afterwards, when she had gone, he had found himself thinking of her. Finding the image of her, there, entangled in his thoughts of other things. How strange that had been. So strange to find himself so vulnerable.

And now this . . .

He went to her and took her arm, coaxing her gently, almost tenderly across, then stood there, one arm holding tightly about her slender waist, the other reaching up to hold the strap. The wind whipped her long, golden hair back and chilled her face, but he made her look.

"There," he said. "Isn't that magnificent?"

He looked sideways at her; saw how she opened her eyes, fighting against the fear she felt; battling with it; trying to see the beauty there in that desolate place.

DeVore's thing. His "gift".

For a moment there was nothing. Then the tiniest of smiles came to her lips, the muscles about her eyes relaxing slightly as she saw.

He shivered, then drew his arm back and up, forcing her head down.

He watched the tiny figure fall away from the craft, twisting silently in the air, a tiny star of darkness against the white, growing smaller by the second, then shuddered again, a strange mixture of pain and incomprehension making him shake his head and moan.

No. There would be no impediments. Not this time. No possessive old women or mad whores with their love children. And certainly no copies.

No. Because he wanted the real Jelka, not some copy. Even if she hated him. Or maybe because she hated him. Yes, that was it perhaps. Because underneath it all she was as strong as him and that strength appealed to him, making her a challenge. A challenge he could not turn his back on.

For you will love me, Jelka Tolonen. You will.

He watched the body hit in a spray of snow then turned away, the roar of the wind abating as he drew the hatch closed behind him.

★ ★ ★

Emily Ascher turned from the door, then caught her breath, the pay-lock key falling from her hand, clattering across the bare ice floor.

"*You . . .*"

DeVore looked back at her from where he sat on the edge of her bed and smiled. "Yes, it's me."

He saw her look from him to the key, judging the distance, assessing the possibility of getting out of the room alive, and smiled inwardly.

She looked back at him, her eyes narrowed. "How did you find me?"

He tilted his head, looking her up and down, his keen eyes searching for the tell-tale bulge of a concealed weapon.

"It wasn't so hard. I've had someone trailing you since that meeting at the meat warehouse. I knew then that you were planning to get out."

"You did?" She laughed, but her face was hard. "That's strange. Because I had no plans to. Not until last night."

He smiled. "Then you got out in good time. They're all dead. Or had you heard?"

He saw the way her breathing changed, how the colour drained from her face.

"And Gesell?"

He nodded, watching her. "I made sure of him myself."

Her lips parted slightly, then she looked down. "I guess it was : . . inevitable." But when she looked back at him he saw the hatred in her eyes and knew he had been right. She was still in love with Gesell.

Such a waste, he thought. Had the worm understood how lucky he had been to share his bed with two such strong women?

No. Probably not. Like all his kind he took things without thinking of their worth.

"Mach helped me," he said, watching her closely now, his hand resting loosely on the gun in his pocket. "He arranged it all."

"Why?" she asked. "I don't understand. He wanted it to work more than any of us."

"He still does. But he wants to start again, without the taint of Bremen. New blood, with new ideals, fresh ideas."

She stared back at him a moment then shook her head. "But still with you, neh?"

"Is that why you got out? Because of my involvement?"

She hesitated, then nodded, meeting the challenge of his eyes. "It changed, after you came. It was different before, sharper, but then . . . well, you saw what happened. It wasn't like that before."

"No . . ." He seemed almost to agree. "Well, that's past, neh?"

"Is it?"

He nodded, sitting back slightly, the gun in his pocket covering her now.

"So what now? What do you want of me?"

His smile broadened. "It's not what I want. It's what Mach wants."

"And?"

"And he wants you dead."

Again that slight tremor of the breasts, that slight change in breathing, quickly controlled. She had guts, that was certain. More, perhaps, than any of them. But he had seen that much at once. Had singled her out because of it.

"I'm unarmed," she said, raising her hands slowly.

"So I see," he said. "So?"

She laughed, almost relaxed. "No . . . It wouldn't worry you at all, would it? To kill an unarmed woman."

"No, it wouldn't. But who said I was going to kill you?"

Her eyes narrowed again. "Aren't you, then?"

He shook his head, then reached into his left pocket and pulled out a wallet. It held a pass, a new set of identity

151

documents, two five hundred *yuan* credit chips and a ticket for the intercontinental jet.

"Here," he said, throwing it to her.

She caught it deftly, opened it, then looked up sharply at him. "I don't understand . . ."

"There's a price," he said. "I promised Mach I'd bring something back. To prove I'd dealt with you. A finger."

He saw the small shiver pass through her. "I see."

"It shouldn't hurt. I'll freeze the hand and cauterise the wound. There'll be no pain. Discomfort, yes, but nothing more."

She looked down, a strangely pained expression on her face, then looked up again. "Why? I mean, why are you doing this? What's your motive?"

"Do I have to have one?"

She nodded. "It's how you are."

He shrugged. "So you've told me before. But you're wrong."

"No strings, then?"

"No strings. You give me a finger and I give you your freedom, and a new life in North America."

She laughed, still not trusting him. "It's too easy. Too . . ." She shook her head.

He stood. "You're wondering why. Why should that cold, calculating bastard DeVore do this for me? What does he want? Well, I'll tell you. It's very simple. I wanted to prove that you were wrong about me."

She studied him a moment, then went across and bent down, recovering the pay-key.

"Well?" he asked. "Have we a deal?"

She looked up at him. "Have I a choice?"

"Yes. You can walk out of here, right now. I'll not stop you. But if you do, Mach will come after you with everything he's got. Because he'll not feel safe until you're dead."

"And you?"

DeVore smiled. "Oh, I'm safe. I'm always safe."

* * *

Slowly the great globe of Chung Kuo turned in space, moving through sunlight and darkness, the blank faces of its continents glistening like ice caps beneath huge swirls of cloud. Three hours had passed by the measure of men and in Sichuan Province, in the great palace at Tongjiang, Li Shai Tung sat with his son in the dim-lit silence of his study, reading through the report General Nocenzi had brought. Li Yuan stood at his father's side, scanning each sheet as his father finished with it.

The report concerned a number of items taken in a raid the previous evening on a gaming club frequented by the sons of several important Company heads. More than a dozen of the young men had been taken, together with a quantity of seditious material: posters and pamphlets, secret diaries and detailed accounts of illicit meetings. Much of the material confirmed what Tolonen had said only the day before. There was a new wave of unrest; a new tide, running for change.

They were good men – exemplary young men, it might be said – from families whose ties to the Seven went back to the foundation of the City. Men who, in other circumstances, might have served his father well. But a disease was rife among them; a foulness which, once infected, could not be shaken from the blood.

And the disease? Li Yuan looked across at the pile of folders balanced on the far side of his father's desk. There were three of them, each bulging with handwritten ice-vellum sheets. He had not had time to compare more than a few paragraphs scattered throughout each text, but he had seen enough to know that their contents were practically identical. He reached across and picked one up, flicking through the first few pages. He had seen the original in Berdichev's papers more than a year ago, amongst the material Karr had brought back with him from Mars, but had never thought to see another.

He read the title page. *The Aristotle File. Being the True History of Western Science. By Soren Berdichev.*

The document had become the classic of dissent for these

153

young men, each copy painstakingly written out in longhand.

His father turned in his seat, looking up at him. "Well, Yuan? What do you think?"

He set the file down. "It is as you said, Father. The thing is a cancer. We must cut it out, before it spreads."

The old T'ang smiled, pleased with his son. "If we can."

"You think it might already be too late?"

Li Shai Tung shrugged. "A document like this is a powerful thing, Yuan." He smiled, then stood, touching his son's arm. "But come . . . let us feed the fish. It is a while since we had the chance to talk."

Li Yuan followed his father into the semi–darkness of the arboretum, his mind filled with misgivings.

Inside, Li Shai Tung turned, facing his son, the carp pool behind him. "I come here whenever I need to think."

Li Yuan looked about him and nodded. He understood. When his father was absent, he would come here himself and stand beside the pool, staring down into the water as if emptying himself into its depths, letting his thoughts become the fish, drifting, gliding slowly, almost listlessly in the water, then rising swiftly to breach the surface, imbued with sudden purpose.

The old T'ang smiled, seeing how his son stared down into the water; so like himself in some respects.

"Sometimes I think it needs a pike . . ."

Li Yuan looked up surprised. "A pike in a carp pool, Father? But it would eat the other fish!"

Li Shai Tung nodded earnestly. "And maybe that is what was wrong with Chung Kuo. Maybe our great carp pool needed a pike. To keep the numbers down and add that missing element of sharpness. Maybe that is what we are seeing now. Maybe our present troubles are merely the consequence of all those years of peace."

"Things decay . . ." Yuan said, conscious of how far

their talk had come; of how far his father's words were from what he normally professed to believe.

"Yes . . ." Li Shai Tung nodded and eased himself back on to the great saddle of a turtle shell that was placed beside the pool. "And perhaps a pike is loose in the depths."

Li Yuan moved to the side of the pool, the toes of his boots overlapping the tiled edge.

"Have you made up your mind yet, Yuan?"

The question was unconnected to anything they had been discussing, but once again he understood. In this sense they had never been closer. His father meant the boy, Kim.

"Yes, Father. I have decided."

"And?"

Yuan turned his head, looking across at his father. Li Shai Tung sat there, his feet spread, the cane resting against one knee. Yuan could see his dead brother, Han Ch'in in that posture of his father's. Could see how his father would have resembled Han when he was younger; as if age had been given him and youth to Han. But Han was long dead and youth with it. Only old age remained. Only the crumbling patterns of their forefathers.

"I was wrong," he said after a moment. "The reports are unequivocal. It hasn't worked out. And now this . . . this matter of the sons and their 'New European' movement. I can't help but think the two are connected – that the boy is responsible for this."

Li Shai Tung's regretful smile mirrored his son's. "It *is* connected, Yuan. Without the boy there would be no file." He looked clearly at his son. "Then you will act upon my warrant and have the boy terminated?"

Li Yuan met his father's eyes, part of him still hesitant, even now. Then he nodded.

"Good. And do not trouble yourself, Yuan. You did all you could. It seems to me that the boy's end was fated."

Li Yuan had looked down; now he looked up again, surprised by his father's words. Li Shai Tung saw this and laughed. "You find it odd for me to talk of fate, neh?"

"You have always spoken of it with scorn."

155

"Maybe so, yet any man must at some point question whether it is chance or fate that brings things to pass; whether he is the author or merely the agent of his actions."

"And you, Father? What do you think?"

Li Shai Tung stood, leaning heavily upon the silver-headed cane he had come to use so often these days; the cane with the dragon's head Han Ch'in had bought him on his fiftieth birthday.

"It is said that in the time of Shang they would take a tortoise shell and cover it with ink, then throw it into a fire. When it dried, a diviner would read the cracks and lines in the scorched shell. They believed, you see, that the tortoise was an animal of great purity – in its hard-soft form they saw the meeting of Yin and Yang, of Heaven and Earth. Later they would inscribe the shells with questions put to their ancestors. As if the dead could answer."

Li Yuan smiled, reassured by the ironic tone of his father's words. For a moment he had thought . . .

"And maybe they were right, Yuan. Maybe it *is* all written. But then one must ask what it is the gods want of us. They seem to give and take without design. To build things up only to cast them down. To give a man great joy, only to snatch it away, leaving him in great despair. And to what end, Yuan? To what end?"

Yuan answered softly, touched to the core by his father's words. "I don't know, Father. Truly I don't."

Li Shai Tung shook his head bitterly. "Bones and tortoise shells . . ." He laughed and touched the great turtle shell behind him with his cane. "They say this is a copy of the great Luoshu shell, Yuan. It was a present to your mother from my father, on the day of our wedding. The pattern on its back is meant to be a charm, you see, for easing childbirth."

Yuan looked away. It was as if his father felt a need to torture himself; to surround himself with the symbols of lost joy.

"You know the story, Yuan? It was in the reign of Yu,

156

oh . . . more than four thousand years ago now, when the turtle crawled up out of the Luo River, bearing the markings on its back."

Yuan knew the story well. Every child did. But he let his father talk, finding it strange that only now should they reach this point of intimacy between them; now when things were darkest, his own life blighted by the failure of his dreams, his father's by ill health.

"Three lines of three figures were marked out there on the shell, as plain as could be seen, the Yin numbers in the corners, the Yang numbers in the centre, and each line – horizontal, vertical and diagonal – adding up to fifteen. Of course, it was hailed at once as a magic square – as a sign that supernatural powers were at work in the world. But we know better, eh, Yuan? We know there are no magic charms to aid us in our troubles – only our reason and our will. And if they fail . . ."

Li Shai Tung heaved a sigh, then sat heavily on the great saddle of the shell. He looked up at his son wearily.

"But what is the answer, Yuan? What might we do that we have not already done?"

Li Yuan looked across at his father, his eyes narrowed. "Cast oracles?"

The T'ang laughed softly. "Like our forefathers, eh?"

The old man looked away; stared down into the depths of the pool. Beyond him the moon was framed within the darkness of the window. The night was perfect, like the velvet worn about the neck of a young girl.

"I hoped for peace, Yuan. Longed for it. But . . ." He shook his head.

"What then, Father? What should we do?"

"Do?" Li Shai Tung laughed; a soft, unfamiliar sound. "Prepare ourselves, Yuan. That's all. Take care our friends are true. Sleep only when we're safe."

It was an uncharacteristically vague answer.

Yuan looked down, then broached the subject he had been avoiding all evening. "Are you well, Father? I had heard . . ."

"Heard? Heard what?" Li Shai Tung turned, his tone suddenly sharp, commanding.

Li Yuan almost smiled, but checked himself, knowing his father's eagle eye was on him. "Only that you were not your best, Father. No more than that. Headaches. Mild stomach upsets. But do not be angry with me. A son should be concerned for his father's health."

Li Shai Tung grunted. "Not my best, eh? Well, that's true of us all after thirty. We're never again at our best." He was silent a moment, then turned, tapping his cane against the tiled floor. "Maybe that's true of all things – that they're never at their best after a while. Men and the things men build."

"Particulars, Father. Particulars."

The old man stared at him a moment, then nodded. "So I've always lectured you, Yuan. You learn well. You always did. You were always suited for this."

There was a long silence between them. Han Ch'in's death lay there in that silence; cold, heavy, unmentionable: a dark stone of grief in the guts of each that neither had managed to pass.

"And Fei Yen?"

It was the first time his father had mentioned the separation. The matter was not yet public knowledge.

Li Yuan sighed. "It's still the same."

There was real pain in Li Shai Tung's face. "You should command her, Yuan. Order her to come home."

Li Yuan shook his head, controlling what he felt. "With great respect, Father, I know what's best in this. She hates me. I know that now. To have her in my home would . . . would weaken me."

Li Shai Tung was watching his son closely, his shoulders slightly hunched. "Ah . . ." He lifted his chin. "I did not know that, Yuan. I . . ." Again he sighed. "I'm sorry, Yuan, but the child. What of the child?"

Li Yuan swallowed, then raised his head again, facing the matter squarely. "The child is not mine. Fei Yen was unfaithful to me. The child belongs to another man."

The old man came closer; came round the pool and stood there, facing his son.

"You know this for certain?"

"No, but I know it. Fei Yen herself . . ."

"No. I don't mean 'know it' in some vague sense, I mean *know* it, for good and certain." His voice had grown fierce, commanding once more. "This is important, Yuan. I'm surprised at you. You should have seen to this."

Li Yuan nodded. It was so, but he had not wanted to face it. Had not wanted to know for good and certain. He had been quite happy accepting her word.

"You must go to her and offer her divorce terms, Yuan. At once. But you will make the offer conditional. You understand?"

Again he nodded, understanding. There would need to be tests. Tests to ascertain the father of the child. Genotyping. Then he would know. Know for good and certain. He gritted his teeth, feeling the pain like a needle in his guts.

"Good," said the T'ang, seeing that what he had wanted was accomplished. "There must be no room for doubt in the future. If your son is to rule, he must be uncontested. *Your* son, not some cuckoo in the nest."

The words stung Li Yuan, but that was their aim. His father knew when to spare and when to goad.

"And then?" Li Yuan felt drained suddenly; empty of thought.

"And then you marry again. Not one wife, but two. Six if need be, Yuan. Have sons. Make the family strong again. *Provide.*"

He nodded, unable to conceive of life with any other woman but Fei Yen, but for now obedient to his father's wishes.

"*Love!*" There was a strange bitterness to his father's voice. An edge. "It's never enough, Yuan. Remember that. It always fails you in the end. Always."

Li Yuan looked up, meeting his father's eyes, seeing the

love and hurt and pain there where for others there was nothing.

"All love?"

The T'ang nodded and reached out to hold his son's shoulder. "All love, Yuan. Even this."

★ ★ ★

There was a pounding at the outer doors. Li Shai Tung woke, drenched in sweat, the dream of his first wife, Lin Yua and that dreadful night so clear that, for a moment, he thought the banging on the doors a part of it. He sat up, feeling weak, disoriented. The banging came again.

"Gods help us . . . what is it now?" he muttered, getting up slowly and pulling on his gown.

He went across and stood there, facing the doors. "Who is it?"

"It is I, *Chieh Hsia*. Your Chancellor, Chung Hu-yan."

He shivered. Chung Hu-yan. As in the dream. As on the night Lin Yua had died, giving birth to his son, Yuan. For a moment he could not answer him.

"*Chieh Hsia*," came the voice again. "Are you all right?"

He turned, looking about him, then turned back. No. He was here. He wasn't dreaming. Seventeen, almost eighteen years had passed and he was here, in his palace, and the knocking on the door, the voice – both were real.

"Hold on, Chung. I'm coming . . ."

He heard how weak his voice sounded, how indecisive, and shivered. Sweat trickled down his inner arms, formed on his forehead. Why was everything suddenly so difficult?

He fumbled with the lock, then drew back the catch. Stepping back, he watched the doors open. Chung Hu-yan stood there, flanked by two guards.

"What is it, Chung?" he said, his voice quavering, seeing the fear in his Chancellor's face.

Chung Hu-yan bowed low. "News has come, *Chieh Hsia*. Bad news."

Bad news . . . He felt his stomach tighten. Li Yuan was dead. Or Tsu Ma. Or . . .

"What is it, Chung?" he said again, unconscious of the repetition.

In answer Chung moved aside. Tolonen was standing there, his face ashen.

"*Chieh Hsia* . . ." the Marshal began, then went down on one knee, bowing his head low. "I have failed you, my lord . . . failed you."

Li Shai Tung half turned, looking to see who was standing behind him, but there was no one. He frowned then turned back. "Failed, Knut? How failed?"

"The Plantations . . ." Tolonen said, then looked up at him again, tears in his eyes. "The Plantations are on fire."

CHAPTER·5

THE BROKEN WHEEL

A huge window filled the end of the corridor where the tunnel turned to the right, intersecting with the boarding hatch. She stood there a moment, looking out across the pre-dawn darkness of the spaceport, barely conscious of the passengers pushing by, knowing that this was probably the last view she would ever have of City Europe – the City in which she had spent her whole life. But that life was over now and a new one lay ahead. Emily Ascher was dead, killed in a fictitious accident three days back. She was Mary Jennings now, a blonde from Atlanta Canton, returning to the eastern seaboard after a two-year secondment to the European arm of her Company.

She had sat up until late learning the brief she had been sent, then snatched three hours before the call came. That had been an hour back. Now she stood, quite literally, on the threshold of a new life, hesitating, wondering even now if she had done the right thing.

Was it really too late to go back – to make her peace with Mach? She sighed and let her fingers move slowly down the dark, smooth surface of the glass. Yes. DeVore might have been lying when he said he had no motive in helping her, but he was right about Mach wanting her dead. She had given Mach no option. No one left the *Ping Tiao*. Not voluntarily, anyway. And certainly not alive.

Even so, wasn't there some other choice? Some other option than putting herself in debt to DeVore?

She looked down at her bandaged left hand then smiled cynically at her reflection in the darkened glass. If there had been she would not be here. Besides, there were things she had to do. Important things. And maybe she could do them just as well in America. If DeVore let her.

It was a big if, but she was prepared to take the chance. The only other choice was death, and while she didn't fear death, it was hardly worth pre-empting things. No. She would reserve that option. Would keep it as her final bargaining counter. Just in case DeVore proved difficult. And maybe she'd even take him with her. If she could.

Her smile broadened, lost its hard edge. She turned, joining the line of boarding passengers, holding out her pass to the tiny Han stewardess, then moved down the aisle towards her seat.

She was about to sit when the steward touched her arm.

"Forgive me, *Fu Jen*, but have you a reserved ticket for that seat?"

She turned, straightening up, then held out her ticket for inspection, looking the man up and down as she did so. He was a squat, broad-shouldered Han with one of those hard, anonymous faces some of them had. She knew what he was at once. One of those minor officials who gloried in their pettiness.

He made a great pretence of studying her ticket, turning it over, then turning it back. His eyes flicked up to her face, then took in her clothes, her lack of jewellery, before returning to her face again – the disdain in them barely masked. He shook his head.

"If you would follow me, *Fu Jen* . . ."

He turned, making his way back down the aisle towards the cramped third- and fourth-class seats at the tail of the rocket, but she stood where she was, her stomach tightening, anticipating the tussle to come.

Realising that she wasn't following him, he came back, his whole manner suddenly, quite brutally antagonistic.

"You must come, *Fu Jen*. These seats are reserved for others."

She shook her head. "I have a ticket."

He tucked the ticket down into the top pocket of his

official tunic. "Forgive me, *Fu Jen*, but there has been a mistake. As I said, these seats are reserved. Paid for in advance."

The emphasis on the last few words gave his game away. For a moment she had thought that this might be DeVore's final little game with her, but now she knew. The steward was out to extract some squeeze from her. To get her to pay for what was already rightfully hers. She glared at him, despising him, then turned and sat. If he just so much as tried to make her budge . . .

He leaned over her, angry now. "*Fu Jen*! You must move! Now! At once! Or I will call the captain!"

She was about to answer him when a hand appeared on the steward's shoulder and drew him back sharply.

It was a big man. A *Hung Mao*. He pushed the Han steward back unceremoniously, a scathing look of contempt on his face. "Have you left your senses, man? The lady has paid for her seat. Now give her her ticket back and leave her alone, or I'll report you to the port authorities – understand me, *hsiao jen*?"

The steward opened his mouth then closed it again, seeing the Security warrant card the man was holding out. Lowering his eyes, he took the ticket from his pocket and handed it across.

"Good!" The man handed it to her with a smile, then turned back, shaking his head. "Now get lost, you little fucker. If I so much as see you in this section during the flight . . ."

The Han swallowed and backed away hurriedly.

The man turned back, looking at her. "I'm sorry about that. They always try it on. A single woman, travelling alone. Your kind is usually good for fifty *yuan* at least."

She looked at her ticket, a small shudder of indignation passing through her, then looked back at him, smiling. "Thank you. I appreciate your help, but I would have been all right."

He nodded. "Maybe. But a mutual friend asked me to look after you."

"Ah . . ." She narrowed her eyes, then tilted her head slightly, indicating the warrant card he still held in one hand. "And that's real?"

He laughed. "Of course. Look, can I sit for a moment? There are one or two things we need to sort out."

She hesitated, then gave a small nod. No strings, eh? But it was just as she'd expected. She had known all along that DeVore would have some reason for helping her out.

"What is it?" she asked, turning in her seat to study him as he sat down beside her.

"These . . ." He handed her a wallet and a set of cards. The cards were in the name of Rachel DeValerian; the wallet contained a set of references for Mary Jennings, including the documentation for a degree in economics, and a letter of introduction to Michael Lever, the director of a company called MemSys. A letter dated two days from then.

She looked up at him. "I don't understand."

He smiled. "You'll need a job over there. Well, the Levers will have a vacancy for an economist on their personal staff. As of tomorrow."

How do you know? she was going to ask, but his smile was answer enough. If DeVore said there was going to be a vacancy, there would be a vacancy. But why the Levers? And what about the other identity?

"What's this?" she asked, holding out the DeValerian cards.

He shrugged. "I'm only the messenger. Our friend said you would know what to do with them."

"I see." She studied them a moment, then put them away. Then DeVore meant her to set up her own movement. To recruit. She smiled and looked up again. "What else?"

He returned her smile, briefly covering her left hand with his right. "Nothing. But I'll be back in a second if you need me. Enjoy the flight." He stood. "Okay. See you in Boston."

"Boston? I thought we were going to New York?"

He shook his head, then leaned forward. "Hadn't you heard? New York is closed. Wu Shih is holding an emergency meeting of the Seven and there's a two-hundred-*li* exclusion zone about Manhattan."

She frowned. "I didn't know. What's up?"

He laughed, then leaned forward and touched his finger to the panel on the seatback in front of her. At once the screen lit up, showing a scene of devastation.

"There!" he said. "That's what's up."

* * *

The two men sat on the high wall of the dyke as the dawn came, looking out across the flat expanse of blackened fields, watching the figures move almost somnolently in the darkness below. The tart smell of burned crops seemed to taint every breath they took, despite the filters both wore. They were dressed in the uniform of reserve corps volunteers, and though only one of the two wore it legitimately, it would have been hard to tell which.

Great palls of smoke lifted above the distant horizon, turning the dawn's light ochre, while, two *li* out, a convoy of transporters sped westwards, heading back towards the safety of the City.

DeVore smiled and sat back. He took a pack of mint drops from his top pocket and offered one to his companion. Mach looked at the packet a moment, then took one. For a while both men were quiet, contemplating the scene, then Mach spoke.

"What now?"

DeVore met Mach's eyes. "Now we melt away. Like ghosts."

Mach smiled. "And then?"

"Then nothing. Not for a long time. You go underground. Recruit. Build your movement up again. I'll provide whatever finance you need. But you must do nothing. Not until we're ready."

"And the Seven?"

DeVore looked down. "The Seven will look to

strengthen their defences. But they will have to spread themselves thin. Too thin, perhaps. Besides, they've their own problems. There's a split in Council."

Mach stared at the other man a moment, wide-eyed, wondering, as he had so often lately, how DeVore came to know so much. And why it was that such a man should want to fight against the Seven.

"Why do you hate them so much?" he asked.

DeVore looked back at him. "Why do you?"

"Because the world they've made is a prison. For everyone. But especially for those lower down."

"And you care about that?"

Mach nodded. "Out here . . . this is real, don't you think? But that inside." He shuddered and looked away, his eyes going off to the horizon. "Well, it's never made sense to me, why human beings should have to live like that. Penned in like meat-animals. Hemmed in by rules. Sorted by money into their levels. I always hated it. Even when I was a child of five or six. And I used to feel so impotent about it."

"But not now?"

"No. Not now. Now I've a direction for my anger."

They were silent again, then Mach turned his head, looking at DeVore. "What of Ascher?"

DeVore shook his head. "She's vanished. I thought we had her, but she slipped through our fingers. She's good, you know."

Mach smiled. "Yes. She was always the best of us. Even Gesell realised that. But she was inflexible. She was always letting her idealism get in the way of practicalities. It was inevitable that she'd break with us."

"So what will you do?"

"Do? Nothing. Oh, I'll cover my back, don't worry. But if I know our Emily, she'll have found some way of getting out of City Europe. She was always talking of setting up somewhere else – of spreading our influence. She's a good organiser. I'd wager good money we'll hear from her again."

DeVore smiled, thinking of her – at that very moment – on the jet to America, and of her left index finger, frozen in its medical case, heading out for Mars. "Yes," he said. "We shall. I'm sure we shall."

* * *

They stood there on the high stone balcony, the seven great lords of Chung Kuo, the sky a perfect blue overhead, the early morning sunlight glistening from the imperial yellow of their silks. Below them the great garden stretched away, flanked by the two great rivers, the whole enclosed within a single, unbroken wall, its lakes and pagodas, its tiny woods and flower beds, its bridges and shaded walkways a pleasure to behold. A curl of red stone steps, shaped like a dragon's tail, led down. Slowly, their talk a low murmur barely discernible above the call of the caged birds in the trees, they made their way down, Wu Shih, their host, leading the way.

At the foot of the steps he turned, looking back. Beyond the gathered T'ang his palace sat atop its artificial mound, firmly embedded, as if it had always been there, its pure white walls topped with steep roofs of red tile, the whole great structure capped by a slender six-storey pagoda that stood out, silhouetted against the sky. He nodded, satisfied, then put out his arm, inviting his cousins into his garden.

There was the soft tinkling of pagoda bells in the wind, the scent of jasmine and forsythia, of gardenia and chrysanthemum wafting to them through the great moon door in the wall. They stepped through, into another world; a world of ancient delights, of strict order made to seem like casual occurrence, of a thousand shades of green contrasted against the grey of stone, the white of walls, the red of tile. It was, though Wu Shih himself made no such claim, the greatest garden in Chung Kuo – the Garden of Supreme Excellence – formed of a dozen separate gardens, each modelled on a famous original.

Their business was done, agreement reached as to the

way ahead. Now it was time to relax, to unburden themselves, and where better than here where symmetry and
disorder, artistry and chance, met in such perfect balance?

Wu Shih looked about him, immensely pleased. The
garden had been built by his great-great-grandfather, but,
like his father and his father's father, he had made his own
small changes to the original scheme, extending the garden
to the north, so that it now filled the whole of the ancient
island of Manhattan.

"It is a beautiful garden, cousin," Wang Sau-leyan said,
turning to him and smiling pleasantly. "There are few
pleasures as sweet in life as that derived from a harmoni-
ously created garden."

Wu Shih smiled, surprised for the second time that
morning at Wang Sau-leyan. It was as if he were a changed
man, all rudeness, all abrasiveness gone from his manner.
Earlier, in Council, he had gone out of his way to assure
Li Shai Tung of his support, even pre-empting Wei Feng's
offer of help by giving Li Shai Tung a substantial amount
of grain from his own reserves. The generosity of the offer
had surprised them all and had prompted a whole spate of
spontaneous offers. The session had ended with the seven
of them grinning broadly, their earlier mood of despon-
dency cast aside, their sense of unity rebuilt. They were
Seven again. Seven.

Wu Shih reached out and touched the young T'ang's
arm. "If there is heaven on earth it is here, in the garden."

Wang Sau-leyan gave the slightest bow of his head, as
if in deference to Wu Shih's greater age and experience.
Again Wu Shih found himself pleased by the gesture.
Perhaps they had been mistaken about Wang Sau-leyan.
Perhaps it was only youth and the shock of his father's
murder, his brother's suicide, that had made him so. That
and the uncertainty of things.

Wang Sau-leyan turned, indicating the ancient, rusted
sign bolted high up on the trunk of a nearby juniper.

"Tell me, Wu Shih. What is the meaning of that sign?
All else here is Han. But that . . ."

"That?" Wu Shih laughed softly, drawing the attention of the other T'ang. "That is a joke of my great-great-grandfather's, cousin Wang. You see, before he built this garden, part of the greatest city of the Americans sat upon this site. It was from here that they effectively ran their great republic of sixty-nine states. And here, where we are walking right now, was the very heart of their financial empire. The story goes that my great-great-grandfather came to see with his own eyes the destruction of their great city and that, seeing the sign, he smiled, appreciating the play on words. After all, what is more Han than a wall? Hence he ordered the sign kept. And so this path is known, even now, by its original name. Wall Street."

The watching T'ang smiled, appreciating the story.

"We would do well to learn from them," Wei Feng said, reaching up to pick a leaf from the branch. He put it to his mouth and tasted it, then looked back at Wang Sau-leyan, his ancient face creased into a smile. "They tried too hard. Their ambition always exceeded their grasp. Like their ridiculous scheme to colonise the stars."

Again Wang Sau-leyan gave the slightest bow. "I agree, cousin. And yet we still use the craft they designed and built. Like much else they made."

"True," Wei Feng answered him. "I did not say that all they did was bad. Yet they had no sense of rightness. Of balance. What they did, they did carelessly, without thought. In that respect we would do well not to be like them. It was thoughtlessness that brought their empire low."

"And arrogance," added Wu Shih, looking about him. "But come. Let us move on. I have arranged for *ch'a* to be served in the pavilion beside the lake. There will be entertainments, too."

There were smiles at that. It had been some time since they had had the chance for such indulgences. Wu Shih turned, leading them along the *lang*, the covered walkway, then up a twist of wooden steps and out on to a broad gallery above a concealed lake.

A low wooden balustrade was raised on pillars above a

tangle of sculpted rock, forming a square about the circle of the lake, the wood painted bright red, the pictogram for immortality cut into it in a repeated pattern. The broad, richly green leaves of lotus choked the water, while, in a thatched *ting* on the far side of the lake, a group of musicians began to play, the ancient sound drifting across to where the Seven sat.

Li Shai Tung sat back in his chair, looking about him at his fellow T'ang. For the first time in months the cloud had lifted from his spirits, the tightness in his stomach vanished. And he was not alone, he could see that now. They all seemed brighter; refreshed and strengthened by the morning's events. So it was. So it had to be. He had not realised how important it was before now; had not understood how much their strength depended on them being of a single mind. And now that Wang Sau-leyan had come to his senses they would be strong again. It was only a matter of will.

He looked across at the young T'ang of Africa, and smiled. "I am grateful for your support, cousin Wang. If there is something I might do for you in return?"

Wang Sau-leyan smiled and looked about him, his broad face momentarily the image of his father's when he was younger, then he looked down. It was a gesture of considerable modesty. "In the present circumstances it is enough that we help each other, neh?" He looked up, meeting Li Shai Tung's eyes. "I am a proud man, Li Shai Tung, but not too proud to admit it when I have been wrong – and I was wrong about the threat from the *Ping Tiao*. If my offer helps make amends I am satisfied."

Li Shai Tung looked about him, a smile of intense satisfaction lighting his face. He turned back to the young T'ang, nodding. "Your kind words refresh me, cousin Wang. There is great wisdom in knowing when one is wrong. Indeed, I have heard it called the first step on the path to true benevolence."

Wang Sau-leyan lowered his head but said nothing. For a while they were quiet, listening to the ancient music.

Servants moved among them, serving *ch'a* and sweet-meats, their pale green silks blending with the colours of the garden.

"Beautiful," said Tsu Ma, when it had finished. There was a strange wistfulness to his expression. "It is some time since I heard that last piece played so well."

"Indeed . . ." began Wu Shih, then stopped, turning as his Chancellor appeared at the far end of the gallery. "Come, Fen . . ." he said, signalling him to come closer. "What is it?"

Fen Cho-hsien stopped some paces from his T'ang, bowing to each of the other T'ang in turn before facing his master again and bowing low. "I would not have bothered you, *Chieh Hsia*, but an urgent message has just arrived. It seems that Lord Li's general has been taken ill."

Li Shai Tung leaned forward anxiously. "Nocenzi, ill? What in the gods' names is wrong with him?"

Fen turned, facing Li Shai Tung, lowering his eyes. "Forgive me, *Chieh Hsia*, but no one seems to know. It seems, however, that he is extremely ill. And not just him, but his wife and children, too. Indeed, if the report is accurate, his wife is already dead, and two of his children."

Li Shai Tung looked down, groaning softly. Gods, was there no end to this? He looked up again, tears in his eyes, the tightness returned to his stomach.

"You will forgive me, cousins, if I return at once?"

There was a murmur of sympathy. All eyes were on the old T'ang, noting his sudden frailty, the way his shoulders hunched forward at this latest calamity. But it was Wang Sau-leyan who rose and helped him from his chair; who walked with him, his arm about his shoulder, to the steps.

Li Shai Tung turned, looking up into the young T'ang's face, holding his arm briefly, gratefully. "Thank you, Sau-leyan. You are your father's son." Then he turned back, going down the twist of steps, letting Wu Shih's Chancellor lead him, head bowed, back down Wall Street to the dragon steps and his waiting craft.

★ ★ ★

Kim woke and lay there in the darkness, strangely alert, listening. For a moment he didn't understand. There was nothing. Nothing at all. Then he shivered. Of course . . . That was it. The silence was too perfect. There was always some noise or other from the corridors outside, but just now there was nothing.

He sat up, then threw back the sheet. For a moment he paused, stretching, working the last traces of the drug from his limbs, then crouched, listening again.

Nothing.

He crossed the room and stood there by the door, his mind running through possibilities. Maybe they had moved him. Or maybe they had closed down the Project and abandoned him. Left him to his fate. But he was not satisfied with either explanation. He reached out, trying the lock.

The door hissed back. Outside, the corridor was dark, empty. Only at the far end was there a light. On the wall outside the guard-room.

He shivered, the hairs on his neck and back rising. The overhead cameras were dead, the red wink of their operational lights switched off. And at the far end of the corridor, beyond the wall-mounted lamp, the door to the Project was open, the barrier up.

Something was wrong.

He stood there a moment, not certain what to do, then let instinct take over. Turning to his left he ran, making for T'ai Cho's room and the labs beyond, hoping it wasn't too late.

T'ai Cho's room was empty. Kim turned, tensing, hearing the soft murmur of voices further along the corridor, then relaxed. They were voices he knew. He hurried towards them, then slowed. The door to the labs was wide open, as if it had been jammed. That too was wrong. It was supposed to be closed when not in use, on a time-lock.

He twirled about, looking back down the dimly lit corridor. The few wall lights that were working were back-ups. Emergency lighting only. The main power system must

173

have gone down. But was that an accident? Or had it been done deliberately?

He stepped inside, cautious now, glancing across to his right where Spatz's office was. He could see the Director through the open doorway, cursing, pounding the keyboard on his desk computer, trying to get some response from it. As he watched, Spatz tried the emergency phone, then threw the handset down angrily.

Then maybe it had just happened. Maybe the shut-down had been what had woken him.

He ducked low and scuttled across the open space between the door and the first row of desks, hoping Spatz wouldn't catch a glimpse of him, then ran along the corridor between the desks until he came to the end. The main labs were to the left, the voices louder now. He could hear T'ai Cho's among them.

He hesitated, turning his head, staring back the way he'd come, but the corridor was empty. He went on, coming out into the labs.

They were seated on the far side, some in chairs, some leaning on the desk. All of them were there except Hammond. They looked round as he entered, their talk faltering.

"Kim!" T'ai Cho said, getting up.

Kim put up his hand, as if to fend off his friend. "You've got to get out! Now! Something's wrong!"

Ellis, the Director's Assistant, smiled and shook his head. "It's all right, Kim. It's only a power failure. Spatz has gone to sort things out."

Kim looked about him. A few of them were vaguely uneasy, but nothing more. It was clear they agreed with Ellis.

"No!" he said, trying to keep the panic from his voice. "It's more than that. The guards have gone and all the doors are jammed open. Can't you see what that means? We've got to get out! Something's going to happen!"

Ellis stood up. "Are you sure? The guards really aren't there?"

174

Kim nodded urgently. He could feel the tension like a coil in him; could feel responses waking in him that he hadn't felt since . . . well, since they'd tried to reconstruct him. He could feel his heart hammering in his chest, his blood coursing like a dark, hot tide in his veins. And above all he could feel all his senses heightened by the danger they were in. It was as if he could hear and see, smell and taste better than before.

He lunged forward, grabbing at T'ai Cho's arm, dragging him back. T'ai Cho began resisting, but Kim held on tenaciously. "Come on!" he begged. "Before they come!"

"What in the gods' names are you talking of, Kim?"

"Come on!" he pleaded. "You've got to come! All of you!"

He could see how his words had changed them. They were looking to each other now anxiously.

"Come on!" Ellis said. "Kim could be right!"

They made for the outer offices, but it was too late. As Kim tugged T'ai Cho around the corner he could see them coming down the corridor, not forty *ch'i* away. There were four of them, dressed in black, suited up and masked, huge lantern guns cradled against their chests. Seeing the tall figure of T'ai Cho, the first of them raised his gun and fired.

Kim pulled T'ai Cho down, then scrambled back, feeling the convected warmth of the gun's discharge in the air, accompanied by a sharp, sweet scent that might almost have been pleasant had it not signalled something so deadly.

"Get back!" he yelled to the others behind him, but even as he said it he understood. They were trapped here. Like the GenSyn apes they had been experimenting upon. Unarmed and with no means of escape.

"Dead . . ." he said softly to himself. *Dead. As if they'd never been.*

* * *

The assassin backed away, shuddering, glad that his mask filtered out the stench of burned flesh that filled the room. He felt a small shiver ripple down his back. He hadn't expected them to act as they had. Hadn't believed that they would just get down on their knees and die, heads bowed.

But maybe that was what made them different from him. Made them watchers, not doers; passive, not active. Even so, the way they had just accepted their deaths made him feel odd. It wasn't that he felt pity for them; far from it – their passivity revolted him. Himself, he would have died fighting for his life, clawing and scratching his way out of existence. But it was the way they made him feel. As if they'd robbed him of something.

He turned away. The others had gone already – had gone to fetch the boy and plant the explosives. Time then to get out. He took a couple of paces then stopped, twisting round.

Nerves, he thought. It's only nerves. It's only one of the apes, scuttling about in its cage. Even so, he went back, making sure, remembering what DeVore had said about taking pains.

He stopped, his right boot almost touching the leg of one of the dead men, and looked about him, frowning. The four apes lay on the floor of their cages, drugged. "Funny . . ." he began. Then, without warning, his legs were grabbed from behind, throwing him forward on to the pile of bodies.

He turned, gasping, his gun gone from him, but the creature was on him in an instant, something hard smashing down into his face, breaking his nose. He groaned, the hot pain of the blow flooding his senses, stunning him.

He put his hands up to his face, astonished. "What the hell?"

This time the blow came to the side of his head, just beside his left eye.

"Kuan Yin!" he screeched, pulling his head back sharply, coughing as the blood began to fill his mouth. He reached out wildly, trying to grasp the creature, but it had moved away. He sat forward, squinting through a blood haze at what looked no more than a child. But not just a child. This was like something out of nightmare.

It stood there, hunched and spindly, the weight held threateningly in one tiny hand, its big, dark, staring eyes fixed murderously on him, its mouth set in a snarl of deadly intent.

"Gods . . ." he whispered, feeling himself go cold. Was this what they were making here? These . . . *things*?

But even as the thought came to him, the creature gave an unearthly yell and leapt on him – leapt high, like something demented – and brought the weight down hard, robbing him of breath.

★ ★ ★

Li Shai Tung turned, angered by what he had seen, and confronted the Chief Surgeon.

"What in the gods' names did this to him, Chang Li?"

Chang Li fell to his knees, his head bent low. "Forgive me, *Chieh Hsia*, but the cause of the General's affliction is not yet known. We are carrying out an autopsy on his wife and children, but as yet . . ."

"The children?" Li Shai Tung took a long breath, calming himself. His eyes were red, his cheeks wet with tears. His right hand gripped at his left shoulder almost convulsively, then let it go, flinging itself outward in a gesture of despair.

"Will he live?"

Again the Chief Surgeon lowered his head. "It is too early to say, *Chieh Hsia*. Whatever it was, it was strong enough to kill his wife and two of his children within the hour. Nocenzi and his other daughter . . . well . . . they're both very ill."

"And you've definitely ruled out some kind of poison in the food?"

Chang Li nodded. "That is so, *Chieh Hsia*. It seems the Nocenzis were eating with friends when they were stricken – sharing from the same serving bowls, the same ricepot.

And yet the three who ate with them are totally unharmed."

Li Shai Tung shuddered, then beckoned the man to get up. "Thank you, Chang Li. But let me know, neh? As soon as anything is known. And do not tell the General yet of the loss of his wife or children. Let him grow stronger before you break the news. I would not have him survive this only to die of a broken heart."

Chang Li bowed his head. "It shall be as you say, *Chieh Hsia*."

"Good." He turned away, making his way across to the great hallway of the hospital, his guards and retainers at a respectful distance. Nocenzi had been conscious when he'd seen him. Even so, he had looked like a ghost of his former self, all his *ch'i*, his vital energy, drained from him. His voice had been as faint as the whisper of a breeze against silk.

"Forgive me, *Chieh Hsia*," he had said, "but you will need a new general now."

He had taken Nocenzi's hand, denying him, but Nocenzi had insisted, squeezing his hand weakly, not releasing it until the T'ang accepted his resignation.

He stopped, remembering the moment, then leaned forward slightly, a mild wash of pain in his arms and lower abdomen making him feel giddy. It passed and he straightened up, but a moment later it returned, stronger, burning like a coal in his guts. He groaned and stumbled forward, almost falling against the tiled floor, but one of his courtiers caught him just in time.

"*Chieh Hsia!*"

There was a strong babble of concerned voices, a thicket of hands reaching out to steady him, but Li Shai Tung was conscious only of the way his skin stung as if it were stretched too tightly over his bones – how his eyes smarted as if hot water had been thrown into them. He took a shuddering breath, then felt the pain spear through him again.

Gods! What was this?

Doctors were hurrying to him now, lifting him with careful, expert hands, speaking soothingly as they helped support him and half carry him back towards the wards.

The pain was ebbing now, the strength returning to his limbs.

"Wait . . ." he said softly. Then, when they seemed not to hear him, he repeated it, stronger this time, commanding them. "Hold there!"

At once they moved back, releasing him, but stayed close enough to catch him if he fell. Chang Li was there now. He had hurried back when he had heard.

"*Chieh Hsia*. . . what is it?"

Li Shai Tung straightened, taking a breath. The pain had left him feeling a little light-headed, but otherwise he seemed all right.

"I'm fine now," he said. "It was but a momentary cramp, that's all. My stomach. Hasty eating and my anxiety for the General's welfare, I'm sure."

He saw how Chang Li looked at him, uncertain how to act, and almost laughed.

"If it worries you so much, Surgeon Chang, you might send two of your best men to accompany me on the journey home. But I must get back. There is much to be done. I must see my son and speak to him. And I have a new general to appoint."

He smiled, looking about him, seeing his smile mirrored uncertainly in thirty faces. "I, above all others, cannot afford to be ill. Where would Chung Kuo be if we who ruled were always being sick?"

There was laughter, but it lacked the heartiness, the sincerity of the laughter he was accustomed to from those surrounding him. He could hear the fear in their voices and understood its origin. And, in some small way, was reassured by it. It was when the laughter ceased altogether that one had to worry. When fear gave way to relief and a different kind of laughter.

He looked about him, his head lifted, his heart suddenly

179

warmed by their concern for him, then turned and began making his way back to the imperial craft.

★ ★ ★

Yin Tsu welcomed the Prince and brought him *ch'a*.

"You know why I've come?" Li Yuan asked, trying to conceal the pain he felt.

Yin Tsu bowed his head, his ancient face deeply lined. "I know, Li Yuan. And I am sorry that this day has come. My house is greatly saddened."

Li Yuan nodded uncomfortably. The last thing he had wished for was to hurt the old man, but it could not be helped. Even so, this was a bitter business. Twice Yin Tsu had thought to link his line with kings, and twice he had been denied that honour.

"You will not lose by this, Yin Tsu," he said softly, his heart going out to the old man. "Your sons . . ."

But it was only half true. After all, what could he give Yin's sons to balance the scale? Nothing. Or as good as.

Yin Tsu bowed lower.

"Can I see her, Father?"

It was the last time he would call him that and he could see the pain it brought to the old man's face. *This was not my doing*, he thought, watching Yin Tsu straighten up then go to bring her.

He was back almost at once, leading his daughter.

Fei Yen sat across from him, her head bowed, waiting. She was more than eight months now, so this had to be dealt with at once. The child might come any day. Even so, he was determined to be gentle with her.

"How are you?" he asked tenderly, concerned for her in spite of all that had happened between them.

"I am well, my lord," she answered, subdued, unable to look at him. She knew how things stood. Knew why he had come.

"Fei Yen, this is . . . painful for me. But you knew when we wed that I was not as other men – that my life, my choices were not those of normal men." He sighed

180

deeply, finding it hard to say what he must. He raised his chin, looking at Yin Tsu, who nodded, his face held rigid in a grimace of pain. "My Family . . . I must ensure my line. Make certain."

These were evasions. He had yet to say it direct. He took another breath and spoke.

"You say it is not my child. But I must be sure of that. There must be tests. And then, if it is so, we must be divorced. For no claim can be permitted if the child is not mine. You must be clear on that, Fei Yen."

Again Yin Tsu nodded. Beside him his daughter was still, silent.

He looked away, momentarily overcome by the strength of what he still felt for her, then forced himself to be insistent.

"Will you do as I say, Fei Yen?"

She looked up at him. Her eyes were wet with tears. Dark, almond eyes that pierced him with their beauty. "I will do whatever you wish, my lord."

He stared at her, wanting to cross the space between them and kiss away her tears; to forgive her everything and start again. Even now. Even after all she had done to him. But she had left him no alternative. This thing could not be changed. In this he could not trust to what he felt, for feeling had failed him. His father was right. What good was feeling when the world was dark and hostile? Besides, his son must be *his* son.

"Then it shall be done," he said bluntly, almost angrily. "Tomorrow."

He stood, then walked across the room, touching the old man's arm briefly, sympathetically. "And we shall speak again tomorrow, Yin Tsu. When things are better known."

* * *

The old Han squatted at the entrance to the corridor, waiting there patiently, knowing the dream had been a true dream; one of those he could not afford to ignore. Beside him, against the wall, he had placed those things he had seen himself use in the dream – a blanket and his old porcelain water-bottle.

This level was almost deserted. The great clothing factory that took up most of it had shut down its operations more than four hours back and only a handful of Security guards and maintenance engineers were to be found down here now. The old man smiled, recalling how he had slipped past the guards like a shadow.

His name was Tuan Ti Fo and, though he squatted like a young man, his muscles uncomplaining under him, he was as old as the great City itself. This knowledge he kept to himself, for to others he was simply Old Tuan, his age, like his origins, undefined. He lived simply, some would say frugally, in his rooms eight levels up from where he now waited. And though many knew him, few could claim to be close to the peaceful, white-haired old man. He kept himself very much to himself, studying the ancient books he kept in the box beside his bed, doing his exercises, or playing himself at *wei chi* – long games that could take a day, sometimes even a week to complete.

The corridor he was facing was less than twenty *ch'i* long; a narrow, dimly lit affair that was little more than a feeder tunnel to the maintenance hatch in the ceiling at its far end. Tuan Ti Fo watched, knowing what would happen, his ancient eyes half-lidded, his breathing unaltered as the hatch juddered once, twice, then dropped, swinging violently on the hinge. A moment later a foot appeared – a child's foot – followed by a leg, a steadying hand. He watched the boy emerge, legs first, then drop.

Tuan Ti Fo lifted himself slightly, staring into the dimness. For a time the boy lay where he had fallen, then he rolled over on to his side, a small whimper – of pain, perhaps, or fear – carrying to where the old Han crouched.

In the dream this was the moment when he had acted.

And so now. Nodding gently to himself, he reached beside him for the blanket.

Tuan Ti Fo moved silently, effortlessly through the darkness. For a moment he knelt beside the boy, looking down at him; again, as in the dream – the reality of it no clearer than the vision he had had. He smiled, then, unfolding the blanket, began to wrap the sleeping boy in it.

The boy murmured softly as he lifted him, then began to struggle. Tuan Ti Fo waited, his arms cradling the boy firmly yet reassuringly against his chest until he calmed. Only then did he carry him back to the entrance.

Tuan Ti Fo crouched down, the boy balanced in his lap, the small, dark, tousled head resting against his chest, and reached out for the water-bottle. He drew the hinged stopper back and put the mouth of the bottle to the child's lips, wetting them. Waiting a moment, he placed it to the boy's mouth again. This time the lips parted, taking in a little of the water.

It was enough. The mild drug in the liquid would help calm him – would make him sleep until the shock of his ordeal had passed.

Tuan Ti Fo stoppered the bottle and fixed it to the small hook on his belt, then straightened up. He had not really noticed before but the boy weighed almost nothing in his arms. He looked down at the child, surprised, as if the boy would vanish at any moment, leaving him holding nothing.

"You're a strange one," he said softly, moving outside the dream a moment. "It's many years since the gods sent me one to tend."

So it was. Many, many years. And why this one? Maybe it had something to do with the other dreams – the dreams of dead, dark lands and of huge, brilliant webs, stretched out like stringed beads, burning in the darkness of the sky. Dreams of wells and spires and falling Cities. Dreams filled with suffering and strangeness.

And what was the boy's role in all of that? Why had the gods chosen *him* to do their work?

Tuan Ti Fo smiled, knowing it was not for him to ask, nor for them to answer. Then, letting his actions be shaped once more by the dream, he set off, carrying the boy back down the broad main corridor towards the guard post and the lift beyond.

★ ★ ★

The doctors were gone, his ministers and advisers dismissed. Now, at last, the great T'ang was alone.

Li Shai Tung stood there a moment, his arm outstretched, one hand resting against the door frame as he got his breath. The upright against which he rested stretched up like a great squared pillar into the ceiling high overhead, white-painted, the simplicity of its design emphasised by the seven pictograms carved into the wood and picked out in gold leaf – the characters forming couplets with those on the matching upright. Servants had opened the two huge, white-lacquered doors earlier; now he stood there, looking into the Hall of Eternal Peace and Tranquillity. To one side, just in view, stood a magnificent funerary couch, the grey stone of its side engraved with images of gardens and pavilions in which ancient scholars sat enthroned while the women of the household wove and prepared food, sang or played the ancient *p'i p'a*. Facing it was a broad, red-lacquered screen, the *Ywe Lung* – the circle of dragons, symbolising the power and authority of the Seven – set like a huge, golden mandala in its centre.

He sighed heavily, then went inside, leaving the great doors ajar, too tired to turn and pull them closed behind him. It was true what they had said; he *ought* to get to bed and rest; *ought* to take a break from his duties for a day or so and let Li Yuan take up his burden as Regent. But it was not easy to break the habits of a lifetime. Besides, there was something he had to do before he rested. Something he had put off far too long.

He crossed the room then slowly lowered himself to his

knees before the great tablet, conscious of how the gold leaf of the *Ywe Lung* seemed to flow in the wavering light of the candles; how the red lacquer of the background seemed to burn. He had never noticed that before. Nor had he noticed how the smoke from the perfumed candles seemed to form words – Han pictograms – in the still, dry air. Chance, meaningless words, like the throw of yarrow stalks or the pattern on a fire-charred tortoise shell.

He shivered. It was cold, silent in the room, the scent of the candles reminding him of the tomb beneath the earth at Tongjiang. Or was it just the silence, the wavering light?

He swallowed drily. The ache in his bones was worse than before. He felt drawn, close to exhaustion, his skin stretched tight, like parchment, over his brittle bones. It would be good to rest. Good to lie there, thoughtless, in the darkness. Yes . . . but he would do this one last thing before he slept.

Reaching out, he took two of the scented sticks from the porcelain jar in front of him and held them in the thread of laser light until they lit. Then, bowing respectfully, he set them in the jar before the tiny image of his great-great-grandfather. At once the image seemed to swell, losing a degree of substance as it gained in size.

The life-size image of the old man seemed to look down at Li Shai Tung, its dark eyes magnificent, its whole form filled with power.

His great-great-grandfather, Li Hang Ch'i, had been a tall, immensely dignified man. For posterity he had dressed himself in the imperial style of one hundred and ten years earlier; a simpler, more brutal style, without embellishment. One heavily bejewelled hand stroked his long, white, unbraided beard, while the other held a silver riding crop – an affectation that was meant to symbolise his love of horses.

"What is it, Shai Tung? Why do you summon me from the dead lands?"

Li Shai Tung felt a faint ripple of unease pass through him.

185

"I . . . I wished to ask you something, Honourable Grandfather."

Li Hang Ch'i made a small motion of his chin, lifting it slightly as if considering his grandson's words; a gesture that Li Shai Tung recognised immediately as his own.

Even in that we are not free, he thought. *We but ape the actions of our ancestors; unconsciously, slavishly, those things we consider most distinctly ours – that strange interplay of mind and nerve and sinew that we term gesture – formed a hundred generations before their use in us.*

Again he shivered, lowering his head, conscious of his own weariness; of how far below his great-great-grandfather's exacting standards he had fallen. At that moment he felt but a poor copy of Li Hang Ch'i.

"Ask," the figure answered. "Whatever you wish."

Li Shai Tung hesitated, then looked up. "Forgive me, most respected Grandfather, but the question I would ask you is a difficult one. One that has plagued me for some while. It is this. Are we good or evil men?"

The hologram's face flickered momentarily, the programme uncertain what facial expression was called for by the question. Then it formed itself into the semblance of a frown, the whole countenance becoming stern, implacable.

"What a question, Shai Tung! You ask whether we are good or evil men. But is that something one can ask? After all, how can one judge? By our acts? So some might argue. Yet are our acts good or evil in themselves? Surely only the gods can say that much." He shook his head, staring down at his descendant as if disappointed in him. "I cannot speak for the gods, but for myself I say this. We did as we had to. How else *could* we have acted?"

Li Shai Tung took a long, shuddering breath. It was as if, for that brief moment, his great-great-grandfather had been there, really there, before him in the room. He had sensed his powerful presence behind the smokescreen of the hologrammic image. Had felt the overpowering certainty of the man behind the words and, again, recognised the echo in himself. So he had once argued. So he had answered his own son, that time when Yuan had come to him with his dream – that awful nightmare he had had of the great mountain of bones filling the plain where the City had been.

Back then he had sounded so certain – so sure of things – but even then he had questioned it, at some deeper level. Had gone to his room afterwards and lain there until the dawn, unable to sleep, Yuan's words burning brightly in his skull. *Are we good or evil men?*

But it had begun before then, earlier that year, when he had visited Hal Shepherd in the Domain. It was then that the seed of doubt had entered him; then – in that long conversation with Hal's son, Ben – that he had begun to question it all.

He sat back, studying the hologram a moment, conscious of how it waited for him, displaying that unquestioning patience that distinguished the mechanical from the human. It was almost solid. Almost. For through the seemingly substantial chest of his great-great-grandfather he could glimpse the hazed, refracted image of the *Ywe Lung*, the great wheel of dragons broken by the planes of his ancestor's body.

He groaned softly and stretched, trying to ease the various pains he felt. His knees ached and there was a growing warmth in his back. I ought to be in bed, he thought, not worrying myself about such things. But he could not help himself. Something urged him on. He stared up into that ancient, implacable face and spoke again.

"Was there no other choice then, Grandfather? No other path we might have taken? Were things as inevitable as they seem? Was it all written?"

Li Hang Ch'i shook his head, his face like the ancient, burnished ivory of a statue, and raised the silver riding crop threateningly.

"There *was* no other choice."

Li Shai Tung shivered, his voice suddenly small. "Then we were right to deny the *Hung Mao* their heritage?"

187

"It was that or see the world destroyed."

Li Shai Tung bowed his head. "Then . . ." He paused, seeing how the eyes of the hologram were on him. Again it was as if something stared through them from the other side. Something powerful and menacing. Something which, by all reason, should not be there. "Then what we did was right?"

The figure shifted slightly, relaxing, lowering the riding crop.

"Make no mistake, Shai Tung. We did as we had to. We cannot allow ourselves the empty luxury of doubt."

"Ah . . ." Li Shai Tung stared back at the hologram a moment longer, then, sighing, he plucked the scented sticks from the offering bowl, and threw them aside.

At once the image shrank, diminishing to its former size.

He leaned back, a sharp sense of anger overwhelming him. At himself for the doubts that ate at him, and at his ancestor for giving him nothing more than a string of empty platitudes. *We did as we had to . . .* He shook his head, bitterly disappointed. Was there to be no certainty for him, then? No clear answer to what he had asked?

No. And maybe that was what had kept him from visiting this place these last five years: the knowledge that he could no longer share their unquestioning certainty. That and the awful, erosive consciousness of his own inner emptiness. He shuddered. Sometimes it felt as if he had less substance than the images in this room. As if, in the blink of an eye, his being would turn to breath as the gods drew the scent sticks from the offering bowl.

He rubbed at his eyes, then yawned, his tiredness returned to him like ashes in the blood. It was late. Much too late. Not only that, but it was suddenly quite hot in here. He felt flushed and there was a prickling sensation in his legs and hands. He hauled his tired bones upright, then stood there, swaying slightly, feeling breathless, a sudden cold washing through his limbs, making him tremble.

It's nothing, he thought. Only my age. Yet for a moment he found his mind clouding. Had he imagined it, or had Chung Hu-yan come to him only an hour back with news of another attack?

He put his hand up to his face, as if to clear the cobwebs from his thoughts, then shrugged. No. An hour past he had been with his Ministers. Even so, the image of Chung Hu-yan waking him with awful news persisted, until he realised what it was.

"Lin Yua . . ." he said softly, his voice broken by the sudden pain he felt. "Lin Yua, my little peach . . . Why did you have to die? Why did you have to leave me all alone down here?"

He shivered, suddenly cold again, his teeth chattering. Yes, he would send for Surgeon Hua. But later – in the morning, when he could put up with the old boy's fussing.

Sleep, he heard a voice say, close by his ear. *Sleep now, Li Shai Tung. The day is done.*

He turned, his eyes resting momentarily upon the dim, grey shape of the funerary couch. Then, turning back, he made a final bow to the row of tiny images. *Like breath*, he thought. *Or flames, dancing in a glass.*

★ ★ ★

It was dark in the room. Li Yuan lay on his back in the huge bed, staring up into the shadows; the woman beside him was sleeping, her leg against his own, warm and strangely comforting.

It was a moment of thoughtlessness, of utter repose. He lay there, aware of the weight of his body pressing down into the softness of the bed, of the rise and fall of his chest with each breath, the flow of his blood. He felt at rest, the dark weight of tension lifted from him by the woman.

In the darkness he reached out to touch the woman's flank, then lay back, closing his eyes.

For a time he slept. Then, in the depths of sleep he heard the summons and pulled himself up, hand over hand, back to the surface of consciousness.

Nan Ho stood in the doorway, his eyes averted. Li Yuan

rose, knowing it was important, letting Master Nan wrap the cloak about his nakedness.

He took the call in his study, beneath the portrait of his grandfather, Li Ch'ing, knowing at once what it was. The face of his father's surgeon, Hua, filled the screen, the old man's features more expressive than a thousand words.

"He's dead," Li Yuan said simply.

"Yes, *Chieh Hsia*," the old man answered, bowing his head.

Chieh Hsia. . . He shivered.

"How did it happen?"

"In his sleep. There was no pain."

Li Yuan nodded, but something nagged at him. "Touch nothing, Surgeon Hua. I want the room sealed until I get there. And Hua, tell no one else. I must make calls first. Arrange things."

"*Chieh Hsia*."

Li Yuan sat there, looking up at the image of his father's father, wondering why he felt so little. He closed his eyes, thinking of his father as he'd last seen him. Of his strength, masked by the surface frailness.

For a moment longer he sat there, trying to feel the sorrow he knew he owed his father, but it was kept from him. It was not yet real. Touch – touch alone – would make it real. Momentarily his mind strayed and he thought of Fei Yen and the child in her belly. Of Tsu Ma and of his dead brother, Han Ch'in. All of it confused, sleep-muddled in his brain. Then it cleared and the old man's face came into focus.

"And so it comes to me," he said quietly, as if to the painting. But the burden of it, the reality of what he had become while he slept, had not yet touched him.

He thought of the calls he must make to tell the other T'ang, but for the moment he felt no impulse towards action. Time seemed suspended. He looked down at his hands, at the prince's ring of power, and frowned. Then, as a concession, he made the call to summon the transporter.

He went back to his room, then out on to the veranda

beyond. The woman woke and came to him, naked, her soft warmth pressed against his back in the cool, pre-dawn air.

He turned to her, smiling sadly. "No. Go back inside."

Alone again, he turned and stared out across the shadowed lands of his estate towards the distant mountains. The moon was a low, pale crescent above one of the smaller peaks, far to his right. He stared at it a while, feeling hollow, emptied of all feeling, then looked away sharply, bitter with himself.

Somehow the moment had no meaning. It should have meant so much, but it was empty. The moon, the mountains, the man – *himself* – standing there in the darkness: none of it made sense to him. They were fragments, broken pieces of some nonsense puzzle, adding to nothing. He turned away, his feeling of anguish at the nothingness of it all overwhelming him. It wasn't death, it was life that frightened him. The senselessness of life.

He stood there a long time, letting the feeling ebb. Then, when it was gone, he returned to his study, preparing himself to make his calls.

* * *

Tolonen stood in the centre of the chaos, looking about him. The floor was cluttered underfoot, the walls black with soot. A pile of dark plastic sacks was piled up against the wall to one side. They were all that remained of the men who had worked here on the Project.

"There were no survivors, Captain?"

The young officer stepped forward and bowed. "Only the tutor, sir. We found him thirty levels down, bound and drugged."

Tolonen frowned. "And the others?"

"Apart from T'ai Cho there were eighteen men on the Project, excluding guards. We've identified seventeen separate corpses. Add to that the other one – Hammond – and it accounts for everyone."

"I see. And the records?"

"All gone, sir. The main files were destroyed in the explosion, but they also managed to get to the back-ups and destroy them."

Tolonen stared at him, astonished. "All of them? Even those held by Prince Yuan?"

"It appears so. Of course, the Prince himself has not yet been spoken to, but his secretary, Chang Shih-sen advises me that the copies he was given on his last visit are gone."

"Gone?" Tolonen swallowed drily. He was still too shocked to take it in. How could it have happened? They had taken the strictest measures to ensure that the Project remained not merely "invisible" in terms of its security profile, but that, in the unlikely event of sabotage, there would be copies of everything. But somehow all their endeavours had come to nothing. The assassins had walked in here as if they owned the place and destroyed everything. Erasing every last trace of the Project.

DeVore. It had to be DeVore. But why? How in the gods' names could he possibly benefit from this?

"Let me see the reports."

The officer turned away, returning a moment later with a clipboard to which were attached the preliminary, hand-written reports. Tolonen took them from him and flicked through quickly.

"Very good," he said finally, looking up. "You've been very thorough, Captain. I . . ."

He paused, looking past the Captain. His daughter Jelka was standing in the doorway at the end of the corridor.

"What is it?"

Jelka smiled uncertainly at him, then came closer. "I wanted to see. I . . ."

Tolonen looked back at her a moment, then shrugged. "All right. But it's not very pleasant."

He watched her come into the room and look about her. Saw how she approached the sacks and lifted one of the labels, then let it fall from her hand with a slight shudder. Even so, he could see something of himself in her; that same hardness in the face of adversity. But there was more than that – it was almost as if she were looking for something.

"What is it?" he said after a moment.

She turned, looking at him, focusing on the clipboard he still held. "Can I see that?"

"It's nothing," he said. "Technical stuff mainly. Assessments of explosive materials used. Post-mortem examinations of remains. That kind of thing."

"I know," she said, coming closer. "Can I see it? Please, Daddy."

Out of the corner of an eye he saw the Captain smile faintly. He had been about to say no to her, but that decided him. After all, she was the Marshal's daughter. He had taught her much over the years. Perhaps she, in turn, could teach the young officer something.

He handed her the file, watching her flick through it quickly, again as if she were looking for something specific. Then, astonishingly, she looked up at him, a great beam of a smile on her face.

"I knew it!" she said. "I sensed it as soon as I came in. He's alive! This proves it!"

Tolonen gave a short laugh then glanced briefly at the Captain, before taking the clipboard back from his daughter and holding it open at the place she indicated. "What in the gods' names are you talking about, Jelka? Who? Who's alive?"

"The boy. Ward. He isn't there! Don't you see? Look at the Chief Pathologist's report. All the corpses he examined were those of adults – of fully grown men. But Kim wasn't more than a child. Not physically. Which means that whoever the seventeenth victim was, he wasn't on the Project."

"And Kim's alive."

"Yes . . ."

He stared back at her, realising what it might mean. The boy had a perfect memory. So good that it was almost impossible for him to forget anything. Which meant . . .

He laughed, then grew still. Unless they'd taken him captive. Unless whoever had done this had meant to destroy everything but him. But then why had they taken the tutor, T'ai Cho and afterwards released him? Or had that been a mistake?

"Gods . . ." he said softly. If DeVore had the boy, he also had the only complete record of the Project's work – the basis of a system that could directly control vast numbers of people. It was a frightening thought. His worst nightmare come true. *If* DeVore had him.

He turned, watching his daughter. She was looking about her, her eyes taking in everything, just as he'd taught her. He followed her through, the young Captain trailing them.

"What is it?" he said quietly, afraid to disturb her concentration. "What are you looking for?"

She turned, looking back at him, the smile still there. "He got out. I know he did."

He shivered, not wanting to know. But she had been right about the other thing, so maybe she was right about this. They went through the ruins of the outer office and into the dark, fire-blackened space beyond where they had found most of the bodies.

"There!" she said, triumphantly, pointing halfway up the back wall. "There! That's where he went."

Tolonen looked. Halfway up the wall there was a slightly darker square set into the blackness. He moved closer, then realised what it was. A ventilation shaft.

"I don't see how . . ." he began, but even as he said it he changed his mind and nodded. Of course. The boy had been small enough, wiry enough. And after all, he had come from the Clay. There was his past record of violence to consider. If anyone could have survived this, it was Kim. So maybe Jelka was right. Maybe he *had* got out this way.

Tolonen turned, looking at the young officer. "Get one of your experts in here now, Captain. I want him to investigate that vent for any sign that someone might have used it to escape."

"Sir!"

He stood there, Jelka cradled against him, his arm about her shoulders, while they tested the narrow tunnel for clues. It was difficult, because the vent was too small for a grown man to get into, but with the use of extension arms and mechanicals they worked their way slowly down the shaft.

After twenty minutes the squad leader turned and came across to Tolonen. He bowed, then gave a small, apologetic shrug.

"Forgive me, Marshal, but it seems unlikely he got out this way. The vent is badly charred. It sustained a lot of fire damage when the labs went up. Besides that, it leads down through the main generator rooms below. He would have been sliced to pieces by the fans down there."

Tolonen was inclined to agree. It was unlikely that the boy had got out, even if DeVore hadn't taken him. But when he looked down and met his daughter's eyes, the certainty there disturbed him.

"Are you sure?"

"I'm certain. Trust me, Father. I know he got out. I just know."

Tolonen sniffed, then looked back at the squad leader. "Go in another five *ch'i*. If there's nothing there we'll call it off."

They waited, Tolonen's hopes fading by the moment. But then there was a shout from one of the men controlling the remote. He looked up from his screen and laughed. "She's right. Damn me if she isn't right!"

They went across and looked. There, enhanced on the screen, was a set of clear prints, hidden behind a fold in the tunnel wall and thus untouched by the blast.

"Well?" said Tolonen, "Are they the boy's?"

There was a moment's hesitation, then the boy's prints were flashed up on the screen, the computer superimposing them over the others.

There was no doubt. They were a perfect match.

"Then he's alive!" said Tolonen. He stared at his daughter, then shook his head, not understanding. "Okay," he said, turning to the Captain, "this is what we'll do. I want you to contact Major Gregor Karr at Bremen Headquarters and get him here at once. And then . . ."

He stopped, staring open-mouthed at the doorway. "Hans . . . what are you doing here?"

Hans Ebert bowed, then came forward. His face was pale, his whole manner unnaturally subdued.

"I've news," he said, swallowing. "Bad news, I'm afraid, Uncle Knut. It's the T'ang. I'm afraid he's dead."

★ ★ ★

Hans Ebert paused on the terrace, looking out across the gardens at the centre of the mansion where the Marshal's daughter stood, her back to him.

Jelka was dressed in the southern Han fashion, a tight silk *sam fu* of a delicate eggshell blue wrapped about her strong yet slender body. Her hair had been plaited and coiled at the back of her head, but there was no mistaking her for Han. She was too tall, too blonde to be anything but *Hung Mao*. And not simply *Hung Mao*, but Nordic. New European.

He smiled then made his way down the steps quietly, careful not to disturb her reverie. She was standing just beyond the bridge, looking down into the tiny stream, one hand raised to her neck, the other holding her folded fan against her side.

His wife. Or soon to be.

He was still some way from her when she turned, suddenly alert, her whole body tensed, as if prepared against attack.

"It's all right," he said, raising his empty hands in reassurance. "It's only me."

He saw how she relaxed – or tried to, for there was still a part of her that held out against him – and smiled inwardly. There was real spirit in the girl; an almost masculine hardness that he admired. His father had been right for once: she would make him the perfect match.

"What is it?" she asked, looking back at him as if forcing herself to meet his eyes. Again he smiled.

"I'm sorry, Jelka, but I have to go. Things are in flux and the new T'ang has asked for me. But please . . . our home is yours. Make yourself comfortable. My *mui tsai*, Sweet Flute, will be here in a while to look after you."

She stared back at him a moment, her lips slightly parted, then gave a small bow of her head. "And my father?"

"He feels it best that you stay here for the moment. As I said, things are in flux and there are rumours of rioting in the lower levels. If it spreads . . ."

She nodded then turned away, looking across at the ancient pomegranate trees, flicking her fan open as she did so. It was a strange, almost nervous gesture and for a moment he wondered what it meant. Then, bowing low, he turned to go. But he had gone only a few paces when she called to him.

"Hans?"

He turned, pleased that she had used his name. "Yes?"

"Will you be General now?"

He took a long breath then shrugged. "If the new T'ang wishes it. Why?"

She made a small motion of her head, then looked down. "I . . . I just wondered, that's all."

"Ah . . ." He stood there a moment longer, watching her, then turned and made his way back along the path towards the house. And if he was? Well, maybe it would be a reason for bringing his marriage forward. After all, a general ought to have a wife, a family, oughtn't he? He grinned, then spurred himself on, mounting the steps two at a time. Yes. He would speak to Tolonen about it later.

★ ★ ★

She stood there after he was gone, her eyes following the slow swirl of a mulberry leaf as it drifted on the artificial current.

So the boy, Kim, was alive. But how had she known?

She shivered and turned, hearing footsteps on the path-way. It was a young woman – a girl little older than herself. The *mui tsai*.

The girl came closer, then stopped, bowing low, her hands folded before her. "Excuse me, *Hsiao Chi*, but my master asked me to see to your every wish."

Jelka turned, smiling at the girl's use of *Hsiao Chi* – Lady – to one clearly no older than herself. But it was obvious that the girl was only trying to be respectful.

"Thank you, Sweet Flute, but I wish only to wait here until my father comes."

The *mui tsai* glanced up at her, then averted her eyes again. "With respect, *Hsiao Chi*, I understand that that might be some while. Would you not welcome some refreshments while you wait? Or perhaps I could summon the musicians. There is a pavilion . . ."

Jelka smiled again, warmed by the girl's manner. Even so, she wanted to be left alone. The matter with the boy disturbed her. The preliminary search of the levels below the Project had found no trace of him.

She sighed, then gave a tiny laugh. "All right, Sweet Flute. Bring me a drink. A cordial. But no musicians. The birds sing sweetly enough for me. And I do wish to be left alone. Until my father comes."

The *mui tsai* bowed. "As you wish, *Hsiao Chi*."

Jelka looked about her, letting herself relax for the first time since she had heard of the attack on the Project, drink-ing in the harmony of the garden. Then she stiffened again.

From the far side of the gardens came a strange, high-pitched keening, like the sound of an animal in pain. For almost a minute it continued, and then it stopped, as abruptly as it had begun.

What in the gods' names?

She hurried across the bridge and down the path, then climbed the wooden steps up on to the terrace. It had come from here, she was sure of it.

She paused, hearing the low murmur of male voices, from the doorway just ahead of her. Slowly, step by step, she crept along the terrace until she stood there, looking in.

There were four of them, dressed in the pale green uniforms of the Ebert household. In the midst of them, a gag tied tightly about her mouth, was a woman. A Han woman in her late twenties.

Jelka watched, astonished, as the woman kicked out wildly and threw herself about, trying to escape her captives, her face dark, contorted. But there was no escaping. As Jelka watched, the men subdued her, forcing her into a padded jacket, the over-long arms of which they fastened at the back.

Shuddering with indignation, she stepped inside. "Stop it! Stop it at once!"

The men turned, disconcerted by her sudden appearance, the woman in their midst suddenly forgotten. She fell and lay there on the floor, her legs kicking impotently.

Jelka took another step, her whole body trembling with the anger she felt. "What in the gods' names do you think you're doing?"

They backed away as she came on, bowing abjectly.

"Forgive us, Mistress Tolonen," one of them said, recognising her, "but we are only acting on our master's orders."

She looked at the man witheringly, then shook her head. "Unbind her. Unbind her at once."

"But, Mistress, you don't understand . . ."

"Quiet, man!" she barked, the strength in her voice surprising him. He fell to his knees, head bowed and stayed there, silent. She shivered, then looked to the others. "Well? Must I ask you again?"

There was a quick exchange of glances, then the men did as she said, unbinding the woman and stepping back, as if afraid of the consequences. But the woman merely rolled over and sat up, easing the jacket from her, calm now, the fit – if that was what it had been – gone from her.

"Good," Jelka said, not looking at them, her attention

fixed upon the strange woman. "Now go. I wish to be alone with the woman."

"But, Mistress . . ."

"*Go!*"

There was no hesitation this time. Bowing furiously, the four men departed. She could hear the dull murmur of their voices outside, then nothing. She was alone with the woman.

Jelka went across and knelt over her, letting her hand rest on the woman's arm. "What is it?"

The woman looked up at her. She was pretty. Very pretty. In some ways more like a child than Jelka herself. "What's your name?" Jelka asked, touched by the expression of innocence in the woman's eyes.

"My baby . . ." the woman said, looking past Jelka distractedly. "Where's my baby?"

Jelka turned, looking about the room, then saw it. A cot, there, on the far side of the room. And as she saw she heard it – a strange, persistent snuffling.

"There," she said gently. "Your baby's there."

She stood to one side as the woman got up and, casting the strait-jacket aside, went across to the cot, bending down over it to lift and cradle the child. "There, there . . ." she heard her say; a mother's softness in her voice. "There, they'll not harm you. I'll see to that, my little darling. Mumma's here now. Mumma's here."

Jelka felt a ripple of relief pass through her. But she was still angry. Angry with Hans, if it really was he who had given the order to subdue the woman. He had no right to torment the woman. She went across, touching the woman's back.

"Let me see . . ."

The woman turned, smiling, offering the child. A small, helpless little bundle, that snuffled and snuffled . . .

Jelka felt herself go cold, then stepped back, shaking her head, her mouth suddenly dry, appalled by what she saw. "No . . ."

It stared up at her, red-eyed, its pink face too thin to be

200

human, the hair that sprouted indiscriminately from its flesh too coarse, despite the silks in which it was wrapped. As she stared at it, one tiny three-toed hand pushed out at her, as if to grasp her hand. She jerked away, feeling the bile rise in her throat.

"Golden Heart!" The voice came from the doorway behind her. "Put that dreadful thing away, right now! What in the gods' names do you think you're doing?"

It was the *mui tsai*, Sweet Flute. She came into the room, setting the drink down on the table, then went across to the woman, taking the bundle from her and setting it back in the cot.

"It's all right," she said, turning back to face Jelka. "I can explain . . ."

But Jelka was no longer there. She was outside, leaning over the balcony, gulping in air, the image of the tiny goat-creature like a mocking demon, burning indelibly in the redness behind her closed lids.

★ ★ ★

Tuan Ti Fo looked up from where he was making *ch'a* to where the boy lay sleeping on the bedroll in the far corner of the room. He had been asleep for some time, physically exhausted after his ordeal, but now he tossed and turned, held fast in the grip of some awful nightmare.

The old man put down the *ch'a* bowl and the cloth then went across to the boy, balancing on his haunches beside him.

The boy seemed in pain, his lips drawn back from his teeth in what was almost a snarl, his whole body hunched into itself, as if something ate at him from within. He threshed this way and that, as if fighting himself, then, with a shudder that frightened the old man, went still.

"*Gweder* . . ." the boy said quietly. "*Gweder* . . ."

It was said softly, almost gently, yet the word itself was hard, the two sounds of which it was made stranger than anything Tuan Ti Fo had ever heard.

For a moment there was silence, then the boy spoke

again, the whole of him gathered up into the movement of his lips.

"*Pandr'a bos ef, Lagasek?*"

This time the voice was harsh, almost guttural. Tuan Ti Fo felt a small ripple of fear pass through him, yet calmed himself inwardly, a still, small voice chanting the *chen yen* to dispense with fear.

"*Travyth, Gweder. Travyth . . .*"

He narrowed his eyes, understanding. Two voices. The first much softer, gentler than the second. Gweder and Lagasek . . . But what did it mean? And what was this language? He had never heard its like before.

He watched, seeing how the face changed, ugly one moment, peaceful, almost innocent the next. Now it was ugly, the mouth distorted. Gweder was speaking again, his voice harsh, spitting out the words in challenge.

"*Praga obery why crenna? Bos why yeyn, Lagasek?*"

The boy shivered violently and the face changed, all spite, all anger draining from it. Softly now it answered, the brittle edges of the words rounded off. Yet there was pain behind the words. Pain and a dreadful sense of loss.

"*Yma gweras yn ow ganow, Gweder . . . gweras . . . ha an pyth bos tewl.*"

The abruptness of the change made him shudder. And the laughter . . .

The laughter was demonic. The face now shone with a dark and greedy malice. With evil.

"*Nyns-us pyth, Lagasek.*"

There was such an awful mockery in that face that it made Tuan Ti Fo want to strike it with his fist.

Slowly, very slowly, the malice sank down into the tissue of the face. Again the boy's features settled into a kinder, more human form.

"*A-dhywar-lur . . .*" it breathed. "*A-dhywar-lur.*" Then, in a cry of anguish, "*My bos yn annown . . . Yn annown!*"

A ragged breath escaped Tuan Ti Fo. He stood abruptly, then crossed the room to the tiny bookshelf. He brought the book back then squatted there again, closing his eyes and opening the pages at random, reading the first thing his eyes opened upon.

He smiled. It was a passage from midway through Book One. One of his favourites. He read, letting his voice be an instrument to soothe the boy.

> Thirty spokes Share one hub. Adapt the nothing therein to the purpose in hand, and you will have the use of the cart. Knead clay in order to make a vessel. Adapt the nothing therein to the purpose in hand, and you will have the use of the vessel. Cut out doors and windows in order to make a room. Adapt the nothing therein to the purpose in hand, and you will have the use of the room. Thus what we gain is Something, yet it is by virtue of Nothing that this can be put to use.

He looked down, seeing how still the boy had become, as if listening to his words, yet he was still asleep.

"Who are you, boy?" he asked softly, setting the book down. He reached across and pulled up the blanket until it covered the boy's chest. *Yes,* he thought, *and what brought you here to me? For the fates as surely directed you to me as they directed my feet this morning to a path I never took before.*

He leaned back, then took up the book and began to read again, letting Lao Tzu's words – words more than two and a half thousand years old – wash over the sleeping boy and bring him ease.

★ ★ ★

"Well?"

Karr stared back morosely at his friend, then set his *ch'a* bowl down.

"Nothing. The trail's gone cold. I tracked the boy as far as the factory, but there it ended. It's as if he vanished. There's no way he could have got past that guard post."

Chen sat down, facing Karr across the table. "Then he's still there. In the factory."

Karr shook his head. "We've taken it apart. Literally. I

had a hundred men in there, dismantling the place back to the bare walls. But nothing.''

"We've missed something, that's all. I'll come back with you. We can go through it again.''

Karr looked down. "Maybe. But I've been through it a dozen, twenty times already. It's as if he was spirited away.''

Chen studied his friend a moment. He had never seen Karr looking so down in the mouth.

"Cheer up,'' he said. "It can't be that bad.''

"No?'' Karr sat back, drawing himself up to his full height. "It seems Ebert's to be appointed General. The old T'ang accepted Nocenzi's resignation before he died. Tolonen was to step back into the job, but it seems the new T'ang wants a new man in the post.''

Chen grimaced, then sat back. "Then our lives aren't worth a beggar's shit.''

Karr stared at him a moment, then laughed. "You think?''

"And you don't?''

Karr stood up. "Let a thousand devils take Hans Ebert. We'll concentrate on finding the boy. After all, that's our job, isn't it – finding people?''

★ ★ ★

Li Yuan was the first to arrive. Walking from the hangar, he felt detached, as if outside himself, watching. The meaning of this death had come to him slowly; not as grief but as nakedness, for this death exposed him. There was no one now but him; a single link from a broken chain.

Outside his father's rooms he stopped, in the grip of a strong reluctance, but the eyes of others were upon him. Steeling himself, he ordered the doors unlocked, then went inside.

The doors closed, leaving him alone with his dead father.

Li Shai Tung lay in his bed, as if he slept, yet his face was pale like carved ivory, his chest still.

Li Yuan stood there, looking down at him. The old

man's eyes were closed, the thin lids veined, mauve leaf patterns on the milky white. He knelt, studying the patterns in the white, but like the rest it meant nothing. It was merely a pattern, a repetition.

He shook his head, not understanding, knowing only that he had never seen his father sleeping. Never seen those fierce, proud eyes closed before this moment.

He put his hand out, touching his father's cheek. The flesh was cold. Shockingly cold. He drew his hand back sharply, then shuddered. Where did it go? Where did all that warmth escape to?

Into the air, he said silently to himself. *Into the air*.

He stood, then drew the covers back. Beneath the silken sheets his father lay there naked, the frailty of his body revealed. Li Yuan looked, feeling an instinctive pity for his father. Not love, but pity. Pity for what time had done to him.

Death had betrayed him. Had found him weak and vulnerable.

His eyes moved down the body, knowing that others had looked before him. Surgeons with their dispassionate eyes; looking, as he looked now.

He shuddered. The body was thin, painfully emaciated, but unmarked. His father had been ill. Badly ill. That surprised him, and he paused a moment before putting back the sheet. It was unlike his father not to comment on his health. Something was amiss. Some element beyond simple senility had been the cause of this.

He had no proof and yet his sense of wrongness was strong. It made him turn and look about him, noting the presence of each object in the room, questioning their function. All seemed well, and yet the sense of wrongness persisted.

He went outside, into the hallway. Surgeon Hua was waiting there with his assistants.

"How has my father been, Hua? Was he eating well?"

The old man shook his head. "Not for some time, *Chieh Hsia*. Not since Han's death. But . . ." he pursed his lips,

205

considering, "well, enough for an old man. And your father *was* old, Li Yuan."

Li Yuan nodded, but he was still troubled. "Was he . . . clear? In his mind, I mean?"

"Yes, *Chieh Hsia*. Even last night." Hua paused, frowning, as if he too were troubled by something. "There was nothing evidently wrong with him. We've . . . examined him and . . ."

"*Evidently?*"

Hua nodded, but his eyes were watchful.

"But you think that appearances might be deceptive, is that it, Hua?"

The old surgeon hesitated. "It isn't something I can put my finger on, *Chieh Hsia*. Just a . . . a *feeling* I have. Confucius says . . ."

"Just tell me, Hua," Li Yuan said, interrupting him; reaching out to hold his arm, his fondness for the old man showing in his face. "No proverbs, please. Just tell me what made you feel something was wrong."

"This will sound unprofessional, *Chieh Hsia*, but as you've asked." Hua paused, clearing his throat. "Well, he was not himself. He was sharp, alert and in a sense no different from his old self, but he was not – somehow – Li Shai Tung. He seemed like an actor, mimicking your father. Playing him exceptionally well, but not . . ."

He faltered, shaking his head, grief overwhelming him.

"Not like the real thing," Li Yuan finished for him.

Hua nodded. "He was . . . uncertain. And your father *never* was uncertain."

Li Yuan considered a moment, then gave his instructions. "I want you to perform an autopsy, Hua. I want you to find out why he died. I want to know what killed him."

* * *

Tsu Ma was dressed in white, his hair tied back in a single elegant bow. The effect was striking in its simplicity, its sobriety, while his face had a gentleness Li Yuan had never seen in it before. He came forward and embraced Li Yuan, holding him to his breast, one hand smoothing the back of his neck. It was this, more than the death, more than the coldness of his father's cheek, that broke the ice that had formed about his feelings. At last he let go, feeling the sorrow rise and spill from him.

"Good, good," Tsu Ma whispered softly, stroking his neck. "A man should cry for his father." And when he moved back, there were tears in his eyes, real grief in his expression.

"And Wei Feng?" Li Yuan asked, wiping his eyes with the back of his hand.

"He's waiting below." Tsu Ma smiled; a friend's strong smile. "We'll go when you're ready."

"I'm ready," Li Yuan answered, straightening, unashamed now of his tears; feeling much better for them. "Let us see our cousin."

Wei Feng was waiting in the viewing room, wearing a simple robe of white, gathered at the waist. As Li Yuan came down the stairs Wei Feng came across and embraced him, whispering his condolences. But he seemed older than Li Yuan remembered him. Much older.

"Are you all right, Wei Feng?" he asked, concerned for the old man's health.

Wei Feng laughed. A short, melodic sound. "As well as could be expected, Yuan." His expression changed subtly. "But your father . . ." He sighed. Wei Feng was the oldest now. By almost twenty years the oldest. "So much has changed, Yuan. So much. And now this. This seems . . ." he shrugged, as if it were beyond words to say.

"I know." Li Yuan frowned, releasing him. "They killed him, Wei Feng."

Wei Feng simply looked puzzled, but Tsu Ma came close, taking his arm. "How do you know? Is there proof?"

"Proof? No. But I *know*. I'm sure of it, Tsu Ma. I've asked Surgeon Hua to . . . to look for something. Maybe that will show something, but even so, I know."

"So what now?" Wei Feng had crossed his arms. His face was suddenly hard, his tiny figure filled with power.

"So now we play their game. Remove the gloves."

Beside him Tsu Ma nodded.

"We know our enemies," Li Yuan said, with an air of finality. "We have only to find them."

"DeVore, you mean?" Tsu Ma looked across at Wei Feng. The old man's face was troubled, but his jaw was set. Determination weighed the heavier in his conflicting emotions. Tsu Ma narrowed his eyes, considering. "And then?"

Li Yuan turned. His eyes seemed intensely black, like space itself; cold, vacant, all trace of life and warmth gone from them. His face was closed, expressionless, like a mask. "Arrange a meeting of the Council, Tsu Ma. Let Chi Hsing host it. We must talk."

Li Yuan was barely eighteen, yet the tone, the small movement of the left hand that accompanied the final words, were uncannily familiar. As if the father spoke and acted through the son.

CHAPTER·6

CHEN YEN

The *ch'a* bowl lay to one side, broken, its contents spilled across the floor. Beside it Tuan Ti Fo crouched, his back to the door, facing the boy.

"*Yn-mes a forth, cothwas!*" the boy snarled, the sound coming from the back of his throat. "*Yn-mes a forth!*"

Tuan Ti Fo felt the hairs rise on the back of his neck. The boy was down on all fours, his face hideously ugly, the features distorted with rage, the chin thrust forward aggressively, his round, dark eyes filled with animal menace. He made small movements with his body, feinting this way and that, gauging Tuan Ti Fo's response to each, a low growling coming from his throat.

It was the third time the boy had tried to get past him, and, as before, he seemed surprised by the old man's quickness; shocked that, whichever way he moved, Tuan Ti Fo was there, blocking his way.

The old man swayed gently on his haunches, then, as the boy threw himself to the left, moved effortlessly across, fending off the child with his palms, using the least force possible to achieve his end. The boy withdrew, yelping with frustration, then turned and threw himself again, like a dog, going for Tuan's throat.

This time he had to fight the boy. Had to strike him hard and step back, aiming a kick to the stomach to disable him. Yet even as the boy fell back, gasping for breath, that strange transformation overcame him again. As Tuan Ti Fo watched, the harshness faded from the boy's features, becoming something softer, more human.

209

"Welcome back, Lagasek," he said, taking a long, shuddering breath. But for how long? He looked about him, noting the broken bowl, the spilled *ch'a*, and shook his head. He would have to bind the boy while he slept, for in time he would have to sleep. He could not guard against this "Gweder" thing for ever.

He moved closer, crouching over the boy. He was peaceful now, his face almost angelic in its innocence. But beneath? Tuan Ti Fo narrowed his eyes, considering, then began to speak, softly, slowly, as if to himself.

"Look at you, child. So sweet you look just now. So innocent. But are you good or evil? Is it Gweder or Lagasek who rules you? And which of them brought you here to my rooms?" He smiled, then got up, moving across to fetch a small towel to mop up the *ch'a*, a brush to gather up the tiny pieces of broken porcelain. And as he did so he continued to speak, letting his voice rise and fall like a flowing stream, lulling the sleeping child.

"Kao Tzu believed that each man, at birth, was like a willow tree, and that righteousness was like a bowl. To become righteous, a man had therefore to be cut and shaped, like the willow, into the bowl. The most base instincts – the desire for food or sex – were, he argued, all that one could ever find in the unshaped man, and human nature was as indifferent to good or evil as free-flowing water is to the shape it eventually fills."

He turned, looking at the child, seeing how the boy's chest now rose and fell gently, as if soothed by his voice, then turned back, smiling, beginning to mop up the spill.

"Meng Tzu, of course, disagreed. He felt that if what Kao Tzu said were true, then the act of becoming righteous would be a violation of human nature – would, in fact, be a calamity. But I have my own reason for disagreeing with Kao Tzu. If it *were* so – if human nature were as Kao Tzu claimed – then why should any goodness come from evil circumstances? And why should evil come from good?" He gave a soft laugh. "Some men *are* water drops and willow-sprouts, it's true, but not all. For there are those

210

who determine their own shape, their own direction, and the mere existence of them demonstrates Kao Tzu's claim to be a misrepresentation."

He finished mopping then carried the towel to the basin in the corner and dropped it in. Returning, he set the two large pieces of the broken bowl to one side then began to sweep the tiny slivers of porcelain into a pile.

"Of course, there is another explanation. It is said that shortly after the Earth was separated from Heaven, Nu Kua created human beings. It appears that she created the first men by patting yellow earth together. She laboured at this a long time, taking great care in the shaping and moulding of the tiny, human forms, but then she grew tired. The work was leaving her little time for herself and so she decided to simplify the task. Taking a long piece of string, she dragged it to and fro through the mud, heaping it up and turning that into men. But these were crude, ill-formed creatures compared to those she had first made. Henceforth, it is said, the rich and the noble are those descended from the creatures who were formed before Nu Kua tired of her task – the men of yellow earth – whereas the poor and the lowly are descendants of the cord-made men – the men of mud."

He laughed quietly then looked up again, noting how restful the boy now was.

"But then, as the *T'ien Wen* says, 'Nu Kua had a body. Who formed and fashioned it?'"

He turned, taking the thin paper box in which the *ch'a* brick had come and set it down, sweeping the fragments up into it, then dropped in the two largest pieces.

"Ah, yes, but we live in a world gone mad. The bowl of righteousness was shattered long ago, when Tsao Ch'un built his City. It is left to individual men to find the way – to create small islands of sanity in an ocean of storms." He looked about him. "This here is such an island."

Or had been. Before the child had come. Before the bowl had been broken, his peace disturbed.

For a moment Tuan Ti Fo closed his eyes, seeking that

inner stillness deep within himself, his lips forming the *chen yen* – the "true words" – of the mantra. With a tiny shudder he passed the hard knot of tension from him ther looked up again, a faint smile at the corners of his mouth

"Food," he said softly. "That's what you need. Something special."

He stood, then went across to the tiny oven set into the wall on the far side of the room and lit it. Taking a cooking bowl from the side he part filled it from the water jar and set it down on the ring.

Tuan Ti Fo turned, looking about him at the simple order of his room. "Chaos. The world is headed into chaos, child, and there is little you or I can do to stop it." He smiled sadly, then went across and took up the basin, carrying it across to the door. He would empty it later, after the child had been fed.

The boy had turned on to his side, the fingers of one hand lightly touching his neck. Tuan Ti Fo smiled and, taking a blanket, took it across and laid it over the child.

He crouched there a moment, watching him. "You know, the Chou believed that Heaven and Earth were once inextricably mixed together in a state of undifferentiated chaos, like a chicken's egg. *Hun tun* they called that state. *Hun tun* . . ."

He nodded, then went back to the oven, taking a jar from the shelf on the wall and emptying out half its contents on to the board beside the oven. The tiny, sac-like dumplings looked like pale, wet, unformed creatures in their uncooked state. Descendants of the mud men. He smiled and shook his head. *Hun tun*, they were called. He had made them himself with the things the girl, Marie, had brought last time she'd come. It was soy, of course, not meat, that formed the filling inside the thin shells of dough, but that was as he wished it. He did not believe in eating flesh. It was not The Way.

As the water began to boil he tipped the dumplings into the bowl and stirred them gently before leaving them to cook. There were other things he added – herbs sent to him from friends on the Plantations, and other, special things. He leaned forward, sniffing the concoction delicately, then nodded. It was just what the child needed. It would settle him and give him back his strength.

That precious strength that "Gweder" spent so thoughtlessly.

He turned, expecting to see the child sitting up, his face transformed again into a snarl, but the boy slept on.

He turned back, for a while busying himself preparing the food. When it was cooked, he poured half of the broth into a small ceramic bowl and took it across.

It was a shame to wake the boy, but it was twelve hours now since he had eaten. And afterwards he would sleep. The herbs in the soup would ensure that he slept.

He set the bowl down, then lifted the boy gently, cradling him in a half-sitting position. As he did so the boy stirred and struggled briefly then relaxed. Lifting the spoon from the bowl, Tuan Ti Fo placed it to the boy's lips, tilting it gently.

"Here, child. I serve you Heaven itself."

The boy took a little of the warm broth, then turned his head slightly. Tuan Ti Fo persevered, following his mouth with the spoon, coaxing a little of the liquid into him each time, until the child's mouth was opening wide for each new spoonful.

At last the bowl was empty. Tuan Ti Fo smiled, holding the boy to him a while, conscious yet again of how insubstantial he seemed. As if he were made of something finer than flesh and bone; finer than yellow earth. And again he wondered about his presence in the dream. What did that mean? For it had to mean something.

He drew a pillow close, then set the boy's head down, covering him with the blanket.

"Maybe you'll tell me, eh? When you wake. That's if that strange tongue is not the only one you speak."

He went back to the oven and poured the remains of the *Hun tun* into the bowl, spooning it down quickly, then took bowls and basin outside, locking the door behind him, going to the washrooms at the far end of the corridor. It didn't take long, but he hurried about his tasks, concerned not to leave the child too long. And when he returned he took care in opening the door, lest "Gweder" should slip out past him. But the boy still slept.

Tuan Ti Fo squatted, his legs folded under him, watching the boy. Then, knowing it would be hours before he woke, he got up and fetched his *wei chi* set, smoothing the cloth "board" out on the floor before him then setting the bowls to either side, the white stones to his left, the black to his right. For a time he lost himself in the game, his whole self gathered up into the shapes the stones made on the board, until it seemed the board was the great Tao and he the stones.

Once he had been The First Hand Supreme in all Chung Kuo, Master of Masters and eight times winner of the great annual championship held in Suchow. But that had been thirty, almost forty years ago. Back in the days when he had yet concerned himself with the world.

He looked up from the board, realising his concentration had been broken. He laughed, a quotation of Ch'eng Yi's coming to mind.

"Within the universe all things have their opposite: when there is the Yin, there is the Yang; where there is goodness, there is evil."

And in the boy? He took a deep breath, looking across at him. Gweder and Lagasek. Yin and Yang. As in all men. But in this one the Tao was at war with itself. Yin and Yang were not complementary but antagonistic. In that sense the child was like the world of Chung Kuo. There too the balance had been lost. Yes, like the boy, Chung Kuo was an entity at war with itself.

But the thought brought with it an insight. Just as this world of theirs had been tampered with, so too had the child. Something had happened to split him and make him fight himself. He had lost his oneness.

Or had it taken from him.

Tuan Ti Fo cleared the board slowly, concerned for the

boy. Yet maybe that was his role in this – to make the boy whole again: to reconcile the animal and the human in him. For what was a man without balance?

"Nothing," he answered himself softly. "Or worse than nothing."

He began again, the shapes of black and white slowly filling the board until he knew there were no more stones to play, nothing left to win or lose.

Tuan Ti Fo looked up. The boy was sitting up, watching him, his dark, over-large eyes puzzling over the shapes that lay there on the cloth.

He looked down, saying nothing, then cleared the board and set up another game. He began to play, conscious now of the boy watching, of him edging slowly closer as the stones were laid, the board filled up again.

Again he laid the final stone, knowing there was no more to be won or lost. He looked up. The boy was sitting there, not an arm's length from him now, studying the patterns of black and white with a fierce intensity, as if to grasp some meaning from them.

He cleared the board and was about to play again when the boy's hand reached out and took a white stone from the bowl to his left. Tuan Ti Fo made to correct him – to make him take from the bowl of black stones – but the boy was insistent. He slapped a stone down, in the corner nearest him on the right. In *tsu*, the north.

They played, slowly at first, then faster, Tuan Ti Fo giving nothing to the boy, punishing him for every mistake he made. Yet when he made to take a line of stones he had surrounded from the board, the boy placed his hand over Tuan's, stopping him, lifting his hand so that he might study the position, his face creased into a frown, as if trying to take in what he had done wrong. Only then did he move his hand back, indicating that Tuan Ti Fo should take the stones away.

The next game was more difficult. The boy repeated none of the simple errors he had made first time round. This time Tuan Ti Fo had to work hard to defeat him. He sat back, his eyes narrowed, staring at the boy, surprised by how well he'd played.

"So," he said. "You can play."

The boy looked up at him, wide-eyed, then shook his head. No, Tuan thought; it's not possible. You *must* have played before.

He cleared the board then sat back, waiting, feeling himself go very still, as if something strange – something wholly out of the ordinary – were about to happen.

This time the boy set the stone down in the south, in *shang*, only a hand's length from Tuan Ti Fo's knee. It was a standard opening – the kind of play that made no real difference to the final outcome – yet somehow the boy made it seem a challenge. An hour later Tuan Ti Fo knew he had been defeated. For the first time in over forty years someone had humbled him on the board he considered his own.

He sat back, breathing deeply, taking in the elegance of the shapes the boy had made, recollecting the startling originality of the boy's strategies – as if he had just re-invented the game. Then he bowed low, touching his forehead almost to the board.

The boy stared back at him a moment, then returned his bow.

So you are *human, after all* Tuan Ti Fo thought, shaking his head, amused by the gesture. *And now I'm certain that the gods sent you.* He laughed. *Who knows? Perhaps you're even one of them.*

The boy sat there, his legs crossed under him, perfectly still, watching Tuan Ti Fo, his eyes narrowed, as if trying to understand why the old man was smiling.

Tuan Ti Fo leaned forward, beginning to clear the board, when a knock sounded at the door. A casual rapping that he knew at once was Marie.

He saw how the boy froze – how his face grew rigid with fear – and reached out to hold his arm.

"It's all right . . ." he whispered. "There!" he said, indicating the blanket. "Get under there, boy, and stay hidden. I'll send them away."

* * *

Marie turned, hearing noises behind her, then broke into a smile, bowing to the two elderly gentlemen who were passing in the corridor. She turned back, frowning. Where was he? It was not like him to delay.

Marie Enge was a tall, good-looking woman in her late twenties with the kind of physical presence that most men found daunting. They preferred their women more delicately made; more deferent. Nor was the impression of physical strength deceptive. She was a powerful woman, trained in the arts of self-defence, but that was not to say that she lacked feminine charm. At a second glance one noticed signs of a softer side to her nature: in the delicate primrose pattern of the edging to her tunic; in the strings of pearl and rose-coloured beads at her wrists; in the butterfly bow on her otherwise masculine-looking pigtail.

She waited a moment longer, then knocked again. Harder this time, more insistent.

"Tuan Ti Fo? Are you there? It's me. Marie. I've come for our game."

She heard a shuffling inside and gave a small sigh of relief. For a moment she had thought he might be ill. She moved back, waiting for the door to open, but it remained firmly shut.

"Tuan Ti Fo?"

The slightest edge of concern had entered her voice now. She moved forward, about to press her ear against the door, when it slid open a little.

"What is it?" the old man said, eyeing her almost suspiciously.

"It's me, *Shih* Tuan. Don't you remember? It's time for our game."

"Ah . . ." He pulled the door a fraction wider, at the same time moving forward, blocking her view into the

217

room. "Forgive me, Marie, I've just woken. I didn't sleep well and . . ."

"You're not ill, are you?" she said, concerned

"No . . ." He smiled, then gave a bow. "However, I do feel tired. So if, for once, you'll excuse me?"

She hesitated, then returned his bow. "Of course, *Shih* Tuan. Tomorrow, perhaps?"

He tilted his head slightly, then nodded. "Perhaps . . ."

She stood back, watching the door slide closed, then turned away. But she had gone only a few paces before she turned and stared back at the door, a strong sense of oddness – of wrongness – holding her in its grip. He had never before spoken of sleepless nights; neither, as far as she knew, had he ever complained of any kind of illness. Indeed, a fitter old boy she had never known. Nor had he ever put her off before. She frowned, then turned away again, moving slowly, reluctantly, away.

For a moment she hesitated, not quite knowing what to do, then she nodded to herself and began to move quicker. She would go straight to the Dragon Cloud. Would ask Shang Chen if she could work an extra hour this end of her shift and leave an hour earlier. Yes. And then she would return.

Just in case the old man needed her.

★ ★ ★

The Dragon Cloud filled one end of Main, dominating the market that spread below its eaves. It was a big, traditional-looking building with a steeply sloping roof of red tile, its five storeys not walled-in but open to the surroundings, each level linked by broad mock-wooden steps. Greenery was everywhere, in bowls and screens and hanging from the open balustrades, giving the teahouse the look of an overgrown garden. Waiters dressed in pale blue gowns – male and female, Han and *Hung Mao* – hurried between the levels, carrying broad trays filled with exquisite ceramics, the bowls and pots a pure white, glazed with a blue marking. At strategic points about the house the *ch'a* masters, specialists in *ch'a shu*, the art of tea, sat at their counters preparing their special infusions.

At a stretch the Dragon Cloud could seat five thousand. More than enough, one would have thought, to cater for the surrounding levels. Even so, it was packed when they got there, not a table free. Chen looked about him, then looked back at Karr.

"Let's go elsewhere, Gregor. It'll be an hour at least before we get a table."

Karr turned, beckoning to one of the waiters. Chen saw how the man came across, wary of Karr, eyeing the big man up and down as if to assess how much trouble he might be. Behind him, at the counter, several of the other waiters, mostly Han, turned, following him with their eyes.

Chen watched; saw Karr press something into the waiter's hand; saw the man look down, then look up again, wide-eyed. Karr muttered something, then pressed a second tiny bundle into the man's hand. This time the waiter bowed. He turned and, summoning two of his fellows across, hurried away, whispering something to his companions.

In a little while the waiter was back, bowing, smiling, leading them up two flights of steps then through to a table at the centre of the house. As they moved between the tables, three elderly Han came towards them, bowing and smiling.

Chen leaned towards Karr, keeping his voice low. "You bought their table?"

Karr smiled, returning the old gentlemen's bows before allowing one of the waiters to pull a chair out for him. When Chen was seated across from him, he answered.

"I've heard that the Dragon Cloud is the cultural centre of these levels. The place where everybody who is anybody comes. Here, if anywhere, we shall hear news of the boy. You understand?"

"Ah . . ." Chen smiled then sat back, relaxing. It was not like Karr to use his privilege so crudely and for a moment he had been concerned by his friend's behaviour.

"Besides," Karr added, accepting the *ch'a* menu the waiter held out to him, "I have heard that the Dragon Cloud is the paragon among teahouses. Its fame spreads far and wide, even to the heavens."

This was said louder, clearly for the benefit of the waiters. The one who had first dealt with Karr bowed his head slightly, responding to Karr's words.

"If the *ch'un tzu* would like something . . . special?"

Karr leaned back. Even seated he was still almost a head taller than the Han.

"You would not have a *hsiang p'ien*, by any chance?"

The waiter bowed his head slightly lower, a smile of pleasure splitting his face. "It is the speciality of the Dragon Cloud, *ch'un tzu*. What kind of *hsiang p'ien* would you like?"

Karr looked across at his friend. "Have you any preference, Kao Chen?"

Chen studied the menu a moment, trying to recognise something he knew amongst the hundred exotic brews, then looked up again, shrugging. "I don't know. I guess I'll have what you have."

Karr considered a moment, then turned his head, looking at the waiter. "Have you a *ch'ing ch'a* with a lotus fragrance?"

"Of course, Master. A *pao yun*, perhaps?"

Karr nodded. "A Jewelled Cloud would be excellent."

The man bowed, then, his head still lowered, took the *ch'a* menus from them. "I will have the girl bring the *ch'a* and some sweetmeats. It will be but a few minutes, *ch'un tzu*." He bowed again, then backed away.

Chen waited a moment, until the man had gone, then leaned across, keeping his voice low. "What in the gods' names is a *hsiang p'ien*?"

Karr smiled, relaxing for the first time in almost twelve hours of searching. "*Hsiang p'ien* are flower *ch'a*. And a *ch'ing ch'a* is a green, unfermented *ch'a*. The one we're having is placed into a tiny gauze bag overnight with the calix of a freshly plucked lotus." He laughed. "Have you not read your Shen Fu, Chen?"

Chen laughed and shook his head. "When would I have time, my friend? With three children there is barely time to shit, let alone read!"

Karr laughed, then studied him a moment. He reached out and touched his arm gently. "Maybe so, Kao Chen, but a man ought to read. I'll give you a copy of Shen Fu some time. His *Six Records Of A Floating Life*. He lived four centuries ago, before the great City was built. It was another age, I tell you, Chen. Cruder, and yet in some ways better than ours. Even so, some things don't change. Human nature, for instance."

Chen lowered his head slightly. So it was. He looked about him, enjoying the strange peacefulness of the place. Each table was cut off from the next by screens of greenery; even so, from where he sat he had a view of what was happening at other tables and on other levels. He turned, looking about him. Above the nearest serving counter a huge banner portrait of the *ch'a* god, Lu Yu, fluttered gently in the breeze of the overhead fans. It was an image that even Chen recognised, flying, as it did, over every teahouse in Chung Kuo.

"Where do we begin?" Chen asked after a moment. "I mean, we can't simply go from table to table asking, can we?"

Karr had been staring away almost abstractedly; now he looked back at Chen. "No. You're quite right, Chen. It must be done subtly. Quietly. If necessary, we will sit here all day, and all tomorrow too. Until we hear something."

"And if we don't?" Chen shook his head. "Besides, I hate all this sitting and waiting. Why don't we just empty this whole deck and search it room by room?"

Karr smiled. "You think that would be a good idea, Chen? And what reason would we give?"

"What reason would we need to give? We are on the T'ang's business, surely?"

Karr leaned towards him, lowering his voice to a

whisper. "And if rumour were to go about the levels that the T'ang has lost something important and would clear a deck to find it? Surely such a rumour would have a price? Would find ears we'd rather it didn't reach?"

Chen opened his mouth then closed it again. "Even so, there must be something else we can do?"

Karr shook his head. "The trail has gone cold. It would not do to rush about blindly elsewhere. The boy is here somewhere. I know he is. The only course now is to wait. To bide our time and listen to the faint whispers from the tables."

Chen leaned forward, about to say something, then sat back again. One of the waiters was approaching their table – a woman this time, a tall, blonde-haired *Hung Mao*. He glanced at her as she set the tray down on the table between them, then frowned, seeing how Karr was staring at her.

"Your *hsiang p'ien*," she said, moving back slightly from the table, her head bowed. "Shall I pour for you, *ch'un tzu*?"

Karr smiled. "That would be most pleasant."

The teapot was square in shape with a wicker handle; a white-glazed, ceramic pot with a blue circular pattern on each side – the stylised pictogram for "long life". Beside it was a *chung*, a lidded serving bowl, and two ordinary *ch'a* bowls. Moving forward, the woman poured some of the freshly brewed *ch'a* into their bowls, then the rest into the *chung*, setting the lid back on.

She was a big woman, yet her movements had been precise, almost delicate. She touched the bowls as if each were alive, while the *ch'a* itself fell daintily, almost musically into the bowls, not a drop splashed or spilled.

Chen, watching Karr, saw a small movement in the big man's face; saw him look up at the woman appreciatively.

"Thank you," Karr said, smiling up at her. "It is good to be served by someone who cares so much for the art."

She looked at him for the first time, then lowered her eyes again. "We try our best to please, *ch'un tzu*."

"And these bowls . . ." Karr continued, as if reluctant

to let her go. "I have rarely seen such elegance, such grace of line, such sobriety of colour."

For the first time she smiled. "They are nice, aren't they? I've often commented how pleasant it is to serve *ch'a* from such bowls. They have . . . *yu ya*, no?"

Karr laughed softly, clearly delighted. "Deep elegance. Yes . . ." He sat back, appraising her more closely. "You know a great deal, *Fu Jen* . . . ?"

Again she lowered her eyes, a faint colour coming to her neck and cheeks. "I had a good teacher. And it is *Hsiao Chieh* Enge, not *Fu Jen*. I am not married, you understand?"

Karr's smile faded momentarily. "Ah . . . forgive me." He sat forward slightly. "Anyway, I thank you again, *Hsiao Chieh* Enge. As I said, it is very pleasing to be served by one who knows so much about the great art of *ch'a shu*."

She bowed one final time, and turned to go. Then, as if changing her mind, she turned back, leaning closer to Karr. "And if it is not too forward, *ch'un tzu*, you might call me Marie. It is how I am known here in these levels. Ask for Marie. Anyone will know me."

Chen watched her go, then turned, looking back at Karr. The big man was still watching her, staring across at where she was preparing her next order.

"You like her, Gregor?"

Karr looked back at him almost blankly, then gave a brief laugh. "I think we have our contact, Chen. What did she say? Anyone will know me. And likewise, she will know anyone, neh?" He raised one eyebrow.

Chen was smiling. "You didn't answer me, Gregor. You like her, don't you?"

Karr stared back at him a moment longer, then shrugged and looked away. As he did so, a commotion started up behind them, at the *ch'a* counter.

Chen turned to look. There were three men – Han, dressed in dark silks with blood-red headbands about their foreheads. He glanced at Karr knowingly, then looked back.

"Triad men," he said quietly. "But what are they doing up this high?"

Karr shook his head. "Things are changing, Chen. They've been spreading their net higher and higher these last few years. The unrest has been their making."

"Even so . . ." He shook his head, angered by what he saw.

Karr reached out and held his arm, preventing him from getting up. "Remember why we're here. We can't afford to get involved."

One of them was shouting at the men behind the counter now; a stream of threats and curses in *Kuo Yu* – Mandarin – while the two behind him looked about them threateningly. It was a classic piece of Triad mischief – an attempt to unsettle the owners of the Dragon Cloud before they moved in in force.

"I'd like to kick their arses out of here," Chen said beneath his breath.

Karr smiled. "It would be fun, neh? But not now. After the boy's found, maybe. We'll find out who's behind it and pay them a visit, neh? In force."

Chen looked at him and smiled. "That would be good."

"In the meantime . . ." Karr stopped, then leaned forward, his eyes suddenly narrowed.

Chen turned and looked across. The leader of the three was still shouting, but now his curses were directed at the woman who was confronting him. Chen stood up, a cry coming to his lips as he saw the bright flash of a knife being drawn.

This time Karr made no attempt to stop him. Rather, Karr was ahead of him, moving quickly between the tables.

Chen saw the knife describe an arc through the air and felt himself flinch. But then the Triad thug was falling backward, the knife spinning away harmlessly through the air. A moment later he saw the second of the men go down with a sharp groan, clutching his balls. The third turned and made to run, but the woman was on him like a tigress, pulling him backward by his hair, her hand chopping down viciously at his chest.

Chen pulled up sharply, almost thudding into Karr who stood there, his hands clenched at his sides, his great chest rising and falling heavily as he stared down at the three prone gangsters.

The woman turned, meeting Karr's eyes briefly, her own eyes wide, her whole body tensed as if to meet some other threat, then she turned away, a faint shudder passing through her, letting her co-workers carry the three men off.

Karr hesitated a moment, then went after her. He caught up with her on the far side of the teahouse, in an area that was roped off for the staff's use only.

She turned, seeing he was following her, and frowned, looking down. "What do you want?"

Karr shook his head. "That was . . . astonishing. I . . ." He shrugged and opened his hands. "I meant to help you, but you didn't need any help, did you?" He laughed strangely. "Where did you learn to fight like that?"

Again she looked at him, almost resentful now; a reaction to the fight beginning to set in. He could see that her hands were trembling faintly and remembered how that felt. He nodded, feeling a mounting respect for her.

"I've never seen a woman fight like that," he began again.

"Look," she said, angry suddenly. "What do you want?"

"I'm looking for someone," he said, trusting her; knowing that she had acted from more than self-interest. "My nephew. He had an accident, you see, and he ran away. He can't remember who he is, but I know he's here somewhere. I tracked him down here, but now he's disappeared."

She stared at him a long while, then shrugged. "So what's that to do with me?"

He swallowed, conscious that others were listening, then pressed on. "It's just that you might be able to help me. You know these levels. Know the people. If anything odd happened, you'd know about it, neh?"

She gave a grudging nod. "I guess so."

"Well, then. You'll help me, neh? He's my dead brother's son and he means a great deal to me. I . . ."

He looked down, as if unable to go on, then felt her move closer.

"All right," she said quietly, touching his arm. "I'll help. I'll listen out for you."

He looked up, meeting her eyes. "Thanks. My name's Karr. Gregor Karr."

She looked back at him a moment longer, then smiled. "Well . . . you'd best get back to your *ch'a*, Gregor Karr. *Hsiang p'ien* tastes awful when it's cold."

★   ★   ★

As before, the old man was slow coming to the door, but this time she was ready for him. This time when he slid the door back, she moved towards him, as if expecting him to let her pass, beginning to tell him about the incident at the Dragon Cloud, the wicker basket of leftovers from the teahouse held out before her.

It almost worked; almost got her into the room, but then, unexpectedly, she found herself blocked.

"I am sorry, Marie, but you cannot stay. It would benefit neither of us to have our session now."

She turned her head, staring at him, noting how he looked down rather than meet her eyes, and knew at once that he was lying to her. It came as a shock, but it was also confirmation of the feeling she had had back at the restaurant when the man, Karr, had spoken to her.

The boy was here. She knew he was. But what was Tuan Ti Fo up to?

"Forgive me," he was saying, the gentle pressure of his hand forcing her slowly back, "but I am in the worst of humours, Marie. And when a man is in an ill humour he is fit company only for himself, neh?"

The faint, apologetic smile was more like the old Tuan Ti Fo.

She tried to look past him, but it was almost impossible to see what or who was in the room beyond. Stalling for time, she pushed the basket at him.

"You will at least take these, Master Tuan. You must eat, after all, bad humour or no."

He looked down at the basket, then up at her, smiling. "I am extremely grateful, Marie, and yes, I would be a foolish old man indeed if I did not welcome your gift."

The small bow he made was all she needed. For that brief moment she could see the room beyond him and there, jutting out from what seemed at first glance to be a pillow beneath the blanket, the naked foot of a youth.

She shivered, then, backing away a step, returned Tuan Ti Fo's bow.

"Tomorrow," he said. "When the mood has passed."

"Tomorrow," she said, watching the door slide shut again. Then, turning away, she began to make her way back to her apartment, confused, a dark uncertainty at the core of her.

* * *

Tuan Ti Fo stood there for some time, staring at the door, the wicker basket resting lightly in his hand. Then, hearing a movement behind him, he turned.

The boy had crawled out from beneath the blanket and knelt there, looking across at Tuan Ti Fo, his eyes wide with fear.

"It was a friend," the old man said reassuringly. "But it seems best not to take any chances, neh?"

He set the basket down on the low table by the oven, then turned back, looking at the boy.

"But we must leave here now. I cannot stall her for ever, and soon she will grow suspicious, if she hasn't already.

She is not a bad woman – quite the contrary – but curiosity can be a destructive thing."

He eyed the boy a moment longer, not certain how much of what he was saying was understood, then gave a small shrug.

"I have lived in this world a long time, child. I have been many things in my time. I have worked in their factories and on their Plantations. I have served in their officialdom and lived among the criminal element down beneath the Net. I know their world. Know it for the madhouse it is. Even so, sometimes the way ahead is uncertain. So it is now. We must leave here. That much is clear. But where should we go?"

"The Clay," the boy answered him, staring back at him with a strange intensity. "Take me down to the Clay. That's where I belong. Where I came from."

"The Clay . . ." he whispered, then nodded, understanding. As in the dream he had had. "Spiders," he said and saw the boy nod his head slowly. Yes, spiders. Tiny, beautiful spiders, infused with an inner light, spinning their vast webs across the endless darkness. He had seen them, their strong yet delicate webs anchored to the Clay. And there – how clearly he remembered it suddenly – *there*, watching them climb into the dark, was the boy, smiling beatifically, his big, dark eyes filled with wonder.

Tuan Ti Fo shivered, awed by the power of the vision.

"What's your name, boy? What did they call you in the Clay?"

The boy looked away, as if the memory disturbed him, then looked back, his eyes searching Tuan Ti Fo's.

"Lagasek," he said finally. "Lagasek, they called me. *Starer.*"

Tuan Ti Fo caught his breath. "And Gweder?"

The boy frowned and looked down, as if he were having trouble recollecting the word. "Gweder? Gweder means mirror. Why? What have I been saying? I . . ." He shuddered and looked about him. "Something happened, didn't it? Something . . ." He shook his head. "I feel funny. My

228

voice – it's . . . different." He stared down at his hands. "And my body, it's . . ."

He looked back at Tuan Ti Fo, puzzled. "It feels like I've been asleep for a long, long time. Trapped in a huge, deep well of sleep. I was working in the Casting Shop. I remember now. Chan Shui was away. And then . . ." His face creased into a fierce frown of concentration, then he let it go, shaking his head. "I don't understand. T'ai Cho was going to . . ."

"T'ai Cho? Who's T'ai Cho?"

The boy looked up again. "Why, T'ai Cho's my friend. My tutor at the Project. He . . ."

The frown came back. Again the boy looked down at his hands, staring at his arms and legs as if they didn't belong to him.

"What's the matter, Lagasek? What's wrong?"

"Laga . . ." The boy stared at him, then shook his head again. "No. It's Kim. My name is Kim. Lagasek was down there."

"In the Clay?"

"Yes, and . . ." he shook his head, "I feel . . . strange. My body . . . It doesn't feel like it's mine. It's as if . . ."

He stopped, staring up at the old man, his face filled with an intent curiosity.

"What did I say? Those words. You must have heard me say them. So what else did I say?"

Tuan Ti Fo met his eyes, remembering the savagery of the face within his face – the face of Gweder, the mirror – then shook his head.

"You said nothing, Kim. Nothing at all. But come. We must pack now and be away from here. Before they find us here."

Kim stood there a moment longer, staring up at the old man. Then, letting his eyes fall, he nodded.

★ ★ ★

"*Shih* Karr! Please . . . stop a moment!"

Karr turned, prepared for trouble, then relaxed, seeing

who it was. "Ah, it's you, Marie Enge. How did you find me?"

She drew one hand back through her hair, then smiled uncertainly. "As I said, I know everyone in these levels. And you . . ." She looked him up and down admiringly. "Well, who could overlook a man like you, *Shih* Karr?"

He laughed. "That's true. But what can I do for you, Marie Enge?"

She seemed to study him a moment before she spoke. "The thing you were talking of . . ."

He was immediately alert. "The boy," he said quietly, leaning towards her. "You know where he is?"

Again she hesitated, but this time he pre-empted her.

"Look. Come inside a moment. I've a private room. We can talk more easily there, if you wish."

She nodded and let herself be led through to his room on the second level of the travellers' hostel. As such places went it was a clean, respectably furnished room, but it was a "transient" all the same and, looking at him, she could not help but think he looked out of place there. She had seen at once, back in the Dragon Cloud, how his brutish exterior concealed a cultured manner.

He offered her the only chair then set himself down on the edge of the bed, facing her. "Well? What do you know?"

She looked away momentarily, thinking of Tuan Ti Fo. Was she doing the right thing in coming to see Karr? Or was this all a mistake? She looked back. "I've heard something. Nothing definite, but . . ."

She saw how Karr narrowed his eyes. Saw him look down, then look back at her, some small change having taken place in his face.

"Can I trust you, Marie Enge?"

The strange openness of his deeply blue eyes took her by surprise. Some quality which had previously been hidden now shone through them. She stared back at him, matching his openness with her own.

"I'm honest, if that's what you mean, *Shih* Karr. And I

can keep a secret if I'm asked. That is, if it's someone I trust."

He lifted his chin slightly. "Ah . . . I understand. You're thinking, can I trust *Shih* Karr? Well, let's see what we can do about that. First I'll take a chance on you. And then, if you still want to help me, maybe you'll trust me, neh?"

She studied him a moment, then nodded.

"Good. Then first things first. My name is Karr, but I'm not *Shih* Karr." He fished into his tunic pocket and took out his ID, handing it across to her. "As you can see, I'm a major in the T'ang's Security forces and my friend, Chen, whom you met earlier, is a captain. The boy we're looking for is not my nephew but we still need to find him. Alive and unharmed."

She looked up from the ID card, then handed it across. "Why do you need to find him? I don't understand. If he's just a boy . . ."

Karr slipped the card back and took out something else – a flat, matt black case – and handed that to her.

"That's a hologram of the boy. You can keep that. I've others. But that'll help you check he's the one we're looking for."

She rested the case on her knee, then pressed her palm on it briefly, the warmth of her flesh activating it. She studied the image a while, then killed it, looking back at Karr.

"He's a strange-looking boy. Why are you interested in him?"

"Because he's the only survivor of a terrorist raid on one of the T'ang's installations. A very important scientific installation. The whole place was destroyed and all Kim's fellow workers killed."

"Kim?"

"That's his name. But as I was saying . . ."

She reached out and touched his arm, stopping him. "I don't follow you. You said 'his fellow workers'. But he's

231

just a boy. What would he be doing on a scientific installation?''

Karr looked down at her hand then sat back slightly. "Don't underestimate him, Marie Enge. He may be just a boy, but he's also something of a genius. Or was, before the attack. And he might be the only surviving link we have to the Project. That's if he's still alive. And if we can get to him before the terrorists find out that he escaped."

She was looking at him strangely. "This is very important, then?''

Karr narrowed his eyes. "You want paying for your help?''

"Did I say that?"

He winced slightly at the sharpness in her voice, then bowed his head. "I'm sorry. It's just . . ."

"It's all right, Major Karr. I understand. You must deal with some unsavoury types in the work you do."

He smiled. "Yes . . . But to answer you – I have the T'ang's own personal authority to find the boy. If I wanted I could tear this place apart to find him. But that's not my way. Besides, I want the boy unharmed. Who knows what he might do if he felt threatened."

"I see . . ." She looked down, suddenly very still.

"Look," he said, "why don't we simplify this? Why don't you act as intermediary? It might be best if you and not one of us were to deal with the boy. He might find it easier to trust you."

She looked back at him, grateful.

Karr smiled. "Then you know where he is."

She caught her breath, a strange little movement in her face betraying the fact that she thought she had been tricked by him. Then she nodded, looking up at him.

"Yes. At least, I think so."

She watched him a moment longer, a lingering uncertainty in her face, then gave a small laugh. "You mean it, then? You'll let me handle it?"

He nodded. "I gave my word to you, didn't I? But take this." He handed her a necklace. "When you're ready, just press the stud on the neck. We'll trace it and come."

Again the uncertainty returned to her face.

He smiled reassuringly. "Trust me, Marie Enge. Please. We will do nothing until you call for us. I shall not even have you followed when you leave this room. But I'm relying on you, so don't let me down. Much depends on this."

"All right." She stood, slipping the necklace over her head. "But what if he's afraid? What if he doesn't want to go back?"

Karr nodded, then reached into his tunic pocket yet again. "Give this to him. He'll understand."

It was a pendant. A beautiful silver pendant. And inside, in the tiny, circular locket, was the picture of a woman. A beautiful, dark-haired woman. She snapped it closed then held it up, watching it turn, flashing, in the light.

She slipped the pendant into her apron pocket and turned to leave, but he called her back. "By the way," he said. "How good are you at *wei chi?*"

She turned in the doorway and looked back at him, smiling. "How good? Well, maybe I'll play you some time and let you find out for yourself, eh, Major Karr?"

Karr grinned. "I'd like that, Marie Enge. I'd like that very much."

★ ★ ★

She was standing there when the door opened. It was just after two in the morning and the corridors were empty. Tuan Ti Fo took one step towards her then stopped, seeing her there in the shadows.

"Marie . . ."

"I know," she said quickly, seeing how he was dressed; how he was carrying his bedroll on his back. Behind him the boy looked out, wide-eyed, wondering what was going on.

He took a breath. "Then you will understand why we must go. The boy is in great danger here."

233

She nodded. "I know that, too. There are men trying to kill him. They killed his friends."

He narrowed his eyes, his voice a whisper. "How do you know all this, Marie?"

"Inside," she said, moving closer. "Please, Tuan Ti Fo. I must talk with you." When he hesitated, she reached out and touched his arm. "Please, Master Tuan. For the boy's sake."

They went inside. The boy had backed away. He was crouched against the back wall, his eyes going from Tuan Ti Fo to the newcomer, his body tensed.

"It's all right, Kim," Tuan Ti Fo said, going across and kneeling next to him. "She's a friend." He half turned, looking back at Marie. "This is Kim. Kim, this is Marie."

She came across, then stood there, shaking her head. "You're the boy, all right, but it doesn't make sense." She looked from him to Tuan Ti Fo. "I was told he was a scientist, a genius, but . . ." She turned back. "Well, he's just a boy. A frightened boy."

Tuan Ti Fo's eyes had widened at her words. Now he laughed. "A boy he may be, but *just* a boy he's certainly not. Do you know something, Marie? He beat me. In only his third game."

"I don't understand you, Master Tuan. Beat you at what?"

"At the game. At *wei chi*. He's a natural."

She stared at Tuan Ti Fo then looked back at the boy, a new respect entering her expression. "He *beat* you?" Her voice dropped to a whisper. "Gods . . ."

"Yes . . ." Tuan Ti Fo chuckled. "And by five stones, no less. Not just beaten, but humiliated." He looked back at Kim and gave him a small bow. "Which makes our friend here unofficial First Hand Supreme of all Chung Kuo, neh?"

She laughed; a small laugh of astonishment. "No wonder they want him back."

Tuan Ti Fo stiffened, his face hardening. "They?"

Marie nodded, suddenly more sober. "Li Yuan. The new T'ang. Kim was working for him."

She explained.

Tuan Ti Fo sighed. "I see . . . And you're certain of this?"

"I . . ." She hesitated, remembering her meeting with Karr, then nodded. "Yes. But there's something I have to give the boy. Something they said would mean something to him."

She took the pendant from her pocket and crouched down, holding it out to the boy.

For a moment he seemed almost not to see the bright silver circle that lay in her palm. Then, a growing wonder filling his eyes, he reached out and touched the hanging chain.

She placed it in his hand, then moved back slightly, watching him.

Slowly the wonder faded, shading into puzzlement. Then, like cracks appearing in the wall of a dam, his face dissolved, a great flood of pain and hurt overwhelming him.

He cried out – a raw, gut-wrenching sound in that tiny room – then pressed the pendant to his cheek, his fingers trembling, his whole face ghastly now with loss.

"T'ai Cho," he moaned, his voice broken, wavering. "T'ai Cho . . . they killed T'ai Cho!"

CHAPTER·7

NEW BLOOD

The statue stood at the centre of the Hall of Celestial Destinies in Nantes spaceport, the huge, bronze figures raised high above the executive-class travellers who bustled like ants about its base. Thrice life-size and magnificently detailed, the vast human figures seemed like giants from some golden age, captured in the holo-camera's trebled eye and cast in bronze.

"Kan Ying bows to Pan Chao after the Battle of Kazatin", read the description, the huge letters cut deep into the two-*ch'i*-thick base, the Mandarin translation given smaller underneath, as though to emphasise the point that the message was aimed at those who had been conquered in that great battle – the *Hung Mao*.

Michael Lever stopped and stared up at it. Kazatin was where the dream of Rome, of the great *Ta Ts'in* emperors, had failed. The defeat of Kan Ying – Domitian as he was known by his own people – had let the Han into Europe. The rest was history.

"What do you make of it?" Kustow, said into his ear. "It looks like more of their crowing to me."

Like Lever, Bryn Kustow was in his late twenties, a tall man with close-cropped blond hair. He wore the same sombre clothes as Lever, a wine red *pau* that made them seem more like clerks than the heirs to great Companies. Facially the two men were very different, Kustow's face blunt, Lever's hawkish, but the similarity of dress and the starkness of their haircuts made them seem like brothers, or members of some strange cult. So, too, the third of them, Stevens, who stood to one side, looking back at the wall-length window and its view of the great circle of the spaceport's landing apron.

They were strangers here. Americans. Young men over here on their fathers' business. Or so their papers claimed. But there were other reasons for coming to City Europe. This was where things were happening just now. The pulsing heart of things. And they had come to feel that pulse. To find out if there was something they could learn from looking around.

Lever turned, smiling back at his best friend. "They say Kan Ying was a good man, Bryn. A strong man and yet fair. Under him the lands of *Ta Ts'in* were fairly governed. Had his sons ruled, they say there would have been a golden age."

Kustow nodded. "A good man, yes, until the great Pan Chao arrived."

The two men laughed quietly, then looked back at the statue.

Kan Ying knelt before Pan Chao, his back bent, his forehead pressed into the bare earth. He was unarmed, while Pan Chao stood above him, legs apart, his great sword raised in triumph, two daggers in his belt. Behind Kan Ying stood his four generals, their arms and insignia stripped from them, their faces gashed, their beards ragged from battle. There was honour in the way they held themselves, but also defeat. Their armies had been slaughtered on the battlefield by the superior Han forces. They looked tired, and the great, empty coffin they carried between them looked too much for their wasted strength to bear.

Nor would it grow any lighter. For, so the story went, Pan Chao had decapitated Kan Ying there and then and sent his body back to Rome where it had lain out in the open in the great square, slowly rotting, waiting for the young Emperor, Ho Ti's triumphal entry into the city three years later.

Two thousand years ago, it had been. And still the Han crowed about it. Still they raised great statues to celebrate the moment when they had laid the *Hung Mao* low.

Lever turned. "Carl! Bryn! Come on! We're meeting Ebert in an hour, don't forget."

Stevens turned, smiling, then hurried across. "I was just watching one of the big interplanetary craft go up. They're amazing. You could feel the floor trembling beneath you as it turned on the power and climbed."

Kustow laughed. "So that's what it was . . . And there was I thinking it was the *chow mein* we had on the flight."

Stevens smiled back at them, then put his arms about their shoulders. He was the eldest of the three; an engineering graduate whose father owned a near-space research and development company. His fascination with anything to do with space and spaceflight bordered upon obsession and he had been horrified when *The New Hope* had been blown out of the sky by the Seven. Something had died in him that day; and, at the same time, something had been born. A determination to get back what had been taken from them. To change the Edict and get out there, into space again, whatever it took.

"We'll be building them one day, I tell you," he said softly. "But bigger than that, and faster."

Kustow frowned. "Faster than that?" He shook his head. "Well, if you say so, Carl. But I'm told some of those craft can make the Mars trip in forty days."

Stevens nodded. "The *Tientsin* can do it in thirty. Twenty-six at perihelion. But yes, Bryn. Give me ten years and I'll make something that can do it in twenty."

"And kill all the passengers! I can see it now. It's bad enough crossing the Atlantic on one of those things, but imagine the g-forces that would build up if you . . ."

"*Please* . . ." Lever interrupted, seeing how things were developing. "Hans will be waiting for us. So let's get on."

They went through to the main City Transfer barrier, ignoring the long queue of passengers formed up at the gates, going directly to the duty officer, a short, broad-shouldered man with neat black hair.

"Forgive me, Captain," Lever began, "but could you

help us?" He took his documentation from his pocket and pushed it into the officer's hand. "We've an appointment with Major Ebert at eleven and . . ."

The officer didn't even look at the card. "Of course, *Shih* Lever. Would you mind following me. You and your two companions. There's a transporter waiting up above. Your baggage will be sent on."

Lever gave a small nod of satisfaction. So Ebert had briefed his men properly. "And the other two in our party?"

The officer smiled tightly. His information was not one hundred per cent perfect then. "They . . . will join you as quickly as possible."

"Good." Lever smiled. No, even Ebert hadn't known he was bringing two experts with him. Nor had he wanted him to know. In business – even in this kind of business – it was always best to keep your opponent wrong-footed; even when your opponent was your friend. To make him feel uncertain, uninformed. That way you kept the advantage.

"Then lead on," he said. "Let's not keep our host waiting."

★ ★ ★

Stevens was the first to note it. He leaned across and touched Lever's arm. "Michael . . . something's wrong."

"What do you mean?"

Stevens leaned closer. "Look outside, through the window. There are mountains down below. And the sun . . . it's to the left. We're heading south. At a guess I'd say we're over the Swiss Wilds."

Lever sat up, staring outward, then turned, looking down the aisle of the transporter.

"Captain? Can you come here a moment?"

The Security officer broke off his conversation with his adjutant and came across, bowing respectfully.

"What is it, *Shih* Lever?"

Lever pointed out at the mountains. "Where are we?"

239

The Captain smiled. "You've noticed. I'm sorry, *ch'un tzu*, but I couldn't tell you before. My orders, you understand. However, *Shih* Stevens is right. We're heading south. And those below are the Swiss Wilds." He reached into his tunic and withdrew a folded, handwritten note, handing it to Lever. "Here, this will explain everything."

Lever unfolded the note and read it quickly. It was from Ebert.

Lever smiled, his fingers tracing the wax seal at the foot of the note, then looked up again. "And you, Captain? What's your role in this?"

The officer smiled, then began to unbutton his tunic. He peeled it off and threw it to one side then sat facing the three Americans.

"Forgive the deception, my friends, but let me introduce myself. My name is Howard DeVore and I'm to be your host for the next eight hours."

★ ★ ★

Lehmann sat at the back of the room, some distance from the others. A huge viewing screen filled the wall at the far end, while to one side, on a long, wide table made of real mahogany, a detailed map of City Europe was spread out, the Swiss Wilds and the Carpathians marked in red, like bloodstains on the white.

DeVore, Lever and the others sat in big leather chairs, drinks in hand, talking. Above them, on the screen, the funeral procession moved slowly through the walled northern garden at Tongjiang: the Li family, the seven T'ang, their generals and their chief retainers. Thirty shaven-headed servants followed, the open casket held high above their heads.

DeVore raised his half-filled glass to indicate the slender, dark-haired figure in white who led the mourners.

"He carries his grief well. But then he must. It's a quality he'll need to cultivate in the days ahead."

DeVore's smile was darkly ironic. Beside him, Lever laughed then leaned forward, cradling his empty glass between his hands. "And look at our friend Hans. A study in solemnity, neh?"

Lehmann watched them laugh, his eyes drawn to the man who sat to the extreme right of the group. He was much older than Lever and his friends, his dark hair tied back in two long pigtails. There was a cold elegance about him that contrasted with the brashness of the others. He was a proud, even arrogant man; the way he sat, the way he held his head, expressed that eloquently. Even so, he was their servant, not they his, and that fact bridled his tongue and kept him from being too familiar with them.

His name was Andrew Curval and he was an experimental geneticist; perhaps the greatest of the age. As a young man he had worked for GenSyn as a commodity slave, his time and talents bought by them on a fifteen-year contract. Twelve years back that contract had expired and he had set up his own Company, but that venture had failed after only three years. Now he was back on contract; this time to Old Man Lever.

Lehmann looked back at the others. Kustow was talking, his deep voice providing a commentary on the proceedings. He was pointing up at Li Yuan, there at the centre of the screen.

"Look at him! He's such an innocent. He hasn't the faintest idea of how things really stand."

"No," Lever agreed. "But that's true of all of them. They're cut off from the reality of what's happening in the Cities. There's real dissent down there, real bitterness, and the Seven simply don't know about it. They're like the emperors of old: they don't like bad news, so their servants make sure the truth never gets through to them. That's bad enough, but, as we all know, the system's corrupt to the core. From the pettiest official to the biggest Minister, there's not one of them you can't put a price to."

The camera closed in. Li Yuan's face, many times its natural size, filled the screen. His fine, dark hair was drawn back tightly from his forehead, secured at the nape in a tiny porcelain bowl of purest white. His skin was unmarked, unlined; the flesh of youth, untouched by time or the ravages of experience.

Even so, he knows, Lehmann thought, looking up into the young T'ang's eyes. He knows we murdered his father. Or, at least, suspects.

Irritated by their arrogance, he stood then went across, filling Lever's glass from the wine kettle.

"I think you underestimate our man," he said quietly. "Look at those eyes. How like his father's eyes they are. Don't misjudge him. He's no fool, this one." He turned, looking directly at DeVore. "You've said so yourself often enough, Howard."

"I agree," said DeVore, eyeing Lehmann sharply. "But there are things he lacks. Things the Seven miss now that Li Shai Tung is dead. Experience, wisdom, an intuitive sense of when and how to act. Those things are gone from them now. And without them . . ." He laughed softly. "Well, without them the Seven are vulnerable."

On the screen the image changed, the camera panning back, the figures diminishing as the larger context was revealed. A grey stone wall, taller than a man, surrounded everything. Beyond it the mountains of the Ta Pa Shan formed faint shapes in the distance. The tomb was to the left, embedded in the earth, the great white tablet stretching out towards its open mouth. To the right was the long pool, still, intensely black, its surface like a mirror. Between stood the seven T'ang and their retainers, all of them dressed in white, the colour of mourning.

"One bomb," said Kustow, nodding to himself. "Just one bomb and it would all be over, neh?" He turned in his seat, looking directly at DeVore. "How do you come by these pictures? I thought these ceremonies were private?"

"They are," DeVore said, taking a sip from his glass. He leaned forward, smiling, playing the perfect host, knowing how important it was for him to win these young men over. "The camera is a standard Security surveillance device. They're all over Tongjiang. I've merely tapped into the system."

242

All three of the Americans were watching DeVore closely now, ignoring what was happening on the screen.

"I thought those systems were discrete," Lever said.

"They are." DeVore set his drink down on the table at his side, then took a small device from his pocket and handed it across. "This was something my friend Soren Berdichev developed at SimFic before they shut him down. It looks and functions like the back-up battery packs they have on those Security cameras, but there's more to it than that. What it does is to send a tight beam of information up to a satellite. There the signal is scrambled into code and re-routed here, where it's decoded."

Lever studied the device then handed it to Kustow. He turned, looking back at DeVore. "Astonishing. But how did you get it into place? I'm told those palaces are tighter than a young whore's arse when it comes to security."

DeVore laughed. "That's true. But whatever system you have, it always relies on men. Individual men. And men can be bought, or won, or simply threatened. It was relatively easy to get these installed."

Lehmann, watching, saw how that impressed the young men, but it was only half true. The device worked exactly as DeVore had said, but the truth was that he had access only to Tongjiang, and that only because Hans Ebert had been daring enough to take the thing in, risking the possibility that an over-zealous officer might search him, Tolonen's favourite or no. Elsewhere his attempts to plant the devices had failed.

They looked back at the screen. Li Yuan stood at the edge of the family tablet, the freshly inscribed name of his father cut into the whiteness there. Behind the young T'ang stood the rest of the Seven, and at their back the generals. Bringing up the rear of this small but powerful gathering stood members of the Li Family: cousins and uncles, wives, concubines and close relations, a hundred in all. The ranks were thin, the weakness of the Family exposed to view, and yet Li Yuan stood proudly, his eyes looking straight ahead, into the darkness of the tomb.

"All the trappings of power," said Kustow, shaking his head as if in disapproval. "Like the Pharaohs, they are. Obsessed with death."

Lehmann studied Kustow a moment, noting the strange mixture of awe and antagonism in his blunt, almost rectangular face. You admire this, he thought. Or envy it, rather. Because you too would like to create a dynasty and be buried in a cloth of gold.

For himself, he hated it all. He would have done with kings and dynasties.

They watched as the casket was carried to the mouth of the tomb. Saw the six strongest carry it down the steps into the candle-lit interior. And then the camera focused once more upon Li Yuan.

"He's strong for one so young."

They were the first words Curval had spoken since he had come into the room. Again Lehmann looked, admiring the manner of the man, his singleness of being. In his face there was a hard, uncompromising certainty about things; in some strange way it reminded Lehmann of Berdichev. Or of how Berdichev had become, after his wife's death.

On the screen Li Yuan bowed to the tablet, then turned, making his slow way to the tomb.

"He *looks* strong," DeVore said after a moment, "but there are things you don't know about him. That outward presence of his is a mask. Inside he's a writhing mass of unstable elements. Do you know that he killed all his wife's horses?"

All eyes were on DeVore, shocked by the news. To kill horses – it was unthinkable!

"Yes," DeVore continued. "In a fit of jealousy, so I understand. So you see, beneath that calm exterior lies a highly unstable child. Not unlike his headstrong brother. And a coward, too."

Lever narrowed his eyes. "How so?"

"Fei Yen, his brother's wife, is heavily pregnant. Rumour has it that it is not his child. The woman has been sent home to her father in disgrace. And they say he knows whose bastard it is. Knows and does nothing."

"I see," Lever said. "But that doesn't necessarily make the man a coward?"

DeVore gave a short laugh. "If you were married you would understand it better, Michael. A man's wife, his child, these things are more than the world to him. He would kill for them. Even a relatively passive man. But Li Yuan holds back, does nothing. That, surely, is cowardice?"

"Or a kind of wisdom?" Lever looked back up at the screen, watching the young T'ang step down into the darkness. "Forgive me, *Shih* DeVore, but I feel your friend here is right. It would not do to underestimate Li Yuan."

"No?" DeVore shrugged.

"Even so," Lever said, smiling, "I take your point. The Seven have never been weaker than they are right now. And their average age has never been younger. Why, we're old men by comparison to most of them!"

There was laughter at that.

DeVore studied the three Americans, pleased by Lever's unconscious echo of his thoughts. It was time.

He raised his hand. At the prearranged signal the screen went dark and a beam of light shone out from above, spot-lighting the table and the map on the far side of the room.

"*Ch'un tzu* . . ." DeVore said, rising to his feet, one arm extended, indicating the table. "You've seen how things stand with the Seven. How things are now. Well, let us talk of how things might be."

Lever stood, studying DeVore a moment, as if to weigh him, then smiled and nodded. "All right, *Shih* DeVore. Lead the way. We're all ears."

★ ★ ★

Back inside, Li Yuan drew Wang Sau-leyan aside.

"Cousin Wang," he said softly. "May I speak to you in private? News has come."

Wang Sau-leyan stared back at him, faintly hostile. "News, cousin?"

Li Yuan turned slightly to one side, indicating the door to a nearby room. Wang hesitated, then nodded and went through. Inside, Li Yuan pulled the doors closed then turned, facing his fellow T'ang.

"Your grain ships . . ." he began, watching Wang Sau-leyan's face closely.

"Yes?" Wang's expression was mildly curious.

"I'm afraid your ships are at the bottom of the ocean, cousin. An hour back. It seems someone blew them up."

Wang's expression of angry surprise was almost comical. He shook his head as if speechless, then, unexpectedly, he reached out and held Li Yuan's arm. "Are you certain, Li Yuan?"

Li Yuan nodded, looking down at the plump, bejewelled hand that rested on the rough cloth of his sleeve. "It's true. Your Chancellor, Hung Mien-lo, has confirmed it."

Wang Sau-leyan let his hand fall. He turned his head away, then looked back at Li Yuan, a strange hurt in his eyes.

"I am so sorry, Li Yuan. So very sorry. The grain was my gift to your father. My final gift to him." He shook his head, pained. "Oh, I can spare more grain – and, indeed, you will have it, cousin – but that's not the point, is it? Someone destroyed my gift! My gift to your father!"

Li Yuan's lips parted slightly in surprise. He had not expected Wang to be so upset, so patently indignant. Nor had he for one moment expected Wang to offer another shipment. No, he had thought this all some kind of clever ruse; some way of shirking his verbal obligation. He frowned, then shook his head, confused.

"Your offer is very generous, cousin, but you are in no way to blame for what has happened. Indeed, I understand that the *Ping Tiao* have claimed responsibility for the act."

"The *Ping Tiao*!" Again there was a flash of anger in Wang's face that took Li Yuan by surprise. "Then the *Ping Tiao* will pay for their insult!"

"Cousin . . ." Li Yuan said softly, taking a step closer. 'The matter is being dealt with, I assure you. The insult will not be allowed to pass."

Wang gave a terse nod. "Thank you, cousin. I . . ."

There was a loud knocking on the door. Li Yuan half turned, then looked back at Wang. "You wished to say . . . ?"

A faint smile crossed Wang's features. "Nothing, cousin. But again, thank you for telling me. I shall instruct my Chancellor to send a new shipment at once."

Li Yuan lowered his head. "I am most grateful."

Wang smiled and returned the bow to the precise degree – tacitly acknowledging their equality of status – then moved past Li Yuan, pulling the door open.

Hans Ebert stood outside, in full dress uniform, his equerry three paces behind him. Seeing Wang Sau-leyan, he bowed low.

"Forgive me, *Chieh Hsia*. I didn't realise . . ."

Wang Sau-leyan smiled tightly. "It is all right, Major Ebert. You may go in. Your master and I have finished now."

* * *

Ebert turned, then, taking a deep breath, stepped into the doorway, presenting himself.

"*Chieh Hsia*?"

Li Yuan was standing on the far side of the room, beside the ceremonial *kang*, one foot up on the ledge of it, his right hand stroking his unbearded chin. He looked across, then waved Ebert in almost casually.

Ebert marched to the centre of the room and came smartly to attention, lowering his head respectfully, waiting for his T'ang to speak.

Li Yuan sighed, then launched into things without preamble. "These are troubled times, Hans. The old bonds must be forged stronger than ever, the tree of State made firm against the storm to come, from root to branch."

Ebert raised his head. "And my role in this, *Chieh Hsia*?"

Li Yuan looked down. "Let me explain. Shortly before his death, my father went to see General Nocenzi in hospital. As you may have heard, he accepted Nocenzi's resignation. There was no other choice. But who was to be general in his place?" He paused significantly. "Well, it was my father's intention to ask Marshal Tolonen to step down from his post of seniority to be general again, and he drafted a memorandum to that effect. There were good reasons for his decision, not least of which was the stability that the old man's presence would bring to the Security forces. He also felt that to bring in a *lao wai* – an outsider – might cause some resentment. Besides which, it takes some time for a new general to adapt to his command, and time was something we did not have."

Li Yuan turned away, silent a moment, then looked back at him. "Don't you agree, Hans?"

Ebert bowed his head. "It is so, *Chieh Hsia*. Moreover, there is no one in all Chung Kuo with more experience than the Marshal. Indeed, I can think of nobody your enemies would less welcome in the post."

He saw Li Yuan smile, pleased by his words. Even so, his sense of disappointment was acute. After what Tolonen had said to him earlier he had hoped for the appointment himself.

Li Yuan nodded, then spoke again. "However, my father's death changes many things. Our enemies will think us weak just now. Will think me callow, inexperienced. We need to demonstrate how wrong they are. Tolonen's appointment as General would certainly help in that regard, but I must also show them that I am my own man, not merely my father's shadow. You understand me, Hans?"

"I understand, *Chieh Hsia*."

Only too well, he thought. Only too well.

"Yes . . ." Li Yuan nodded thoughtfully. "In that we are alike, neh, Hans? We know what it is to have to wait. To be our fathers' hands. Yet in time we must become them, and more, if we are to gain the respect of the world."

248

"It is so," Ebert said quietly.

"Besides which," Li Yuan continued, "things are certain to get worse before they get better. In consequence we must grow harder, more ruthless than we were in the days of ease. In that, Wang Sau-leyan is right. It is a new age. Things have changed, and we must change with them. The days of softness are past."

Ebert watched Li Yuan's face as he spoke the words and felt a genuine admiration for the young T'ang. Li Yuan was much harder, much more the pragmatist than his father; his ideas about the Wiring Project were proof of that. But Ebert was too far along his own road now to let that colour his thinking; too deeply committed to his own dream of inheritance.

One day he would have to kill this man, admire him or not. It was that or see his own dream die.

"Trust," Li Yuan said. "Trust is the cornerstone of the State. In that, as in many things, my father was right. But in an age of violent change who should the wise man trust? Who *can* he trust?" He looked back at Ebert, narrowing his eyes. "I'm sorry, Hans. It's just that I must talk this through. You understand?"

Ebert bowed his head. "I am honoured that you feel you can talk so freely in my presence, *Chieh Hsia*."

Li Yuan laughed, then grew serious again. "Yes, well . . . I suppose it is because I consider you almost family, Hans. Your father was chief amongst my father's counsellors since Shepherd's illness and will remain among my council of advisers. However, it is not about your father that I summoned you today, it is about you."

Ebert raised his head. "*Chieh Hsia*?"

"Yes, Hans. Haven't you guessed, or have I been too indirect? I want you for my general – my most trusted man. I want you to serve me as Tolonen served my father. To be my sword arm and my scourge, the bane of my enemies and the defender of my children."

Ebert's mouth had fallen open. "But, *Chieh Hsia*, I thought . . ."

249

"Oh, Tolonen is appointed temporarily. As caretaker general. He agreed an hour past. But it is you I want to stand behind me at my coronation three days from now. You who will receive the ceremonial dagger that morning."

Ebert stared at him, open-mouthed, then fell to his knees, bowing his head low. "*Chieh Hsia*, you do me a great honour. My life is yours to command."

He had rehearsed the words earlier, yet his surprise at Li Yuan's sudden reversal gave them force. When he glanced up, he could see the pleasure in the young T'ang's face.

"Stand up, Hans. Please."

Ebert got to his feet slowly, keeping his head bowed.

Li Yuan came closer. "It might surprise you, Hans, but I have been watching you for some time now. Seeing how well you dealt with your new responsibilities. It did not escape my notice how loyal your officers were to you. As for your courage . . ." He reached out and touched the metal plate on the back of Ebert's head, then moved back again. "Most important of all, though, you have considerable influence among the élite of First Level. An important quality in a general."

Li Yuan smiled broadly. "Your appointment will be posted throughout the levels, tonight at twelfth bell. But before then I want you to prepare a plan of action for me."

"A plan, *Chieh Hsia*?"

Li Yuan nodded. "A plan to eradicate the *Ping Tiao*. To finish off what my father began. I want every last one of them dead, a month from now. Dead and their bodies lain before me."

Ebert stood there, his mouth fallen open again. Then he bowed his head. But for a moment he had almost laughed. Eradicate the *Ping Tiao*? Little did Li Yuan know. It was done already! And done by Li Yuan's chief enemy, DeVore!

Li Yuan touched his shoulder. "Well . . . go now, Hans. Go and tell your father. I know he will be proud. It was what he always wanted."

Ebert smiled, then bowed his head again, surprised by the pride he felt. To be this man's servant – what was there to be proud in that? And yet, strangely enough, he was. He turned, making to leave, but Li Yuan called him back.

"Oh, and Hans . . . we found the boy."

Ebert turned back, his stomach tightening. "That's excellent, *Chieh Hsia*. How was he?"

Li Yuan smiled. "It could not have been better, Hans. He remembered everything. Everything . . ."

★ ★ ★

DeVore took his eye from the lens of the electron-microscope and looked across at the geneticist, smiling, impressed by what he'd seen.

"It's clever, *Shih* Curval. Very clever indeed. And does it always behave like that, no matter the host?"

Curval hesitated a moment, then turned back, reaching across DeVore to take the sealed slide from the microscope, handling it with extreme delicacy. As indeed he ought, for the virus it contained was deadly. He looked back at DeVore.

"If the host has had the normal course of immunisation, then yes, it should follow near enough the same evolutionary pattern. There will be slight statistical variations, naturally, but such 'sports' will be small in number. For all intents and purposes you could guarantee a one hundred per cent success rate."

DeVore nodded thoughtfully. "Interesting. So, in effect, what we have here is a bug that evolves. That's harmless when it's first passed on, but which, in only a hundred generations, evolves into a deadly virus. A brainkiller." He laughed. "And what's a hundred generations in the life of a bug?"

For the first time, Curval laughed. "Exactly . . ."

DeVore moved back, letting the scientist past, his mind reeling with an almost aesthetic delight at the beauty of the thing. "Moreover, the very thing that triggers this evolutionary pattern is that which is normally guaranteed

251

to defend the body against disease – the immunisation programme!"

"Exactly. The very thing that every First Level child has pumped into their system as a six-month foetus."

DeVore watched him place the sealed slide back into the padded, shocksafe case and draw another out.

"Come . . . here's another. Slightly different this time. Same principle, but more specific."

DeVore leaned forward, fascinated. "What do you mean, more specific?"

Curval slipped the slide into the slot, then stood back. "Just watch. I'll trigger it when you're ready."

He put his eye to the lens. Again he saw the thing divide and grow and change, like the ever-evolving pattern in a kaleidoscope, but this thing was real, *alive* – as alive as only a thing whose sole purpose was to kill could be.

DeVore looked up. "It looks the same."

Curval looked at him closely. "You noticed no difference then?"

DeVore smiled. "Well, there were one or two small things, midway through. There was a brief stage when the thing seemed a lot bigger than before. And afterwards, there was a slight colour change. Then it normalised. Was the same as before."

Curval laughed. "Good. So you did see."

"Yes, but what did I see?"

Curval took out the slide – it seemed not as carefully as before – and set it down on the table beside him.

"This . . ." he tapped it almost carelessly, "is as harmless to you or me as spring water. We could take in a huge dose of it and it wouldn't harm us one tiny little bit. But to a Han . . ."

DeVore's eyes widened.

Curval nodded. "That's right. What you saw was the virus priming itself genetically, like a tiny bacteriological time-bomb, making itself racially specific."

DeVore laughed, then reached across to pick it up. The slide seemed empty, yet its contents could do untold damage. Not to him or his kind, but to the Han. He smiled broadly. "Wonderful! That's wonderful!"

Curval laughed. "I thought you'd like it. You know, I had you in mind constantly while I was making it. I would sit there late nights and laugh, imagining your reaction."

DeVore looked at him a moment, then nodded. The two had known each other more than twenty years, ever since their first fateful meeting at one of Old Mar Ebert's parties. Curval had been restless even then – wanting to break out on his own, burdened by the remaining years of his contract. It had been DeVore who had befriended him. DeVore who had found him his first, important contacts in City America. DeVore who had shown him the top-security files detailing the deals Klaus Ebert had struck with various Companies to destroy Curval's own enterprise. DeVore who had arranged the deal whereby he worked for the Levers and yet had his own private laboratories.

And now Curval was returning the favour. With only one string attached. A minor thing. DeVore could have the virus, but first he must promise to kill Old Man Ebert.

He had agreed.

"Does Michael know about this?"

Curval smiled. "What do you think? Michael Lever is a nice young man for all his revolutionary fervour. He wants to change things – but fairly. He'll fight if he must, but he won't cheat. He'd kill me if he knew I'd made something like this."

DeVore considered that a while then nodded. "You're sure of that?"

Curval laughed sourly. "I know that young man too well. He seems different, but underneath it all he's the same as the rest of them. They've had it too easy, all of them. What fires them isn't ambition but a sense of bitterness. Bitterness that their fathers still treat them as children. For all they were saying back there in the screen-room, they don't want change. Not real change like you and I want. When they talk of change what they mean is a change of leadership. They'd as soon relinquish their privileges as the Seven."

"Maybe," DeVore said, watching Curval pack up the microscope. "By the way, has the virus a name?"

Curval clicked the case shut and turned, looking back at DeVore. "Yes, as a matter of fact it does. I've named it after the viral strain I developed it from. That too was a killer, though not as lethal or efficient as mine. And it was around for centuries before people managed to find a cure for it. Syphilis they called it. What the Han call *yang mei ping*, 'willow-plum sickness'."

DeVore laughed, surprised. "So it's sexually transmitted?"

Curval stared at DeVore, then laughed quietly. "Of course! I thought you understood that. It's the only way to guarantee that it will spread, and spread widely. Fucking . . . it's the thing the human race does most of and says least about. And when you consider it, it's the perfect way of introducing a new virus. After all, they're all supposed to be immune to sexual disease. From birth."

DeVore touched his tongue against his top teeth, then nodded. Errant husbands and their unfaithful wives, bored concubines and their casual lovers, lecherous old men and randy widows, singsong girls and libertine young sons – he could see it now, spreading like the leaves and branches of a great tree, until the tree itself rotted and fell. He laughed, then slapped Curval on the back.

"You've done well, Andrew. Very well."

Curval looked at him. "And you, Howard? You'll keep your promise?"

DeVore squeezed his shoulder. "Of course. Have I ever let you down? But come, let's go through. Our young friends will be wondering why we've been gone so long. Besides, I understand our friend Kustow has brought his *wei chi* champion with him and I fancied trying myself out against him."

Curval nodded. "He's good. I've seen him play."

DeVore met his eyes. "As good as me?"

254

Curval turned and took the tiny, deadly slide from off the table. "They say he might even challenge for the championship next year."

DeVore laughed. "Maybe so, but you still haven't answered me. You've seen me play. Would you say he's as good as me?"

Curval slotted the slide back into the case and secured the lid, then looked back at DeVore, hesitant, not certain how he'd take the truth.

"To be honest with you, Howard, yes. Every bit as good. And maybe a lot better."

DeVore turned away, pacing the tiny room, lost in his own thoughts. Then he turned back, facing Curval again, a smile lighting his face.

"Our friend Kustow . . . do you know if he likes to gamble?"

★ ★ ★

DeVore looked up from the board, then bowed to his opponent, conceding the game. It was the fifth the two had played and the closest yet. This time he had come within a stone of beating the Han. Even so, the result of the tournament was conclusive: Kustow's champion had triumphed five-nil, two of those games having been won by a margin of more than twenty stones.

"Another five?" Kustow said, smiling. He had done well by the contest – DeVore had wagered five thousand *yuan* on each game and a further ten thousand on the tournament.

DeVore looked back at him, acknowledging his victory. "I wish there were time, my friend, but you must be at the Ebert Mansion by nine and it's six already. I'll tell you what, though. When I come to America, I'll play your man again. It will give me the opportunity to win my money back."

Lever leaned forward in his chair. "You plan to come to America, then, *Shih* DeVore? Wouldn't that be rather dangerous for you?"

DeVore smiled. "Life *is* dangerous, Michael. And whilst it pays to take care, where would any of us be if we did not take risks?"

Lever looked to his two friends. "True. But one must choose one's friends well in these uncertain times."

DeVore bowed his head slightly, understanding what was implied. They were inclined to work with him, but had yet to commit themselves fully. He would need to give them further reasons for allying with him. "And one's lieutenants. My man Mach, for instance. He served me well in the attack on the T'ang's Plantations."

Lever gave a laugh of surprise. "That was you? But I thought . . ."

"You thought as everyone was meant to think. That it was the *Ping Tiao*. But no, they were my men."

"I see. But why? Why not claim credit for yourself?"

"Because sometimes it suits one's purpose to make one's enemies believe the truth is other than it is. You see, the *Ping Tiao* is now defunct. I destroyed the last vestiges of that organisation two days back. Yet as far as the Seven are concerned, it still exists – still poses a threat to them. Indeed, the new T'ang, Li Yuan, plans to launch a major campaign against them. He has given instructions to his new General to use whatever force it takes to destroy them, and at whatever cost. Such a diversion of funds and energies is to be welcomed, wouldn't you say?"

Lever laughed. "Yes! And at the same time it draws attention away from your activities here in the Wilds. I like that."

DeVore nodded, pleased. Here were young men with fire in them. They were not like their European counterparts. Their anger was pure. It had only to be channelled.

He stood, and, with one final bow to his opponent, came round the table, facing the three young men.

"There's one more thing before you go from here. Something I want to give you."

Lever looked to his friends, then lowered his head. "We

thank you, *Shih* DeVore, but your hospitality has been reward enough."

DeVore understood. Lever was accustomed to the use of gifts in business to create obligations. It was a trick the Han used a great deal. He shook his head. "Please, my friends, do not mistake me; this gift carries no obligation. Indeed, I would feel greatly offended if you took it otherwise. I am no trader. I would not dream of seeking any material advantage from our meeting. Let this be a simple token of our friendship, neh?"

He looked to each of them; to Lever, Kustow and finally to Stevens, seeing how each had been won by the simplicity of his manner.

"Good. Then wait here. I have it in the other room."

He left them, returning a moment later with a bulky, rectangular parcel wrapped in red silk.

"Here," he said, handing it to Lever. "You are to open it later – on the flight to Ebert's if you must, but later. And whatever you finally decide to do with it, bear in mind that great sacrifices have been made to bring this to you. Let no one see it whom you do not trust like a brother."

Lever stared at the parcel a moment, his eyes burning with curiosity, then looked up again, smiling.

"I've no idea what this is, but I'll do as you say. And thank you, Howard. Thank you for everything. You must be our guest when you come to America."

DeVore smiled. "That's kind of you, Michael. Very kind indeed."

★ ★ ★

"Well, Stefan, what do you think?"

Lehmann stood there a moment longer at the one-way mirror, then turned back, looking at DeVore. He had witnessed everything.

"The contest . . . You lost it deliberately, didn't you?"

DeVore smiled, pleased that Lehmann had seen it.

"I could have beaten him. Not at first, maybe, but from the third game on. There's a pattern to his game. So with these Americans. There's a pattern to their thinking and I feel as if I'm beginning to discern it. Which is why I have to go there myself. Europe is dead as far as we're concerned. We've milked it dry. If we want to complete the fortresses, we've got to get funds from the Americans. We've got to persuade them to invest in us – to make them see us as the means by which they can topple the Seven."

"And Curval? You promised him you'd kill Old Man Ebert. Is that wise?"

DeVore laughed. "If the gods will it that the old man dies in the next six months, he will die, and I will claim the credit. But I shall do nothing to aid them. I have no great love for Klaus Ebert – I think he's a pompous old windbag, to tell the truth – but he is Hans's father. Kill him and we risk all. No, we will leave such things to fate. And if Curval objects . . ." He laughed. "Well, we can deal with that as and when, neh? As and when."

CHAPTER·8

MIRRORS

It was night. Li Yuan stood there on the bridge, staring down into the lake, watching the full moon dance upon the blackness. Tongjiang was quiet now, the guests departed. Guards stood off at a distance, perfectly still, like statues in the silvered darkness.

It had been a long and busy day. He had been up at four, supervising the final arrangements for his father's funeral, greeting the mourners as they arrived. The ceremony had taken up the best part of the morning, followed by an informal meeting of the Seven. Interviews with ministers and various high officials had eaten up the rest of the afternoon as he began the task of tying up the loose strands of his father's business and making preparations for his own coronation ceremony three days hence. And other things. So many other things.

He felt exhausted, yet there was still more to do before he retired.

He turned, looking back at the palace, thinking how vast and desolate it seemed without his father's presence. There was only him now – only Li Yuan, second son of Li Shai Tung. The last of his line. The last of the house of Li.

A faint wind stirred the reeds at the lake's edge. He looked up, that same feeling of exposure – that cold, almost physical sense of isolation – washing over him again. Where were the brothers, the cousins he should have had? Dead, or never born. And now there was only him.

A thin wisp of cloud lay like a veil across the moon's bright face. In the distance a solitary goose crossed the sky, the steady beat of its wings carrying to where he stood.

He shivered. Today he had pretended to be strong; had made his face thick, like a wall against his inner feelings. And so it had to be, from this time on, for he was T'ang now, his life no longer his own. All day he had been surrounded by people – countless people, bowing low before him and doing as he bid – and yet he had never felt so lonely.

No, never in his life had he felt so desolate, so empty.

He gritted his teeth, fighting back what he felt. Be strong, he told himself: harden yourself against what is inside you. He took a deep breath, looking out across the lake. His father had been right. Love was not enough. Without trust – without those other qualities that made of love a solid and substantial thing – love was a cancer, eating away at a man, leaving him weak.

And he could not be weak, for he was T'ang now, Seven. He must put all human weakness behind him. Must mould himself into a harder form.

He turned away, making his way quickly down the path towards the palace.

At the door to his father's rooms he stopped, loath to go inside. He looked down at the ring that rested, heavy and unfamiliar, on the middle finger of his right hand, and realised that nothing could have prepared him for this. His father's death and the ritual of burial had been momentous occasions, yet neither was quite as real as this simpler, private moment.

How often had he come in from the garden and found his father sat there at his desk, his secretaries and ministers in attendance? How often had the old man looked up and seen him, there where he now stood, and, with a faint, stern smile, beckoned him inside?

And now there was no one to grant him such permission. No one but himself.

Why, then, was it so difficult to take that first small step into the room? Why did he feel an almost naked fear at the thought of sitting at the desk – of looking back at where he was now standing?

Perhaps because he knew the doorway would be empty.

Angry with himself, he took a step into the room, his heart hammering in his chest as if he were a thief. He laughed uncomfortably then looked about him, seeing it all anew.

It was a long, low-ceilinged room, furnished in the traditional manner, his father's desk, its huge scrolled legs shaped like dragons, raised up on a massive plinth at the far end of the chamber, a low, gold-painted balustrade surrounding it, like a room within a room, the great symbol of the *Ywe Lung* set into the wall behind. Unlike his own, it was a distinctly masculine room, no hanging bowls, no rounded pots filled with exotic plants breaking up its rich Yang heaviness; indeed, there was not a single trace of greenery, only vases and screens and ancient wall hangings made of silk and golden thread.

He moved further in, stopping beside a huge bronze cauldron. It was empty now, but he recalled when it had once contained a thousand tiny objects carved from jade; remembered a day when he had played there on his father's floor, the brightly coloured pieces – exquisite miniatures in blue and red and green – scattered all about him. He had been four then, five at most, but still he could see them vividly; could feel the cool, smooth touch of them between his fingers.

He turned. On the wall to his right was a mirror; an ancient, metallic mirror of the T'ang dynasty, its surface filled with figures and lettering, arrayed in a series of concentric circles emanating outwards from the central button. Li Yuan moved closer, studying it. The button – a simple unadorned circle – represented the indivisibility of all created things. Surrounding it were the animals of the Four Quadrants: the Tiger, symbol of the west and of magisterial dignity, courage and martial prowess; the Phoenix, symbol of the south and of beauty, peace and prosperity; the Dragon, symbol of the east, of fertility and male

vigour; and the Tortoise, symbol of the north, of longevity, strength and endurance. Beyond these four were
the Eight Trigrams and surrounding those the Twelve Ter-
restrial Branches of the zodiac – rat, ox and tiger, hare,
dragon and serpent, horse, goat and monkey, cock, dog
and boar. A band of twenty-four pictograms separated that
from the next circle of animals – twenty-eight in all –
representing the constellations.

He looked past the figures a moment, seeing his face
reflected back at him through the symbols and archetypes
of the Han universe. Such a mirror was *hu hsin ching* and
was said to have magic powers, protecting its owner from
evil. It was also said that one might see the secrets of
futurity in such a mirror. But he had little faith in what
men said. Why, he could barely see his own face, let alone
the face of the future.

He turned his head away, suddenly bitter. Mirrors: they
were said to symbolise conjugal happiness, but his own
was broken now, the pieces scattered.

He went across to the desk. Nan Ho had been in earlier
to prepare it for him. His father's things had been cleared
away and his own set in their place: his ink block and
brushes, his sandbox and the tiny statue of Kuan Ti, the
God of War, which his brother, Han Ch'in, had given him
on his eighth birthday. Beside those were a small pile of
folders and one large, heavy-bound book, its thick spine
made of red silk decorated with a cloud-pattern of gold
leaf.

Mounting the three small steps he stood there, his hands
resting on the low balustrade, his head almost brushing the
ceiling, looking across at the big, tall-backed chair. The
great wheel of seven dragons – the *Ywe Lung* or Moon
Dragon – had been burned into the back of the chair, black
against the ochre of the leather, mirroring the much larger
symbol on the wall behind. This chair had been his father's
and his father's father's before that, back to his great-
great-great-grandfather in the time of Tsao Ch'un.

And now it was his.

Undoing the tiny catch, he pushed back the gate and entered this tiny room-within-a-room, conscious of how strange even that simple action felt. He looked about him again, then lowered himself into the chair. Sitting there, looking out into the ancient room, he could feel his ancestors gathered close: there in the simple continuity of place, but there also in each small movement that he made. They lived, within him. He was their seed. He understood that now. Had known it even as they had placed the lid upon his father's casket.

He reached across and drew the first of the folders from the pile. Inside was a single sheet, from Klaus Ebert at GenSyn: a document relinquishing thirteen patents granted in respect of special food production techniques. Before his father's death, Ebert had offered to release the patents to his competitors to help increase food production in City Europe. They were worth an estimated two hundred and fifty million *yuan* on the open market, but Ebert had given them freely, as a gift to his T'ang.

Li Yuan drew the file closer, then reached across and took his brush, signing his name at the bottom of the document.

He set the file aside and took another from the pile. It was the summary of the post-mortem report he had commissioned on his father. He read it through, then signed it and set it atop the other. Nothing. They had found nothing. According to the doctors, his father had died of old age. Old age and a broken heart.

Nonsense, he thought. Utter nonsense.

He huffed out his impatience, then reached across for the third file, opening it almost distractedly. Then, seeing what it was, he sat back, his mouth gone dry, his heart beating furiously. It was the result of the genotyping test he had had done on Fei Yen and her child.

He closed his eyes, in pain, his breathing suddenly erratic. So now he would know. Know for good and certain who the father was. Know to whom he owed the pain and bitterness of the last few months.

He leaned forward again. It was no good delaying. No good putting off what was inevitable. He drew the file closer, forcing himself to read it; each word seeming to cut and wound him. And then it was done.

He pushed the file away and sat back. So . . .

For a moment he was still, silent, considering his options, then reached across, touching the summons bell.

Almost at once the door to his right swung back. Nan Ho, his Master of the Inner Chambers, stood there, his head bowed low.

"*Chieh Hsia*?"

"Bring *ch'a*, Master Nan. I need to talk."

Nan Ho bobbed his head. "Should I send for your Chancellor, *Chieh Hsia*?"

"No, Master Nan, it is you I wish to speak with."

"As you wish, *Chieh Hsia*."

When he had gone, Li Yuan leaned across and drew the large, heavy-bound book towards him. A stylised dragon and phoenix – their figures drawn in gold – were inset into the bright red silk of the cover. Inside, on the opening page, was a handwritten quotation from the *Li Chi*, the ancient Book of Rites, the passage in the original Mandarin.

> The point of marriage is to create a union between two persons of different families, the object of which is to serve, first, the ancestors in the temple, and, second, the generation to come.

He shivered. So it was. So it had always been amongst his kind. Yet he had thought it possible to marry for love. In so doing he had betrayed his kind. Had tried to be what he was not. For he was Han. Han to the very core of him. He recognised that now.

But it was not too late. He could begin again. Become what he had failed to be. A good Han, leaving all ghosts of other selves behind.

He flicked through the pages desultorily, barely seeing

the faces that looked up at him from the pages. Here were a hundred of the most eligible young women, selected from the Twenty-Nine, the Minor Families. Each one was somewhat different from the rest, had some particular quality to recommend her, yet it was all much the same to him. One thing alone was important now – to marry and have sons. To make the family strong again, and fill the emptiness surrounding him.

For anything was better than to feel like this. Anything.

He closed the book and pushed it away, then sat back in the chair, closing his eyes. He had barely done so when there was a tapping on the door.

"*Chieh Hsia?*"

"Come!" he said, sitting forward again, the tiredness like salt in his blood, weighing him down.

Nan Ho entered first, his head bowed, the tray held out before him. Behind him came the *She t'ou* – the "tongue", or taster. Li Yuan watched almost listlessly as Nan Ho set the *ch'a* things down on a low table, then poured, offering the first bowl to the *She t'ou*.

The man sipped, then offered the bowl back, bowing gracefully, a small smile of satisfaction crossing his lips. He waited a minute, then turned to Li Yuan and bowed low, kneeling, touching his head against the floor before he backed away.

Nan Ho followed him to the door, closing it after him, then turned, facing Li Yuan.

"Shall I bring your *ch'a* up to you, *Chieh Hsia?*"

Li Yuan smiled. "No, Nan Ho. I will join you down there." He stood, yawning, stretching the tiredness from his bones, then leaned forward, picking up the heavy-bound volume.

"Here," he said, handing it to Nan Ho, ignoring the offered bowl.

Nan Ho set the bowl down hastily, then took the book from his T'ang. "You have decided, then, *Chieh Hsia?*"

Li Yuan stared at Nan Ho a moment, wondering how

much he knew – whether he had dared look at the genotyping – then, dismissing the thought, he smiled.

"No, Master Nan. I have not decided. But you will."

Nan Ho looked back at him, horrified. "*Chieh Hsia?*"

"You heard me, Master Nan. I want you to choose for
me. Three wives, I need. Good, strong, reliable women.
The kind that bear sons. Lots of sons. Enough to fill the
rooms of this huge, empty palace."

Nan Ho bowed low, his face a picture of misery. "But
Chieh Hsia. . . It is not my place to do such a thing. Such
responsibility . . ." He made to shake his head, then fell
to his knees, his head pressed to the floor. "I beg you,
Chieh Hsia. I am unworthy for such a task."

Li Yuan laughed. "Nonsense, Master Nan. If anyone,
you are the very best of men to undertake such a task for
me. Did you not bring Pearl Heart and Sweet Rose to my
bed? Was your judgment so flawed then? No! So, please,
Master Nan, do this for me, I beg you."

Nan Ho looked up, wide-eyed. "*Chieh Hsia*. . . you
must not say such things! You are T'ang now."

"Then do this thing for me, Master Nan," he said
tiredly. "For I would be married the day after my coronation."

Nan Ho stared at him a moment longer, then bowed his
head low again, resigned to his fate. "As my lord wishes."

"Good. Now let us drink our *ch'a* and talk of other
things. Was I mistaken or did I hear that there was a message from Hal Shepherd?"

Nan Ho set the book down beside the table, then picked
up Li Yuan's bowl, turning back and offering it to him,
his head bowed.

"Not Hal, *Chieh Hsia*, but his son. Chung Hu-yan dealt
with the matter."

"I see. And did the Chancellor happen to say what the
message was?"

Nan Ho hesitated. "It was . . . a picture, *Chieh Hsia*."

"A picture? You mean, there were no words? No actual
message?"

"No, *Chieh Hsia*."

"And this picture – what was in it?"

"Should I bring it, *Chieh Hsia*?"

"No. But describe it, if you can."

Nan Ho frowned. "It was odd, *Chieh Hsia*. Very odd indeed. It was of a tree – or rather, of twinned apple trees. The two were closely intertwined, their trunks twisted about each other, yet one of the trees was dead, its leaves shed, its branches broken and rotting. Chung Hu-yan set it aside for you to look at after your coronation." He averted his eyes. "He felt it was not something you would wish to see before then."

Like the gift of stones his father had tried to hide from him – the white *wei chi* stones DeVore had sent to him on the day he had been promised to Fei Yen.

Li Yuan sighed. For five generations the Shepherds had acted as advisers to his family. Descended from the original architect of the City, they lived beyond its walls, outside its laws. Only they, in all Chung Kuo, stood equal to the Seven. "Chung Hu-yan acted as he felt he ought, but in future any message – worded or otherwise – that comes from the Shepherds must be passed directly to me, at once, Master Nan. This picture – you understand what it means?"

"No, *Chieh Hsia*."

"No. And nor, it seems, does Chancellor Chung. It means that Hal Shepherd is dying. The tree was a gift from my father to him. I must go and pay my respects at once."

"But *Chieh Hsia* . . ."

Li Yuan shook his head. "I know, Master Nan. I have seen my schedule for tomorrow. But the meetings will have to be cancelled. This cannot wait. He was my father's friend. It would not do to ignore such a summons, however strangely couched."

"A summons, *Chieh Hsia*?"

"Yes, Master Nan. A summons."

He turned away, sipping at his *ch'a*. He did not look forward to seeing Hal Shepherd in such a state, yet it would be good to see his son again; to sit with him and talk.

A faint, uncertain smile came to his lips. Yes, it would be good to speak with him, for in truth he needed a mirror just now: someone to reflect him back clearly to himself. And who better than Ben Shepherd? Who better in all Chung Kuo?

★ ★ ★

The man staggered past him, then leaned against the wall unsteadily, his head lowered, as if drunk. For a moment he seemed to lapse out of consciousness, his whole body hanging loosely against his outstretched arm, then he lifted his head, stretching himself strangely, as if shaking something off. It was only then that Axel realised what he was doing. He was pissing.

Axel looked away, then turned back, hearing the commotion behind him. Two burly-looking guards – Han, wearing the dark green of GenSyn, not the powder blue of Security – came running across, batons drawn, making for the man.

They stood either side of the man as he turned, confronting him.

"What the fuck you think you do?" one of them said, prodding him brutally, making him stagger back against the wall.

He was a big man, or had been, but his clothes hung loosely on him now. They were good clothes, too, but, like those of most of the people gathered there, they were grime-ridden and filthy. His face, too, bore evidence of maltreatment. His skin was blotched, his left eye almost closed, a dark, yellow-green bruise covering the whole of his left cheek. He stank, but again that was not uncommon, for most were beggars here.

He looked back at the guards blearily, then lifted his head in a remembered but long-redundant gesture of pride.

"I'm here to see the General," he said uncertainly, his pride leaking from him slowly until his head hung once again. "You know . . ." he muttered, glancing up apologetically, the muscle in his cheek ticking now. "The hand-out . . . I came for that. It was on the newscast. I heard it. Come to this place, it said, so I came."

The guard who had spoken grunted his disgust. "You shit bucket," he said quietly. "You fucking shit bucket. What you think you up to, pissing on the T'ang's walls?" Then, without warning, he hit out with his baton, catching the beggar on the side of the head.

The man went down, groaning loudly. As he did, the two guards waded in, standing over him, striking him time and again on the head and body until he lay still.

"Fucking shit bucket!" the first guard said as he stepped back. He turned, glaring at the crowd that had formed around him. "What you look at? Fuck off! Go on! Fuck off! Before you get same!" He raised his baton threateningly, but the message had got through already. They had begun to back off as soon as he had turned.

Axel stood there a moment longer, tensed, trembling with anger, then turned away. There was nothing he could do. Nothing, at least, which would not land him in trouble. Two he could have handled, but there were more than fifty of the bastards spread out throughout the hall, jostling whoever got in their way and generally making themselves as unpleasant as they could. He knew the type. They thought themselves big men – great fighters, trained to take on anything – but most of them had failed basic training for Security or had been recruited from the Plantations, where standards were much lower. In many cases their behaviour was simply a form of compensation for the failure they felt at having to wear the dark green of a private security force and not the imperial blue.

He backed away, then turned, making his way through the crowd towards the end of the hall, wondering how much longer they would be forced to wait. They had started queuing three hours back, the corridors leading to the main transit packed long before Axel had arrived. For a brief while he had thought of turning back – even the smell of the mob was enough to make a man feel sick –

but had stayed, determined to be among the two thousand "fortunates" who would be let into the grounds of the Ebert Mansion for the celebrations.

He had dressed specially. Had gone out and bought the roughest, dirtiest clothes he could lay his hands on. Had put on a rough workman's hat – a hard shell of dark plastic, like an inverted ricebowl – and dirtied his face. Now he looked little different from the rest. A beggar. A shit-bucket bum from the lowest of the levels.

He looked about him, his eyes travelling from face to face, seeing the anger there and the despair, the futility and the incipient madness. There was a shiftiness to their eyes, a pastiness to their complexions, that spoke of long years of deprivation. And they were thin, every last one of them; some of them so painfully undernourished that he found it difficult to believe that they were still alive, still moving their wasted, fragile limbs. He stared at them, fascinated, his revulsion matched by a strong instinctive pity for them; for many, he knew, there had been no choice. They had fallen long before they were born, and nothing in this world could ever redeem them. In that he differed. He too had fallen, but for him there had been a second chance.

Lowering his head, he glanced at the timer at his wrist, keeping it hidden beneath the greasy cuff of his jacket. It was getting on towards midnight. They would have to open the gates soon, surely?

Almost at once he felt a movement in the crowd, a sudden surge forward, and knew the gates had been opened. He felt himself drawn forward, caught up in the crush.

Hei were manning the barriers, the big GenSyn half-men herding the crowd through the narrow gates. Above the crowd, on a platform to one side, a small group of Han officials looked on, counting the people as they went through.

Past the gates, crush barriers forced the crowd into semi-orderly lines, at the head of which more officials –

many of them masked against the stench and the possibility of disease – processed the hopeful.

As movement slowed and the crush grew more intense, he heard a great shouting from way back and knew the gates had been closed, the quota filled. But he was inside.

The pressure on him from all sides was awful, the stink of unwashed bodies almost unbearable, but he fought back his nausea, reminding himself why he was there. To bear witness. To see for himself the moment when Hans Ebert was declared General-elect.

As he passed through the second barrier, an official drew him aside and tagged his jacket with an electronic trace, then thrust a slice of cake and a bulb of drink into his hands. He shuffled on, looking about him, seeing how the others crammed their cake down feverishly before emptying the bulb in a few desperate swallows. He tried a mouthful of the cake, then spat it out. It was hard, dry and completely without flavour. The drink was little better. Disgusted, he threw them down, and was immediately pushed back against the wall as those nearby fought for what he had discarded.

The big transit lift was just ahead of them now. Again *Hei* herded them into the space, cramming them in tightly, until Axel felt his breath being forced from him. Like the others surrounding him, he fought silently, desperately, for a little space – pushing out with his elbows, his strength an asset here.

The doors closed, the huge elevator – used normally for goods, not people – began its slow climb up the levels. As it did, a voice sounded overhead, telling them that they must cheer when the masters appeared on the balcony; that they would each receive a five *yuan* coin if they cheered loud enough.

"The cameras will be watching everyone," the voice continued. "Only those who cheer loudly will get a coin."

The journey up-level seemed to last an eternity. Two hundred and fifty levels they climbed, up to the very top of the City.

Coming out from the transit was like stepping outside into the open. Overhead was a great, blue-black sky, filled with moonlit cloud and stars, the illusion so perfect that for a moment Axel caught his breath. To the right, across a vast, landscaped park, was the Ebert Mansion, its imposing façade lit up brilliantly, the great balcony festooned with banners. A barrier of *Hei* prevented them from going that way – the brute, almost porcine faces of the guards lit grotesquely from beneath. All around him people had slowed, astonished by the sight, their eyes wide, their mouths fallen open, but masked servants hurried them on, ushering them away to the left, into an area that had been fenced off with high transparent barriers of ice.

They stumbled on, only a low murmur coming from them now, most of them awed into silence by the sight of such luxury, intimidated by the sense of openness, by the big sky overhead. But for Axel, shuffling along slowly in their midst, it reminded him of something else – of that day when he and Major DeVore had called upon Representative Lehmann at his First Level estate. And he knew, almost without thinking it, that there was a connection between the two. As if such luxury bred corruption.

Stewards herded them down a broad gravel path and out into a large space in front of the mansion. Here another wall barred their way, the translucent surface of it coated with a non-reflective substance that to the watching cameras would make it seem as if there were no wall – no barrier – between the Eberts and the cheering crowd.

As the space filled up, he noticed the stewards going out into the crowd, handing out flags and streamers – the symbols of GenSyn and the Seven distributed equally – before positioning themselves at various strategic points. Turning, he sought out one of the stewards and took a banner from him, aiming to conceal himself behind it when the cheering began. It was unlikely that Hans Ebert would study the film of his triumph that closely, but it was best to take no chances.

He glanced at his timer. It was almost twelve. In a few moments . . .

The stewards began the cheering, turning to encourage the others standing about them. "Five *yuan!*" they shouted. "Only those who shout will get a coin!"

As the Eberts stepped out on to the balcony, the cheering rose to a crescendo. The cameras panned about the crowd, then focused on the scene on the balcony again. Klaus Ebert stood there in the foreground, a broad beam of light settling on him, making his hair shine silver-white, his perfect teeth sparkle.

"Friends!" he began, his voice amplified to carry over the cheering. "A notice has been posted throughout our great City. It reads as follows." He turned and took a scroll from his secretary, then turned back, clearing his throat. Below the noise subsided as the stewards moved among the crowd, damping down the excitement they had artificially created.

Ebert opened out the scroll, then began.

"I, Li Yuan, T'ang designate of *Ch'eng Ou Chou*, City Europe, declare the appointment of Hans Joachim Ebert, currently Major in my Security services, as Supreme General of my forces, this appointment to be effective from midday on the fifteenth day of September in the year two thousand two hundred and seven."

He stepped back, beaming with paternal pride.

There was a moment's silence and then a ragged cheer went up, growing stronger as the stewards whipped the crowd into a fury of enthusiasm.

Up on the balcony, Hans Ebert stepped forward, his powder blue uniform immaculate, his blond hair perfectly groomed. He grinned and waved a hand as if to thank them for their welcome, then stepped back, bowing, all humility.

Axel, watching from below, felt a wave of pure hatred pass through him. If they knew – if they only knew all he had done. The cheating and lying and butchery; the foulness beneath the mask of perfection. But they knew nothing. He looked about him, seeing how caught up in it they suddenly were. They had come for the chance of food and drink and for the money, but now they were here their enthusiasm was genuine. Up there they saw a king – a man so high above them that to be at such proximity was a blessing. Axel saw the stewards look among themselves and wink, laughing, sharing the joke, and felt more sick than he had ever felt among the unwashed mass. They, at least, did not pretend that they were clean. One could smell what they were. But Ebert?

Axel looked past the fluttering banner; saw how Ebert turned to talk to those behind him, so at ease in his arrogance, and swore again to bring him low. To pile the foul truth high, burying his flawless reputation.

He shuddered, frightened by the sheer intensity of what he felt; knowing that had he a gun and the opportunity, he would have tried to kill the man, right there and then. Up on the balcony, the Eberts turned away, making their way back inside. As the doors closed behind them the lights went down, leaving the space before the mansion in darkness.

The cheering died. Axel threw the banner down. All about him the crowd was dispersing, making for the barriers. He turned, following them, then stopped, looking back. Was it that? Was it excess of luxury that corrupted a man? Or were some men simply born evil and others good?

He looked ahead, looked past the barriers to where small knots of beggars had gathered. Already they were squabbling, fighting each other over the tiny pittance they had been given. As he came closer he saw one man go down and several others fall on him, punching and kicking him, robbing him of the little he had. Nearby the guards looked on, laughing among themselves.

Laughing . . . He wiped his mouth, sickened by all he'd seen, then pushed past the barrier, ignoring the offered coin.

* * *

Inside the mansion the celebrations were about to begin.
At the top of the great stairway, Klaus Ebert put his arm
about his son's shoulders and looked out across the gathering that filled the great hall below.

"My good friends!" he said, then laughed. "What can I
say? I am so full of pride! My son . . ."

He drew Hans closer and kissed his cheek, then looked
about him again, beaming and laughing, as if he were
drunk.

"Come, Father," Hans said in a whisper, embarrassed
by his father's sudden effusiveness. "Let's get it over with.
I'm faint with hunger."

Klaus looked back at him, smiling broadly, then
laughed, squeezing his shoulder again. "Whatever you say,
Hans." He turned back, putting one arm out expansively.
"Friends! Let us not stand on formalities tonight. Eat,
drink, be merry!"

They made their way down the stairs, father and son,
joining the crowd gathered at the foot. Tolonen was
amongst those there, lean and elegant in his old age, his
steel-grey hair slicked back, the dress uniform of General
worn proudly for the last time.

"Why, Knut," Klaus Ebert began, taking a glass from a
servant, "I see you are wearing Hans's uniform!"

Tolonen laughed. "It is but briefly, Klaus. I am just
taking the creases out of it for him!"

There was a roar of laughter at that. Hans smiled and
bowed, then looked about him. "Is Jelka not here?"

Tolonen shook his head. "I'm afraid not, Hans. She took
an injury in her practice session this morning. Nothing
serious – only a sprain – but the doctor felt she would be
better off resting. She was most disappointed, I can tell
you. Why, she'd spent two whole days looking for a new
dress to wear tonight!"

Hans lowered his head respectfully. "I am sorry to hear
it, Father-in-law. I had hoped to dance with her tonight.
But perhaps you would both come here for dinner – soon,
when things have settled."

Tolonen beamed, delighted by the suggestion. "That would be excellent, Hans. And it would make up for her disappointment, I am sure."

Hans bowed and moved on, circulating, chatting with all his father's friends, making his way slowly towards a small group on the far side of the hall, until, finally, he came to them.

"Michael!" he said, embracing his old friend.

"Hans!" Lever held Ebert to him a moment, then stood back. They had been classmates at Oxford in their teens, before Lever had gone on to Business College and Ebert to the Academy. But they had stayed in touch all this time.

Ebert looked past his old friend, smiling a greeting to the others.

"How was your journey?"

"As well as could be expected!" Lever laughed, then leaned closer. "When in the gods' names are they going to improve those things, Hans? If you've any influence with Li Yuan, make him pass an amendment to the Edict to enable them to build something more comfortable than those transatlantic rockets."

Ebert laughed, then leaned closer. "And my friend? Did you enjoy his company?"

Lever glanced at his companions, then laughed. "I can speak for us all in saying that it was a most interesting experience. I would never have guessed . . ."

Ebert smiled. "No. And let's keep it that way, neh?" He turned, looking about him, then took Lever's arm. "And his gift?"

Lever's eyes widened. "You knew about that?"

"Of course. But come. Let's go outside. It's cool in the garden. We can talk as we go. Of Chung Kuo and *Ta Ts'in* and dreams of empire."

Lever gave a soft laugh then bowed his head. "Lead on . . ."

* * *

It was just after four when the last of the guests left the Ebert Mansion. Hans, watching from the balcony, stifled a yawn, then turned and went back inside. He had not been drinking and yet he felt quite drunk – buoyed up on a vast and heady upsurge of well-being. Things had never been better. That very evening his father had given over a further sixteen companies to him, making it almost a quarter of the giant GenSyn empire that he now controlled. Life, at last, was beginning to open to him. Earlier he had taken Tolonen aside to suggest that his marriage to Jelka be brought forward, and while, at first, the old man had seemed a little put out, when Hans had spoken of the sense of stability it would bring him, Tolonen had grown quite keen – almost as if the idea had been his own.

Ebert went down the stairs and out into the empty hall, standing there a moment, smiling, recollecting Tolonen's response.

"Let me speak to her," Tolonen had said, as he was leaving. "After the coronation, when things have settled a little. But I promise you, Hans, I'll do my best to persuade her. After all, it's in no one's interest to delay, is it?"

No, he thought. Especially not now. At least, not now that they had come to an arrangement with the Americans.

He went out and said goodnight to his father and mother, then came back, running across the hall and out through the back doors into the garden. The night seemed fresh and warm and for the briefest moment he imagined himself outside, beneath a real moon, under a real sky. Well, maybe that would happen soon. In a year, two years perhaps. When he was King of Europe.

On the ornamental bridge he slowed, looking about him. He felt a great restlessness in his blood; an urge to do something. He thought of the *mui tsai*, but for once his restlessness was pure, uncontaminated by a sense of sexual urgency. No, it was as if he needed to go somewhere, do something. All of this waiting – for his inheritance, his command, his wife – seemed suddenly a barrier to simple *being*. Tonight he wanted to *be*, to *do*. To break heads or ride a horse at breakneck speed.

He kicked out, sending gravel into the water below, watching the ripples spread. Then he moved on, jumping down the steps to the path and vaulting up on to the balcony above. He turned, looking back. A servant had stopped, watching him. Seeing Ebert turn, he moved on hurriedly, his head bowed, the huge bowl he held making slopping sounds in the silence.

Ebert laughed. There were no heads to break, no horses here to ride. So maybe he would fuck the *mui tsai* anyway. Maybe that would still his pulse and purge the restlessness from his system. He turned, making his way along to his suite of rooms. Inside he began to undress, unbuttoning his tunic. As he did so, he went over to the comset and touched in the code.

He turned away, throwing his tunic down on a chair, then went across and tapped on the inner door. At once a servant popped his head around the door.

"Bring the *mui tsai* to my room, then go. I'll not need you any more tonight, Lo Wen."

The servant bowed and left. Ebert turned back, looking at the screen. There were a great number of messages for once, mainly from friends, congratulating him on his appointment. But amongst them was one he had been expecting. DeVore's.

He read it through then laughed. So the meeting with the Americans had gone well. Good. The introduction was yet another thing DeVore owed him for. What's more, DeVore wanted him to do something else.

He smiled, then sat down, pulling off his boots. Slowly, by small degrees, DeVore was placing himself in his debt. More and more he had come to rely on him – for little things at first, but now for ever larger schemes. And that was good. For he would keep account of all.

There was a faint tapping at the inner door.

He turned in the chair, looking across. "Come in," he said softly.

The door slid back. For a moment she stood there, naked, looking in at him, the light behind her. She was so beautiful, so wonderfully made that his penis grew hard simply looking at her. Then she came across, fussing about him, helping him with the last few items of his clothing.

Finished, she looked up at him from where she knelt on the floor in front of him. "Was your evening good, master?"

He pulled her up on to his lap, then began to stroke her neck and shoulder, looking up into her dark and liquid eyes, his blood inflamed now by the warmth of her flesh against his own. "Never better, Sweet Flute. Never in my whole life better."

★   ★   ★

DeVore slipped the vial back into its carrying case, sealed the lid, and handed it to Lehmann.

"Don't drop it, Stefan, whatever else you do. And make sure that Hans knows what to do with it. He knows it's coming, but he doesn't properly know what it is. He'll be curious, so it's best if you tell him something, if only to damp down his curiosity."

The albino slipped the cigar-shaped case into his inner pocket, then fastened his tunic tight. "So what should I say?"

DeVore laughed. "Tell him the truth for once. Tell him it kills Han. He'll like that."

Lehmann nodded, then bowed and turned away.

He watched Lehmann go, then went across and took his furs from the cupboard in the corner. It was too late now to sleep. He would go hunting instead. Yes, it would be good to greet the dawn on the open mountain-side.

DeVore smiled, studying himself in the mirror as he pulled on his furs, then, taking his crossbow from the rack on the wall, went out, making his way towards the old tunnels; taking the one that came out on the far side of the mountain beside the ruins of the ancient castle.

As he walked along he wondered, not for the first time, what Lever had made of the gift he'd given him.

The Aristotle File. A copy of Berdichev's original, in his own handwriting. The true history of Chung Kuo. Not the altered and sanitised version the Han peddled in their schools, but the truth, from the birth of Western thought in Aristotle's Yes/No logic, to the splendours of space travel, mass communications and artificial intelligence systems. A history of the West systematically erased by the Han. Yes, and that was another kind of virus. One, in its own way, every bit as deadly for the Han.

DeVore laughed, his laughter echoing down the tunnel. All in all it had been a good day. And it was going to get better. Much better.

★ ★ ★

It was exactly ten minutes past five when the scouts moved into place on the mountainside, dropping the tiny gas pellets into the base's ventilation outlets. At the entrance to the hangar, four masked men sprayed ice-eating acids on to the snow-covered surface of the doors. Two minutes later, Karr, wearing a mask and carrying a lightweight air canister, kicked his way inside.

He crossed the hangar at a quick march, then ran down the corridor linking it to the inner fortress, his automatic searching this way and that, looking for any sign of resistance, but the colourless, odourless gas had done its work. Guards lay slumped in several places. They would have had no chance to issue any kind of warning.

He glanced down at his timer, then turned, looking back. Already the first squad were busy, binding and gagging the unconscious defenders before the effects of the gas wore off. Behind them a second squad was coming through, their masked faces looking from side to side, double-checking as they came along.

He turned back, pushing on, hyper-alert now, knowing

that it would not be long before he lost the advantage of surprise.

There were four lifts, spaced out along a single broad corridor. He stared at them a moment then shook his head. A place like this, dug deep into the mountainside, would be hard to defend unless one devised a system of independent levels, and of bottlenecks linking them – bottlenecks which could be defended like the barbican in an ancient castle – the killing ground. So here. These lifts – seemingly so innocuous – were their barbican. But unlike in a castle there would be another way into the next level of the fortress. There had to be, because if the power ever failed, they had to have some way of ensuring that they still got air down in the lower tunnels.

There would be shafts. Ventilation shafts. As above.

Karr turned and beckoned the squad leader over.

"Locate the down shafts. Then I want one man sent down each of them straight away. They're to secure the corridors beneath the shafts while the rest of the men come through. Understand?"

The young lieutenant bowed, then hurried away, sending his men off to do as Karr had ordered. He was back a moment later.

"They're sealed, Major Karr."

"Well? Break the seals!"

"But they're alarmed. Maybe even boobytrapped."

Karr grunted, impatient now. "Show me!"

The shaft was in a tiny corridor leading off what seemed to be some kind of storeroom. Karr studied it a moment, noting its strange construction, then, knowing he had no alternative, raised his fist and brought it down hard. The seal cracked but didn't break. He struck it again, harder this time, and it gave, splintering into the space below.

Somewhere below he could hear a siren sounding, security doors slamming into place.

"Let's get moving. They know we're here now. The sooner we hit them the better, neh?"

He went first, bracing himself against the walls of the

narrow tunnel as he went down, his shoulders almost too wide for the confined space. Others followed, almost on top of him.

Some five *ch'i* above the bottom seal he stopped and brought his gun round, aiming it down between his legs. He opened fire. The seal shattered with a great upward hiss of air, tiny splinters thrown up at him.

He narrowed his eyes, then understood. The separate levels were kept at different pressures, which meant there were air-locks. But why? What were they doing here?

He scrambled down, then dropped. As he hit the floor he twisted about. A body lay to one side of the shaft's exit point, otherwise the corridor was empty.

It was a straight stretch of corridor, sixty *ch'i* long at most, ending in a T-junction at each end. There were no doors, no windows and, as far as he could make out, no cameras.

Left or right? If the groundplan followed that of the level above, the lifts would be somewhere off to the left, but he didn't think it would be that simple. Not if DeVore had designed this place.

Men were jumping down behind him, forming up either side, kneeling, their weapons raised to their shoulders, covering both ends of the corridor.

Last down was the squad leader. Karr quickly despatched him off to the left with six men, while he went right with the rest.

He had not gone more than a dozen paces when there was a loud clunk and a huge metal firedoor began to come down.

From the yells behind him, he knew at once that the same was happening at the other end of the corridor. No cameras, eh? How could he have been so naïve!

He ran, hurling himself at the diminishing gap, half sliding, half rolling beneath the door just before it slammed into the floor. As he thudded into the end wall he felt his gun go clattering away from him, but there was no time to think of that. As he came up from the floor the first of them was on him, slashing down with a knife the length of his forearm.

Karr blocked the blow and counter-punched, feeling the man's jaw shatter. Behind him, only a few paces off, a second guard was raising his automatic. Karr ducked, using the injured guard as a shield, thrusting his head into the man's chest as he began to fall, pushing him upward and back, into the second man.

Too late, the guard opened fire, the shells ricocheting harmlessly off the end wall as he stumbled backwards.

Karr kicked him in the stomach, then stood over him, chopping down savagely, finishing him off. He stepped back, looking about him. His gun was over to the right. He picked it up and ran on, hearing voices approaching up ahead.

He grinned fiercely. The last thing they would expect was a single man coming at them. Even so, it might be best to give himself some additional advantage.

He looked up. As he'd thought, they hadn't bothered to set the pipework and cabling into the rock, but had simply secured it to the ceiling of the tunnel with brackets. The brackets looked firm enough – big metallic things – but were they strong enough to bear his weight?

There was only one way to find out. He tucked his gun into his tunic and reached up, pulling himself up slowly. Bringing his legs up, he reached out with his boots to get a firmer grip. So far so good. If he could hold himself there with his feet and one hand he would be above them when they came into view. The rest should be easy.

They were close now. At any moment they would appear at the end of the corridor. Slowly he drew the gun from his tunic, resting the stock of it against his knee.

There! Four of them, moving quickly but confidently, talking among themselves, assuming there was no danger. He let them come on four, five paces, then squeezed the trigger.

As he opened fire, the bracket by his feet jerked, then came away from the wall. At once a whole section of cabling slewed towards him, his weight dragging it down. Along the whole length of the ceiling the securing brackets gave, bringing down thick clouds of rock and debris.

Karr rolled to one side, freeing himself from the tangle, bringing his gun up to his chest. Through the dust he could see that two of them were down. They lay still, as if dead, pinned down by the cables. A third was getting up slowly, groaning, one hand pressed to the back of his head where the cabling had struck him. The fourth was on his feet, his gun raised, looking straight at Karr.

There was the deafening noise of automatic fire. Shells hammered into the wall beside him, cutting into his left arm and shoulder, but he was safe. His own fire had ripped into the guards an instant earlier, throwing them backwards.

Karr got up slowly, the pain in his upper arm intense, the shoulder wound less painful but more awkward. The bone felt broken – smashed probably. He crouched there a moment, feeling sick, then straightened up, gritting his teeth, knowing there was no option but to press on. It was just as it had been in the Pit all those years ago. He had a choice. He could go on and he could live, or he could give up and let himself be killed.

A choice? He laughed sourly. No, there had never really been a choice. He had always had to fight. As far back as he could remember, it had always been the same. It was the price for being who he was, for living where he'd lived, beneath the Net.

He went on, each step jolting his shoulder painfully, taking his breath. The gun was heavy in his right hand. Designed for two-handed use, its balance was wrong when used one-handed, the aim less certain.

Surprise. It was the last card left up his sleeve. Surprise and sheer audacity.

He was lucky. The guard outside the control-room had his back to Karr as he came out into the main corridor. There was a good twenty *ch'i* between them, but his luck held. He was on top of the man before he realised he was there, smashing the stock of the gun into the back of his head.

As the man sank to his knees, Karr stepped past him into the doorway and opened fire, spraying the room with shells. It was messy – not the way he'd normally have done it – but effective. When his gun fell silent again, there were six corpses on the floor of the room.

One wall had been filled with a nest of screens, like those they'd found in the Overseer's House in the Plantation. His gunfire had destroyed a number of them, but more than three-quarters were still functioning. He had the briefest glimpse of various scenes, showing that fighting was still going on throughout the fortress, and then the screens went dead, the overhead lights fading.

He turned, listening for noises in the corridor, then turned back, knowing his only hope was to find the controls that operated the doors and let his men into this level.

He scanned the panels quickly, cursing the damage he'd done to them, then set his gun down beside a keyboard inset into the central panel. Maybe this was it.

The keyboard was unresponsive to his touch. The screen stayed blank. Overhead a red light began to flash. Karr grabbed his gun and backed out. Not before time. A moment later a metal screen fell into place, sealing off the doorway.

What now?

Karr turned, looking to his left. It was the only way. But did it lead anywhere? Suddenly he had a vision of DeVore sitting somewhere, watching him, laughing as he made his way deeper and deeper into the labyrinth he had built; knowing that all of these tunnels led nowhere. Nowhere but into the cold, stone heart of the mountain.

He shuddered. The left side of his tunic was sodden now, the whole of his left side warm, numb yet tingling, and he was beginning to feel light-headed. He had lost a lot of blood and his body was suffering from shock, but he had to go on. It was too late now to back off.

He went on, grunting with pain at every step, knowing

he was close to physical collapse. Every movement pained him, yet he forced himself to keep alert, moving his head from side to side, his whole body tensed against a sudden counter-attack.

Again his luck held. The long corridor was empty, the rooms leading off deserted. But did it go anywhere?

Karr slowed. Up ahead the wall lighting stopped abruptly, but the tunnel went on, into the darkness.

He turned, looking back, thinking he'd heard something, but there was nothing. No one was following him. But how long would it be before someone came? He had to keep going on.

Had to.

He threw off his mask then pulled the heat-sensitive glasses down over his eyes and went on.

After a while the tunnel began to slope downwards. He stumbled over the first of the steps and banged his damaged shoulder against the wall. For a moment he crouched there, groaning softly, letting the pain ease, then went on, more careful now, pressing close to the right-hand wall in case he fell.

At first they were not so much steps as broad ledges cut into the rocky floor, but soon that changed as the tunnel began to slope more steeply. He went on, conscious of the sharp hiss of his breathing in the silent darkness.

Partway down he stopped, certain he had made a mistake. The wall beside him was rough, as if crudely hacked from the rock. Moreover, the dank, musty smell of the place made him think that it was an old tunnel, cut long before DeVore's time. For what reason he couldn't guess, but it would explain the lack of lighting, the very crudeness of its construction.

He went on, slower now, each step an effort, until, finally, he could go no further. He sat, shivering, his gun set down beside him in the darkness.

So this was it? He laughed painfully. It was not how he had expected to end his days – in the cold, dank darkness at the heart of a mountain, half his shoulder shot away –

but if this was what the gods had fated, then who was he to argue? After all, he could have died, ten years back, had Tolonen not bought out his contract, and they had been good years. The very best of years.

Even so, he felt a bitter regret wash over him. Why now? Now that he had found Marie. It made no sense. As if the gods were punishing him. And for what? For arrogance? For being born the way he was? No . . . it made no sense. Unless the gods were cruel by nature.

He pulled the heat-sensitive glasses off, then leaned back a little, seeking some posture in which the pain would ease, but it was no good. However he sat, the same fierce, burning ache would seize him again after a few moments, making him feel feverish, irrational.

What then? Go back? Or go on, ever down?

The question was answered for him. Far below he heard a heavy rustling noise, then the sharp squeal of an unoiled door being pushed back. Light spilled into the tunnel. Someone was coming up, hurriedly, as if pursued.

He reached beside him for his gun, then sat back, the gun laid across his lap, its barrel facing down towards the light.

It was too late now to put his glasses back on, but what the hell? Whoever it was, they had the light behind them, while he sat in total darkness. Moreover, he knew they were coming, while they had no idea he was there. The advantages were all his. Even so, his hand was trembling so badly now that he wondered if he could even pull the trigger.

Partway up the steps the figure stopped, moving closer to the right-hand wall. There was a moment's banging, then it stopped, the figure turning towards him again. It sniffed the air, then began to climb the steps, slower now, more cautiously, as if it sensed his presence. Up it came, closer and closer, until he could hear the steady pant of its breath, not twenty *ch'i* below.

Now! he thought, but his fingers were dead, the gun a heavy weight in his lap.

He closed his eyes, awaiting the end, knowing it was only a matter of time. Then he heard it. The figure had stopped; now it was moving back down the steps. He heard it try the lock again and opened his eyes.

For a moment his head swam, then, even as his eyes focused, the door below creaked open, spilling light into the dimly lit passageway.

Karr caught his breath, praying the other wouldn't turn and see him there. Yet even as the figure disappeared within, he recognised the profile.

DeVore. It had been DeVore.

CHAPTER·9

IN THE TEMPLE OF HEAVEN

The tower was built into the side of the mountain; a small, round, two-storey building, dominated by a smooth, grey overhang of rock. Beneath it only the outlines of ancient walls remained, huge rectangles laid out in staggered steps down the mountainside, the low brickwork overgrown with rough grasses and alpine flowers.

Lehmann stood there at the edge of the ruins, looking out across the broad valley towards the east. There was nothing human here; nothing but the sunlit mountains and, far below, the broad stretch of the untended meadows, cut by a slow-moving river. Looking at it, he could imagine it remaining so a thousand years, while the world beyond the mountains tore itself apart.

And so it would be. Once the disease of humanity had run its course.

He looked across. On the far side of the valley bare rock fell half a *li* to the green of the valley floor, as if a giant had cut a crude path through the mountains. Dark stands of pine crested the vast wall of rock, then, as the eye travelled upwards, that too gave way – to snow and ice and, finally, to the clear, bright blue of the sky.

He shivered. It was beautiful. So beautiful it took his breath. All else – all art, however fine – was mere distraction compared to this. This was real. Was like a temple. A temple to the old gods. A temple of rock and ice, of tree and stream, thrown up into the heavens.

He turned, looking back at Reid. The man was standing by the tower, hunched into himself, his furs drawn tight

289

about him, as if unaware of the vast mystery that surrounded him. Lehmann shook his head then went across.

It was only a hunch, but when he had seen the Security craft clustered on the slopes, his first thought had been of the old tunnel. He'll be there, he'd thought. Now, an hour later, he wasn't quite so sure.

"What are we doing?" Reid asked anxiously. He too had seen the extent of the Security operation; had seen the rows of corpses stretched out in the snow.

Lehmann stared back at him a moment, then climbed the narrow path to the tower. The door frame was empty. He went inside and stood there, looking about him. The tower was a shell, the whole thing open to the sky, but the floor was much newer. The big planks there looked old, but that was how they were meant to look. At most they were ten years old.

Reid came and stood there in the doorway, looking in at him. "What is this? Are we going to camp here until they've gone?"

Lehmann shook his head, then turned and came out, searching the nearby slope. Then, with a grunt of satisfaction, he crouched down, parting the spiky grasses with his gloved hands.

"Here," he said. "Give me a hand."

Reid went across. It was a hatch of some kind. An old-fashioned circular metal plate less than a *ch'i* in circumference. There were two handles set into either side of the plate. Lehmann took one, Reid the other. Together they heaved at the thing until it gave.

Beneath was a shallow shaft. Lehmann leaned inside, feeling blindly for something.

"What are you doing?" Reid asked, looking out past him, afraid that a passing Security craft would spot them.

Lehmann said nothing, simply carried on with his search. A moment later he sat back, holding something in his hand. It looked like a knife. A broad, flat knife with a circular handle. Or a spike of some kind.

Lehmann stood, then went back to the tower.

He went inside and crouched down, setting the spike down at his side. Groaning with the effort, he pushed one of the planks back tight against the far wall, revealing a small depression in the stonework below, its shape matching that of the spike perfectly. Lehmann hefted the spike a moment, then slotted it into the depression. Reid, watching from the open doorway, laughed. It was a key.

Lehmann stepped back into the doorway. As he did so there was a sharp click and the whole floor began to rise, pushing up into the shell of the tower, until it stopped, two *ch'i* above their heads.

It was a lift. Moreover, it was occupied. Reid made a small sound of surprise, then bowed his head hurriedly. It was DeVore.

"About time!" DeVore said, moving out past the two men, his face livid with anger. "Another hour and they'd have had me. I could hear them working on the seal at the far end of the tunnel."

"What happened?" Lehmann asked, following DeVore out into the open.

DeVore turned, facing him. "Someone's betrayed us! Sold us down the fucking river!"

Lehmann nodded. "They were Security," he said. "The craft I saw were special élite. That would take orders from high up, wouldn't you say?"

There was an ugly movement in DeVore's face. His incarceration in the tunnel had done nothing for his humour. "Ebert! But what's the bastard up to? What game's the little fucker playing now?"

"Are you sure it's him?"

DeVore looked away. "No. I can't see what he'd gain from it. But who else could it be? Who else knows where we are? Who else could hit me without warning?"

"So what are you going to do?"

DeVore laughed sourly. "Nothing. Not until I've spoken to the little weasel. But if he hasn't got a bloody good explanation then he's dead. Useful or not, he's dead, hear me?"

★ ★ ★

Hal Shepherd turned his head, looking up at the young T'ang, his eyes wet with gratitude.

"Li Yuan . . . I'm glad you came."

His voice was thin, almost transparently so, matching perfectly the face from which it issued: a thin-fleshed, ruined face that was barely distinguishable from a skull. It pained Li Yuan to see him like this. To see all the strength leeched from the man and death staring out from behind his eyes.

"Ben sent me a note," he said gently, almost tenderly. "But you should have sent for me before now. I would have spared the time. You know I would."

The ghost of a smile flickered on Shepherd's lips. "Yes. You're like Shai Tung in that. It was a quality I much admired in him."

It took so long for him to say the words – such effort – that Li Yuan found himself longing for him to stop. To say nothing. Simply to lie there, perhaps. But that was not what Shepherd wanted. He knew his death lay but days ahead of him and, now that Li Yuan was here, he wanted his say. Nor was it in Li Yuan's heart to deny him.

"My father missed you greatly after you returned here. He often remarked how it was as if he had had a part of him removed." Li Yuan looked aside, giving a small laugh. "You know, Hal, I'm not even sure it was your advice he missed, simply your voice."

He looked back, seeing how the tears had formed again in Shepherd's eyes, and found his own eyes growing moist. He looked away, closing his eyes briefly, remembering another time, in the long room at Tongjiang, when Hal had shown him how to juggle. How, with a laugh, he had told him that it was the one essential skill a ruler needed. So he always was – part playful and part serious, each game of his making a point, each utterance the distillation of a wealth of unspoken thought. He had been the very best of counsellors to his father. In that the Li Family had always been fortunate, for who else, among the Seven, could draw from such a deep well as they did with the Shepherds? It was what gave them their edge. Was why the other Families always looked to Li for guidance.

But now that chain was broken. Unless he could convince Hal's son otherwise.

He looked back at Shepherd and saw how he was watching him, the eyes strangely familiar in that unrecognisably wasted face.

"I'm not a pretty sight, I realise, Yuan. But look at me. Please. I have something important to say to you."

Li Yuan inclined his head. "Of course, Hal. I was . . . remembering."

"I understand. I see it all the time. In Beth. You grow accustomed to such things."

Shepherd hesitated, a brief flicker of pain passing across his face, then went on, his voice a light rasp.

"Well . . . let me say it simply. Change has come, Yuan, like it or not. Now you must harness it and ride it like a horse. I counselled your father differently, I know, but things were different then. Much has changed, even in this last year. You must be ruthless now. Uncompromising. Wang Sau-leyan is your enemy. I think you realise that. But do not think he is the only one who will oppose you. What you must do will upset friend as well as foe, but do not shrink from it merely because of that. No. You must steer a hard course, Yuan. If not there is no hope. No hope at all."

Hal lay there afterwards, quiet, very still, until Yuan realised that he was sleeping. He sat there, watching him a while. There was nothing profound in what Hal had said; nothing he had not heard a thousand times before. No. What made it significant was that it was Hal who had said it. Hal, who had always counselled moderation, even during the long War with the Dispersionists. Even after they had seeded him with the cancer that now claimed him.

He sat there until Beth came in. She looked past him, seeing how things were, then went to the drawer and fetched another blanket, laying it over him. Then she turned, looking at Li Yuan.

"He's not . . . ?" Li Yuan began, suddenly concerned.

Beth shook her head. "No. He does this often now. Sometimes he falls asleep in mid-sentence. He's very weak now, you understand. The excitement of you coming will have tired him. But please, don't worry about that. We're all pleased that you came, Li Yuan."

Li Yuan looked down, moved by the simplicity of her words. "It was the least I could do. Hal has been like a father to me." He looked up again, meeting her eyes. "You don't know how greatly it pains me to see him like this."

She looked away, only a slight tightening of her cheek muscles revealing how much she was holding back. Then she looked back at him, smiling.

"Well . . . let's leave him to sleep, neh? I'll make some *ch'a*."

He smiled, then gave the smallest bow, understanding now why his father had talked so much about his visit here. Hal's pending death or no, there was contentment here. A balance.

And how find that for himself? For the wheel of his own life was broken, the axle shattered.

He followed her, out down the narrow twist of steps, then stood there, staring out through the shadows of the hallway at the garden – at a brilliant square of colour framed by the dark oak of the doorway.

He shivered, astonished by the sight; by the almost hallucinatory clarity of what could be seen within that frame. It was as if, in stepping through, one might enter another world. Whether it were simply a function of the low ceiling and the absence of windows here inside and the contrasting openness of the garden beyond he could not say, but the effect took away his breath. It was like nothing he had ever seen. The light seemed embedded in the darkness, like a lens. So vivid it was. As if washed clean. He went towards it, his lips parted in wonder, then stopped, laughing, putting his hand against the warm wood of the upright.

"Ben?"

The young man was to the right, in the kitchen garden, close by the hinged door. He looked up from where he was kneeling at the edge of the path, almost as if he had expected Li Yuan to appear at that moment.

"Li Yuan . . ."

Li Yuan went across and stood there over him, the late morning sunlight warming his neck and shoulders. "What are you doing?"

Ben patted the grass beside him. "I'm playing. Won't you join me?"

Li Yuan hesitated, then, sweeping his robes beneath him, knelt at Ben's side.

Ben had removed a number of the rocks from the border of the flowerbeds, exposing the dark earth beneath. Its flattened surface was criss-crossed with tiny tunnels. On the grass beside him lay a long silver box with rounded edges, like an over-long cigar case.

"What's that?" Li Yuan asked, curious.

Ben laughed. "That's my little army. I'll show you in a while. But look. It's quite extensive, isn't it?"

The maze of tiny tunnels spread out several *ch'i* in each direction.

"It's part of an ants' nest," Ben explained. "Most of it's down below, under the surface. A complex labyrinth of tunnels and levels. If you could dig it out in one big chunk it would be huge. Like a tiny City."

"I see," said Li Yuan, surprised by Ben's interest. "But what are you doing with it?"

Ben leaned forward slightly, studying the movement in one of the tracks. "They've been pestering us for some while. Getting in the sugar jar and scuttling along the back of the sink. So Mother asked me to deal with them."

"Deal with them?"

Ben looked up. "Yes. They can be a real nuisance if you

don't deal with them. So I'm taking steps to destroy their nest."

Li Yuan frowned, then laughed. "I don't understand, Ben. What do you do – use acid or something?"

Ben shook his head. "No. I use these." He picked up the silver case and handed it across to the young T'ang.

Li Yuan opened the case and immediately dropped it, moving back from it sharply.

"It's all right," Ben said, retrieving the case. "They can't escape unless I let them out."

Li Yuan shivered. The box was full of ants. Big, red, brutal-looking things. Hundreds of them, milling about menacingly.

"You use them?"

Ben nodded. "Amos made them. He based them on *polyergus* – Amazon ants as they're known. They're a soldier caste, you see. They go into other ants' hives and enslave them. These are similar, only they don't enslave, they simply destroy."

Li Yuan shook his head slowly, horrified by the notion.

"They're a useful tool," Ben continued. "I've used them a lot out here. We get new nests every year. It's a good job Amos made a lot of these. I'm for ever losing half a dozen or so. They get clogged up with earth and stop functioning, or, just occasionally, the real ants fight back and take them apart. Usually, however, they encounter very little resistance. They're utterly ruthless, you see. Machines, that's all they are. Tiny, super-efficient little machines. The perfect gardening tool."

Ben laughed, but the joke was lost on Li Yuan.

"Your father tells me I must be ruthless."

Ben looked up from the ants and smiled. "It was nothing you didn't know."

Li Yuan looked back at Ben. As on the first occasion they had met – the day of his engagement to Fei Yen – he had the feeling of being with his equal; of being with a man who understood him perfectly.

"Ben? Would you be my counsellor? My Chief Adviser?

Would you be to me what your father was to my father?"

Ben turned, looking out across the bay, as if to take in his surroundings, then he looked back at Li Yuan.

"I am not my father, Li Yuan."

"Nor I mine."

"No." Ben sighed and looked down, tilting the case, making the ants run this way and that. There was a strange smile on his lips. "You know, I didn't think it would tempt me, but it does. To try it for a while. To see what it would be like." He looked up again. "But no, Li Yuan. It would simply be a game. My heart wouldn't be in it. And that would be dangerous, don't you think?"

Li Yuan shook his head. "You're wrong. Besides, I need you, Ben. You were bred to be my helper, my adviser . . ."

He stopped, seeing how Ben was looking at him.

"I can't be, Li Yuan. I'm sorry, but there's something else I have to do. Something more important."

Li Yuan stared at him, astonished. Something more important? How could *anything* be more important than the business of government?

"You don't understand," Ben said. "I knew you wouldn't. But you will. It may take twenty years, but one day you'll understand why I said no today."

"Then I can't persuade you?"

Ben smiled. "To be your Chief Adviser – to be what my father was to Li Shai Tung – that I can't be. But I'll be your sounding board if you ever need me, Li Yuan. You need only come here. And we can sit in the garden and play at killing ants, neh?"

Li Yuan stared back at him, not certain whether he was being gently mocked, then let himself relax, returning Ben's smile.

"All right. I'll hold you to that promise."

Ben nodded. "Good. Now watch. The best bit is always at the start. When they scuttle for the holes. They're like hounds scenting blood. There's something pure – some- thing utterly pure – about them."

Li Yuan moved back, watching as Ben flipped back the transparent cover to the case, releasing a bright red spill. They fell like sand on to the jet black earth, scattering at once into the tiny tracks, the speed at which they moved astonishing. And then they were gone, like blood-soaked water drained into the thirsty earth, seeking out their vic- tims far below.

It was as Ben had said; there was something pure – something quite fascinating – about them. Yet at the same time they were quite horrifying. Tiny machines, they were. Not ants at all. He shuddered. What in the gods' names had Amos Shepherd been thinking when he made such things? He looked at Ben again.

"And when they've finished . . . what happens then?"

Ben looked up at him, meeting his eyes. "They come back. They're programmed to come back. Like the *Hei* you use beneath the Net. It's all the same, after all. All very much the same."

* * *

Hans Ebert sat back in his chair, his face dark with anger.

"Karr did *what*?"

Scott bowed his head. "It's all here, Hans. In the report."

"*Report*?" Ebert stood and came round the desk, snatch- ing the file from the Captain. He opened it, scanning it a moment, then looked back at Scott.

"But this is to Tolonen."

Scott nodded. "I took the liberty of making a copy. I knew you'd be interested."

"You did, eh?" Ebert took a breath, then nodded. "And DeVore?"

"He got away. Karr almost had him, but he slipped through the net."

Ebert swallowed, not knowing what was worse:

DeVore in Karr's hands or DeVore loose and blaming him for the raid.

He had barely had time to consider the matter when his equerry appeared in the doorway.

"There's a call for you, sir. A *Shih* Beattie. A business matter, I understand."

He felt his stomach tighten. Beattie was DeVore.

"Forgive me, Captain Scott. I must deal with this matter rather urgently. But thank you. I appreciate your prompt action. I'll see that you do not go unrewarded for your help."

Scott bowed then left, leaving him alone. For a moment he sat there, steeling himself, then leaned forward.

"Patch *Shih* Beattie through."

He sat back, watching as the screen containing DeVore's face tilted up from the desk's surface, facing him. He had never seen DeVore so angry.

"What the fuck are you up to, Hans?"

Ebert shook his head. "I only heard five minutes back. Believe me, Howard."

"Crap! You must have known something was going on. You've got your finger on the pulse, haven't you?"

Ebert swallowed back his anger. "It wasn't *me*, Howard. I can prove it wasn't. And I didn't know a fucking thing until just now. All right? Look . . ." He held up the file, turning the opening page so that it faced the screen.

DeVore was silent a moment, reading through, then he swore.

"You see?" Ebert said, glad for once that Scott had acted off his own initiative. "Tolonen ordered it. Karr carried it out. Tsu Ma's troops were used. I was never, at any stage, involved."

DeVore nodded. "All right. But why? Have you asked yourself that yet, Hans? Why were you excluded from this?"

Ebert frowned. He hadn't considered it. He had just assumed that they had done it because he was so busy, preparing to take over the generalship. But now that he thought about it, it was odd. Very odd indeed. Tolonen, at the very least, ought to have let him know that *something* was going on.

"Do you think they suspect some kind of link?"

DeVore shook his head. "Tolonen would not have recommended you, and Li Yuan certainly wouldn't have appointed you. No, this has to do with Karr. I'm told his men were poking about the villages recently. I was going to deal with that, but they've pre-empted me."

"So what do we do?"

DeVore laughed. "That's very simple. You'll be General in a day or so. Karr, instead of being your equal, will be your subordinate."

Ebert shook his head. "That's not strictly true. Karr is Tolonen's man. He always was. He took a direct oath to the old man when he joined Security eleven years ago. He's only technically in my command."

"Then what about that friend of his. Kao Chen? Can't you start court martial proceedings against him?"

Ebert shook his head, confused. "Why? What will that achieve?"

"They're close. Very close, so I've heard. If you can't get at Karr, attack his friends. Isolate him. I'm sure you can rig up enough evidence to convict the Han. You've friends who would lie for you, haven't you, Hans?"

Hans laughed. More than enough. Even so, he wasn't sure he wanted to take on Karr. Not just yet.

"Isn't there an alternative?"

"Yes. You might have Karr killed. And Tolonen, too, while you're at it."

"Kill Tolonen?" Ebert sat forward, startled by the suggestion. "But he's virtually my father-in-law!"

"So? He's dangerous. Can't you see that, Hans? He almost had me killed last night. And where would we have been then, neh? Besides, what if he discovers the link between us? No, Hans, this is no time to play *Shih* Conscience. If you don't have him killed, I will."

Ebert sat back, a look of sour resignation on his face. "All right. I take your point. Leave it with me."

"Good. And Hans . . . congratulations. You'll make a good general. A very good general."

Ebert sat there afterwards, thinking back on what had been said between them. To kill Karr: he could think of nothing more satisfying, nor – when he considered it – more difficult. In contrast, having Tolonen killed would be all too easy, for the old man trusted him implicitly.

He understood DeVore's anger – understood and even agreed with the reasons he had given – yet the thought of killing the old man disturbed him. Oh, he had cursed the old man often enough for a fool, but he had never been treated badly by him. No, Tolonen had been like a father to him these past years. More of a father than his own. At some level he rather liked the old dog. Besides, how could he marry Jelka, knowing he had murdered her father?

He stood, combing his fingers back through his hair, then came out from behind his desk.

And yet, if he didn't, DeVore would. And that would place him at a disadvantage in his dealings with the Major. Would place him in his debt. He laughed bitterly. In reality there was no choice at all. He had to have Tolonen killed. To keep the upper hand. And to demonstrate to DeVore that, when it came to such matters, he had the steel in him to carry through such schemes.

He paused, contemplating the map. As from tomorrow, all this was his domain. Across this huge continent he was the arbiter, the final word, speaking with the T'ang's tongue. Like a prince, trying out the role before it became his own.

There was a tapping on the door behind him. He turned. "Come!"

It was the Chancellor, Chung Hu-yan.

"What is it Chung? You look worried?"

Chung held out a sheaf of papers to him, the great seal of the T'ang of Europe appended to the last of them.

"What are these?"

Chung shook his head, clearly flustered. "They are my orders for the coronation ceremony tomorrow, Major Ebert. They outline the protocol I am to follow."

Ebert frowned. "So what's the problem? You follow protocol. What is unusual in that?"

"Look!" Chung tapped the first sheet. "Look at what he wants them all to do."

Ebert read the passage Chung was indicating, then looked up at him, wide-eyed. "He wants them to do *that*?"

Chung nodded vigorously. "I tried to see him, this morning, but he is not at the palace. And the rehearsal is to be in an hour. What shall I do, Major Ebert? Everyone who is to be there tomorrow is attending – the very cream of the Above. They are bound to feel affronted by these demands. Why, they might even refuse."

Ebert nodded. It was a distinct possibility. Such a ritual had not been heard of since the tyrant Tsao Ch'un's time, and he had modelled it upon the worst excesses of the Ch'ing dynasty – the Manchu.

"I feel for you, Chung Hu-yan, but we are our masters' hands, neh? And the T'ang's seal is on that document. My advice to you is to follow it to the letter."

Chung Hu-yan stared at the sheaf of papers a moment longer, then quickly furled them and, with a bow to Ebert, turned, hurrying away. Ebert watched him go, amused by how ruffled the normally implacable Chancellor was. Even so, he had to admit to a small element of unease on his own account. What Li Yuan was asking for was a radical departure from the traditional ceremony and there was bound to be resentment, even open opposition. It would be interesting to see how he dealt with that. Very interesting indeed.

* * *

The big man mounted the steps, pressing his face close to the Chancellor's, ignoring the guards who hurried to intercede.

"Never!" he said, his voice loud enough to carry to the

back of the packed hall. "I'd as soon cut off my own bol-
locks as agree to that!"

There was laughter at that, but also a fierce murmur of
agreement. They had been astonished when Chung
Hu-yan had first read Li Yuan's instructions to them. Now
their astonishment had turned to outrage.

Chung Hu-yan waved the guards back, then began
again. "Your T'ang instructs you . . ." but his words were
drowned out by a roar of disapproval.

"*Instructs* us?" the big man said, turning now, looking
back into the hall. "By what right does he instruct us?"

"You must do as you are told," Chung Hu-yan began
again, his voice quavering. "These are the T'ang's orders."

The man shook his head. "It is unjust. We are not *hsiao
jen* – little men. We are the masters of this great City. It is
not right to try to humiliate us in this manner."

Once more a great roar of support came from the packed
hall. Chung Hu-yan shook his head. This was not his
doing. Not his doing at all. Even so, he would persist.

"You must step down, *Shih* Tarrant. These are the
T'ang's own instructions. Would you disobey them?"

Tarrant puffed out his huge chest. "You've heard what
I have to say, Chancellor Chung. I'll not place my neck
beneath any man's foot, T'ang or no. Nor will anyone in
this room, I warrant. It is asking too much of us. Too
much by far!"

This time the noise was deafening. But as it faded the
great doors behind Chung Hu-yan swung back and the
T'ang himself entered, a troop of his élite guards behind
him.

A hush fell upon the crowd.

Li Yuan came forward until he stood beside his Chancellor, looking back sternly at the big man, unintimidated
by his size.

"Take him away," he said, speaking over his shoulder
to the captain of the guard. "What he has said is in defiance
of my written order. Is *treason*. Take him outside at once
and execute him."

There was a hiss of disbelief. Tarrant stepped back, his face a picture of astonishment, but four of the guards were on him at once, pinning his arms behind his back. Shouting loudly, he was frogmarched past the T'ang and out through the doors.

Li Yuan turned his head slowly, looking out across the sea of faces in the hall, seeing their anger and astonishment, their fear and surprise.

"Who else will defy me?" he demanded. "Who else?"

He paused, looking about him, seeing how quiet, how docile they had become. "No. I thought not."

"This is a new age," he said, lifting his chin commandingly. "And a new age demands new rules, new ways of behaving. So do not mistake me for my father, *ch'un tzu*. I am Li Yuan, T'ang of City Europe. Now bow your heads."

★ ★ ★

He was like the sun, stepping down from the *Tien Tan*, the Temple of Heaven. His arms were two bright flashes of gold as he raised the imperial crown and placed it on his brow. Sunlight beat from his chest in waves as he moved from side to side, looking out across the vast mass of his subjects who were stretched out prone before him in the temple grounds.

No one looked. Only the cameras took this in. All other eyes were cast into the dust, unworthy of the sight.

"This is a new age," Li Yuan said softly to himself. "A new time. But old are the ways of power. As old as Man himself."

One by one his servants came to him, stretched out on the steps beneath him, their heads turned to one side, the neck exposed. And on each proferred neck he trod, placing his weight there for the briefest moment before releasing them. His vassals. This time they'd learn their lesson. This time they would know whose beasts they were.

Officers and Administrators, Representatives and Company Executives, Ministers and Family Heads; all bowed before him and exposed their necks, each one acknowledging him their lord and master.

Last was Tolonen. Only here did Li Yuan's reluctance take a shape, his naked sole touching the old man's neck as if he kissed it, no pressure behind the touch.

Then it was done. The brute thing made manifest to all. He was an emperor, like the emperors of old, powerful and deadly. And afterwards he saw how changed they were by this; how absolute he'd made them think his power. He almost smiled, wondering what his father would have made of this. So powerful was this ritual, so naked its meaning.

You are mine, it said, *to crush beneath my heel, or raise to prominence.*

The ceremony over, he dismissed all but those closest to him, holding audience in the great throne-room. First to greet him there were his fellow T'ang. They climbed the marble steps to bow their heads and kiss his ring, welcoming him to their number. Last of these was Wei Feng, wearing the white of mourning. Wei's eyes were filled with tears, and when he had kissed the ring, he leaned forward to hold Li Yuan to him a moment, whispering in his ear.

Li Yuan nodded and held the old man's hands a moment, then relinquished them. "I shall," he said softly, moved deeply by the words his father's friend had uttered.

Others came, pledging loyalty in a more traditional way. And last of all his officers, led by General Tolonen.

The General knelt, unsheathing his ceremonial dagger and offering it up to his T'ang, hilt first, his eyes averted. Li Yuan took it from him and laid it across his lap.

"You served my father well, Knut. I hope you'll serve me just as well in future. But new lords need new servants. I must have a general to match my youth."

The words were a formality, for it was Tolonen who had pushed to have Ebert appointed. The old man nodded and lifted his head. "I wish him well, *Chieh Hsia*. He is as a son to me. I have felt honoured to have served, but now my time is done. Let another serve you as I tried to serve your father."

Li Yuan smiled then summoned the young man forward.

Hans Ebert came towards the throne, his head bowed, his shoulders stooped, and knelt beside Tolonen. "I am yours," he said ritually, lowering his forehead to touch the step beneath the throne, once, twice and then a third time. The sheath at his belt was empty. No mark of rank lay on his powder blue uniform. He waited, abased and "naked" before his lord.

"Let it begin here," said Li Yuan, speaking loudly over the heads of the kneeling officers to the gathered eminences. "My trust goes out from me and into the hands of others. So it is. So it must be. This is the chain we forge; the chain that links us all."

He looked down at the young man, speaking more softly, personally now. "Raise your head, Hans Ebert. Look up at your lord, who is as the sun to you and from whom you have your life. Look up and take from me my trust."

Ebert raised his head. "I am ready, *Chieh Hsia*," he said, his voice steady, his eyes meeting those of Li Yuan unflinchingly.

"Good." Li Yuan nodded, smiling. "Then take the badge of your office."

He lifted the dagger from his lap and held it out. Ebert took it carefully, then sheathed it, curtly lowering his head once more. Then both he and Tolonen backed down the steps, their eyes averted, their heads bowed low.

★ ★ ★

That same evening they met in a room in the Purple Forbidden City: the Seven who ruled Chung Kuo. One thing remained before they went from there; one final task to set things right.

Tsu Ma stood before Li Yuan, grasping his hands firmly,

meeting him eye to eye. "You're sure you want this?"

"The genotyping is conclusive. It must be done now, before the child is born. Afterwards is too late."

Tsu Ma held him a moment longer, then released his hands. "So be it then. Let us all sign the special Edict."

Each signed his name and sealed it with his ring, in the old manner. Later it would be confirmed with retinal prints and ECG patterning, but for now this was sufficient.

Wei Feng was last to sign and seal the document. He turned, looking back at the new T'ang. "Good sits with ill this day, Li Yuan. I would not have thought it of her."

"Nor I," said Li Yuan, staring down at the completed Edict. And so it was done. Fei Yen was no longer his wife. The child would not inherit.

"When is the marriage to be?" Tsu Ma stood close. His voice was gentle, sympathetic.

"Tomorrow," Yuan answered, grateful for Tsu Ma's presence. "How strange that is. Tonight I lose a wife. And tomorrow . . ."

"Tomorrow you gain three." Tsu Ma shook his head. "Do you know who it was, Yuan? Whose son Fei Yen is carrying?"

Li Yuan looked at him, then looked away. "That does not concern me," he said stiffly. Then, relenting, he laid his hand on Tsu Ma's arm. "It was a mistake ever to have begun with her. My father was right. I know that now. Only my blindness kept it from me."

"Then you are content?"

Li Yuan shook his head. "Content? No. But it is done."

* * *

Tolonen turned from the screen and the image of the boy and faced the Architect.

"From what I've seen, the experience seems not to have done Ward too much harm, but what's your opinion? Is he ready for this yet, or should we delay?"

The Architect hesitated, remembering the last time,

years before, when he had been questioned about the boy's condition. Then it had been Berdichev, but the questions were much the same. How is the boy? Is he ready to be used? He smiled tightly, then answered Tolonen.

"It's too early to know what the long-term effects are going to be, but in the short term you're right. He's emerged from this whole episode extremely well. His reaction to the attack – the trauma and loss of memory – seems to have been the best thing that could have happened to him. I was concerned in case it had done lasting damage, particularly to his memory, but if anything the experience seems to have" – he shrugged – "toughened him up, I guess you'd say. He's a resilient little creature. Much tougher than we thought. The psychological blocks we created during his restructuring four years ago seem to have melted away – as if they'd never been. But instead of regressing to that state of savagery in which we first encountered him, he appears to have attained a new balance. I've never seen anything like it, to be honest. Most minds are too inflexible – too set in their ways – to survive what Kim has been through without cracking. He, on the other hand, seems to have emerged stronger, saner than ever."

Tolonen frowned. "Maybe. But you say that the psychological blocks have gone. That's a bad thing, surely? I thought they were there to prevent the boy from reverting into savagery."

"They were."

"Then there's a chance he might still be dangerous?"

"There's a chance. But that's true of anyone. And I mean anyone. We've all of us a darker side. Push us just so far and we'll snap. I suspect now that that was what happened the first time; that Kim was simply responding to extreme provocation from the other boy. My guess is that unless Kim were pushed to the same extreme again he'd be perfectly safe. After all, he's not a bomb waiting to go off, he's only a human being, like you or I."

"So what you're saying is that, in your opinion, he's not

308

dangerous. He won't be biting people's ears off or clawing out their eyes?"

The Architect shook his head. "I doubt it. The fact that his friend survived has helped greatly. Their reunion was a major factor in his recuperation. If T'ai Cho had been killed our problems might have been of a different order, but as it is, I'd say Kim's fine. As fine as you or I."

Tolonen turned, looking back at the screen. "Then you think he's up to it?"

The Architect laughed. "I do. In fact, I think it would be positively good for him. He has a mind that's ever-hungry for new things and an instinct for seeking them out. From what I've heard of it, the North American scene should prove a good hunting ground in that regard."

Tolonen frowned, not certain he liked the sound of that, but it was not in his brief to query what was happening in Wu Shih's City; his job was to find out whether Kim were fit to travel to North America, and from all indications he was.

He sniffed deeply, then nodded, his mind made up. "Good. Then prepare the boy at once. There's a flight from Nantes spaceport at tenth bell. I want Ward and his tutor on it."

"And the wire? Shall we remove that now that our tests are finished?"

Tolonen looked away. "No. Leave it in. It won't harm, after all." He looked back at the Architect, his face a mask. "Besides, if something does go badly wrong – if he goes missing again – we'd be able to trace him, wouldn't we?"

The Architect looked down, beginning to understand what was really happening. "Of course. Of course . . ."

* * *

"Would you like anything, sir?"

The boy looked up, startled, his dark eyes wide, then settled back in his seat again, shaking his head.

"Nothing . . . I . . . I'm all right."

The Steward backed off a pace, noting how tense the bodyguards had grown, and bowed his head. "Forgive me, sir, but if you change your mind you have only to press the summons button."

The boy returned a tense smile. "Of course."

He moved on, settling the passengers, checking they were securely strapped into the seats, asking if there was anything he could do for them before the launch, but all the while his mind was on the boy.

Who was he? he wondered. After all, it wasn't every day they received an order direct from Bremen; nor was it customary for Security to reserve a whole section of the cabin for a single passenger. Knowing all this he had expected some high-ranking Han – a Minor Family prince at the very least, or a Minister – so the boy's appearance had surprised him. At first he had thought he might be a prisoner of some kind, but the more he thought about it the more that seemed ridiculous. Besides, he wasn't bound in any way, and the men with him were clearly bodyguards, not warders. He had only to ask for something and one of them would go running.

No. Whoever he was, he was important enough to warrant the kind of treatment reserved only for the very highest of the Above – the *Supernal*, as they were known these days – and yet he seemed merely a boy, and a rather odd, almost ugly little boy at that. There was a curious angularity to his limbs, a strange darkness in his over-large eyes.

The Steward came to the end of the walkway and turned, looking back down the cabin. It was five minutes to take-off. The young Americans were settled now. Like so many of their kind they were almost totally lacking in manners. Only the quiet one – Lever – had even seemed to notice he was there. The rest had snapped their fingers and demanded this and that, as if he were not Steward but

310

some half-human creature manufactured in the GenSyn vats. It was things like that that he hated about this new generation. They were not like their fathers. No, not at all. Their fathers understood that other men had their own pride, and that it was such pride that held the vast fabric of society together. These youngsters had no idea. They were blind to such things. And one day they would pay – and pay dearly – for their blindness.

He turned and went through the curtain. The Security Captain was sitting there, the file open on his knee. He looked up as the Steward came in, giving him a brief smile.

"Are they all settled?"

The Steward nodded. "Even the two women. I had to give them a sedative each, but they seem all right now." He shook his head. "They shouldn't let women travel. I've nothing but trouble with them."

The Captain laughed, closing the file. "And the boy?"

"He's fine. I wondered . . ."

The Captain shook his head. "Don't ask me. All I was told was that there was to be a special guest on board. A guest of the T'ang himself. But who he is or what . . ." He shrugged, then laughed again. "I know. I'm as curious as you. He's a strange one, neh?"

The Steward nodded, then moved away, satisfied that the Captain knew no more than him. Even so, he thought he had glimpsed a picture of the boy, earlier, when he had first come back behind the curtain – in the file the Captain was reading. He could have been mistaken, but . . .

"Are you on business?" he asked, pulling the webbing harness out from the wall behind the Captain.

"Liaison," the Captain answered, moving forward in his seat, letting himself be fastened into the harness. "My job is to increase co-operation between the two Cities."

The Steward smiled politely. "It sounds very interesting. But I'd have thought there was little need."

"You'd be surprised. The days of isolation are ended for the Cities. The Triads have spread their nets wide these days. And not only the Triads. There's a lot of illicit trade

311

goes on. Some of it via these rockets, I've no doubt!"

The Steward stared at him a moment, then turned away. "Anyway, I'll leave you now. I have one last check to make before I secure myself."

The Captain nodded, then called him back. "Here. I almost forgot. I was told to deliver this to the boy before we took off." He handed the Steward a sealed envelope. "It was in my file. Along with a picture of the boy. All very mysterious, neh?"

The Steward stared at the envelope a moment, then nodded. He turned away, disappearing through the curtain once again.

DeVore watched the man go, breathing a sigh of relief. Then he laughed. It was easy – all so bloody easy. Why, he could have taken the boy out earlier, in the lobby, if he'd wished. He'd had a clear shot. But that wasn't what he wanted. No, he wanted the boy. Besides, Li Yuan was up to something. It would be interesting to find out what.

He smiled then opened the file again, picking up from where he'd left off. After a moment he looked up, nodding thoughtfully. Ebert had done him proud. There was everything here. Everything. The report Tolonen had made on the attack on the Project, the medical and psychological reports on Ward and a full transcript of the debriefing. The only thing missing – and it was missing only because it didn't exist – was something to indicate just why Li Yuan had decided to ship the boy off to North America.

Well, maybe he could clarify things a little over the next few days. Maybe he could find out – through the Levers – what it was Li Yuan wanted. And at the same time he might do a little business on his own account: would take up young Lever's invitation to meet his father and have dinner.

Yes, and afterwards he would put his proposal to the son. Would see just how deep his enthusiasm for change was. And then . . . ?

He smiled and closed the file. And then he would begin again, building new shapes on a new part of the board;

constructing his patterns until the game was won. For it would be won. If it took him a dozen lifetimes he would win it.

CHAPTER·10

<u>GHOSTS</u>

It was a cold, grey morning, the sky overcast, the wind whipping off the surface of the West Lake, bending back the reeds on the shoreline of Jade Spring Island. In front of the great pavilion – a huge, circular, two-tiered building with tapered roofs of vermilion tile – the thousand bright red and gold dragon banners of the T'ang flapped noisily, the ranks of armoured bearers standing like iron statues in the wind, their red capes fluttering behind them.

To the south of the pavilion a huge platform had been built, reaching almost to the lake's edge. In its centre, on a dais high above the rest, stood the throne, a great canopy of red silk shielding it from the rain that gusted intermittently across the lake.

Li Yuan sat there on the throne, his red silks decorated with tiny golden dragon and phoenix emblems. Behind him, below the nine steps of the great dais, his retainers and Ministers were assembled, dressed in red.

Facing Li Yuan, no more than a hundred *ch'i* distant, a wide bridge linked the island to the eastern shore. It was an ancient bridge, built in the time of the Song dynasty, more than a thousand years before, its white stone spans decorated with lions and dragons and other mythical beasts.

Li Yuan stared at it a moment, then turned his head, looking out blank-eyed across the lake, barely conscious of the great procession that waited on the far side of the bridge. News had come that morning. Fei Yen had had her child. A boy, it was. A boy.

The music of the ceremony began, harsh, dissonant – bells and drums and cymbals. At once the New Confucian officials came forward, making their obeisance to him before they backed away. On the eastern shore the procession started forward, a great tide of red, making its slow way across the bridge.

He sighed and looked down at his hands. It was only two days since he had removed her wedding ring. Two days . . . He shivered. So simple it had been. He had watched himself remove it from his finger and place it on the gold silk cushion Nan Ho held out to him. Had watched as Nan Ho turned and took it from the room, ending the life he had shared with her, destroying the dream for good and all.

He took a shuddering breath then looked up again. This was no time for tears. No. Today was a day for celebrations, for today was his wedding day.

He watched them come. The heads of the three clans walked side by side at the front of the procession: proud old men, each bearing his honour in his face like a badge. Behind them came the ranks of brothers and cousins, sisters and wives, many hundreds in all, and beyond them the *lung t'ing* – the "dragon pavilions" – each one carried by four bare-headed eunuch servants. The tiny sedan chairs were piled high with dowry gifts for the T'ang: bolts of silk and satin, boxes of silver, golden plates and cups, embroidered robes, delicate porcelain, saddles and fans and gilded cages filled with songbirds. So much, indeed, that this single part of the procession was by far the longest, with more than a hundred *lung t'ing* to each family.

An honour guard was next. Behind that came the three *feng yu*, the phoenix chairs, four silver birds perched atop each canopy, each scarlet and gold sedan carried aloft by a dozen bearers.

His brides . . .

He had told Nan Ho to get the Heads of the three clans to agree to waive the preliminary ceremonies – had insisted that the thing be done quickly if at all – yet it had not been possible to dispense with this final ritual. It was, after all, a matter of face. Of pride. To marry a T'ang – that was not done without due celebration; without due pomp and ceremony. And would the T'ang deny them that?

He could not. For to be T'ang had its obligations as well as its advantages. And so here he was, on a cold, wet, windy morning, marrying three young women he had never seen before this day.

Necessary, he told himself. *For the Family must be strong again*. Even so, his heart ached and his soul cried out at the wrongness of it.

He watched them come, a feeling of dread rising in him. These were the women he was to share his life with. They would bear his sons; would lie beneath him in his bed. And what if he came to hate them? What if they hated him? For what was done here could not easily be undone.

No. A man was forgiven one failure. But any more and the world would condemn him, wherever lay the fault.

Wives. These strangers were to be his wives. And how had this come about? He sat there, momentarily bemused by the fact. Then, as the music changed and the chant began below, he stood and went to the top of the steps, ready for the great ceremony to begin.

An hour later it was done. Li Yuan stepped back, watching as his wives knelt, bowing low, touching their foreheads to the floor three times before him.

Nan Ho had chosen well; had shown great sensitivity, for not one of the three reminded him in the least of Fei Yen and yet each was, in her own way, quite distinct. Mien Shan, the eldest and officially his First Wife, was a tiny thing with a strong build and a pleasantly rounded face. Fu Ti Chang, the youngest, just seventeen, was also the tallest; a shy, elegant willow of a girl. By way of contrast, Lai Shi seemed quite spirited; she was a long-faced girl, hardly a beauty, but there was a sparkle in her eye that made her by far the most attractive of the three. Li Yuan had smiled when she'd pulled back her veil, surprised to find an interest in her stirring in himself.

Tonight duty required him to visit the bed of Mien Shan. But tomorrow?

He dismissed his wives, then turned, summoning Nan Ho to him.

"*Chieh Hsia?*"

He lowered his voice. "I am most pleased with this morning's events, Master Nan. You have done well to prepare things so quickly."

Nan Ho bowed low. "It was but my duty, *Chieh Hsia.*"

"Maybe so, but you have excelled yourself, Nan Ho. From henceforth you are no longer Master of the Inner Chamber but Chancellor."

Nan Ho's look of amazement was almost comical. "*Chieh Hsia!* But what of Chung Hu-yan?"

Li Yuan smiled. "I am warmed by your concern, Nan Ho, but do not worry. I informed Chung yesterday evening. Indeed, he confirmed my choice."

Nan Ho's puzzlement deepened. "*Chieh Hsia?*"

"I should explain, perhaps, Master Nan. It was all agreed long before my father's death. It was felt that I would need new blood when I became T'ang, new men surrounding me. Men I could trust. Men who would grow as I grew and would be as pillars, supporting me in my old age. You understand?"

Nan Ho bowed his head. "I understand, *Chieh Hsia*, and am honoured. Honoured beyond words."

"Well . . . Go now. Chung Hu-yan has agreed to stay on as your adviser until you feel comfortable with your new duties. Then he is to become my counsellor."

Nan Ho gave the briefest nod, understanding. Counsellor. It would make Chung virtually an uncle to Li Yuan; a member of Li Yuan's inner council, discussing and formulating policy. No wonder he had not minded relinquishing his post as Chancellor.

"And when am I to begin, *Chieh Hsia?*"

Li Yuan laughed. "You began two days ago, Master Nan, when you came to my room and took the book of brides from me. I appointed you then, in here." He tapped his forehead. "You have been my Chancellor ever since."

★ ★ ★

Jelka was standing at her father's side, among the guests in the great pavilion, when Hans Ebert came across and joined them.

"Marshal Tolonen . . ." Ebert bowed to the old man, then turned, smiling, to Jelka. In his bright red dress uniform he looked a young god, his golden hair swept back neatly, his strong, handsome features formed quite pleasantly. Even his eyes, normally so cold, seemed kind as he looked at her. Even so, Jelka hardened herself against the illusion, reminding herself of what she knew about him.

He lowered his head, keeping his eyes on her face. "It's good to see you here, Jelka. I hope you're feeling better."

His enquiry was soft-spoken, his words exactly what a future husband ought to have said, yet somehow she could not accept them at face value. He was a good actor – a consummately good actor, for it seemed almost as if he really liked her – but she knew what he was beneath the act. A shit. A cold, self-centred shit.

"I'm much better, thank you," she said, lowering her eyes, a faint blush coming to her cheeks. "It was only a sprain."

The blush was for the lie she had told. She had not sprained her ankle at all. It was simply that the idea of seeing Hans Ebert made general in her father's place had been more than she could bear. To have spent the evening toasting the man she most abhorred! – she could think of nothing worse.

She kept her eyes averted, realising the shape her thoughts had taken. Was it really that bad? Was Hans Ebert really so abhorrent? She looked up again, meeting his eyes, noting the concern there. Even so, the feeling persisted. To think of marrying this man was a mistake. A horrible mistake.

His smile widened. "You will come and dine with us, I hope, a week from now. My father is looking forward to it greatly. And I. It would be nice to speak with you, Jelka. To find out who we are."

"Yes . . ." She glanced up at him, then lowered her eyes again, a shiver of revulsion passing through her at the thought. Yet what choice had she? This man was to be her husband – her life partner.

Ebert lifted her hand, kissing her knuckles gently before releasing it. He smiled then bowed, showing her the deepest respect. "Until then . . ." He turned slightly, bowing to her father, then turned away.

"A marvellous young man," Tolonen said, watching Ebert make his way back through the crowd towards the T'ang. "Do you know, Jelka, if I'd had a son, I'd have wished for one like Hans."

She shivered. The very thought of it made her stomach tighten; reminded her of the mad girl in the Ebert Mansion and of that awful pink-eyed goat-baby. A son like Hans . . . She shook her head. No! It could never be!

* * *

In the sedan travelling back to Nanking, Jelka sat there, facing her father, listening to him, conscious, for the first time in her life, of how pompous, how vacuous his words were. His notion that they were at the beginning of a new "Golden Age", for instance. It was a nonsense. She had read the special reports on the situation in the lower levels and knew how bad things were. Every day brought growing disaffection from the Seven and their rule – brought strikes and riots and the killing of officials – yet he seemed quite blind to all that. He spoke of growth and stability and the glorious years to come. Years that would recapture the glory of his youth.

She sat there a long while, simply listening, her head lowered. Then, suddenly, she looked up at him.

"I can't."

He looked across at her, breaking off. "Can't what?"

She stared back into his steel-grey eyes, hardening herself against him. "I can't marry Hans Ebert."

He laughed. "Don't be silly, Jelka. It's all arranged. Besides, Hans is General now."

"I don't care!" she said, the violence of her words surprising him. "I simply *can't* marry him!"

He shook his head, then leaned forward. "You mustn't say that, Jelka. You mustn't!"

She glared back at him defiantly. "Why not? It's what I feel. To marry Hans would kill me. I'd shrivel up and die."

"Nonsense!" he barked, angry now. "You're being ridiculous! Can't you see the way that boy looks at you? He's besotted with you!"

She looked down, shaking her head. "You don't understand. You really don't understand, do you?" She shuddered, then looked up at him again. "I don't *like* him, Daddy. I . . ." She gave a small, pained laugh. "How can I possibly marry someone I don't like?"

He had gone very still, his eyes narrowed. "Listen, my girl, you *will*, and sooner than you think. I've agreed a new date for the wedding. A month from now."

She sat back, open-mouthed, staring at him.

He leaned closer, softening his voice. "It's not how I meant to tell you, but there, it's done. And no more of this nonsense. Hans is a fine young man. The very best of young men. And you're a lucky girl, if only you'd get these silly notions out of your head. You'll come to realise it. And then you'll thank me for it."

"*Thank* you?" The note of incredulity in her voice made him sit back, bristling.

"Yes. *Thank* me. Now no more. I insist."

She shook her head. "You don't know him, Father. He keeps a girl in his house – a mad girl whose baby he had killed – and I've heard . . ."

"*Enough!*"

Tolonen got to his feet, sending the sedan swaying. As it slowed, he sat again, the colour draining slowly from his face.

"I won't hear another word from you, my girl. Not

another word. Hans is a fine young man. And these
lies . . ."

"They're not lies. I've seen her. I've seen what he did to
her."

"*Lies* . . ." he insisted, shaking his head. "Really . . . I
would not have believed it of you, Jelka. Such behaviour.
If your mother were alive . . ."

She put her head down sharply, trembling with anger.
Gods! To talk of her mother at such a time. She slowed
her breathing, calming herself, then said it one more time.

"I *can't*."

She looked up and saw how he was watching her: coldly,
so far from her in feeling that it was as if he were a stranger
to her.

"You will," he said. "You will because I say you will."

* * *

The doctor was still fussing over Karr's shoulder when
they brought the man in. Karr turned, wincing, waving
the doctor away, then leaned across the desk, studying the
newcomer.

"You're sure this is him?" he asked, looking past the
man at Chen.

Chen nodded. "We've made all the checks. He seems to
be who he claims he is."

Karr smiled, then sat back, a flicker of pain passing
across his face. "All right. So you're Reid, eh? Thomas
Reid. Well, tell me, *Shih* Reid, why are you here?"

The man looked down, betraying a moment's fear, then
he girded up his courage again and spoke.

"I was there, you see. After you raided the fortress. I
was there with the Man's lieutenant . . ."

"The Man?"

"DeVore. That's what we call him. The Man."

Karr glanced at Chen. "And?"

"Just that I was there, afterwards. Lehmann and I . . ."

"Lehmann?"

321

"Stefan Lehmann. The albino. Under-Secretary Lehmann's son."

Karr laughed, surprised. "And he's DeVore's lieutenant?"

"Yes. I was with him, you see. We'd been off to deliver something for the Man. But when we got back, shortly after eight, we saw your transporters from some distance away and knew there had been trouble. We flew south then doubled back, crossing the valley on foot, then climbed up to the ruins."

"The ruins?"

"Yes, there's a castle . . . or, at least, the remains of one. It's on the other side of the mountain to the base. There's an old system of tunnels beneath it. The Man used them when he built the base. Linked up to them."

"Ah . . ." The light of understanding dawned in Karr's eyes. "But why did you go there?"

"Because Lehmann had a hunch. He thought DeVore might be there, in the old tunnel."

"And was he?"

"Yes."

Karr looked to Chen. It was as he'd said. But now they knew for sure. DeVore had got out: was loose in the world to do his mischief.

"Do you know where he is?"

Reid shook his head.

"So why are you here? What do you want?"

Reid looked aside. "I was . . . afraid. Things were getting desperate out there. Out of hand. DeVore, Lehmann . . . they're not people you can cross."

"And yet you're here. Why?"

"Because I'd had enough. And because I felt that you, if anyone, could protect me."

"And why should I do that?"

"Because I know things. Know where the other bases are."

Karr sat back, astonished. *Other bases* . . . "But I thought . . ." He checked himself and looked at Chen,

322

seeing his own surprise mirrored back at him. They had stumbled on to the Landek base by complete chance in the course of their sweep of the Wilds, alerted by its heat emission patterns. They had blessed their luck, but never for an instant had they thought there would be others. They assumed all along that DeVore was working on a smaller scale: that he'd kept his organisation much tighter.

This changed things. Changed them dramatically.

Reid was watching Karr. "I know how things are organised out there. I was in charge of several things in my time. I've pieced things together in my head. I know where their weak spots are."

"And you'll tell us all of this in return for your safety?"

Reid nodded. "That and ten million *yuan*."

Karr sat back. "I could have you tortured. Could wring the truth from you."

"You could. But then, Ebert might come to know about it, mightn't he? And that would spoil things for you. I understand he's already instigated a special investigation into your activities."

Karr jerked forward, grimacing, the pain from his shoulder suddenly intense. "How do you know this?"

Reid smiled, amused by the effect his words had had. "I overheard it. The Man was speaking to Ebert. It seems the new General plans a purge of his ranks. And you and your friend, Kao Chen, are top of the list."

"But ten million. Where would I get hold of ten million *yuan*?"

Reid shrugged. "That's your problem. But until you agree to my terms I'm telling you nothing. And the longer you wait, the more likely it is that Ebert will close you down."

Chen broke his silence. "And what good would that do you, *Shih* Reid?"

Reid turned, facing Chen. "The way I figure it, Kao Chen, is that I'm either dead or I'm safe and very, very rich. It's the kind of choice I understand. The kind of risk

I'm willing to take. But how about you? You've children, Kao Chen. Can you look at things so clearly?"

Chen blanched, surprised that Reid knew so much. It implied that DeVore had files on them all: files that Ebert, doubtlessly, had provided. It was a daunting thought. The possibility of Wang Ti and the children being threatened by DeVore made him go cold. He looked past Reid at Karr.

"Gregor . . ."

Karr nodded then looked back at Reid, his expression hard. "I'll find the money, *Shih* Reid. I give you my word. You'll have it by this evening. But you must tell me what you know. Now. While I can still act on it. Otherwise my word won't be worth a dead whore's coonie."

Reid hesitated, then nodded. "All right. Get me a detailed map of the Wilds. I'll mark where the bases are. And then we'll talk. I'll tell you a story. About a young General and an ex-Major, and about a meeting the two had at an old skiing lodge a year ago."

* * *

Li Yuan sat in his chair in the old study at Tongjiang, the package on the desk before him. He looked about him, remembering. Here he had learned what it was to shoulder responsibility; to busy himself with matters of State. Here he had toiled – his father's hands – until late into the night, untangling the knotted thread of event to find solutions to his father's problems.

And now those problems were his. He looked down at the package and sighed.

He turned, looking across at the big communications screen. "Connect me with Wu Shih," he said, not even glancing at the overhead camera. "Tell him I have something urgent to discuss."

There was a short delay and then the screen lit up, the T'ang of North America's face filling the screen, ten times life-size.

"Cousin Yuan. I hope you are well. And congratulations. How are your wives?"

"They are wives, Wu Shih. But listen. I have been considering that matter we talked about and I believe I have a solution."

Wu Shih raised his eyebrows. Some weeks before, his Security sources had discovered the existence of a new popular movement, "The Sons of Benjamin Franklin". Thus far there was nothing to link them to anything even resembling a plot against the Seven, nor could any acts of violence or incitement be laid at their door. In that respect they kept scrupulously within the letter of the law. However, the mere existence of such a secret society – harking, as its name implied, back to a forbidden past – was cause for grave concern. In other circumstances he might simply have rounded up the most prominent figures and demoted them. But these were no ordinary hotheads. The "Sons" were, without exception, the heirs to some of the biggest Companies in North America. Wu Shih's problem was how to curtail their activities without alienating their powerful and influential fathers. It was a tricky problem, made worse by the fact that because no "crime" had been committed, there was also no pretext upon which he might act.

"A solution, Li Yuan? What kind of solution?"

"I have sent someone into your City, Wu Shih. As my envoy, you might say, though he himself does not know it."

Wu Shih frowned and sat forward slightly, his image breaking up momentarily, then reforming clearly. "An envoy?"

Li Yuan explained.

Afterwards Wu Shih sat back, considering. "I see. But why do you think this will work?"

"There is no guarantee that it will, but if it fails we have lost nothing, neh?"

Wu Shih smiled. "That sounds reasonable enough."

"And you will look after the boy for me?"

"Like my own son, Li Yuan."

"Good. Then I must leave you, Wu Shih. There is much to do before this evening."

Wu Shih laughed. "And much to do tonight, neh?"

There was a momentary hesitation in Li Yuan's face, then he returned Wu Shih's smile tightly, bowing his head slightly to his fellow T'ang before he cut contact.

Tonight. He shivered. Tonight he wished only to be alone. But that was not his fate. He was married now. He had duties to his wives. And to his ancestors. For it was up to him now to provide a son. To continue the line. So that the chain should remain unbroken, the ancestral offerings made, the graves tended.

Even so, his heart felt dead in him. Ever since this morning he had kept thinking of the new child, seeing it in his mind, resting in Fei Yen's arms as she lay there propped up in bed on her father's estate.

He shook his head, then stood. It hurt. It hurt greatly, but it was behind him now. It had to be. His life lay ahead of him, and he could not carry his hurt about like an open wound. Nor could he wait for time to heal the scars. He must press on. For he was T'ang now. T'ang.

He stood with his hands resting against the edge of the desk, staring down at the package, still undecided whether he should send it, then leaned forward, pressing the summons bell. "Send in Nan Ho."

The boy's debriefing had proved more successful than any of them had dared hope and had put the lie to what Director Spatz had said about Ward's "nil contribution" to the Project. Ward had remembered everything. In fact, the extent of his knowledge about the Wiring Project had surprised them all. With what he had given them, they would be able to reconstruct the facility within months. A facility which, in theory anyway, would be far more advanced than the one Spatz had so spectacularly mismanaged.

This time he would do it right. Would ensure that the right men were appointed; that it was adequately funded and properly protected. No, there would be no mistakes this time.

Mistakes. He shook his head. He had misjudged things badly. He ought to have trusted to his instinct about the boy, but he had been off-balance. That whole business with Fei Yen had thrown him. He had been unable to see things clearly. But now he could put things right. Could reward the boy. Indeed, what better way was there of making Ward loyal to him than through the ties of gratitude? And he needed the boy to be loyal. He saw that now. Saw what he had almost lost through his inadvertence.

Such talent as Kim possessed appeared but rarely in the world. It was a priceless gift. And whoever had the use of it could only benefit. Change was coming to Chung Kuo, like it or not, and they must find a way to harness it. Ward's skills – his genius, if you like – might prove effective, not in preventing Change – for who could turn back the incoming tide – but in giving it a shape better suited to the wishes of the Seven.

For now, however, Li Yuan would use him in a different role. As an eye, peering into the darkness of his enemies' hearts. As an ear, listening to the rhythms of their thought. And then, when he was done with that, he would fly him on a long leash, like a young hawk, giving him the illusion of freedom, letting him stretch his wings, even as he restrained and directed him.

There was a faint knock. "Come," he said.

"You sent for me, *Chieh Hsia*?"

He picked up the package and offered it to his Chancellor. "Have this sent to *Shih* Ward at once. I want it to be in his room when he returns tonight."

"Of course, *Chieh Hsia*." Nan Ho hesitated. "Is that all?"

As ever, he had read Li Yuan's mood. Had understood without the need for words.

"One thing, Nan Ho. You will carry a note for me. Personally. To Fei Yen. To wish her well."

Nan Ho bowed his head. "Forgive me, *Chieh Hsia*, but

327

is that wise? There are those who might construe such a note to mean . . ."

Li Yuan cut him off. "Nan Ho! Just do it. Wise or not, I *feel* it must be done. So please, take my message to her and wish her well. I would not be bitter about the past, understand me? I would be strong. And how can I be strong unless I face the past clear-eyed, understanding my mistakes?"

Nan Ho bowed, impressed by his master's words. "I will go at once, *Chieh Hsia*."

"Good. And when you return you will find me a new Master of the Inner Chambers. A man who will serve me as well as you have served me."

Nan Ho smiled. "Of course, *Chieh Hsia*. I have the very man in mind."

★ ★ ★

It was after midnight and Archimedes Kitchen was packed. The club was dimly lit, like the bottom of the ocean, the air heavy with exotic scents. As one stepped inside, under the great arch, the deep growl of a primitive bass rhythm obliterated all other sound, like a slow, all-pervasive heart-beat, resonating in everything it touched.

The architecture of the club was eccentric but deliberate. All things Han were absent here. Its fashions looked back-wards, to the last years of the American Empire, before the Great Collapse.

From its position at the top edge of the City, the Kitchen overlooked the dark green, island-strewn waters of Buz-zard Bay. Through the vast, clear windows of the upper tiers you could, on a clear day, see the south-western tip of Martha's Vineyard, distant and green, unspoiled by any structure. Few were so inclined. For most of the time the magnificent view windows were opaqued; arabesques of vivid colour swirling across their blinded surfaces.

Inside, the place was cavernous. Tier after tier spiralled up about the central circle of the dance floor, a single, broad ramp ascending smoothly into the darkened heights.

Along the slowly winding length of this elegantly carpeted "avenue", tables were set. Ornate, impressive tables, in "Empire" style, the old insignia of the sixty-nine States carved into the wooden surfaces, bronzed eagles stretching their wings across the back of each chair. Gold-and-black-suited waiters hovered – literally hovered – by the rail to take orders. Their small backpack jets, a memory of the achievements of their technological past, flaunted the Edict. Like bees, they tended the needs of the crowded tiers, fetching and carrying, issuing from the darkness high above their patrons' heads.

In the centre of all was a huge light sculpture, a twisting double band of gold stretching from floor to ceiling. It was a complex double helix, detailed and flowing, pulsing with the underlying bass rhythm, by turns frail and intense, ghostly thin and then broad, sharply delineated, like a solid thing. This, too, bordered on the illicit; was a challenge of sorts to those who ruled.

Membership of the Kitchen was exclusive. Five, almost six thousand members crowded the place on a good night – which this was – but five times that number were members and twenty times that were on the club's waiting list. More significantly, membership was confined to just one section of the populace. No Han were allowed here, nor their employees. In this, as in so many other ways, the club was in violation of statutes passed in the House some years before, though the fact that every one of the North American Representatives was also a member of the Kitchen had escaped no one's notice.

It was a place of excess. Here, much more was permitted than elsewhere. Eccentricity seemed the norm, and naked-ness, or a partial nakedness that concealed little of impor-tance, was much in evidence. Men wore their genitalia dressed in silver, small fins sprouting from the sides of their drug-aroused shafts. The women were no less overt in their symbolism; many wore elaborate rings of polished metal about their sex – space gates, similar in form to the docking apertures on spacecraft. It was a game, but there was a meaning behind its playfulness.

Of those who were dressed – the majority, it must be said – few demonstrated a willingness to depart from what was the prevalent style: a style which might best be described as Techno–Barbarian, a mixture of space suits and ancient chain-mail. Much could be made of the curious opposition of the fine, in some cases beautiful aristocratic faces and the brutish, primitive dress. It seemed a telling contrast, illustrative of some elusive quality in the society itself. Of the unstated yet ever-present conflict in their souls. Almost a confession.

It was almost two in the morning when Kim arrived at the "Gateway" and presented his invitation. The sobriety of his dress marked him out as a visitor, just as much as his diminutive status. People stared at him shamelessly as he was ushered through the crowded tunnel and out into the central space.

He boarded a small vehicle to be taken to his table – a replica of the four-wheeled, battery-powered jeep that had first been used on the moon two hundred and thirty-eight years before. At a point halfway up the spiral it stopped. There was an empty table with spaces set for five. Nearby two waiters floated, beyond the brass and crystal rail.

Kim sat beside the rail, looking down at the dance floor more than a hundred *ch'i* below. The noise was not so deafening up here. Down there, however, people were thickly pressed, moving slowly, sensuously to the stimulus of a Mood Enhancer. Small firefly clouds of hallucinogens moved erratically amongst the dancers, sparking soundlessly as they made contact with the moist warmth of naked flesh.

Kim looked up. His hosts had arrived. They stood there on the far side of the table: two big men, built like athletes, dressed casually in short business *pau*, as if to make him more at ease.

The older of the two came round the table to greet him.

330

"I'm glad you could come," he said, smiling broadly. "My name is Charles Lever."

"I know," Kim said simply, returning his smile.

Old Man Lever; he was Head of the biggest pharmaceuticals company in North America, possibly in the whole of Chung Kuo. The other man, his personal assistant, was his son, Michael. Kim shook Lever's hand then looked past him at his son, noting how alike they were.

They sat, the old man leaning towards him across the table. "Do you mind if I order for you, Kim? I know the specialties of this place."

Kim nodded and looked around, noting the occupants of the next table down. His eyes widened in surprise. Turning, he saw it was the same at the next table up.

A group of aristocrats now sat at each table. They had not been there before, so they must have slipped into their places after the Levers had arrived. There was nothing especially different about the way they dressed, yet they were immediately noticeable. They were bald. That absence of hair first drew the eye, but then another detail held the attention: a cross-hatching of scars, fine patterns like a wiring grid in an ancient circuit. These stood out, blue against the whiteness of each scalp – like some alien code.

Kim studied them a moment, fascinated, not certain what they were, then looked back to find Old Man Lever watching him, a faint smile of amusement on his lips.

"I see you've noticed my friends."

Lever rose and went from table to table, making a show of introducing them. Kim watched, abstracted from the reality of what was happening, conscious only of how uniform they seemed despite a wide variation of features; of how this one thing erased all individuality in their faces, making *things* of them.

"What you see gathered here, Kim, is the first stage of a grand experiment. One I'd like you to help me in." The old man stood there, his arms folded against his broad chest, relaxed in his own power and knowledge, confident of Kim's attention. "These here are the first to benefit from a breakthrough in ImmVac's research programme. Trailblazers, you might call them. Pioneers of a new way of living."

Kim nodded, but he was thinking how odd it was that Lever should do this all so publicly; should choose this way of presenting things.

"These," Lever paused and smiled broadly, as if the joke was all too much for him. "These are the first immortals, Kim. The very first."

Kim pursed his lips, considering, trying to anticipate the older man. He was surprised. He hadn't thought anyone was close enough yet. But if it was so, then what did it mean? Why did Lever want to involve him? What was the flaw that needed ironing out?

"Immortals," the old man repeated, his eyes afire with the word. "What Mankind has always dreamed of. The defeat of death itself."

There was a whisper from the nearby tables, like the rustle of paper-thin metal streamers in a wind. At Kim's back the coiled and spiralling threads of light pulsed and shimmered, while waiters floated between the levels. The air was rich with distracting scents. It all seemed dreamlike, almost absurd.

"Congratulations," he said. "I assume . . ."

He paused, holding the old man's eyes. What *did* he assume? That it worked? That Lever *knew* he was flouting the Edict? That it *was* "what Mankind had always dreamed of"? All of these, perhaps, but he finished otherwise. "I assume you'll pay me well for my help, *Shih* Lever."

The son turned his head sharply and looked at Kim, surprised. His father considered a moment, then laughed heartily and took his seat again.

"Why, of course you'll be paid well, *Shih* Ward. Very well indeed. *If* you can help us."

The waiters arrived, bringing food and wine. For a moment all speech was suspended as the meal was laid out. When it was done Kim reached across and poured himself a glass of water from the jug, ignoring the wine. He sipped the ice-cool liquid, then looked across at Old Man Lever again.

"But why all this? Why raise the matter here, in such a *public* place?"

Lever smiled again and began to tuck into his starter. He chewed for a while, then set his fork down. "You aren't used to our ways yet, are you? All this . . ." he gestured with his knife. "It's a marketplace. And these," he indicated his friends, "these are my product." He grinned and pointed at Kim with his knife. "You, so I'm told on good authority, come with a reputation second to none. Forget connections." There was a brief flicker in the corner of one eye. "By meeting you here, like this, I signal my intention to work with you. The best with the best." He took a second forkful and chewed and swallowed. Beside him his son watched, not eating.

"So it's all publicity?"

"Of a kind." The son spoke for the father. "It does our shares no harm. Good rumour feeds a healthy company."

Old Man Lever nodded. "Indeed. So it is, Kim. And it won't harm your own career one jot to be seen in harness with ImmVac."

Yes, thought Kim, unless the Seven start objecting to what you're doing and close you down. Aloud he said, "You know I've other plans."

The old man nodded. "I know everything about you, Kim."

It sounded ominous and Kim looked up from his plate, momentarily alarmed, but it was only a form of words. *Not everything*, he thought.

"It would be . . . theoretical work," continued Lever. "The sort of thing I understand you're rather good at. *Synthesising*."

Kim tilted his head, feeling uneasy, but not knowing quite why he had the feeling. Perhaps the words had simply thrown him. He didn't like to be *known* so readily.

"We have a drug that works. A stabiliser. Something

333

that in itself prevents the *error catastrophe* that creates ageing in human beings. But we don't want to stop there. Longevity shouldn't just be for the young, eh, Kim?" There was a slight nervousness in his laughter that escaped no one at the table. The son looked disconcerted by it, embarrassed. To Kim, however, it was the most significant thing Lever had said. He knew now what it was that drove him.

You want it for yourself. And the drug you have won't give it to you. It doesn't reverse the process, it only holds it in check. You want to be young again. You want to live for ever. And right now you can't have either.

"And your terms?"

Again Lever laughed, as if Kim were suddenly talking his own language. "Terms we'll discuss, when we meet. For now just enjoy this marvellous food. Tuck in, Kim. Tuck in. You've never tasted anything like this fish, I guarantee."

Kim took a bite and nodded. "It's good. What is it?"

There was laughter at the surrounding tables. Lever raised a hand to silence it, then leaned across the table towards the boy. "They only serve one kind of fish here. Shark."

Kim looked across at the watchful faces of the new immortals, then back at the Levers, father and son, seeing how much they enjoyed this little joke.

"Like Time," he said.

"How's that?" asked the old man, sitting back in his chair, one arm curled about the eagle's wing.

"Time," said Kim, slowly cutting a second mouthful from the fish steak in front of him. "It's like a shark in a bloodied sea."

He saw their amusement fade, the biter bit, a flicker in the corner of the old man's eye. And something else. Respect. He saw how Lever looked at him, measuring him anew. "Yes," he said, after a moment. "So it is, boy. So it is."

* * *

Tolonen climbed the twist of stairs easily, two at a time, like a man half his age, yet as he turned to say something to the leader of the honour guard, he realised he was alone. The stairs behind were empty, the door at their foot closed. Up ahead the corridor was silent, dimly lit, doors set off either side. At the far end a doorway led through to the central control room.

"What in hell . . ." he began, then fell silent. Something had not been right. His instincts prickled, as if to alert him. Something about their uniforms . . .

He reacted quickly, turning to shoot the first of them as they came through the far door, but they were moving fast and the second had aimed his knife before Tolonen could bring him down.

He fell to his knees, crumpled against the right-hand wall, blood oozing from his left arm, his gun arm, his weapon fallen to the floor. He could hear shooting from below, from back the way he'd come, but there was no time to work out what it meant. As he pulled the knife from his arm and straightened up, another of the assassins appeared at the far end of the corridor.

Grabbing up the gun he opened fire right-handed, hitting the man almost as he was on him. The assassin jerked backwards then lay there, twitching, his face shot away, the long knife still trembling in his hand.

He understood. They had instructions to take him alive. If not, he would have been dead already. But who was it wanted him?

He barely had time to consider the question when he heard the door slide open down below and footsteps on the stairs. He swung round, a hot stab of pain shooting up his arm as he aimed his gun down into the stairwell.

It was Haavikko. Tolonen felt a surge of anger wash through him. "You bastard!" he hissed, pointing his gun at him.

"*No!*" Haavikko said urgently, putting his hands out at his sides, the big automatic he carried pointing away from the Marshal. "You don't understand! The honour guard. Their chest patches . . . Think, Marshal! Think!"

Tolonen lowered his gun. That was right. The recognition band on their chest patches had been the wrong colour. Had been the green of an African banner, not the orange of a European one.

Haavikko started up the steps again. "Quick! We've got to get inside."

Tolonen nodded, then turned, covering the corridor as Haavikko came alongside.

"I'll check the first room out," Axel said into his ear. "We can hole up there until help comes. It'll be easier to defend than this."

The old man nodded, gritting his teeth against the pain in his arm. "Right. Go. I'll cover you."

He moved out to the right, covering the doorway and the corridor beyond as Haavikko tugged the door open and stepped inside. Then Haavikko turned back, signalling for him to come.

Inside, the room was a mess. This whole section was supposed to be a "safe area" – a heavily guarded resting place for visiting Security staff – but someone had taken the place apart. The mattresses were ripped, the standing lockers kicked over. Papers littered the floor.

Haavikko pointed across the room. "Get behind there – between the locker and the bed. I'll take up a position by the door."

Tolonen didn't argue. His arm was throbbing painfully now and he was beginning to feel faint. He crossed the room as quickly as he could then slumped against the wall, a wave of nausea sweeping over him.

It was not a moment too soon. Tolonen heard the door slam further down the corridor and the sound of running men. Then Haavikko's big gun opened up, deafening in that confined space.

Haavikko turned, looking back at him. "There are more of them coming. Down below. Wait there. I'll deal with them."

Through darkening vision, Tolonen saw him draw the grenade from his belt and move out into the corridor. It was a big thing: the kind they used to blast their way through a blocked Seal. He closed his eyes, hearing the grenade clatter on the steps.

And then nothing.

* * *

Axel crossed the room swiftly, throwing himself on top of the locker, shielding the Marshal with his body. It was not a moment too soon. An instant later the blast shook the air, ripping at his back, rocking the whole room.

He pulled himself upright. There was a stinging pain in his right shoulder and a sudden warmth at his ear and neck. He looked down. Tolonen was unconscious now and the wound in his arm was still seeping blood, but the blast seemed not to have harmed him any further.

Axel turned. The room was slowly filling with smoke and dust. Coughing, he half lifted the old man then dragged him across the room and out into the corridor. He stopped a moment, listening, then hauled the old man up on to his shoulder, grunting with the effort, his own pain forgotten. Then, half-crouching, the gun strangely heavy in his left hand, he made his way along the corridor, stepping between the fallen bodies. At the far end he kicked the door open, praying there were no more of them.

The room was empty, the door on the far side open. Taking a breath he moved on, hauling the old man through the doorway. He could hear running feet and shouts from all sides now, but distant, muted, as if on another level.

Ping Tiao? If so, he had to get the Marshal as far away as possible.

The Marshal was breathing awkwardly now, erratically. The wound in his arm was bad, his uniform soaked with blood.

He carried the old man to the far side of the room then set him down gently, loosening his collar. He cut a strip of cloth from his own tunic and twisted it into a cord, then bound it tightly about the Marshal's arm, just above the wound. The old man hadn't been thinking. Pulling the knife out had been the worst thing he could have done. He should have left it in. Now it would be touch and go.

He squatted there on his haunches, breathing slowly, calming himself, the gun balanced across his knee, one hand combing back his thick blond hair. Waiting . . .

Seconds passed. A minute . . . He had almost relaxed when he saw it.

The thing scuttled along the ceiling at the far end of the corridor. Something new. Something he had never seen before. A probe of some kind. Slender, camouflaged, it showed itself only in movement, in the tiny shadows it cast.

It came a few steps closer then stopped, focusing on them. Its tiny camera eye rotated; the smallest of movements of the lens.

He understood at once. This was the assassin's "eyes". The man himself would be watching, out of sight, ready to strike as soon as he knew how things stood.

Axel threw himself forward, rolling, coming up just as the assassin came round the corner.

The tactic worked. It gave him the fraction of a second that he needed. He was not where the man thought he'd be, and in that split second of uncertainty the assassin was undone.

Axel stood over the dead man, looking down at him. His limbs shook badly now, adrenalin changed to a kind of naked fear, realising how close it had been.

He turned away, returning to Tolonen. The bleeding had stopped, but the old man was still unconscious, his breathing slow, laborious. His face had an unhealthy pallor.

Axel knelt astride the Marshal, tilting his head backward, lifting his neck. Then, pinching the Marshal's nostrils closed, he breathed into his mouth.

Where was the back-up? Where was the regular squad? Or had the *Ping Tiao* taken out the entire deck?

He shuddered and bent down again, pushing his breath into the old man, knowing he was fighting for his life.

And then there was help. People were milling about behind him in the room – special élite Security and medics. Someone touched his arm, taking over from him. Another drew him aside, pulling him away.

"The Marshal will be all right now. We've regularised his breathing."

Haavikko laughed. Then it had failed! The assassination attempt had failed! He made to turn, to go over to Tolonen and tell him, but as he moved a huge wave of blackness hit him.

Hands grabbed for him as he keeled over, cushioning his fall, then settled him gently against the wall.

"Kuan Yin!" said one of them, seeing the extent of his burns. "We'd better get him to a special unit fast. It's a wonder he got this far."

* * *

Ten thousand *li* away, on the far side of the Atlantic, DeVore was sitting down to breakfast at the Lever Mansion. The Levers – father and son – had come straight from Archimedes Kitchen. DeVore had got up early to greet them, impressed by the old man's energy. He seemed as fresh after a night spent wining and dining as he had when he'd first greeted DeVore more than thirty hours before.

While servants hurried to prepare things, they went through to the Empire Room. It was a big, inelegant room, its furnishings rather too heavy, too overbearing for DeVore's taste. Even so, there was something impressive about it, from the massive pillars that reached up into the darkness overhead to the gallery that overlooked it on all four sides. The table about which they sat was huge – large enough to sit several dozen in comfort – and yet it had been set for the three of them alone. DeVore sat back in the tall-backed chair, his hands resting on the polished oak of the arms, looking down the full length of the table at Lever.

The old man smiled, raising a hand to summon one of his servants from the shadows. "Well, Howard? How did you get on?"

DeVore smiled. Lever was referring to the return-match against Kustow's *wei chi* champion.

"I was very fortunate. I lost the first two. But then . . ."

Lever raised an eyebrow. "You *beat* him?"

DeVore lowered his head, feigning modesty, but it had been easy. He could have won all five. "As I say, I was fortunate."

Michael Lever stared at him, surprised.

"Your friends were most hospitable," DeVore said. "They're good fellows, Michael. I wish we had their like in City Europe."

"And you, Howard? Did you win your money back?"

DeVore laughed. "Not at all. I knew how weak Kustow's man was. It would not have been fair to have wagered money on the outcome."

Michael Lever nodded "I see . . ." But it was clear he was more impressed than he was willing to say. So it had been with the others last night: their eyes had said what their mouths could not. He had seen the new respect with which they looked at him. Ten stones he had won by, that last game. Kustow's champion would never live it down.

The old man had been watching them from the far end of the table. Now he interrupted.

"It's a shame you're not staying longer, Howard. I would have liked to have taken you to see our installations."

DeVore smiled. He had heard rumours of how advanced they were; how openly they flouted the Edict's guidelines. But then, the War with the Dispersionists which had so completely and devastatingly crushed the Above in City Europe had barely touched them here. Many of the Dispersionists' natural allies here had kept out of that war. As a result, things were much more buoyant, the Company Heads filled with a raw self-confidence that was infectious. Everywhere he'd been there was a sense of optimism; a sense that here, if nowhere else, change could be forced through, Seven or no.

He looked back at Old Man Lever, bowing his head. "I would have liked that, Charles. But next time, perhaps? I've been told your factories are most impressive: a good few years ahead of their European counterparts."

Lever laughed, then leaned forward. "And so they should be! I've spent a great deal of money rebuilding them these past few years. But it hasn't been easy. No. We've had to go backward to go forward, if you see what I mean."

DeVore nodded, understanding. Indeed, if he needed any further clue to what Lever meant, he had only to look about him. Mementoes of the American Empire were everywhere in the room, from the great spread eagles on the backs of the chairs to the insignia on the silverware. Most prominent of all was the huge map on the wall behind Old Man Lever: a map of the American Empire at its height in 2043, five years after the establishment of the sixty-nine States. The year of President Griffin's assassination and the Great Collapse.

On the map, the red, white and blue of the Empire stretched far into the southern continent. Only the triple alliance of Brazil, Argentina and Uruguay had survived the massive American encroachments, forming the last outposts of a one-time wholly Latin continent, while to the north the whole of Canada had been swallowed up, its vastness divided into three huge administrative areas.

He looked down. To him such maps were vivid testimonies to the ephemerality of empires: to the certain dissolution of all things human in the face of Time. But to Lever and his kind they were something different. To them the map represented an ideal; a golden age to which they must return.

America. He had seen how the word lit them from within; how their eyes came alive at its sound. Like their European cousins, they had been seduced by the great dream of return. A dream that his gift of the Aristotle File was sure to feed, like coals on the fire of their disaffection, until this whole vast City erupted in flames.

He sighed. Yes, the day would come. And he would be there when it did. To see the Cities in flames, the Seven cast down.

He turned in his chair, taking a coffee from the servant, then looked across again, meeting Lever's eyes. "And the boy? How was your dinner? I understand you took him to the Kitchen."

Lever smiled thoughtfully. "It went well. He's sharp, that one. Very sharp. And I'm grateful for your introduction, Howard. It could prove a most valuable contact."

"That's what I thought . . ."

"However," Lever interrupted, "I've been wondering."

DeVore took a sip of his coffee then set the cup down, pushing it away from him. "Wondering?"

"Yes. Think a moment. If the boy is so valuable, then why has Li Yuan sent him here? Why hasn't he kept him close at hand, in Europe, where he can use him?"

DeVore smiled. "To be honest with you, Charles, I'm not sure. I do know that the old T'ang intended to have the boy terminated. Indeed, if it wasn't for the attack on the Project, the boy wouldn't be here now. It seems Li Yuan must have reconsidered."

"Yes. But what's he up to now?"

DeVore laughed. "That's what we'd all like to know, neh? But to be serious, I figure it like this. The boy suffered a great shock. Certain psychological blocks that were induced in him during his personality reconstruction aren't there any longer. In a very real sense he's not the same person he was before the attack. Li Yuan has been told that. He's also been told that, as a result, the boy is not one hundred per cent reliable. That he needs a rest and maybe a change of setting. So what does he do? He ships the boy off here, with a complete medical back-up, hoping that the trip will do him good and that he'll return refreshed, ready to get to work again."

Lever nodded thoughtfully. "So you think Li Yuan will use him, after all?"

DeVore raised his eyebrows. "Maybe. But then maybe not. I have heard rumours."

"Rumours?"

DeVore smiled, then shrugged apologetically. "More I can't say just yet. But when I hear more I'll let you know, I promise you."

Lever huffed impatiently, then turned in his chair, snapping his fingers. "Come! Quickly now! I'm starving."

Across from him his son laughed. "But, Father, you only ate three hours back. How can you be starving?"

Lever stared back at his son a moment, then joined his laughter. "I know. But I am, all the same." He looked back at DeVore. "And you, Howard, what will you eat?"

DeVore smiled. *The world*, he thought. *I'll eat the world*. But aloud he said, "Coffee will do me fine, Charles. I've no appetite just now. Maybe later, neh?"

He turned, looking at the son. "Are you eating, Michael, or can I interest you in a breath of air?"

The young man sat back, drawing one hand through his short blond hair. "I was going to get a few hours' sleep, but half an hour won't make much difference." He turned, looking across. "You'll excuse us, Father?"

Lever nodded. "That's fine, Michael. But remember there's a lot still to be done before Friday night."

Young Lever smiled. "It's all in hand."

"Good!" Lever lifted his fork, pointing at DeVore. "Why don't you change your mind and stay over, Howard? We're holding a Thanksgiving Ball. You could see how we Americans celebrate things. Besides, there'll be a lot of interesting and important people there. People you ought to meet."

DeVore bowed his head. "Thanks, but I really must get back tonight. Another time, perhaps?"

Lever shrugged, then waved them away, lowering his head as he dug into his breakfast.

Outside it was cooler. Subtle lighting gave the

impression that it really was morning; that they really were walking beneath a fresh, early autumn sky, a faint breeze whispering through the branches of the nearby trees.

DeVore, watching the younger Lever, saw how he changed once out of his father's presence; how the tense pose of formality slipped from him.

"Was I right?" he asked, as soon as they were out of earshot of the mansion.

Lever turned. "You're a clever man, Howard, but don't underestimate my father."

"Maybe. But was I right?"

Lever nodded. "It was all he talked about. But then, that's not surprising. It's an obsession with him. Immortality . . ." He shook his head.

DeVore put his hand on the young man's arm. "I understand how you must feel, Michael. I've not said anything before now – after all, it would hardly be good manners to talk of it in front of your father – but to you I can speak freely. You see, I find the idea of living for ever quite absurd. To think that we could outwit death – that we could beat the old Master at his own game!" He laughed and shook his head ruefully, seeing how he had struck a chord in the other man. "Well, I'm sure you agree. The very idea is ludicrous. Besides, why perpetuate the weakness of the old creature – the *mei yu jen wen*? Why not strive to make some better, finer being?"

"What do you mean?"

DeVore lowered his voice. "You've seen what I've achieved so far. Well, much more has yet to be done. The fortresses are but a small part of my scheme. It's my belief that we must look beyond the destruction of the Seven and anticipate what happens afterwards. And not merely anticipate. The wise man seeks to shape the future, surely?"

Lever nodded thoughtfully. "It's what I've always said."

"Good. Then hear me out, for I've a plan that might benefit us both."

"A plan?"

"Yes. Something that will keep everyone happy."

Lever laughed. "That's a tall order."

"But not impossible. Listen. What if we were to set up an Immortality Research Centre in the Wilds?"

Lever started. "But I thought you said . . . ?"

"I did. And I meant what I said. But look at it this way: you want one thing, your father another. However, he has the power – the money, to be precise – and you have nothing. Or as good as."

He could see from the sourness in the young man's face that he had touched a raw nerve.

"Well, why not channel a little of that money into something for yourself, Michael?"

Lever's eyes widened, understanding. "I see. When you talk of a research centre, you don't mean that, do you? You're talking of a front. A way of channelling funds."

"Of course."

"You're asking me to fool my father. To draw on his obsession, hoping he'll be blind to what I'm doing."

DeVore shook his head. "I'm asking nothing of you, Michael. You'll act as you choose to act. And if that accords with what I want, then all well and good. If not . . ." He shrugged and smiled pleasantly, as if it didn't matter.

"And what *do* you want?"

DeVore hesitated. He had been asked that question so many times now that he had even begun to ask it of himself. For a brief moment he was tempted to spell it out – the whole grand scheme he carried in his head – then changed his mind.

"I think you know what I want. But let me just ask you this, Michael. If your father got his dearest wish – if he finally found a way of becoming immortal – what then? Wouldn't that simply prove a curse to all involved? After all, if he *were* to live for ever, when would you inherit?"

Lever met DeVore's eyes briefly, then looked away. But DeVore, watching, had seen how his words had touched him to the quick. It was what he feared – what his whole generation feared. To be a son for ever, bound by a living ghost.

Lever shivered, then shook his head. "And this centre . . . how would you go about selling the idea to my father?"

DeVore smiled, then took the young man's arm again, leading him on, beginning to outline his plan. But the most difficult part now lay behind him. The rest would be easy.

Immortality. It was a nonsense, but a useful nonsense. And he would milk it to the last drop. But before then he would carry out a few last schemes of his own. To tidy things up, and settle a few last scores.

*   *   *

It was after six when Kim got back to the high-security complex where he was staying. The guards checked his ID then passed him through.

The apartment was in darkness, only the faint glow of the console display showing from the room at the far end of the hallway. He stood there a moment, feeling uneasy. His bedroom was just up a little on the right. He went through, closing the door behind him, then turned on the bedside lamp.

He stiffened, then turned slowly, looking about him. The red silk package on the bedside table had not been there when he had left. Someone had been into the room.

He stared at it a moment, wondering what to do. If it were a bomb it might already be too late – merely coming into the room could have triggered the timer. Then he saw the note, poking out from beneath, and smiled, recognising the hand.

He sat, placing the package beside him on the bed while he read the note. It was in Mandarin, the black ink characters formed with confident, fluent strokes. At the foot of the small, silken sheet was the young T'ang's seal, the

Ywe Lung impressed into the bright gold wax. He read it quickly.

> *Shih* Ward,
>
> At our first meeting I said that if you did as I wished I would tear up my father's warrant. You have more than fulfilled your part of our agreement, therefore I return my father's document, duly enacted.
>
> I would be honoured if you would also accept these few small gifts with my sincere gratitude for your help in restoring the Project.
>
> I look forward to seeing you on your return from my cousin's City.
>
> > With deepest respect,
> > Li Yuan.

Kim looked up. The note was most unusual. *With deepest respect*. These were not words a T'ang normally used to a subject. No, he knew enough of the social mechanics of Chung Kuo to know that this was exceptional behaviour on the young T'ang's part. But why? What did he want from him?

Or was that fair? Did Li Yuan *have* to want something?

He set the note down and picked up the package. Beneath the silk wrapping was a tiny box: a black, lacquered box, the letters of Kim's name impressed into the lid in bright gold lettering. He felt a tiny tremor of anticipation ripple through him, then opened it. Inside the box, wrapped in the torn pieces of Li Shai Tung's warrant, were four small cards. He spilled them on to the bed. They were little different from the computer cards that were in use everywhere throughout Chung Kuo: multipurpose cards that served to store information in every shape and form. There was no guessing what these were until he fed them into a comset. They might be credit chips, for instance, or holograms, or special programmes of some kind. The only clue he had was the number Li Yuan had handwritten on each.

He scooped them up and went through to the end room, putting on the desk lamp beside the console before slipping the first of the cards – numbered *yi* – one – into the slot in front of him.

He sat back, waiting.

There was the sound of a tiny bell being rung, the note high and pure, then a word appeared on the screen.

PASS-CODE?

He placed his hand palm down on the touch-pad and leaned forward over the dark, reflective surface, opening his eyes wide, letting the machine verify his retinal print. He spoke four words of code, then sat back.

There was a fraction of a second's delay before the response came up on the screen.

AUDIO OR VISUAL?

"Visual," he said softly.

The surface rippled in acknowledgment, like the calm surface of a pool disturbed by a single small stone falling cleanly into its centre. A moment later the screen lifted smoothly from the desktop, tilting up to face him.

He gave the code again. At once the screen filled with information. He scanned through quickly, then sat back. It was an amended copy of his contract with SimFic, buying out their interest in him. And the new owner? It was written there at the foot of the contract. Kim Ward. For the first time in his life he owned himself.

He shivered, then took the file from the slot, replacing it with the one marked *er* – two.

As the screen lit up again, he nodded to himself. Of course. It would have meant nothing being his own master without this – his citizenship papers. But Li Yuan had gone further: he had authorised an all-levels pass. That gave Kim clearance to travel anywhere within the seven Cities, and few – even among the Above – were allowed that.

Two more . . . He stared at the tiny cards a moment, wondering, then placed the third – marked *san* – into the slot

At first he didn't understand. Maybe one of Li Yuan's

servants had made a mistake and placed the wrong card in the package. Then, as the document scrolled on, he caught his breath, seeing his name, there in the column marked "Registered Head".

A company! Li Yuan had given him his own company – complete with offices, patents and enough money to hire staff and undertake preliminary research. He shook his head, bewildered. All this . . . he didn't understand.

He closed his eyes. It was like a dream, a dream he would shortly wake from, yet when he opened his eyes again, the information was still there on the screen, Li Yuan's personal verification codes rippling down the side of the file.

But why? Why had Li Yuan given him all this? What did he want in return?

He laughed strangely, then shook his head again. It always came back to that. He had grown so used to being owned – to being *used* – that he could not think of such a gesture in any other way. But what if Li Yuan wanted nothing? What if he meant what he had said in his note? What had he to lose in making such a gesture?

And what gain?

He frowned, trying to see through the confusion of his feelings to the objective truth – but for once it proved too difficult. He could think of no reason for Li Yuan's generosity. None but the one his words appeared to give.

He removed the file, then placed the last of the cards – *si* – into the slot.

What now? What else could Li Yuan possibly give him?

It was a different kind of file – he saw that at once. For a start, Li Yuan's personal code was missing. But it was more than that. He could tell by the length and complexity of the file that it had been prepared by experts.

He gave the access code. At once the screen filled with brilliant colours, like a starburst, quickly resolving itself into a complex diagram. He sat back, his mouth wide open. It was a genotyping.

No. Not just a genotyping. He knew at once what it

was without needing to be told. It was *his* genotyping.

He watched, wide-eyed, as the programme advanced, one detail after another of the DNA map boldly emphasised on the screen. Then, lifting the details from the flat screen one by one, it began to piece the building blocks together until a holo-image of a double helix floated in the air above the desk, turning slowly in the darkness.

He studied the slow turning spiral, memorising it, his heart pounding in his chest, then gave the verbal cue to progress the file.

The next page gave a full probability set. It numbered just short of six billion possible candidates: the total number of adult male *Hung Mao* back in 2190. He shivered, beginning to understand, then cued the file again. The next display itemised close-match candidates. Ten names in all. He scanned the list, his mouth fallen open again. His father . . . One of these was his father.

One by one he was given details of the ten: genotypes; full face portraits; potted biographies; each file quite frightening in its detail.

When the last had faded from the screen he called hold, then sat back, his eyes closed, his breathing shallow. He felt strange, as if he were standing on the edge of a deep well, ill-balanced, about to fall. He shivered, knowing he had never felt like this before. Knowledge had always been an opening – a breaching of the dark – but this . . .

For once he was afraid to know.

He let the giddiness pass then opened his eyes again, steeling himself. "All right. Move on . . ."

There was a full second's hesitation and then the screen lit up. This time it gave details of the known movements of the ten candidates over a three-month period in the winter of 2190; details compiled from Security files.

It narrowed things down to a single candidate. Only one of the ten had visited the Clay during that period. Only one, therefore, could possibly have been his father.

He swallowed drily, then cued the file again.

The image appeared immediately, as sharp as if it had

been made earlier that day. A youngish man in his late twenties or early thirties; a tall, slightly built man, fine-boned and elegant, with distinctly aristocratic features. His light brown hair was cut neatly but not too severely and his dark green eyes seemed kind, warm. He was dressed simply but stylishly in a dark red *pau*, while about both of his wrists were a number of slender *tiao tuo* – bracelets of gold and jade.

Kim narrowed his eyes, noticing an oddity about the man. It was as if his head and body were parts of two different, separate beings; the head too large, somehow, the chin and facial features too strong for the slender, almost frail body that supported them. Kim frowned, then mouthed his father's name.

"*Edmund . . . Edmund Wyatt.*"

It was an old image. Looking at it, he felt something like regret that he would never meet this man or come to know him, for, as the file indicated, Edmund Wyatt had been dead eight years – executed for the murder of the T'ang's minister, Lwo Kang. A crime for which he had later, privately, been pardoned.

Kim shuddered. Was *that* the reason for Li Yuan's generosity? To square things up somehow? Or was a T'ang above such moral scruples?

He leaned forward, about to close the file, when the image of Wyatt vanished. For a moment the screen was blank, then it lit up again.

GENOTYPE PREDICT: FEMALE SOURCE.

He called hold, his voice almost failing him, his heart hammering once more.

For a long time he sat there, hunched forward in his chair, staring at the heading, then, in a voice that was almost a whisper, he gave the cue.

First came the genotype: the puzzle pieces of DNA that would interlock with Edmund Wyatt's to produce his own. He watched as they formed a double helix in the air. Then, dramatically, they vanished, replaced not by further figures, but by a computer graphics simulation – a full-length 3–D portrait of a naked woman.

He gasped, then shook his head, not quite believing what he saw. It was his mother. Though he had not seen her in almost a dozen years, he knew at once that it was her. But not as she had been. No, this was not at all like the scrawny, lank-haired, dugless creature he had known.

He almost laughed at the absurdity of the image, but a far stronger feeling – that of bitterness – choked back the laughter.

He moaned and looked away, the feeling of loss so great that, for a moment, it threatened to unhinge him.

"Mother . . ." he whispered, his eyes blurring over. "Mother . . ."

The computer had made assumptions. It was programmed to assume a normal Above diet, normal Above life-expectations. These it had fed into its simulation, producing something that, had such conditions prevailed down there in the Clay, would have been quite accurate. But as it was . . .

Kim looked at the image again: staring open-mouthed at a portrait of his mother as she might have been: at a dark-haired beauty, strong-limbed and voluptuous, full-breasted and a good two *ch'i* taller than she had been in life. A strong, handsome woman.

He shuddered, angered – it was awful, like some dreadful mockery – then shook his head. No. The reality – the truth – *that* was grotesque. And this?

He hesitated, afraid to use the word; but there was no other way of describing the image that floated there in the darkness.

It was beautiful. *Beautiful.*

The image was a lie. And yet it *was* his mother. There was no doubt of that. He had thought her gone from mind, all trace of her erased. After all, he had been little more than four when the tribe had taken him. But now the memories came back, like ghosts, taunting, torturing him.

He had only to close his eyes and he could see her

crouched there beneath the low stone wall, just after they had escaped from the Myghtern's brothel, her eyes bright with excitement. Could see her lying beside him in the darkness, reaching out to hold him close, her thin arms curled about him. Could see her, later, scrambling across the rocks in the shadow of the Wall, hunting, her emaciated form flexing and unflexing as she tracked some pallid, rat-like creature. Could see her turn, staring back at him, a smile on her lips and in her dark, well-rounded eyes.

Could *see* her . . .

He covered his eyes, pressing his palms tight into the sockets as if to block out these visions, a single, wavering note of hurt – a low, raw, animal sound, unbearable in its intensity – welling up from deep inside him.

For a time there was nothing but his pain. Nothing but the vast, unendurable blackness of loss. Then, as it ebbed, he looked up once more; and, with a shuddering breath, reached out to touch her.

His fingers brushed the air; passed through the beautiful, insubstantial image.

He sighed. Oh, he could see her now. Yes. And not only as she was but as she should have been. Glorious. Wonderful . . .

He sat back, wiping the wetness from his cheeks, then shook his head, knowing that it was wrong to live like this, the City above, the Clay below. Knowing, with a certainty he had never felt before, that something had gone wrong. Badly wrong.

He leaned forward, closing the file, then sat back again, letting out a long, shuddering breath. Yes, he knew it now. Saw it with a clarity that allowed no trace of doubt. Chung Kuo was like himself: motherless, ghost-haunted, divided against itself. It might seem teeming with life, yet in reality it was a great, resounding shell, its emptiness echoing down the levels.

Kim picked up the four tiny cards and held them a moment in his palm. Li Yuan had given him back his life. More than that, he had given him a future. But who would

CHAPTER·11

THE TIGER'S MOUTH

Ebert looked about him, then turned back to Mu Chua, smiling.

"You've done well, Mu Chua. I'd hardly have recognised the place. They'll be here any time now, so remember, these are important business contacts and I want to impress them. Are the new girls dressed as I asked?"

Mu Chua nodded.

"Good. Well, keep them until after my entrance. These things must be done correctly, neh? One must whet their appetites before giving them the main course."

"Of course, General. And may I say again how grateful I am that you honour my humble house. It is not every day that we play host to the nobility."

Ebert nodded. "Yes . . . but more is at stake than that, Mother Chua. If these *ch'un tzu* like what they see then it is more than likely you will receive an invitation."

"An invitation?"

"Yes. To a *chao tai hui* – an entertainment – at one of the First Level mansions. This afternoon, I am told, there is to be a gathering of young princes. And they will need . . . how shall I put it? . . . special services."

Mu Chua lowered her head. "Whatever they wish. My girls are the very best. They are *shen nu*. . . god girls."

Again Ebert nodded, but this time he seemed distracted. After a moment he looked back at Mu Chua. "Did the wine from my father's cellar arrive?"

"It did, Excellency."

"Good. Then you will ensure that our guests drink that

and nothing else. They are to have nothing but the best."

"Of course, General."

"I want no deceptions, understand me, Mu Chua. Carry this off for me and I will reward you handsomely. Ten thousand *yuan* for you alone. And a thousand apiece for each of your girls. That's on top of your standard fees and expenses."

Mu Chua lowered her head. "You are too generous, Excellency . . ."

Ebert laughed. "Maybe. But you have been good to me over the years, Mother Chua. And when this proposition was put before me, my first thought was of you and your excellent house. 'Who better,' I said to myself, 'than Mu Chua at entertaining guests.'" He smiled broadly at her, for once almost likeable. "I am certain you will not let me down."

Mu Chua lowered her head. "Your guests will be transported . . ."

He laughed. "Indeed . . ."

After Ebert had gone, she stood there a moment, almost in a trance at the thought of the ten thousand *yuan* he had promised. Together with what she would milk from this morning's entertainment, it would be enough. Enough, at last, to get out of here. To pay off her contacts in the Above and climb the levels.

Yes. She had arranged it all already. And now, at last she could get away. Away from Whiskers Lu and the dreadful seediness of this place. Could find somewhere up-level and open up some small, discreet, cosy little house. Something very different, with its own select clientele and its own strict rules.

She felt a little shiver of anticipation pass through her, then stirred herself, making the last few arrangements before the two men came, getting the girls to set out the wine and lay a table with the specially prepared sweetmeats.

She had no idea what Ebert was up to, but it was clear that he set a great deal of importance on this meeting. Only two days ago his man had turned up out of the blue and handed her twenty-five thousand *yuan* to have the house redecorated. It had meant losing custom for a day, but she had still come out of it ahead. Now it seemed likely that she would gain much more.

Even so, her suspicions of Hans Ebert remained. If he was up to something it was almost certain to be no good. But was that her concern? If she could make enough this one last time she could forget Ebert and his kind. This was her pass out. After today she need never compromise again. It would be as it was, before the death of her protector, Feng Chung.

The thought made her smile; made her spirits rise. Well, as this was the last time, she would make it special. Would make it something that even Hans Ebert would remember.

She busied herself, arranging things to perfection, then called in the four girls who were to greet their guests. Young girls, as Ebert had specified; none of them older than thirteen.

She looked at herself in the mirror, brushing a speck of powder from her cheek, then turned, hearing the bell sound out in the reception room. They were here.

She went out, kneeling before the two men, touching her forehead against her knees. Behind her, the four young girls did the same, standing at the same time that she stood. It was a calculated effect, and she saw how much it pleased the men.

Ebert had briefed her fully beforehand; providing her with everything she needed to know about them, from their business dealings down to their sexual preferences. Even so, she was still surprised by the contrast the two men made.

Hsiang K'ai Fan was a big, flabby-chested man, almost effeminate in his manner. Treble-chinned and slack-jowled, his eyes seemed to stare out of a landscape of flesh, yet his movements were dainty and his dress sense exquisite. His lavender silks followed the fashion of the Minor Families – a fashion which was wholly and deliberately out of step with what was being worn elsewhere in the Above – with long, wide sleeves and a flowing gown that hid his booted feet. Heavily perfumed, he was nonetheless restrained in his use of jewellery, the richest item of his apparel being the broad, red velvet *ta lian*, or girdle pouch, that he wore about his enormous waist, the two clasps of which were studded with rubies and emeralds in the shape of two butterflies. His nails were excessively long, in the manner of the Families; the ivory-handled fan he held moved slowly in the air as he looked about him.

An Liang-chou, on the other hand, was a tiny, rat-like man, stringily built and astonishingly ugly even by the standard of some of the clients Mu Chua had entertained over the years. Flat-faced and beady-eyed, he was as nervy as Hsiang was languid; his movements jerky, awkward. Meeting his eyes, Mu Chua smiled tightly, trying to keep the aversion she felt from showing. Rumour had it that he fucked all six of his daughters – even the youngest, who was only six. Looking at him, it was not hard to imagine. She had seen at once how his eyes had lit up at the sight of her girls. How a dark, lascivious light had come to them: the kind of look a predatory insect gives its victim before it pounces.

Unlike Hsiang, An Liang-chou seemed to have no taste at all when it came to dress. His gaudily coloured *pau* hung loose on him, as if he had stolen it from another. Like Hsiang he was heavily perfumed, but it was an unpleasantly sickly scent, more sour than sweet, as if mixed with his own sweat. She saw how his hand – the fingers thickly crusted with jewelled rings – went to his short ceremonial dagger; how his lips moved wetly as he considered which girl he would have first.

"My lords . . . you are welcome to my humble house," she said, lowering her head again. "Would you care for something to drink?"

Hsiang seemed about to answer, but before he could do so, An Liang-chou moved past her and, after pawing two of the girls, chose the third. Gripping her upper arm tightly he dragged her roughly after him, through the beaded curtain and into the rooms beyond.

Mu Chua watched him go, then turned back to Hsiang, smiling, all politeness.

"Would the Lord Hsiang like refreshments?"

Hsiang smiled graciously and let himself be led through. But in the doorway to the Room of Heaven he stopped and turned to look at her.

"Why, this is excellent, Mu Chua. The General was not wrong when he said you were a woman of taste. I would not have thought such a place could have existed outside First Level."

She bowed low, immensely pleased by his praise. "Ours is but a humble house, Excellency."

"However," he said, moving on, into the room, "I had hoped for . . . well, let us not prevaricate, eh? . . . for *special* pleasures."

She saw how he looked at her and knew at once that she had misjudged him totally. His silken manners masked a nature far more repugnant than An Liang-chou's.

"Special pleasures, Excellency?"

He turned, then sat in the huge, silk-cushioned chair she had bought specially to accommodate his bulk, the fan moving slowly, languidly in his hand.

He looked back at her, his tiny eyes cold, calculating amidst the flesh of his face. "Yes," he said smoothly. "They say you can buy anything in the Net. Anything at all."

She felt herself go cold. Ebert had said nothing about this. From what he'd said, Hsiang's pleasures were no more unnatural than the next man's. But this . . .

She waved the girls away, then slid the door across and turned back, facing him, reminding herself that this was her passage out, the last time she would have to deal with his kind.

"What is it you would like?" she asked, keeping her voice steady. "We cater for all tastes here, my lord."

He smiled, a broad gap opening in the flesh of his lower

face, showing teeth that seemed somehow too small to fill the space. His voice was silken, like the voice of a young woman.

"My needs are simple, Mu Chua. Very simple. And the General promised me that you would meet them."

She knelt, bowing her head. "Of course, Excellency. But tell me, what *exactly* is it that you want?"

He clicked the fan shut, then leaned forward slightly, beckoning her across.

She rose, moving closer, then knelt, her face only a hand's width from his knees. He leaned close, whispering, a hint of aniseed on his breath.

"I have been told that there is a close connection between sex and death. That the finest pleasure of all is to fuck a woman at the moment of her death. I have been told that the death throes of a woman bring on an orgasm so intense . . ."

She looked up at him, horrified, but he was looking past her, his eyes lit with an intense pleasure, as if he could see the thing he was describing. She let him spell it out, barely listening to him now, then sat back on her heels, a small shiver passing through her.

"You want to kill one of my girls, is that it, Lord Hsiang? You wish to slit her throat while you are making love to her?"

He looked back at her, nodding. "I will pay well."

"Pay well . . ." She looked down. It was not the first time she had had such a request. Even in the old days there had been some like Hsiang who linked their pleasure to the pain of others, but even under Whiskers Lu there had been limits to what she would allow. She had never had one of her girls die while with a client, intentionally or otherwise, and it was on her tongue to tell this bastard, Prince or no, to go fuck himself. But . . .

She shuddered, then looked up at him again, seeing how eagerly he awaited her answer. To say no was to condemn herself at best to staying here, at worst to incurring the anger of Hans Ebert. And who knew what he would do to her if she spoiled things for him now? But to say yes was to comply with the murder of one of her girls. It would be as if she herself had held the knife and drawn it across the flesh.

"What you ask . . ." she began, then hesitated.

"Yes?"

She stood, then turned away, moving towards the door before turning back to face him again. "You must let me think, Lord Hsiang. My girls . . ."

"Of course," he said, as if he understood. "It must be a special girl."

His laughter chilled her blood. It was as if what he was discussing were a commonplace. As for the girl herself . . . In all her years she had tried to keep it in her mind that what her clients bought was not the girl, but the services of the girl, as one bought the services of an accountant or a broker. But men like Hsiang made no such distinction. To them the girl was but a thing; to be used and discarded as they wished.

But how say no? What possible excuse could she give that would placate Hsiang K'ai Fan? Her mind raced, turning back upon itself time and again, trying to find a way out, some way of resolving this impossible dilemma. Then she relaxed, knowing, at last, what to do.

She smiled and moved closer, taking Hsiang's hands gently and raising him from his chair.

"Come," she said, kissing his swollen neck, her right hand moving down his bloated flank, caressing him. "You wanted special pleasures, Hsiang K'ai Fan, and special pleasures you will have. Good wine, fine music, the very best of foods . . ."

"And after?" He stared at her, expectantly.

Mu Chua smiled, letting her hand rest briefly on the hard shape at his groin, caressing it through the silk. "After, we shall do as you wish."

★ ★ ★

Charles Lever's son, Michael, sat at his desk, facing Kim across the vastness of his office.

"Well? Have you seen enough?"

Kim looked about him. Huge tapestries filled the walls to the left and right of him: broad panoramas of the Rockies and the great American plains, while on the end wall, beyond Lever's big oak desk and the leather-backed swivel chair, was a bank of screens eight deep and twenty wide. In the centre of the plushly carpeted room, on a big, low table, under glass, was a 3–D map of the east coast of City North America, ImmVac's installations marked in blue. Kim moved closer, peering down through the glass.

"There's an awful lot to see."

Lever laughed. "That's true. But I think you've seen most of the more interesting parts."

Kim nodded. They had spent the day looking over ImmVac's installations, but they had still seen only a small fraction of Old Man Lever's vast commercial empire. More than ever, Kim had been conscious of the sheer scale of the world into which he had come. Down there, in the Clay, it was not possible to imagine the vastness of what existed *a wartha* – up Above. At times he found himself overawed by it all; wishing for somewhere smaller, darker, cosier in which to hide. But that feeling never lasted long. It was, he recognised, residual; part of the darker self he had shrugged off. No, this was his world now. The world of vast, continent-spanning Cities and huge Corporations battling for their share of Chung Kuo's markets.

He looked up. Lever was searching in one of the drawers of his desk. A moment later he straightened, clutching a bulky folder. Closing the drawer with his knee, he came round, thumping the file down beside Kim.

"Here. This might interest you."

Kim watched as Lever crossed the room and locked the big double doors with an old-fashioned key.

"You like old things, don't you?"

Lever turned, smiling. "I've never thought about it really. We've always done things this way. Handwritten research files, proper keys, wooden desks. I guess it makes us . . . different from the other North American Companies. Besides, it makes good sense. Computers are untrustworthy, easily accessed and subject to viruses. Likewise doorlocks and recognition units. But a good, old-fashioned key can't be beaten. In an age of guile, people are reluctant to use force – to break down a door or force open a drawer. The people who'd be most interested in our product have grown too used to sitting at their own desks to commit their crimes. To take the risk of entering one of our facilities would be beyond most of them." He laughed. "Besides, it's my father's policy to keep them happy with a constant flow of disinformation. Failed research, blind alleys, minor spin-offs of more important research programmes – that kind of thing. They tap into it and think they've got their finger on the pulse."

Kim grinned. "And they never learn?"

Lever shook his head, amused. "Not yet they haven't."

Kim looked down at the file. "And this?"

"Open it and see. Take it across to my desk if you want."

Kim flipped back the cover and looked, then turned his head sharply, staring at Lever. "Where did you get this?"

"You've seen it before?"

Kim looked down at it again. "I have . . . of course I have, but not in this form. Who . . . ?" Then he recognised the handwriting. The same handwriting that had been on the copy of the cancelled SimFic contract he had been given by Li Yuan. "Soren Berdichev . . ."

Lever was looking at him strangely now. "You knew?"

Kim gave a small, shuddering breath. "Six years ago. When I was on the Project."

"You met Berdichev there?"

"He bought my contract. For his Company, SimFic."

"Ah . . . Of course. Then you knew he'd written the File?"

Kim laughed strangely. "You think *Berdichev* wrote this?"

"Who else?"

Kim looked away. "So. He claimed it for his own."

Lever shook his head. "Are you trying to tell me he stole it from someone?"

In a small voice, Kim began to recite the opening of the File: the story of the pre-Socratic Greeks and the establishment of the Aristotelian Yes/No mode of thought. Lever stared back at him with mounting surprise.

"Shall I continue?"

Lever laughed. "So you do know it. But how? Who showed it to you?"

Kim handed it back. "I know because I wrote it."

Lever looked down at the folder then back at Kim, giving a small laugh of disbelief. "No," he said quietly. "You were only a boy."

Kim was watching Lever closely. "It was something I put together from some old computer records I unearthed. I thought Berdichev had had it destroyed. I never knew he'd kept a copy."

"And yet you knew nothing about the dissemination?"

"The dissemination?"

"You mean, you *really* didn't know?" Lever shook his head, astonished. "This here is the original, but there are a thousand more copies back in Europe, each one of them like this, handwritten. Now we're going to do the same over here – to disseminate them amongst those sympathetic to the cause."

"The cause?"

"The Sons of Benjamin Franklin. Oh, we'd heard rumours about the File and its contents some time back, but until recently we'd never seen it. Now, however . . ." he laughed, then shook his head again in amazement. "Well, it's like a fever in our blood. But you understand that, don't you, Kim? After all, you *wrote* the bloody thing!"

Kim nodded, but inside he felt numbed. He had never imagined . . .

"Here, look . . ." Lever led Kim over to one of the

364

tapestries. "I commissioned this a year ago, before I'd seen the file. We put it together from what we knew about the past. It shows how things were before the City."

Kim looked at it then shook his head. "It's wrong."

"Wrong?"

"Yes, all the details are wrong. Look." He touched one of the animals on the rocks in the foreground. "This is a lion. But it's an African lion. There never were any lions of this kind in America. And those wagons, crossing the plains, they would have been drawn by horses. The petrol engine was a much later development. And these tents here – they're Mongol in style. Red Indian tents were different. And then there are these pagodas . . ."

"But in the File it says . . ."

"Oh, it's not that these things didn't exist, it's just that they didn't exist at the same time nor in the same place. Besides, there were Cities even then – here on the east coast."

"Cities . . . but I thought . . ."

"You thought the Han invented Cities? No. Cities have been in Man's blood since the dawn of civilisation. Why, Security Central at Bremen is nothing more than a copy of the great zigurrat at Ur, built more than five thousand years ago."

Lever had gone very still. He was watching Kim closely, a strange intensity in his eyes. After a moment he shook his head, giving a soft laugh.

"You really *did* write it, didn't you?"

Kim nodded, then turned back to the tapestry. "And this . . ." he bent down, indicating the lettering at the foot of the picture, ". . . this is wrong, too."

Lever leaned forward, staring at the lettering. "How do you mean?"

"AD. It doesn't mean what's written here. That was another of Tsao Ch'un's lies. He was never related to the Emperor Tsao He, nor to any of them. So all of this business about the Ancestral Dynasties is a complete nonsense. Likewise BC. It doesn't mean 'Before the Crane'. In fact,

Tsao He, the 'Crane', supposedly the founder of the Han dynasty and ancestor of all subsequent dynasties, never even existed. In reality, Liu Chi-tzu, otherwise known as P'ing Ti, was Emperor at the time – and he was twelfth of the great Han dynasty emperors. So, you see, the Han adapted parts of their own history almost as radically as they changed that of the West. They had to – to make sense of things and keep it all consistent."

"So what do they really mean?"

"AD . . . that stands for *Anno Domini*. It's Latin – *Ta Ts'in* – for 'The Year of our Lord'."

"Our Lord?"

"Jesus Christ. You know, the founder of Christianity."

"Ah . . ." But Lever looked confused. "And BC? Is that Latin, too?"

Kim shook his head. "That's 'Before Christ'."

Lever laughed. "But that doesn't make sense. Why the mixture of languages? And why in the gods' names would the Han adopt a Christian dating for their calendar?"

Kim smiled. When one thought about it, it didn't make a great deal of sense, but that was how it was – how it had been for more than a hundred years before Tsao Ch'un arrived on the scene. It was the *Ko Ming* – the Communists – who had adopted the western calendar, and Tsao Ch'un, in rewriting the history of Chung Kuo, had found it easiest to keep the old measure. After all, it provided his historians with a genuine sense of continuity, especially after he had hit upon the idea of claiming that it dated from the first *real* Han dynasty, ruled, of course, by his ancestor, Tsao He, "the Crane".

"Besides . . ." Lever added, "I don't understand the importance of this Christ figure. I know you talk of all these wars fought in his name, but if he was so important why didn't the Han incorporate him into their scheme of things?"

Kim looked down, taking a long breath. So . . . they had read it but they had not understood. In truth, their reading of the File was, in its way, every bit as distorted as Tsao Ch'un's retelling of the world. Like the tapestry, they would put the past together as they wanted it, not as it really was.

He met Lever's eyes. "You forget. I didn't invent what's in the File. That's how it was. And Christ . . ." he sighed. "Christ was important to the West, in a way he wasn't to the Han. To the Han he was merely an irritation. Like the insects, they didn't want him in their City, so they built a kind of Net to keep him out."

Lever shivered. "It's like that term they use for us – *T'e an tsan* – 'innocent Westerners'. All the time they seek to denigrate us. To deny us what's rightfully ours."

"Maybe . . ." But Kim was thinking about Li Yuan's gifts. He, at least, had been given back what was his.

* * *

Ebert strode into the House of the Ninth Ecstasy, smiling broadly, then stopped, looking about him. Why was there no one here to greet him? What in the gods' names was the woman up to?

He called out, trying to keep the anger from his voice – "Mu Chua! Mu Chua, where are you?" – then crossed the room, pushing through the beaded curtain.

His eyes met a scene of total chaos. There was blood everywhere. Wine glasses had been smashed underfoot, trays of sweetmeats overturned and ground into the carpet. On the far side of the room a girl lay face down, as if drunk or sleeping.

He whirled about, drawing his knife, hearing sudden shrieking from the rooms off to his left. A moment later a man burst into the room. It was Hsiang K'ai Fan.

Hsiang looked very different from when Ebert had last seen him. His normally placid face was bright – almost incandescent – with excitement; his eyes popping out from the surrounding fat. His clothes, normally so immaculate, were dishevelled, the lavender silks ripped and spattered with blood. He held his ceremonial dagger out before him, the blade slick, shining wetly in the light, while, as if in some obscene parody of the blade, his penis poked out from between the folds of the silk, stiff and wet with blood.

"Lord Hsiang . . ." Ebert began, astonished by this transformation. "What has been happening here?"

Hsiang laughed: a strange, quite chilling cackle. "Oh, it's been wonderful, Hans . . . simply wonderful! I've had such fun. Such glorious fun!"

Ebert swallowed, not sure what to make of Hsiang's "fun", but quite sure that it spelt nothing but trouble for himself.

"Where's An Liang-chou? He's all right, isn't he?"

Hsiang grinned insanely, lowering the dagger. His eyes were unnaturally bright, the pupils tightly contracted. He was breathing strangely, his flabby chest rising and falling erratically. "An's fine. Fucking little girls, as usual. But Hans . . . your woman . . . she was magnificent. You should have seen the way she died. Oh, the orgasm I had. It was just as they said it would be. Immense it was. I couldn't stop coming. And then . . ."

Ebert shuddered. "You *what*?" He took a step forward. "What are you saying? Mu Chua is *dead*?"

Hsiang nodded, his excitement almost feverish now, his penis twitching as he spoke. "Yes, and then I thought . . . why not do it again. And again . . . After all, as she said, I could settle with Whiskers Lu when I was done."

Ebert stood there, shaking his head. "Gods . . ." He felt his fingers tighten about his dagger, then slowly relaxed his hand. If he killed Hsiang it would all be undone. No, he had to make the best of things. To make his peace with Whiskers Lu and get Hsiang and An out of here as quickly as possible. Before anyone else found out about this.

"How many have you killed?"

Hsiang laughed. "I'm not sure. A dozen. Fifteen. Maybe more . . ."

"Gods . . ."

Ebert stepped forward, taking the knife from Hsiang. "Come on," he said, worried by the look of fierce bemusement in Hsiang's face. "Fun's over. Let's get An and go home."

Hsiang nodded vaguely, then bowed his head, letting himself be led through.

Towards the back of the house things seemed almost normal. But as Ebert came to the Room of Heaven, he slowed, seeing the great streaks of blood smeared down the door frames, and guessed what lay within.

He pushed Hsiang aside, then went inside. A girl lay to one side, dead, her face bloody, her abdomen ripped open, the guts exposed, while, on the far side of the room lay Mu Chua, naked, face up, on the huge bed, her throat slit from ear to ear. Her flesh was ashen, as if bleached, the sheets beneath her dark with her blood.

He stood there, looking down at her a moment, then shook his head. Whiskers Lu would go mad when he heard about this. Mu Chua's house had been a key part of his empire, bringing him a constant flow of new contacts from the Above. Now, with Mu Chua dead, who would come?

Ebert took a deep breath. Yes, and Lu Ming-shao would blame him – for making the introduction. For not checking up on Hsiang before he let him go berserk down here. *If he had known* . . .

He twirled about, his anger bubbling over. "Fuck you, Hsiang! Do you know what you've done?"

Hsiang K'ai Fan stared back at him, astonished. "I b . . . beg your pardon?" he stammered.

"*This!*" Ebert threw his arm out, indicating the body on the bed, then grabbed Hsiang's arm and dragged him across the room. "What the fuck made you want to do it, eh? Now we've a bloody war on our hands! Or will have, unless you placate the man."

Hsiang shook his head, bewildered. "What man?"

"Lu Ming-shao. Whiskers Lu. He's the big Triad boss around these parts. He owned this place. And now you've gone and butchered his Madam. He'll go berserk when he finds out. He'll hire assassins to track you down and kill you."

369

He saw how Hsiang swallowed at that, how his eyes went wide with fear, and felt like laughing. But no, he could use this. Yes, maybe things weren't quite so bad after all. Maybe he could turn this to his advantage.

"Yes, he'll rip your throat out for this, unless . . ."

Hsiang pushed his head forward anxiously. "Unless . . . ?"

Ebert looked about him, considering. "This was one of his main sources of income. Not just from prostitution, but from other things too – drugs, illicit trading, blackmail. It must have been worth, oh, fifteen, twenty million *yuan* a year to him. And now it's worth nothing. Not since you ripped the throat out of it."

"I didn't know . . ." Hsiang shook his head, his hands trembling. His words came quickly now, tumbling from his lips. "I'll pay him off. Whatever it costs. My family is rich. Very rich. You know that, Hans. You could see this Whiskers Lu, couldn't you? You could tell him that. Please, Hans. Tell him I'll pay him what he asks."

Ebert nodded slowly, narrowing his eyes. "Maybe. But you must do something for me, too."

Hsiang nodded eagerly. "Anything, Hans. You only have to name it."

He stared at Hsiang contemptuously. "Just this. I want you to throw your party this afternoon – your *chao tai hui* – just as if nothing happened here. You understand? Whatever you or An did or saw here must be forgotten. Must never, in any circumstances, be mentioned. It must be as if it never was. Because if news of this gets out there will be recriminations. Quite awful recriminations. Understand?"

Hsiang nodded, a look of pure relief crossing his face.

"And Hsiang. This afternoon . . . don't worry about the girls. I'll provide *them*. You just make sure your friends are there."

Hsiang looked down, chastened, the madness gone from him. "Yes . . . As you say."

"Good. Then find your friend and be gone from here.

Take my sedan if you must, but go. I'll be in touch."

Hsiang turned, making to go, but Ebert called him back one last time.

"And Hsiang . . ."

Hsiang stopped and turned, one hand resting against the blood-stained upright of the door. "Yes?"

"Do this again and I'll kill you, understand?"

Hsiang's eyes flickered once in the huge expanse of flesh that was his face, then he lowered his head and backed away.

Ebert watched him go, then turned, looking down at Mu Chua again. It was a shame. She had been useful – very useful – over the years. But what was gone was gone. Dealing with Whiskers Lu was the problem now. That and rearranging things for the party later.

It had all seemed so easy when he'd spoken to DeVore earlier, but Hsiang had done his best to spoil things for him. Where, at this late stage, would he find another fifteen girls – special girls of the quality Mu Chua would have given him?

Ebert sighed, then, seeing the funny side of it, began to laugh, remembering the sight of Hsiang standing there, his penis poking out stiffly, for all the world like a miniature of his rat-like friend, An Liang-chou, staring out from beneath the fat of Hsiang's stomach.

Well, they would get theirs. They and all their friends. But he would make certain this time. He would inject the girls he sent to entertain them.

He smiled. Yes, and then he'd watch, as one by one they went down. Princes and cousins and all; every last one of them victims of the disease DeVore had bought from his friend, Curval.

How clever, he thought, to catch them that way. For who would think that that was what it was. He laughed. Syphilis . . . it had not been heard of in the Above for more than a century. Not since Tsao Ch'un had had his own son executed for giving it to his mother. No, and when they did find out it would be too late. Much too

371

late. By then the sickness would have spread throughout the great tree of the Families, infecting root and branch, drying up the sap. And then the tree would fall, like the rotten, stinking thing it was.

He shivered, then put his hand down, brushing the hair back from the dead woman's brow, frowning.

"Yes. But why did you do it, Mother? Why in hell's name did you let him do it to you? It can't have been the money . . ."

Ebert took his hand away, then shook his head. He would never understand – never in ten thousand years. To lie there while another cut your throat and fucked you. It made no sense. And yet . . .

He laughed sourly. That was exactly what his kind had done for the last one hundred and fifty years. Ever since the time of Tsao Ch'un. But now all that had changed. From now on things would be different.

He turned and looked across. Three of Mu Chua's girls were standing in the doorway, wide-eyed, huddled together, looking in at him.

"Call Lu Ming-shao," he said, going across, holding the eldest by the arm. "Tell him to come at once, but say nothing more. Tell him Hans Ebert wants to talk to him. About a business matter."

He let her go, then turned, facing the other two, putting his arms about their shoulders. "Now, my girls. Things seem uncertain, I know, but I've a special task for you, and if you do it well . . ."

* * *

Hsiang Wang leaned his vast bulk towards the kneeling messenger and let out a great huff of annoyance.

"What do you mean, my brother's ill? He was perfectly well this morning. What's happened to him?"

The messenger kept his head low, offering the handwritten note. "He asks you to accept his apologies, Excellency, and sends you this note."

Hsiang Wang snatched the note and unfolded it. For a

moment he grew still, reading it, then threw it aside, making a small, agitated movement of his head, cursing beneath his breath.

"He says all has been arranged, Excellency," the messenger continued, made uncomfortable by the proximity of Hsiang Wang's huge, trunk-like legs. "The last of the girls – the special ones – were hired this morning."

The messenger knew from experience what a foul temper Hsiang K'ai Fan's brother had and expected at any moment to be on the receiving end of it, but for once Hsiang Wang bridled-in his anger. Perhaps it was the fact that his guests were only a few *ch'i* away, listening beyond the wafer-thin wall, or perhaps it was something else: the realisation that, with his elder brother absent, he could play host alone. Whatever, it seemed to calm him and, with a curt gesture of dismissal, he turned away, walking back towards the great double doors that led through to the Hall of the Four Willows.

Hsiang Wang paused in the doorway, taking in the scene. From where he stood, five broad, grass-covered terraces led down, like crescent moons, to the great willow-leaf-shaped pool and the four ancient trees from which the hall derived its name. There were more than a hundred males from the Minor Families here this afternoon, young and old alike. Most of the Twenty-Nine were represented, each of the great clans distinguishable by the markings on the silk gowns the princes wore, but most were from the five great European Families of Hsiang and An, Pei, Yin and Chun. Girls went amongst them, smiling and laughing, stopping to talk or rest a gentle hand upon an arm or about a waist. The party had yet to begin and for the moment contact was restrained, polite. The sound of *erhu* and *k'un ti* – bow and bamboo flute – drifted softly in the air, mixing with the scents of honeysuckle and plum blossom.

Low tables were scattered about the terraces. The young princes surrounded these, lounging on padded couches, talking or playing *Chou*. On every side tall shrubs and plants and lacquered screens – each decorated with scenes of forests and mountains, spring pastures and moonlit rivers – broke up the stark geometry of the hall, giving it the look of a woodland glade.

Hsiang Wang smiled, pleased by the effect, then clapped his hands. At once doors opened to either side of him and servants spilled out down the terraces, bearing trays of wine and meats and other delicacies. Leaving the smile on his lips, he went down, moving across to his right, joining the group of young men gathered about Chun Wu-chi.

Chun Wu-chi was Head of the Chun Family; the only Head to honour the Hsiang clan with his presence this afternoon. He was a big man in his seventies, long-faced and bald, his pate polished like an ancient ivory carving, his sparse white beard braided into two thin plaits. Coming close to him, Hsiang Wang knelt, in *san k'ou*, placing his forehead to the ground three times before straightening up again.

"You are most welcome here, Highness."

Chun Wu-chi smiled. "I thank you for your greeting, Hsiang Wang, but where is your elder brother? I was looking forward to seeing him again."

"Forgive me, Highness," Hsiang said, lowering his head, "but K'ai Fan has been taken ill. He sends his deep regards and humbly begs your forgiveness."

Chun looked about him, searching the eyes of his close advisers to see whether this could be some kind of slight; then, reassured by what he saw, he looked back at Hsiang Wang, smiling, putting one bejewelled hand out towards him.

"I am sorry your brother is ill, Wang. Please send him my best wishes and my most sincere hope for his swift recovery."

Hsiang Wang bowed low. "I will do so, Highness. My Family is most honoured by your concern."

Chun gave the smallest nod, then looked away, his eyes searching the lower terraces. "There are many new girls here today, Hsiang Wang. Are there any with . . . *special* talents?"

Hsiang Wang smiled inwardly. He had heard of Chun Wu-chi's appetites. Indeed, they were legendary. When he was younger, it was said, he had had a hundred women, one after the other, for a bet. It had taken him three days, so the story went, and afterwards he had slept for fifty hours, only to wake keen to begin all over. Now, in his seventies, his fire had waned. Voyeurism had taken the place of more active pursuits.

"There is one girl, Highness . . ." he said, remembering what K'ai Fan had said. "I have been told that she can manage the most extraordinary feats."

"Really?" Chun Wu-chi's eyes lit up.

Hsiang Wang smiled. "Let me bring her, Highness." He looked about him at the younger men. "In the meantime, if the *ch'un tzu* would like to entertain themselves?"

On cue the lights overhead dimmed, the music grew more lively. From vents overhead subtle, sweet-scented hallucinogens wafted into the air.

As he made his way down to the pool, he saw how quickly some of the men, eager not to waste a moment, had drawn girls down on to the couches next to them, while one – a prince of the Pei family – had one girl massaging his neck and shoulders while another knelt between his legs.

Hsiang Wang laughed softly. There would be more outrageous sights than that before the day was done. Many more. He slowed, looking about him, then saw the girl and lifted his hand, summoning her.

She came across and stopped, bowing before him. A dainty little thing, her hair cut in swallow bangs. She looked up at him, revealing her perfect features, her delicate rosebud lips. "Yes, Excellency?"

He reached in his pocket and took out the thousand *yuan* chip he had stashed there earlier, handing it to her. "You know what to do?"

She nodded, a smile coming to her lips.

"Good . . . then go and introduce yourself. I'll have the servants bring the beast."

He watched her go, glad that he had gone through all this with his brother two days before.

Sick. What a time for K'ai Fan to fall sick! Surely he knew how important this occasion was for the Family? Hsiang Wang shuddered, then threw off his irritation. It could not be helped, he supposed. And if he could please Old Chun, who knew what advantages he might win for himself?

He hurried back in time to see the servants bring the beast. The Ox-man stood there passively, its three-toed hands at its sides, looking about it nervously, its almost-human eyes filled with anxiety. Seeing it, some of the younger princes laughed among themselves and leaned close to exchange words. Hsiang Wang smiled and moved closer, standing at Chun's shoulder. At once another girl approached and knelt at Chun's side, her flank against his leg, one hand resting gently on his knee.

Chun looked down briefly, smiling, then looked back, studying the girl and the beast, one hand tugging at his beard, an expression of interest on his long, heavily lined face.

Hsiang raised his hand. At once the servants came forward, tearing the fine silks from the Ox-man's back, tugging down its velvet trousers. Then they stood back. For a moment it stood there, bewildered, trembling, its big, dark-haired body exposed. Then, with a low, cow-like moan, it turned its great head, as if looking to escape.

At once the girl moved closer, putting one hand up to its chest, calming it, whispering words of reassurance. Again it lowed, but now it was looking down, its eyes on the girl.

From the couches to either side of Chun Wu-chi came laughter. Laughter and a low, excited whisper.

Slowly she began to stroke the beast, long, sensuous strokes that began high up in the beast's furred chest and ended low down, between its heavily muscled legs. It was not long before it was aroused, its huge member poking up stiffly into the air, glistening, long and wet and pinky-red in the half-light – a lance of quivering, living matter.

As the girl slipped her gown from her shoulders, there was a low murmur of approval. Now she stood there, naked, holding the beast's huge phallus in one hand, while with the other she continued to stroke its chest.

Its lowing now had a strange, inhuman urgency to it. It turned its head from side to side, as if in pain, its whole body trembling, as if at any moment it might lose control. One hand lifted, moving towards the girl, then withdrew.

Then, with a small, teasing smile at Chun Wu-chi, the girl lowered her head and took the beast deep into her mouth.

There was a gasp from all round. Hsiang, watching, saw how the girl he had assigned to Chun was working the old man, burrowed beneath his skirts, doing to him exactly what the other was doing to the Ox-man. He smiled. From the look of pained pleasure on the old man's face, Chun Wu-chi would not forget this evening quickly.

* * *

It was just after nine and in the great Hall of Celestial Destinies at Nantes spaceport a huge crowd milled about. The eight twenty rocket from Boston had come in ten minutes back and the final security clearances were being made before its passengers were passed through into the hall.

Lehmann stood at the base of the statue in the centre of the hall, waiting. DeVore had contacted him an hour and a half back to say he would be on the eight twenty. He had sounded angry and irritable, but when Lehmann had pressed him about the trip, he had seemed enthusiastic. It was something else, then, that had soured his mood – something that had happened back here, in his absence – and there was only one thing that could have done that: the failure of the assassination attempt on Tolonen.

Was that why DeVore had asked him to meet him here?

To try again? It made sense, certainly, for despite all their "precautions" the last thing Security *really* expected was a new attempt so shortly after the last.

He turned, looking up at the giant bronze figures. He knew that the composition was a lie, part of the Great Lie the Han had built along with their City; even so there was an underlying truth to it, for the Han *had* triumphed over the *Ta Ts'in*. Kan Ying *had* bowed before Pan Chao. Or at least, their descendants had. But for how much longer would the dream of Rome be denied?

For himself, it was unimportant. Han or *Hung Mao*, it did not matter who ruled the great circle of Chung Kuo. Even so, in the great struggle that was to come, his ends would be served. Whoever triumphed, the world would be no longer as it was. Much that he hated would, of necessity, be destroyed, and in that process of destruction – of purification – a new spirit would be unleashed. New and yet quite ancient. Savage and yet pure, like an eagle circling in the cold clear air above the mountains.

He looked away. A new beginning, that was what the world needed. A new beginning, free of all this.

Lehmann looked about him, studying those making their way past him, appalled by the emptiness he saw in every face. Here they were, all the half-men and half-women and all their little halflings, hurrying about their empty, meaningless lives. On their brief, sense-dulled journey to the Oven Man's door.

And then?

He shivered, oppressed suddenly by the crush, by the awful perfumed stench of those about him. This now – this brief moment of time before it began – was a kind of tiger's mouth; that moment before one surrounded one's opponent's stone, robbing it of breath. It was a time of closing options. Of fast and desperate plays.

There was a murmuring throughout the hall as the announcement boards at either end showed that the passengers from the eight twenty Boston rocket were coming through. Lehmann was about to go across when he noticed two men making their way through the crowd, their faces set, their whole manner subtly different.

Security? No. For a start they were Han. Moreover, there was something fluid, almost rounded about their movements; something one never found in the more rigorously and classically trained Security élite. No. These were more likely Triad men. Assassins. But who were they after? Who else was on DeVore's flight? Some Company head? Or was this a gang matter?

He followed them surreptitiously, interested; wanting to observe their methods.

The gate at the far end of the hall was open now and passengers were spilling out. Looking past the men he saw DeVore, his neat, tidy figure making its way swiftly but calmly through the press. The men were exactly halfway between him and DeVore, some ten or fifteen *ch'i* in front of him, when he realised his mistake.

"Howard!"

DeVore looked up, alerted, and saw at once what was happening. The two assassins were making directly for him now, less than two body lengths away, their blades out, slashing at anyone who got in their way, intent on reaching their quarry. Beyond them Lehmann was pushing his way through the crowd, yelling at people to get out of his way, but it would be several seconds before he could come to DeVore's aid.

DeVore moved forward sharply, bringing the case he was carrying up into the face of the first man as he came out of the crowd in front of him. Hampered by a woman at his side, the assassin could only jerk his head back, away. At once DeVore kicked out, making him stagger back. But even as he did, the second assassin was upon him, his notched knife swinging through the air at DeVore's head.

The speed at which DeVore turned surprised the man. One hand countered the knife blow at the wrist while the other punched to the ribs. The assassin went down with a sharp cry.

DeVore turned, facing the first assassin, feinting once,

twice with his fists before he twisted and kicked. The assassin moved back expertly, but before he could counter, he sank to his knees, Lehmann's knife embedded in his back.

There was shouting and screaming from all sides of them now.

"Come away," Lehmann said quietly, taking DeVore's arm. "Before Security come!" But DeVore shrugged him off, going over to the second man.

The would-be assassin lay there, helpless, clutching his side, gasping with pain. DeVore had shattered his rib-cage, puncturing his lung. He crouched close, over the man, one hand at his throat.

"Who sent you?"

The man pushed his face up at DeVore's and spat.

DeVore wiped the bloodstained phlegm from his cheek and reached across to pick up the assassin's blade. Then, as the man's eyes widened, he slit open his shirt and searched his torso for markings.

DeVore turned, looking up at Lehmann, a fierce anger in his face. "He's not Triad and he's not Security, so who the fuck . . . ?"

The third man came from nowhere.

DeVore had no time to react. It was only accident that saved him. As Lehmann turned, he moved between DeVore and the man, glancing against the assassin's knife arm. The knife, which would have entered DeVore's heart, was nudged to one side, piercing DeVore between neck and shoulder.

The assassin jerked the serrated knife out savagely from DeVore's flesh, but before he could strike again, Lehmann had lashed out, punching his nose up into his skull. The man fell and lay still.

DeVore sank to his knees, holding one hand over the wound, a look of astonishment on his bloodless face. This time Lehmann didn't ask. With a single blow he finished off the second man, then turned and did the same to the third. Then, lifting DeVore on to his shoulder, ignoring the shouts of protest from all about him, he began to carry him towards the exit and the safety of the transit, praying that their man in Security could hold his fellows off a minute longer.

As for DeVore's question, he had his answer now, for that last man had been a *Hung Mao*, a face they'd seen often in the past: one of several who had always been there in the background at their meetings with the *Ping Tiao*. A guard. One of the ones who had defected to the *Yu*.

So it was Mach, Jan Mach, who'd tried to have them killed.

CHAPTER·12

WILLOW-PLUM SICKNESS

On the open, windswept hillside the small group gathered about the grave. Across the valley, cloud shadow drew a moving line that descended, crossing the water, then came swiftly up the slope towards them.

Ben watched the shadow sweep towards him, then felt the sudden chill as the sun passed behind the cloud.

So it is, he thought. *As swift as that it comes.*

The wooden casket lay on thick silken cords beside the open grave. Ben stood there, facing the casket across the darkness of the hole, his feet only inches from the drop.

Earth. Dark earth. It had rained and tiny beads of moisture clung to the stems of grass overhanging the grave. In the sunlight they seemed strange, incongruous.

It was still unreal. Or not yet real. He felt no grief as yet, no strong feeling for what he had lost, only a vacancy, a sense of his own inattentiveness. As if he had missed something . . .

They were all in black, even Li Yuan. Blackness for death. The old Western way of things. His mother stood beside the casket, her face veiled, grieving heavily. Beside him stood his sister, and next to her Li Yuan's Chancellor, Nan Ho.

A cold wind gusted from the south across the hilltop, blowing his hair into his eyes. A sea breeze, heavy with brine. He combed strands back into place with his fingers, then left his hand there, the fingers buried in his fine, thick hair, his palm pressed firmly against his forehead. Like an amnesiac. A sleeper.

He felt like an actor, the outer shell dissociated from the inner core of himself: the "boy in black" at the graveside. An impostor. Neither loving nor dutiful. Cuckoo in the nest. Too distanced from things to be his father's son, his brother's brother.

Had he ever even said he loved him?

Two of Li Yuan's men came and lifted the casket on its cords.

Ben moved back as they lowered the casket into the earth. A cassette of death, slotting into the hillside.

And no rewind . . . no playback. Hal Shepherd existed only in the memories of others now. And when they in their turn died? Was it all simply a long process of forgetting? Of blinded eyes and decaying images? Maybe . . . but it didn't have to be.

The earth fell. He closed his eyes and could see it falling, covering the pale wood of the casket. Could hear the sound of the earth tumbling against the wood. A hollow, empty sound.

He opened his eyes. The hole was a shallow depression of uneven darkness. The T'ang's men had ceased shovelling.

He felt the urge to bend down and touch the cold, dark earth. To crush it between his fingers and feel its gritty texture, its cool, inanimate substance. Instead he watched as Li Yuan stepped forward and pressed the young tree into the pile of earth, firming it down, then moving back to let the servants finish their task.

No words. No graven stones. This was his father's wish. Only a tree. A young oak.

Ben shivered, his thoughts drawn elsewhere. What was the darkness like on the other side of being? Was it *only* a nothingness? *Only* blank, empty darkness?

They walked back along the path, down to the cottage by the bay, Li Yuan holding his mother's arm, consoling her, Nan Ho walking beside his sister. Ben came last, alone, several paces behind.

His father's death. Expected so long, it had nonetheless

come like a blow of evil fate to his mother. He had heard her crying in the night: a sound that could not be described, only heard and remembered. A wordless noise, connected to the grieving animal deep within the human – a sound drawn from the great and ancient darkness of our racial being. An awful, desolate sound. Once heard it could never be forgotten.

He turned and looked back. There was no sign of the grave, the fledgling tree. Banks of iron grey cloud were massed above the hillside. In a while it would rain.

He turned and looked down the slope at the cottage and the bay beyond, seeing it all anew. Where was its paradigm? Where the designer of all this? The shaping force?

Death had unlocked these questions, forcing his face relentlessly against the glass.

He sighed, then walked on, making his slow way down.

* * *

Li Yuan stood in the centre of Ben's room, looking about him. Ben was hunched over his desk, working, making notations in a huge, loose-leafed book, the pages of which were covered in strange diagrams.

It was not what Li Yuan had expected. The room was cluttered and untidy, totally lacking, it seemed, in any organisational principle. Things were piled here, there and everywhere, as if discarded and forgotten, while one whole wall was taken up by numerous half-completed pencil sketches depicting parts of the human anatomy.

He looked back at Ben, seeing how tense he was, crouched over the big, square-paged book, and felt a ripple of unease pass through him. It did not seem right, somehow, to be working on the day of his father's funeral. Li Yuan moved closer, looking over Ben's shoulder at the diagram he was working on – seeing only a disorganised mess of lines and shapes and coded instructions, set down in a dozen brilliant colours on the underlying grid, like the scribblings of a child.

"What is that?"

Ben finished what he was doing, then turned, looking up at the young T'ang.

"It's a rough."

"A rough?" Li Yuan laughed. "A rough of what?"

"No . . . that's what I call it. All of these are instructions. The dark lines – those in brown, orange and red, mainly, are instructions to the muscles. The small circles in blue, black and mauve – those are chemical input instructions; the nature of the chemical and the dosage marked within the circle. The rectangular blocks are just that – blocks. They indicate when no input of any kind is passing through the particular node."

"Nodes?" Li Yuan was thoroughly confused by this time.

Ben smiled. "*Pai pi*. You know, the old artificial reality experiments. I've been working on them these last fifteen months. I call them Shells. This here is an input instruction diagram. As I said, a rough. These eighty-one horizontal lines represent the input points, and these forty vertical lines represent the dimension of time – twenty to a second."

Li Yuan frowned. "I still don't understand. Inputs into what?"

"Into the recipient's body. Come. I'll show you. Downstairs."

They went down, into the basement workrooms. There, at one end of the long, low-ceilinged room, almost hidden by the clutter of other machinery, was the Shell. It was a big, elaborately decorated casket; like something one might use for an imperial lying-in-state, the lid lacquered a midnight black.

Ben stood beside it, looking back at Li Yuan. "The recipient climbs in here and is wired up – the wires being attached to eighty-one special input points both in the brain and at important nerve-centres throughout the body. That done, the casket is sealed, effectively cutting the recipient off from all external stimuli. That absence of stimuli is an unnatural state for the human body: if denied sensory input for too long the mind begins to hallucinate. Using this well-documented receptivity of the sensory apparatus to false stimuli, we can provide the mind with a complete alternative experience."

Li Yuan stared at the apparatus a moment longer, then looked back at the Shepherd boy. "Complete? How complete?"

Ben was watching him, as a hawk watches a rabbit. An intense, predatory stare.

"As complete as the real thing. If the art is good enough."

"The art . . . I see." Li Yuan frowned. It seemed such a strange thing to want to do. To create an art that mimicked life so closely. An art that *supplanted* life. He reached out and touched the skeletal frame that hung to one side, noting the studded inputs about head and chest and groin. Eighty-one inputs in all. "But why?"

Ben stared at him as if he didn't understand the question, then handed him a book similar to the one he had been working on in his room. "These, as I said, are the roughs. They form the diagrammatic outline of an event-sequence – a story. Eventually those lines and squiggles and dots will become events. Sensory actualities. Not real, yet indistinguishable from the real."

Li Yuan stared at the open page and nodded, but it still didn't explain. Why this need for fictions? For taking away what was and filling it with something different? Wasn't life itself enough?

Ben was leaning close now, looking into his face, his eyes filled with an almost insane intensity, his voice a low whisper.

"It's like being a god. You can do whatever you want. Create whatever you want to create. Things that never happened. That never *could* happen."

Li Yuan laughed uncomfortably. "Something that never happened? But why should you want to do that? Isn't there enough diversity in the world as it is?"

Ben looked at him curiously, then looked away, as if disappointed. "No. You miss my point."

It was said quietly, almost as if it didn't matter. As if, in that brief instant between the look and the words he had made his mind up about something.

"Then what *is* the point?" Li Yuan insisted, setting the book down on the padded innards of the casket.

Ben looked down, his hand reaching out to touch the apparatus. For the first time Li Yuan noticed that the hand was artificial. It seemed real, but the deeply etched ridge of skin gave it away. Once revealed, other signs added to the impression. There was an added subtlety of touch; a deftness of movement just beyond the human range.

"Your question is larger than you think, Li Yuan. It questions not merely what I do, but all art, all fiction, all dreams of other states. It asserts that 'what is' is enough. My argument is that 'what is' is insufficient. We need more than 'what is'. Much more."

Li Yuan shrugged. "Maybe. But this takes it too far, surely? It seems a kind of mockery. Life is good. Why seek this false perfection?"

"Do you really believe that, Li Yuan? Are you sure there's nothing my art could give you that life couldn't?"

Li Yuan turned away, as if stung. He was silent for some time, then he looked back, a grim expression of defiance changing his features. "Only illusions, my friend. Nothing real. Nothing solid and substantial."

Ben shook his head. "You're wrong. I could give you something so real, so solid and substantial that you could hold it in your arms – could taste it and smell it and never for a moment know that you were only dreaming."

Li Yuan stared at him, aghast, then looked down. "I don't believe you," he said finally. "It could never be that good."

"Ah, but it will."

Li Yuan lifted his head angrily. "Can it give you back your father? Can it do that?"

387

The boy did not flinch. His eyes caught Li Yuan's and held them. "Yes. Even that, if I wanted it."

★ ★ ★

Li Yuan arrived at Tongjiang two hours later to find things in chaos, the audience hall packed with his ministers and advisers. While the T'ang changed, Nan Ho went among the men, finding out what had been happening in their brief absence.

When Li Yuan returned to his study, Nan Ho was waiting for him, his face flushed, his whole manner extremely agitated.

"What is it, Nan Ho? What has got my ministers in such a state?"

Nan Ho bowed low. "It is not just your ministers, *Chieh Hsia*. The whole of the Above is in uproar. They say that more than two hundred are ill already, and that more than a dozen have died."

Li Yuan sat forward. "Ill? *Died?* What do you mean?"

Nan Ho looked up at him. "There is an epidemic, *Chieh Hsia*, sweeping through the Minor Families. No one knows quite what it is . . ."

Li Yuan stood angrily and came round his desk. "No one knows? Am I to believe this? Where are the Royal Surgeons? Have them come to me at once."

Nan Ho lowered his head. "They are outside, *Chieh Hsia*, but . . ."

"No buts, Master Nan. Get them in here now. If there is an epidemic we must act fast."

Nan Ho brought them in, then stood back, letting his T'ang question the men directly.

The eight old men stood there, their ancient bodies bent forward awkwardly.

"Well?" he said, facing the most senior of them. "What has been happening, Surgeon Yu? Why have you not been able to trace the source of this disease?"

"*Chieh Hsia* . . ." the old man began, his voice quavering. "Forgive me, but the facts contradict themselves."

"Nonsense!" Li Yuan barked, clearly angry. "Do you know the cause of the disease or not?"

The old man shook his head, distressed. "Forgive me, *Chieh Hsia*, but it is not possible. The Families are bred immune. For more than one hundred and fifty years . . ."

Li Yuan huffed impatiently. "Impossible? *Nothing* is impossible! I've just come from Hal Shepherd's funeral. They killed him, remember? With a cancer. Something that, according to you, was quite impossible. So what have they come up with now?"

The old man glanced sideways at his colleagues, then spoke again. "It seems, from our first tests, that what the victims are suffering from is what we term *yang mei ping*, 'Willow-plum sickness'."

Li Yuan laughed. "A fancy name, Surgeon Yu, but what does it mean?"

Nan Ho answered for the old man. "It is syphilis, *Chieh Hsia*. A sexually transmitted disease that affects the brain and drives its victims insane. This strain, apparently, is a particularly virulent and fast-working one. Besides sidestepping the natural immunity of its victims, it has a remarkably short incubation period. Many of its victims are dead within thirty hours of getting the dose."

Surgeon Yu looked at Nan Ho gratefully, then nodded. "That is so, *Chieh Hsia*. However, it seems that this particular strain affects only those of Han origin. As far as we can make out, no *Hung Mao* are affected."

Li Yuan turned away, recognising at once the implications of the thing. Willow-plum sickness . . . He had a vague recollection of reading about the disease. It was one of those many sicknesses the *Hung Mao* had brought with them when they had first opened China up, in the seventeenth and eighteenth centuries. But this was worse, far worse than anything those ancient seatraders had spread among the port women, because this time his kind had no natural immunity to it. None at all.

He turned back. "Are you certain, Surgeon Yu?"

"As certain as we can be, *Chieh Hsia*."

"Good. Then I want you to isolate each victim and question them as to who they have slept with in the past thirty days. Then I want all contacts traced and isolated. Understand?"

He looked past Yu at his Chancellor. "Nan Ho . . . I want you to contact all the heads of the Minor Families and have them come here, at once. By my express order."

Nan Ho bowed. "*Chieh Hsia* . . ."

And meanwhile he would call his fellow T'ang. For action must be taken. Immediate action, before the thing got out of hand.

★ ★ ★

Karr was buttoning his tunic when Chen came into the room, barely stopping to knock. He turned from the mirror, then stopped, seeing the look of delight on Chen's face.

"What is it?"

Chen handed Karr a file. "It's our friend. There's no doubt about it. These are stills taken from a Security surveillance film thirty-two hours back at Nantes spaceport."

Karr flipped the folder open and flicked through the stills a moment, then looked back at Chen, his face lit up. "Then we've got him, neh?"

Chen's face fell. He shook his head.

"*What?*"

"I'm afraid not. It seems his man, Lehmann, just picked him up and carried him out of there."

"And no one intercepted him? Where were Security?"

"Waiting for orders."

Karr made to speak, then understood. "Gods . . . *Again?*"

Chen nodded.

"And the Security Captain. He committed suicide, neh?"

Chen sighed. "That's right. It fits the pattern. I checked back in their surveillance records. The computer registers that a man matching DeVore's description passed through Nantes spaceport four times in the past month."

"And there was no Security alert?"

"No. Nor would there have been. The machine was reprogrammed to ignore the instruction from Bremen. As he was wearing false retina, the only way they could have got him was by direct facial recognition, and because they rely so heavily on computer-generated alerts, the chance of that was minimal."

"So how did we get these?"

Chen laughed. "It seems there was a fairly high-ranking Junior Minister on the same flight as DeVore. He complained about the incident direct to Bremen, and when they discovered they had no record of the event they instigated an immediate enquiry. This resulted."

Karr sat down heavily, then, setting the file to one side, began to pull on his boots. For a moment he was quiet, thoughtful, then he looked up again.

"Do we know where he'd been?"

"Boston. But who he saw there or what he was doing we don't yet know. Our friends in North American Security are looking into it right now."

"And the assassins?" Karr asked, pulling on the other boot. "Do we know who they were?"

Chen shrugged. "The two Han look like Triad assassins, but the third . . . well, we have him on record as a probable *Ping Tiao* sympathiser."

Karr looked up, raising his eyebrows. "*Ping Tiao?* But they don't exist any longer. At least, that's what our contacts down below tell us. Our friend Ebert is supposed to have wiped them out."

Chen nodded. "You don't think . . . ?"

Karr laughed. "Even Ebert wouldn't be stupid enough to try to work with the *Ping Tiao*. DeVore wouldn't let him."

"So what do you think?"

Karr shook his head. "We don't know enough, that's clear. Who, beside ourselves, would want DeVore dead?"

"Someone he's crossed?"

Karr laughed. "Yes. But that could be anyone, neh? Anyone at all."

* * *

Li Yuan looked out across the marbled expanse of the Hall of the Seven Ancestors and nodded to himself, satisfied. The space between the dragon pillars was packed. More than two thousand men – all the adult males of the Twenty-Nine – were gathered here this afternoon. All, that was, but those who had already succumbed to the sickness.

He sat there on the High Throne, dressed in the dragon robe of imperial yellow edged with blue. In one hand he held the Special Edict, in the other the bamboo cane with the silver cap that had been his brother's present to his father.

There was the faintest murmur from below, but when he stood the hall fell silent, followed a moment later by a loud rustling of expensive silks as, in a single movement, the great crowd knelt, touching their heads to the floor three times in the ritual *liu k'ou*. Li Yuan smiled bleakly, remembering another day, nine years ago – the day when his father had summoned the leaders of the Dispersionists before him, here in this very hall, and humbled them, making their leader, Lehmann, give up his friend, Wyatt. Much had changed since then, but once again the will of the T'ang had to be imposed. By agreement it was hoped, but by force, if necessary.

Li Yuan came down, stopping three steps from the bottom, facing the five elderly men who stood at the front of the crowd. His Chancellor, Nan Ho, stood to the right, the list scrolled tightly in one hand. Behind him, just beyond the nearest of the dragon pillars, a troop of élite guards waited, their shaven heads bowed low.

He looked past the five Family heads at the great press of men behind them. All had their heads lowered, their eyes averted, acknowledging his supremacy. Right now they were obedient, but would they remain so when they knew his purpose? Would they understand the need for this, or would they defy him? He shivered, then looked back at the five who stood closest.

He saw how the hands of nephews and cousins reached from behind Chun Wu-chi, supporting him, keeping him from falling; saw how frail his once-father-in-law, Yin Tsu, had become; how the first signs of senility had crept into the eighty-three-year-old face of Pei Ro-hen. Only An Sheng and Hsiang Shao-erh, both men in their fifties, seemed robust. Even so, the Minor Families had thrived — a dozen, fifteen sons not uncommon amongst them — while the Seven had diminished. Why was that? he wondered for the first time. Was it merely the pressures of rule, the depredations of war and politics, or was it symptomatic of some much deeper malaise?

There was silence in the hall, but behind it he could feel the invisible pressure of their expectations. Many of them had heard rumours of the sickness; even so, most were wondering why he had summoned them. Why, in this unprecedented manner, they were standing here in the Great Hall at Tongjiang, waiting for him to speak.

Well, now they would know. He would put paid to all speculation.

"Ch'un tzu!" he began, his voice resonant, powerful. "I have summoned you here today because we face a crisis — perhaps the greatest crisis the Families have ever faced."

Li Yuan looked across the sea of lowered heads, aware of the power he exercised over these men, but conscious also of what that power rested upon. They obeyed him because they had agreed among themselves to obey him. Take away that agreement — that mandate — and what followed?

He took a breath then continued.

"More than fifty of our number are dead. Another three hundred, I am told, are sick or close to death. And the cause of this mysterious illness? Something we thought we had rid ourselves of long ago – *yang mei ping*. Willow-plum sickness!"

There was an audible murmur of surprise and a number of heads moved agitatedly, but as yet no one dared meet his eyes. He moved on, keeping his voice calm, letting the authority of his position fill his words.

"In the past, I am told, the disease would have killed only after long months of suffering, leading to blindness and eventual madness, but this is a new, more virulent strain – one that our Families are no longer immune to. It is a brain-killer. It can strike down a healthy man – or woman – in less than thirty hours, though, as is the way of such diseases, not all succumb immediately to the virus but become carriers. That, in itself, is horrible enough, but this strain, it seems, is particularly vile, for it is racially specific. It affects only we Han."

Shocked faces were looking up at him now, forgetting all propriety. Deliberately ignoring this lapse, Li Yuan pressed on, saying what must be said.

"Such are the facts. What we must now ask ourselves is what must we do to combat this disease? There is no cure nor is there time to find one. No cure, that is, but the most drastic of preventative measures."

Hsiang Shao-erh was looking up at him, his eyes half-lidded, deeply suspicious. "What do you mean, *Chieh Hsia?*"

Li Yuan met the older man's gaze firmly. "I mean that we must test everyone in this hall. Wives and children too. And then we must find those outside the Families – man or woman – who have been in contact with anyone from the Families."

"In contact, *Chieh Hsia?*"

The words were framed politely, but he noted Hsiang's hostility. Hsiang had already lost his eldest son to the virus and it was clear that he saw the drift of Li Yuan's speech.

He answered unflinchingly. "In *sexual* contact. How else do you think the disease was spread?"

Again he felt the ripples of shock pass through the Hall.

Despite his reference to Willow-plum sickness, many had simply not understood until that moment. A low buzz ran from one end of the hall to the other.

"But surely, *Chieh Hsia* . . . ?"

Li Yuan cut Hsiang off sharply, his patience snapping. "Silence! All of you, be silent now! I have not finished."

The hall fell silent, heads were lowered again, but only a pace or so from him, Hsiang glared back at him, bristling with anger. Li Yuan looked past him, addressing the great mass.

"We must test everyone. We must track down every last victim – especially the carriers – of this disease."

"And then?" The voice was Hsiang Shao-erh's. Stubborn, defiant.

Li Yuan looked back at him. "And then they must die."

The hall erupted. Li Yuan looked out across the seething crowd, seeing the angry opposition, but also the strong agreement, his words had engendered. Arguments raged on every side. Just beneath him, Hsiang Shao-erh and An Sheng were protesting loudly, their arms gesticulating, their faces dark with anger, while Yin Tsu and Pei Ro-han attempted to remonstrate with them. For a while he let it go on, knowing that this violent flood of feelings must be allowed its channel, then he raised one hand, palm outward. Slowly the hall fell silent again.

He looked down at Hsiang Shao-erh. "You wish to say something, cousin?"

Hsiang took a pace forward, placing one foot on the first step of the High Throne, seeming almost to threaten his T'ang. He spat the words out angrily.

"I protest, *Chieh Hsia*! You cannot do this! We are Family, not *hsiao jen*! Never in our history have we been subjected to such humiliation! To make us take this test of yours would be to undermine our word, our honour as *ch'un tzu*! Why, it is tantamount to saying that we are all fornicators and cheats on our wives!"

Li Yuan shook his head. "And the deaths? The spread

of the disease? Are these things mere ghosts and idle rumours?"

"There are a few, I admit. Young bucks . . . but even so . . ."

"A *few*!" Li Yuan spat the words back angrily, almost contemptuously, taking a step forward, almost pushing his face into Hsiang's, forcing him to take a step back. "You are a fool, Hsiang, to think of face at such a time! Do you really believe I would do this if it were not necessary? Do you think I would risk damaging my relationship with you, my cousins, if there were not some far greater threat?"

Hsiang opened his mouth, then closed it again, taken aback by the unexpected violence of Li Yuan's counter-attack.

"This is a war," Li Yuan said, looking past him again, addressing the massed sons and cousins. "And upon its outcome depends how Chung Kuo will be in years to come. Whether there will be good, stable rule – the rule of Seven and Twenty-Nine – or chaos. To think that we can fight such a war without losses – without sacrifices – is both ridiculous and untenable."

He looked back directly at Hsiang. "Do not mistake me, Hsiang Shao-erh. Face, honour, a man's word – these are the very things that bind our society in times of peace, and I would defend them before any man, yet in times of war we must let go sometimes of our high ideals, if but briefly. We must bow, like the reeds before the wind, or go down, like a great tree in a storm."

Hsiang lowered his eyes. "*Chieh Hsia* . . ."

"Good. Then you will sign the paper, Hsiang Shao-erh?"

Hsiang looked up again. "The paper?"

Nan Ho brought the scroll across. Li Yuan turned, offering it to Hsiang. "Here. I have prepared a document. I would not have it said that the compact between Seven and Twenty-Nine was broken. There must be agreement between us, even in this matter."

Li Yuan stood there, holding the document out towards Hsiang Shao-erh. As his father had, so he now seemed the very embodiment of imperial power; unyielding, like the famous rock in the Yellow River which, for centuries, had withstood the greatest of floods.

Hsiang stared at the scroll, then looked up at his T'ang, his voice smaller suddenly, more querulous. "And if any here refuse?"

Li Yuan did not hesitate. "Then the compact is ended, the Great Wheel broken."

Hsiang shuddered. For a moment longer he stood there, hesitant, staring at the document. Then, suddenly, he lowered his head. "Very well, *Chieh Hsia*. I will sign."

★ ★ ★

Afterwards, while the Families were queuing to be tested, Nan Ho went to Li Yuan in his study.

"Forgive me, *Chieh Hsia*," he said, bowing low, "but I did not understand. Why did Hsiang Shao-erh oppose you just now? I would have thought, with his eldest son dead, he would have been the first to sanction your actions – to prevent the deaths of more of his sons."

Li Yuan sighed. "So it would have been, I'm sure, Master Nan, but the *chao tai hui* where the sickness was originally spread was held on Hsiang's estate. Oh, he had nothing to do with the organisation of the affair – that was all his son, K'ai Fan's doing – nor was Hsiang Shao-erh responsible for the sickness itself. However, he *feels* responsible. Many among the Twenty-Nine blame him, irrational as that is. As a consequence he has lost great face. That display today was an attempt to regain his face. Unfortunately, I could not allow it. Now, I am afraid, I have made an enemy."

"Things can be smoothed over, surely, *Chieh Hsia*? A gift, perhaps . . ."

Li Yuan shook his head. "I made him challenge me. And then I broke him before his equals. It had to be done, but there is no repairing it. No, so we must watch ourselves from that quarter from henceforth. Wang Sau-leyan is sure to hear of what happened here today. No doubt he will try to exploit the division between Hsiang and me."

The Chancellor shook his head, then looked up again. "Forgive me, *Chieh Hsia*, but do you not think death too extreme a penalty? After all, it was not their fault that they picked up this sickness. Have you not considered, perhaps, castrating those found with the virus. Those, that is, who would not die of it anyway."

"No, Master Nan. Had they been servants we might well have done that, but these are Family. Such a humiliation would have been worse than death for them. Besides, what of the women they have infected? What are we to do with them? Sew them up?"

Nan Ho gave a brief, uncomfortable laugh, then bowed his head. "I had not thought, *Chieh Hsia.*"

Li Yuan smiled sadly. "Never mind. Go now, Nan. Go and supervise the screening. I will expect you three hours from now to give your report on the proceedings."

"*Chieh Hsia . . .*"

Li Yuan sat back. There were other things to consider now; other sicknesses to rid the world of. The Young Sons, for instance, and the virus of the Aristotle File. He sighed and leaned forward again, punching in the code that would connect him with Tsu Ma in Astrakhan.

It was time to act. Time to draw in the nets and see what fish they had caught.

* * *

Wu Shih, T'ang of North America, raised his eyes from the small screen inset into his desk and looked across at the huge image of Li Yuan's face that filled the facing wall.

He gave a deep sigh, then placed his hands palm down on the desk, clearly disturbed by what he had just seen.

"Well, cousin. I must thank you. The tape is quite conclusive. Even so, I feel nothing but sadness that it has come to this. I had hoped that I could persuade them somehow from their folly, but it is much more than mere folly, isn't it? More than boredom or high spirits. This can lead to one thing only – rebellion and the overthrow of the Seven. I have to act. You understand that?"

Li Yuan nodded. "Of course," he said sympathetically. "Which is why I have already spoken with Tsu Ma. He agrees. And the sooner the better. The Sons of Benjamin Franklin are not the only group. There are similar factions in the other Cities, linked to the Young Sons. If we are to act, it would be best if we acted in concert, neh? Tonight, if possible. At twelfth bell."

"And the other T'ang?"

Li Yuan shook his head. "There's no time for that. Besides, if Wang Sau-leyan were to learn, it's likely there would be no one there to arrest. He has a funny way with 'secrets'."

Wu Shih looked down, considering, then nodded. "All right. Twelfth bell. And you will act elsewhere? You and Tsu Ma?"

"At twelfth bell." He made to cut connection.

"Li Yuan! Wait! What of the boy? Do you think they will suspect his role in this?"

Li Yuan laughed. "How could they? Even he doesn't know what he has been these past few days."

Wu Shih gave a small laugh. "Even so, should I take steps to get him out?"

Li Yuan shook his head. "No. Any such move might alert them. Ensure only that your men do not harm him by mistake."

Wu Shih lowered his head slightly, a mark of respect that he had often made to Yuan's father, Li Shai Tung, and an implicit acknowledgment of where the real leadership lay within the Seven.

Li Yuan smiled. "Then goodnight, cousin. We shall speak in the morning. Once things are better known."

★ ★ ★

The Lever Mansion was a huge, two-storey house with gables, standing in its own wooded grounds. Outside it was dark, the house lights reflected brightly in the dark waters of the nearby lake. In the centre of the mansion's bold façade was a pillared entrance, its wide, double doors open, light spilling out on to a gravel drive. Dark sedans, some antique, some reproduction, lined the entrance road, their runners dressed in a black-suited livery that matched the ancient crest on the sides of the sedans. All evening they had gone back and forth, ferrying guests between the house and the transit, almost a *li* away.

The illusion was almost perfect. The darkness hid the walls of the surrounding decks, while above, a thick, dark blue cloth masked the ice of the stack's uppermost floor, like a starless night sky.

Kim stood there between the trees, in darkness, looking back at the house. This was the third time he had come to Richmond, to the Lever Mansion, but it was the first time he had seen the house in darkness. Tonight they were throwing a ball. A party for the élite of their City – the *Supernal*, as they called themselves. It was the first time he had heard the term used and it amused him to think of himself, so *low* in birth, mixing in such *high* company. He was not drunk – he took care never to touch alcohol or drugs – but merely mixing in the atmosphere of the house was enough to create a mild euphoria. The air was chill, sharp. In the trees nearby the leaves rustled in a mild, artificial breeze. Kim smiled, enjoying the strangeness of it all, and reached out to touch the smooth bark of one of the pines.

"Kim?"

A tall, elegant young man in old-fashioned evening dress stood at the edge of the gravel, calling him. It was Michael Lever.

"I'm here," he said, stepping out from the trees. "I was just getting some air."

Lever greeted him, more than a *ch'i* taller than him, straight-backed and blond, an *American* . . .

"Come on through," he said, smiling. "Father was asking after you."

Kim let himself be ushered inside once more, through reception room and ballroom and out into a smaller, quieter space beyond. Leather doors closed behind him. The room was dimly lit, pervaded by the tart smell of cigar smoke. Old Man Lever was sitting on the far side of the room, beside the only lamp, his friends gathered about him in high-backed leather chairs. Old men, like himself. By the window stood a group of younger men. Michael joined them, accepting a drink from one, then turned back, looking across at Kim.

Charles Lever lit up a new cigar, then beckoned Kim over. "Here, Kim. Take a seat." He indicated the empty chair beside him. "There are some people here – friends of mine – I want you to meet."

Old men. The thought flashed through Kim's mind. *Old men, afraid of dying.*

He sat in the huge, uncomfortable chair, ill at ease, nodding acknowledgment to each of the men in turn; noting each face and placing it. These were big men. Powerful men. Each of them Lever's equal. So what had Lever said? What had Lever promised he could do for them?

"We were talking," Lever said, turning in his chair to look at Kim. "Chewing things over among ourselves. And I was telling my friends here about your new company. About *Chih Chu*. Potentially a nice little outfit, but small, undercapitalised."

Kim looked down, surprised that Lever knew already.

Lever cleared his throat, then nodded, as if satisfied by his own evaluation of things. "And I was saying what a shame it was. Because I've seen your like before, Kim. A hot property with plenty of good, strong ideas and lots of get-up-and-go, but nothing to back it up. There's a pattern to it, too. I've seen how they've built things up – how they've grown real fast. Up to a certain point. And then . . ." He shook his head and looked down at the cigar smouldering between his fingers. "Then they've tried to move up a league. Into manufacturing. Because it's a shame to let the big industrials take so large a share of the cut. Galling, even."

The young men by the window were watching him intently, almost suspiciously. Kim could feel their eyes on him; could almost sense what they were thinking. What would this mean for them? For if their fathers lived for ever . . .

"I've seen them try to take that step," Lever continued. "And I've seen them flounder, unable to cope with the sheer size of the market. I've watched the big Companies move in, like those sharks we were talking of, and gobble up the pieces. Because that's what it's really all about, Kim. Not ideas. Not potential. Not get-up-and-go. But money. Money and power."

He paused and sucked at his cigar. All about him the old men nodded, but their eyes never left Kim's face.

"So I was saying to my friends here, let's make things happen a little differently this time. Use some of *our* money, *our* power to help this young man. Because it's a shame to see potential go to waste. A damn shame, if you ask me."

He leaned back, drawing on the cigar, then puffed out a narrow stream of smoke. Kim waited, silent, not knowing what to say. He wanted nothing from these men. Neither money, nor power. But that was not the point. It was what they wanted from him that mattered here.

"CosTech has offered for your contract. Right?"

Kim opened his mouth, then snapped it shut. Of course Lever would know. He had spies, hadn't he? They all had spies. It was how things worked at this level. You weren't in business unless you knew what the competition was up to.

"Yes. But I haven't decided yet," he lied, wanting to hear what they were going to offer. "I'm meeting them again in two weeks to talk terms."

Lever smiled, but it was a smile tinged with sourness. "Working for the competition, eh?" He laughed. "Rather you than me, boy."

There was laughter from the gathered circle. Only by the window was there silence.

"But why's this, Kim? Why would you want to waste a year of your life slaving for CosTech when you could be pushing *Chih Chu* on to bigger things?"

Make your offer, Kim thought. Spell it out. What you want. What you're offering. Make a deal, old man. Or would that embarrass you, being so direct?

"You know what they've offered?" he asked.

Lever nodded. "It's peanuts. An insult to your talent. And it ties you. Limits what you could do."

Ah, thought Kim, that's more to the point. Working for CosTech he could not work for ImmVac. And they needed him. The old men needed him, because, after a certain age, it was not possible to stop the ageing process. Not as things stood. They had to catch it before the molecular signal that triggered it. Afterwards was no good. What ImmVac had developed was no good for any of these men. The complex system of cell replication began to break down, slowly at first, but exponentially, until the genetic damage was irreparable. And then senility.

And what good was money or power against senility and death?

"I'm a physicist," he said, looking at the old man directly. "What good am I to you? You want a biochemist. Someone working in the field of defective protein manufacture. In cell repair. Not an engineer."

Lever shook his head. "You're good. People say you're the best. And you're young. You could learn. Specialise in self-repair mechanisms." He stared at Kim fiercely. The cigar in his hand had gone out. "We'll pay what you ask. Provide whatever you need."

Kim rubbed at his eyes. The cigar smoke had made them sore. He wanted to say no and have an end to it, but knew these were not men he could readily say no to.

"Two weeks, *Shih* Lever. Give me two weeks, then I'll let you know."

Lever narrowed his eyes, suspicious of the young, child-like man. "Two weeks?"

"Yes. After all, you're asking me to change the direction of my life. And that's something I have to think about. I've got to consider what it means. What I might lose and what gain. I can't see it right now. Which is why I need to think it through."

But he had thought it through already and dismissed it. He knew what he wanted; had known from the first moment he had glimpsed the vision of the web. Death – what was death beside that vision?

Lever looked to the other men in the room, then nodded his agreement. "All right, *Shih* Ward. Two weeks it is."

* * *

It was late. The crowd in the ballroom had thinned out, but the dancing went on. On the balcony overlooking the hall, a ten-man orchestra played a slow waltz, their bows rising and falling in the fragmented light. Kim stood at the back of the hall, beside Michael Lever, watching the couples move about the floor, realising that this too was an illusion; a dream of agelessness. As if time could be restored, its flow reversed.

"I love their dresses," he said, looking up at the tall young man. "They're like jellyfish."

Lever roared, then turned to his friends and repeated Kim's comment. In a moment their laughter joined his own. Lever turned back to Kim, wiping his eyes with the back of his hand.

"That's rich, Kim. Marvellous! Like jellyfish!" And again he burst into laughter.

Kim looked at him, surprised. What had he said? It was true, wasn't it? The bobbing movement of their many-layered dresses were like those of jellyfish in the ocean, even down to the frilled edges.

"I was only saying . . ." he began, but he never finished the sentence. At that moment the main lights came up. The orchestra played on for a moment or two, then ended in sudden disarray. The dancers stopped circling and stood there, looking towards the doorway at the far end of the ballroom. Suddenly it felt much colder in the hall. There was the sound of shouting from outside.

"What in hell's name?" Lever said, starting to make his way towards the doors. Then he stopped abruptly. Soldiers had come out on to the balcony above the dance floor. More came into the ballroom through the doorway. Security troops in powder blue fatigues, black-helmeted, their visors down.

Kim felt his mouth go dry. Something was wrong.

The soldiers formed a line along the edge of the balcony and along the lower walls, covering the dancers with their weapons. Only a few of their number went among the dancers, their visors up, looking from face to face. Up above, on the balcony, a lieutenant began to read out a warrant for the arrest of fifteen men.

In the ballroom there was disbelief and anger. One young man jostled a Security guard and was brought down by a sharp blow with a rifle butt. When the soldiers went from the hall they took more than a dozen young men, Lever and his friends amongst them.

Kim, watching, saw the anger in surrounding faces after the soldiers had gone. More anger than he'd ever seen. And different, very different from the anger of the Clay. This anger smouldered like red-hot ashes fanned by a breath. It was a deep-rooted, enduring anger.

Beside Kim a young man's face was distorted; black with rage. "He'll pay! The bastard will pay for this!" Others gathered about him, shouting, their fists clenched, the dance forgotten.

Kim stood there a moment longer, then turned away, going quickly from the hall. Things had changed. Suddenly, dramatically, the rules had changed, and he was no longer safe here. He passed through, glancing from side to side, seeing only outrage on the faces of those he passed. Outside he walked past the waiting sedans and on, out across the darkness towards the transit.

In a sober moment they would remember. Old Man Lever would remember. And in his anger, who knew how he would act? It was a time for taking sides, and he was Li Yuan's man.

He saw soldiers up ahead, guarding the transit entrance, and began to run, knowing his safety lay with them. But nearer the barrier he turned and looked back at the house, remembering the dresses bobbing to the music, the swish of lace in the air. And a circle of old men, offering him the earth.

CHAPTER·13

I<small>N</small> T<small>HE</small> O<small>PEN</small>

Tolonen stood there at Haavikko's bedside, looking down at him, a faint smile on his lips. It was only two days since his own operation and he was still feeling weak, but he had had to come.

A nurse brought him a chair and he sat, content to wait until the young man woke. His new arm ached at the shoulder, despite the drugs, but it was feeling better than it had.

Besides, he was alive. Thanks to Haavikko he was alive.

The nurse hovered but he waved her away, then settled to watch the sleeping man.

All his life he had been self-reliant. All his life he had fought his own fights, keeping himself always one step ahead of his enemies. But now he was growing old. At last he had proof of it. His old eyes had missed the discrepancy of the colour codings on the soldiers' chests – his reactions had been just that fraction of a second too slow – and he had lost his arm as a result. Almost his life.

He smiled, studying the young man. Haavikko was cradled in bandages, special healants creating new skin growth on his badly burned shoulder and back.

Tolonen shook his head as if to clear it, feeling both sad and happy at once. He had been told what Haavikko had done for him, like a son for a father; risking himself when all bonds of duty or obligation had long ago been severed between them.

Yes, he had sorely misjudged the boy.

Haavikko stirred and opened his eyes. "Marshal . . ."

He made to sit up, then winced and eased back, closing his eyes again. The blast had removed most of the skin at the top of his back and taken off his ear.

"Lie still, boy. Please. You need your rest."

Haavikko opened his eyes again and looked up at the Marshal. "Your arm . . ." he said, clearly pained by the sight.

Tolonen laughed gruffly. "You like it? It hurts a bit just now, but that doesn't matter. I'm alive, that's the thing." He sat back, his right hand reaching up to scratch at the stubble on his left cheek; an awkward, embarrassed gesture, indicative of just how hard the old man found it to deal with this. The warmth he felt towards the other man – that depth of reawakened feeling – brought him close to tears. He looked away a moment, controlling himself, then finished what he had meant to say. "Thanks to you, Axel. Thanks to you."

Axel smiled. His hands lay above the sheets. Long, fine hands, undamaged in the incident. Tolonen took one and squeezed it.

"I misjudged you, boy. I . . ."

Haavikko shook his head, a slight grimace of pain crossing his face. "It doesn't matter. Really, sir. I . . ." He turned his head slightly, looking across the room to where his clothes hung on a peg. "But there's something you must know. Something important."

Tolonen smiled. "Rest, my boy. There's plenty of time for other things . . ."

"No . . ." Haavikko swallowed drily. "Over there, in my tunic, there's a package. I was bringing it to you when it happened. I'd pieced it all together."

Tolonen shook his head, puzzled. "Pieced what together?"

Haavikko looked up, pleading with his eyes. "Just look. Please, sir. You don't have to read it all right now. Later, perhaps, when you feel up to it. But promise me you'll read it. Please, Marshal."

Tolonen let go of Haavikko's hand, then got up heavily

and went across. Just as Haavikko had said, there was a small package in the inner pocket of the tunic. He tugged at it until it came free, then went back, taking his seat again.

He held the package out, a query in his eyes. "So what is this?"

Haavikko swallowed again and Tolonen, taking the hint, set the package down and picked up the glass by the bedside, giving Haavikko a few sips.

"Well?"

"Long ago you asked me to do something for you – to make a list of people who might have been involved in the assassination of Minister Lwo Kang. Do you remember?"

Tolonen laughed. "Gods! That must have been eleven years ago. And you did that?"

Haavikko made the smallest movement of his head. "That's how it began. But I extended it. I kept a record of anything I felt wasn't right – anything that didn't quite make sense to me. Then, recently, I teamed up with Kao Chen and your man Karr."

"Good men," Tolonen said, nodding his approval.

"Yes," Haavikko smiled then grew serious again. "Anyway, what you have there is the result of our investigations. My original list, my notes and a few other things. Computer files. Hologram images."

Tolonen lifted the package and turned it in his hand, then set it down on his knee and reached out to take Haavikko's hand again. "And you want me to look at it?"

"Yes . . ."

Tolonen considered a moment. He had promised Jelka he would dine with her later on, but maybe he would cancel that. He could always say he was tired. Jelka would understand. He smiled broadly at Haavikko. "Of course. It's the very least I could do."

Haavikko looked back at him, his eyes moist. "Thank you," he said, his voice almost a whisper. "Thank you, sir."

Tolonen sat there, clasping the young man's hand. The

ache in his left shoulder was much stronger now. It was probably time for his medication, but he felt loath to leave the young man.

"I must go now," he said softly. "But I promise you I'll look at your files. Later. When it's quiet."

Haavikko smiled, his eyes closed. Slowly his mouth relaxed. In a moment he was sleeping.

Tolonen placed the young man's hand gently back on the sheets then got to his feet stiffly. Twice lucky, he thought, remembering the attack at Nanking spaceport. He made his way across, then turned, looking back, noticing for the first time just how pale Haavikko was. He stood there a moment longer, absently scratching at the dressing at his shoulder, then desisted, annoyed with himself.

He looked down at the silver arm and sighed, remembering how Jelka had fussed when she'd first seen it. But there was steel in her too. She had borne up bravely. So too this young man. Oh, he would make things up. He was determined on it. Would find a way of making things right again.

Tolonen yawned, then, smiling sadly to himself, turned away, leaving the young officer to sleep.

* * *

Tsu Ma lifted the dish and brushed his thumb across its silken, contoured surface. It was a perfect piece: black lacquer carved with two water fowls against a background of lotus. Fourteenth century, from the last years of the Yuan dynasty. He smiled to himself, then turned to face Li Yuan.

"Two years they would labour to make one of these. Two years of a master craftsman's life. And at the end, this. This small fragment of dark perfection."

Li Yuan looked across at him, turning from the view of the bay and the sugarloaf mountain beyond. He had not been listening, but he saw the lacquered dish in Tsu Ma's hands and nodded. "That piece is beautiful. Hou Ti had many fine things."

Tsu Ma held his eyes a moment. "These days some think of them as primitive, ignorant men. Barbarians. But look at this. Is this barbarian?" He shook his head slowly, his eyes returning to the dish. "As if the mere passage of years could make our species more sophisticated."

Li Yuan laughed and came closer. "Your point, Tsu Ma?"

Behind them, at the far side of the long room, the rest of the Seven were gathered, talking among themselves.

Tsu Ma set the dish down, letting his fingers rest in its shallow bowl, then looked up at Li Yuan again. "Just that there are those here who think the future better than the past simply because it is the future. Who believe that change is good simply because it is change. They have no time for comparisons. Nor for the kind of values expressed in the simplicity of this dish. No time for craft, control or discipline." He lowered his voice a fraction. "And I find that disturbing, Li Yuan. Dangerous, even."

Li Yuan studied him a moment, then gave the barest nod of agreement. They had covered much ground that morning, but nothing yet of true significance. On the matters of the stewardships and the new immortality drugs he had bowed like the reed before the wind, not pushing his own viewpoint, merely ensuring that these matters were not finalised. Let them play their games of evading death, he thought; death would find them anyway, wherever they hid. As for the other, there was time enough to force his view on that.

"How deep is this feeling?"

Tsu Ma considered a moment, then leaned towards Li Yuan. "Deep, cousin. Deep enough to trouble me." He looked past the younger man, out beyond the window glass, seeing how the space between the bowl of hills was plugged with the white of the City's walls. "They would do away with certain restraints." He stretched his long neck, lifting his chin, then looked directly at Li Yuan. "You'll see. This afternoon . . ."

The early afternoon sunlight fell across Li Yuan's arm

411

and shoulder. "It is the illness of our time. Change and the desire for Change. But I had not thought . . ." Yuan smiled and broke off, seeing Chi Hsing, the T'ang of the Australias approach.

The two men nodded, acknowledging the newcomer.

"Are you not eating, cousins?" Chi Hsing smiled and turned, summoning the waiters, then turned back. "Before we resume, there is a matter I must raise with you. A change has been proposed to the scheduled itinerary."

"A *change*?" Li Yuan said, raising his eyebrows slightly, but heavily emphasising the word. Beside him Tsu Ma kept his amusement to himself, staring back mask-like at his fellow T'ang.

Chi Hsing was known for neither his intelligence nor his subtlety. In that regard he was much more his mother's child than his father's. He was a father now himself, of course. Two young sons, the eldest barely two, had blessed his first marriage, changing him considerably. He was less rash now than he'd been, and though he had secretly applauded Li Yuan's purge of the *Ping Tiao*, he also had misgivings about such actions. He feared for his sons, remembering what had happened in the War with the Dispersionists. Vengeance was fine, but now he wished only for peace.

Peace. So that he might see his sons grow to be men. Strong, fine men, as his father had been.

"Wang Sau-leyan has made a request," he began, his eyes searching both their faces. "And there are others here who wish to speak on the matter." His eyes grew still, focused on Li Yuan.

"Go on, cousin."

Chi Hsing bowed his head slightly. "He wishes to discuss the arrests. The action you took in league with Wu Shih against the young sons."

It was clear, by the way Chi Hsing stood there, that he expected Li Yuan to refuse. Indeed, it was within Li Yuan's rights to refuse Wang's request, as his father had done once before. But Li Yuan only smiled politely.

"I have no objection to that. Do you, Tsu Ma?"

"Not I."

Li Yuan reached out and touched Chi Hsing's shoulder. "It is best, after all, if these things are aired between us. In the open."

Chi Hsing nodded, still hesitant, as if he expected Li Yuan to change his mind at any moment. Then, realising he had achieved his end, he smiled.

"Good. That's very good, Li Yuan. As you say, it is best. In the open." He nodded again, this time decisively, then turned and went across to where Wang Sau-leyan and their host, Hou Tung-po, T'ang of South America, were standing. Wang listened a moment, then looked across at Li Yuan, bowing his head slightly.

"In the open," said Tsu Ma beneath his breath. "You're like your father, Yuan. Devious."

Li Yuan turned, surprised, then laughed, seeing the humour beneath the surface of Tsu Ma's words. "Words are words, Tsu Ma. We must bend and shape them to our needs."

Tsu Ma nodded, pleased with that. "So it is in these troubled times, cousin. But history shall judge us by our actions."

★ ★ ★

Wang Sau-leyan was leaning forward in his seat, his hands folded in his lap, his big, moon face looking from one to another as he spoke. He seemed calm, relaxed, his voice soft and deep, persuasive in its tones. Thus far he had said little that had not been said before, but now he turned the conversation.

"In this room, as in the rooms of the Twenty-Nine and the mansions of the Supernal, there are those who are questioning recent events. Some with anger, some with sadness and misgivings. Others fearfully, remembering things not long past. But every last one of them is concerned, wondering where it will stop. For myself, I believe it has already gone too far."

Wu Shih made to interrupt, but Wang raised his hand "You will have your say, Wu Shih, and I shall listen. But first hear me out. This must be said, before it is too late for words."

Tsu Ma reached into the pocket of his jacket and took out a slender silver case. "Then talk, cousin. Let us hear what you have to say."

There was an unconcealed hostility in the words that surprised Li Yuan. He watched Tsu Ma take a cheroot from the case then close it and slip it back into his pocket

"Thank you, cousin," said Wang, watching the older man light the cheroot and draw the first breath from it He smiled tightly, then let his face fall blank again. "As I said, there is anger and sadness and a great deal of fear Unhealthy symptoms. Signs of a deep and bitter hostility towards us."

Wu Shih grunted indignantly, but kept his silence. His cheeks burned red and his eyes bored into the side of Wang's softly rounded face.

"We have sown a harvest of discontent," Wang went on. "And I say we, because this affects us all. And yet I hesitate to use that plural, because it suggests consensus on our part. Suggests a commonly agreed-upon set of actions discussed and debated here, in Council, as has always been our way." He paused and looked about him, shaking his head. "Instead I wake to find the world a different place from when I slept. And myself every bit as surprised as those who came begging audience, saying, 'Why is my son arrested?'"

In the chair beside him, Hou Tung-po nodded his head vigorously. "So it was for me. I was not notified, Li Yuan Not consulted before you and Wu Shih acted. A poor choice was left to me – to seem a scoundrel or look a fool Relations are bad between us and the Above. As bad as at any time during the last ten years. We must act to defuse this situation before it gets out of hand. We must make some gesture to placate the Above."

There was a moment's silence, then Li Yuan spoke, his

anger at Wang Sau-leyan's criticism barely contained.

"When a man saves his brother's life, does he say first, 'Excuse me, brother, I would save your life, is that all right with you?' No, he acts, pushing his brother aside, out of the way of the falling rock. He *acts*! I make no apologies for my actions. Nor for the lack of consultation. Surprise was a necessity. I could not risk informing *anyone.*"

He stood, going to the centre of their informal circle, looking down at Wang Sau-leyan.

"Perhaps you relish death, cousin Wang. For myself I would grow old in peace, no dagger to my throat."

Wang laughed; a short, bitter laugh. "Oh yes, Li Yuan, you act like one destined to live long. For while your enemies multiply, your friends diminish."

Li Yuan smiled back at him tightly. "So it is in this world. But it is better to trust one's friends and know one's enemies. To act than to prevaricate."

Wang Sau-leyan glared back at Li Yuan, infuriated by his words, all pretence of calm gone from him. "*Ai ya!* – but must we all suffer for your rashness, cousin? Must *we* reap what *you* sow? You sound like your dead brother – hot-headed!"

For a moment there was a tense silence, then Li Yuan gave a soft laugh. "Hot-headed, you say?" He shook his head. "Not so, cousin. Not so. You ask for something to placate the Above, like a woman begging for her son's life. Has it come to that? Are we so weak we must *beg* for our existence? Are we not to crush what seeks to destroy us? It seems you have changed your tune, Wang Sau-leyan, for once you sought to lecture *us* . . ."

Wang was shaking his head. "Young men, Li Yuan, that's all they are. Young men. Misguided, over-enthusiastic, that's all." Wang looked beyond Li Yuan, a faint smile resting on his lips. "It would defuse things if we let them go, and in time this thing would certainly blow over."

"Blow over?" Li Yuan shook his head in disbelief. "What must they do before you see it, *cousin*? Must they hold the gun to your head? This is no act of high spirits. This is revolution. Open rebellion. Don't you understand? It begins with ideas and it ends with bloodshed." He paused, then took a step closer, pointing down at Wang. "They would kill you, Wang Sau-leyan, T'ang of Africa, and set themselves up in your place. Just as they killed your eldest brothers. Or do you forget?"

Li Yuan stood there, breathing deeply, staring down at Wang Sau-leyan, forcing him to meet his eyes.

"Well? Do you still want appeasement?"

Wang nodded.

"And who else?" He looked at Hou Tung-po, then across to Chi Hsing. Both nodded, though neither met his eyes.

"And you, Wei Feng? What do you counsel?" He turned, facing the aged T'ang of East Asia. "You, surely, know the depths of this problem."

"You speak as if I had the casting vote, Li Yuan."

"You have." It was Tsu Ma who answered for Li Yuan. Beside him Wu Shih looked across, bowing his head in assent.

Wei Feng sighed and looked down. "You know what I feel," he began, his low, toneless voice picking out each word slowly, meticulously. "You know my dislikes, my prejudices." He looked up at Li Yuan. "You must know, then, that what you did pleased me greatly." He smiled sourly. "However, that is not what is at issue here. What's at issue is our manner of conducting ourselves, Li Yuan. Not the action itself – with which I basically agree and on which I would support you at any other time – but the *way* in which you acted. As Wang Sau-leyan says, you acted without consulting us."

He paused, considering, then spoke again. "We are Seven, Li Yuan. Not One, but Seven. In that lies our strength. For seven generations now, our strength and the reason for peace in the world. For the strength of our society. Break that cohesion and you break it all."

"You defer then, Wei Feng?"

Wei Feng nodded. "I say free the young men. Then do as Wang says. Make the best of a bad lot and seek conciliation."

For a moment longer Li Yuan stood there, then he shrugged. "So be it," he said, looking across at Wang. "I will hand my prisoners over to you, cousin, to do with as you will."

He looked away, leaving it there, but in his head the words resounded. *Not One, but Seven. In that lies our strength.* He had never questioned it before, but now, standing there amidst his peers, he asked himself if it was really so.

He glanced at Wu Shih, seeing how the T'ang of North America was looking down, his anger unexpressed, and had his answer. The days of unanimity were gone, and what had made the Seven such a force had gone with them. What Wei Feng had said, that had been true once, back in his father's time, but now?

Seven . . . the word was hollow now, the Great Wheel broken. It had died with his father. Four against three – that was the new reality. He looked across at Wang Sau-leyan, seeing the gleam of triumph in his eyes and knew. It was finished. Here, today, it had ended. And now they must find another path, another way of governing themselves. That was the truth. But the truth could not be spoken. Not yet, anyway, and certainly not here, in Council.

He smiled, suddenly relaxing, as if a great weight had been taken from his shoulders and turned his head, meeting Tsu Ma's eyes; seeing the light of understanding there.

"Shall we move on?" he said, looking about the circle of his fellow T'ang. "Time presses and there's much to do."

Yes, he thought; but none of it matters now. From now on this is merely play, a mask to hide our real intentions. For all the real decisions will henceforth be made in secret.

Out in the open. He laughed, recognising finally the full irony of what he had said earlier, then turned, looking at

417

Tsu Ma, and smiled, seeing his smile returned strongly. Yes. So it would be from now on. *In the open . . .*

* * *

It had been summer in Rio. In Tongjiang it was winter.

Li Yuan stood on the terrace, looking out over the frozen lake. He wore furs and gloves and thick leather boots, but his head was bare, snowflakes settling in his fine, dark hair. Below him the slope was deep in snow while on the far shore the trees of the orchard formed stark, tangled shapes against the white.

He looked up past the gentle slopes towards the distant mountains. Vast, sharp-edged escarpments of rock speared the colourless sky. He shivered then turned away, finding the bleakness of the view too close to his present mood.

He looked across at the palace, the stables beyond. His men were waiting on the veranda, talking amongst themselves beneath the great, shuttered windows. They did not like it here, he knew. This openness appalled them. They felt exposed, naked to all the primal things the City shut out behind its walls, but for him only this was real. The rest was but a game.

He had expected to find her here, or at least the memory of her, but there was nothing. Only the place itself remained, robbed of its scents, its vivid greenness, all human presence gone. As if all that had happened here had never been.

He shivered and looked down at his feet. A leaf clung to the ankle of his right boot. He removed his glove then stooped to pluck the wet and blackened leaf, then straightened up, feeling the icy cold against his flesh, the wetness in his palm. What did it all mean? He brushed the leaf away and pulled his glove back on, turning to walk back to the palace and the waiting transit.

Nothing, he decided. *It meant nothing.*

He flew south-west, over unbroken whiteness. Not snow this time but the endless City, three thousand *li* without a break, until they reached Kuang Chou, ancient

418

Canton, at the mouth of the Pei River. Then, for a while, there was the blue of the South China Sea, before Hong Kong and, to its south-east, the island of T'ai Yueh Shan, where Yin Tsu had his estate.

He had put this off too long. But now it was time to see the child. To bestow his gift upon his past-wife's son.

Coded signals passed between the ship and the estate's defence system, then they came down, Yin Tsu greeting him in the hangar. He was kneeling, his forehead pressed to the cold metal of the grid as Li Yuan stepped down.

Li Yuan had changed on the flight down, shedding his furs and gloves and heavy boots in favour of thin satins of a fiery orange and slippers of the finest kid. Approaching the old man he stopped, lifting his foot.

Yin Tsu took the offered foot with care and kissed it once, then once more before releasing it.

"Yin Tsu, once-father, please." He reached down and took the old man's hand, helping him up. Only then did Yin Tsu look at him.

"I am honoured by your visit, *Chieh Hsia*. What may I do for you?"

"Fei Yen . . . Is she still here with you?"

The old man nodded, his thin lips forming the faintest of smiles. "Yes, *Chieh Hsia*. She is here. And the child."

"Good. Good." He hesitated a moment, feeling awkward, then spoke again. "I'd like to see her. And . . . the child too. If she would see me."

"Please. Come through." Yin Tsu led the way, half turned towards Li Yuan in courtesy as he walked, bowed low, his hands held out but pressed together in an attitude of the deepest respect.

While he waited for her, he thought of what he would say. He had not seen her since the day he had insisted on the tests. Had she forgiven him for that?

He gritted his teeth, thinking on it, then turned to find her standing there. She was wearing a pale lemon-coloured dress, her dark hair hanging loose about her shoulders. The child was not with her.

"I . . ." he began, but the sight of her struck him dumb. She seemed more beautiful than ever, her face stronger, her breasts much fuller than he remembered them. As he had turned to face her she had bowed and now rested on one knee, her head lowered, awaiting his command.

"Fei Yen," he said, but the words came out so softly that she did not hear them. He went across and touched her gently on the crown of her head, wanting to kiss her there, his cheek muscle twitching with the tension he felt this close to her. He stepped back, straightening up. "Get up, Fei Yen. Please . . ."

She got up slowly, her dark eyes filled with awe of him. She had seen how powerful he was; how his servants laid their necks down for him to tread upon. Had seen and was afraid. This was not the boy she had known. No, he was no longer a child, but a man: the cub a lion now, dressed in flame.

"You look well," he said, aware of the inadequacy of the words.

"I wondered when you'd come. I knew you would."

He nodded, surprised by how subdued she sounded. So different from before. "And the child?"

"He's fine." She looked away, biting her lip. "He's sleeping now. Do you want to see him?" She glanced at him, aware of his hesitation. "You don't have to. I know how you feel about all this."

Do you? he thought; but he kept silent and simply nodded.

"Han," she said. "I called him Han. As you wished."

She was watching him; trying to see what he made of it. His cheek muscle twitched once more and then lay still, his face a mask.

"Come," she said after a moment, then led him through, down a high-ceilinged corridor to the nursery.

A girl sat beside the cot, her hands in her lap. At the entrance of her mistress she got up and bowed. Then she saw Li Yuan and abased herself, as Yin Tsu had done. Fei

Yen dismissed her hurriedly, then turned to face Li Yuan again.

"Don't wake him, Yuan. He needs his sleep."

He nodded and went close, looking down at the baby from the side of the cot.

The child lay on its side, one hand up to its mouth, the other resting lightly against the bars at the side of the cot. A fine, dark down of hair covered its scalp, while about its neck lay a monitoring strip, the milky white band pulsing quickly, in time with the baby's heartbeat.

"But he's so . . . so *tiny*!" Li Yuan laughed, surprised. The baby's hands, his tiny, perfectly formed feet were like fine sculpture. Like miniatures in tarnished ivory.

"He's not six weeks yet," she said, as if that explained the beauty of the child. Li Yuan wanted to reach out and hold one of those tiny hands; to feel its fingers stretch and close about his thumb.

He turned, looking at her, and suddenly all of the old bitterness and love were there, impurely mixed in what he was feeling. He hated her for this. Hated her for making him feel so much. Frustration made him grit his teeth and push past her, the feeling overwhelming him, making him want to cry out for the pain he felt.

As at first, he realised. It had always hurt him to be with her. She took too much. Left him so little of himself. And that was wrong. He could not be a T'ang and feel like this. No, it was better to feel nothing than to feel so much. He stood with his back to her, breathing deeply, trying to calm himself, to still the turmoil in his gut and put it all back behind the ice.

Where it belonged. Where it had to belong.

She was silent, waiting for him. When he turned back all trace of feeling had gone from his face. He looked across at the cot and the sleeping child, then back at her, his voice quiet, controlled.

"I want to give you something. For you and the child. It will be his when he comes of age, but until that time it is yours to administer."

She lowered her head obediently.

"I want him to have the palace at Hei Shui."

She looked up, wide-eyed with surprise. "Li Yuan . . ." But he had raised his hand to silence her.

"The documents are drawn up. I want no arguments, Fei Yen. It's little enough compared to what he might have had."

She turned her head away, unable to disguise the moment's bitterness, then nodded her acquiescence.

"Good." He turned, looking at the cot once more. "There will be an allowance, too. For both of you. You will not want for anything, Fei Yen. Neither you nor he."

"My father . . ." she began, pride creeping back into her voice, but she cut it off, holding her tongue. She knew he need do nothing. The terms of the divorce were clear enough. Hers was the shame. In her actions lay the blame for how things were.

"Let it be so, then," he said finally. "Your father shall have the documents. And Han . . ." he said the name; said it and breathed deeply afterwards, a muscle jumping in his cheek. "Han shall have Hei Shui."

* * *

Tolonen looked up, his long face ashen, his grey eyes filled with a deep hurt. For a time he stared sightlessly at the wall, then, slowly, shook his head.

"I can't believe it," he said quietly, pushing the file away from him. "I just can't believe it. Hans . . ." His mouth creased into a grimace of pain. "What will I say . . . What will his father say?" Then he thought of Jelka and the betrothal and groaned. "Gods, what a mess. What a stinking, horrible mess this is."

The file on Hans Ebert was a slender dossier, not enough to convict a man in law, but enough to prove its case by any other measure. To an advocate it would have been merely a mass of circumstantial evidence, but that evidence pointed in one direction only.

Tolonen sighed, then rubbed at his eyes. Hans had been

clever. Too clever, in fact, for the sum total of his cleverness was a sense of absence: of shadow where there should have been substance. Discrepancies in GenSyn funds. Payments to fellow officers. Unexplained absences in Ebert's service record – missing hours and days that, in three cases, linked up with dates given them by DeVore's man, Reid. Misplaced files on five of the eighteen younger sons arrested on Li Yuan's instructions only a day or so ago, all of which had, at some point, passed through Ebert's hands. Then there was the statement given by the girl in the Ebert household, Golden Heart, and, finally, the holograms.

The holograms seemed, on the surface of it, to be the most conclusive evidence, though in law, he knew, they held no real significance. It had been successfully claimed long ago that photographic and holographic evidence was unreliable, since GenSyn could make a perfect duplicate of anyone. This and the whole question of image-verification had relegated such "information" to a secondary status in law.

But this was not something that would ever see a courtroom. Wider issues were at stake here. And older codes of conduct.

In one of the holograms Hans could be seen standing on the veranda of a skiing lodge, looking down at a figure on the snow below him. That figure was DeVore. They were grainy shots, taken from a narrow triangulation – perhaps as little as twenty degrees – and consequently the far side of the three-dimensional image blurred into perfect whiteness, but that incompleteness itself suggested that it was genuine, taken with two hand-helds from a distance, who knew for what purpose – maybe blackmail. The holograms had been found in storage in DeVore's stronghold, almost as though they had been left to be found. In itself this might have led Security to discount them as a subtle attempt to undermine Ebert's position, but added to the other matters they were significant.

No, there was no *real* proof, but the circumstantial evidence was considerable. Ebert had been working with the rebels; providing them with funds; meeting with them; passing on information, and covering their tracks where necessary.

Tolonen closed the file, then sat back, his hands trembling. He had always trusted Ebert. When he had asked Haavikko to investigate he had been thinking of three other officers. For him the question of Hans Ebert's loyalty had never arisen. Not until this evening.

He shook his head. There were tears in his eyes now; tears running down his furrowed cheeks. He gritted his teeth, tightening the muscles in his face, but still the tears came. There was only one thing to do. He would have to go and see Klaus. After all, this was Family. A matter of honour.

He let out a shuddering sigh, then shook his head, remembering. Jelka . . . He had promised Jelka that he would dine with her at home tonight. He glanced at the timer on the wall, then pulled himself up out of the chair, throwing the file down on the bed. He was late already, but she would understand. He would call Helga and explain. And maybe send Jelka a note by messenger.

He shivered, feeling old beyond his years. He had been so wrong. So very wrong. And not just once but twice now. First with DeVore and then . . .

"Ach . . ." he muttered, then turned, angry with himself for his weakness, pressing the button to summon his aide. He would bathe and dress and go to see his old friend. For a father should know his son. Whatever kind of creature he was.

* * *

It was just after three when Jelka woke. The apartment was in darkness, silent. For a while she lay there, trying to settle back into sleep, then abandoned the idea.

She slipped on a robe and went through to her father's room, forgetting for a moment. His bed was empty, the room tidy. Of course . . . She moved on, pausing outside her aunt and uncle's room, hearing their soft snoring from within. In the kitchen she found a handwritten note rested against the coffee machine. The sheet was folded in half, her name written on the front in her father's neat, upright hand. She sat up to table and read it through then smiled, thinking of him. She always felt such fear for him when he was out on business. More so since the latest attempt on his life.

She looked about her at the dark forms of the kitchen, feeling suddenly tense, restless. That sense of restlessness seemed almost her natural state these days. That and an underlying desire to break things. But she told no one of these feelings. She knew they had to do with Hans and the forthcoming marriage, but there was little she could do to salve them.

One thing she *could* do, however, was exercise. The gym was locked, but, unknown to her father, she had memorised the combination. She punched it in then went through, into darkness, the doors closing behind her automatically.

They had strengthened the walls since the attack on her and put in a special locking system, but otherwise the gym was much as it had been before the attack. She went across to the panel on the wall and switched on three of the spotlights over the wallbars, then shrugged off her robe and began to exercise, knowing that no one could hear her once the doors were closed.

There was a wall-length mirror at the far end of the gym. As she went through her routine, she caught glimpses of her naked figure as it moved between the three separate beams of light, her limbs flashing like spears of ice, her body twisting and turning intricately. And as she danced she felt the tension drain from her, deriving a definite pleasure from her body's precise and disciplined movements. Faster she went and faster, like a dervish, crying out in delight as her feet pounded the floor, flicking her over in a somersault, then into a tight, high leap.

And afterwards she stood there, breathing deeply, trying

not to laugh. *If he could only see me now* . . . She shook her head, then drew her hair back from her face.

She had begun a second routine when something caught her eye. She slowed, then stopped, facing the door, her whole body tensed.

The panel above the door was pulsing steadily. A feverish, silent pulse that meant one thing only. There were intruders in the apartment.

★　★　★

Lehmann read the note quickly, then crumpled it in his hand and threw it aside. Tolonen led a charmed life. Three times they had tried for him now and three times they had failed. Tonight, for instance, Ebert had assured him that he would be home, but for some reason he had not come. Lehmann cursed softly, then turned, going through to where they held the two captives.

They lay on the bed, face down, their plumply naked bodies bound at hand and foot. Beside them the two Han waited.

"Anything?" he asked, seeing the huge welts on the prisoners' backs, the burns on their arms where they had been tortured.

"Nothing," one of the Han answered him. "Nothing at all."

Lehmann stood there a moment, wondering if he should try something more persuasive, then shrugged and gave the order, turning away, letting them get on with it.

Outside, in the corridor, he paused and looked about, sniffing the air. Something nagged at him. They had searched the apartment thoroughly and there was no sign of the girl, so maybe she *had* gone. But then why the note?

He turned and looked down the corridor at the door to the gym. In there? he wondered. It was unlikely, but then so too was the possibility that the girl had gone. Her bed had been slept in, even if the covers were cold.

He stood at the control panel, studying it. It was a new doorlock, specially strengthened. Without the code there was no way of opening it. He was about to turn away when he realised that he didn't have to get inside to find out if she was there. There was a security viewscreen. Which meant that there were cameras inside.

It took only a moment to work out how to operate the screen, then he was staring into darkness, the cameras looking for forms amongst the shadows. He scanned the whole room once, then went back carefully, double-checking. Nothing. There was no one in the room.

He switched off the screen, satisfied now that she had gone. It was a shame. She would have made the perfect hostage. But as it was the death of Tolonen's brother and sister-in-law would hurt the old man badly.

He went back through to where his men were waiting. They had finished now and were ready to go. He looked down at the corpses dispassionately, feeling nothing for them. Directly or indirectly they served a system that was rotten. This, then, was their fate. What they deserved. He leaned forward and spat in the face of the dead man, then looked up, meeting the eyes of the Han.

"All right. We've finished here. Let's go."

They nodded, then filed out past him, their weapons sheathed, their eyes averted. Lehmann stood, looking about him, then drew his knife and followed them, out into the corridor.

★ ★ ★

Jelka waited in the darkness, fearing the worst, her cheeks wet, her stomach tight with anxiety. This was the night-mare come again. And this time it was much worse than before, for this time she could do nothing. Nothing but crouch there by the locked door, waiting.

In the past hour she learned how dreadful a thing inaction was – far worse than the terror of hiding. When she had been balanced on the perch above the camera it had been somehow easier – much easier – than the awful limbo of not-knowing that came afterwards. Then she could think to herself, In a few moments this will be over,

427

the cameras will stop moving and I can drop to the floor again. But the waiting was different. Horribly different. The very quality of time changed subtly, becoming the implement by which she tortured herself, filling the darkness with her vile imaginings.

In the end her patience broke and she went out, afraid that they would still be there, waiting silently for her, but unable to stay in the gym a moment longer.

Outside it was dark, silent. A strange smell hung in the air. She went slowly down the corridor, feeling her way, crouching warily, prepared to strike out with hand or foot, but there was nothing. Only her fear.

At the first door she stopped, sniffing the air. The smell was stronger here, more sickly than in the corridor. She gritted her teeth and went inside, placing her feet carefully, staring into the darkness, trying to make out forms.

There were vague shapes on the floor close to her. She leaned towards them, then jerked her head back, giving a small cry, unable to stop herself. Even in the darkness she could tell. Could see the wire looped tightly about their throats.

She backed away, horrified, gasping for breath, her whole body shaking violently, uncontrollably. They were dead . . .

She turned and made to run, but her legs betrayed her. She stumbled and her outstretched hands met not the hard smoothness of the floor but the awful, yielding softness of dead flesh. She shrieked and scrambled up, then fell again, her horror mounting as she found herself tangled amongst the bodies that littered the floor.

She closed her eyes and reached out, taking the wall as her guide, small sounds of brute disgust forming at the back of her throat as she forced herself to tread over them.

She went out into the dimly lit corridor. The outside barrier was unmanned, the lift empty. She stood there a moment, beside the open doors, then went inside and pressed to go down. It was the same at the bottom of the deck. There were no guards anywhere, as if the whole contingent had been withdrawn. She went through, into the control centre for the deck and sat at the console, trying to work out how to operate the board. Her first few attempts brought no response, then the screen lit up and a soft MekVoc asked for her Security code.

She stammered the number her father had made her memorise, then repeated it at the machine's request. At once a face filled the central screen.

"*Nu shi* Tolonen," the duty officer said, recognising her at once. "What is it? You look . . ."

"Listen!" she said, interrupting him. "There are no guards. The apartment has been attacked. They've . . ." She bit it off, unable to say, yet it seemed he understood.

"Stay where you are. I'll inform the General at once. We'll get a special unit over to you within the next ten minutes." He was leaning out of screen as he spoke, tapping a scramble code into the machine next to him. Then he turned back, facing Jelka again. "All right. They're on their way. The General will contact you directly. Stay by the board." He paused and drew a breath. "How long ago did this happen?"

"About an hour." She shuddered, trying not to think of what she had left back up the levels. "I think they've gone now. But there are . . ." She swallowed drily, then continued, steeling herself to say it. "There are bodies. My aunt and uncle. Some others. I don't know who." She took a shuddering breath, so close to tears again that she found it difficult to control herself.

"Listen to me, Jelka. Do exactly what I say. There should be a medical cupboard in the rest room next to you. You'll find some tranquillisers there. Take two. Only two. Then come back to the board and stay there. All right?"

She nodded and went off to do as she was told, but then she stopped and turned, looking back at the screen. Why was there no one here? Where *was* the guard unit? The pattern was all too familiar. Like the attack on the Wiring Project that time.

It hit her suddenly. This wasn't like the other attack on

429

her. This had been set up. From inside. Someone had given
the order for the unit to pull out. Someone at the top.

Which meant that she had to get out. Right away. Before
they came for her.

Even as she turned and looked, the picture on the screen
changed. Hans Ebert's face appeared, red-eyed, his cheeks
unshaven. He had been summoned from his bed. "Jelka?
Is that you? Come closer. Come over to the board."

In a trance she went across and stood there, staring down
at the screen.

"Stay where you are. And don't worry. I'll be with you
just as soon as I can."

She stood there, a cold certainty transfixing her. Then,
as his face vanished from the screen, she reached across and
cut the connection. She laughed: a cold bitter laughter,
then, not looking back, made her way across to the transit
and went inside, pressing the down button.

* * *

It was ten minutes after four when Tolonen got to the
Ebert Mansion. One of the goat-creatures greeted him and
ushered him through to the study. It bowed low, then, in
a deep, burred voice, excused itself while it went to fetch
its master. A moment later another of the creatures entered
the room; taller, gaunter than the first, its dress immaculate. It came across to where the Marshal stood and asked
him what he would have to drink.

"Nothing, thank you," he answered, not looking at the
beast.

"Would you like something to eat, Marshal?"

It stood close to him, almost at his elbow. He could hear
its breathing, smell its heavy musk beneath the artifice of
its cologne.

"No. Now leave me," he said, waving it away.

"Is there anything I can do for you, Excellency?" it persisted, seeming not to have heard what he had said, nor
seen his gesture of dismissal.

Tolonen turned and shook his head, meeting the

creature's pink eyes. He had not noticed before how repulsive the creatures were; how vile their combination of sophistication and brutality. "I'm sorry," he said tightly, controlling the irritation he was feeling, "but please leave me alone. I want nothing, I assure you."

He watched it go, then shuddered, wondering if this would be the last time he would come here; whether by this he ended it all between himself and his oldest friend. He looked around, trying to distract himself, aware that the moment was drawing close, but it was no good: the words he had come to say ran on inside his head, like an awful, unrelenting litany.

He hadn't long to wait. Klaus Ebert had doused his face, put on a robe and come down. He pushed the far doors open and strode into the room, smiling, his arms out to welcome his friend.

"You're damned early, Knut, but you're as welcome as ever."

Ebert clasped Tolonen to him, then released him, standing back.

"What brings you here at this hour, Knut? All's well with you and yours, I hope?"

Tolonen smiled wanly, touched more than ever by the warmth and openness of the greeting, but the smile was fragile. Underlying it was a bitterness that he found hard to contain. He nodded, then found his voice. "They were well when I left them, Klaus."

He drew a breath, then shook his head once, violently, his face muscles tightening into a grimace. "I rehearsed the words, but I can't . . ." He straightened his back, controlling his emotions. Then, with his right hand, he took the file from beneath his artificial arm and handed it across.

Ebert frowned. "What's this, Knut?" He searched his friend's face for explanations, troubled now, but could find nothing there. His broad lips formed a kind of shrug, then he turned and went to his desk, pulling open the top drawer and taking out a small case. He sat, setting the file down on the broad desktop, then opened the case and drew

431

out a pair of old-fashioned spectacles, settling them on the bridge of his nose.

He opened the file and began to read.

Tolonen went across and stood there on the far side of the desk, watching Ebert's face as he read. He had written out a copy of the file in his own hand, taking direct responsibility for the matter.

After a moment Ebert looked up at him, his eyes half-lidded. "I don't understand this, Knut. It says . . ." He laughed briefly, awkwardly, then shook his head, watching Tolonen carefully all the while. "You wouldn't . . ."

He looked down, then immediately looked up again, his mouth making the first motion of speech but saying nothing. There was a strange movement in his face as he struggled towards realisation; a tightening of his lips, a brief flash of pain in his eyes.

Tolonen stood there silently, his right fist clenched tight, the nails digging into the soft palm, his own face taut with pain, waiting.

Ebert looked down again, but now there was a visible tremor in his hand as it traced the words, and after a moment a tear gathered then fell from his nose on to the sheet below. He turned the page and read on, the trembling spreading to his upper arms and shoulders. When he had finished he closed the folder slowly and took off his glasses before looking up at Tolonen. His eyes were red now, tear-rimmed, and his face had changed.

"Who else knows of this, Knut?"

Ebert's voice was soft. His eyes held no hatred of his old friend, no blame, only a deep, unfathomable hurt.

Tolonen swallowed. "Three of us now."

"And Li Yuan? Does he know yet?"

Tolonen shook his head. "This is Family, Klaus. Your son."

The man behind the desk considered that, then nodded slowly, a small sad smile forming on his lips. "I thank you, Knut. I . . ." The trembling in his hands and arms returned. Then something broke in the old man and his face crumpled, his mouth opening in a silent howl of pain, the lower jaw drawn back. He pressed his palms into the desk's surface, trying to still the shaking, to control the pain that threatened to tear him apart. "*Why?*" he said at last, looking up at the Marshal, his eyes beseeching him. "What could he possibly have wanted that he didn't have?"

Tolonen shrugged. He had no answer to that. No understanding of it.

At that moment the door at the far end of the study opened. One of the goat-creatures stood there, a tray of drinks in one hand. For a second or two Klaus Ebert did nothing, then he turned in his seat and yelled at the beast.

"Get out, you bloody thing! *Get out!*"

It blanched, then turned and left hurriedly. There was the sound of breaking glass in the hallway outside.

Ebert turned back to face the Marshal, breathing deeply, his face a deep red. "How long have I, Knut? How long before Li Yuan has to know?"

Tolonen shivered. They both knew what had to be done. "Two days," he said quietly. "I can give you two days."

Ebert nodded, then sat back in his chair, clasping his hands together tightly. "Two days," he repeated, as if to himself, then looked up at Tolonen again. "I'm sorry, Knut. Sorry for Jelka's sake."

"And I."

Tolonen watched him a moment longer, then turned and left, knowing that there was nothing more to be said. His part in this was ended, his duty discharged, but for once he felt anything but satisfaction.

★ ★ ★

There were fires on the hillside. Bodies lay unmoving on the snow. In the skies above the mountains the dark, knife-like shapes of Security battleships moved slowly eastward, searching out any trace of warmth in the icy wasteland.

In the control room of the flagship sat Hans Ebert, Li Yuan's General. He was unshaven and his eyes were red-rimmed from lack of sleep. His uniform was undone at the collar and he had his feet up on the console in front of him. Above him a bank of nine screens showed the landscape down below. Over the image on the central screen ran bright red lines of data. From time to time a map would flash up, showing the current extent of the sweep.

Hans watched the screens vacantly, tired to the core. There were drugs he might have taken to ameliorate his condition, but he had chosen to ignore them, feeding his bitter disappointment.

There were five others in the low-ceilinged room with him, but all were silent, wary of their commander's dark mood. They went about their tasks deftly, quietly, careful not to draw his attention.

Eight strongholds had been taken. Another five had been found abandoned. DeVore's network was in tatters, more than three thousand of his men dead. What Karr had begun, he, in the space of six short hours, had finished. Moreover, Jelka was gone, probably dead, and all his dreams with her. His dreams of being king. King of the world.

"The lodge is up ahead, sir!"

He looked up sharply, then took his feet down from the desk. "Good!" He bit the word out savagely, then relented. He turned, looking at the young officer who had reported it to him. "Thanks . . ."

The officer saluted and turned smartly away. Ebert sat there a moment longer then hauled himself up on to his feet and went down the narrow corridor and out into the cockpit. Staring out through the broad, thickly slatted screen he could see the mountain up ahead, the lodge high up on its western slopes.

It was a mere twelve months since he had met DeVore here, and now he was forced to return, the architect of his own undoing, following his T'ang's explicit orders. Silently he cursed Li Yuan. Cursed the whole damn business, his irritation and frustration rising to fever pitch as he stood there, watching the lodge draw closer.

They touched down less than half a *li* away, the twin turrets of the battleship pointed towards the lodge. Hans suited up then went down, on to the snow. He crossed the space slowly, a lonely figure in black, holding the bulky gun with both hands, the stock tucked into his shoulder. Fifty paces from the veranda he stopped, balancing the gun's barrel across his left forearm and flicking off the safety. Then, without a word, he emptied the cartridge into the side of the lodge.

The explosions were deafening. In seconds the lodge was a burning ruin, debris falling everywhere, sizzling in the snow as it fell, the concussions echoing back and forth between the mountains, starting small slides. He waited a moment longer, the weapon lowered, watching the flames, then turned and walked back, the heavy gun resting loosely on his shoulder.

CHAPTER·14

THE SHATTERED LAND

Klaus Ebert waited in his study for his son. He had dismissed his servants and was alone in the huge, dimly lit room, his face expressionless. The file lay on the desk behind him, the only object on the big leather-topped desk. It had been fifteen hours since Tolonen's visit and he had done much in that time; but they had been long, dreadful hours, filled with foul anticipation.

Hans had been summoned twice. The first time he had sent word that he was on the T'ang's business and could not come, the second that he would be there within the hour. Between the two had been the old man's curtly worded message: *"Come now, or be nothing to me."*

A bell rang in the corridor outside, the signal that his son had arrived. Ebert waited, his feet apart, his hands clasped behind his back. He was the picture of strength, of authority, his short grey hair combed back severely from his high forehead, but his grey-green eyes were lifeless.

There were footsteps on the tiled floor outside then a knock on the great oak door. Hans entered, followed by two young lieutenants. He crossed the room and stood there, only an arm's length from his father. The two officers stood by the door, at ease.

"Well, Father?" There was a trace of impatience, almost of insolence in the young man's tone.

Klaus Ebert narrowed his eyes and looked past his son at the two lieutenants. "This is Family business," he said to them. "Please leave us."

There was a moment's uncertainty in their faces. They

looked to each other but made no move to go. Ebert stared at them a moment then looked to his son for explanation.

"They're under my direct orders, Father. They're not to leave me. Not for a moment." His voice was condescending now, as if he were explaining something to an inferior.

Ebert looked at his son, seeing things he had never noticed before: the arrogance of his bearing; the slight surliness in the shapes his mouth formed; the lack of real depth in his clear blue eyes. It was as if he looked *at* you, but not into you. He saw only surfaces; only himself, reflected in others.

He felt something harden at the core of him. This was his son. This . . . *creature*. He hissed out a long breath, his chest feeling tight, then started forward, shouting at the two officers. "Get *out*, damn you! Now! Before I throw you out!"

There was no hesitation this time. They jerked as if struck then turned, hurrying from the room. Klaus stared at the closed door a moment then turned, looking at his son.

"There was no need for that . . ."

"There was *every* need!" he barked, and saw his son flinch slightly. "I summon you and you excuse yourself. And then you have the nerve to bring your popinjay friends . . ."

"They're officers . . ." Hans began, interrupting, but the old man cut him off with a sharp gesture of his hand.

"Your . . . *friends*." He turned to face his son, no longer concealing his anger. He bit the words out. "To bring them *here*, Hans." He pointed at the floor. "Here, where only we come." He took a breath, calming himself, then moved away, back to the desk. From there he turned and looked back at his son.

Hans was looking away from him, his irritation barely masked. "Well? What *is* it, Father?"

The words were sharp, abrasive. Hans glanced at his father then resumed his rigid stance, his whole manner sullen, insolent, as if answering to a superior officer he detested.

So it has come to this? Ebert thought, growing still, studying his son. He looked down at the file and gritted his teeth. But he didn't need the Marshal's carefully documented evidence. All that he needed was there, before him, for his own eyes to read.

"Well?" the young man insisted. "You've summoned me from my duties, threatened to withhold from me what is mine by right and insulted my officers. I want to know why, Father? What have I done to warrant this treatment?"

Ebert laughed bitterly. "My *son*," he said, weighting the second word with all the irony he could muster, but what he felt was hurt – a deep, almost overwhelming feeling of hurt – and a sense of disillusionment that threatened to unhinge his mind. He stood up, then moved away from the desk, circling his son until he stood there with his back to the door.

"What have you done, Hans? What have you done?"

The young man turned, facing his father, his fists clenched at his sides. He seemed barely in control of himself. "Yes, what *have* I done?"

Ebert pointed across at the desk. "See that file?"

"So?" Hans made no move to look. "You could have sent it to me. I would have read it."

Ebert shook his head. "No, Hans. I want you to read it now."

There was a small movement in the young man's face, a moment's doubt, and then it cleared. He nodded and turned, taking his father's seat.

Ebert went across and locked the door, slipping the key into his pocket.

Hans was reading the first page, all colour drained from his face.

Why? the old man asked himself for the thousandth time that day. But in reality he knew. Selfishness. Greed. A cold self-interest. These things were deeply rooted in his son. He looked at him, his vision doubled, seeing both his

438

son and the stranger who sat there wearing the T'ang's uniform. And, bitterly, he recognised the source.

Berta, he thought. *You're Berta's child.*

Hans closed the file. For a moment he was silent, staring down at the unmarked cover of the folder, then he looked up, meeting his father's eyes. "So . . ." he said. There was sober calculation in his eyes: no guilt or regret, only a simple cunning. "What now, Father?"

Ebert kept the disgust he felt from his voice. "You make no denial?"

"Would you believe me if I did?" Hans sat back, at ease now.

The old man shook his head.

Hans glanced at the file then looked back at his father. "Who else knows, beside Tolonen?"

"His one-time lieutenant, Haavikko." Ebert moved slowly, crossing the room in a half-circle that would bring him behind his son.

"Then Li Yuan has yet to be told?"

He nodded.

Hans seemed reassured. "That's good. Then I could leave here this evening." He turned in his seat, watching his father's slow progress across the room towards him. "I could take a ship and hide out amongst the Colony planets."

Ebert stopped. He was only paces from his son. "That's what you want, is it? Exile? A safe passage?"

Hans laughed. "What else? I can't argue with this." He brushed the file with the fingertips of his left hand. "Li Yuan would have me killed if I stayed."

Ebert took another step. He was almost on top of his son now. "And what if I said that that wasn't good enough? What if I said no? What would you do?"

The young man laughed uncomfortably. "Why should you?" He leaned back, staring up at his father, puzzled now.

Ebert reached out, placing his hand gently on his son's shoulder.

"As a child I cradled you in my arms, saw you learn to walk and utter your first, stumbling words. As a boy you were more to me than all of this. You were my joy. My delight. As a man I was proud of you. You seemed the thing I'd always dreamed of."

Hans licked at his top lip, then looked down. But there was no apology. "Shall I go?"

The old man ignored the words. The pressure of his hand increased. His fingers gripped and held. Reaching out, he placed his other hand against Hans's neck, his thumb beneath the chin. Savagely, he pushed Hans's head up, forcing him to look into his face. When he spoke the words were sour, jagged-edged. "But now all that means nothing." He shook his head, his face brutal, pitiless. "*Nothing! Do you hear me, Hans?*"

Hans reached up to free himself from his father's grip, but the old man was unrelenting. His left hand slipped from the shoulder to join the other about his son's neck. At the same time he leaned forward, bearing down on the younger man, his big hands tightening their grip, his shoulder muscles straining.

Too late, the young man realised what was happening. He made a small, choked sound in his throat, then began to struggle in the chair, his legs kicking out wildly, his hands beating, then tearing at his father's arms and hands, trying to break the vice-like grip. Suddenly the chair went backward. For a moment Hans was free, sprawled on the floor beneath his father's body, but then the old man had him again, his hands about his throat, his full weight pressing down on him, pushing the air from the young man's lungs.

For one frozen moment the old man's face filled the younger man's vision, the mouth gasping as it strained, spittle flecking the lips. The eyes were wide with horror, the cheeks suffused with blood. Sweat beaded the brow. Then, like a vast, dark wave, the pain became immense. His lungs burned in his chest and his eyes seemed about to burst.

And then release. Blackness . . .

He gasped air into his raw throat, coughing and wheezing, the pain in his neck so fierce that it made him groan aloud; a hoarse, animal sound.

After a moment he opened his eyes again and pulled himself up on to one elbow. His father lay beside him, dead, blood gouting from the hole in the back of his head.

He looked about, expecting to see his lieutenants, but they were not in the room. The door to his father's private suite was open, however, and there was movement inside. He called out – or tried to – then struggled up into a sitting position, feeling giddy, nauseous.

At the far end of the room a figure stepped into the doorway: tall as a man, but not a man. Its white silk jacket was spattered with blood, as were its trousers. It looked at the sitting man with half-lidded eyes; eyes that were as red as the blood on its clothes. Over one arm was a suit of Hans' father's clothes.

"Here, put these on," said the goat-creature in its soft, animal voice. It crossed the room and stood there over him, offering the clothes.

He took them, staring at the beast, not understanding yet, letting it help him up and across the study to his father's room. There, in the doorway, he turned and looked back.

His father lay face down beside the fallen chair, the wound at the back of his head still wet and glistening in the half-light.

"We must go now," said the beast, its breath like old malt.

He turned and met its eyes. It was smiling at him, showing its fine, straight teeth. He could sense the satisfaction it was feeling. Years of resentment had culminated in this act. He shuddered and closed his eyes, feeling faint.

"We have an hour, two at most," it said, its three-toed hand moving to the side of Ebert's neck, tracing but not touching the welt-like bruise there. For a moment its eyes seemed almost tender.

He nodded and let it take him through. There was nothing for him here now. Nothing at all.

★　★　★

Karr looked up over his glass and met the young officer's eyes. "What is it, Captain?"

"Forgive me, sir. I wouldn't normally come to you on a matter of this kind, but I think this will interest you."

He held out a slender dossier. Karr stared at it a moment, then took it from him. Setting down his glass, he opened it. A moment later, he started forward, suddenly alert.

"When did this come in?"

"Twenty minutes back. Someone said you were down here in the Mess, sir, so I thought . . ."

Karr grinned at him fiercely. "You did well, Captain. But what put you on to this?"

"The name sir. Mikhail Boden. It was one of the names we had as a suspect for the murder of a *Fu jen* Maitland six years ago. It seems she was Under-Secretary Lehmann's wife at one time. She was burned to death in her rooms. An incendiary device. Boden was there shortly before she died. His retinal print was in the door camera which survived the blaze. When it appeared again, I thought I'd have a look at the visual image and see if it was the same man. As you can see, it wasn't."

"No . . ." Karr got to his feet. The camera stills were of two quite different men, yet the retinal print was the same. "But how come the computer allowed the match?"

"It seems that the only detail it has to have a one hundred per cent mapping on is the retinal pattern. That's unchanging. The rest – facial hair, proportion of muscle and fat in the face – changes over the years. The computer is programmed to ignore those variations. As long as the underlying bone structure is roughly the same the computer will recognise it as being the same face."

Karr laughed. "And you know who this is?"

The young officer smiled back at Karr. "I read my files, sir. It's DeVore, isn't it?"

"Yes. And he entered Salzburg *hsien* twenty, twenty-five minutes back, right?"

"Yes, sir."

"Good. And you're tracking him?"

"Yes, sir. I've put two of my best men on to the job."

"Excellent."

Karr looked down at the dossier again. The gods knew why DeVore had made such an elementary mistake, but he had, so praise them for it. Taking the handset from his pocket, he tapped in Chen's combination, then, as Chen came on line, gave a small laugh. "It's DeVore, Chen. I think we've got him. This time I really think we've got him!"

★   ★   ★

Tolonen was crouched in the middle of the room. The corpses were gone now, his men finished here, but still the room seemed filled with death. He looked up at the young officer, his face pulled tight with grief, his eyes staring out at nothing. "I should have killed him . . . while I had the chance." He shuddered and looked down at his big, square hands. "If only I had known what mischief he was up to."

"We'll track him, sir. Bring him back," the officer offered, watching his Marshal, a deep concern in his clear grey eyes.

The old man shook his head then looked down again. Something had broken in him in the last few hours. His shoulders sagged, his hands – real and artificial – rested on his knees limply. All of the anger, all of the old blind rage that had fired him as a man, had gone. There was no avenging this, whatever he said. The young officer had seen how the old man had looked, such tenderness and agony in his face as he bent and gently touched the wire about his brother's neck. It was awful to see such things. More than could be borne.

The young man swallowed, his voice a sympathetic whisper. "Can I get you anything, sir?"

Tolonen looked up at him again, seeming to see him for

the first time. There was a faint smile on his lips, but it was only the smallest flicker of warmth in the wasteland of his features.

"Is there any news?"

The young man shook his head. There was no trace of Jelka. It was as if she had vanished. Perhaps she was dead, or maybe Ebert had her after all. He hoped not. But she was nowhere in the City. An eighteen-hour Security trawl had found no trace of her.

He went through to the living-room, returning a moment later with two brandies. "Here," he said, handing one to the Marshal. "This will help."

Tolonen took the glass and stared at it a while, then drained it at a gulp. He looked up at the young officer, his face expressionless.

"Telling Li Yuan was hard." His wide brow furrowed momentarily. "I felt I had failed him. Betrayed him. It was bad. Worse than Han Ch'in's death. Much worse."

"It wasn't your fault . . ."

Tolonen met his eyes a moment, then looked away, shaking his head. "If not mine, then whose? I knew and didn't act. And this . . ." His mouth puckered momentarily and his fists clenched. He took a deep breath, then looked up again. "*This* is the result."

He was about to answer the Marshal, to say something to alleviate the old man's pain, when a three-tone signal sounded in his head. There was news. He narrowed his eyes, listening, then smiled; a huge grin of a smile.

"What is it?" Tolonen asked, getting to his feet.

"It's Viljanen, from Jakobstad. He says to tell you that Jelka is there. And safe."

★ ★ ★

Jelka stood at the end of the old stone jetty, waiting for him. Waves crashed against the rocks across the bay. Above her the slate grey sky was filled with huge thunderheads of cloud, black and menacing.

The island was in winter's grip. Snow covered everything. She stood there, above the deep green swell of the sea, wrapped in furs against the cold, only her face exposed to the bitter air. The boat was small and distant, rising and falling as she watched, labouring against the elements. Beyond it, its scale diminished by the distance, lay the cliff-like whiteness of the City, its topmost levels shrouded by low cloud.

Only as the boat came nearer could she hear the noise of its engine, a thin thread of regularity amidst the swirling chaos of wind and wave. Entering the bay the engine noise changed, dropping an octave as the boat slowed, turning in towards the jetty. She saw him on the deck, looking across at her, and lifted her arm to wave.

They embraced on the path above the water, the old man hugging her to him fiercely, as if he would never again let her go. He pushed back her hood and kissed her on the crown, the brow, the lips, his hot tears coursing down her frozen face, cooling in her lashes and on her cheeks.

"Jelka . . . Jelka . . . I was so worried."

She closed her eyes and held on to him. Snow had begun to fall, but he was warm and close and comforting. The familiar smell of him eased her tortured mind. She let him turn her and lead her back to the house.

He built a fire in the old grate, then lit it, tending it until it was well ablaze. She sat, watching him in the half-light from the window, her hand clasping the pendant at her neck, the tiny *kuei* dragon seeming to burn against her palm.

Still kneeling, he half turned towards her, his face a mobile mask of black and orange, his grey hair glistening in the flickering light.

"How did you get here?" he asked gently. "My men were looking for you everywhere."

She smiled but did not answer him. Desperation creates its own resources, and she had been desperate to get here. Besides, she wasn't sure. It was as if she had dreamed her journey here. She had known. Known that while the storm

might rage on every side, here was safety, here the eye.
And she had run for the eye. Here, where it was warm
and safe.

He watched her a moment longer, his moist eyes filled
with the fire's wavering light, then stood. He was old.
Old, and weary to the bone. She went across and held
him, laying her cheek against his neck, her arm about his
waist. For a moment he rested against her, thoughtless,
unmoving, then he shifted slightly, looking down into her
face.

"But why here? Why did you come here?"

In her head there had been the memory of brine and
leather and engine oils, the strong scent of pine; the
memory of a circle of burned and blackened trees in the
woods; of an ancient stone tower overlooking a boiling
sea. These things, like ghosts, had summoned her.

She smiled. "There was nowhere else."

He nodded, then sighed deeply. "Well . . . It's over
now."

"Over?"

His hand went to her face, holding her where the jawbone came down beneath the ear, his thumb stroking the
soft flesh of her cheek. His own face was stiff, his chin
raised awkwardly.

"I was wrong, Jelka. Wrong about many things, but
most of all wrong to try to force you into something you
didn't want."

She knew at once what he meant. Hans. She felt herself
go cold, thinking of him.

"I was blind. Stupid." He shook his head slowly. His
face muscles clenched and unclenched, then formed a
grimace. This pained him. As much as the deaths.

She opened her lips to speak, but her mouth was dry.
She nodded. She had tried to tell him.

"He's gone," he said, after a moment. "Hans has gone."

For a moment she said nothing. Her face was blank, her
eyes puzzled. "Gone?"

Her father nodded. "So it's over. Finished with."

For a moment longer she held herself there, tensed against the news, afraid to believe him. Then, suddenly, she laughed, relief flooding her. She shivered, looking away from her father. *Gone. Hans was gone.* Again she laughed, but then the laughter died. She looked up suddenly, remembering.

"He told me to stay there. He was coming for me."

She shivered again, more violently this time, her arm tightening about her father's waist, her hands gripping him hard. She looked up fiercely into his face.

"He would have killed me."

"I know," he said, pulling her face down against his neck, his arms wrapped tightly about her. His voice was anxious now, filled with sorrow and regret. "I was wrong, my love. So very wrong. Gods forgive me, Jelka, I didn't know. I just didn't know . . ."

★ ★ ★

That night Jelka dreamed. The sky pressed down upon her head, solid and impenetrable. Voices clawed at her with hands of ragged metal, screeching their elemental anger. It was dark; a darkness laced with purple. She was alone on the tilted, broken land, the storm raging at every corner of the earth.

Each time the lightning struck, she felt a tremor pass through her from head to toe, as sharp as splintered ice. And when the thunder growled it sounded in her bones, exploding with a suddenness that made her shudder.

Through the dark, its progress marked in searing flashes of sudden light, came the tower, its eyes like shattered panes of glass, its wooden spider limbs folding and stretching inexorably, bringing it closer.

She stood there, unable to move, watching it come. It seemed malefic, evil, its dark mouth crammed with splintered bone. She could hear it grunt and wheeze as it dragged its weight across the jagged, uneven ground. Closer it came, climbing the hill on which she stood, picking its way through the darkness.

447

In the sudden light she saw it, close now and laughing horribly, its crooked mouth smiling greedily at her. Its breath was foul, rolling up the hill to where she stood. The scent of rottenness itself.

As the darkness enfolded her again she cried out, knowing she was lost. Her cry rang out, louder than the storm, and for a moment afterwards there was silence. Light leaked slowly into that silence, as if her cry had cracked the darkness open at its seams.

Things took a shadowy form. The tower had stopped. It stood there, not far below her. She could hear its wheezing, scraping voice as it whispered to itself. Her sudden cry had startled it. Then, as she stared into the half-dark, the earth between her and the tower cracked and split. For a moment the land was still and silent and then something small and dark crawled from the dark mouth of the earth. A stooped little creature with eyes that burned like coals. Its wet, dark skin shone with an inner light and its limbs were short but strong, as though it had dug its way to the surface. As she watched, it climbed up on to its legs and stood there, facing the tower. In one hand it held a circle of glass backed with silver. Holding it up before it, it advanced.

Light flashed from the circle and where it touched the tower small leaves of bright red flame blossomed. The tower shrieked and stumbled backward, but the small, dark creature kept advancing, light flashing from the circle in its hand, the tiny fires spreading, taking hold.

Screeching, the tower turned and began to run, its thin legs pumping awkwardly. Thick black smoke billowed up into the air above it, gathering in a dense layer beneath the solid sky. The noise of the tower burning, splitting, was fierce. Great cracks and pops filled the bright-lit silence.

The creature turned, looking at her, the glass lowered now. Its fiery eyes seemed both kind and sad. They seemed to see right through her, to the bone and the darkness beneath the bone.

She stared back at it as the darkness slowly returned, filling the space between the sky and the cracked and shattered land, until all she could see was the fallen tower, blazing in the distance, and, so close she could feel their warmth, two jewels of fire set into the soft and lambent flesh of the creature.

As she watched, it smiled and bowed its head to her. Then, its movements quick and fluid, it returned to the open crack and slipped down into the darkness of the earth.

* * *

For eighteen hours DeVore hadn't settled, but had moved on constantly, as if he knew that his only salvation lay in flight. His disguises had been tenuous at best and he had cashed in old friendships at a frightening rate, but all the while Karr had kept close on his tail. Then, suddenly, Karr had lost him. That was in Danzig. It might have ended there, but DeVore got careless. For the second time that day he doubled up on an identity.

As a back-up, Karr had programmed the Security pass computer to "tag" all past known aliases of DeVore – eight in all – with special priority "screamers". If DeVore used any of them, alarm bells would ring. It was the slimmest of chances and no one expected it to work, but for once it did. A day after Karr had lost the trail, DeVore gave himself away. A screamer sounded on one Joseph Ganz, who had moved up-level in one of the Amsterdam stacks. A random Security patrol had checked on his ID and passed him through, unaware of the "tag".

Karr was there in less than an hour. Chen was waiting for him, with a full Security battalion. He had sealed off all the surrounding stacks and put Security guards at every entrance to the transit lifts. The fast-track bolts were shut down and they were ready to go in.

There was no possibility that DeVore had gone far. All the local Security posts had been alerted at once. If DeVore was coming out, it would be by force this time, not guile. He had worn his last disguise.

Karr smiled fiercely and rubbed his big hands together.

"I have you now, old ghost. You won't slip away this time."

There were five decks to check out. Chen planned to move through them carefully, one at a time, from the bottom up – fifty levels in all – but Karr knew already where he would find DeVore. At the very top of the City. He left Chen in charge of the sweep and went on up, alone, taking the transit to the uppermost deck.

He was an impressive sight, coming out of the transit: a seven *ch'i* giant, in full combat dress and carrying a fearsome array of weaponry. He walked slowly, searching faces, but knowing that he wouldn't find DeVore there, in the corridors. His quarry would be higher up, holed up somewhere in one of the penthouse apartments. With an old friend, perhaps.

Karr lowered his visor and pressed out a code into his wrist comset. On to the transparent visor came a read-out. He thumbed it through as he walked, until he came upon a name he knew. *Stefan Cherkassky*. An old associate of DeVore's and a retired Security officer. Karr checked habitation details, moving towards the inter-level lifts. Cherkassky's apartment was on the far side of the deck and at the highest level. Just as he'd thought.

DeVore would be there.

Karr took a deep breath, considering. It would not be easy. DeVore was one of the best. He had been an excellent Security Major. In time he would have been General. But he'd had more ambitious plans than that. Karr had studied his file carefully and viewed training films of him in action. Karr respected few men, but DeVore demanded respect. Speed, size and age were on Karr's side, but DeVore was cunning. And strong too. A fox with the strength of a tiger.

People moved hurriedly out of Karr's way as he strode along. The lift emptied at his bark of command and he went up. He thumbed for a map, then thumbed again for Cherkassky's service record. The man might have retired, but he could still be dangerous. It did not pay to make assumptions.

Cherkassky, Stefan. The file extract appeared after a two-second delay. He took in the details at a glance, then cleared his visor and stopped.

He hadn't realised . . . This gave things a new complexion. The old man had been specially trained. Like Karr, he was an assassin.

Karr checked his guns, all the while staring down the wide, deserted corridor. He was less than a hundred *ch'i* from Cherkassky's apartment now. If they were being careful – and there was no reason to expect otherwise – they would know he was coming. There would have been an "eye" close by the transit; someone to report back at once.

Which meant they would be waiting for him.

He switched to special lenses. At once his vision changed. Using lenses he could pick out the shape of a tiny insect at five hundred *ch'i*. Squeezing the corners of his eyes he adjusted them to medium range and checked all the surfaces ahead for signs of anti-personnel devices. It seemed clear, but for once he decided not to trust the visual scan. He set one of his hand lasers to low charge and raked it along the walls and floors, then along the ceiling. Nothing. Yet he still felt ill at ease. Some instinct held him back. He waited, breathing shallowly, counting to twenty in his head, then heard a sound behind him – so faint that it would have been easy to miss it. The faintest clicking, like a claw gently tapping the side of a porcelain bowl.

He tensed, listening, making sure, then turned fast and rolled to one side, just as the machine loosed off a burst of rapid fire. The wall exploded beside him as the heavy shells hit home. He cursed and fired back, the first few rounds wild, the next deadly accurate. The machine sputtered, then blew apart, hot fragments flying everywhere. A piece embedded itself in his side, another cracked the front of his visor.

There was no time to lose now. The machine was like

the one they had used to attack Tolonen, but more deadly. A remote. Which meant they had seen him. Seen how good he was. He was using up his advantage.

He considered the situation as he ran. They knew he was coming. Knew what he was like, how fast, how agile he was. There was one of him and two of them. Older, yes, but more experienced than him. A Security Major and a special services assassin, now sixty-eight, but still fit and active, he was certain. On those facts alone it might seem he had little chance of succeeding. But there was one final factor: something they didn't know; that DeVore couldn't know, because it had never got on to Karr's service record. In his teens – before he had become a blood – he had been an athlete; perhaps the finest athlete the Net had ever produced. And he was better now. At twenty-nine he was fitter and faster than he'd ever been.

Karr slowed as he neared the end of the corridor. There was no tape to break this time, even so, his time was close to nine seconds. They wouldn't think . . .

He fired ahead of him, letting momentum take him through the door, rolling and springing up, turning in the next movement to find Cherkassky on the ceiling above the door, held there in an assassin's cradle. He was turning with his feet, but it wasn't fast enough. Karr shot away the strands, making Cherkassky tumble to the floor, all the while his eyes darting here and there, looking for DeVore. He skipped over the rubble and crouched above the winded assassin.

"Where is he? Tell me where he is."

The old man laughed, then coughed blood. Karr shot him through the neck. DeVore had gone. Had traded on his final friendship. But he could not have gone far. Cherkassky hadn't been operating the machine. So . . .

Quickly, carefully, he checked the rest of the apartment. There was no sign of the controls here, so DeVore had them elsewhere. Somewhere close by. But where?

He pushed his helmet out into the corridor, then, a moment later, popped his head round the corner to look.

Nothing. There was a high-pitched screaming from a nearby apartment but he ignored it, stepping out into the corridor again. There was no way out overhead. The roof was sealed here. He had checked on that earlier. No. The only way out was down.

He glanced at his timer. It was only three minutes and forty-eight seconds since he had stood at the far end of the corridor. Was that time enough for DeVore to get to the lift? Possibly. But Karr had a hunch that he hadn't done that. DeVore would want to make sure he was safe, and that meant getting back at his pursuer.

He walked slowly down the corridor, keeping to the wall, the largest of his guns, an antique Westinghouse-Howitzer, pressed tight against his chest. He would take no chances with this bastard.

' He was about to go on when he paused, noticing the silence. The screaming had stopped, suddenly, almost abruptly, in mid-scream. It had taken him a second or two to notice it, but then it hit him. He turned, lowering himself on to his haunches, as if about to spring. Two doors down the corridor, it had been. He went back slowly, his finger trembling against the hair-line trigger, making a small circle of the door until he stood on its far side, his back to Cherkassky's apartment.

He had two options now: to wait or to go in. Which would DeVore expect him to do? Was he waiting for Karr to come in, or was he about to come out? For a moment Karr stood there, tensed, considering, then he smiled. There was a third option: burn away the wall and see what lay behind it. He liked that. It meant he didn't have to go through a door.

He lay down, setting the big gun up in front of him, ejecting the standard explosive shells and slipping a cartridge of ice-penetrating charges into the loader. Then he squeezed the trigger, tracing a line of shells first up the wall, then along the top of it. The partition shuddered, like something alive, and began to peel away from where the charges had punctured holes in it. There was no sound from the other side of the wall; only silence and the roiling smoke.

He waited, easing his finger back and forth above the hair-trigger as the ice curled back, revealing the shattered room. Karr's eyes took in each and every detail, noting and discarding them. A young woman lay dead on the lounger, her pale limbs limp, her head at an odd angle, garrotted by the look of it. There was no sign of DeVore, but he had been there. The woman had been alive only a minute before.

Karr crawled into the room. A siren had begun to sound in the corridor. It would bring Chen and help. But Karr wanted to finish this now. DeVore was his. He had pursued him for so long now. And, orders or no, he would make sure of things this time.

He stopped, calling out.

"Surrender yourself, DeVore. Put your hands up and come out. You'll get a fair trial."

It was a charade. Part of the game they had to play. But DeVore would pay no heed. They both knew now that this could only end in death. But it had to be said. Like the last words of a ritual.

His answer came a moment later. The door to the right hissed open a fraction and a grenade was lobbed into the room. Karr saw it curl in the air and recognised what it was. Dropping his gun he placed his hands tight over his ears and pushed his face down into the floor. It was a concussion grenade. The shock of it ripped a hole in the floor and seemed to lift everything in the room into the air.

In a closed room it would have been devastating, but much of the force of it had gone out into the corridor. Karr got up, stunned but unhurt, his ears ringing. And then the door began to iris open.

Reactions took over. Karr buckled at the knees and rolled forward, picking up his gun on the way. DeVore was halfway out of the door, the gun at his hip already firing, when the butt of Karr's gun connected with his head. It was an ill-aimed blow which glanced off the side of his jaw, just below the ear, but the force of it was enough to send DeVore sprawling, the gun flying from his hands. Karr went across, his gun raised to aim another blow, but it was already too late. DeVore was dead, his jaw shattered, fragments of it pushed up into his brain.

Karr stood there a moment, looking down at his old enemy, all of the fierce indignation and anger he felt welling up in him again. He shuddered, then, anger getting the better of him, brought the gun down, once, twice, a third time, smashing the skull apart, spilling DeVore's brains across the floor.

"You bastard . . . You stinking, fucking bastard!"

Then, taking the small cloth bag from his top pocket, he undid the string and spilled the stones over the dead man. Three hundred and sixty one black stones.

For Haavikko's sister, Vesa, and Chen's friend, Pavel; for Kao Jyan and Han Ch'in, Lwo Kang and Edmund Wyatt, and all the many others whose deaths were down to him.

Karr shuddered, then threw the cloth bag down. It was done. He could go home now and sleep.

★ ★ ★

Li Yuan stood in the deep shadow by the carp pool, darkness wrapped about him like a cloak. It had been a long and tiring day, but his mind was sharp and clear. He stared down through layers of darkness, following the languid movements of the carp. In their slow, deliberate motions it seemed he might read the deepest workings of his thoughts.

Much had happened. Out there, in the chill brightness of his study, all had seemed chaos. DeVore was dead and his warren of mountain fortresses destroyed. But Klaus Ebert was also dead and his son, the General, had fled. That had come as a shock to him, undermining his new-found certainty.

Here, in the darkness, however, he could see things in

a better light. He had survived the worst his enemies could do. Fei Yen and young Han were safe. Soon he would have a General he could trust. These things comforted him. In the light of them, even Wang Sau-leyan's concessions to the Young Patriots seemed a minor thing.

For a while he let these things drift from him; let himself sink into the depths of memory, his mood dark and sorrowful, his heart weighed down by the necessities of his life. He had companionship in Tsu Ma and three wives to satisfy his carnal needs. Soon he would have a child – an heir, perhaps. But none of this was enough. So much was missing from his life. Fei Yen herself. Han Ch'in, so deeply missed that sometimes he would wake from sleep, his pillow wet with tears. Worst were the nightmares: images of his father's corpse, exposed, defenceless in its nakedness, painfully emaciated, the skin stretched pale across the frame of bone.

The fate of kings.

He turned and looked across at the single lamp beside the door. Its light was filtered through the green of fern and palm, the smoky darkness of the panels, as if through depths of water. He stared at it, reminded of something else – of the light on a windswept hillside in the Domain as a small group gathered about the unmarked grave. Sunlight on grass and the shadows in the depths of the earth. He had been so certain that day: certain that he didn't want to stop the flow of time and have the past returned to him, fresh, new again. But had Ben been right? Wasn't that the one thing men wanted most?

Some days he ached to bring it back. To have it whole and perfect. To sink back through the years and have it all again. The best of it. Before the cancer ate at it. Before the worm lay in the bone.

He bowed his head, smiling sadly at the thought. To succumb to that desire was worse than the desire itself. It was a weakness not to be tolerated. One had to go on, not back.

The quality of the light changed. His new Master of the

Inner Chambers, Chan Teng, stood beside the doorway, silent, waiting to be noticed.

"What is it, Master Chan?"

"Your guest is here, *Chieh Hsia*."

"Good." He lifted a hand to dismiss the man, then changed his mind. "Chan, tell me this. If you could recapture any moment from your past – if you could have it whole, perfect in every detail – would you want that?"

The middle-aged man was silent a while, then answered.

"There are, indeed, times when I wish for something past, *Chieh Hsia*. Like all men. But it would be hard. Hard living in the 'now' if 'what was' were still to hand. The imperfection of a man's memories is a blessing."

It was a good answer. A satisfactory answer. "Thank you, Chan. There is wisdom in your words."

Chan Teng bowed and turned to go, but at the door he turned back and looked across at his master.

"One last thing, *Chieh Hsia*. Such a gift might well prove useful. Might prove, for us, a blessing."

Li Yuan came out into the light. "How so?"

Chan lowered his eyes. "Might its very perfection not prove a cage, a prison to the mind? Might we not snare our enemies in its sticky web?"

Li Yuan narrowed his eyes. He thought he could see what Chan Teng was saying, but he wanted to be sure. "Go on, Chan. What are you suggesting?"

"Only this. That desire is a chain. If such a thing exists it might be used, not as a blessing but a curse. A poisoned gift. It would be the ultimate addiction. Few men would be safe from its attractions. Fewer still would recognise it for what it was. A drug. A way of escaping from what is here and now and real."

Li Yuan took a deep breath, then nodded. "We shall speak more on this, Chan. Meanwhile, ask my guest to come through. I shall see him here, beside the pool."

Chan Teng bowed low, then turned away. Li Yuan stared down at the naked glow of the lamp, then moved his hand close, feeling its radiant warmth, tracing its rounded shape. How would it feel to live a memory? Like this? As real as this? He sighed. Perhaps, as Chan said, there was a use for Shepherd's art: a way of making his illusions serve the real. He drew his hand away, seeing how shadows formed between the fingers, how the glistening lines of the palm turned dull and lifeless.

To have Han and Fei again. To see his father smiling.

He shook his head, suddenly bitter. Best nothing. Better death than such sweet torture.

There was movement in the corridor outside. A figure appeared in the doorway. Li Yuan looked up, meeting Shepherd's eyes.

"Ben . . ."

Ben Shepherd looked about him at the room, then looked back at the young T'ang, a faint smile on his lips. "How are you, Li Yuan? With all that's happened, I wasn't sure you'd remember our meeting."

Li Yuan smiled and moved forward, greeting him. "No. I'm glad you came. Indeed, our meeting is fortuitous, for there's something I want to ask you. Something only you can help me with."

Ben raised an eyebrow. "As mirror?"

Li Yuan nodded, struck once again by how quick, how penetrating Ben Shepherd was. He, if anyone, could make things clear to him.

Ben went to the edge of the pool. For a moment he stared down into the darkness of the water, following the slow movements of the fish, then he looked back at Li Yuan.

"Is it about Fei Yen and the child?"

Li Yuan shivered. "Why should you think that?"

Ben smiled. "Because, as I see it, there's nothing else that only I could help you with. If it were a matter of politics, there are a dozen able men to whom you might talk. Whereas the matter of your ex-wife and the child. Well . . . who could you talk to of that within your court? Who could you trust not to use what was said to gain some small advantage?"

Li Yuan bowed his head. It was true. He had not thought of it in quite such a calculated manner, but it was so.

"Well?" he said, meeting Ben's eyes.

Ben moved past him, crouching down to study the great tortoise shell with its ancient markings.

"There's an advantage to being outside of things," Ben said, his eyes searching the surface of the shell, tracing the fine patterning of cracks beneath the transparent glaze. "You see events more clearly than those taking part in them. What's more, you learn to ask the right questions." He turned his head, looking up at Li Yuan. "For instance. Why, if Li Yuan knows who the father of his child is, has he not acted on that knowledge? Why has he not sought vengeance on the man? Of course, the assumption has always been that the child is not Li Yuan's. But why should that necessarily be the case? It was assumed by almost everyone that Li Yuan divorced Fei Yen to ensure the child of another man would have no legitimate claim upon the dragon throne, but why should that be so? What if that were merely a pretext? After all, it is not an easy thing to obtain a divorce when one is a T'ang. Infidelity, whilst a serious enough matter in itself, would be an insufficient reason. But to protect the line of inheritance . . ."

Li Yuan had been watching Ben, mesmerised, unable to look away. Now Ben released him and he drew back a pace, shuddering.

"You always saw things clearly, didn't you, Ben?"

"To the bone."

"And was I right?"

"To divorce Fei Yen? Yes. But the child . . . Well, I'll be frank and say that that puzzles me somewhat. I've thought about it often lately. He's *your* son, isn't he, Li Yuan?"

Li Yuan nodded.

"Then why disinherit him?"

Li Yuan looked down, thinking back to the evening when he had made that awful decision, recollecting the turmoil of his feelings. He had expected the worst – had steeled himself to face the awful fact of her betrayal – but then, when he had found it was his child, unquestionably *his*, he was surprised to find himself not relieved but appalled, for in his mind he had already parted from her. Had cast her from him, like a broken bowl. For a long time he had sat there in an agony of indecision, unable to see things clearly. But then the memory of Han Ch'in had come to him – of his dead brother, there beside him in the orchard, a sprig of white blossom in his jet black hair – and he had known, with a fierce certainty, what he must do.

He looked back at Ben, tears in his eyes. "I wanted to protect him. Do you understand that, Ben? To keep him from harm. He was Han, you see. Han Ch'in reborn." He shook his head. "I know that doesn't make sense, but it's how I felt. How I still feel, every time I think about the child. It's . . ."

He turned away, trying for a moment to control – to wall in – the immensity of his suffering. Then turned back, his face open, exposed to the other man, all of his grief and hope and suffering there on the surface for Ben's eyes to read.

"I couldn't save Han Ch'in. I was too young, too power-less. But my son . . ." He swallowed, then looked aside. "If one good thing can come from my relationship with Fei Yen, let it be this: that my son can grow up safe from harm."

Ben looked down, then, patting the shell familiarly, he stood. "I see." He walked back to the edge of the pool, then turned, facing Li Yuan again. "Even so, you must have sons, Li Yuan. Indeed, you have taken wives for that very purpose. Can you save them all? Can you keep them all from harm?"

Li Yuan was staring back at him. "They will be sons . . ."

"And Fei's son, Han? Is he *so* different?"

Li Yuan looked aside, a slight bitterness in his face. "Don't tease me, Ben. I thought you of all people would understand."

Ben nodded. "Oh, I do. But I wanted to make sure that you did. That you weren't trying to fool yourself over your real motives. You say the boy reminds you of Han. That may be so, and I understand your reasons for wanting to keep him out of harm's way. But it's more than that, isn't it? You still love Fei Yen, don't you? And the child . . . the child is the one real thing that came of your love."

Li Yuan looked back at him gratefully.

Ben sighed. "Oh, I understand clear enough, Li Yuan. You wanted to be her, didn't you? To *become* her. And the child . . . that's the closest you'll ever come to it."

Li Yuan shivered, acknowledging the truth of what Ben had said. "Then I was right to act as I did?"

Ben turned, looking down, watching the dark shapes of the carp move slowly in the depths. "You remember the picture I drew for you, the day of your betrothal ceremony?"

Li Yuan swallowed. "I do. The picture of Lord Yi and the ten suns – the ten dark birds in the *fu sang* tree."

"Yes. Well, I saw it then. Saw clearly what would come of it."

"To the bone."

Ben looked back at the young T'ang, seeing he understood. "Yes. You remember. Well, the mistake was made back there. You should never have married her. You should have left her as your dream, your ideal." He shrugged. "The rest, I'm afraid, was inevitable. And unfortunate, for some mistakes can never be rectified."

Li Yuan moved closer, until he stood there facing Ben, his hand resting loosely on Ben's arm, his eyes boring into Ben's, pleading for something that Ben could not give him.

"But what else *could* I have done?"

"Nothing," Ben said. "There was nothing else you could have done. But still it isn't right. You tried to shoot the moon, Li Yuan, like the great Lord Yi of legend. And what but sorrow could come of that?"

★ ★ ★

461

It was dawn in the Otzalen Alps and a cold wind blew down the valley from the north. Stefan Lehmann stood there on the open mountainside, his furs gathered tight about him, the hood pulled up over his head. He squinted into the shadows down below, trying to make out details, but it was hard to distinguish anything, so much had changed.

Where there had been snow-covered slopes and thick pine forest was now only barren rock – rock charred and fused to a glossy hardness in places. Down there where the entrance had been was now a crater almost a *li* across and half a *li* deep.

He went down, numbed by what he saw. Where the land folded and rose slightly he stopped, resting against a crag. All about him were the stumps of trees, charred and splintered by the explosions that had rent the mountain. He shuddered and found he could scarcely catch his breath. "All gone," he said, watching his words dissipate into the chill air.

All gone . . .

A thin veil of snow began to fall, flecks on the darkness below where he stood. He made himself go on, clambering down the treacherous slope until he stood there at the crater's edge, looking down into the great circle of its ashen bowl.

Shadow filled the crater like a liquid. Snowflakes drifted into that darkness and seemed to blink out of existence, their glistening brightness extinguished in an instant. He watched them fall, strangely touched by their beauty. For a time his mind refused to acknowledge what had been done. It was easier to stand there, emptied of all thought, all enterprise, and let the cold and delicate beauty of the day seep into the bones, like ice into the rock. But he knew that the beauty of it was a mask, austere and terrible. Inhumanly so. For, even as he watched, the whiteness spread, thickening, concealing the dark and glassy surface.

At his back the mountains thrust high into the thin, cold air. He looked up into the greyness of the sky, then turned, looking across at the nearest peaks. The early daylight threw them into sharp relief against the sky. Huge, jagged shapes they were, like the broken, time-bared jawbone of a giant. Beneath, the rest lay in shadow, in vast depths of blue shading into impenetrable darkness. Cloud drifted in between, casting whole slopes of white into sudden shade, obscuring the crisp, paleocrystic forms. He watched, conscious of the utter silence of that desolate place, his warm breath pluming in the frigid air. Then, abruptly, he turned away, beginning to climb the slope again.

The rawness of the place appalled some part of him that wanted warmth and safety, yet the greater part of him – that part he termed his "true self" – recognised itself in all of this. It was not a place for living, yet living things survived here, honed to the simplest of responses by the savagery of the climate; made lithe and fierce and cunning by necessity. So he then. Rather this than the deadness of the City – that sterile womb from which nothing new came forth.

He reached the crest and paused, looking back. The past and all its complex schemes was gone. It lay behind him now. From here on he would do it his way; would become a kind of ghost, a messenger from the outside, flitting between the levels, singular and deadly.

A bleak smile came to his albinic eyes, touched the corners of his thin-lipped mouth. He felt no grief for what had happened, only a new determination. This had not changed things so much as clarified them. He knew now what to do; how to harness all the hatred that he felt for them. Hatred enough to fill the whole of Chung Kuo with death.

The cloud moved slowly south. Suddenly he was in sunlight again. He turned to his right, looking up towards the summit. There, at the top of the world, an eagle circled the naked point of rock, its great wings extended fully. The sight was unexpected yet significant; another sign for him to read. He watched it for some time then moved on, descending into the valley, heading north again towards

DRAGON'S TEETH

———————

"Without preparedness superiority is not real superiority and there can be no initiative either. Having grasped this point, a force which is inferior but prepared can often defeat a superior enemy by surprise attack."

– Mao Tse-tung, *On Protracted War*, May 1938

DRAGON'S TEETH

It was dusk on Mars. On the Plain of Elysium it was minus seventy-six degrees and falling. Great swathes of shadow lay to the north, beneath the slopes of Chaos, stretching slowly, inexorably towards the great dome of Kang Kua City. Earth lay on the horizon, a circle of pure whiteness, backlit by the sun. The evening star, they called it here. Chung Kuo. The place from which they had come, centuries before.

DeVore stood at the window of the tower, looking out across the great dome of Kang Kua towards the northern desert and the setting sun. The messenger had come an hour back, bringing news from Earth. He smiled. And so it had ended, his group surrounded, his pieces taken from the board. Even so, he was pleased with the way his play had gone. It was not often that one gained so much for so small a sacrifice.

He turned, looking back into the room. The morph sat at the table, its tautly muscled skin glistening in the dull red light. It was hunched forward, its hands placed either side of the board, as if considering its next play. So patient it was; filled with an inhuman watchfulness, with an inexhaustible capacity for waiting.

He went across and sat, facing the faceless creature. This was the latest of his creations; the closest yet to the human. Closest and yet furthest, for few could match it intellectually or physically.

He took a white stone from the bowl and leaned

forward, placing it in *shang*, the south, cutting the line of black stones that extended from the corner.

"Your move," he said, sitting back.

Each stone he placed activated a circuit beneath the board, registering in the creature's mind. Even so, the illusion that the morph had actually seen him place the stone was strong. Its shoulders tensed as it leaned closer, seeming to study the board, then it nodded and looked up, as if meeting his eyes.

Again it was only the copy – the counterfeit – of a gesture, for the smooth curve of its head was unmarked; like unmoulded clay, or a shell waiting to be formed.

So too its personality.

He looked away, a faint smile on his lips. Even in those few moments it had grown much darker. The lights of the great dome, barely evident before, now glowed warmly, filling the cold and barren darkness.

"Did you toast my death, Li Yuan?" he asked the darkness softly. "Did you think it finally done between us?"

But it wasn't done. It was far from being done.

He thought back, remembering the day when he had sent the "copy" out, two weeks after the assassination squad. It had never known; never for a moment considered itself anything but real. DeVore, it had called itself, fancying that that was what it had always been. And so, in a sense, it had. Was it not his genetic material, after all, that had gone into the being's making? Were they not his thoughts, his attitudes that had gone to shape its mind? Well then, perhaps, in a very real sense, it *was* himself. An imperfect copy, perhaps, but good enough to fool all those it had had to face; even, when it turned to face the mirror, itself.

He watched the morph lay its stone, shadowing his own one line out while at the same time protecting the connection between its groups. He smiled, pleased. It was the move he himself would have made.

Shadowing . . . it was an important part of the game. As important, perhaps, as any of the final skirmishes. One had to sketch out one's territory well in advance, while at the same time plotting to break up one's opponent's future schemes: the one need balanced finely against the other.

DeVore leaned across and took a stone from the bowl, holding it a moment between his fingers, finding its cool, polished weight strangely satisfying, then set it down in *p'ing*, the east, beginning a new play.

He stood and went to the window again, looking out across the lambent hemisphere of the dome to the darkness beyond.

He had never returned from Mars. What had landed at Nanking ten years ago had been a copy – a thing so real that to call it artificial questioned definition – while he had remained here, perfecting his plays, watching – from this cold and distant world – how the thing he had made fared in his place.

It was impressive. Indeed, it had exceeded all expectations. Whatever doubts he had harboured about its ability had quickly vanished. By all reports it had inherited his cunning along with many other of his traits. But in the end its resources had proved insufficient. It was but a single man, fragile in all the ways a single man is fragile. Karr's rifle butt had split its skull and ended all its schemes. And so it was if one *were* single. But to amend the forgotten poet Whitman's words, he would contain multitudes: would be like the dragon's teeth which, when planted from the dragon's severed head would sprout, producing a harvest of dragons, each fiercer, finer than its progenitor.

He breathed deeply then turned, looking at the morph again. Soon it would be time. They would take this unformed creature and mould it, mind and body, creating a being superior to those it would face back on Chung Kuo. A quicker, more cunning beast, unfettered by pity or love or obligation. A new model, better than the last.

But this time it would have another's face.

He went across, placing his hand on the creature's shoulder. Its flesh was warm, but the warmth was of the kind that communicated itself to the senses only after a moment or two: at first it had seemed cold, dead almost. Well, so it was, and yet, when they had finished with it, it would think itself alive; would defy God himself had He said, "I *made* you."

But whose face would he put to this one? Whose personality would furnish the empty chambers of its mind? He leaned across the creature to play another stone, furthering his line in *p'ing*, extending out towards *tsu*, the north. A T'ang? A general? Or something subtler? – something much more unexpected?

DeVore smiled and straightened up, squeezing the creature's arm familiarly before he moved away. It would be interesting to see what they made of this one, for it was different in kind from the last. Was what his own imperfect copy had dreamed of. An *inheritor*. The first of a new species. A cleaner, purer being.

A dragon's tooth. A seed of destruction, floated across the vacuum of space. The first stone in a new, more terrifying game. He laughed, sensing the creature move behind him in the semi-dark, responding to the noise. Yes, the first . . . but not the last.

THE WHITE MOUNTAIN

———— · ————

Chi K'ang Tzu asked Confucius about government, say-ing, "What would you think if, in order to move closer to those who possess the Way, I were to kill those who do not follow the Way?"

Confucius answered, "In administering your govern-ment, what need is there for you to kill? Just desire the good in yourself and the common people will be good. The virtue of the gentleman is like wind; the virtue of the small man is like grass. Let the wind blow over the grass and it is sure to bend."

— Confucius, *The Analects*, Book XII

"All warfare is based on deception."

— Sun Tzu, *The Art Of War*, Book I, Estimates

CHAPTER·15

BETWEEN LIGHT AND SHADOW

Chen knelt patiently before the mirror as Wang Ti stood over him, brushing out his hair and separating it into bunches. He watched her fasten three of them at the scalp, her fingers tying the tiny knots with a practised deftness. Then, with a glancing smile at his reflection, she began to braid the fourth into a tight, neat queue. As ever, he was surprised by the strength of her hands, their cleverness, and smiled to himself. A good woman, she was. The best a man could have.

"What are you thinking?" she asked, her fingers moving on to the second of the bunches, her eyes meeting his in the mirror.

"Just that a man needs a wife, Wang Ti. And that if all men had wives as good as mine this world would be a better place."

She laughed; her soft, rough-edged peasant's laugh which, like so many things she did, made him feel warm deep down inside. He lowered his eyes momentarily, thinking back. He had been dead before he met her. Or as good as. Down there, below the Net, he had merely existed, eking out a living day by day, like a hungry ghost, tied to nothing, its belly filled with bile.

And now? He smiled, noting the exaggerated curve of her belly in the mirror. In a month – six weeks at most – their fourth child would be born. A girl, the doctors said. A second girl. He shivered and turned his head slightly, trying to look across at the present he had bought her only the day before, but she pulled his head back firmly.

"Keep still. A minute and I'll be done."

He smiled and held still, letting her finish.

"There," she said, stepping back from him, satisfied. "Now put on your tunic. It's on the bed, freshly pressed. I'll come and help you with your leggings in a while."

Chen turned, about to object, but she had already gone to see to the children. He could hear them in the living-room, their voices competing with the trivee, his second son, the six-year old Wu, arguing with the "baby" of the family, Ch'iang Hsin, teasing her, as he so often did.

Chen laughed. Things were good. No, he thought; things had never been better. It was as if the gods had blessed him. First Wang Ti. Then the children. And now all this. He looked about him at the new apartment. Eight rooms they had. Eight rooms! And only four stacks out from Bremen Central! He laughed, surprised by it all, as if at any moment he might wake and find himself back there, beneath the Net, that all-pervading stench filling his nostrils, some pale, blind-eyed bug crawling across his body while he had slept. Back then, simply to be out of that hell had been the sum total of his ambitions. While this – this apartment that he rented in the upper third; in Level 224 – had seemed as far beyond his reach as the stars in the midnight sky.

He caught his breath, remembering, then shook his head. That moment on the roof of the solarium – how long ago had that been now? Ten years? No, twelve. And yet he remembered it as if it were yesterday. That glimpse of the stars, of the snow-capped mountains in the moon-light. And afterwards, the nightmare of the days that fol-lowed. Yet here he was, not dead like his companion, Kao Jyan, but alive: the T'ang's man, rewarded for his loyalty.

He pulled on his tunic, then looked at himself in the mirror. It was the first time he had worn the azurite-blue ceremonial tunic and he felt awkward in it.

"Where's that rascal, Kao Chen?" he asked his image, noting how strange his hair looked now that it was braided, how odd his blunt, nondescript face seemed set against such elegant clothes.

"You look nice," Wang Ti said from the doorway. "You should wear your dress uniform more often, Chen. It suits you."

He fingered the chest patch uncomfortably, tracing the shape of the young tiger there – the symbol of his rank as Captain in the T'ang's Security forces – then shook his head. "It doesn't feel right, Wang Ti. I feel over-dressed. Even my hair."

He sniffed-in deeply, then shook his head again. He should not have let Wang Ti talk him into having the implants. For all his adult life he had been happy shaving his scalp, wearing its bareness like a badge, but for once he had indulged her, knowing how little she asked of him. It was four months now since the operation had given him a full head of long, glistening black hair. Wang Ti had liked it from the first, of course, and for a while that had been enough for him, but now his discontent was surfacing again.

"Wang Ti . . . ?" he began, then fell silent.

She came across, touching his arm, her smile of pride for once making him feel uncomfortable. "What is it, husband?"

"Nothing . . ." he answered. "It's nothing . . ."

"Then hold still. I'll do your leggings for you."

* * *

The woman was leaning over the open conduit, reaching in with the fine-wire to adjust the tuning, when Leyden, the elder of the two Security men, came up with a bulb of *ch'a* for her. She set the wire down, looking across at him as she peeled off her elbow-length gloves.

"Thanks," she said softly, and sipped at the steaming lip of the bulb.

"How much longer, Chi Li?"

Ywe Hao looked up, responding to the false name on her ID badge, then smiled. It was a beautiful smile; a warm, open smile that transformed her plain, rather narrow face. The old guard, seeing it, found himself smiling in return, then turned away, flustered. She laughed, knowing what he was thinking, but there was nothing mocking in her laughter, and when he turned back, a trace of red lingering in the paleness of his neck, he too was laughing.

"If you were my daughter . . ." he began.

"Go on. What would you do?" The smile remained, but fainter, a look of unfeigned curiosity in the young woman's eyes. Still watching him, she tilted her head back and ran one hand through her short dark hair. "Tell me, Wolfgang Leyden. If I were your daughter . . ." And again there was laughter – as if she hadn't said this a dozen times before.

"Why . . . I'd lock you up, my girl. That's what I'd do!"

"You'd have to catch me first!"

He looked at her, the web of wrinkles about his eyes momentarily stark in the brightness of the overhead light, then he nodded, growing quieter. "So I would . . . So I would . . ."

Their nightly ritual over, they grew silent. She drained the bulb, then pulled on her gloves and got back to work, crouching there over the conduit while he knelt nearby, watching her clever hands search the tight cluster of filaments with the fine-wire, looking for weak signals.

There was a kind of natural fellowship between them. From the first – almost three weeks ago now – he had sensed something different in her; in the way she looked at him, perhaps. Or maybe simply because she, twenty years his junior, *had* looked at him; had noticed him and smiled her beautiful smile, making him feel both young and old, happy and sad. From that first day had come their game – the meaningless banter that, for him at least, was too fraught with meaning to be safe.

"There!" she said, looking up. "One more of the fiddly little buggers done!"

Leyden nodded, but he was still remembering how her top teeth pulled down the pale flesh of her lower lip when

476

she concentrated; how her eyes filled with a strange, almost passionate intensity. As if she saw things differently. Saw more finely, clearly than he.

"How many more?"

She sat back on her heels and drew in a deep breath. "Eighty-seven junctions, one hundred and sixteen conduits, eleven switches and four main panels." She smiled. "Three weeks' work at the outside."

She was part of a team of three sent in to give the deck its biannual service. The others were hard at work elsewhere – checking the transportation grid for faults; repairing the basic plumbing and service systems; cleaning out the massive vents that threaded these upper decks like giant cat's cradles. Their jobs were important, but hers was the vital one. She was the communications expert. In her hands rested the complex network of computer links that gave the deck its life. There were backups, of course, and it was hard to cause real damage, but it was still a delicate job – more like surgery than engineering.

"It's like a huge head," she had told him. "Full of fine nerves which carry messages. And it has to be treated like a living mind. Gently, carefully. It can be hurt, you know." And he recalled how she had looked at him, a real tenderness and concern in her face, as if the thing really were alive.

But now, looking at her, he thought, *Three weeks. Is that all? And what then? What will I do when you're gone?* Seeing him watching her, she leaned across and touched his arm gently.

"Thanks for the *ch'a*, but shouldn't you be checking on things?"

He laughed. "As if anything ever happens." But he sensed that he had outstayed his welcome and turned to go, stopping only at the far end of the long, dark shaft to look back at her.

She had moved on, further in towards the hub. Above her the overhead lamp, secure on its track and attached to her waist by a slender, web-like thread, threw a bright, golden light over her dark, neat head as she bent down, working on the next conduit in the line. For a moment longer he watched her, her head bobbing like a swimmer's between light and shadow, then turned, sighing, to descend the rungs.

★ ★ ★

Chen sat there, watching the screen in the corner while Wang Ti dressed the children. The set was tuned to the local MidText channel and showed a group of a dozen or so dignitaries on a raised platform, a great mass of people gathered in the Main in front of them. It was a live broadcast, from Hannover, two hundred *li* to the south-east.

At the front of the group on-screen was the T'ang's Chancellor, Nan Ho, there on his Master's behalf to open the first of the new Jade Phoenix Health Centres. Behind him stood the *Hsien L'ing*, the Chief Magistrate of Hannover *Hsien*, Shou Chen-hai, a tall man with a patrician air and a high-domed head which shone damply in the overhead lights. The Chancellor was speaking, a great scroll held out before him, outlining Li Yuan's "new deal" for the Lowers, dwelling in particular upon the T'ang's plan to build one hundred and fifty of the new Health Centres throughout the lower third.

"About time," said Wang Ti, not looking up from where she sat, lacing-up her young daughter's dress. "They've neglected things far too long. You remember the problems we had when Jyan was born. Why, I almost gave birth to him in the reception hall. And that was back then. Things have got a lot worse in the years since."

Chen grunted, remembering; yet he felt uneasy at the implied criticism of his T'ang. "Li Yuan means only well," he said. "There are those who would not do one tenth as much."

Wang Ti looked across at him, a measured look in her eyes, then looked away. "I'm sure that's so, but there are rumours . . ."

Chen turned his head abruptly, the stiff collar of his

jacket chafing his neck. "*Rumours*? About the T'ang?"

Wang Ti laughed, pushing Ch'iang Hsin away from her. "No. Of course not. And yet his hands . . ."

Chen frowned. "His hands?"

Wang Ti got up slowly, putting a hand to her lower back. "They say that some grow fat on the T'ang's generosity, while others get but the crumbs from his table."

"I don't follow you, Wang Ti."

She indicated the figures on the screen. "Our friend, the *Hsien L'ing*. It is said he has bought himself many things these past six months. Bronzes and statues and silks for his concubines. And more besides . . ."

Chen's face had hardened. "You *know* this, Wang Ti? For a certainty?"

"No. But the rumours . . ."

Chen stood, angered. "Rumours! Kuan Yin preserve us! Would you risk all this over some piece of ill-founded tittle-tattle?"

The three children were staring up at him, astonished. As for Wang Ti, she lowered her head, her whole manner suddenly submissive.

"Forgive me, husband, I . . ."

The sharp movement of his hand silenced her. He turned, agitated, and went to the set, jabbing a finger angrily at the power button. At once the room was silent. He turned back, facing her, his face suffused with anger.

"I am surprised at you, Wang Ti. To slander a good man like Shou Chen-hai. Do you know for a fact what the *Hsien L'ing* has or hasn't bought? Have you been inside his Mansion? Besides, he is a rich man. Why should he not have such things? Why are you so quick to believe he has used the T'ang's money and not his own? What evidence have you?"

He huffed impatiently. "Can't you see how foolish this is? How dangerous? Gods, if you were to repeat to the wrong ear what you've just said to me, we would all be in trouble! Do you want that? Do you want us to lose all we've worked so long and hard to build? Because it's still a crime to damage a man's reputation with false allegations. Demotion, that's what I'm talking about, Wang Ti. Demotion. Back below the Net."

Wang Ti gave a tiny shudder, then nodded. "Forgive me, Kao Chen. I was wrong to say what I did. I will say no more about the *Hsien L'ing*."

Chen stared at her a moment longer, letting his anger drain from him, then nodded, satisfied. "Good. Then we'll say no more. Now hurry or we'll be late. I promised Karr we'd be there by second bell."

★ ★ ★

Shou Chen-hai looked about him nervously, then, satisfied that everything was prepared, forced himself to relax.

The T'ang's Chancellor had departed an hour past, but though Nan Ho was high, high enough to have the ear of a T'ang, Shou's next guest – a man never seen on the media – was in many ways more important.

For Shou it had begun a year back, when he had been appointed to the Chair of the Finance Committee for the new Health Centre. He had seen then where it might lead . . . *if* he was clever enough, audacious enough. He had heard of the merchant some time before and, his mind made up, had gone out of his way to win his friendship. But it was only when *Shih* Novacek had finally called on him, impressed more by his persistence than his gifts or offers of help, that he had had a chance to win him to his scheme. And now, this afternoon, that friendship would bear its first fruit.

Novacek had briefed him fully on how to behave. Even so, Shou's hands trembled with a mixture of fear and excitement at the thought of entertaining a Red Pole, a real-life 426, like on the trivee serials. He called the Chief Steward over and wiped his hands on the towel the man held out for him, dabbing his forehead nervously. When he had first considered all this he had imagined a meeting with the Big Boss, the 489 himself, but Novacek had quickly disillusioned him. The Triad bosses rarely met the people they dealt with. They were careful to use intermediaries. Men like Novacek, or like their Red Poles, the 'Executioners' of the Triads; cultured, discreet men with the manners of Mandarins and the instincts of sharks.

The curtains at the far end of the long room swished back and four young, muscular-looking Han entered, Novacek just behind. They wore yellow headbands with a wheel – the symbol of the Big Circle Triad – embroidered in blue silk above the forehead. Novacek looked across and smiled reassuringly. Again, Shou had been prepared for this – even so, the thought of being 'checked out' by the Red Pole was faintly disturbing.

They worked with an impressive thoroughness, as if it were much more than simple precaution. But then, if what *Shih* Novacek said were true, theirs was a cut-throat world down there, and those who succeeded were not merely the strongest but the most careful.

Novacek came across, bowing to Shou Chen-hai. "You have done well, *Hsien L'ing* Shou," he said, indicating the spread Shou had prepared.

Shou returned Novacek's bow, immensely gratified by the merchant's praise. "It is but the humblest fare, I am afraid."

Novacek came closer, lowering his voice. "Remember what I said. Do not smile at our friend when he comes. Nor should you show any sign of familiarity. Yao Tzu, like most Red Poles, is a proud man – he has great face – but understandably so. One does not become a Red Pole through family influence or by sitting exams. The *Hung Mun*, the Secret Societies, are a different kind of school – the very toughest of schools, you might say, and our friend, the Red Pole, is its finest graduate. If any other man were qualified for the job, then *he* would be Red Pole and our friend, Yao Tzu would be dead. You understand?"

Shou Chen-hai bowed his head, swallowing nervously, made aware once again of the risks he was taking even in meeting this man. His eyes went to the *Hung Mao*'s face. "You will sit beside me, *Shih* Novacek?"

Novacek smiled reassuringly. "Do not worry, *Hsien L'ing* Shou. Just do as I've said and all will be well."

Shou Chen-hai gave a tiny shudder, then bowed again, grateful that the merchant had agreed to this favour. It would cost him, he knew, but if his scheme succeeded it would be a small price to pay.

At the entrance to the kitchen one of the runners appeared again, giving a brief hand-signal to one of his compatriots. At once the young man turned and disappeared through the curtain.

"All's well, it seems," Novacek said, turning back. "Come, let's go across. Our friend, the Red Pole will be here any moment now."

Little was said during the meal. Yao Tzu sat, expressionless, facing Shou Chen-hai across the main table, one of his henchmen seated either side of him. If what Novacek said were true, the Red Pole himself would be unarmed, but that didn't mean that he was unprepared for trouble. The henchmen were big, vicious-looking brutes who sat there, eating nothing. They merely stared at Shou; stared and stared until his initial discomfort became something else – a cold, debilitating dread that seeped into his bones. It was something Novacek had not prepared him for and he wondered why. But he let nothing show. His fear and discomfort, his uncertainty and self-doubt were kept hidden behind the thickness of his face.

He watched the Red Pole wipe at his lips delicately with the cloth, then look across at him. Yao Tzu had tiny, almost child-like features; his nose and ears and mouth dainty, like those of a young woman, his eyes like two painted marbles in a pock-marked face that was almost *Hung Mao* in its paleness. He stared at Shou Chen-hai with an impersonal hostility that seemed of a piece with the rest of him. Meeting that gaze, Shou realised that there was nothing this man would not do. Nothing that could ever make him lose a moment's sleep at night. It was this that made him so good at what he did – that made him a 426, an Executioner.

He almost smiled, but stopped himself, waiting, as he'd been told, for Yao Tzu to speak first. But instead of speaking, the Red Pole half-turned in his seat and clicked his fingers. At once one of his men came across and placed a slender case on the table by Yao Tzu's left hand.

Yao Tzu looked up, then pushed the case towards him.

Shou glanced at Novacek, then drew the case closer, looking to the Red Pole for permission to open it. At the man's brief nod, he undid the catches and lifted the lid. Inside, embedded in bright red padded silk, were three rows of tiny black-wrapped packages, Han pictograms embossed on the wrappings in red and blue and yellow – a row of each colour. He stared at them a moment, then looked up, meeting the Red Pole's eyes. Again he had to fight down the impulse to smile – to try to make some kind of personal contact with the man facing him – but he felt exultant. If these were what he thought they were . . . He glanced at Novacek for confirmation, then looked back at the Red Pole, bowing his head.

For the first time in over an hour, Yao Tzu spoke.

"You understand, then, Shou Chen-hai? You have there the complete range of our latest drugs, designed to suit every need, manufactured to the very highest quality in our laboratories. At present there is nothing like them in the whole of Chung Kuo. We will supply you with whatever you require for the first two months, free of charge, and you in turn will provide the capsules without payment to your contacts in the Above. After that time, however, we begin to charge for whatever we supply. Not much, of course – nothing like what you will be charging your friends, neh? – but enough to keep us both happy."

Shou Chen-hai gave the smallest nod, his throat dry, his hands trembling where they rested either side of the case. "And my idea?"

Yao Tzu looked down. "Your scheme has our approval, *Hsien L'ing* Shou. Indeed, we had been looking for some while to move in this direction. It is fortunate for us both that our interests coincide so closely, neh?"

"And the other bosses . . . they'll not contest you?"

It was his deepest worry – the one thing that had kept him sleepless night after night – and now he had blurted it out. For a moment he thought he had said the wrong thing, but beside him Novacek was silent, and there was no sign in the Red Pole's face that he had been offended; even so, Shou sensed a new tension about the table.

"It will be dealt with," Yao Tzu answered stiffly, meeting his eyes. "When the well is deep, many can draw from it, neh? Besides, it is better to make money than fight a war. I am certain the other bosses will feel the same."

Shou let the tension drain from him. Then it was agreed. Again he felt a wave of pure elation wash through him.

Yao Tzu was watching him coldly. "You, of course, will be responsible for your end of things. You will take care of recruitment and marketing. You will also provide all tea money."

Shou bowed his head, concealing his disappointment. He had hoped they would help him out in respect of "tea money" – bribes; had assumed that they would pay well to buy his contacts, but it was clear they saw things differently. His funds were large, admittedly, since he had tapped into the Health Project finances, but they were far from infinite and he had had extensive experience already of dealing with officials. They were like whores, only whores were cheap.

He looked up, meeting the Red Pole's stare with a sudden confidence, knowing he had not been wrong all those months back. He, Shou Chen-hai, was destined for great things. And his sons would be great men, too. Maybe even Ministers.

When they had gone he sat there, studying the contents of the case. If what he had heard were true, this lot alone was worth half a million. He touched his tongue to his teeth thoughtfully, then lifted one of the tiny packages from its bed.

It was identical in size to all the others, its waxy, midnight black wrapper heat-sealed on the reverse with the blue wheel logo of the Big Circle. The only difference was the marking on the front. In this instance the pictograms were in red. *Pan shuai ch'i*, it read – "half-life". The others had similarly strange names. He set it in its place and sat back, staring thoughtfully into the distance. He was still sitting there when Novacek came back.

"What are these?"

Novacek hesitated, then laughed. "You know what they are."

"I know they're drugs, but why are they so different? He said there was nothing like them in Chung Kuo. Why? I need to know if I'm going to sell them."

Novacek studied him a moment, then nodded. "Okay, Shou Chen-hai. Let me tell you what's happening . . . what's *really* happening here."

* * *

"It's all pipes now," said Vasska, his voice coming from the darkness close by. "The shit goes down and the water comes up. Water and shit. Growth and decay. Old processes, but mechanised now. Forced into narrow pipes."

A warm, throaty laughter greeted Vasska's comment. "Don't we just know it," said Erika, her knees rubbing against Ywe Hao's in the cramped space.

"They fool themselves," Vasska continued, warming to his theme. "But it isn't a real living space, it's a bloody machine. Switch it off and they'd die, they're so cut off from things."

"And we're so different?"

Ywe Hao's comment was sharp, her irritation with Vasska mixed up with a fear that they might be overheard. They were high up here, at the very top of the stack, under the roof itself, but who knew what tricks acoustics played in the ventilation system? She glanced at the faintly glowing figure at her wrist and gritted her teeth.

"Yes, we're different," said Vasska, leaning closer, so that she could feel his breath on her cheek. "We're different

485

because we want to tear it down. To level it all and get back to the earth."

It was close to an insult. As if she had forgotten – she, who had been in the movement a good five years longer than this . . . this *boy*! Nor was it what she had really meant. They too were cut off. They too had lived their lives inside the machine. So what if they only *thought* they were different?

She was about to respond, but Erika leaned forward, touching her arm. "How much longer, Chi Li? I'm stifling."

It was true. The small space at the hub hadn't been designed for three.

"Another five at least," she said, covering Erika's hand with her own. She liked the woman, for all her faults, whereas Vasska . . . Vasska was a pain. She had met his sort before. Zealots. Bigots. They used the *Yu* ideology as a substitute for thinking. The rest was common talk. Shit and water. Narrow pipes. These were the catch-phrases of the old *Ping Tiao* intelligentsia. As if *she* needed such reminders.

She closed her eyes a moment, thinking. The three of them had been together as a team for only six weeks now – the first three of those in training and in what they termed 'assimilation'. Vasska, Erika – those weren't their real names, any more than her own was Chi Li, the name on her ID badge. Those were the names of dead men and women in the Maintenance Service; men and women whose identities the *Yu* had stolen for their use. Nor would she ever learn their real names. They were strangers, brought in from other *Yu* cells for this mission. Once they were finished here she would never see them again.

It was a necessary system, and it worked, but it had its drawbacks. From the start Vasska had challenged her. He had never said as much, but it was clear that he resented her leadership. Even though there was a supposed equality between men and women in the movement, the men still expected to be the leaders – the doers and the thinkers, the formulators of policy and the agents of what had been decided. Vasska was one such. He stopped short of open dissent, but not far. He was surly, sullen, argumentative. Time and again she had been forced to give him explicit orders. And he, in return, had questioned her loyalty to the cause and to the underlying dogma of the *Yu* ideology; questioned it until she, in her quiet moments, had begun to ask herself, "*Do* I believe in what I'm doing? *Do* I believe in Mach's vision of the new order that is to come once the City has been levelled?" And though she did, it had grown harder than ever to say as much – as though such lip-service might make her like Vasska.

For a while there was only the sound of their breathing and the faint, ever-present hum of the life-systems. Then, prefacing his remark with an unpleasantly insinuating laugh, Vasska spoke again. "So how's your boyfriend, Chi Li? How's . . . *Wolf*-gang?" And he made the older man's name sound petty and ridiculous.

"Shut up, Vasska," said Erika, defusing the sudden tension. Then, leaning closer to Ywe Hao, she whispered, "Open the vent. Let's look. It's almost time."

In the dark Ywe Hao smiled, grateful for Erika's intervention, then turned and slipped the catch. Light spilled into the cramped, dark space, revealing the huddle of their limbs.

"What can you see?"

For a moment it was too bright. Then, when her eyes had focused, she found she was looking down into Main from a place some fifty or sixty *ch'i* overhead. It was late and the day's crowds had gone from Main, leaving only a handful of revellers and one or two workers, making their way to their night-shift occupations. Ywe Hao looked beyond these to a small doorway to her left at the far end of Main. It was barely visible from where she was, yet even as her eyes went to it, a figure stepped out, raising a hand in parting.

"That's him!" she said in an urgent whisper. "Vasska, get going. I want that lift secured." Dismissing him, she turned, looking into the strong, feminine face close to her own. "Well? What do you think?"

Erika considered, then nodded, a tight, tense smile lighting her features. "If it's like last time we've thirty minutes, forty at the outside. Time enough to secure the place and get things ready."

"Good. Then let's get moving. There won't be another opportunity as good as this."

* * *

Ywe Hao looked about her, then nodded, satisfied. The rooms looked normal, no sign of the earlier struggle visible. Four of the servants were locked away in the pantry, bound hand and foot and sedated. In another room she had placed the women and children of the household, taking care to administer the exact dosage to the boys. Now she turned, facing the fifth member of the household staff, the Chief Steward, the number *yi* – one – emblazoned in red on the green chest patch he wore on his pure white *pau*. He stared back at her, his eyes wide with fear, his head slightly lowered, wondering what she would do next. Earlier she had taped a sticky-bomb to the back of his neck, promising him that at the slightest sign or word of warning, she would set it off.

"Remember," she said reassuringly, "it's not you we want, Steward Wong. Do as I say and you'll live. But Shou Chen-hai must suspect nothing. He'll be back from seeing the girl soon, so run his bath and tend to him as normal. But remember, we shall be watching your every movement."

The Steward bowed his head.

"Good." She turned, double-checking the room, then patted the pocket of her tunic. The papers were inside – the pamphlet explaining their reasons for the execution and the official death warrant, signed by all five members of the High Council of the *Yu*. These would be left on Shou's body for Security to find. Meanwhile, friends sympathetic to the cause would be distributing copies of the pamphlet throughout the Lowers. More than fifty million in all, paid for from the coffers of the long-defunct *Ping Tiao*. Money that Mach had sifted away after Helmstadt and before the débâcle at Bremen that had brought about the *Ping Tiao*'s demise.

"Okay. You know what to say? Good. Then get to work. I want things prepared for when he returns."

She joined Erika at the desk in the tiny surveillance room. At once she picked up the figure of the Chief Steward as he made his way down the corridor to the main bathroom. Keeping an eye on what he did, she glanced at the other screens, once more appalled by the luxury, by the sheer waste of what she saw. Shou Chen-hai's family was no bigger than many in the Mids and Lowers, and yet he had all this: twenty-four rooms, including no less than two kitchens and three private bathrooms. It was disgraceful. An insult to those he was meant to serve. But that was not why she was here, for there were many who lived as Shou Chen-hai lived, unaware of the suffering their greed relied upon. No, there were specific reasons for singling out Shou Chen-hai.

She shuddered, indignation fuelling her anger. Shou Chen-hai was a cheat. And not just any cheat. His cheating was on a grand scale and would result in untold suffering: in children not receiving treatment for debilitating diseases; in good men bleeding to death in overcrowded Accident Clinics; in mothers dying in childbirth because the facilities promised by the T'ang had not been built. She laughed coldly. That ceremony earlier had been a sham. The T'ang's Chancellor had been shown around the new wards and operating theatres as if they were typical of what existed in the rest of the facility. But she had seen. With her own eyes she had seen the empty wards, the un-built theatres, the empty spaces where real and solid things ought to have been. Only a fifth of the promised facility had been built. The rest did not exist – would *never* exist – because Shou Chen-hai and his friends had taken the allocated funds and spent them on their own personal schemes. She shook her head slowly, still astonished by the scale of the deception. It was not unheard of for officials to take ten, even fifteen per cent of any project. It was even, in this crazy world of theirs, *expected*. But eighty per cent! Four *billion* yuan! Ywe Hao gritted her teeth. No. It could not be tolerated. Shou Chen-hai had to be made an example of, else countless more would suffer while such as Shou grew bloated on their suffering.

She turned, looking at Erika. "Who is Shou seeing?"

Erika smiled, her eyes never leaving the screen. "One of his underling's daughters. A young thing of thirteen. The mother knows but condones it. And who can blame her?"

"No . . ." Yet Ywe Hao felt sick at the thought. It was another instance of Shou's rottenness; of his corrupt use of the power given him. Power . . . that was what was at fault here. Power, given over into the hands of petty, unscrupulous men. Men who were not fit to run a brothel, let alone a *Hsien*.

She drew her knife and stared at it, wondering what it would feel like to thrust it into Shou Chen-hai, and whether that would be enough to assuage the anger she felt. No. She could kill a million Shous and it would not be enough. Yet it was a start. A sign, to be read by High and Low alike.

She turned the knife in her hand, tested the sharpness of the edge, then sheathed it again. "Are you ready?"

Erika laughed. "Don't worry about me. Just worry whether Vasska's done his job and covered the lifts."

"Yes . . ." she said, then tensed, seeing the unmistakable figure of Shou Chen-hai at the far end of the approach corridor. "Yes. But first our man . . ."

* * *

The ceremony was far advanced. In the small and crowded room there was an expectant silence as the New Confucian official turned back, facing the couple.

Karr was dressed in his ceremonial uniform, the close-

490

fitting azurite-blue tunic emphasising his massive frame. His close-cropped head was bare, but about his neck hung the huge golden dragon pendant of the *chia ch'eng*. It had been awarded to him by the T'ang himself at a private ceremony only two months earlier and Karr wore it now with pride, knowing it was the highest honour a commoner could attain outside of government, making him Honorary Assistant to the Royal Household.

Beside Karr, soon to be his wife, stood the woman he had met at the Dragon Cloud teahouse six months before, Marie Enge. In contrast to Karr she wore bright scarlet silks, a simple one-piece, tied at the waist. The effect, though simple, was stunning. She looked the perfect mate for the big man.

Karr turned, meeting her eyes briefly, smiling, then turned back to face the official, listening attentively as the wizen-faced old man spelt out the marriage duties.

"I must remind you that in public it is neither seemly nor appropriate to show your love. Your remarks must be restrained and considerate to the feelings of those about you. Love must be kept in bounds. It must not be allowed to interfere with the husband's work nor with his duties to the family. As for you, Marie Enge, you must perform your household duties as a good wife, without reproach or complaint. In social gatherings you should not sit with your husband but should remain aloof. As a wife, all ties of blood are broken. You will become part of your husband's household."

The old man paused, becoming, for a moment, less formal.

"I am told that among the young it has become unfashionable to view things in this light, but there is much to be said for our traditions. They bring stability and peace, and peace breeds contentment and happiness. In your particular cases, Gregor Karr and Marie Enge, I realise that there are no families to consider. For you the great chain of family was broken, from no fault of your own. And yet these traditions are still relevant, for in time you will have children. You will be family. And so the chain will be re-forged, the ties re-made. By this ceremony you re-enter the great tidal flow of life in Chung Kuo. By taking part in these most ancient of rituals, you reaffirm their strength and purpose."

Chen, looking on from Karr's left, felt a tiny shiver ripple down his spine at the words. So it had been for him when he had married Wang Ti. It had been like being re-born. No longer simply Chen, but *Kao* Chen, Head of the Kao family, linked to the future by the sons he would have. Sons who would sweep his grave and enact the rituals. In marrying he had become an ancestor. He smiled, feeling deeply for Karr at that moment, enjoying the way the big man looked at his bride, knowing that this was a marriage made in heaven.

Afterwards he went across, holding Karr to him fiercely. "I am so pleased for you, Gregor. I always hoped . . ." He stopped, choked by the sudden upsurge of feeling.

Karr laughed, then pushed him back to arm's length. "What's this, my friend? Tears? No . . . this is a time for joy, for today my heart is fuller than it has ever been."

He turned, raising a hand. At the signal the doors behind him were thrown open, revealing a long, high-ceilinged room, all crystal and lace, the tables set for two hundred guests.

"Well, dear friends, let us go through. There is food and drink, and later there will be dancing." He looked across at his bride, smiling broadly, holding out his hand until she joined him. "So . . . welcome, everyone. Tonight we celebrate!"

* * *

The golden eye of the security camera swivelled in its dragon-mouth socket, following Shou Chen-hai as he approached. Moments later the door hissed back. Beyond it, in the tiled entrance hall, the Chief Steward was waiting, head bowed, a silken indoor robe over one arm.

Shou Chen-hai let Wong Pao-yi remove his outside garments and help him on with the lightweight *pau*. He breathed deeply, enjoying the cool silence of the anteroom, then turned, looking at his servant. "Where is everyone?"

Wong Pao-yi lowered his head. "Your first wife, Shou Wen-lo is visiting her mother, Excellency. She will be back in the morning. Your second wife, Shou He has taken the boys to buy new robes. She called not long ago to say she would be another hour."

Shou nodded, satisfied. "And Yue Mi?"

The old servant hesitated. "She is asleep, Excellency. Would you have me wake her and send her to your room?"

Shou laughed. "No, Steward Wong. Later, perhaps. Just now I'd like a bath."

Wong Pao-yi bowed his head again. "It is already poured, Excellency. If you will come through, I will see to your needs personally."

"There's no need. Just bring me a drink."

Alone in the bathroom, he kicked off his thin briefs, then set the wine cup down and peeled the *pau* over his head. Naked, he stretched, feeling good, then lifted his wine cup, toasting himself. The girl had been good. Much less tense than before. Much more willing to please him. Doubtless that was her mother's doing. Well, perhaps he would reward the mother. Send her some small gift to encourage her. Or maybe he would have them both next time, mother and daughter, in the same bed.

The thought made him laugh, but as he turned he slowed, sensing another presence in the corridor outside.

"Wong Pao-yi? Is that you?"

He took a step forward, then stopped, the heavy porcelain wine cup falling from his hand, clattering against the side of the bath.

"What the fuck . . . ?"

It was a man, dressed in the orange and yellow work fatigues of Maintenance, standing there, a handgun raised and pointed at him.

"Wong Pao-yi!" Shou called, staring back at the man,

conscious of his nakedness, his vulnerability. "Wong Pao-yi, where are you?"

The man laughed softly and shook his head. "Been having fun, Shou Chen-hai? Been fucking little girls, have we?"

Anger made Shou take two more steps before he remembered the gun. He stopped, frowning, seeing the odd look of enjoyment on the man's face.

"What do you want?" he asked. "All I have is in the safe in the study. Cards, cash, a few other bits and pieces . . ."

"I'm no thief, Shou Chen-hai. If I were, I'd have taken you earlier, in the corridors."

Shou nodded, forcing himself to stay calm. If this were one of the rival Triad bosses trying to muscle-in on the deal he had made with the Big Circle, then it would not do to show any fear in front of one of their messenger boys. He puffed out his chest, wearing his nakedness like a badge of courage.

"Who sent you? Fat Wong? Li the Lidless? Or was it Whiskers Lu?"

The man waved the gun impatiently and thrust a piece of paper at him. Shou Chen-hai turned his head slightly, not understanding, but at second prompting took the paper. Looking down at it, his stomach turned over.

It was a terrorist pamphlet. Itemising his crimes. Saying why they had had to kill him.

"Look, I . . ." Shou began. But there was no arguing with this. No way of dealing with these bastards. His only chance was to jump the man. But as if he knew this, the man took a step backwards, pulling back the safety. He was watching Shou intently, his eyes gloating now.

"Been having *fun*?" the man insisted, jerking the gun forward, making Shou jump and give a tiny whimper of fright. "Been fucking little girls?"

Was that it? Was it someone hired by his underling, Fang Shuo? And was all this business with the pamphlets merely a cover? He put out one hand, as if to fend off the man.

"I'll pay you. Pay you lots. Much more than Fang Shou paid you. Look, I'll take you to the safe now. I'll . . ."

494

"Shut up!"

The man's mouth was formed into a snarl, but his eyes were cold and pitiless and Shou Chen-hai knew at once he had been mistaken. He was a terrorist. There was no mistaking that mad gleam, that uncompromising fanaticism.

"Your kind revolt me," he said, raising the gun and pointing it at Shou's forehead. "You think you can buy anything. You think . . ." He stopped and turned abruptly, following Shou's eyes.

A second figure had come into the corridor. She too wore the orange and yellow of Maintenance. Taking one look at how things were, she raised her gun and came forward.

"What the fuck do you think you're doing?"

The man gave a visible shudder of anger then turned back, facing Shou Chen-hai. Even so, his face had changed; had lost its look of hideous amusement. Shou could see immediately how things stood between the two – could sense the acid resentment in the man – and at once began working on a way to use it. But it was too late.

Ywe Hao pointed her gun and fired, twice, then, a moment later, a third time, standing over the slumped, lifeless body to make sure it was dead. There was blood on the ceramic tiles. Blood in the glass-like water of the bath. She turned and looked at Vasska, her anger making her voice shrill.

"You fucking idiot! I've had to send Erika to do what you should have done. Now go! Go and link up with her. Now!"

The man huffed out his resentment, but lowered his gun and began to turn away. He was two steps across the room when he stopped and turned back.

"Someone's coming! I can hear footsteps!"

She looked up at him, shaking her head. He was such a fool. Such a bloody amateur. Why had she had to get him on her team? Quickly she placed the papers on the corpse. Then, straightening up, she went out past Vasska and into the corridor. At the far end a man had come into view –

barefoot, it seemed, and in his indoor clothes. As he came closer, she recognised who it was. It was the Security guard, Leyden.

"No . . ." she said softly. "Please no . . ." But he kept coming. A few paces from her, he stopped.

"Chi Li . . . What's going on? I thought I heard shots. I . . ."

His voice tapered off. He was frowning and looking at the gun in her hand, part of him understanding, another part refusing to understand.

She shook her head. There wasn't time to tie him up. No time even to argue with him. Training and instinct told her to shoot him and get out, but something held her back. Vasska, coming alongside her, looked at the man and raised his gun.

"No . . ." she said, reaching out to restrain his hand. "Let him go. He's not armed."

Vasska laughed. "You're a fool. Soft, too," he sneered, forgetting what she had done in the other room. "Let's kill him and get out."

Leyden was looking frightened now. He glanced from one to the other and began to back away. Vasska stepped forward, throwing off Ywe Hao's arm, and aimed his gun. But he didn't have a chance to fire it. Two more shots rang out and he fell forward, dead.

Leyden looked at Ywe Hao, his eyes wide, his mouth open.

"Go!" she said, her eyes pleading with him. "Go, before I have to kill you, too!" And she raised her gun at him – the gun that had killed Shou Chen-hai and Vasska. He hesitated only a moment, then turned and ran, back up the corridor. She watched him go – heard his footsteps sound long after he was out of sight – then, stepping over Vasska's corpse, walked slowly down the corridor, the gun held out in front of her.

★ ★ ★

The lights had been dimmed in the reception room, a space cleared for dancing. A small troupe of Han musicians had set up their instruments in one corner and were playing a sprightly tune, their faces beaming as they watched the dancers whirl about the floor.

Chen stood to one side, watching as Karr led his new wife through the dance. He had never seen the big man so happy; never seen that broad mouth smile so much, those blue eyes sparkle so vividly. Marie, facing him, seemed almost breathless with happiness. She gasped and laughed and threw her head back, screeching with delight. And all about them the crowd pressed close, sharing their happiness. Chen grinned and turned his head, looking across at his own family. Jyan and young Wu were sitting at a nearby table, sipping at their drinks through straws, their eyes taking in everything. Beside them sat Wang Ti, her heavily-swollen belly forcing her to sit straight-backed, her legs apart. Even so, she seemed not to notice her discomfort as she held Ch'iang Hsin's hands, twirling her baby daughter this way and that to the rhythms of the music.

Chen smiled, then took a deep swig of his beer. It felt good to be able to let go. To relax and not have to worry about what the morning would bring. The last six months had been murderously busy, getting the new squad ready for active service, but after tonight both Karr and he were on a week's furlough. Chen yawned, then put his hand up to smooth his head, surprised, for the briefest moment, that his fingers met not flesh but a soft covering of hair. He lowered his hand, frowning. A lifetime's habits were hard to shift. He was always forgetting . . .

He made his way back, catching Karr's eye as he circled the dance floor, lifting his glass in salute.

"Are you all right?" he asked Wang Ti, crouching at her side. "If you're feeling tired . . . ?"

She smiled. "No, I'm fine. Just keep an eye on the boys. Make sure they don't drink anything they shouldn't. Especially Wu. He's a mischievous little soul."

Chen grinned. "Okay. But if you want anything, just let me know, eh? And if you get tired . . ."

"Don't nag me, husband. Who's carrying this thing – you or me? I'll tell you straight enough when I want to go. All right?"

Chen nodded, satisfied, then straightened up. As he did, the door at the far end swung open and a uniformed guard came into the room. Chen narrowed his eyes, noting at once that the man was a special services courier. In one hand he held a Security folder. As he came into the room he looked about him, then swept off his cap, recognising Karr.

Chen went across, intercepting him. "I am Captain Kao," he said, standing between Karr and the man. "What is your business here?"

The courier bowed. "Forgive me, Captain, but I have sealed orders for Major Karr. From Marshal Tolonen I was told to give them directly into the Major's hands."

Chen shook his head. "But this is his wedding night. Surely . . . ?" Then he caught up with what the man had said. *From Tolonen* . . . He frowned. "What has been happening?"

The courier shrugged. "Forgive me, Captain, but I am unaware of the contents, only that it is a matter of the most extreme urgency."

Chen stood back, letting the man pass, watching as he made his way through the dancers to stand before Karr.

Karr frowned, then, with a shrug, tore open the wallet and pulled out the printed documents. For a moment he was still, reading; then, grim-faced, he came across.

"What is it?" Chen asked, disturbed by the sudden change in Karr's mood.

Karr sighed, then handed Chen the photostat of the terrorist pamphlet. "I'm sorry, Chen, but we've work to do. It looks like the *Ping Tiao* are active again. They've assassinated a senior official. A man named Shou Chen-hai."

"Shou Chen-hai . . ." Chen looked up from the pamphlet, his mouth fallen open. "The *Hsien L'ing* from Hannover?"

Karr's eyes widened. "That's right. You knew him?"

But Chen had turned and was looking at Wang Ti, remembering what she had said only that morning – the argument they had had over the rumours of the man's corruption. And now the man was dead; murdered by assassins. He turned back. "But your wedding night . . . ?"

Karr smiled. "Marie will understand. Besides, it will be sweeter for the waiting, neh?" And, turning away, the big man went across.

* * *

The first corpse lay where it had fallen, on its back on the bathroom floor. The face was unmarked, the eyes closed, as if sleeping, but the chest was a mess. The first two high-velocity shells had torn the rib-cage apart and spattered the heart and most of the left lung over the far wall, but whoever had killed him had wanted to make absolutely sure. A third shot had been fired into the man's gut after he had fallen, haemorrhaging the stomach and large intestine and destroying the left kidney.

Chen had already seen the computer simulation produced by the Medical Examiner on the scene, but he had wanted to see the damage for himself; to try to picture what had happened. He knelt there a moment longer, studying the dead man, fingering the fine silk of his bathrobe then looked across at the fallen wine cup, the faintly pink water of the low-edged marble bath. The medical report showed that Shou Chen-hai had recently had sex. As for the wine, he had barely sipped at the cup before he had dropped it, presumably in surprise, for it lay some way from the body, the thick stoneware chipped.

He stood and took a step back, taking in the whole of the scene, then turned, looking out into the hallway where the second corpse lay, face down, the back of the orange and yellow Maintenance worksuit stained red in a figure-of-eight where the wounds had overlapped. Chen shook his head, trying to piece it together, but as yet it made no sense. The second corpse was supposedly a terrorist. His ID was faked and, as expected, they had found a fish pendant about his neck, a copy of the pamphlet in his pocket. But was that what they had been meant to find? Was this, in fact, a Triad killing and the rest of it a front, meant to send them off on the wrong track? It would certainly make sense of the explicit mention in the pamphlet of Shou's dealings with the Big Circle. If a rival Triad boss wanted to discredit Iron Mu, or, more likely, to frighten off those who might think of dealing with him, what better way than to resurrect old fears of fanatical terrorists who struck like ghosts between the levels?

Because the *Ping Tiao* were ghosts. They had been destroyed – their cells smashed, their leaders killed – less than six months ago. It was not possible that they could have rebuilt themselves in such a short time.

Chen took the copy of the pamphlet from his tunic pocket and unfolded it. There was no mention of the *Ping Tiao* anywhere on the pamphlet, but the Han pictogram for the word "fish" – *Yu* – the symbol of the old *Ping Tiao* was prominent in several places, and the printing and style of the pamphlet were familiar. Even if the *Ping Tiao* itself had not survived, part of it – one man, perhaps, the brain and eye behind the original organisation – had come through. Unless this were an intricate fake: a mask, designed to confuse them and throw them off the scent. But why do that?

He walked through, skirting the corpse. First Level was meant to be immune from attack – a haven from such violence. But that myth had just been blown. Whoever it was, *Ko Ming* or Triad, had just sent a ripple of fear throughout the whole of City Europe.

Karr was coming out of a room to his right. Seeing Chen, he beckoned him inside.

They had set up an Operations Room here by the main entrance. The room had been a store-cupboard, but they had cleared it and moved in their own equipment. Karr's desk was at one end of the tiny room, piled high with tapes and papers. In a chair in front of it sat a middle-aged man wearing the uniform of Deck Security.

"This is Wolfgang Leyden," Karr said, taking his seat on the far side of the desk. "It seems he knew the team who were responsible for this. More than that, he was witness to one of the killings."

Chen stared at the man in disbelief. "I don't understand."

Karr looked to the man. "Leyden, tell Captain Kao what you just told me."

Slowly, and with a faint tremor in his voice, Leyden repeated his story.

"Well?" said Karr. "Have you ever heard the like?"

Chen shook his head. "No. But it makes sense. I had begun to think this was some kind of Triad operation. One of the big bosses cutting-in on another's deals, but now . . ." Now he understood. The *Ping Tiao* really were back. Or something like them. "What else have we got?"

Karr looked up. "Surprisingly little. The woman did a thorough job on the deck communications system. For the three weeks they were here there's no visual record of them."

Chen laughed. "That isn't possible."

"That's what I thought. You've got Security guards checking the screens all the time. They'd notice if anything were being blanked out, neh? But that's not what she did. The cameras were working, but nothing was being stored by the deck computer. The term for it is a 'white-out'. It would only get noticed if someone wanted to refer back to something on the tapes, and with so little happening at this level, it's rare that Security have to make checks. I looked at their log. It was almost nine weeks since they last called anything from memory. You see, there's no crime this high up. At least, nothing that would show as being crime."

Chen frowned. "You said 'she' just then when you were talking about the tampering with the computer system. How do we know that?"

Leyden spoke up. "She was good. I've seen them before, many times, but none of them were as good as her. I sat and watched her while she was at work. It was like she was part of the system." He paused, looking away, a sudden wistfulness in his face. "She was such a nice girl. I . . . I don't understand."

Chen leaned towards him. "You're certain it happened as you said. The other . . . Vasska, you say his name was . . . he had already drawn his gun when she shot him?"

Leyden nodded. "He was going to kill me, but she wouldn't let him. His gun was pointed at me. At my head." He looked up, his eyes searching Chen's face. "You'll kill her, won't you? You'll track her down and kill her."

Chen looked down, disturbed by the accusation in Leyden's voice.

"I've read their pamphlet," Leyden went on, "and it's true. I've seen them come here for meetings. Businessmen. And others. Others who had no legitimate business to be here. And I've seen the things he's bought these past eight months. Things beyond his means. So maybe they were right . . ."

Karr raised a hand. "Take care what you say, friend. Captain Kao here and I . . . we understand how you feel. The girl saved your life and you're grateful to her. But there are others who will be less understanding. They will take your gratitude for sympathy with the girl's ideals. I would advise you to keep your opinion of the *Hsien L'ing* to yourself, *Shih* Leyden. As for your account . . ."

Karr hesitated, noting the guard who had appeared at the door. "Yes?"

The guard snapped to attention, bowing his head. "Forgive me, Major, but an official from the *T'ing Wei* has arrived."

"Shit," Karr said under his breath. "So soon?"

The *T'ing Wei* was the Superintendent of Trials, and his department was responsible for keeping the wheels of justice turning in City Europe, yet it was in the department's other role – as the official mouthpiece of the State – that it was most active.

Karr turned to Leyden. "Forgive me, but I must attend to this. However, as I was about to say, your account will be entered in the official record and, if the matter comes to trial, will be offered in mitigation of the woman's crime. That said, I'm afraid I can't vouch that she'll ever come to trial. State policy towards terrorism is, and must be, of the severest kind. To have exposed Shou Chen-hai would have been one thing, to have murdered him is another."

Leyden shuddered, then stood, bowing his head first to Karr and then to Chen. As he left, Chen looked across at Karr.

"The *T'ing Wei* were bloody quick getting here. What do you think they want?"

Karr snorted in disgust. "To meddle in things, as ever. To bugger things up and muddy the clearest of streams. What else are they good for?"

Chen laughed. "Then we'll be giving them our full cooperation?"

Karr nodded. "And dropping our pants for good measure, neh?"

The two men roared with laughter. They were still laughing when the official from the *T'ing Wei* entered, trailing four youthful, effeminate-looking assistants. All five were Han, and all had that unmistakable air of self-contained arrogance that was the hallmark of the *T'ing Wei* – a kind of brutal elegance that was reflected in their clothes and manners.

The official looked about him distastefully, then began to speak, not deigning to look at Karr.

"I understand that a pamphlet has been circulated linking the *Hsien L'ing* with certain nefarious organisations."

Karr picked up a copy of the pamphlet and made to offer it, but the official ignored him.

"Our task here is to make sure that the truth is known. That this scurrilous tissue of lies is revealed for what it is and the reputation of the late Shou Chen-hai returned to its former glorious condition."

Karr stared at the official a moment, then laughed. "Then I'm afraid you have your work cut out, *Shih* . . . ?"

"My name is Yen T'ung," the official answered coldly, turning to take a folder from one of his assistants, "and I am Third Secretary to the Minister, Peng Lu-Hsing."

"Well, Third Secretary Yen, I have to inform you that it seems the accusations are true. Our friend, the *Hsien L'ing* has been having meetings with people with whom a man of his . . . reputation . . . ought not to have associated. As for the funds relating to the Phoenix Health Centre . . ."

Yen T'ung stepped forward, placing the folder carefully, almost delicately, on the edge of Karr's desk.

"Forgive me, Major Karr, but inside you will find the official report on the murder of Shou Chen-hai. It answers all of the points raised as well as several others. Moreover it paints a full and healthy picture of the dead man." Yen T'ung stepped back, brushing his left hand against his silks, as if to cleanse it. "Copies of the report will be distributed to the media at twelfth bell tomorrow. Shortly afterwards I shall be making a statement regarding the capture of those responsible for this heinous crime."

"A statement?" For once Karr looked nonplussed. "Are you saying that we have until twelfth bell tomorrow to find the culprits?"

Yen T'ung snapped his fingers. At once another of his assistants opened the case he was carrying and handed him a scroll. With a flourish, Yen T'ung unfurled it and read.

"We have been informed by our Security sources that the four man Triad assassination squad responsible for the murder of the *Hsien L'ing* of Hannover, Shou Chen-hai, were, in the early hours of this morning, surrounded by forces loyal to the T'ang and, after a brief struggle, subdued and captured."

"I see," Karr said, after a moment. "Then we're to let things drop?"

"Not at all, Major Karr. Your investigations will continue as before, but from henceforth any discoveries made will be screened by my office. I have the authority to that effect right here." He took a document from another of his assistants and handed it across.

Karr studied the authority a moment, then looked up again. "Then we're to paint black white, is that it?"

Yen T'ung was silent, a fixed smile on his lips.

"And the guard, Leyden's account?"

Yen T'ung raised an eyebrow in query.

"We have a witness who saw exactly what happened. His account . . ."

". . . will be screened by this office. Now, if you will excuse me, Major Karr, there is much to be done."

Karr watched the Third Secretary and his retinue depart, then sat back heavily, looking up at Chen.

"Can you believe that? The arrogance of the little shit. And they've got it all worked out beforehand. Every last little detail."

Chen shook his head. "It won't work. Not this time."

"Why not? The *T'ing Wei* are pretty good at their job, and even if you and I don't like what they do or the way they go about it, it is necessary. Terrorist propaganda has to be countered. It softens public opinion and that makes our job easier."

"Maybe, but this time I've a feeling that they're up against people who are better at this than them."

Karr narrowed his eyes. "What do you mean?"

Chen hesitated, then said what had been on his mind all along. "Wang Ti. She knew about Shou Chen-hai. When we were getting ready this morning, she commented upon him – on his corruption. It was most unlike her. Usually she has nothing to do with such tittle-tattle, but it seems that the rumours were unusually strong. I suspect someone seeded them long before the assassination. And then there are the pamphlets."

Karr nodded. Yes, it would be hard to counter the effect of the pamphlets. In the past they had been circulated on a small scale, but reports were coming in that millions of the things had been distributed throughout the Lowers. All of which spoke of a much larger scale of activity than before. And the assassination itself was far more subtle, far better planned than previous *Ping Tiao* attacks. Far more audacious. Whoever was behind this had learned a great deal from past mistakes.

Chen had gone to the door. He pulled it shut then turned, looking back at Karr. "So what now? Where do we begin?"

Karr lifted the pamphlet. "We begin with this. I want to know how much of it is true and I want to know how our friends the terrorists got hold of the information."

"And the two women?"

Karr smiled. "We've good descriptions on both of them from several sources – Leyden, the wives and servants, the three guards who tried to intercept them at the lift. We'll get one of our experts to run a face match and see what comes out of the files. Then we'll dig a little deeper. See what turns up."

"And then?"

It seemed an innocuous question, but Karr knew what Chen meant. If they got to the girl, what would they do? Would they kill her? Would they hand her over, to be tortured and disposed of at the whim of the *T'ing Wei* official, Yen T'ung? Or was there something else they might do? Something which was not strictly by the book?

Karr sat back, sighing heavily. "I don't know, Chen. Let's find her first, neh? Then we'll decide."

★ ★ ★

It was a dark and empty place, echoing silent, its ceiling lost in the blackness overhead. They were gathered at one end, a single lamp placed at the centre of the circle of chairs. There were nine of them, including Ywe Hao, and they spoke softly, leaning towards the lamp, their faces moving from darkness into light, features forming from the anonymity of shadow. Just now the one called Edel was speaking.

"Is there any doubt?" he said, looking across at Ywe Hao as he spoke. "There are many who have heard the guard's story. How she killed my brother – shot him in the back – and spared the guard."

"So you say," said Mach, his long, thin face stretching towards the light. "But have you witnesses to bring forward? Written statements?"

Edel laughed scathingly, moving back into shadow. "As if they'd come here! As if they'd risk their names on paper to satisfy a *Yu* court!"

"No *Yu*, even? Or is it only your say-so? Chi Li denies your charge. Without proof it is her word against yours."

"Send someone. Get proof."

A woman leaned forward, one of the Council of Five. Her face, etched in the light like a woodcut, showed strong, determined features. Her voice, when she spoke, was hard, uncompromising. "You know we cannot do that. You know also that you broke our strictest orders by going yourself."

"He was my *brother*!"

"We are all brothers."

"Not *all*, it seems. Some are murderers."

There was a moment's silence, then Mach leaned forward. "You asked for this hearing, Edel. As was your right. But you have made accusations without supporting evidence. You have brought the reputation of a good and proven comrade into question. She has answered your charges fully and still you persist. Such, one might argue, is your duty as a brother. But do not add insolence to the list of things against you."

Edel stood. His voice boomed, echoing in the dark and empty space. "So it's *wrong* to want justice, is it? Wrong to want to unmask this murdering bitch?"

His finger pointed unerringly across the circle at Ywe Hao, who kept her head lowered, the lamplight shining in the crown of her dark, neat hair. This tableau held for a moment, then, without another word, Edel sat back again, putting his trembling hands on his knees. From the fierce look of hatred in his eyes there was no doubting he believed what he said.

"Chi Li?" asked the woman, looking at her. "You stand by your account?"

Ywe Hao looked up, the lamp's light catching in her dark, liquid eyes. "Vasska was a fool. Erika and I barely got out alive. There was a patrol at the lift he should have secured. We had to shoot our way out. Erika was badly wounded. These are facts. If I could, I would have killed him for that. For risking others' lives. But I didn't. Shou Chen-hai killed him. Killed him before I could get to him."

So ran the official Security report, given to the media. Edel had done nothing, provided nothing, to seriously counter this. His evidence was rumour, hearsay, the kind of romantic legend that often attached itself to this kind of event. The Five made their decision and gave it.

"I find no case proven," said Mach, standing. "You must apologise, Edel, or leave the *Yu*. That is our law."

Edel also stood, but there was no apology. Instead he leaned forward and spat across the lamp at Ywe Hao. It fell short, but at once Veda, the female Council member, stepped forward and pushed Edel back. She spoke quickly, harshly.

"That's it. You have proved there's no place for you here. Go! And say nothing, do nothing to harm the *Yu*. The merest word and we shall hear of it. And then . . ." She raised one finger to her throat and drew it across.

Sullenly, glaring back at Ywe Hao, Edel left the circle and walked slowly across the factory floor, stopping only in the brightness of the doorway at the far end to look back, as if to say it wasn't over yet.

When he'd gone, Mach signalled to one of the men at his side to follow Edel. "Best do it now, Klaus. Veda's warning will have no effect on him. He is past reasoning."

The man nodded, then ran across the dark floor, following Edel, his knife already drawn. Mach turned, facing Ywe Hao.

"I'm sorry, Chi Li. This has been a sad day for us all."

But Ywe Hao was watching the man disappear in pursuit of Edel and asking herself if her lie had been worth the life of another man; if this barter, his life for hers, could in any way be justified. And as if in answer, she saw Leyden again, standing there, terrified, facing Edel's brother, the man she had only known as Vasska, and knew she had been right to spare the guard and kill her comrade. As right as she had been in killing Shou Chen-hai.

Veda came and stood by her, taking her hand, her words soft, comforting. "It's all right, Chi Li. It wasn't your fault."

But the thing was, she had enjoyed killing Vasska. Had wanted to kill him. And how could she live with that?

"Listen," said Mach, coming close, turning her to face him. "I have another task for you. There's a place the younger sons use. A place called the Dragonfly Club . . ."

CHAPTER·16

DRAGONFLIES

The Pavilion of Elegant Sound rested on a great spur of pale rock, the delicately carved tips of its six sweeping gables spread out like the arms of white-robed giants raised in supplication to Heaven. To either side twin bridges spanned the ravine, the ancient wood of the hand-rails worn smooth like polished jade by a million pilgrims' hands.

A dark, lush greenery clothed the flank of Mount Emei about the ancient building, filtering the early morning sunlight, while below, long, twisted limbs of rock reached down to a shadowed gorge, their dark, eroded forms slick with the spray of the two tiny falls that met in a frenzy of mist and whiteness at their foot. Farther out, a great heart-shaped rock, as black as night itself, sat peacefully amidst the chill, crystal-clear flow.

Standing at the low, wooden balustrade, Li Yuan looked down into the waters. For more than a thousand years travellers had stopped here on their long journey up the sacred mountain, to rest and contemplate the perfection of this place. Here two rivers met, the black dragon merging with the white, forming a swirl of dark and light – a perfect, natural *tai ch'i*.

He turned, looking across. Tsu Ma stood by the table on the far side of the Pavilion, pouring wine. They were alone, the nearest servants five hundred *ch'i* distant, guarding the approaches. From the gorge below came the melodious sound of the falls, from the trees surrounding them the sweet, fluting calls of wild birds. Li Yuan

510

breathed in deeply, inhaling the heady scent of pine and cypress that filled the air. It was beautiful: a place of perfect harmony and repose. He smiled. It was like Tsu Ma to choose such a place for their meeting.

Tsu Ma came across, handing Li Yuan one of the cups. For a moment he stood there, looking out past Li Yuan at the beauty of the gorge, then turned to face him, placing a hand lightly on his shoulder. "Life is good, neh, Yuan?"

Li Yuan's smile broadened. "Here one might dream of an older, simpler age."

Tsu Ma grunted. "Things have never been simple for those who have to rule. Some problems are eternal, neh? Why, it is said that even the great Hung Wu, founder of the Ming dynasty, slept poorly at night. Population pressures, famines, civil unrest, the corruption of Ministers, court intrigues, the ambitions of rivals – these were as much his problems as they are ours. Nor was he much more successful at solving them."

Li Yuan frowned. "Then you think we should do nothing?"

"On the contrary. As T'ang, it is our purpose in this life to attempt the impossible – to try to impose some kind of order on the chaos of this world. There would be no justification for our existence were it not so. And where would we be then?"

Li Yuan laughed, then took a sip of wine, growing serious again. "And in Council tomorrow? How are we to play that?"

Tsu Ma smiled. Tomorrow's was an important meeting; perhaps the most important since Li Shai Tung's death nine months earlier.

"With regard to GenSyn, I think you are right, Yuan. Wang Sau-leyan's proposal must be opposed. His idea of a governing committee of seven – one member appointed by each T'ang – whilst fair in principle would prove unworkable in practice. Wang's appointment would be but a front for his own guiding hand. He would seize upon the slightest excuse – the most petty of internal divisions

511

on policy – to use his veto. It would have the effect of closing GenSyn down, and as few of GenSyn's facilities are based in City Africa, our cousin would escape relatively unscathed, while you would be harmed greatly. Which is why I shall support your counter-proposal of a single independent stewardship."

"And my candidate?"

Tsu Ma smiled. "I can see no reason why Wang should object to Wei Feng's man, Sheng, taking charge. No. It's the perfect choice. Wang would not dare suggest that Minister Sheng is unsuited for the post. It would be tantamount to a slur on Sheng's master, the T'ang of East Asia! And even our moon-faced cousin would not dare risk that."

Li Yuan joined in with Tsu Ma's laughter, but deep down he was not so sure. Wang Sau-leyan made much of his power to offend. His sense of *hsiao* – of filial submission – was weak. If the man *had* dared to have his father killed, his brother driven to suicide, what else might he not do? And yet the question of GenSyn was the least of the items that were to be discussed. As Tsu Ma knew, Li Yuan was prepared to concede ground in this instance if Wang would give way on more important matters.

"Do you think the balance of Council will be against us on the other measures?"

Tsu Ma stared into his cup, then shrugged. "It is hard to say. I have tried to sound Wu Shih and Wei Feng on the question of the changes, but they have been strangely reticent. On any other matter we might guarantee their support, but on this I am afraid they see things differently."

Li Yuan huffed, exasperated. Without those concessions provided by the changes to the Edict and the reopening of the House, there was no chance of striking a deal with the Above over population controls. The three items worked as a package or not at all. The Edict changes were the sweetener, creating new prosperity for the merchant classes, whereas the reopening of the House would not only satisfy the growing call for proper representation of the Above in government, but would provide the vehicle for the passage of new laws. Laws controlling the number of children a man might have. Laws that the Seven might find it difficult to implement without Above support.

Tsu Ma looked at Yuan ruefully. "And the perversity of it is that Wang Sau-leyan will oppose us not because he disagrees – after all, he has made it quite clear that he would like to see changes to the Edict, the House reopened – but because it is his will to oppose us."

Li Yuan nodded. "Maybe so. But there is something else, cousin Ma. Something I have not mentioned before now."

Tsu Ma smiled, intrigued. "Which is?"

Li Yuan laughed quietly, but his expression was sombre, almost regretful. "First fill my cup, then I will tell you a tale about a nobleman and a T'ang and a scheme they have hatched to make all plans of mine mere idle talk."

*   *   *

It was all much dirtier than she remembered it. Dirtier and more crowded. Ywe Hao stood there, her back to the barrier, and breathed out slowly. Two boys, no taller than her knee, stood beside her, looking up at her. Their faces were black with dirt, their heads covered in sores and stubble. Their small hands were held up to her, palms open, begging. They said nothing, but their eyes were eloquent. Even so, she shooed them from her, knowing that to feed two would bring a hundred more.

Main had become a kind of encampment. The shops she remembered from her childhood had been turned into sleeping quarters, their empty fronts covered with sheets. There was rubbish everywhere, and the plain, clean walls she had glimpsed in memory were covered with graffiti and posters for a hundred different political groupings.

There was no sign anywhere of Security, but men wearing armbands stood at the intersections and about Main itself, wielding ugly-looking clubs. Against the walls families huddled or lay, mother and father on the outside, children between. These last were mainly Han. They called them "little t'ang" down here, the irony savage, for these t'ang had nothing – only the handouts from Above. And an unfair share of that.

It had been only eight years since she had come from here. How could it have changed so much in that brief time?

Ywe Hao pushed across Main, jostled by surly, ill-featured men who looked at her with undisguised calculation. One of them came across and grabbed her arm. She shook herself free and reached out with a quicksilver movement that surprised him. "Don't . . ." she warned, pushing him away. He backed off, understanding what she was. Others saw it too and a whisper went out, but she was gone by then, down a side corridor that, unlike the rest, seemed little changed. At the far end was her mother's place.

The room was squalid. Three families were huddled into it. She knew none of them. Angry, worried, she came out into the corridor and stood there, her heart pounding. *She hadn't thought . . .*

From across the corridor an old man called to her. "Is that you, Ywe Hao? Is that really you?"

She laughed and went across. To either side people were watching her, standing in doorways, or out in the corridor itself. There was no privacy anywhere down here.

It was her Uncle Chang. Her mother's brother. She went to him and held him tightly to her, so glad to see him that for the moment she forgot they had parted badly.

"Come in, girl! Come in out of the way!" He looked past her almost haughtily at the watching faces, sniffing loudly before ushering her inside and sliding back the panel.

It was quieter inside. While her uncle crouched at the *k'ang*, preparing *ch'a*, she looked about her. Most of the floor was taken up by three bed rolls, made neatly, tidily. To her left, beside the door panel, was a small table containing holos and 2-Ds of the family. In a saucer in front of them was the stub of a burnt candle. The room smelled of cheap incense.

"Where's Mother?"

Her uncle looked round at her and smiled. "At market. With Su Chen."

"Su Chen?"

He looked away, embarrassed. "My wife," he said. "Didn't you hear?"

She almost laughed. Hear? How would she hear? For years she hadn't known a thing. Had lived in fear of anyone finding out anything about them. But she had never stopped thinking of them. Wondering how they were.

"And how is she?"

"Older," he answered distractedly, then grunted his satisfaction at getting the *k'ang* to work. Ywe Hao could see he did little here. There was a vid unit in the corner, but it was dead. She looked at it, then back at him, wondering how he filled his days.

She had been right to get out. It was like death here. Like slow suffocation. The thought brought back the memory of the last time she had been here. The argument. She turned her face away, gritting her teeth.

The tiny silver fish hung on a chain about her neck, resting between her breasts, its metal cool against her flesh. It was like a talisman against this place; the promise of something better.

Her uncle finished pottering about and sat back on the edge of the nearest bed roll. "So how are you?" His eyes looked her up and down. Weak, watery eyes, watching her from an old man's face. He had been younger, stronger, when she'd last seen him, but the expression in the eyes was no different. They wanted things.

He was a weak man, and his weakness made him spiteful. She had lived out her childhood avoiding his spitefulness; avoiding the wanting in his eyes. From his pettiness she had forged her inner strength.

"I'm fine," she said. And what else? That she was an

515

expert killer now? One of the most wanted people in the City?

"No man? No children, then?"

Again she wanted to laugh at him. He had never understood.

"No. No man. No children," she said, after a moment. "Only myself."

She crouched beside the table, studying the small collection of portraits. There was one of her, much younger, there beside her dead brother.

"I thought Mother didn't need this."

"She gets comfort from it. You'd not deny her that?"

There was a holo of her father; one she had never seen before. No doubt her mother had bought the image from the public records. There was a file date at the foot of it which told her that the holo had been made almost eight years before she had been born. He would have been – what? – twenty. She shivered and straightened up, then turned, looking down at her uncle. "Do you need money?"

She saw at once that she had been too direct. He avoided her eyes, but there was a curious tenseness in him that told her he had been thinking of little else. But to admit it . . . that was something different. He was still her uncle. In his head she was still a little girl, dependent on him. He shrugged, not meeting her eyes. "Maybe . . . It would be nice to get a few things."

She was about to say something more when the panel behind her slid back and her mother stepped into the room. "Chang, I . . ."

The old woman paused, then turned to face Ywe Hao, confused. At first it didn't register, then her face lit up. She dropped the package she was carrying and opened her arms wide. "Hao! My little Hao!"

Ywe Hao laughed and hugged her mother tightly, stooping to do so. She had forgotten how small her mother was. "Mama . . ." she said, looking into her eyes and laughing again. "How have you been?"

"How have *I* been?" The old lady shook her head. Her

eyes were brimming with tears and she was trembling with emotion. "Oh, dear gods, Hao, it's so good to see you. All these years . . ." There was a little sob, then, with another laugh and a sniff, she pointed to the beds. "Sit down. I'll cook you something. You must be hungry."

Ywe Hao laughed, but did as she was told, squatting beside her uncle on the bedroll. From the doorway Su Chen, unintroduced, looked on bewildered. But no one thought to explain things to her. After a while she pulled the door closed and sat on the far side of her husband. Meanwhile, the old lady pottered at the *k'ang*, turning every now and then to glance at her daughter, wiping her eyes before turning back, laughing softly to herself.

Later, after eating, they sat and talked, and for a time, it seemed almost as though the long years of parting had not happened; that this day and the last were stitched together like points on a folded cloth. But when, finally, she left them, she knew at last that there was no returning. She had gone beyond this, to a place where even a mother's love could not keep her.

Looking back at Main she saw the changes everywhere. Time had injured this place, and there seemed no way to heal it. Best then to tear it down. Level by level. Maybe then they would have a chance. Once they had rid themselves of Cities.

Shivering, more alone now than she had been for many years, she turned from it and stepped into the transit, going up, away from her past.

* * *

The dark, heart-shaped rock was embedded deep into the earth beneath the pool, like the last tooth in an ancient's jaw. Its surface was scored and pitted, darker in places than in others, its long flank, where it faced the Pavilion, smoother than those that faced away; like a dark, polished glass, misted by the spray from the tiny falls. At its foot the cold, clear waters of the pool swirled lazily over an uneven surface of rock, converting the white-water turbulence of the two rivers' convergence into a single, placid flow.

From the rock one could see the two figures in the Pavilion; might note their gestures and hear the murmur of their words beneath the hiss and rush of the falling water. Tsu Ma was talking now, his hand moving to his mouth every so often, a thin thread of dark smoke rising in the air. He seemed intensely agitated, angered even, and his voice rose momentarily, carrying over the sound of the falls.

"It is all very well *knowing*, Yuan, but how will you get proof? If this is true, it is most serious. Wang Sau-leyan must be called to account for this. His conduct is outrageous!"

Li Yuan turned to face his fellow T'ang. "No, cousin Ma. Think what damage it would do to confront Wang openly. At best he might be forced to abdicate, and that would leave us with the problem of a successor – a problem that would make the GenSyn inheritance question a mere trifle, and the gods know that is proving hard enough! At worst he might defy us. If he did, and Hou Tung-po and Chi Hsing backed him, we could find ourselves at war among ourselves."

"That cannot be."

"No. But for once the threat to expose Wang might prove more potent than the actuality. If so, we might still use this to our benefit."

Tsu Ma sniffed. "You mean, as a bargaining counter?"

Li Yuan laughed; a hard, clear laughter. "Nothing so subtle. I mean we blackmail the bastard. Force him to give us what we want."

"And if he won't?"

"He will. Like us all, he enjoys being a T'ang. Besides, he knows he is too weak, his friends in Council unprepared for such a war. Oh, he will fight if we push him to it, but only if he must. Meanwhile he plays his games and bides his time, hoping to profit from our failures. But this once he has over-stretched himself. This once we have him."

Tsu Ma nodded. "Good. But how do you plan to use this knowledge?"

Li Yuan looked outward. "First we must let things take their course. Hsiang Shao-erh meets with our cousin Wang on his estate in Tao Yuan an hour from now. My friend in Wang's household will be there at that meeting. By tonight I will know what transpired. And tomorrow, after Council, we can confront Wang with what we know. That is, if we need to. If we haven't already achieved what we want by other, more direct means."

"And your . . . *friend*? Will he be safe? Don't you think Wang might suspect there is a spy in his household?"

Li Yuan laughed. "That is the clever part. I have arranged to have Hsiang Shao-erh arrested on his return home. It will seem as if he had . . . *volunteered* the information. As, indeed, he will."

Tsu Ma nodded thoughtfully. "Good. Then let us get back. All this talking has given me an appetite."

Li Yuan smiled, then looked about him, conscious once more of the beauty of the shadowed gorge, the harmony of tree and rock and water. And yet that beauty was somehow insufficient.

He grasped the smooth wood of the rail, looking out at the great, heart-shaped rock that rested, so solid and substantial, at the centre of the flow, and felt a tiny tremor pass through him. This place, the morning light, gave him a sense of great peace, of oneness with things, and yet, at the same time, he was filled with a seething mass of fears and expectations and hopes. And these, coursing like twin streams in his blood, made him feel odd, distanced from himself. To be so at rest and yet to feel such impatience, was that not strange? And yet, was that not the condition of all things? Was that not what the great Tao taught? Maybe, but it was rare to feel it so intensely in the blood.

Like a dragonfly hovering above the surface of a stream.

Tsu Ma was watching him from the bridge. "Yuan? Are you coming?"

Li Yuan turned, momentarily abstracted from the scene,

then, with the vaguest nod, he moved from the rail, following his friend.

And maybe peace never came. Maybe, like life, it was all illusion, as the ancient Buddhists claimed. Or maybe it was himself. Maybe it was his own life that was out of balance. On the bridge he turned, looking back, seeing how the great swirl of white drifted out into the black, how its violent energy was stilled and channelled by the rock.

Then turned back, walking on through the shadow of the trees, the dark image of the rock embedded at the centre of his thoughts.

* * *

It was midday and the sky over Northern Hunan was the cloudless blue of early spring. In the garden of the palace at Tao Yuan, Wang Sau-leyan sat on a tall throne, indolently picking from the bowls of delicacies on the table at his side while he listened to the man who stood, head bowed, before him.

The throne was mounted on an ancient sedan, the long arms carved like rearing dragons, the thick base shaped like a map of the ancient Middle Kingdom, back before the world had changed. Wang had had them set him down at the very heart of the garden, the elegant whiteness of the three-tiered Pagoda of Profound Significance to his right, the stream, with its eight gently arching bridges, partly concealed beyond a stand of ancient junipers to his left.

To one side Sun Li Hua, newly promoted to Master of the Royal Household, stood in the shadow of the junipers, his arms folded into his powder-blue sleeves, his head lowered, waiting to do his Master's bidding.

The man who stood before Wang was a tall, elegant-looking Han in his mid-fifties. His name was Hsiang Shao-erh and he was Head of the Hsiang family of City Europe, Li Yuan's bondsman – his blood vassal. But today he was here, speaking to his Master's enemy. Offering him friendship. And more . . .

For an hour Hsiang had prevaricated; had talked of many things, but never of the one thing he had come to raise. Now, tiring of his polite evasions, Wang Sau-leyan looked up, wiping his fingers on a square of bright red silk as he spoke.

"Yes, cousin, but why are you here? What do you want from me?"

For the second time that day Hsiang was taken aback. Earlier, when Wang had invited him outdoors to talk, his mouth had flapped uselessly, trying to find the words which would not offend the T'ang; that might make clear this was a matter best discussed behind closed doors or not at all. But Wang had insisted and Hsiang had had to bow his head and follow, concealing his discomfort.

Now, however, Hsiang was feeling much more than simple discomfort. He glanced up, then looked away, troubled by Wang Sau-leyan's directness. For him this was a major step. Once taken, it could not be reversed. Even to be here today was a kind of betrayal. But this next . . .

With a tiny shudder, Hsiang came to the point.

"Forgive me, *Chieh Hsia*, but I am here because I can do you a great service." He lifted his head slightly, meeting Wang's eyes tentatively. "There is one we both . . . dislike immensely. One who has offended us gravely. He . . ."

Wang raised an eyebrow. "Go on, Hsiang Shao-erh . . ."

Hsiang looked down. "You know what happened, *Chieh Hsia*?"

Wang nodded, a faint smile on his lips. He did indeed. And, strangely enough, it was one of the few things he actually admired Li Yuan for. Faced with similar circumstances – with an outbreak of a deadly strain of syphilis – he would have acted exactly as Li Yuan had done, even to the point of offending his own Family Heads. But that was not the issue. Hsiang Shao-erh was here because – quite rightly – he assumed Wang hated Li Yuan as much as he

521

did. But though Hsiang's loss of face before his peers had been a great thing, it was as nothing beside this act of betrayal.

Hsiang looked up, steeling himself, his voice hardening as he recalled his humiliation; his anger momentarily overcoming the fear he felt. "Then you understand why I am here, *Chieh Hsia*."

Wang shook his head. "You will have to be less opaque, cousin. You talk of one who has offended us both. Can you be more specific?"

Hsiang was staring at him now. But Wang merely turned aside, picking a lychee from one of the bowls and chewing leisurely at the soft, moist fruit before looking back at Hsiang.

"Well?"

Hsiang shook his head slightly, as if waking, then stammered his answer. "Li Yuan. I mean Li Yuan."

"Ah . . ." Wang nodded. "But I still don't follow you, cousin. You said there was some great service you could do me."

Hsiang's head fell. He had clearly not expected it to be so hard. For a time he seemed to struggle against some inner demon, then he straightened, pushing out his chest exaggeratedly, his eyes meeting Wang's.

"We are tied, you and I. Tied by our hatred of this man. There must be some way of using that hatred, surely?"

Wang's eyes narrowed slightly. "It is true. I dislike my cousin. Hatred may be too strong a word, but . . ." He leaned forward, spitting out the seeds. "Well, let me put it bluntly, Hsiang Shao-erh. Li Yuan is a T'ang. My equal and your Master. So what are you suggesting?"

It could not have been put more explicitly, and Wang could see how Hsiang's eyes widened fearfully before he looked down again. Wang reached out and took another fruit, waiting, enjoying the moment. Would Hsiang dare take the next step, or would he draw back?

"I . . ." Hsiang shuddered. His hands pulled at the silk over his thighs. Then, after another titanic inner struggle, he looked up again. "There is a substance I have heard of. An illegal substance that was developed, I am told, in the laboratories of SimFic."

"A substance?"

Hsiang moved his head uncomfortably. "Yes, *Chieh Hsia*. Something which destroys the female's ability to produce eggs."

"Ah . . ." Wang sat back, staring up into the blueness. "And this substance? You have it, I take it?"

Hsiang shook his head. "No, *Chieh Hsia*. It was taken in a raid on one of *Shih* Berdichev's establishments. Your late father's Security forces undertook that raid, I believe, yet the substance . . ."

"Was destroyed, I should think," Wang said brusquely. "But tell me, cousin. Had it existed – had there been some of this substance remaining, held, perhaps, illegally, in defiance of the Edict – what would you have done with it?"

Again it was too direct. Again Hsiang shied back like a frightened horse. Yet the desire for revenge – that burning need in him to reverse the humiliation he had suffered at Li Yuan's hands – drove him on. He spoke quickly, nervously, forcing the words out before his courage failed.

"I plan to hold a party, *Chieh Hsia*. In celebration of Li Yuan's official birthday. He will accept, naturally, and his wives will accompany him. It is there that I will administer this substance to them."

Wang Sau-leyan had been sitting forward, listening attentively. Now he sat back, laughing. "You mean, they will sit there calmly while you spoon it down their throats?"

Hsiang shook his head irritably. "No, *Chieh Hsia*. I . . . The substance will be in their drinks."

"Oh, of course!" Wang let out another burst of laughter. "And the *She tou*, the official taster – what will he have been doing all this while?"

Hsiang looked down, biting back his obvious anger at Wang Sau-leyan's mockery. "I am told this substance is tasteless, *Chieh Hsia*. That even a *She tou* would be unable to detect any trace of its presence."

Wang sat forward, suddenly more conciliatory. He looked across at Sun Li Hua, then back at Hsiang Shao-erh, smiling.

"Let me make this absolutely clear, Hsiang Shao-erh. What you are suggesting is that I provide you with a special substance – an illegal substance – that you will then administer secretly to Li Yuan's three wives. A substance that will prevent them from ovulating."

Hsiang swallowed deeply, then nodded. "That is it, *Chieh Hsia*."

"And if our young friend marries again?"

Hsiang laughed uneasily. "*Chieh Hsia?*"

"If Li Yuan casts off these three and marries again?"

Hsiang's mouth worked uselessly.

Wang shook his head. "No matter. In the short term your scheme will deny Li Yuan sons. Will kill them even before they are born, neh?"

Hsiang shuddered. "As he killed mine, *Chieh Hsia.*"

It was not strictly true. Hsiang's sons had killed themselves. Or, at least, had fallen ill from the *yang mei ping* – the Willow-plum sickness – that had spread among the Minor Families after the entertainment at Hsiang's estate. If Li Yuan had helped Hsiang's sons end their worthless lives a few days earlier than otherwise, that was more to his credit than to theirs. They had been fated anyway. But Wang was unconcerned with such sophistry. All that concerned him was how he might use this. Hsiang's sense of humiliation made him useful, almost the perfect means of getting back at Li Yuan. *Almost.*

Wang Sau-leyan leaned forward, thrusting out his right hand, the matt black surface of the *Ywe Lung*, the ring of power, resting like a saddle on the index finger.

Hsiang stared at it a moment, not understanding, then, meeting Wang's eyes, he quickly knelt, drawing the ring to his lips and kissing it once, twice, a third time before he released it, his head remaining bowed before the T'ang of Africa.

* * *

Karr had washed and put on a fresh uniform ready for the meeting. He turned from the sink and looked across. Marie was in the other room, standing before the full-length mirror. In the lamp's light her skin was a pale ivory, the long line of her backbone prominent as she leaned forward.

For a moment he was perfectly still, watching her, a tiny thrill of delight rippling through him. She was so strong, so perfectly formed. He felt his flesh stir and gave a soft laugh, going across.

He closed his eyes, embracing her from behind, the warm softness of her skin, that sense of silk over steel, intoxicating. She turned, folding into his arms, her face coming up to meet his in a kiss.

"You must go," she said, smiling.

"Must I?"

"Yes, you must. Besides, haven't you had enough?"

He shook his head, his smile broadening. "No. But you're right. I must go. There's much to be done."

Her smile changed to a look of concern. "You should have slept . . ."

He laughed. "And you'd have let me?"

She shook her head.

"No. And nor could I with you beside me."

"The time will come . . ."

He laughed. "Maybe. I can't imagine it, but . . ."

She lifted her hand. "Here."

He took the two pills from her and swallowed them down. They would keep him awake, alert, for another twelve to fifteen hours – long enough to get things done. Then he could sleep. If she'd let him.

"Is it important?" Marie asked, a note of curiosity creeping into her voice.

"It is the T'ang's business," he answered cryptically, stone-faced, then laughed. "You must learn patience, my love. There are things I have to do . . . well, they're not always pleasant . . ."

She put a finger to his lips. "I understand. Now go. I'll be here, waiting, when you get back."

He stood back from her, at arm's length, his hands kneading her shoulders gently, then bent forward, kissing her breasts. "Until then . . ."

She shivered, then came close again, going up on tiptoe to kiss the bridge of his nose. "Take care, my love, whatever it is."

★ ★ ★

"Okay, Major Karr. You can take off the blindfold."

Karr looked about him, genuinely surprised. "Where are we? First Level?"

The servant lowered his head respectfully, but there was a smile on his face. He was too wary, too experienced in his Master's service, to be caught by such a blatant attempt to elicit information, but he was also aware that, blindfolded as he was, Karr knew he had been taken down the levels, not up.

"If you would follow me . . ."

Karr smiled and followed, taken aback by the elegance of the rooms through which they passed. He had not thought such luxury existed here just above the Net, but it was not really that surprising. He had read the report on the United Bamboo; had seen the financial estimates for the last five years. With an annual turnover of one hundred and fifteen billion *yuan*, Fat Wong, the big boss of United Bamboo, could afford luxuries like these. Even so, it was unexpected to find them in such a setting. Like finding an oasis on Mars.

Karr looked down, noting that the floor mosaic mirrored that of the ceiling overhead. Nine long, thick canes of bamboo were gripped by a single, giant hand, the ivory yellow of the canes and the hand contrasted against the brilliant emerald green of a paddy field. Karr smiled, thinking of how often he had seen that symbol, on the headbands of dead runners trapped in Security ambushes, or on the packaging of illicitly smuggled goods that had made their way up from the Net. And now he was to meet the head behind that grasping hand – the 489 himself.

The servant had stopped. Now he turned, facing Karr again, and bowed deeply. "Forgive me, Major Karr, but I must leave you here. If you would go through, my Master will be with you in a while."

Karr went through, past a comfortably-furnished ante-room and out into a long, spacious gallery with a moon door at each end. Here, on the facing walls, were displayed the banners of the thirty or more minor Triads that the United Bamboo had conquered or assimilated over the centuries. Karr made his way down the row, stopping at the last of the banners.

He reached up, touching the ancient silk gently, delicately, conscious that it was much older than the others hung there. The peacock blue of the banner had faded, but the golden triangle at its centre still held something of its former glory. In the blue beside each face of the triangle was embroidered a Han word, the original red of the pictograms transformed by time into a dull mauvish-brown, like ancient bloodstains. He gave a little shudder, then offered the words softly to the air.

"Tian. Nan Jen. Tu."

Heaven. Man. Earth. He turned, then stopped, noticing the figure that stood inside the moon door at the far end of the gallery.

"You walk quietly, Wong Yi-sun. Like a bird."

Fat Wong smiled, then came forward, his cloth-clad feet making no sound on the tiles.

"I am delighted to meet you, Major Karr. Your reputation precedes you."

Contrary to public expectations, Fat Wong was not fat at all. Quite the contrary – he was a compact, wiry-looking man who, in his peach silks and bound white feet, looked more like a successful First Level businessman than the reputedly savage leader of one of the seven biggest Triads in City Europe. Karr had read the file and seen holos of Wong; even so, he found himself unprepared for the soft-spokenness of the man, for the air of sophistication that seemed to emanate from him.

"I am honoured that you would see me, Wong Yi-sun. A thousand blessings upon your sons."

"And yours, Major. I understand you are recently married. A fine, strong woman, I am told." Wong's smile broadened. "I am happy for you. Give her my best regards. A man needs a strong wife in these unhappy times, neh?"

Karr bowed his head. "Thank you, Wong Yi-sun. I will pass on your kind words."

Fat Wong smiled and let his eyes move from Karr's figure for the first time since he had entered the room. Released from his gaze, Karr had a better opportunity of studying the man. Seen side-on, one began to notice those qualities that had made Wong Yi-sun a 489. There was a certain sharpness to his features, a restrained tautness, that equated with reports on him. When he was younger, it was said, he had gone into a rival's bedroom and cut off the man's head with a hatchet, even as he was making love to his wife, then had taken the woman for his own. Later, he had taken the name Fat Wong, because, he claimed, the world was a place where worm ate worm, and only the biggest, fattest worm came out on top. From then on he had worked day and night to be that worm – to be the fattest of them all. And now he was. Or almost.

"I noticed you were admiring the ancient silk, Major. Do you know the history of the banner?"

Karr smiled. "I have heard something of your history, Wong Yi-sun, but of that banner I am quite ignorant. It looks very old."

Wong moved past Karr, standing beneath the banner, then turned, smiling up at the big man.

"It is indeed. More than four hundred years old, in fact. You say you know our history, Major Karr, but did you realise just how old we are? Before the City was, we were. When the City no longer is, we shall remain."

Wong Yi-sun moved down the row of banners, then turned, facing Karr again.

"People call us criminals. They say we seek to destroy the social fabric of Chung Kuo, but they lie. Our roots are deep. We were founded in the late seventeenth century by the five monks of the Fu Chou monastery – honourable, *loyal* men, whose only desire was to overthrow the Ch'ing, the Manchu – and replace them with the rightful rulers of Chung Kuo, the Ming. Such was our purpose for a hundred years. Before the Manchu drove us underground, persecuting our members and cutting off our resources. After that we were left with no choice. We had to improvise."

Karr smiled inwardly. *Improvise.* It was a wonderfully subtle euphemism for the crudest of businesses: the business of murder and prostitution, gambling, drugs and protection.

"So you see, Major Karr, we have always been loyal to the traditions of Chung Kuo. Which is why we are always pleased to do business with the Seven. We are not their enemies. All we wish is to maintain order in those lawless regions which have escaped the long grasp of the T'ang."

"And the banner?"

Fat Wong smiled. "The banner comes from Fu Chou monastery. It is the great ancestor of all such banners. And whoever leads the Great Council holds the banner."

Wong turned slightly, his stance suggesting that Karr should join him. Karr hesitated, then went across, his mind racing. Fat Wong *wanted* something. Something big. But to ask for help directly was impossible for Wong: for to admit to any weakness – to admit that there was something, *anything* beyond his grasp – would involve him in an enormous loss of face. And face was everything down here. As Above.

Karr shivered, filled with a sudden certainty. Yes. Something was happening down here. In that veiled allusion to the Triad Council and the banner, Fat Wong had revealed more than he'd intended. Karr looked at him in profile and knew he was right. Fat Wong was under pressure. But from whom? From inside his own Triad, or from without – from another of the 489s?

He followed Wong through, up a broad flight of steps and out into a huge, subtly-lit room.

Steps led down into a sunken garden, at the centre of which was a tiny, circular pool. Within the pool seven golden fish seemed to float, as if suspended in glass. But the garden and the pool were not the most striking things about the room, for the eye was drawn beyond them to where one whole wall – a wall fifty *ch'i* in length, ten in height – seemed to look out onto the West Lake at Hang Chou, providing a panoramic view of its pale, lace-like bridges and pagodas, its willow-strewn islands and ancient temples. Here it was perpetually spring, the scent of jasmine and apple blossom heavy in the cool, moist air.

From somewhere distant, music sounded, carried on the breeze that blew gently through the room. For a moment the illusion was so perfect that Karr held himself still, enthralled by it. Then, realising Wong was watching him, he went down the steps and stood at the edge of the pool.

"You know why I have come here, Wong Yi-sun?"

"I understand you want some information. About the *Ko Ming* who assassinated the *Hsien L'ing*."

"We thought you might know something about this group – for instance, whether or not they were related to the *Ping Tiao*."

"Because they share the same symbol?" Wong sniffed, his face suddenly ugly. "I don't know what your investigations have thrown up, Major Karr, but let me tell you this, the *Hsien L'ing* was meddling in things he ought never to have been involved in."

Karr kept his face a mask, but behind it he felt an intense curiosity. What was Shou Chen-hai involved in that could possibly anger Fat Wong? For there was no doubting that Wong Yi-sun was furious.

"And the *Ko Ming*?"

Fat Wong gulped savagely at his drink then took a deep

breath, calming himself. "Your assassins are called the *Yu*. Beyond that I cannot say. Only that their name echoes throughout the Lowers."

Karr nodded thoughtfully. "That is unusual, neh?"

Wong met Karr's eyes steadily. "You are right, Major Karr. They are something different. We have not seen their like for many years. I . . ."

Wong paused, looking beyond Karr, towards the arched doorway. "Come," he said brusquely, one hand waving the servant on.

The servant handed Wong something, then leaned close, whispering.

For a moment Wong stared at the three tiny packages, his hand trembling with anger, then he thrust his hand out, offering them to Karr.

"These are yours, I understand."

Karr nodded. "We found them in the *Hsien L'ing*'s apartment. I thought they might interest you."

Wong narrowed his eyes. "You know what was in them?"

Again Karr nodded. They had had them analysed and knew they were something special. But what did Fat Wong know about them? Karr watched the movement in his face and began to understand. Wong hadn't been sure. He had only suspected until he had seen the packages. But now he knew.

Wong turned away and stood there, as if staring out across the lake. A wisp of his jet black hair moved gently in the breeze. "They have overstretched themselves this time. They have sought to destroy the balance . . ."

Then, as if he realised he had said too much, he turned back, giving a tiny shrug. But, though Fat Wong smiled, his eyes gave him away. This was what had been worrying him. This was the big something he could not deal with on his own. He had been the biggest, fattest worm until now. The keeper of the ancient banner. But now the Big Circle were making their bid to oust him; a bid financed by the revenue from new drugs, new markets.

But what did Fat Wong want? Did he want help to crush the Big Circle? Or did he want something else – some other arrangement that would keep the Big Circle in their place while keeping him supreme? And, beyond that, what would his own master, Li Yuan, want from such a deal? That was, if he wanted anything but to keep the Triads in their place.

Fat Wong closed his hand over the three tiny packets then threw them down, into the water. Reaching inside his silks, he withdrew a slender envelope.

"Give this to your T'ang," he said, handing it across.

"And what am I to say?"

"That I am his friend. His very good friend."

★ ★ ★

On the table by the bed was a holo plinth. Mach knelt, then placed his hand on the pad. Nothing. He turned slightly, looking up at Ywe Hao, curious. She leaned across him, holding her fingertips against the pad. At once two tiny figures formed in the air above the plinth.

"My brother," she explained. "He died in an industrial accident. At least, that's what the official enquiry concluded. But that's not the story his friends told at the time. He was a union organiser. Eighteen he was. Four years older than me. My big brother. They say the *pan chang* threw him from a balcony. Eight levels he fell, into machinery. There wasn't much left of him when they pulled him out. Just bits."

Mach took a breath, then nodded. For a moment longer Ywe Hao stared at the two tiny images, then drew her hand back, the pain in her eyes sharp, undiminished by the years.

"I wanted to see," he said, looking about him again. "I wanted to be sure."

"Sure?"

"About you."

"Ah . . ."

He smiled. "Besides which, I've got to brief you."

She frowned, then stood, moving back slightly. "About what?"

"The attack on the Dragonfly Club. We're bringing it forward." He went over to his pack and took out a hefty-looking folder, handing it to her.

She looked down at the folder, then back at Mach. "What's this?"

"It's a full dossier. It's not pleasant reading, I'm afraid, but then, it's not meant to be. But you have to understand why we need to do this."

"And the raid? When do we go in?"

"Tonight."

"*Tonight?* But I thought you said it would take at least a week to set this up."

"That's what I thought. But our man is on duty tonight."

She frowned. "But we've not had time to rehearse things. We'd be going in blind."

Mach shook his head. "Let me explain. When I gave you this assignment I had already allocated a team leader. But after what happened I wanted to give you a chance. An opportunity to prove yourself."

She made to speak, but he silenced her.

"Hear me out. I know what happened the other day. I know you killed Vasska. But it doesn't matter. You were right. The other matter . . . his brother . . . that's unfortunate, but we'll deal with it. What was important was that you did the right thing. If you'd let him kill the guard . . . well, it would have done us great harm, neh?"

She hesitated, then nodded, but he could see she was unhappy with his over-simplification of events. Which was good. It showed that she hadn't acted callously. He took the folder from her lap and opened it up, turning one of the still photographs towards her.

"This is why we're going in tonight. To put an end to this kind of thing. But it has to be done carefully. That's why I've drafted you in to lead the team. Not to organise the raid – your team know exactly what they have to do.

No, your role is to keep it all damped down. To make sure the right people are punished. I don't want anyone getting over-excited. We have to get this right. If we get it wrong, we're fucked, understand me?"

She nodded, but her eyes stayed on the photo of the mutilated child. After a moment she looked up at him, the disgust in her eyes touched with a profound sadness. "What makes them do this, Jan? How in the gods' names could anyone do this to a little boy?"

He shook his head. "I don't know. It's how they are." He put his hand gently to her cheek. "All I know is that all that anger you feel, all that disgust and indignation . . . well, it's a healthy thing. I want to harness that. To give it every opportunity to express itself."

He let his hand fall away. "You know, you remind me of an old friend. She was like you. Strong. Certain about what she did."

Ywe Hao shivered, then looked down again. "What about my cover?"

Mach smiled, impressed by her professionalism, then turned, pointing across at the pack beside the door. "It's all in there. All you need to do is read the file. Someone will come for you at eleven. You go in at second bell."

He sat back. "There's a lot there, but read it all. Especially the statements by the parents. As I said, you need to know why you're there. It'll make it easier to do what you have to do."

She nodded.

"Good. Now I must go. My shift begins in an hour and I've got to get back and change. Good luck, Ywe Hao. May Kuan Yin smile on you tonight."

* * *

In the torch-lit silence of the Hall of Eternal Peace and Tranquillity, Li Yuan knelt on the cold stone tiles, facing the hologram of his father. Thin threads of smoke from the offering sticks drifted slowly upwards, their rosewood scent merging with the chill dampness of the ancient room.

Beyond the ghostly-radiant figure of the dead T'ang, the red lacquer of the carved screen seemed to shimmer, as if it shared something of the old man's insubstantiality, the *Ywe Lung* at its centre flickering, as if, at any moment, it might vanish, leaving a smoking circle of nothingness.

Li Shai Tung stood there as in life, the frailty of his latter days shrugged off, the certainty he had once professed shaping each ghostly gesture as he spoke.

"Your dreams have meaning, Yuan. They are like the most loyal of ministers. They tell us not what we would have them say, but that which is true. We can deny them, can banish them to the farthest reaches of our selves, but we cannot kill them, not without killing ourselves."

Li Yuan looked up, meeting his dead father's eyes. "And is that what we have done? Is that why things are so wrong?"

Li Shai Tung sniffed loudly, then leaned heavily on his cane, as if considering his son's words, but tonight Yuan was more than ever conscious of what lay behind the illusion. In the slender case beneath the image, logic circuits had instantly located and selected from a score of possible responses, pre-programmed guidelines determining their choice. It seemed spontaneous, yet the words were given – were as predetermined as the fall of a rock or the decay of atoms. And the delay? That too was deliberate; was a machine-created mimicry of something that had once been real.

Even so, the sense of his father was strong. And though the eyes were blank, unseeing – were not eyes at all, but mere smoke and light – they seemed to see right through him; through to the tiny core of unrest that had robbed him of sleep and brought him here at this unearthly hour.

"Father?"

The old man lifted his head slightly, as if, momentarily, he had been lost in his thoughts. Then, unexpectedly, he gave a soft laugh.

"Dreams. Maybe that's all we have, Yuan. Dreams. The City itself, was that not a dream? The dream of our ancestors made tangible. And our long-held belief in peace, in order and stability, was that not also a dream? Was any of it ever real?"

Li Yuan frowned, disturbed by his father's words. For a moment his mind went back to the evening of his father's death, recalling how sickly thin his body had been, how weak and vulnerable death had found him.

"But what does it mean, Father? How am I to read my dream?"

The dead T'ang stared at his son, then gave a tiny shudder. "You say you dreamt of dragonflies?"

Li Yuan nodded. "Of great, emerald green dragonflies, swarming on the river bank. Thousand upon thousand of them. Beautiful creatures, their wings like glass, their bodies like burnished jade. The sun shone down on them and yet the wind blew cold. And as I watched, they began to fall, first one, and then another, until the river was choked with their struggling forms. And even as I watched they stiffened and the brilliant greenness was leached from their bodies, until they were a hideous grey, their flesh flaking from them like ash. And still the wind blew, carrying the ash away, covering the fields, clogging every pool and stream, until all was grey and ashen."

"And then?"

"And then I woke, afraid, my heart pounding."

"Ah . . ." The T'ang put one hand to his beard, his long fingers pulling distractedly at the tightly-braided strands, then shook his head. "That is a strange and powerful dream, *erh tzu*. You ask me what it means, yet I fear you know already." He looked up, meeting his son's eyes. "Old glassy, he is the very symbol of summer, neh? And the colour green symbolises spring. Furthermore it is said that when the colour green figures in a dream, the dream will end happily. Yet in your dream the green turns to ash. Summer dies. The cold wind blows. How are you to read this but as an ill omen?"

Li Yuan looked down sharply, a cold fear washing through him. He had hoped against hope that there was some other way to read his dream, but his father's words merely confirmed his own worst fears. The dragonfly, though the emblem of summer, was also a symbol of weakness and instability, of all the worst excesses of a soft and easy life. Moreover it was said that they swarmed in vast numbers just before the storm.

Yet was the dream anything more than a reflection of his innermost fears? He thought of his father's words – of dreams as loyal ministers, uttering truths that could not otherwise be faced. Was that the case here? Had this dream been sent to make him face the truth?

"Then what am I to do?"

The dead T'ang looked at him and laughed. "*Do*, Yuan? Why, you must wear stout clothes and learn to whistle in the wind. You must look to your wives and children. And then . . ."

"And then, Father?"

The old man looked away, as if he'd done. "Spring will come, *erh tzu*. Even in your darkest hour, remember that. Spring always comes."

Li Yuan hesitated, waiting for something more, but his father's eyes were closed now, his mouth silent. Yuan leaned forward and took the burning spills from the porcelain jar. At once the image shrank, taking its place beside the other tiny, glowing images of his ancestors.

He stood, looking about him at the torch-lit stillness of the Hall – at the grey stone of the huge, funerary couch to his right, at the carved pillars and tablets and lacquered screens – then turned away, angry with himself. There was so much to be done – the note from Minister Heng, the packet from Fat Wong, the last few preparations for Council – yet here he was, moping like a child before his dead father's image. And to what end?

He clenched his fist, then slowly let it open. No. His anger could not be sustained. Nor would the dream be denied that easily. If he closed his eyes he could see them – a thousand bright, flickering shapes in the morning sunlight, their wings like curtains of the finest lace. Layer upon layer of flickering, sunlit lace . . .

"*Chieh Hsia* . . ."

Li Yuan turned, almost staggering, then collected himself, facing his Chancellor.

"Yes, Chancellor Nan. What is it?"

Nan Ho bowed low. "News has come, *Chieh Hsia*. The news you were waiting for."

He was suddenly alert. "From Tao Yuan? We have word?"

"More than that, *Chieh Hsia*. A tape has come. A tape of the meeting between Wang and Hsiang."

"A tape . . ." Li Yuan laughed, filled with a sudden elation that was every bit as powerful as his previous mood of despair. "Then we have him, neh? We have him where we want him."

★   ★   ★

The doorman had done his job. The outer door slid back at her touch. Inside it was pitch black, the security cameras dead. Ywe Hao turned, then nodded, letting the rest of the team move past her silently.

The doorman was in the cubicle to the left, face down on the floor, his hands on his head. One of the team was crouched there already, binding him at hand and foot.

She went quickly to the end of the hallway, conscious of the others forming up to either side of the door. She waited until the last of them joined her, then stepped forward, knocking loudly on the inner door.

There was a small eye-hatch near the top of the reinforced door. She faced it, clicking on the helmet lamp and holding up her ID. The call had gone out half an hour ago, when the outer power had "failed", so they were expecting her.

The hatch cover slid back, part of a face staring out from the square of brightness within.

"Move the card closer."

She did as she was told.

"Shit . . ." The face moved away; spoke to someone inside. "It's a fuckin' woman."

"Is there a problem?"

The face turned back to her. "Well, it's like this. This is a men's club. Women ain't supposed to come in."

She took a breath, then nodded. "I understand. But look. I've only got to cut the power from the box inside. I can do the repairs out here in the hallway."

The guard turned, consulting someone inside, then turned back. "Okay, but be quick, neh? And keep your eyes to yourself or there'll be a report going in to your superior."

Slowly the door slid back, spilling light into the hallway. The guard moved back, letting Ywe Hao pass, his hand coming up, meaning to point across at the box, but he never completed the gesture. Her punch felled him like a sack.

She turned, looking about her, getting her bearings. It was a big, hexagonal room, corridors going off on every side. In its centre was a circular sunken pool of bright red tile, five steps leading down into its depths.

The young men in the pool seemed unaware of her entrance. There were eight of them, naked as newborns. One of them was straddling another over the edge of the pool, his buttocks moving urgently, but no one seemed to care. Behind him the others played and laughed with an abandon that was clearly drug-induced.

She took it all in at a glance, but what she was really looking for was the second guard – the one her fallen friend had been speaking to. She felt the hairs on her neck rise, unable to locate him, then she saw movement, a brief flash of green between the hinges of the screen to her right.

She fired twice through the screen, the noise muted by the thick carpeting underfoot, the heavy tapestries that adorned the walls, but it was loud enough to wake the young men from their reverie.

The others stood behind her now, masked figures

clothed from head to toe in black. At her signal they fanned out, making for the branching corridors.

She crossed the room slowly, the gun held loosely in her hand, until she stood on the tiled lip of the pool. They had backed away from her, the drug-elation dying in their eyes as they began to realise what was happening. The copulating couple had drawn apart and were staring wide-eyed at her, signs of their recent passion still evident. Others had raised their hands in the universal gesture of surrender.

"Out!" she barked, lifting the gun sharply.

They jerked at the sound of her voice, then began to scramble back, abashed now at their nakedness, fear beginning to penetrate the drug-haze of their eyes.

She knew them all. Faces and names and histories. She looked from face to face, forcing them to meet her gaze. They were so young. Barely out of childhood, it seemed. Even so, she felt no sympathy for them, only disgust.

There were noises from the rest of the club now; thumps and angry shouts and a brief snatch of shrieking that broke off abruptly. A moment later one of the team reappeared at the entrance to one of the corridors.

"Chi Li! Come quickly . . ."

"What is it?" she said as calmly as she could, tilting her head slightly, indicating her prisoners.

He looked beyond her, understanding, then came across, lowering his voice. "It's Hsao Yen. He's gone crazy. You'd better stop him." He drew the gun from his belt. "Go on. I'll guard these."

She could hear Hsao Yen long before she saw him, standing over the young man in the doorway, a stream of obscenities falling from his lips as he leaned forward, striking the prisoner's head and shoulders time and again with his rifle butt.

"Hsao Yen!" she yelled. "*Ai ya!* What are you doing!"

He turned, confronting her, his face livid with anger, then jerked his arm out, pointing beyond the fallen man.

She moved past him, looking into the room, then drew

back, shuddering, meeting Hsao Yen's eyes almost fearfully. "He did that?"

Hsao Yen nodded. "Yes . . ."

He made to strike the fallen man again, but Ywe Hao stopped his hand, speaking to him gently. "I understand. But let's do this properly, neh? After all, that's what we came here for. To put an end to this."

Hsao Yen looked down at the bloodied figure beneath him and shivered. "All right. As you say."

She nodded, then looked past him, torn by what she saw. "And the boy? He's dead, I take it."

Hsao Yen shuddered, his anger transformed suddenly to pain. "How could he do that, Chi Li? How could he do that to a child?"

She shook her head, unable to understand. "I don't know, Hsao Yen. I simply don't know."

They were lined up beside the pool when she returned, three dozen of them, servants included. The masked figures of the *Yu* stood off to one side, their automatic pistols raised. She had two of their number hold up their beaten fellow, then went down the line, separating out the servants.

"Tu Li-shan, Rooke . . . . take them through to the kitchens. I want them gagged and bound. But don't harm them. Understand?"

Ywe Hao turned back, facing the remaining men. There were twenty-three of them. Less than she had hoped to find here. Looking down the line she noted the absence of several of the faces from the files. A shame, she thought, looking at them coldly. She would have liked to have caught them all; every last one of the nasty little bastards. But this would do.

"Strip off!" she barked angrily, conscious that more than half of them were naked already, then turned away, taking the thickly wadded envelope from within her tunic. These were the warrants. She unfolded them and flicked through, taking out those that weren't needed and slipping them back into the envelope, then turned back, facing them again.

They were watching her, fearful now, several of them crying openly, their limbs trembling badly. She went slowly down the line, handing each of them a single sheet of paper; watching as they looked down, then looked back up at her again, mouths open, a new kind of fear in their eyes.

They were death warrants, individually drafted, a photograph of the condemned attached to each sheet. She handed out the last, then stood back, waiting, wondering if any of them would have the balls at the last to say something, to try to argue their way out of this, perhaps even to fight. But one glance down the line told her enough.

For a moment she tried to turn things round; to see it from their viewpoint; maybe even to elicit some small trace of sympathy from deep within herself. But there was nothing. She had seen too much; read too much: her anger had hardened to something dark, impenetrable. They were evil, gutless little shits. And what they had done here – the suffering they had caused – was too vast, too hideous, to forgive.

Ywe Hao pulled the mask aside, letting them view her face for the first time, letting them see the disgust she felt, then walked back to the end of the line and stood facing the first of them. Taking the paper from his shaking hands, she began, looking directly into his face, not even glancing at the paper, reciting from memory the sentence of the *Yu* inner council, before placing the gun against his temple and pulling the trigger.

* * *

Fifth bell was sounding as Wang Sau-leyan stood at the head of the steps, looking down into the dimly-lit cellar. It was a huge, dark space, poorly ventilated and foul-smelling. From its depths came a steady groaning, a distinctly human sound, half-articulate with pained confession. The semblance of words drifted up to him, mixing with the foul taste in his mouth, making him shudder with distaste and spread his fan before his face.

Seeing him there, Hung Mien-lo tore himself away from the bench and hurried across.

"*Chieh Hsia*," he said, bowing low. "We are honoured by your presence."

The T'ang descended the uneven steps slowly, with an almost finicky care. At the bottom he glared at his Chancellor, as if words could not express the vulgarity of this.

It was old-fashioned and barbaric, yet in that lay its effectiveness. Torture was torture. Sophistication had nothing to do with it. Terror was of the essence. And this place, with its dank, foul-smelling miasma, was perfect for the purposes of torture. It stank of hopelessness.

The bench was an ordinary workman's bench from an earlier age. Its hard wooden frame was scrubbed clean and four dark iron spikes – each as long as a man's arm – jutted from the yellow wood, one at each corner, the polished metal thick at the base, tapering to a needle-sharp point. The prisoner's hands and feet were secured against these spikes with coils of fine, strong chain that bit into the flesh and made it bleed. Across his naked chest a series of heated wires had been bound, pulling tight and searing the flesh even as they cooled, making the prisoner gasp and struggle for each breath; each painful movement chafing the cutting wires against the blood-raw flesh.

One eye had been put out. Burned in its blackened socket. The shaven head was criss-crossed with razor-fine scars. Both ears had been severed. All four limbs were badly scarred and bruised, broken bone pushing through the skin in several places. There were no nails on hands or feet and the tendons of each finger had been cut neatly, individually, with a surgeon's skill. Lastly, the man's genitals had been removed and the amputation sealed with a wad of hot tar.

Wang Sau-leyan looked, then turned away, moving his fan rapidly before his face, but Hung Mien-lo had seen, mixed in with the horror, the revulsion, a look of genuine satisfaction.

The prisoner looked up, his one good eye moving between the two men. Its movements seemed automatic, intent only on knowing where the pain would come from next. All recognition was gone from it. It saw only blood and heat and broken bone. Wang Sau-leyan, looking down at it, knew it from childhood. It was the eye of his father's Master of the Royal Household, Sun Li Hua.

"You have his confession?"

"Yes, *Chieh Hsia*," Hung answered, one hand resting lightly on the bench. "He babbled like a frightened child when I first brought him down. He couldn't take much pain. Just the thought of it and the words spilled from him like a songbird."

And yet he's still alive, Wang thought. *How can he still be alive when all this has been done to him?* Even so, he deserved no pity. Sun Li Hua had sold him to another. To Li Yuan, his enemy.

Just as he sold my father to me.

Wang leaned over and spat on the scarred and wounded body. And the eye, following the movement, was passive, indifferent to the gesture, as though to say, "Is that all? Is there to be no pain this time?"

They moved on, looking at the other benches. Some were less damaged than Sun Li Hua, others were barely alive – hacked apart piece by piece, like hunks of animal product on a butcher's table. They were all old and trusted servants; all long-serving and "loyal" men of his father's household. And Li Yuan had bought them all. No wonder the bastard had been able to anticipate him in Council these last few times.

Wang turned, facing his Chancellor.

"Well, *Chieh Hsia*?" Hung Mien-lo asked. "Are you pleased?"

There was an unpleasant smile on the Chancellor's features, as if to say there was nothing he liked better than inflicting pain on others. And Wang Sau-leyan, seeing it, nodded and turned quickly away, mounting the steps in twos, hurriedly, lest his face betray his true feelings.

It was a side of Hung Mien-lo he would never have suspected. Or was there another reason? It was said that Hung and Sun had never got on. So maybe it was that. Whatever, there would come a time of reckoning. And then Hung Mien-lo would really learn to smile. As a corpse smiles.

* * *

Li Yuan stood at the window, letting himself be dressed. Outside the garden lay half in shadow, half in light, the dew-misted top leaves of the nearby rhododendron bushes glittering in the dawn's first light. He held himself still as the maid drew the sashes tight about his waist, then turned, facing his Master of the Inner Chambers.

"And have you no idea what they want, Master Chan?"

Chan Teng bowed low. "None at all, *Chieh Hsia*. Only that the Marshal said it was of the utmost urgency. That I was to wake you if you were not awake already."

Li Yuan turned away, hiding the smile that came to his lips at the thought of Tolonen's bluntness. Even so, he felt a ripple of trepidation run down his spine.

They were waiting in his study. Impatient to hear what had happened, he crossed the room quickly and stood before them.

"Well, Knut? What is it?"

Tolonen held out a file. Li Yuan took it and flicked it open. After a moment he looked up, giving a small, strange laugh. "How odd. Only last night, I dreamed of dragonflies. And now this . . ." He studied Tolonen a moment, his eyes narrowed. "But why show me this? It's nasty, certainly, but it is hardly the kind of thing to wake a T'ang about, surely?"

Tolonen bowed his head, acceding the point. "In ordinary circumstances that would be so, *Chieh Hsia*. But this is a matter of the utmost importance. The beginning of something we would do well to take very seriously indeed."

Li Yuan turned, looking at his Chancellor. "So what makes this different?"

Nan Ho lowered his head again. "This, *Chieh Hsia*."

Li Yuan set the file down on a nearby chair, then took the pamphlet from his Chancellor. It was a single large sheet that had been folded into four, the ice-paper no more than a few mols thick, the print poor, uneven. He realised at once that it had been hand set; that whoever had produced this had wanted to avoid even the slightest chance of being traced through the computer network.

He shrugged. "It's interesting, but I still don't understand."

Nan Ho smiled tautly. "Forgive me, *Chieh Hsia*, but it is not so much the pamphlet, as the numbers in which it has been distributed. It's hard to estimate exactly how many copies went out, but latest Security estimates place it at between a quarter of a billion and a billion."

Li Yuan laughed. "Impossible! How would they print that number? How distribute them? Come to that, how on earth would they finance it?"

And yet he saw how grave the old man looked.

"This is something new, *Chieh Hsia*. Something dangerous. Which is why we must deal with it at once. That is why I came. To seek your permission to make the elimination of this new group our number one priority."

Li Yuan stared at his Marshal a moment, then turned away. A billion pamphlets. If that were true it was certainly something to be concerned about. But was Tolonen right to be so worried, or was he over-reacting? He went to his desk and sat, considering things.

"What is Major Karr doing right now?"

Tolonen smiled. "Karr is on their trail already, *Chieh Hsia*. I put him in charge of investigating the murder of the *Hsien L'ing*, Shou Chen-hai."

"And?"

Tolonen shook his head. "And nothing, I'm afraid. Our investigations have so far drawn a blank."

"All right. But I want Karr in charge, Knut, and I want a daily report on my desk concerning any and every development. You will make sure he gets whatever resources he needs."

"Of course, *Chieh Hsia.*"

He watched Tolonen go, then turned his attention to his Chancellor.

"Was there something else?"

The Chancellor hesitated, as if weighing something up, then came forward, taking a small package from within his robes and offering it to his T'ang, his head lowered, his eyes averted. "I was not certain whether to give this to you, *Chieh Hsia.*"

Li Yuan took the package, smiling, then felt his breath catch in his throat. There was the faintest scent from the silk. The scent of *mei hua.* Of plum blossom.

"Thank you, Nan Ho. I . . ."

But the Chancellor had already gone. Even as Li Yuan looked up, the door was closing on the far side of the room.

He sat back, staring at the tiny package on his desk. It was from her. From Fei Yen. Though there were no markings on the wrapping, he knew no other would have used that scent. No one else would have used his Chancellor as a messenger.

He shuddered, surprised by the intensity of what he felt. Then, leaning forward, his hand trembling, he began to unfasten the wrappings, curious and yet afraid of what was inside.

There was a note, and beneath the note a tiny tape. He unfolded it and read the brief message, then lifted the tape gingerly, his eyes drawn to the gold leaf pictograms embossed into the black of the casing. *Han Ch'in*, they read. His son.

He swallowed, then closed his eyes. What did she want? Why was she doing this to him? For a moment he closed his hand tightly on the tiny cassette, as if to break it, then loosened his grip. No. He would have to see it. Suddenly he realised just how much he had wanted to go to the estate at Hei Shui and simply stand there, unobserved, watching his child at play.

Even so, the question still remained. What did she want? He went to the long window. Already the sun was higher, the shadows on the eastern lawn much shorter. He breathed deeply, watching the sunlight flicker on the surface of the pond, then shook his head. Maybe she didn't know. Maybe she didn't understand what power she had over him, even now. Maybe it *was* a simple act of kindness . . .

He laughed quietly. No. Whatever it was, it wasn't that. Or not simply that. He turned, looking across at the tape, the note, then turned back again, staring outward. Whatever, it would have to wait. Right now he must prepare himself, clearing his mind of everything but the struggle ahead. Tonight, after Council, he could relax; might let himself succumb to his weakness. But not before. Not until he had dealt with Wang Sau-leyan.

He sighed and turned from the window, making his way back to his rooms and the waiting maids.

Out on the pond, in the early morning light, a dragonfly hovered over the water, its wings flickering like molten sunlight, its body a bright iridescent green.

CHAPTER·17

IN A DARKENED EYE

It was just after seven in the morning, but in the Black Heart business was brisk. At the huge centre table a crowd of men pressed close, taking bets on the two tiny contestants crouched in the tight beam of the spotlight.

They were mantises, brought up from the Clay, their long, translucent bodies raised threateningly, switchblade forelegs extended before their tiny, vicious-looking heads as they circled slowly. To Chen, watching from the edge of the crowd, it was an ugly, chilling sight. He had seen men – Triad gangsters – behave in this manner, their every movement suggestive of a deadly stillness. Men whose eyes were dead, who cared only for the perfection of the kill. Here, in these cold, unsympathetic creatures, was their model; the paradigm of their behaviour. He shuddered. To model oneself on such a thing – what made a man reduce himself so much?

As he watched, the larger of the creatures struck out, its forelegs moving in a blur as it tried to catch and pin its opponent. There was a roar of excitement from the watching men, but the attack faltered, the smaller mantis struggling free. It scuttled back, twitching, making small, answering feints with its forelegs.

Chen looked about him, sickened by the glow of excitement in every face, then came away, returning to the table in the corner.

"So what's happened?"

Karr looked up from the map, smiling wearily. "It's

gone cold. And this time even our Triad friends can't help us."

Chen leaned across, putting his finger down where the map was marked with a red line – a line that ended abruptly at the entrance to the stack in which the Black Heart was located. "We've tracked them this far, right? And then there's nothing. It's a white-out, right?"

Karr nodded. "The cameras were working, but the storage system had been tampered with. There was nothing on record but white light."

"Right. And there's no trace of either of them coming out of this stack, correct? The records have been checked for facial recognition?"

Again Karr nodded.

"Then what else remains? No one broke the seals and went down to the Net, and no one got out by flyer. Which means they *must* be here."

Karr laughed. "But they're not. We've searched the place from top to bottom and found nothing. We've taken the place apart."

Chen smiled enigmatically. "Which leaves what?"

Karr shrugged. "Maybe they were ghosts."

Chen nodded. "Or maybe the images on the tape were. What if someone tampered with the computer storage system down the line?" He traced the red line back with his finger, stopping at the point where it took a sixty degree turn. "What if our friends turned off earlier? Or went straight on? Have we checked the records from the surrounding stacks?"

"I've done it. And there's nothing. They just disappeared."

At the gaming table things had changed dramatically. Beneath the spotlight's glare the smaller mantis seemed to be winning. It had pinned the larger creature's forelegs to the ground, trapping it, but it could not take advantage of its position without releasing its opponent. For a long time it was still, then, with a suddenness that surprised the hushed watchers, it moved back, meaning to strike at once and cripple its enemy. But the larger beast had waited for that moment. The instant it felt the relentless pressure of the other's forelegs lapse, it snapped back, springing up from the floor, its back legs powering it into the smaller insect. The snap of its forelegs was followed instantly by the crunch of its opponent's brittle flesh. It was over. The smaller mantis was dead.

For a moment they looked across, distracted by the uproar, then Karr turned back, his blue eyes filled with doubt. "Come . . . there's nothing here."

They were getting up as a messenger came across; one of the Triad men they had met earlier. Bowing, he handed Karr a sheet of computer printout – a copy of a Security report timed at 4.24 a.m.

Karr studied it a moment, then laughed. "Just when I thought it had died on us. Look, Chen! Look what the gods have sent us!"

Chen took the printout. It was a report on a new terrorist attack. On a place called the Dragonfly Club. The details were sketchy, but one fact stood out – a computer face-recognition match. Chen stared at Karr. "It's the woman! Chi Li, or whatever her real name is!"

"Yes," Karr laughed, his gloom dispelled for the first time in two days. "So let's get there, neh? Before the trail goes cold."

* * *

Ywe Hao woke, her heart pounding, and threw back the sheet. Disoriented, she sat up, staring about her. What in the gods' names . . . ?

Then she saw it – the winking red light of the warning circuit. Its high-pitched alarm must have woken her. She span about, looking to see what time it was. 7.13. She had been asleep less than an hour.

Dressing took fifteen seconds, locating and checking her gun another ten. Then she was at the door, breathing deeply, preparing herself, as the door slid slowly back.

The corridor was empty. She walked quickly, her gun

held out before her, knowing they would have to use this corridor.

At the intersection she slowed, hearing footsteps, but they were from the left. The warning had come from her friends – the two boys at the lift – which meant her assailants would be coming from that direction; from the corridor directly ahead. She put the gun away and let the old man pass, then went to the right, breaking into a run, heading for the inter-level steps.

There was urgent whispering in the corridor behind her at the intersection. She flattened herself against the wall, holding her breath. Then the voices were gone, heading towards her apartment.

Vasska's brother, Edel. She was certain of it.

She was eight, nine steps up the flight when she remembered the case. She stopped, annoyed with herself. But there hadn't been time. If she'd have stopped to dig it out from the back of the cupboard she would have lost valuable seconds. Would have run into them in the corridor. Even so, she couldn't leave it there. The dossier on the raid was in it.

A group of Han students passed her on the steps, heading for their morning classes, their sing-song chatter filling the stairwell briefly. Then she was alone again. For a moment longer she hesitated, then she went up, heading for the maintenance room at the top of the deck.

* * *

Karr looked about him at the ruins. It was the same pattern as before – broken security cameras, deserted guard-posts, secured lifts, the terrorists' trail cleverly covered by whiteouts. All spoke of a highly-organised operation, planned well in advance and carried out with a professionalism that even the T'ang's own élite would have found hard to match.

Not only that, but the *Yu* chose their targets well. Even here, amidst this chaos, they had taken care to identify their victims. Twenty-four men had died here, all but one of them – a guard – regular members of the club, each of them 'tagged' by the *Yu*, brief histories of their worthless lives tied about their necks. The second guard had simply been beaten and tied up, while the servants had again been left unharmed. Such discrimination was impressive and the rumour of it – passed from mouth to ear, in defiance of the explicit warnings of the *T'ing Wei* – had thus far served to discredit every effort of that Ministry to portray the terrorists as uncaring, sadistic killers, their victims as undeserving innocents.

He shook his head, then went across. "Anything new?" he asked, looking past Chen at the last of the corpses.

"Nothing," Chen answered, his weary smile a reminder that they had been on duty more than thirty hours. "The only remarkable thing is the similarity of the wounds. My guess is that there was some kind of ritual involved."

Karr grimaced. "Yes. These men weren't just killed, they were executed. And, if our *Ko Ming* friends are right, for good reason."

Chen looked away, a shudder of disgust passing through him. He too had seen the holos the assassins had left – studies of their victims with young boys taken from the Lowers. Scenes of degradation and torture. Scenes that the *T'ing Wei* were certain to keep from popular consumption.

Which was to say nothing of the mutilated corpse of the child they had found in the room at the far end of the club.

Karr leaned across, touching Chen's arm. "We're waiting on lab reports, word from our Triad contacts. There's little we can do just now, so why don't you go home? Spend some time with that wife of yours, or take young Jyan to the Palace of Dreams. They tell me there's a new Historical."

Chen laughed. "And Marie? I thought this was supposed to be your honeymoon?"

Karr grinned. "Marie understands. It's why she married me."

Chen shook his head. "And I thought *I* was mad." He

laughed. "Okay. But let me know as soon as something happens."

Karr nodded. "All right. Now go."

He watched Chen leave, then stood, feeling the emotional weight of what had happened here bearing down on him. It was rare that he was affected by such scenes, rarer still that he felt any sympathy for the perpetrators, but for once he was. The *Yu* had done society a great service here tonight. Had rid Chung Kuo of the kind of scum he had met so often below the Net.

He breathed out heavily, recalling Chen's disgust, knowing, at the very core of him, that this was what all healthy, decent men *ought* to feel. And yet the *T'ing Wei* would try to twist it, until these good-for-nothing perverts, this shit masquerading as men, were portrayed as shining examples of good citizenship.

Yes, he had seen the holos. Had felt his guts wrenched by the distress in the young boys' eyes, by that helpless, unanswered plea. He shuddered. The Oven Man had them now. And no evidence remained, but for that small, pathetic corpse and these mementoes – these perverse records of a foul desire.

And was he to watch it being whitewashed? Made pure and sparkling by a parcel of lies? He spat, angered by the injustice of it. Was this why he had become Tolonen's man? For *this*?

Everywhere he looked he found the signature of decadence; of sons given everything by their fathers – everything but time and attention. No wonder they turned out as they did, lacking any sense of value. No wonder they pissed their time away, drinking and gambling and whoring – for inside them there was nothing. Nothing *real*, anyway. Some of them were even clever enough to realise as much, yet all their efforts to fill that nothingness were pointless. The nothingness was vast, unbounded. To fill it was like trying to carry water in a sieve.

Karr sighed, angered by the sheer waste of it all. He had seen enough to know that it was not even their fault; they had had no choice but to be as they were – spoilt and corrupt, vacuous and sardonic. They had been given no other model to emulate, and now it was too late.

He found the sheer sumptuousness of the room abhorrent. His own taste was for the simple, the austere. Here, confronted by its opposite, he found himself baring his teeth, as if at an enemy. Then, realising what he was doing, he laughed uncomfortably and turned, forcing himself to be still.

It would be no easy task tracking down the *Yu*, for they were unlike any of the other *Ko Ming* groups currently operating in City Europe. They were fuelled not by simple hatred – by that obsessive urge to destroy that had fired the *Ping Tiao* and their like – but by a powerful indignation and a strong sense of injustice. The first *Ko Ming* emperor, Mao Tse-tung, had once said something about true revolutionaries being the fish that swam in the great sea of the people. Well, these *Yu* – these "fish" – were certainly that. They had learned from past excesses. Learned that the people cared who died and who was spared. Discrimination – *moral* discrimination – was their most potent tool, and they took great pains to be in the right. At least, from where he stood, it looked like that, and the failure of the *T'ing Wei* to mould public opinion seemed to confirm his gut instinct.

And now this. Karr looked about him. Last night's raid – this devastatingly direct strike against the corrupt heart of the Above – would do much to bolster the good opinion of the masses. Yes, he could imagine the face of the *T'ing Wei*'s Third Secretary, Yen T'ung, when he learned of this. Karr laughed, then fell silent, for his laughter, like the tenor of his thoughts, were indicative of a deep inner division.

His duty was clear. As Tolonen's man he owed unswerving loyalty. If the Marshal asked him to track down the *Yu*, he would track them down. But for the first time ever he found himself torn, for his instinct was for the *Yu*, not against them. If one of those boys had been *his* son . . .

But he was Tolonen's man; bound by the strongest of

555

oaths. Sworn to defend the Seven against *Ko Ming* activity, of whatever kind.

He spoke softly to the empty room. "Which is why I must find you, Chi Li, even if, secretly, I admire what you have done here. For I am the T'ang's man, and you are the T'ang's enemy. A *Ko Ming*."

And when he found her? Karr looked down, troubled. When he found her he would kill her. Swiftly, mercifully, and with honour.

* * *

The first of them was facing Ywe Hao as she came through the door. He fell back, clutching his ruined stomach, the sound of the gun's detonation echoing in the corridor outside. The second came out of the kitchen. She shot him twice in the chest, even as he fumbled for his weapon. Edel was behind him. He came at her with a small butcher's knife, his face twisted with hatred. She blew his hand off, then shot him through the temple. He fell at her feet, his legs kicking impotently.

She looked about her. There had been five of them according to her lookouts. So where were the others?

There was shouting outside. Any time now Security would investigate. She went through to the kitchen, then came back, spotting the case on the bed. Good. They'd taken nothing. It was only when she lifted it that she realised she was wrong. They *had* taken something. The case was empty.

"Shit . . ."

She looked about her, trying to work out what to do. Where would they have taken the dossiers? What would they have wanted them for?

There were footsteps, coming down the corridor.

She threw the case down and crossed the room, standing beside the open door, clicking the spent clip from the handle of her gun. Outside the footsteps stopped.

"Edel? Is that you?"

She nodded to herself, then slipped a new clip into the

handle. The longer she waited, the more jittery they'd get. At the same time, they might just be waiting for her to put her head round the door.

She smiled. It was the kind of dilemma she understood.

She counted. At eight she turned and went low, the gun kicking noisily in her hand as she moved out into the corridor.

* * *

Overhead, tiny armies, tens of thousands strong, fought against a hazed background of mountains, the roar of battle faint against the hubbub of noise in the crowded Main. The giant hologram was suspended in the air above the entrance to the Golden Emperor's Palace of Eternal Dreams.

Crowds were pushing out from the Holo-Palace while others queued to get in, their necks – young and old alike – craned back to watch the battle overhead. As Kao Chen pushed through, ushering his son before him, he smiled, seeing how his head strained up and back, trying to glimpse the air-show.

"Well, Jyan? What did you think?"

The ten-year-old looked up at his father and beamed a smile. "It was wonderful! That moment when Liu Pang raised his banner and the whole army roared his name. That was great!"

Chen laughed. "Yes, wasn't it? And to think he was but Ch'en She, a poor man, before he became Son of Heaven! Liu Pang, founder of the great Han dynasty!"

Jyan nodded eagerly. "They should teach it like that at school. It's far more interesting than all that poetry."

Chen smiled, easing his way through the crowds. "Maybe, but not all poetry is bad. You'll understand that when you're older."

Jyan made a face, making Chen laugh. He too had always preferred history to poetry, but then he'd never had Jyan's chances, Jyan's education. No, things would be different for Jyan. Very different.

He slowed, then leaned close again. "Do you want to eat out, Jyan, or shall we get back?"

Jyan hesitated, then smiled. "Let's get back, neh? Mother will be waiting, and I want to tell her all about it. That battle between Liu Pang and the Hegemon King was brilliant. It was like it was really real. All those horsemen and everything!"

Chen nodded. "Yes . . . it was, wasn't it? I wonder how they did that?"

"Oh, it's easy," Jyan said, pulling him on by the hand. "We learned all about it in school ages ago. It's all done with computer images and simulated movement."

"Simulated movement, eh?" Chen laughed, letting himself be pulled through the crowds and into one of the quieter corridors. "Still, it seemed real enough. I was wincing myself once or twice during some of those close-up fight scenes."

Jyan laughed, then fell silent, slowing to a halt.

"What is it?" Chen said, looking up ahead.

"Those two . . ." Jyan whispered. "Come. Let's go back. We'll take the south corridor and cut through."

Chen glanced at Jyan, then looked back down the corridor. The two young men – Han, in their mid-teens – were leaning against the wall, pretending to be talking.

Chen bent down, lowering his voice. "Who are they?"

Jyan met his eyes. "They're senior boys at my school – part of a *tong*, a gang. They call themselves the Green Banner Guardians."

"So what do they want?"

"I don't know. All I know is that they're trouble."

"You've not done anything, then, Jyan? Nothing should know of?"

Jyan looked back at him clear-eyed. "Nothing, Father. I swear to you."

"Good. Then we've nothing to fear, have we?" He straightened up. "Do you want me to hold your hand?"

Jyan shook his head.

Chen smiled, understanding. "Okay. Then let's go."

They were almost level with the two when they turned and stepped out, blocking their way. "Where do you think you're going, shit-brains?" the taller of them said, smirking at Jyan.

"What do you want?" Chen asked, keeping the anger from his voice.

"Shut your mouth, *lao jen*," said the second of them, moving closer. "We've business with the boy. He owes us money."

Chen made himself relax. So that was it. They were out of funds and thought they could shake down one of the junior boys. He smiled and touched the tiny eye on his tunic's lapel, activating it. "I don't think my son has any business with you, friend. So be on your way."

The first youth laughed; a false, high laugh that was clearly a signal. At the sound of it, four more youths stepped out from doorways behind him.

"As I said, the boy owes us money. Twenty *yuan*."

Chen put his left arm out, moving Jyan back, behind him. "You have proof of this?"

"Not on me," the first youth said, his face ugly now, his body movements suddenly more menacing. "But he does. And I want it. So unless you want to call me a liar . . ."

Chen smiled, moving his body slightly, so that the camera would capture all their faces. "Oh, I'm sure there's no need for that, friend. But I'm afraid my son doesn't have a single *fen* on him, let alone twenty *yuan*."

The youth's eyes flickered to the side, then looked back at Chen, a smile coming to his lips. "Well, what about you, *lao jen*? They say a father is responsible for his son's debts. I reckon you're good for twenty *yuan*."

Chen smiled and shook his head, taking a step back. "I've spent my money, friend. Now let us pass. Our home is up ahead."

There was a peel of mocking laughter from behind the two youths. The taller of them stepped forward, resting his hand lightly on Chen's shoulder.

"I'm sorry . . . *friend*. . . but I don't believe you. I saw the note you paid with at the picture house. You can't have spent it all, can you?"

Chen looked at the hand on his shoulder. It was a thin, ugly hand. It would be easy – and immensely satisfying – to take it from his shoulder and crush it. But he could not do that. He was an officer of the T'ang. And besides, Jyan had to learn the right way of doing things.

Chen took a breath, then bowed his head, taking the slender, crumpled note from his pocket and handing it to the youth.

"Good . . ." The youth squeezed Chen's shoulder reassuringly, then turned, holding the note up triumphantly for his friends to see. They whooped and jeered, making hand gestures at Chen. Then, with a final, mocking bow, the youth turned and strolled arrogantly away, his friends parting before him, one of them turning to send a final gesture of contempt.

Chen watched them go, then turned, looking down at his son. Jyan was standing there sullenly, his head turned away, held stiffly.

"I had to . . ." Chen began, but Jyan shook his head violently.

"You let them piss on us!"

Chen felt himself go still. He had never heard Jyan swear in front of him before. Nor had he ever heard that tone of anger – of hurt and fierce disapproval.

"There were six of them. Someone would have got hurt."

Jyan looked up, glaring at him. "*You*, you mean!"

It wasn't what he'd meant, but he didn't argue. He took a breath, spelling it out clearly, trying to make his son understand. "I am an officer of the T'ang's Security forces, Jyan, and I am off duty. I am not empowered to brawl in the corridors."

"They pissed on us," Jyan said again, glaring at his father, close to tears now. "And you let them get away

560

with it. You just handed the money over to them, like some low-level oaf!"

Chen lifted his hand abruptly, then let it fall. "You don't understand, Jyan. I've got it all on camera. I . . ."

Jyan gave a huff of derision and turned, beginning to walk away.

"*Jyan!* Listen to me!"

The boy shook his head, not looking back. "You let them piss on us!"

Chen stood there a moment longer, watching him, shaking his head, then began to follow.

Back at the apartment, he went through to the end bedroom. Wang Ti was seated on the bed, packing his kit.

"Where is he?" he said quietly.

She looked up at him, then pointed to the closed door of Jyan's room. *There*, she mouthed. *But leave him be.*

He looked at her, then looked down, sighing heavily. Seeing that, she stopped and came across, holding him to her. "What is it?" she asked quietly.

He closed the door behind him, then told her what had happened, explaining what he planned to do. If he acted now, they could trace the note to the youths. That and the evidence of the camera eye would be enough to have the boys demoted to a lower deck. It was the proper way of doing things. The effective way, for it rid the level of that kind of scum. But for once he felt a strong sense of dissatisfaction.

"You were right, Chen," she said softly. "And what you did was right. There must be laws. We cannot live as they did in the old days. It would be like the Net up here if it were otherwise."

"I know," he said, "but I let him down. I could see it in his face. He thinks I am a coward."

Wang Ti shook her head, pained. "And you, Chen? Do you consider yourself a coward? No. You are *kwai*, husband. Whatever clothes you wear, you will always be *kwai*. But sometimes it is right to avoid trouble. You have said so yourself. Sometimes one must bend like a reed."

"*Ai ya* . . ." He turned his head aside, but she drew it gently back.

"Let him be, Chen. He'll come round. Just now his head is filled with heroics. That film you took him to see. His imagination was racing with it. But life is not like that. Sometimes one must concede to get one's way."

He stared back at her, knowing she was right, but some part of him couldn't help thinking that he should have acted. Should have crushed the boy's hand and broken a few of their hot heads. To teach them a lesson.

And impress his son . . .

He looked down. "It hurts, Wang Ti. To have him look at me like that. To have him say those things . . ."

She touched his cheek tenderly, her caress, like her voice, a balm. "I know, my love. But that too is a kind of bravery, no? To face that hurt and conquer it. For the good. Knowing you did right." She smiled. "He'll come round, Chen. I know he will. He's a good boy and he loves you. So just leave him be a while, neh?"

He nodded. "Well . . . I'd best get Deck Security on to it. I've got to report back in a few hours, so there's not much time."

She smiled and turned away, returning to her packing. "And, Chen?"

"Yes?" he said, turning at the door, looking back at her.

"Don't do anything silly. Remember what I said. You know what you are. Let that be enough."

He hesitated, then nodded. But even as he turned away he knew it wasn't. *Damn them!* he thought, wondering what it was that twisted men's souls so much that they could not exist without tormenting others.

* * *

In the long, broad hallway that led to the Hall of the Serene Ultimate it was cool and silent and dimly lit. From the dark, animal mouths of cressets set high in the blood red walls, naked, oil-fed flames gave off a thin, watery glow that flickered on the tiled mosaic of the floor and gave a dozen wavering shadows to the slender pillars that lined each side. The long shapes of dragons coiled upwards about these pillars in alternating reds and greens, stretching towards the heavens of the ceiling where, in the flicker of dark and light, a battle between gods and demons raged in bas-relief.

Between the pillars stood the guards, unmoving, at attention. Light glimmered dimly on their burnished armour, revealing the living moistness of their eyes. They faced the outer doors prepared, their lives a wall, defending their lords and masters.

At their back was a second double door, locked now. Beyond it, the Seven sat in conference. There it was warmer, brighter. Each T'ang sat easy in a padded chair, relaxed, their ceremonial silks the only outward sign of ritual. Wang Sau-leyan, host of this Council, was talking, discussing the package of proposals Li Yuan had set before them.

Li Yuan sat facing Wang, a hard knot of tension in his chest. Earlier, he had been taken aback by the unexpected warmth of the young T'ang of Africa's greeting. He had come expecting coldness, even an overt hostility, but Wang's embrace, his easy laughter, had thrown him. And so now. For while his words seemed fair – seemed to endorse, even to embrace Li Yuan's scheme for the days ahead – Li Yuan could not shed the habit of suspicion. Wang Sau-leyan was such a consummate actor – such a *natural* politician – that to take anything he did or said at face value was to leave oneself open, unguarded, vulnerable to the next twist or turn of his mood.

Li Yuan eased back into the cushions, forcing himself to relax, trying to see through the veil of Wang's words. Beside him, he could sense Tsu Ma shift in his chair.

"And so . . ." Wang said, looking across at Li Yuan again, his smile clear, untroubled, "my feeling is that we must support Li Yuan's ideas. To do otherwise would be unwise, maybe even disastrous." He looked about him, raising his plump hands in a gesture of acceptance. "I realise that I have argued otherwise in the past, but in the last six months I have come to see that we must face these problems, *now*, before it is too late. That we must deal with them, resolutely, with the will to overcome all difficulties."

Li Yuan was aware of how closely Wang's words echoed his father's. But was that deliberate on Wang's part or mere unconscious echo?

He looked up, noting how Wang was watching him, and nodded.

"Good," Wang said, turning to face Wu Shih and Wei Feng, understanding that only those two alone remained to be convinced. "In that case, I propose that we draft a much fuller document to be agreed and ratified by us at the next meeting of this Council."

Li Yuan looked to Tsu Ma, surprised. Was that it? Was there to be no sting in the tail?

Tsu Ma leaned forward, a soft laugh forming a prologue to his words. "I am glad that we see eye to eye on this matter, cousin, but let me make this clear. Are you proposing that we adopt Li Yuan's package of measures, or are you suggesting some . . . *alteration* of their substance?"

Wang Sau-leyan's smile was disarming. "In essence I see nothing wrong with Li Yuan's proposals, yet in matters of this kind we must make sure that the fine detail – the drafting of the laws themselves – are to our satisfaction, neh? To allow too little would be as bad as to allow too much. The changes to the Edict must be regulated finely, as must the laws on population growth. The *balance* must be right, would you not agree, Wei Feng?"

Wei Feng, addressed unexpectedly, considered the matter a moment. He was looking old these days, markedly tired, and for the last meeting he had let his eldest son, Wei Chan Yin sit in for him. But this time, in view of the importance of the meeting, he had decided to attend in person. He sat forward slightly, clearly in pain, and nodded.

"That is so, Wang Sau-leyan. And I am gratified to hear

you talk of balance. I have heard many things today that I thought not to hear in my lifetime, yet I cannot say you are wrong. Things have changed these last ten years. And if it takes this package of measures to set things right, we must pursue this course, as my cousin Wang says, resolutely and with the will to overcome all difficulties. Yet we would do well to take our own counsel on the extent and nature of these changes before we make them. We must understand the likely outcome of our actions."

Wang bowed his head respectfully. "I agree, honoured cousin. There is great wisdom in your words. And that is why I propose that a joint committee is set up to investigate the likely consequences of such measures. Moreover, might I suggest that my cousin, Wei Feng's man, Minister Sheng, be appointed Head of that committee, reporting back directly to this Council with his findings."

Li Yuan stared at Tsu Ma, astonished. Minister Sheng! It was Sheng whom he and Tsu Ma had planned to propose as the new Steward for GenSyn – Sheng who was the linchpin of their scheme to keep the company from financial ruin – but somehow Wang Sau-leyan had found out, and now he had pre-empted them, robbing them of their candidate, knowing they had prepared no other. Wei Feng was nodding, immensely pleased by the suggestion. A moment later a vote had carried the decision unanimously, bringing them on to the next piece of business, the question of GenSyn and how it was to be administered.

"But first let us eat," Wang said, lifting his bulky figure from the chair. "I don't know about you, cousins, but I could eat an ox, raw if necessary."

There was laughter, but it was not shared by Li Yuan or Tsu Ma – they were still reeling from the shock of Wang's final twist. Li Yuan looked across, meeting Wang's eyes. Before they had been clear, but now there was a hardness, a small gleam of satisfaction in them.

Li Yuan bit back his anger, then leaned forward and picked up the silk-bound folder, gripping it tightly as he made his way across and out on to the balcony. Only minutes ago he had decided not to use what he knew, but now he was determined.

No. He was not finished yet. Let Wang Sau-leyan savour his tiny victory, for this day would see him humbled, his power in Council broken for all time.

And nothing – *nothing* – would stop him now.

★ ★ ★

At that moment, twenty thousand *li* away, at Nanking spaceport, a tall Han, wearing the outworld fashions of the Mars Colony, was stepping down from the interplanetary craft *Wuhan*. He had been through one exhaustive security check on board the ship, but another lay ahead. Ever since the attempt on Marshal Tolonen's life, security had been tight at Nanking.

He joined the queue, staring out across the massive landing pit dispassionately. The tests inside the ship had interested him. They were looking for abnormalities; for differences in the rib structure and the upper chest; signs of unusual brain-scan patterns. He had had to produce a sample of his urine and his faecal matter. Likewise he had had to spit into a small ceramic dish. And afterwards the guard had looked up at him and smiled. 'It's all right,' he'd said, laughing, as if he'd cracked the joke a thousand times, 'you're human.'

As if that meant anything.

"Tuan Wen-ch'ang . . ."

He stepped forward, presenting his papers. The guard ignored them, taking his hand and placing it on to a lit-up pad on the desk in front of him. After a moment the guard released his hand, then brought round a swivel arm. Tuan put his eye to the cup at the end, holding there a moment longer than was necessary for the machine to take a retinal scan.

"Okay," the guard said, then leaned across, taking Tuan's papers. Holding them under the high-density light he looked for signs of tampering or falsification. Satisfied, he slipped the pass into the slim black box at his side. A moment later it popped out again. At Security Central in Bremen the computer had entered Tuan Wen-ch'ang's personal details into the mainframe.

"All right. You're authorised for unobstructed passage in the four Cities in which you have business, full access granted between Level 150 and First Level."

Tuan gave the slightest bow then walked on, pocketing his papers.

Deep inside he felt a mild amusement. It had been much easier than he had expected. But he understood why. This whole society had been conditioned not to anticipate; to think of how things were and had always been, not of their potential. Their security procedures, for instance. They were testing for something that was already redundant; that was as outmoded as the tests they used to find it. On Mars things were different. There the pace was faster. Things had moved on.

He climbed aboard the courtesy train and sat there, waiting, his patience inexhaustible, his path through the great labyrinth of the City mapped out clearly in his head, as if already travelled. It was four hours by bolt to Luo Yang, then another hour and a half north to Yang Ch'ian on the edge of the City, only a hundred *li* from Wang Sau-leyan's palace at Tao Yuan. But the central computer records would show something else; would show him travelling south down the coast to catch the inter-continental shuttle from Fuchow to Darwin. And if the central computer said it were so, who would argue with it? Who would bother to check whether it reflected anything real – anything happening in the solid, physical world?

Outwardly Tuan Wen-ch'ang's face remained placid, almost inscrutable in its mask-like quality, yet deep down he was smiling. Yes, they had had all kinds of things bred out of them down here. Things which the species needed if it were to evolve beyond its present state. And that was why he was here. To remind them of what could be done. To shake them up a little.

And to push things one stage further.

★ ★ ★

567

Beyond the one-way glass the two youths sat, their backs to the wall, their hands bound. The preliminary interrogation was over. Now it was time to take things further.

Chen followed the sergeant through, watching how the two boys glanced at him, seeing the uniform, then looked again, their eyes widening as they recognised who he was.

"*Ai ya . . .*" the younger of them murmured beneath his breath, but the tall, thin youth – the ringleader – was silent.

"Well, my friends," the sergeant said, a warm, ironic tone to his voice. "You've met your accuser before, but I don't think you knew his name. So let me present Captain Kao of the T'ang's special élite force."

The thin youth's eyes came up, meeting Chen's briefly.

Good, thought Chen. *So now you understand.*

"All right," he said brusquely. "You have had your chance to confess. Now you will be taken before a specially-convened panel of judges who will decide the matter." He paused. "Your families will be present."

He saw the sudden bitterness in the thin youth's face. "You bastard," the boy said quietly. "You fucking bastard."

Again, he let it pass. He was the T'ang's man, after all.

They took them down, under armed escort, to the meeting hall at the far end of the deck. There, in closed session, the three judges were waiting, seated behind their high lecterns. To one side of the hall, on chairs set apart from the rest, sat the four accomplices. Behind them were the families – men, women and children – numbering several hundred in all.

All this, Chen thought, looking about him, surprised by the size of the gathering. *All this because I willed it. Because I wanted things to be done properly.*

And yet it didn't feel right. He should have broken the little bastard's hand. Should have given him a simple lesson in power. Whereas this . . .

It began. Chen sat there, to the side, while the judges went through the evidence, questioning the boys and noting down their replies. It was a cold, almost clinical process. Yet when Chen stood to give his statement, he could feel the silent pressure of all those eyes, accusing him, angry at him for disturbing the balance of their lives. He felt his face grow numb, his heart begin to hammer, but he saw it through. He was *kwai*, after all. Besides, it was not he who had threatened another; who had extorted money and then lied about it.

He stared at the two youths, the desire to lash out – to smash their ugly little faces – almost too much for him. The darkness afterwards came as a relief. He sat there, barely conscious of the film being shown on the screen behind the judges – the film he had taken only hours before – yet when the lights came up again, it was hard to turn and confront that wall of hostile faces.

He listened carefully as the senior judge summed up the case, then, steeling himself, stood for the verdict. There was a moment's silence, then an angry murmur of disapproval as the two ringleaders were sent down, demoted fifty levels, their families fined heavily, their accomplices fined and ordered to do one hundred days' community service.

Chen looked across, conscious of the pointing fingers, the accusing eyes, and even when the senior judge admonished the families, increasing the fines and calling upon the Heads to bring their clans to order, he felt no better. Maybe they were right. Maybe it was too harsh. But that wasn't really the point. It was the kind of punishment, not the degree, that felt wrong.

As the families left, Chen stood there by the door, letting them jostle him as they filed past, staring back at his accusers, defying them to understand.

You saw what your sons did. You have seen what they've become. Why blame me for your children's failings?

And yet they did.

Ts'ui Wei, father of the ringleader, came across, leaning

menacingly over Chen. "Well, Captain Kao, are you *satisfied* with what you have done here today?"

Chen stared back at him silently.

Ts'ui Wei's lips curled slightly, the expression the mirror image of his son's disdainful sneer. "I am sure you feel proud of yourself, Captain. You have upheld the law. But you have to live here, neh? You have children, *neh*?"

Chen felt himself go cold with anger. "Are you threatening me, *Shih* Ts'ui?"

Ts'ui Wei leaned back, smiling; a hideously cynical smile. "You misunderstand me, Captain. I am a law-abiding man. But one must live, neh?"

Chen turned away, biting back his anger, leaving before he did something he would regret. As Wang Ti said, he should be content to have done his part and helped cleanse his level. Yet as he made his way back it was anger, not satisfaction that he felt. That and a profound sense of wrongness. And as he walked, his hand went to his queue, feeling the thick braid of hair then tugging at it, as if to pull it from his head.

★ ★ ★

It was after three when they called Karr from his bed. There had been a shoot-out at one of the stacks east-south-east of Augsburg *Hsien*. Five men were dead, all visitors to the stack. That alone would not have been significant enough to wake him, but, some hours later, a sack had been found near one of the inter-deck lifts. A sack containing a full *Yu* dossier on the Dragonfly Club.

Now, less than thirty minutes later, Karr stood in the bedroom of the two-roomed apartment, trying to work out what had happened.

As he stood there the deck's duty officer knocked and entered. He bowed and handed Karr two printouts.

"Ywe Hao . . ." Karr mouthed softly, studying the flat, black and white image of the apartment's occupant; noting at once how like the artist's impression of the *Yu* terrorist,

Chi Li, she was. This was her. There was no doubting it. But who were the others?

The security scans on the five victims had revealed little. They were from various parts of the City – though mostly from the north-central *hsien*. All were engineers or technicians in the maintenance industries: occupations that allowed them free access at this level. Apart from that their past conduct had been exemplary. According to the record, they were fine, upstanding citizens, but the record was clearly wrong.

So what was this? A rival faction, muscling in on the action? Or had there been a split in the ranks of the *Yu* – some internal struggle for power, culminating in this? After all he'd seen of such *Ko Ming* groups it would not have surprised him, but for once the explanation didn't seem to fit.

"What do the cameras show?"

"They're being processed and collated, sir. We should have them in the next ten to fifteen minutes."

"And the woman – this Ywe Hao – she's on them, neh?"

"I sent a squad up to where she was last seen by the cameras, but there was no sign of her, sir. She vanished."

"Vanished?" Karr shook his head. "How do you mean?"

The man glanced away uneasily. "Our cameras saw her enter the maintenance room at the top of the deck. After that there's no sign of her. Neither of the cameras on the main conduit picked her up."

"So she must be there, neh?"

"No, sir. I had my men check that straight away. The room's empty and there's no sign of her in the conduit itself."

Karr sighed. It was clear he would have to look for himself. "You said earlier that she may have been warned – that there was a lookout of some kind . . . ."

"Two young boys, sir."

"I see. And you've traced them, neh?"

"They're in custody, sir. Would you like to see them?"

Karr looked about him at the mess. "Your men have finished here, I take it?"

The Captain nodded.

"Good. Then clear this up first. Remove the corpses and put some cloths down. I don't want our young friends upset, understand me?"

"Sir!"

"Oh, and Captain . . . have one of your men run a file on the movements of our friend Ywe Hao over the last three months. With particular attention to those occasions when she doesn't show up on camera."

The Captain frowned but nodded. "As you wish, Major."

"Good. And bring me some *ch'a*. A large *chung* if you have one. We may be here some while."

★ ★ ★

Chen stood there in the doorway, looking about him at the carnage. "Kuan Yin! What happened here?"

Karr smiled tiredly. "It looks like some kind of inter-factional rivalry. As to whether it's two separate groups or a struggle within the *Yu*, maybe that's something we'll discover, if and when we find the woman. As for the woman herself, I'm certain she was involved in both the Hannover assassination and the attack on the Dragonfly Club. I've asked for files on her movements over the last three months. If I'm right about her, then there ought to be blanks on the tape corresponding with the white-outs surrounding the terrorist incidents. We've no next of kin details, which is unusual, but you can do a little digging on that, neh? Oh yes, and the Duty Captain is going to bring two young boys here. They were the woman's look-outs. I want you to question them and find out what they know about her. But be easy on them. I don't think they understood for a moment what they were in on."

"And you, Gregor? What will you be doing?"

Karr straightened up, then laughed. "First I'm going to

finish this excellent *ch'a*, then I'm going to find out how a full-grown woman can disappear into thin air."

* * *

"And so, cousins, we come to the question of the GenSyn inheritance." Wang looked about him, his eyes resting briefly on Li Yuan and Tsu Ma before they settled on the ageing T'ang of East Asia, Wei Feng. "As I see it, this matter has been allowed to drag on far too long. As a result the company has been harmed, its share price reduced dramatically on the Index. Our immediate concern, therefore, must be to provide GenSyn with a stable administrative framework, thus removing the uncertainties that are presently plaguing the company. After that . . ."

Li Yuan cleared his throat. "Forgive me for interrupting, cousin, but, before we debate this matter at any length, I would like to call for a further postponement."

Wang laughed, a small sound of disbelief. "Forgive me, cousin, but did I hear you correctly? A *further* postponement?"

"If it would please my cousins. It is clear that we need more time to find a satisfactory solution. Another month or two."

Wang sat forward, his face suddenly hard. "Forgive me, cousin, but I do not understand. Since Klaus Ebert's death, this matter has been brought before this Council twice. On both occasions there was a unanimous agreement to postpone. For good reason, for no solution was forthcoming. But now we have the answer. Hou Tung-po's proposal is the solution we were looking for."

Tsu Ma's laugh was heavily sardonic. "You call that a solution, cousin? It sounds to me like a bureaucratic nightmare – a recipe not for stability but for certain financial disaster."

Hou Tung-po sat forward, his face red with anger, but Wang's raised hand silenced him.

"Had this matter not been raised before, Tsu Ma, and were there not already a satisfactory solution before us –

one you will have a full opportunity to debate – I would understand your desire to look for other answers, but the time for prevarication is past. As I was saying, we must act now or see the company damaged, perhaps irreparably."

Wang paused, looking to Wei Feng, appealing to the old man directly. As things stood, Hou Tung-po and Chi Ling would support Wang, while Tsu Ma and Wu Shih would line up behind Li Yuan. If it came to a fight, Wei Feng held the casting vote.

Wang smiled, softening his stance.

"Besides, what objections could my cousins possibly have to the idea of a ruling committee? Would that not give us each a fair say in the running of the company? Would that not demonstrate – more clearly than anything – that the Seven have full confidence in the continuing prosperity of GenSyn?"

Li Yuan looked away. Whilst in terms of holdings it was second behind the giant MedFac company on the Hang Seng Index, GenSyn was, without doubt, the single most important commercial concern on Chung Kuo, and, as Tsu Ma had rightly said, any weakening of the Company would affect him far more than it did Wang Sau-leyan.

But that could not be said. Not openly. For to say as much would give Wang the chance to get back at Li Yuan for his family's special relationship with GenSyn – a relationship which, though it had existed for a century or more, was, in truth, against the spirit of the Seven.

Li Yuan sat back, meeting Tsu Ma's eyes. They would have to give way. Minister Sheng had been their winning card, and Wang had already taken him from their hand.

"Cousin Wang," he said coldly. "I concede. Let us adopt cousin Hou's proposal. As you say, what possible objection could we have to such a scheme?"

He drew a breath, finding comfort in the presence of the silk-bound folder in his lap – in the thought of the humiliation he would shortly inflict on Wang. Then – from nowhere, it seemed – a new thought came to him. He leaned forward again, the sheer outrageousness of the idea making him want to laugh aloud.

"Indeed," he said softly, "let me make my own proposal. If the Council permits, I would like to suggest that Marshal Tolonen be replaced in his high post and appointed as Head of the ruling committee of GenSyn." He looked at Wang directly. "As my cousin argued so eloquently, we need to boost the market's confidence, and what clearer sign could we give than to make a man of such experience and integrity the head of our committee?"

He saw the movement in Wang's face and knew he had him. Wang could object, of course, but on what grounds? On the unsuitability of the candidate? No. For to argue that would be to argue that their original ratification of Tolonen as Marshal had been wrong, and that he could not – *would not* – do.

Li Yuan looked about him, seeing the nods of agreement from all sides – even from Wang's own allies – and knew he had succeeded in limiting the damage. With Tolonen in charge there was a much greater chance of things getting done. It would mean a loss of influence in the Council of Generals, but that was as nothing beside the potential loss of GenSyn's revenues.

He met Wang's eyes, triumphant, but Wang had not finished.

"I am delighted that my cousin recognises the urgency of this matter. However, I am concerned whether my cousin really means what he says. It would not, after all, be the first time that he has promised this Council something, only to go back on his word."

Li Yuan started forward, outraged by Wang's words. All around him there was a buzz of astonishment and indignation. But it was Wei Feng who spoke first, his deeply-lined face grown stern and rock-like as he sat stiffly upright in his chair. His gruff voice boomed, all sign of frailty gone from it.

"You had best explain yourself, Wang Sau-leyan, or withdraw your words. I have never heard the like!"

"No?" Wang stood in a flurry of silks, looking about him defiantly. "Nor would you have, cousin, had there not been good reason. I am talking of Li Yuan's promise to this Council that he would release the young sons – a promise that my cousins, Wu Shih and Tsu Ma were also party to." He shifted his bulk, looking about the circle of his fellow T'ang. "It is six months since they gave that promise and what has happened? Are the sons back with their fathers? Is the matter resolved, the grievance of those high citizens settled? No. The fathers remain unappeased, rightfully angry that – after giving our word – their sons remain imprisoned."

Li Yuan stood, facing Wang. "There is good reason why the sons have not been released, and you know it."

"Know it?" Wang laughed contemptuously. "All I know is that you gave your word. Immediately, you said."

"And so it would have been had the paperwork gone smoothly."

"*Paperwork* . . . ?" Wang's mocking laughter goaded Wu Shih to rise and stand beside Li Yuan, his fists clenched, his face livid.

"You know as well as any of us why there have been delays, Wang Sau-leyan! Considering the gravity of the circumstances, the terms of release were laughable. All we asked of the fathers was that they should sign a bond of good behaviour. It was the very minimum we could have asked for, and yet they refused, quibbling over the wording of the papers."

"With every right, if what I've heard is true . . ."

Wu Shih bristled. "And what *have* you heard, *cousin*?"

Wang Sau-leyan half turned, then turned back, moving a step closer, his face thrust almost into Wu Shih's. "That it has been your officials and not the fathers who have quibbled over the precise wording of these . . . *bonds*. That they have dragged their heels and delayed until even the best man's patience would be frayed. That they have found every excuse – however absurd – not to come to terms. In short, that they have been ordered to delay matters."

"*Ordered?*" Wu Shih shuddered with rage, then lifted his hand, as if to strike Wang, but Li Yuan put out his arm, coming between them.

"Cousins . . ." he said urgently, "let us remember where we are." He turned his head, staring fiercely at Wang. "We will achieve nothing by hurling insults at each other."

"You gave your word," Wang said, defiantly, meeting his eyes coldly. "All three of you. Immediately, you said. Without conditions." He took a breath, then turned away, taking his seat.

Wu Shih glared at Wang a moment longer then stepped back, his disgust at his cousin no longer concealed. Li Yuan stood there, feeling the tensions that flowed like electric currents in the air about him and knew – for the first time knew beyond all doubt – that this was a breach that could never be healed. He took his seat again, leaning down to lift the folder from where it had fallen.

"Wang Sau-leyan," he began, looking across at his moon-faced cousin, calm now that he had taken the first step. "There is a small matter I would like to raise before we continue. A matter of . . . etiquette."

Wang Sau-leyan smiled. "As you wish, cousin."

Li Yuan opened the folder, looking down at the wafer-thin piece of black plastic. It was the template of a holo-grammic image: the image of Wang Sau-leyan in the garden at Tao Yuan, meeting with Li Yuan's bondsman, Hsiang Shao-erh. There were other things in the folder – a taped copy of their conversation, and the testimony of Wang's Master of the Royal Household, Sun Li Hua, but it was the holo that was the most damning piece of evidence.

He made to offer it to Wang, but Wang shook his head. "I know what it is, Li Yuan. You have no need to show me."

Li Yuan gave a small laugh of astonishment. What was this? Was Wang admitting his treachery?

With what seemed like resignation, Wang pulled himself up out of the chair and went to the double doors, unlocking them and throwing them open. At his summons a servant approached, head bowed, bearing a large, white lacquered box. Wang took it and turned, facing his fellow T'ang.

"I wondered when you would come to this," he said, approaching to within an arm's length of where Li Yuan was sitting. "Here. I was saving this for you. As for the traitor, Sun, he has found peace. After telling me everything, of course."

Li Yuan took the box, his heart pounding.

He opened it and stared, horrified. From within the bright red wrappings of the box Hsiang Shao-erh stared back at him, his eyes like pale grey, bloated moons in an unnaturally white face, the lids peeled back. And then, slowly, very slowly, as in a dream, the lips began to move.

"Forgive . . . me . . . *Chieh* . . . *Hsia*. . . I . . . confess . . . my . . . treachery . . . and . . . ask . . . you . . . not . . . to . . . punish . . . my . . . kin . . . for . . . my . . . abject . . . unworthiness . . ." There was a tiny shudder from the severed head, and then it went on, the flat, almost gravelly whisper like the voice of stone itself. "Forgive . . . them . . . *Chieh* . . . *Hsia*. . . I . . . beg . . . you . . . Forgive . . . them . . ."

Li Yuan looked up, seeing his horror reflected in every face but one. Then, with a shudder of revulsion he dropped the box, watching it fall, the frozen head roll unevenly across the thick pile of the carpet until it lay still, resting on its cheek beside Wang Sau-leyan's foot. Bending down, the T'ang of Africa lifted it and held it up, offering it to Li Yuan, the smile on his face like the rictus of a corpse.

"This is yours, I believe, cousin." Then he began to laugh, his laughter rolling from him in great waves. "Yours . . ."

★ ★ ★

"What's your name?"

"Kung Lao."

"And yours?"

"Kung Yi-lung."

"You're brothers, then?"

The nine-year-old, Yi-lung shook his head. "Cousins," he said quietly, still not sure of this man who, despite his air of kindness, wore the T'ang's uniform.

Chen sat back slightly, smiling. "Okay. You were friends of Ywe Hao's, weren't you? You helped her when those men came, didn't you?"

He saw how the younger of the two, Lao, looked to his cousin before he nodded.

"Good. You probably saved her life."

He saw how they looked down at that; how, again, they glanced at each other, still not sure what this was all about.

"She must have been a very good friend for you to do that for her, Yi-lung. Why was that? How did you come to be friends?"

Yi-lung kept his head lowered. "She was kind to us," he mumbled, the words offered reluctantly.

"Kind?" Chen gave a soft laugh, recalling what Karr had said about the guard, Leyden, and how she had probably spared his life. "Yes, I can imagine that. But how did you meet her?"

No answer. He tried another tack.

"That's a nice machine she's got. A MedRes Network-6. I'd like one like that, wouldn't you? A top-of-the-range machine. It was strange, though. She was using it to record news items."

"That was our project," the younger boy, Lao, said without thinking, then fell quiet again.

"Your project? For school, you mean?"

Both boys nodded. Yi-lung spoke for them. "She was helping us with it. She always did. She took the time. Not like the rest of them. Any time we had a problem we could go to her."

Chen took a deep breath. "And that's why you liked her?"

Both boys were looking at him now, a strange earnestness in their young faces.

"She was funny," Lao said reflectively. "It wasn't all

work with her. She made it fun. Turned it all into a game. We learned a lot from her, but she wasn't like the teachers."

"That's right," Yi-lung offered, warming to things. "They made everything seem dull and grey, but she brought it all alive for us. She made it all make sense."

"Sense?" Chen felt a slight tightening in his stomach. "How do you mean, Yi-lung? What kind of things did she use to say to you?"

Yi-lung looked down, as if he sensed there was some deeper purpose behind Chen's question. "Nothing," he said evasively.

"Nothing?" Chen laughed, letting go, knowing he would get nothing if he pushed. "Look, I'm just interested, that's all. Ywe Hao's gone missing and we'd like to find her. To help her. If we can find out what kind of woman she was . . ."

"Are you tracking her down?"

Chen studied the two a moment, then leaned forward, deciding to take them into his confidence. "Ywe Hao's in trouble. Those men who came tried to kill her, but she got away. So yes, Kung Lao, we have to find her. Have to track her down, if that's how you want to put it. But the more we know – the more good things we know about her – the better it will be for her. That's why you have to tell me all you can about her. To help her."

Lao looked at his cousin, then nodded. "Okay. We'll tell you. But you must promise, Captain Kao. Promise that once you find her you'll help her all you can."

He looked back at the two boys, momentarily seeing something of his own sons in them, then nodded. "I promise. All right? Now tell me. When did you first meet Ywe Hao, and how did you come to be friends?"

* * *

The maintenance room was empty, the hatch on the back wall locked, the warning light beside it glowing red in the half-light. Karr crouched down, squeezing through the low doorway, then stood there, perfectly still, listening, sniffing the air. There was the faintest scent of sweat. And something else . . . something he didn't recognise. He went across, putting his ear against the hatch. Nothing. Or almost nothing. There was a faint hum – a low, pulsing vibration.

He paused a moment, studying the hatchway, realising it would be a tight squeeze; that he would be vulnerable momentarily if she was waiting just the other side. But the odds were that she was far away by now.

He ducked into the opening backwards, head first, forcing his shoulders through the narrow space diagonally, then grabbed the safety bar overhead and heaved himself up, twisting sideways. He dropped and span round quickly, his weapon out, but even as he turned, he had to check himself, staggering, realising suddenly that the platform was only five *ch'i* in width and that beyond . . .

Beyond was a drop of half a *li*.

He drew back, breathing slowly. The conduit was fifty *ch'i* across, a great diamond-shaped space, one of the six great hollowed columns which stood at the corners of the stack, holding it all up. Pipes went up into the darkness overhead, massive pipes twenty, thirty times the girth of a man, each pipe like a great tree, thick branches stretching off on every side, criss-crossing the open space. Service lights speckled the walls of the great conduit above and below, but their effect was not so much to illuminate the scene as to emphasise its essential darkness.

It was a cold, sombre place, a place of shadows and silence. Or so it seemed in those first few moments. But then he heard it – the sound that underlay all others throughout the City – the sound of great engines, pushing the water up the levels from the great reservoirs below, and of others, filtering what came down. There was a palpable hum, a vibration in the air itself. And a trace of that same indefinable scent he had caught a hint of in the room earlier, but stronger here. Much stronger.

Poking his head out over the edge he looked down, then

moved back, craning his neck, trying to see up into the shadows.

Which way? Had she gone up or down?

He looked about him, locating the cameras, then frowned, puzzled. There was no way the cameras wouldn't have seen her come out of the room and onto the platform. No chance at all. Which meant that either she hadn't gone into the maintenance room in the first place or those cameras had been tampered with. And she *had* gone into the room.

For a moment Karr stared at the camera just across from him, then, struck by the absurdity of it, he laughed. It was all too bloody easy. Since the City had first been built Security had been dependent on their eyes – their security cameras – to be their watchdogs and do most of their surveillance work for them, not questioning for a moment how satisfactory such a system was, merely using it, as they'd been taught. But the *Yu* had recognised how vulnerable such a network was – how easily manipulated. They had seen just how easy it was to blind an eye or feed it false information. All they needed was access. And who had access? Technicians. Maintenance technicians. Like the five dead men. And the girl. And others. Hundreds of others. Every last one of them tampering with the network, creating gaps in the vision of the world.

False eyes they'd made. False eyes. Like in *wei chi*, where a group of stones was only safe if it had two eyes, and where the object was to blind an eye and take a group, or to lull one's opponent into a false sense of security, by letting them think they had an eye, whereas in fact . . .

Pulling his visor down, he leaned out, searching the walls for heat traces.

Nothing. As he'd expected, the trail was cold. He raised the visor, sighing heavily. What he really needed was sleep. Twelve hours if possible, four if he was lucky. The drugs he was taking to keep awake had a limited effect. Thought processes deteriorated, reflexes slowed. If he didn't find her soon . . .

He leaned back, steadying himself with one hand, then stopped, looking down. His fingers were resting in something soft and sticky. He raised them to his mouth, tasting them. It was blood, recently congealed.

Hers? It had to be. No one else had come here in the last few hours. So maybe she'd been wounded in the fire-fight. He shook his head, puzzled. If that were so, why hadn't they found a trail of blood in the corridors outside? Unless they hadn't looked.

He went to the edge of the platform, feeling underneath, his fingers searching until, at the top of the service ladder, three rungs down, they met a second patch of stickiness.

Down. She had gone down.

Karr smiled, then, drawing his gun, turned and clambered over the edge, swinging out, his booted feet reaching for the ladder.

* * *

Towards the bottom of the shaft it became more difficult. The smaller service pipes that branched from the huge arterials proliferated, making it necessary for Karr to clamber out, away from the wall, searching for a way down.

The trail of blood had ended higher up, on a platform thirty levels down from where he had first discovered it. He had spent twenty minutes searching for further traces, but there had been nothing. It was only when he had trusted to instinct and gone down that he had found something – the wrapping of a field-dressing pad, wedged tightly into a niche in the conduit wall.

It was possible that she had gone out through one of the maintenance hatches and into the deck beyond. Possible but unlikely. Not with all the nearby stacks on special security alert. Neither would she have doubled back. She had lost a lot of blood. In her weakened state the climb would have been too much.

Besides which, his instinct told him where he would find her.

Karr moved on, working his way down, alert for the

smallest movement, the least deviation in the slow, rhythmic pulse that filled the air. That sound seemed to grow in intensity as he went down, a deep vibration that was as much within his bones as in the air. He paused, looking up through the tangled mesh of pipework, imagining the great two-*li*-high conduit as a giant flute – a huge *k'un-ti* – reverberating on the very edge of audibility: producing one single, unending note in a song written for Titans.

He went down, taking greater care now, conscious that the bottom of the shaft could not be far away. Even so, he was surprised when, easing his way between a nest of overlapping pipes, his feet met nothing. For a moment he held himself there, muscles straining, as his feet searched blindly for purchase, then drew himself up again.

He crouched, staring down through the tangle of pipework. Below him there was nothing. Nothing but darkness.

In all probability she was down there, in the darkness, waiting for him. But how far down? Twenty *ch'i*? Thirty? He pulled his visor down and switched to ultra-violet. At once his vision was filled with a strong red glow. Of course . . . he had felt it earlier – that warmth coming up from below. That was where the great pumps were – just beneath. Karr raised the visor and shook his head. It was no use. She could move about as much as she wanted against that bright backdrop of warmth, knowing that she could not been seen. Nor could he use a lamp. That would only give his own position away, long before he'd have the chance to find her.

What then? A flash bomb? A disabling gas?

The last made sense, but still he hesitated. Then, making up his mind, he turned, making his way across to the wall.

There would be a way down. A ladder. He would find it and descend, into the darkness.

He went down, tensed, listening for the slightest movement from below, his booted feet finding the rungs with a delicacy surprising in so big a man. His body was half-turned towards the central darkness, his weapon drawn, ready for use. Even so, it was a great risk he was taking and he knew it. She didn't have night-sight – he was fairly sure of that – but, if she *was* down there, there was the distinct possibility that she would see him first, if only as a shadow against the shadows.

He stopped, crouching on the ladder, one hand going down. His foot had met something. Something hard but yielding.

It was a mesh. A strong security mesh, stretched across the shaft. He reached out, searching the surface. Yes, there! – the raised edge of a gate, set into the mesh. He traced it round. There was a slight indentation on the edge farthest from the ladder, where a spanner-key fitted, but it was locked. Worse, it was bolted from beneath. If he was to go any further he would have to break it open.

He straightened up, gripping the rung tightly, preparing himself, then brought his foot down hard. With a sharp crack it gave, taking him with it, his hand torn from the rung, his body twisting about.

He fell. Instinctively, he curled into a ball, preparing for impact, but it came sooner than he'd expected, jarring him.

He rolled to one side, then sat up, sucking in a ragged breath, his left shoulder aching.

If she was there . . .

He closed his eyes, willing the pain to subside, then got up on to his knees. For the briefest moment he felt giddy, disoriented, then his head cleared. His gun . . . he had lost his gun.

In the silent darkness he waited, tensed, straining to hear the click of a safety or the rattle of a grenade, but there was nothing, only the deep, rhythmic pulse of the pumps, immediately beneath. And something else – something so faint he thought at first he was imagining it.

Karr got to his feet unsteadily, then, feeling his way blindly, he went towards the sound.

The wall was closer than he'd thought. For a moment his hands searched fruitlessly, then found what they'd been looking for. A passageway – a small, low-ceilinged tunnel barely broad enough for him to squeeze into. He stood there a moment, listening. Yes, it came from here. He could hear it clearly now.

Turning side-on, he ducked inside, moving slowly down the cramped passageway, his head scraping the ceiling. Halfway down he stopped, listening again. The sound was closer now, its regular pattern unmistakable. Reaching out, his fingers connected with a grill. He recognised it at once. It was a storage cupboard, inset into the wall, like those they had in the dormitories.

Slipping his fingers through the grill, he lifted it, easing it slowly back and up into the slot at the top. He paused, listening again, his hand resting against the bottom edge of the niche, then began to move his fingers inward, searching . . .

Almost at once they met something warm. He drew them back a fraction, conscious of the slight change in the pattern of the woman's breathing. He waited for it to regularise, then reached out again, exploring the shape. It was a hand, the fingers pointing to the left. He reached beyond it, searching, then smiled, his fingers closing about a harder, colder object. Her gun.

For a moment he rested, his eyes closed, listening to the simple rhythm of the woman's breathing, the deep reverberation of the pumps. In the darkness they seemed to form a kind of counterpoint and for a moment he felt himself at ease, the two sounds connecting somewhere deep within him, Yin and Yang, balancing each other.

The moment passed. Karr opened his eyes into the darkness and shivered. It was a shame. He would have liked it to have ended otherwise, but it was not to be. He checked the gun, then pulled his visor down, clicking on the lamp. At once the cramped niche filled with light and shadow.

Karr caught his breath, studying the woman. She lay on her side, her face towards the entrance, one hand folded across her breasts. In the pearled glow of the lamp she was quite beautiful, her Asiatic features softened in sleep, her strength – the perfect bone structure of her face and shoulders – somehow emphasised. Like Marie, he thought, surprised by the notion. As he watched she stirred, moving her head slightly, her eyes flickering beneath the lids in dream.

Again he shivered, recalling what the guard, Leyden, had said about her, and what the two boys had told Chen. At the same time he could see the murdered youth at the Dragonfly Club and the soft, hideous excess of that place, and for a moment he was confused. Was she *really* his enemy? Was this strong, beautiful creature really so different from himself?

He looked away, reminding himself of the oath of loyalty he had made to his T'ang. Then, steeling himself, he raised the gun, placing it a mere finger's length from her sleeping face and clicking off the safety.

The sound woke her. She smiled and stretched, turning towards him. For a moment her dark eyes stared out dreamily, then, with a blink of realisation, she grew still.

He hesitated, wanting to explain, wanting, just this once, for her to understand. "I . . ."

"Don't . . ." she said quietly. "Please . . ."

The words did something to him. He drew the gun back, staring at her, then, changing its setting, he leaned forward again, placing it to her temple.

Afterwards he stood there, out in the darkness of the main shaft, the mesh overhead glittering in the upturned light from his visor, and tried to come to terms with what he'd done. He had been resolved to kill her; to end it cleanly, honourably. But, faced with her, hearing her voice, he had found himself unmanned – incapable of doing what he'd planned.

He turned, looking back at the shadowed entrance to the passageway. All this while he had been operating under a communications blackout, so in theory he might still kill her or let her go and no one would be the wiser. But he knew now that he would do what his duty required of him and deliver her, stunned, her wrists and ankles bound, into captivity.

Whether it felt right or not. Because that was his job – the thing Tolonen had chosen him to do all those years ago.

Karr sighed, then, raising his right hand, held down the two tiny blisters on the wrist, reactivating the inbuilt comset.

"Kao Chen," he said softly, "can you read me?"

There was a moment's silence, then the reply came, sounding directly in his head. "Gregor . . . thank the gods. Where are you?"

He smiled, comforted by the sound of Chen's voice. "Listen. I've got her. She's bound and unconscious, but I don't think I can get her out of here on my own. I'll need assistance."

"Okay. I'll get on to that straight away. But where are you? There's been no trace of you for almost two hours. We were worried."

Karr laughed quietly. "Wait. There's a plaque here somewhere." He lowered his visor, looking about, then went across. "All right. You'll need two men and some lifting equipment – pulleys and the like."

"Yes," Chen said, growing impatient. "I'll do all that. But tell me where you are. You must have some idea."

"It's Level 31," Karr said, turning back, playing the beam on to the surface of the plaque, making sure. "Level 31, Dachau *Hsien*."

CHAPTER·18

THE DEAD BROTHER

Li Yuan stood on the high terrace at Hei Shui, looking out across the lake. He had come unannounced. Behind him stood his eight retainers, their black silks merging with the shadows.

A light breeze feathered the surface of the lake, making the tall reeds at the shoreline sway, the cormorants bob gently on the water. The sky was a perfect blue, the distant mountains hard, clear shapes of black. Sunlight rested like a honeyed gauze over everything, glinting off the long sweep of steps, the white stone arches of the bridge. On the far bank, beyond the lush green of the water meadow, Fei Yen's maids moved among the trees of the orchard, preparing their mistress for the audience.

From where he stood he could see the child's cot – a large, sedan-like thing of pastel-coloured cushions and veils. Seeing it had made his heart beat faster, the darkness at the pit of his stomach harden like a stone.

He turned, impatient. "Come," he said brusquely, then turned back, skipping down the broad steps, his men following like shadows on the white stone.

They met on the narrow bridge, a body's length separating them. Fei Yen stood there, her head lowered. Behind her came her maids, the cot balanced between four of them.

As Li Yuan took a step closer, Fei Yen knelt, touching her head to the stone. Behind her her maids did the same.

"Chieh Hsia . . ."

She was dressed in a simple *chi pao* of pale lemon,

embroidered with butterflies. Her head was bare, her fine, dark hair secured in a tightly braided bun at the crown. As she looked up again, he noticed a faint colour at her neck.

"Your gift . . ." he began, then stopped, hearing a sound from within the cot.

She turned her head, following his gaze, then looked back at him. "He's waking."

He looked at her without recognition, then looked back at the cot. Stepping past, he moved between the kneeling maids and, crouching, drew back the veil at the side of the cot. Inside, amidst a downy nest of cushions, young Han was waking. He lay on his side, one tiny, delicate hand reaching out to grip the edge of the cot. His eyes – two tiny, rounded centres of perfect, liquid blackness – were open, staring up at him.

Li Yuan caught his breath, astonished by the likeness. "Han Ch'in . . ." he said softly.

Fei Yen came and knelt beside him, smiling down at the child, evoking a happy gurgle of recognition. "Do you wish to hold him, *Chieh Hsia*?"

He hesitated, staring down at the child, engulfed by a pain of longing so strong it threatened to unhinge him, then nodded, unable to form the words.

She leaned past, brushing against him, the faint waft of her perfume, the warmth of the momentary contact, bringing him back to himself, making him realise that it was her there beside him. He shivered, appalled by the strength of what he was feeling, knowing suddenly that it had been wrong for him to come. A weakness. But now he had no choice. As she lifted the child and turned towards him, he felt the pain return, sharper than before.

"Your son," she said, so faintly that only he caught the words.

The child nestled in his arms contentedly, so small and frail and vulnerable that his face creased with pain at the thought that anyone might harm him. Nine months old, he was – a mere thirty-nine weeks – yet already he was the image of Yuan's brother, Han Ch'in, dead these last ten years.

Li Yuan stood, then turned, cradling the child, cooing softly to him as he moved between the kneeling maids. Reaching the balustrade, he stood there, looking down at the bank, his eyes half-lidded, trying to see. But there was nothing. No younger self stood there, his heart in his throat, watching as a youthful Han Ch'in strode purposefully through the short grass, like a proud young animal, making towards the bridge and his betrothed.

Li Yuan frowned then turned, staring across the water meadow, but again there was nothing. No tent, no tethered horse or archery target. It had gone, all of it, as if it had never been. And yet there was the child, so like his long-dead brother that it was as if he had not died but simply been away, on a long journey.

"*Where have you been, Han Ch'in?*" he asked softly, almost inaudibly, feeling the warm breeze on his cheek; watching it stir and lift the fine dark hair that covered the child's perfect, ivory brow. "*Where have you been all these years?*"

Yet even as he uttered the words he knew he was deluding himself. This was not Tongjiang, and his brother Han Ch'in was dead. He had helped bury him himself. No, this was someone else. A stranger to the great world. A whole new cycle of creation. His son, fated to be a stranger.

He shivered again, pained by the necessity of what he must do, then turned, looking back at Fei Yen.

She was watching him, her hands at her neck, her eyes misted, moved by the sight of him holding the child, all calculation gone from her. That surprised him – that she was as unprepared for this as he. Whatever she had intended by her gift – whether to wound him or provoke a sense of guilt – she had never expected this.

Beyond her stood his men, like eight dark statues in the late morning sunlight, watching, waiting in silence for their lord.

He went back to her, handing her the child. "He is a good child, neh?"

She met his eyes, suddenly curious, wondering what he meant by coming, then lowered her head. "Like his father," she said quietly.

He looked away, conscious for the first time of her beauty. "You will send me a tape each year, on the child's birthday. I wish . . ." He hesitated, his mouth suddenly dry. He looked back at her. "If he is ill, I want to know."

She gave a small bow. "As you wish, *Chieh Hsia*."

"And Fei Yen . . ."

She looked up, her eyes momentarily unguarded. "*Chieh Hsia?*"

He hesitated, studying her face, the depth of what he had once felt for her there again, just below the surface, then shook his head. "Just that you must do nothing beyond that. What was between us is past. You must not try to rekindle it. Do you understand me clearly?"

For a moment she held his eyes, as if to deny him, then, with a familiar little motion of her head, she looked away, her voice harder than before.

"As you wish, *Chieh Hsia*. As you wish."

★ ★ ★

A screen had been set up between the pillars at the far end of the Hall, like a great white banner gripped between the teeth of dragons. Wang Sau-leyan's Audience Chair had been set before it, some twenty *ch'i* back. He went to it and climbed up, taking his place, then looked across at his Chancellor. "Well?"

Hung Mien-lo shuddered, then, turning towards the back of the Hall, lifted a trembling hand.

At once the lights in the Hall faded. A moment later the screen was lit with a pure white light. Only as the camera panned back slightly did Wang Sau-leyan realise that he was looking at something – at the pale stone face of something. Then, as the border of green and grey and blue came

592

into stronger focus, he realised what it was. A tomb. The door to a tomb.

And not just any tomb. It was his family's tomb at Tao Yuan, in the walled garden behind the eastern palace. He shivered, one hand clutching at his stomach, a tense feeling of dread growing in him by the moment. "What . . . ?"

The query was uncompleted. Even as he watched, the faintest web of cracks formed on the pure white surface of the stone. For the briefest moment these darkened, broadening, tiny chips of whiteness falling away as the stone began to crumble. Then, with a suddenness that made him jerk back, the door split asunder, revealing the inner darkness.

He stared at the screen, horrified, his throat constricted, his heart hammering in his chest. For a moment there was nothing – nothing but the darkness – and then the darkness moved, a shadow forming on the ragged edge of stone. It was a hand.

Wang Sau-leyan was shaking now, his whole body trembling, but he could not look away. Slowly, as in his worst nightmare, the figure pulled itself up out of the darkness of the tomb, like a drowned man dragging himself up from the depths of the ocean bed. For a moment it stood there, faintly outlined by the morning sunlight, a simple shape of darkness against the utter blackness beyond, then it staggered forward, into the full brightness of the sun.

Wang groaned. "*Kuan Yin* . . ."

It was his brother, Wang Ta-hung. His brother, lain in a bed of stone these last twenty months. But he had grown in the tomb, becoming the man he had never been in life. The figure stretched in the sunlight, earth falling from its shrouds, then looked about it, blinking into the new day.

"It cannot be," Wang Sau-leyan said softly, breathlessly. "I had him killed, his copy destroyed."

"And yet his vault was empty, *Chieh Hsia*."

The corpse stood there, swaying slightly, its face up to the sun. Then, with what seemed like a drunken lurch, it started forward again, trailing earth.

"And the earth?"

"Is real earth, *Chieh Hsia*. I had it analysed."

Wang stared at the screen, horrified, watching the slow, ungainly procession of his brother's corpse. There was no doubting it. It was his brother, but grown large and muscular, more like his elder brother than the weakling he had been in life. As it staggered across the grass towards the locked gate and the watching camera, the sound of it – a hoarse, snuffling noise – grew louder step by step.

The gate fell away, the seasoned wood shattering as if rotten, torn brutally from its solid, iron hinges. Immediately the image shifted to another camera, watching the figure come on, up the broad pathway beside the eastern palace and then down the steps, into the central gardens.

"Did no one try to stop it?" Wang asked, his mouth dry.

Hung's voice was small. "No one knew, *Chieh Hsia*. The first time an alarm sounded was when it broke through the main gate. The guards there were petrified. They ran from it. And who can blame them?"

For once Wang Sau-leyan did not argue. Watching the figure stumble on he felt the urge to hide – somewhere deep and dark and safe – or to run and keep running, even to the ends of the earth. The hair stood up on his neck, and his hands shook like those of an old man. He had never felt so afraid. Never, even as a child.

And yet it could not be his brother. Even as he feared it, a part of his mind rejected it.

He put his hands out, gripping the arms of the chair, willing himself to be calm, but it was hard. The image on the screen was powerful, more powerful than his reasoning mind could bear. His brother was dead – he had seen that with his eyes; touched the cold and lifeless flesh – and yet here he was once more, reborn – a new man, his eyes agleam with life, his body glowing with a strange, unearthly power.

He shuddered, then tore his eyes from the screen, looking down into the pale, terrified face of his Chancellor.

"So where is it now, Hung? Where in the gods' names is it now?"

Hung Mien-lo looked up at him, wide-eyed, and gave the tiniest shrug. "In the hills, *Chieh Hsia*. Somewhere in the hills."

*   *   *

Ywe Hao was standing with her back to Karr, naked, her hands secured behind her back, her ankles bound. To her right, against the bare wall, was an empty examination couch. Beyond the woman, at the far end of the cell, two medical staff were preparing their instruments at a long table.

Karr cleared his throat, embarrassed, even a touch angry, at the way they were treating her. It had never worried him before – normally the creatures he had to deal with deserved such treatment – but this time it was different. He glanced at the woman uneasily, disturbed by her nakedness, and, as he moved past her, met her eyes briefly, conscious once more of the strength there, the defiance, even, perhaps, a slight air of moral superiority.

He stood by the table, looking at the instruments laid out on the white cloth. "What are these for, Surgeon Wu?"

He knew what they were for. He had seen them used a hundred, maybe a thousand times. But that was not what he meant.

Wu looked up at him, surprised. "Forgive me, Major . . . ?"

Karr turned, facing him. "Did anyone instruct you to bring these?"

The old man gave a short laugh. "No, Major Karr. But it is standard practice at an interrogation. I assumed . . ."

"You will assume nothing," Karr said, angry that his explicit instructions had not been acted on. "You'll pack them up and leave. But first you'll give the prisoner a full medical examination."

"It is most irregular, Major . . ." the old man began, affronted by the request, but Karr barked at him angrily.

"This is *my* investigation, Surgeon Wu, and you'll do as I say! Now get to it. I want a report ready for my signature in twenty minutes."

Karr stood by the door, his back turned on the girl, while the old man and his assistant did their work. Only when they'd finished did he turn back.

The girl lay on the couch, naked, the very straightness of her posture, like the look in her eyes, a gesture of defiance. Karr stared at her a moment, then looked away, a feeling of unease eating at him. If the truth were told, he admired her. Admired the way she had lain there, suffering all the indignities they had put her through, and yet had retained her sense of self-pride. In that she reminded him of Marie.

He looked away, disturbed at where his thoughts had led him. Marie was no terrorist, after all. Yet the thought was valid. He had only to glance at the girl – at the way she held herself – and he could see the similarities. It was not a physical resemblance – though both were fine, strong women – but some inward quality that showed itself in every movement, every gesture.

He went across and opened one of the store cupboards on the far side of the room, then returned, laying the sheet over her, covering her nakedness. She stared up at him a moment, surprised, then looked away.

"You will be moved to another cell," he said, looking about him at the appalling bareness of the room. "Somewhere more comfortable than this."

He looked back at her, seeing how her body was tensed beneath the sheet. She didn't trust him. But then why should she? He was her enemy. He may have shown her some small kindness now, but ultimately it was his role to destroy her, and she knew that.

Maybe this was just as cruel. Maybe he should just have let this butcher, Wu, get on with things. But some instinct in him cried out against that. She was not like the others he had had to act against – not like DeVore or Berdichev. There he had known exactly where he stood, but here . . .

He turned away, angry with himself. Angry that he found himself so much in sympathy with her; that she reminded him so much of his Marie. Was it merely that? – that deep resemblance? If so, it was reason enough to ask to be taken off the case. But he wasn't sure it *was*. Rather, it was some likeness to himself; the same thing he had seen in Marie, perhaps – that had made him want her for his mate. Yet if that were so, what did it say about him? Had things changed so much – had *he* changed so much – that he could now see eye to eye with his master's enemies?

He looked back at her – at the clear, female shape of her beneath the sheet – and felt a slight tremor pass through him. Was he deluding himself – making it harder for himself – by seeing in her some reflection of his own deep-rooted unease? Was it that? For if it were . . .

"Major Karr?"

He turned. Surgeon Wu stood there, the medical report on the table beside him.

Karr picked it up, studying it carefully, then took the pen and signed, giving the under-copy to the surgeon.

"Okay. You can go now, Wu. I'll finish off here."

Wu's lips and eyes formed a brief, knowing smile. "As you wish, Major Karr." Then, bowing his head, he departed, his assistant – silent, colourless, like a pale shadow of the old man – following two paces behind.

Karr turned back to the woman. "Is there anything you need?"

She looked at him a moment. "My freedom? A new identity, perhaps?" She fell silent, a look of sour resignation on her face. "No, Major Karr. There's nothing I need."

He hesitated, then nodded. "We'll move you in the next hour or so. Then, later, I'll be back to question you. We know a great deal anyway, but it would be best for you . . ."

"*Best* for me?" She stared back at him, a look of disbelief in her eyes. "Do what you must, Major Karr, but never

tell me what's best for me. Because you just don't know.
You haven't an idea."

He felt a shiver pass through him. She was right. This
much was fated. Was like a script from which they both
must read. But best . . . ? He turned away. This was their
fate, but at least he could make it easy for her once they
had done – make it painless and clean. That much he could
do, little as it was.

★   ★   ★

In Tao Yuan, in the walled burial ground of the Wang
clan, it was raining. Beneath a sky of dense grey-black
cloud, Wang Sau-leyan stood before the open tomb, his
cloak pulled tight about him, staring wide-eyed into the
darkness below.

Hung Mien-lo, watching from nearby, felt the hairs rise
on the back of his neck. So it was true. The tomb had been
breached from within, the stone casket that had held Wang
Ta-hung shattered like a plaster god. And the contents?

He shuddered. There were footprints in the earth, traces
of fibre, but nothing conclusive. Nothing to link the missing corpse with the damage to the tomb. Unless one
believed the film.

On the flight over from Alexandria they had talked it
through, the T'ang's insistence bordering on madness. The
dead did not rise, he argued, so it was something else.
Someone had set this up, to frighten him and try to undermine him. But how? And who?

Li Yuan was the obvious candidate – he had most to
gain from such a move – but equally, he had had least
opportunity. Hung's spies had kept a close watch on the
young T'ang of Europe and no sign of anything relating
to this matter had emerged – not even the smallest hint.

Tsu Ma, then? Again, he had motive enough, and it
was true that Hung's spies in the Tsu household were less
effective than in any other of the palaces, but somehow it
seemed at odds with Tsu Ma's nature. With Tsu Ma even
his deviousness had a quality of directness to it.

So who did that leave? Mach? The thought was pre-
posterous. As for the other T'ang, they had no real motive
– even Wu Shih. Sun Li Hua had had motive enough, but
he was dead, his family slaughtered, to the third generation.

All of which made the reality of this – the shattered
slabs, the empty casket – that much more disturbing.
Besides which, the thing was out there somewhere, a
strong, powerful creature, capable of splitting stone and
lifting a slab four times the weight of a man.

Something inhuman.

He watched the T'ang go inside and turned away, looking about him at the lay-out of the rain-swept garden.
Unless it was the real Wang Ta-hung, it would have had
to get inside the tomb before it could break out so spectacularly, so how would it have done that?

Hung Mien-lo paced to and fro slowly, trying to work
things out. It was possible that the being had been there a
long time – placed there at the time of Wang Ta-hung's
burial ceremony, or before. But that was unlikely. Unless
it was a machine it would have had to eat, and he had yet
to see a machine as lifelike as the one that had burst from
the tomb.

So how? How would something have got into the tomb
without them seeing it?

He called the Head of the team across and questioned
him. It seemed that the security cameras here worked on
a simple principle. For most of the time the cameras were
inactive, but at the least noise or sign of movement they
would focus on the source of the disturbance, following it
until it left their field of vision. In the dark it was programmed to respond to the heat traces of intruders.

The advantage of such a system was that it was easy to
check each camera's output. There was no need to reel
through hours of static film; one had only to look at what
was there.

Hung could see how that made sense . . . normally. Yet

what if, just this once, something cold and silent had crept in through the darkness?

He went across, looking down into the tomb. At the foot of the steps, in the candle-lit interior, Wang was standing beside the broken casket, staring down into its emptiness. Sensing Hung there, above him, Wang Sau-leyan turned, looking up. "He's dead. I felt him. He was cold."

The T'ang's words sent a shiver down his spine. *Something cold. . .* He backed away, bowing low, as Wang came up the steps.

"You'll find out who did this, Master Hung. And you'll find that thing . . . whatever it is. But until you do, you can consider yourself demoted, without title. Understand me?"

Hung met the T'ang's eyes, then let his head drop, giving a silent nod of acquiescence.

"Good. Then set to it. This business makes my flesh creep."

And mine, thought Hung Mien-lo, concealing the bitter anger he was feeling. *And mine*.

* * *

Since the fire that had destroyed it, Deck Fourteen of Central Bremen stack had been rebuilt, though not to the old pattern. Out of respect for those who had died here, it had been converted into a memorial park, landscaped to resemble the ancient water gardens – the Chuo Cheng Yuan – at Su Chou. Guards walked the narrow paths, accompanied by their wives and children, or alone, enjoying the peaceful harmony of the lake, the rocks, the delicate bridges and stilted pavilions. From time to time one or more would stop beside the great *t'ing*, named 'Beautiful Snow, Beautiful Clouds' after its original, and stare up at the great stone – the Stone of Enduring Sorrow – that had been placed there by the young T'ang only months before, reading the red-painted names cut into its broad, pale grey flank. The names of all eleven thousand

and eighteen men, women and children who had been killed here by the *Ping Tiao*.

Further down, on the far side of the lotus lake, a stone boat jutted from the bank. This was the teahouse, "Travelling by Sea". At one of the stone benches near the prow Karr sat, alone, a *chung* of the house's finest *ch'a* before him. Nearby two of his guards made sure he was not disturbed.

From where Karr sat, he could see the Stone, its shape partially obscured by the willows on the far bank, its top edge blunted like a filed tooth. He stared at it a while, trying to fit it into the context of recent events.

He sipped at his *ch'a*, his unease returning, stronger than ever. However he tried to argue it, it didn't feel right. Ywe Hao would never have done this. Would never, for a moment, have countenanced killing so many innocent people. No. He had read what she had written about her brother and been touched by it. Had heard what the guard, Leyden, had said about her. Had watched the tape of Chen's interview with the two boys – her young lookouts – and seen the fierce love for her in their eyes. Finally he had seen with his own eyes what had happened at the Dragonfly Club, and in his heart of hearts he could find no wrong in what she had done.

She was a killer, yes, but then so was he, and who was to say what justified the act of killing, what made it right or wrong? He killed to order, she for conscience's sake, and who could say which of those was right, which wrong?

And now this – this latest twist. He looked down at the scroll on the table beside the *chung* and shook his head. He should have killed her while he still had the chance. No one would have known. No one but himself.

He set his bowl down angrily, splashing the *ch'a*. Where the hell was Chen? What in the gods' names was keeping him?

But when he turned, it was to find Chen there, moving past the guards to greet him.

"So what's been happening?"

"This . . ." Karr said, pushing the scroll across to him. Chen unfurled it and began to read.

"They've taken it out of our hands," Karr said, his voice low and angry. "They've pushed us aside, and I want to know why."

Chen looked up, puzzled by his friend's reaction. "All it says here is that we are to hand her over to the *T'ing Wei*. That is strange, I agree, but not totally unheard of."

Karr shook his head. "No. Look further down. The second to last paragraph. Read it. See what it says."

Chen looked back at the scroll, reading the relevant paragraph quickly, then looked up again, frowning. "That can't be right, surely? SimFic? They are to hand her over to SimFic? What is Tolonen thinking of?"

"It's not the Marshal. Look. There at the bottom of the scroll. That's the Chancellor's seal. Which means Li Yuan must have authorised this."

Chen sat back, astonished. "But why? It makes no sense."

Karr shook his head. "No. It makes sense. It's just that we don't know how it fits together yet."

"And you want to know?"

"Yes."

"But isn't that outside our jurisdiction? I mean . . ."

Karr leaned towards him. "I've done a bit of digging and it seems that the *T'ing Wei* are to hand her over to SimFic's African operation."

Chen frowned. "Africa?"

"Yes. It's strange, neh? But listen to this. It seems she's destined for a special unit in East Africa. A place named Kibwezi. The gods alone know what they do there or why they want her, but it's certainly important – important enough to warrant the T'ang's direct intervention. And that's why I called for you, Chen. You see, I've another job for you – another task for our friend Tong Chou."

Tong Chou was Chen's alias. The name he had used in the Plantations when he had gone in there after DeVore.

Chen took a long breath. Wang Ti was close to term:

the child was due some time in the next few weeks and he
had hoped to be there at the birth. But this was his duty.
What he was paid to do. He met Karr's eyes, nodding.
"All right. When do I start?"

"Tomorrow. The documentation is being prepared.
You're to be transferred to Kibwezi from the European
arm of SimFic. All the relevant background information
will be with you by tonight."

"And the woman? Ywe Hao? Am I to accompany her?"

Karr shook his head. "No. That would seem too circumstantial, neh? Besides which, the transfer won't be made
for another few days yet. It'll give you time to find out
what's going on over there."

"And how will I report back?"

"You won't. Not until you have to come out."

Chen considered. It sounded dangerous, but no more
dangerous than before. He nodded. "And when I have to
come out – what do I do?"

"You'll send a message. A letter to Wang Ti. And then
we'll come in and get you out."

"I see . . ." Chen sat back, looking past the big man
thoughtfully. "And the woman, Ywe Hao . . . am I to
intercede?"

Karr dropped his eyes. "No. Not in any circumstances.
You are to observe, nothing more. Our involvement must
not be suspected. If the T'ang were to hear . . ."

"I understand."

"Good. Then get on home, Kao Chen. You'll want to
be with Wang Ti and the children, neh?" Karr smiled.
"And don't go worrying. Wang Ti will be fine. I'll keep
an eye on her while you're gone."

Chen stood, smiling. "I am grateful. That will ease my
mind greatly."

"Good. Oh, and before you go . . . what did you find
out down there? Who had Ywe Hao been meeting?"

Chen reached into his tunic pocket and took out the two
framed pictures he had taken from the uncle's apartment;
the portraits of Ywe Hao's mother with her husband, and

that of Ywe Hao with her brother. He looked at them a moment, then handed them across.

Karr stared at the pictures, surprised. "But they're dead. She told me they were dead."

Chen sighed. "The father's dead. The brother too. But the mother is alive, and an uncle. That's who she went to see. Her family."

Karr stared at them a moment longer, then nodded. "All right. Get going, then. I'll speak to you later."

When Chen had gone, Karr got up and went to the prow of the stone boat, staring out across the water at the Stone. He could not save her. No. That had been taken out of his hands. But there was something he could do for her: one small but significant gesture, not to set things right, but to make things better – maybe to give her comfort at the last.

He looked down at the portraits one last time, then let them fall into the water, smiling, knowing what to do.

★ ★ ★

Li Yuan looked about him at the empty stalls, sniffing the warm darkness. On whim, he had summoned the Steward of the Eastern Palace and had him bring the keys, then had gone inside, alone, conscious that he had not been here since the day he had killed the horses.

Though the stalls had been cleaned and disinfected, the tiled floors cleared of straw, the scent of horses was strong; was in each brick and tile and wooden strut of the ancient building. And if he closed his eyes . . .

If he closed his eyes. . . He shivered and looked about him again, seeing how the moonlight silvered the huge square of the entrance; how it lay like a glistening layer of dew on the end posts of the stalls.

"I must have horses . . ." he said softly, speaking to himself. "I must ride again and go hawking. I have kept too much to my office. I had forgotten . . ."

Forgotten what? he asked himself.

How to live, came the answer. *You sent her away, yet still she holds you back. You must break the chain, Li Yuan. You*

604

must learn to forget her. You have wives, Li Yuan – good wives.
And soon you will have children.

He nodded, then went across quickly, standing in the doorway, holding on to the great wooden upright, looking up at the moon.

The moon was high and almost full. As he watched, a ragged wisp of cloud drifted like a net across its surface. He laughed, surprised by the sudden joy he felt and looked to the north-east, towards Wang Sau-leyan's palace at Tao Yuan, fifteen hundred *li* in the distance.

"Who hates you more than I, cousin Wang? Who hates you enough to send your brother's ghost to haunt you?"

And was it that which brought this sudden feeling of well-being. No, for the mood seemed unconnected to event – was a sea change, like the sunlight on the waters after the violence of the storm.

He went out on to the gravelled parade ground and turned full circle, his arms out, his eyes closed, remembering. It had been the morning of his twelfth birthday and his father had summoned all the servants. If he closed his eyes he could see it; could see his father standing there, tall and imperious, the grooms lined up before the doors, the Chief Groom, Hung Feng-chan, steadying the horse and offering him the halter.

He stopped, getting back his breath. Had that happened? Had that been him, that morning, refusing to mount the horse his father had given him, claiming his brother's horse instead? He nodded slowly. Yes, that had been him.

He walked on, stopping where the path fell away beneath the high wall of the East Gardens, looking out towards the hills and the ruined temple, remembering.

For so long now he had held it all back, afraid of it. But there was nothing to be afraid of. Only ghosts. And he could live with those.

A figure appeared on the balcony of the East Gardens, above him and to his left. He turned, looking up. It was his First Wife, Mien Shan. He went across and climbed the steps, meeting her at the top.

"Forgive me, my lord," she began, bowing her head low, the picture of obedience. "You were gone so long. I thought . . ."

He smiled and reached out, taking her hands. "I had not forgotten, Mien Shan. It was just that it was such a perfect night I thought I would walk beneath the moon. Come, join me."

For a time they walked in silence, following the fragrant pathways, holding hands beneath the moon. Then, suddenly, he turned, facing her, drawing her close. She was so small, so daintily made, the scent of her so sweet that it stirred his blood. He kissed her, crushing her body against his own, then lifted her, laughing at her tiny cry of surprise.

"Come, my wife," he said, smiling down into her face, seeing how two tiny moons floated in the darkness of her eyes. "I have been away from your bed too long. Tonight we will make up for that, neh? And tomorrow . . . Tomorrow we shall buy horses for the stables."

* * *

The morph stood at the entrance to the cave, looking out across the moonlit plain below. The flicker of torches, scattered here and there across the darkened fields, betrayed the positions of the search parties. All day it had watched them, as they criss-crossed the great plain, scouring every last copse and stream on the estate. They would be tired now and hungry. If it amplified its hearing it could make out their voices, small and distant on the wind – the throaty encouragement of a sergeant or the muttered complaints of a guard.

It turned, focusing on the foothills just below where it stood. Down there among the rocks, less than a *li* away, a six-man party was searching the lower slopes, scanning the network of caves with heat-tracing devices. But they would find nothing. Nothing but the odd fox or rabbit, that was. For the morph was cold, almost as cold as the

606

rocks surrounding it, its body heat shielded beneath thick layers of insulating flesh.

In the centre of the plain, some thirty *li* distant, was the palace of Tao Yuan. Extending its vision, it looked, searching, sharpening its focus until it found what it was looking for – the figure of the Chancellor, there in the south garden, crouched over a map table in the flickering half-light of a brazier, surrounded by his men.

"Keep looking, Hung Mien-lo," it said quietly, coldly amused by all this activity. "For your master will not sleep until I'm found."

No, and that would suit its purpose well. For it was not here to hurt Wang Sau-leyan, but to engage his imagination, like a seed, planted in the soft earth of the young T'ang's mind. It nodded to himself, remembering DeVore's final words to it on Mars.

You are the first stone, Tuan Wen-ch'ang. The first in a whole new game. And whilst it may be months, years even, before I play again in that part of the board, you are nonetheless crucial to my scheme, for you are the stone within, placed deep inside my opponent's territory – a single white stone, embedded in the darkness of his skull, shining like a tiny moon.

It was true. He was a stone, a dragon's tooth, a seed. And in time the seed would germinate and grow, sprouting dark tendrils in the young T'ang's head. And then, when it was time . . .

The morph turned, its tautly muscled skin glistening in the silvered light, the smooth dome of its near-featureless head tilted back, its pale eyes searching for handholds, as it began to climb.

CHAPTER·19

<u>WHITE MOUNTAIN</u>

The rocket came down at Nairobi, on a strip dominated by the surrounding mountains. It was late afternoon, but the air was dry and unbearably hot after the coolness of the ship. Chen stood there a moment, then made hurriedly for the shelter of the buildings a hundred *ch'i* off. He made it, gasping from the effort, his shirt soaked with sweat.

"Welcome to Africa!" one of the guards said, then laughed, taking Chen's ID.

They took a skimmer south-east, over the old, deserted town, heading for Kibwezi. Chen stared out through one of the skimmer's side windows. Below him was a rugged wilderness of green and brown, stretching to the horizon in every direction. Huge bodies of rock thrust up from the plain, their sides creased and ancient-looking, like the flanks of giant, slumbering beasts. He shivered and took a deep breath. It was all so raw. He had been expecting something like the Plantations. Something neat and ordered. He had not imagined it would be so primitive.

Kibwezi Station was a collection of low buildings surrounded by a high wire fence, guard towers standing like machine-sentinels at each corner. The skimmer came in low over the central complex and dropped on to a small, hexagonal landing pad. Beside the pad was an incongruous-looking building; a long, old-fashioned construction made of wood, with a high, steeply-sloping roof. Two men stood on the verandah, watching the skimmer land. As it settled one of them came down the open, slatted steps and out on to the pad; a slightly-built *Hung Mao* in

608

his late twenties. As Chen stepped down, the man moved between the guards and took his pack, offering a hand.

"Welcome to Kibwezi, Tong Chou. I'm Michael Drake. I'll be showing you the ropes. But come inside. This damned heat . . ."

Chen nodded, looking around him at the low, featureless buildings. Then he saw it. "*Kuan Yin!*" he said, moving out of the skimmer's shadow. "What's that?"

Drake came and stood beside him. "Kilimanjaro, they call it. The White Mountain."

Chen stared out across the distance. Beyond the fence the land fell away. In the late afternoon it seemed filled with blue, like a sea. Thick mist obscured much of it, but from the mist rose up a giant shape of blue and white, flat-topped and massive. It rose up and up above that mist, higher than anything Chen had ever seen. Higher, it seemed, than the City itself. Chen wiped at his brow with the back of his hand and swore.

Drake smiled and touched his arm familiarly. "Anyway, come. It's far too hot to be standing out here."

Inside, Chen squinted into shadow, then made out the second man, seated behind a desk at the far end.

"Come in, Tong Chou. Your appointment came as something of a surprise – we're usually given much more notice – but you're welcome all the same. So . . . take a seat. What's your poison?"

"My . . . ?" Then he understood. "Just a beer, if you have one. Thanks." He crossed the room and sat in the chair nearest the desk, feeling suddenly disoriented, adrift from normality.

There was a window behind the desk, but like all the windows in the room it had a blind, and the blind was pulled down. The room was chill after the outside, the low hum of the air-conditioning the only background noise. The man leaned forward, motioning to Drake to bring the drink, then switched on the old-fashioned desk lamp.

"Let me introduce myself. My name is Laslo Debrenceni and I'm Acting Administrator of Kibwezi Station."

The man half rose from his chair, extending his hand.

Debrenceni was a tall, broad-shouldered *Hung Mao* in his late forties, a few strands of thin blond hair combed ineffectually across his sun-bronzed pate. He had a wide, pleasant mouth and soft green eyes above a straight nose.

Drake returned with the drinks, handing Chen a tall glass beaded with chill drops of water. Chen raised his glass in a toast, then took a long sip, feeling refreshed.

"Good," said Debrenceni, as if he had said something. "The first thing to do is get you acclimatised. You're used to the City. To corridors and levels and the regular patterning of each day. But here . . . Well, things are different." He smiled enigmatically. "Very different."

★ ★ ★

The White Mountain filled the sky. As the skimmer came closer it seemed to rise from the very bowels of the earth and tower over them. Chen pressed forward, staring up through the cockpit's glass, looking for the summit, but the rock went up and up, climbing out of sight.

"How big is it?" he asked, whispering, awed by the great mass of rock.

Drake looked up from the controls and laughed. "About twelve *li* at the summit, but the plateau is less . . . no more than ten. There are actually two craters – Kebo and Mawensi. The whole thing is some five *li* across at the top, filled with glaciers and ice sheets."

"Glaciers?" Chen had never heard the term before.

"A river of ice – real ice, I mean, not plastic. It rests on top like the icing on some monstrous cake." He looked down at the controls again. "You can see it from up to four hundred *li* away. If you'd known it was here you could have seen it from Nairobi."

Chen looked out, watching the mountain grow. They were above its lower slopes now, the vast fists of rock below them like speckles on the flank of the sleeping mountain.

"How old is it?"

"Old," said Drake, softer than before, as if the sheer scale of the mountain was affecting him too. "It was formed long before Mankind came along. Our distant ancestors probably looked at it from the plains and wondered what it was."

Chen narrowed his eyes.

"We'll need breathing apparatus when we're up there," Drake continued. "The air's thin and it's best to take no chances when you're used to air-conditioning and corridors."

Again there was that faint but good-natured mockery in Drake's voice that seemed to say, 'You'll find out, boy, it's different out here.'

* * *

Masked, Chen stood in the crater of Kebo, looking across the dark throat of the inner crater towards the crater wall and, beyond it, the high cliffs and terraces of the northern glacier. No, he thought, looking out at it, not a river but a city. A vast, tiered city of ice, gleaming in the midday sun.

He had seen wonders enough already: perfect, delicate flowers of ice in the deeply-shadowed caves beneath the shattered rocks at the crater's rim, and the yellowed, steaming mouths of fumeroles, rank-smelling crystals of yellow sulphur clustered obscenely about each vent. In one place he had come upon fresh snow, formed by the action of wind and cold into strange fields of knee-high and razor-sharp fronds. *Neige penitant*, Drake had called it. *Snow in prayer*. He had stood on the inner crater's edge, staring down into its ashen mouth, four hundred *ch'i* deep, and tried to imagine the forces that had formed this vast, unnatural edifice. And failed. He had seen wonders, all right, but this, this over-towering wall of ice, impressed him most.

"Five more minutes and we'd best get back," Drake said, coming over and standing next to him. "There's more to show you, but it'll have to wait. There are some things back at Kibwezi you need to see first. This . . ." he raised an arm, indicating the vastness of the mountain, "is an exercise in perspective, if you like. It makes the rest easier. Much easier."

Chen stared at him, not understanding. But there was a look in the other's masked face that suggested discomfort, maybe even pain.

"If you ever need to, come here. Sit a while and think. Then go back to things." Drake turned, staring off into the hazed distance. "It helps. I know. I've done it myself a few times now."

Chen was silent a while, watching him. Then, as if he had suddenly tired of the place, he reached out and touched Drake's arm. "Okay. Let's get back."

★ ★ ★

The guards entered first. A moment later two servants entered the cell, carrying a tall-backed sedan chair and its occupant. Four others – young Han dressed in the blue of officialdom – followed, the strong, acridly-sweet scent of their perfume filling the cell.

The sedan was set down on the far side of the room, a dozen paces from where Ywe Hao sat, her wrists and ankles bound.

She leaned forward slightly, tensed. From his dress – from the cut of his robes and the elaborate design on his chest patch – she could tell this was a high official. And from his manner – from the brutal elegance of his deportment – she could guess which Ministry he represented. The *T'ing Wei*, the Superintendency of Trials.

"I am Yen T'ung," the official said, not looking at her, "Third Secretary to the Minister, and I am here to give judgment on your case."

She caught her breath, surprised by the suddenness of his announcement, then gave the smallest nod, her head suddenly clear of all illusions. They had decided her fate already, in her absence. That was what Mach had warned her to expect. It was just that that business with Karr – his

612

kindness and the show of respect he had made to her – had muddied the clear waters of her understanding. But now she knew. It was War. Them and us. And no possibility of compromise. She had known that since her brother's death. Since that day at the hearing when the overseer had been cleared of all blame, after all that had been said.

She lifted her head, studying the official, noting how he held a silk before his nose, how his lips formed the faintest moue of distaste.

The Third Secretary snapped his fingers. At once one of the four young men produced a scroll. Yen T'ung took it and unfurled it with a flourish. Then, looking at her for the first time, he began to read.

"I, Ywe Hao hereby confess that on the seventh day of June in the year two thousand two hundred and eight I did, with full knowledge of my actions, murder the honourable Shou Chen-hai, *Hsien L'ing* to his most high eminence, Li Yuan, Grand Counsellor and T'ang of City Europe. Further, I confess that on the ninth day of the same month I was responsible for the raid on the Dragonfly Club and the subsequent murder of the following innocent citizens . . ."

She closed her eyes, listening to the list of names, seeing their faces vividly once more, the fear or resignation in their eyes as they stood before her, naked and trembling. And, for the first time since that evening, she felt the smallest twinge of pity for them – of sympathy for their suffering in those final moments.

The list finished, Yen T'ung paused. She looked up and found his eyes were on her; eyes that were cruel and strangely hard in that soft face.

"Furthermore," he continued, speaking the words without looking at the scroll. "I, Ywe Hao, daughter of Ywe Kai-chang and Ywe Sha . . ."

She felt her stomach fall away. Her parents . . . Kuan Yin! How had they found that out?

". . . confess also to the charge of belonging to an illegal organisation and to plotting the downfall of his most high eminence . . ."

She stood, shouting back at him. "This is a lie! I have confessed nothing!"

The guards dragged her down on to the stool again. Across from her Yen T'ung stared at her as one might stare at an insect, with an expression of profound disgust.

"What you have to say has no significance here. You are here only to listen to your confession and to sign it when I have done."

She laughed. "You are a liar, Yen T'ung, in the pay of liars, and nothing in heaven or earth could induce me to sign your piece of paper."

There was a flash of anger in his eyes. He raised a hand irritably. At the signal one of his young men crossed the room and slapped her across the face, once, then again; stinging blows that brought tears to her eyes. With a bow to his master, the man retreated behind the sedan.

Yen T'ung sat back slightly, taking a deep breath. "Good. Now you will be quiet, woman. If you utter another word I will have you gagged."

She glared back at him, forcing her anger to be pure, to be the perfect expression of her defiance. But he had yet to finish.

"Besides," he said softly, "there is no real need for you to sign."

He turned the document, letting her see. There at the foot of it was her signature – or, at least, a perfect copy of it.

"So now you understand. You must confess and we must read your confession back to you, and then you must sign it. That is the law. And now all that is done, and you, Ywe Hao, no longer exist. Likewise your family. All data has been erased from the official record."

She stared back at him, gripped by a sudden numbness. Her mother . . . they had killed her mother. She could see it in his face.

In a kind of daze she watched them lift the chair and carry the official from the room.

"You bastard!" she cried out, her voice filled with pain. "She knew nothing . . . nothing at all."

The door slammed. *Nothing . . .*

"Come," one of the guards said softly, almost gently. "It's time."

★　★　★

Outside was heat – fifty *ch'i* of heat. Through a gate in the wire fencing, a flight of a dozen shallow steps led down into the bunkers. There the icy coolness was a shock after the thirty-eight degrees outside. Stepping inside was like momentarily losing vision. Chen stopped there, just inside the doorway, his heart pounding from exertion, waiting for his vision to normalise, then moved on slowly, conscious of the echo of his footsteps on the hard concrete floor. He looked about him at the bareness of the walls, the plain unpainted metal doors, and frowned. Bracket lights on the long, low-ceilinged walls gleamed dimly, barely illuminating the intense shadow. His first impression was that the place was empty, but that, like the loss of vision, was only momentary. A floor below – through a dark, circular hole cut into the floor – were the cells. Down there were kept a thousand prisoners, fifty to a cell, each shackled to the floor at wrist and ankle, the shortness of the chains making them crouch on all fours like animals.

It was Chen's first time below. Drake stood beside him, silent, letting him judge things for himself. The cells were simple divisions of the open-plan floor – no walls, only lines of bars, each partitioned space reached by a door of bars set into the line. All was visible at a glance, all the misery and degradation of these thin and naked people. And that, perhaps, was the worst of it – the openness, the appalling openness. Two lines of cells, one to the left and one to the right. And between, not recognised until he came to them, were the hydrants. To hose down the cells and swill the excrement and blood, the piss and vomit, down the huge, grated drains that were central to the floor of each cell.

Chen looked on, mute, appalled, then turned to face Drake. But Drake had changed. Or, rather, Drake's face had changed; had grown harder, more brutish, as if in coming here he had cast off the social mask he wore above, to reveal his true face; an older, darker, more barbaric face.

Chen moved on, willing himself to walk, not to stop or turn back. He turned his head, looking from side to side as he walked down the line of cells, seeing how the prisoners backed away – as far as their chains allowed. Not knowing him, yet fearing him. Knowing him for a guard.

At the end he turned and went to the nearest cell, standing at the bars and staring into the gloom, grimacing with the pain and horror he was feeling. He had thought at first there were only men, but there were women too, their limbs painfully emaciated, their stomachs swollen, signs of torture and beatings marking every one of them. Most were shaven-headed. Some slouched or simply lay there, clearly hurt, but from none came even the slightest whimper of sound. It was as if the very power to complain, to cry out in anguish against what was being done to them, had been taken from them.

He had never seen . . . never imagined . . .

Shuddering, he turned away, but they were everywhere he looked, their pale, uncomplaining eyes watching him. His eyes looked for Drake and found him there, at the far end.

"Is . . . ?" he began, then laughed strangely and grew quiet. But the question remained close to his tongue and he found he had to ask it, whether these thousand witnesses heard him or not. "Is *this* what we do?"

Drake came closer. "Yes," he said softly. "This is what we do. What we're *contracted* to do."

Chen shivered violently, looking about him, freshly appalled by the passive suffering of the prisoners; by the incomprehensible acceptance in every wasted face. "I don't understand," he said, after a moment. "Why? What are we trying to do here?"

His voice betrayed the true depth of his bewilderment. He was suddenly a child again, innocent, stripped bare before the sheer horror of it.

"I'm sorry," Drake said, coming closer. His face was less brutish now, almost compassionate; but his compassion did not extend beyond Chen. "There's no other way. You have to come down here and see it for yourself, unprepared." He shrugged. "What you're feeling now . . . we've all felt that. Deep down we still do. But you have to have that first shock. It's . . . necessary."

"*Necessary?*" Chen laughed, but the sound seemed inappropriate. It died in his throat. He felt sick, unclean.

"Yes. And afterwards . . . once it's sunk in . . . we can begin to explain it all. And then you'll see."

But Chen *didn't* see. He looked at Drake afresh, as if he had never seen him before that moment, and began to edge round him, towards the steps and the clean, abrasive heat outside, and when Drake reached out to touch his arm, he backed away, as if the hand that reached for him were something alien and unclean.

"This is vile. It's . . ."

But there wasn't a word for it. He turned and ran, back up the steps and out – out through icy coolness to the blistering heat.

★ ★ ★

It was late night. A single lamp burned in the long, wood-walled room. Chen sat in a low chair across from Debrenceni, silent, listening, the drink in his hand untouched.

"They're dead. Officially, that is. In the records they've already been executed. But here we find a use for them. Test out a few theories." He cleared his throat. "We've been doing it for years, actually. At first it was all quite unofficial. Back in the days when Berdichev ran things there was a much greater need to be discreet about these things. But now . . ."

617

Debrenceni shrugged, then reached out to take the wine jug and refill his cup. There was a dreadful irony in his voice – a sense of profound mistrust in the words even as he offered them. He sipped at his cup then sat back again, his pale green eyes resting on Chen's face.

"We could say no, of course. Break contract and find ourselves dumped one morning in the Net, brain-wiped and helpless. That's one option. The moral option, you might call it. But it's not much of a choice, wouldn't you say?" He laughed; a sharp, humourless laugh.

"Anyway . . . we do it because we must. Because our 'side' demands that someone does it, and we've been given the short straw. Those we deal with here are murderers, of course – though I've found that that helps little when you're thinking about it. After all, what are we? I guess the point is that they started it. They began the killing. As for us, well, I guess we're merely finishing what they began."

He sighed. "Look, you'll find a dozen rationalisations while you're here. A hundred different ways of evading things and lying to yourself. But trust to your first instinct, your first response. Never – whatever you do – question that. Your first response was the correct one. The natural one. It's what we've grown used to here that's unnatural. It may *seem* natural after a while, but it isn't. Remember that in the weeks to come."

"I see."

"Some forget," Debrenceni said, leaning forward, his voice lowered. "Some even *enjoy* it."

Chen breathed in deeply. "Like Drake, you mean?"

"No. There you're wrong. Michael feels it greatly, more than any of us, perhaps. I've often wondered how he's managed to stand it. The mountain helps, of course. It helps us all. Somewhere to go. Somewhere to sit and think things through, *above* the world and all its pettiness."

Chen gave the barest nod. "Who are they? The prisoners, I mean. Where do they come from?"

Debrenceni smiled. "I thought you understood. They're

618

terrorists. Hot-heads and troublemakers. This is where they send them now. All of the State's enemies."

★　★　★

Kibwezi Station was larger than Chen had first imagined. It stretched back beneath the surface boundary of the perimeter fence and deep into the earth, layer beneath layer. Dark cells lay next to stark-lit, cluttered rooms, while bare, low-ceilinged spaces led through to crowded guard rooms, banked high with monitor screens and the red and green flicker of trace lights. All was linked somehow, interlaced by a labyrinth of narrow corridors and winding stairwells. At first it had seemed very different from the City, a place that made that greater world of levels seem spacious – open-ended – by comparison, and yet, in its condensation and contrasts, it was very much a distillation of the City. At the lowest level were the laboratories and operating theatres – the "dark heart of things", as Drake called it, with that sharp, abrasive laugh that was already grating on Chen's nerves. The sound of a dark, uneasy humour.

It was Chen's first shift in the theatres. Gowned and masked he stood beneath the glare of the operating lights and waited, not quite knowing what to expect, watching the tall figure of Debrenceni washing his hands at the sink. After a while two others came in and nodded to him, crossing the room to wash up before they began. Then, when all were masked and ready, Debrenceni turned and nodded to the ceiling camera. A moment later two of the guards wheeled in a trolley.

The prisoner was strapped tightly to the trolley, his body covered with a simple green cloth, only his shaved head showing. From where Chen stood he could see nothing of the man's features, only the transparency of the flesh, the tight knit of the skull's plates in the harsh overhead light. Then, with a small jerk of realisation that transcended the horrifying unreality he had been experiencing since coming into the room, he saw that the man was still conscious. The head turned slightly, as if to try to see what was behind it. There was a momentary glint of brightness, of a moist, penetratingly blue eye, straining to see, then the neck muscles relaxed and the head lay still, kept in place by the bands that formed a kind of brace about it.

Chen watched as one of the others leaned across and tightened the bands, bringing one loose-hanging strap across the mouth and tying it, then fastening a second across the brow, so that the head was held rigid. Satisfied, the man worked his way round the body, tightening each of the bonds, making sure there would be no movement once things began.

Dry-mouthed, Chen looked to Debrenceni and saw that he too was busy, methodically laying out his scalpels on a white cloth. Finished, the Administrator looked up and, smiling with his eyes, indicated that he was ready.

For a moment the sheer unreality of what was happening threatened to overwhelm Chen. His whole body felt cold and his blood seemed to pulse strongly in his head and hands. Then, with a small, embarrassed laugh, he saw what he had not noticed before. It was not a man. The prisoner on the trolley was a woman.

Debrenceni worked swiftly, confidently, inserting the needle at four different points in the skull and pushing in a small amount of local anaesthetic. Then, with a deftness Chen had not imagined him capable of, Debrenceni began to cut into the skull, using a hot-wire drill to sink down through the bone. The pale, long hands moved delicately, almost tenderly over the woman's naked skull, seeking and finding the exact points where he would open the flesh and drill down towards the softer brain beneath. Chen stood at the head of the trolley, watching everything, seeing how one of the assistants mopped and staunched the bleeding while the other passed the instruments. It was all so skilful and so gentle. And then it was done, the twelve slender filaments in place, ready for attachment.

Debrenceni studied the skull a moment, his fingers checking his own work. Then he nodded and, taking a spray from the cloth, coated the skull with a thin, almost plastic layer that glistened wetly under the harsh light. It had the sweet, unexpected scent of some exotic fruit.

Chen came round and looked into the woman's face. She had been quiet throughout and had made little movement, even when the tiny, hand-held drill let out its high, nerve-tormenting whine. He had expected screams, the outward signs of struggle, but there had been nothing; only her stillness, and that unnerving silence.

Her eyes were open. As he leant over her her eyes met his and the pupils dilated, focusing on him. He jerked his head back, shocked after all to find her conscious and undrugged, and looked across at Debrenceni, not understanding. *They had drilled into her skull . . .*

He watched, suddenly frightened. None of this added up. Her reactions were wrong. As they fitted the spiderish helmet, connecting its filaments to those now sprouting from the pale, scarred field of her skull, his mind feverishly sought its own connections. He glanced down at her hands and saw, for the first time, how they were twitching, as if in response to some internal stimulus. For a moment it seemed to mean something – to *suggest* something – but then it slipped away, leaving only a sense of wrongness – of things not connecting properly.

When the helmet was in place, Debrenceni had them lower the height of the trolley and sit the woman up, adjusting the frame and cushions to accommodate her new position. In doing this the cover slipped down, exposing the paleness of her shoulders and arms, her small firm breasts, the smoothness of her stomach. She had a young body. Her face, in contrast, seemed old and abstract, the legs of the metal spider forming a cage about it.

Chen stared at her, as if seeing her anew. Before he had been viewing her only in the abstract. Now he saw how frail and vulnerable she was; how individual and particular her flesh. But there was something more – something that made him turn from the sight of her, embarrassed. He had been aroused. Just looking at her he had felt a strong, immediate response. He felt ashamed, but the fact was there and, turned from her, he faced it. Her helpless exposure had made him want her. Not casually or coldly, but with a sudden fierceness that had caught him off guard.

Beneath his pity for her was desire. Even now it made him want to turn and look at her – to feast his eyes on her helpless nakedness. He shuddered, loathing himself. It was hideous; more so for being so unexpected, so incontestable.

When he turned back his eyes avoided the woman. But Debrenceni had seen. He was watching Chen pensively, the mask pulled down from his face. His eyes met Chen's squarely, unflinchingly.

"They say a job like this dehumanises the people who do it, Tong Chou. But you'll learn otherwise here. I can see it in you now, as I've seen it in others who've come here. Piece by piece it comes back to us. What we *really* are. Not the ideal but the reality. The full, human reality of what we are. Animals that think, that's all. Animals that think."

Chen looked away, hurt – inexplicably hurt. Not knowing why. As if even Debrenceni's understanding were suddenly too much to bear. And, for the second time since his arrival, he found himself stumbling out into the corridor, away from something which, even as he fled it, he knew he could not escape.

★ ★ ★

Up above, the day had turned to night. It was warm and damp and a full moon bathed the open space between the complex and the huts with a rich, silvery light. In the distance the dark shadow of Kilimanjaro dominated the skyline, an intense black against the velvet blue.

Debrenceni stood there, taking deep breaths of the warm, invigorating air. The moonlight seemed to shroud him in silver and for the briefest moment he seemed insubstantial, like a projection cast against a pure black backcloth. Chen made to put out his hand, then drew it back, feeling foolish.

622

Debrenceni's voice floated across to him. "You should have stayed. You would have found it interesting. It's not an operation I've done that often and this one went very well. You see, I was wiring her."

Chen frowned. Many of the senior officers in Security were wired – adapted for linking-up to a comset – or, like Tolonen, had special slots surgically-implanted behind their ears so that tapes could be direct-inputted. But this had been different.

Debrenceni saw the doubt in Chen's face and laughed. "Oh, it's nothing so crude as the usual stuff. No, this is the next evolutionary step. A pretty obvious one, but one that – for equally obvious reasons – we've not taken before now. This kind of wiring needs no input connections. It uses a pulsed signal. That means the connection can be made at a distance. All you need is the correct access code."

"But that sounds . . ." Chen stopped. He had been about to say that it sounded an excellent idea, but some of its ramifications had struck him. The existence of a direct-input connection gave the subject a choice. They could plug in or not. Without that there was no choice. He – or she – became merely another machine, the control of which was effectively placed in the hands of someone else.

He shivered. So *that* was what they were doing here. That was why they were working on sentenced prisoners and not on volunteers. He looked back at Debrenceni, aghast.

"Good," Debrenceni said, yet he seemed genuinely pained by Chen's realisation.

Chen looked down, suddenly tired of the charade, wishing he could tell Debrenceni who he really was and why he was there; angry that he should be made a party to this vileness. For a moment his anger extended even to Karr for sending him in here, knowing nothing; for making him have to feel his way out of this labyrinth of half-guessed truths. Then, with a tiny shudder, he shut it out.

Debrenceni turned, facing Chen fully. Moonlight

silvered his skull, reduced his face to a mask of dark and light. "An idea has two faces. One acceptable, the other not. Here we experiment not only on perfecting the wiring technique, but on making the idea of it acceptable."

"And once you've perfected things?" Chen asked, a tightness forming at the pit of his stomach.

Debrenceni stared back at him a moment, then turned away, his moonlit outline stark against the distant mountain's shape. But he was silent. And Chen, watching him, felt suddenly alone and fearful and very, very small.

★ ★ ★

Chen watched them being led in between the guards; three men and two women, loosely shackled to each other with lengths of fine chain, their clothes unwashed, their heads unshaven.

She was there, of course, hanging back between the first two males, her head turned from him, her eyes downcast.

Drake took the clipboard from the guard and flicked through the flimsy sheets, barely glancing at them. Then, with a satisfied nod, he came across, handing the board to Chen.

"The names are false. As for the rest, there's probably nothing we can use. Security still think it's possible to extract factual material from situations of duress, but we know better. Hurt a man and he'll confess to anything. But it doesn't really matter. We're not really interested in who they were or what they did. That's all in the past."

Chen grunted, then looked up from the clipboard, seeing how the prisoners were watching him, as if, by handing him the board, Drake had established him as the man in charge. He handed the clipboard back and took a step closer to the prisoners. At once the guards moved forward, raising their guns, as if to intercede, but their presence did little to reassure him. It wasn't that he was afraid – he had been in far more dangerous situations, many a time – yet he had never had to face such violent hatred, such open hostility. He could feel it emanating from the five. Could see it burning in their eyes. And yet they had never met him before this moment.

"Which one first?" Drake asked, coming alongside.

Chen hesitated. "The girl," he said finally. "The one who calls herself Chi Li."

His voice was strong, resonant. The very sound of it gave him a sudden confidence. He saw at once how his outward calm, the very tone of his voice, impressed them. There was fear and respect behind their hatred now. He turned away, as if he had done with them.

He heard the guards unshackle the girl and pull her away. There were murmurs of protest and the sounds of a brief struggle, but when Chen turned back she was standing away from the others, at the far end of the cell.

"Good," he said. "I'll see the others later."

The others were led out, a single guard remaining inside the cell, his back to the door.

He studied the girl. Without her chains she seemed less defiant. More vulnerable. As if sensing his thoughts she straightened up, facing him squarely.

"Try anything and I'll break both your legs," he said, seeing how her eyes moved to assess how things stood. "No one can help you now but yourself. Cooperate and things will be fine. Fight us and we'll destroy you."

The words were glib – were the words Drake had taught him to say in this situation – but they sounded strangely sinister now that things were real. Rehearsing them, he had thought them stagey, melodramatic, like something out of an old Han opera, but now, alone with the prisoner, they had a potency which chilled him as he said them. He saw the effect they had on her. Saw the hesitation as she tensed and then relaxed. He wanted to smile, but didn't. Karr was right. She was an attractive woman, even with that damage to her face. Her very toughness had a beauty to it.

"What do you want to do?" Drake asked.

Chen took a step closer. "We'll just talk for now."

The girl was watching him uncertainly. She had been

beaten badly. There were bruises on her arms and face, unhealed cuts on the left side of her neck. Chen felt a sudden anger. All this had been done since she'd been released to SimFic. Moreover there was a tightness about her mouth that suggested she had been raped. He shivered, then spoke the words that had come into his head.

"Have they told you that you're dead?"

Behind him Drake drew in a breath. The line was impromptu. Was not scripted for this first interview.

The girl looked down, smiling, but when she looked up again Chen was still watching her, his face unchanged.

"Did you think this was just another Security cell?" he asked, harsher now, angry, his anger directed suddenly at her – at the childlike vulnerability beneath her outward strength; at the simple fact that she was there, forcing him to do this to her.

The girl shrugged, saying nothing, but Chen could see the sweat beading her brow. He took a step closer; close enough for her to hit out at him, if she dared.

"We do things here. Strange things. We take you apart and put you back together again. But different."

She was staring at him now, curiosity getting the better of her. His voice was calm, matter-of-fact, as if what he was saying to her was quite ordinary, but the words were horrible in their implication and the very normality of his voice seemed cruel.

"Stop it," she said softly. "Just do what you're going to do."

Her eyes pleaded with him, like the hurt eyes of a child; the same expression Ch'iang Hsin sometimes had when he teased her. That similarity – between this stranger and his youngest child – made him pull back; made him realise that his honesty was hurting her. Yet he was here to hurt. That was his job here. Whether he played the role or not, the hurt itself was real.

He turned from her, a small shiver passing down his spine.

Drake was watching him strangely, his eyes half-lidded. *What are you up to?* he seemed to be saying.

Chen met his eyes. "She'll do."

Drake frowned. "But you've not seen the others . . ."

Chen smiled. "*She'll do.*" He was still smiling when she kicked him in the kidneys.

★　★　★

She was beaten and stripped and thrown into a cell. For five days she languished there, in total darkness. Morning and night a guard would come and check on her, passing her meal through the hatch and taking the old tray away. Otherwise she was left alone. There was no bed, no sink, no pot to crap into, only a metal grill set into one corner of the floor. She used it, reluctantly at first, then with a growing indifference. What did it matter, after all? There were worse things in life than having to crap into a hole.

For the first few days she didn't mind. After a lifetime spent in close proximity to people it was something of a relief to be left alone, almost a luxury. But from the third day on it was hard.

On the sixth day they took her from the cell, out into a brightness that made her screw her eyes tight, tiny spears of pain lancing her head. Outside, they hosed her down and disinfected her, then threw her into another cell, shackling her to the floor at wrist and ankle.

She lay there for a time, letting her eyes grow accustomed to the light. After the foetid darkness of the tiny cell she had the sense of space about her, yet when finally she looked up, it was to find herself eye to eye with a naked man. He was crouched on all fours before her, his eyes lit with a feral glint, his penis jutting stiffly from between his legs. She drew back sharply, the sudden movement checked by her chains. And then she saw them.

She looked about her, appalled. There were forty, maybe fifty naked people in the cell with her, men and women both. All were shackled to the floor at wrist and ankle. Some met her eyes, but it was without curiosity, almost without recognition. Others simply lay there, listless. As she watched, one of them raised herself on her haunches and let loose a bright stream of urine, then lay still again, like an animal at rest.

She shuddered. So this was it. This was her fate, her final humiliation, to become like these poor souls. She turned back, looking at her neighbour. He was leaning towards her, grunting, his face brutal with need, straining against his chains, trying to get at her. One hand was clutched about his penis, jerking it back and forth urgently.

"Stop it," she said softly. "Please . . ." But it was as if he was beyond the reach of words. She watched him, horrified; watched his face grow pained, his movements growing more frantic, and then, with a great moan of pain, he came, his semen spurting across the space between them.

She dropped her eyes, her face burning, her heart pounding in her chest. For a moment – for the briefest moment – she had felt herself respond; had felt something in her begin to surface, as if to answer that fierce, animal need in his face.

She lay there, letting her pulse slow, her thoughts grow still, then lifted her head, almost afraid to look at him again. He lay quietly now, no more than two *ch'i* from her, his shoulders rising and falling gently with each breath. She watched him, feeling an immense pity, wondering who he was and what crime he had been sent here for.

For a time he lay still, soft snores revealing he was sleeping, then, with a tiny whimper, he turned slightly, moving on to his side. As he did she saw the brand on his upper arm; saw it and caught her breath, her soul shrivelling up inside her.

It was a fish. A stylised fish.

* * *

Chen stood in the doorway to the Mess, looking into the deeply shadowed room. There was the low buzz of conversation, the smell of mild euphorics. Sitting at the bar, alone, a tall glass at his elbow, was Debrenceni. Seeing Chen, he lifted his hand and waved him across.

"How are the kidneys?"

Chen laughed. "Sore, but no serious damage. She connected badly."

"I know. I saw it." Debrenceni was serious a moment longer, then he smiled. "You did well, despite that. It looked as if you'd been doing the job for years."

Chen dropped his head. He had been in the sick bay for the last six days, the first two in acute pain.

"What do you want to drink?"

Chen looked up. "I'd best not."

"No. Maybe not." Debrenceni raised his glass, saluting Chen. "You were right about the girl, though."

"I know." He hesitated, then. "Have you wired her yet?"

"No. Not yet." Debrenceni sat back a little on his stool, studying him. "You know, you were lucky she didn't kill you. If the Security forces hadn't worked her over before we'd got her, she probably would have."

Chen nodded, conscious of the irony. "What happened to her?"

"Nothing. I thought we'd wait until you got back on duty."

It was not what Chen had expected. "You want me to carry on? Even after what happened?"

"No. *Because* of what happened." Debrenceni laid his hand lightly on Chen's shoulder. "We see things through here, Tong Chou. To the bitter, ineluctable end."

"Ineluctable?"

"Ineluctable," repeated Debrenceni solemnly. "That from which one cannot escape by struggling."

"Ah . . ." In his mind Chen could see the girl and picture the slow working-out of her fate. *Ineluctable.* Like the gravity of a black hole, or the long, slow process of entropy. Things his son, Jyan, had told him of. He gave a tiny, bitter laugh.

Debrenceni smiled tightly, removing his hand from Chen's shoulder. "You understand, then?"

Chen looked back at him. "Do I have a choice?"

"No. No one here has a choice."

"Then I understand."

"Good. Then we'll start in the morning. At six sharp. I want you to bring her from the cells. I'll be in the theatre. Understand?"

* * *

It was late when Chen returned to his room. He felt frayed and irritable. More than that, he felt ashamed and – for the first time since he'd come to Kibwezi – guilty of some awfulness that would outweigh a lifetime's atonement. He sat heavily on his bed and let his head fall into his hands. Today had been the day. Before now he had been able to distance himself from what had been happening. Even that last time, facing her in the cell, it had not really touched him. It had been something abstract; something happening to someone else – Tong Chou, perhaps – who inhabited his skin. But now he knew. It was himself. No one else had led her there and strapped her down, awaiting surgery. It was no stranger who had looked down at her while they cut her open and put things in her head.

"That was *me*," he said, shuddering. "That was *me* in there."

He sat up, drawing his feet under him, then shook his head in disbelief. And yet he had to believe. It had been too real – too *personal* – for disbelief.

He swallowed deeply. Drake had warned him. Drake had said it would be like this. One day fine, the next the whole world totally different; like some dark, evil trick played on your eyesight, making you see nothing but death. Well, Drake was right. Now he too could see it. Death. Everywhere death. And he a servant of it.

There was a knocking at the door.

"Go away!"

The knocking came again. Then a voice. "Tong Chou? Are you all right?"

He turned and lay down, facing the wall. "Go away . . ."

* * *

Ywe Hao had never run so far, nor been so afraid. As she ran she seemed to balance two fears in the pit of her stomach: her fear of what lay behind outweighing her fear of the dark into which she ran. Instinct took her towards the City. Even in the dark she could see its massive shape against the skyline, blotting out the light-scattered velvet backdrop.

It was colder than she had ever thought it could be. And darker. As she ran she whimpered, not daring to look back. When the first light of morning coloured the sky at her back she found herself climbing a gradual slope. Her pace had slowed, but still she feared to stop and rest. At any moment they would discover her absence. Then they would be out, after her.

As the light intensified, she slowed, then stopped and turned, looking back. For a while she stood there, her mouth open. Then, as the coldness, the stark openness of the place struck her, she shuddered violently. It was so open. So appallingly open. Another kind of fear, far greater than anything she had known before, made her take a backward step.

The whole of the distant horizon was on fire. Even as she watched, the sun's edge pushed up into the sky; so vast, so threatening, it took her breath. She turned, away from it, horrified, then saw, in the first light, what lay ahead.

At first the ground rose slowly, scattered with rock. Then it seemed to climb more steeply until, with a suddenness that was every bit as frightening as anything she had so far seen, it ended in a thick, choking veil of whiteness. Her eyes went upward . . . No, not a veil, a *wall*. A solid wall of white that seemed soft, almost insubstantial.

Again she shuddered, not understanding, a deep-rooted, primitive fear of such things making her crouch into herself. And still her eyes went up until, beyond the wall's upper lip, she saw the massive summit of the shape she had run towards throughout the night. The City . . .

Again she sensed a wrongness to what she saw. The shape of it seemed . . . Seemed what? Her arms were making strange little jerking movements and her legs felt weak. Gritting her teeth, she tried to get her mind to work, to triumph over the dark, mindless fear that was washing over her, wave after wave. For a moment she seemed to come to herself again.

What was wrong? What in the gods' names was it?

And then she understood. The shape of it was wrong. The rough, tapered, irregular look of it. Whereas . . . Again her mouth fell open. But if it wasn't the City . . . then what in hell's name was it?

For a moment longer she stood there, swaying slightly, caught between two impulses, then, hesitant, glancing back at the growing circle of fire, she began to run again. And as she ran – the dark image of the sun's half circle stamped across her vision – the wall of mist came down to meet her.

★ ★ ★

It was just after dawn when the two cruisers lifted from the pad and banked away over the compound, heading north-west, towards the mountain. Chen was in the second craft, Drake at the controls beside him. On Chen's wrist, scarcely bigger than a standard Security field comset, was the tracer unit. He glanced at it, then stared steadily out through the windscreen, watching the grassy plain flicker by fifty *ch'i* below.

"We're going to kill her, aren't we?"

Drake glanced at him. "She was dead before she came here. Remember that."

Chen shook his head. "That's just words. No, what I mean is that *we* are going to kill *her*. Us. Personally."

"In a manner of speaking."

Chen looked down at his hands. "No. Not in a manner of speaking. This is real. We're going out to kill her. I've been trying not to think about it, but I can't help it. It seems . . ." He shook his head. "It's just that some days I can't believe it's me, doing this. I'm a good man. At least, I thought I was."

Drake was silent, hunched over the controls as if concentrating, but Chen could see he was thinking; chewing over what he'd said.

"So?" Chen prompted.

"So we set down, do our job, get back. That's it."

Again Chen stared at Drake for a long time, not sure even what he was looking for. Whatever it was, it wasn't there. He looked down at the tiny screen. Below the central glass were two buttons. They looked innocuous enough, but he wasn't sure. Only Drake knew what they were for.

He looked away, holding his tongue. Maybe it was best to see it as Drake saw it. As just another job to be done. But his disquiet remained, and, as the mountain grew larger through the front screen, his sense of unreality grew with it.

It was all so impersonal. As if what they were tracking was a thing; another kind of machine – one that ran. But Chen had seen her close; had looked into her eyes and stared down into her face while Debrenceni had been operating. He had seen just how vulnerable she was.

How human . . .

* * *

He had put on the suit's heater and pulled the helmet visor down – even so, his feet felt like ice and his cheeks were frozen. A cold breeze blew across the mountain now, shredding the mist in places, but generally it was thick, like a flaw in seeing itself.

There was a faint buzz on his headset, then a voice came through. "It's clearing up here. We can see right up the mountain now, to the summit."

Chen stared up the slope, as if to penetrate the dense mist, then glanced back at Drake. "What now?"

Drake nodded distractedly, then spoke into his lip-mike. "Move to within a hundred *ch'i*. It looks like she's stopped. Gustaffson, you go to the north of where she is. Palmer, come round to the east. Tong Chou and I will take the other points. That way we've got a perfect grid."

Drake turned, looking up the mountain. "Okay. Let's give this thing a proper test."

Chen spoke to Drake's back. "The trace ought to be built into a visor display, This thing's vulnerable when you're climbing. Clumsy, too."

"You're right," Drake answered, beginning to climb. "It's a bloody nuisance. It should be made part of the standard Security headgear, with direct computer input from a distance."

"You mean wire the guards, too?"

Drake paused, mist wreathing his figure. "Why not? That way you could have the coordinator at a distance, out of danger. It would make the team less vulnerable. The runner couldn't get at the head – the brains behind it. It makes sense, don't you think?"

Halfway up, Drake turned, pointing across. "Over there. Keep going until you're due south of her. Then wait. I'll tell you what to do."

Chen went across, moving slowly over the difficult terrain, then stopped, his screen indicating that he was directly south of the trace, approximately a hundred *ch'i* down. He signalled back, then waited, listening as the others confirmed they were in place. The mist had cleared up where he was and he had eye contact with both Gustaffson and Palmer. There was no sign of the runner.

Drake's voice sounded in his headset. "You should be clear any minute. We'll start when you are."

Chen waited, while the mist slowly thinned out around him. Then, quite suddenly, he could see the mountain above him, the twin peaks of Kebo and Mawensi white against the vivid blue of the sky. He shivered, looking across, picking out the others against the slope.

"I see you," Drake said, before he could say anything. "Good. Now come up the slope a little way. We'll close to fifty now. Palmer, Gustaffson, you do the same."

Chen walked forward slowly, conscious of the others as they closed on him. Above him was a steep shelf of bare earth. As he came closer he lost sight, first of Drake, then of the other two.

"I'll have to come up," he said into his lip-mike. "I can't see a thing from down here."

He scrambled up and stood there, on the level ground above the shelf, where the thick grass began. He was only twenty *ch'i* from the trace signal now. The others stood back at fifty, watching him.

"Where is she?" he said, softer than before.

"Exactly where the trace shows she is," said Drake into his head. "In that depression just ahead of you."

He had seen it already, but it looked too shallow to hide a woman.

"Palmer?" It was Drake again. Chen listened. "I want you to test the left-hand signal on your handset. Turn it slowly to the left."

Chen waited, watching the shallow pit in front of him. It seemed as if nothing had happened.

"Good," said Drake. "Now you, Gustaffson. I want you to press both your controls at the same time. Hold them down firmly for about twenty seconds. Okay?"

This time there was a noise from the depression. A low moaning that increased as the seconds passed. Then it cut off abruptly. Chen shuddered. "What was that?"

"Just testing," Drake answered. "Each of our signals is two-way. They transmit, but they also have a second function. Palmer's cuts off all motor activity in the cortex. Gustaffson's works on what we call the pain gate, stimulating nerves at the stem of the brain."

"And yours?" asked Chen. He could hear the breathing of the others on the line as they listened in.

"Mine's the subtlest. I can talk to our runner. Directly. Into her head."

The line went silent. From the depression in front of Chen came a sudden whimper of pure fear. Then Drake was speaking again. "Okay. You can move the signal back to its starting position. Our runner is ready to come out."

There was a tense moment of waiting, then, from the front of the shallow pit a head bobbed up. Wearily, in obvious pain, the woman pulled herself up out of the deep hole at the front lip of the shallow depression. As her head came up and round she looked directly at Chen. For a moment she stood there, swaying, then she collapsed and sat back, pain and tiredness etched in her ravaged face. She looked ragged and exhausted. Her legs and arms were covered in contusions and weeping cuts.

Drake must have spoken to her again, for she jerked visibly and looked round, finding him. Then she looked about her, seeing the others. Her head dropped and for a moment she just sat there, breathing heavily, her arms loose at her sides.

"Okay," Drake said. "Let's wrap things up."

Chen turned and looked across at Drake. In the now brilliant sunlight, he seemed a cold and alien figure. His suit, like all of them, was non-reflective. Only the visor sparkled menacingly. Just now he was moving closer in. Twenty *ch'i* from the woman he stopped. Chen watched as Drake made Palmer test his signal again. As it switched off, the woman fell awkwardly to one side. Then, moments later, she pushed herself up again, looking round, wondering what had happened to her. Then it was Gustaffson's turn. He saw how the woman's face changed, her teeth clamped together, her whole body arching as she kicked out in dreadful pain.

When she sat up again, her face twitched visibly. Something had broken in her. Her eyes, when they looked at him now, seemed lost.

He looked across at Drake, appalled, but Drake was talking to her again. Chen could see his lips moving, then looked back and saw the woman try to cover her ears, a look of pure terror on her face.

Slowly, painfully, she got up and, looking straight at Chen, clambered over the lip and began to make her way towards him, almost hopping now, each touch of her damaged leg against the ground causing her face to buckle in pain. But still she came.

He made to step back, but Drake's voice was suddenly in his headset, on the discreet channel. "Your turn," it said. "Just hold down the left hand button and touch the right."

She was less than two body-lengths away from him now, reaching out to him. He looked down at the tiny screen, then held and touched.

The air was filled with a soft, wet sound of exploding matter. As if someone had fired a gun off in the middle of a giant fruit. And there, where the signal had been, there was nothing.

He looked up. The body was already falling, the shoulders and upper chest ruined by the explosion that had taken off the head. He turned away, sickened, but the stench of burned flesh was in his nostrils and gobbets of her ruptured, bloodied flesh were spattered all over his suit and visor. He stumbled and almost went down the steep, bare bank, but stopped there on the edge, swaying, keeping his balance, telling himself quietly that he would not be sick, over and over again.

After a while he turned and, looking past the body, met Drake's eyes. "You bastard . . . why did she come at me? What did you say to her?"

Drake pulled off his helmet and threw it down. "I told her you'd help her," he said, then laughed strangely. "And you did. You bloody well did."

CHAPTER·20

FLAMES IN A GLASS

"Wang Ti?"

Chen stood just inside the door, surprised to find the apartment in darkness. He put out his hand, searching the wall, then slowly brought up the lights. Things looked normal, everything in its place. He released a breath. For the briefest moment . . .

He went out into the kitchen and filled the kettle, then plugged it in. As he turned, reaching up to get the *ch'a* pot, he heard a noise. A cough.

He went out, into the brightness of the living-room. "Wang Ti?" he called softly, looking across at the darkened doorway of their bedroom. "Is that you?"

The cough came again, a strong, racking cough that ended with a tiny moan.

He went across and looked into the room. It was Wang Ti beneath the covers, he could see that at once. But Wang Ti as he had never seen her before; her hair unkempt, her brow beaded with sweat. Wang Ti, who had never suffered a day's illness in her life.

"*Wang Ti?*"

She moaned, turning her head slightly on the pillow. "Nmmm . . ."

He looked about him, conscious that something was missing, but not knowing what. "Wang Ti?"

Her eyes opened slowly. Seeing him, she moaned and turned away, pulling the sheet up over her head.

"Wang Ti?" he said gently, moving closer. "Where are the children?"

638

Her voice was small, muffled by the sheets. "I sent them below. To Uncle Mai."

"Ahh . . ." He crouched down. "And you, my love?"

She hesitated, then answered in that same small, frightened voice. "I am fine, husband."

Something in the way she said it – in the way her determination to be a dutiful, uncomplaining wife faltered before the immensity of her suffering – made him go cold inside. Something awful had happened.

He pulled back the sheet, studying her face in the half light. It was almost unrecognisable. Her mouth – a strong mouth, made for laughter – was twisted into a thin-lipped grimace of pain. Her eyes – normally so warm and reassuring – were screwed tightly shut as if to wall-in all the misery she felt, the lids heavy and discoloured. Pained by the sight, he put his fingers to her cheek, wanting to comfort her, then drew them back, surprised. She had been crying.

There was a moment's blankness, then he felt his stomach fall away. "The child . . ."

Wang Ti nodded, then buried her face in the pillow, beginning to sob, her body convulsing under the sheets.

He sat on the bed beside her, holding her to him, trying to comfort her, but his mind was in shock. "No . . ." he said, after a while. "You have always been so strong. And the child was well. Surgeon Fan said so."

She lay there quietly – so quiet that it frightened him. Then it was true. She had lost the child.

"When was this?" he asked, horrified.

"A week ago."

"A week! *Ai ya!*" He sat back, staring sightlessly into the shadows, thinking of her anguish, her suffering, and him not there. "But why wasn't I told? Why didn't Karr send word. I should have been here."

She put out a hand, touching his chest. "He wanted to. He begged me to, but I would not let him. Your job . . ."

He looked back at her. She was watching him now, her

639

puffed and blood-red eyes filled with pity. The sight of her – of her concern *for him* – made his chest tighten with love. "Oh, Wang Ti, my little pigeon . . . what in the gods' names happened?"

She shuddered and looked away again. "No one came," she said quietly. "I waited, but no one came . . ."

He shook his head. "But the Surgeon . . . We paid him specially to come."

"There were complications," she said, afraid to meet his eyes. "I waited. Three hours I waited, but he never came. Jyan tried . . ."

"Never came?" Chen said, outraged. "He was notified and never came?"

She gave a tight little nod. "I got Jyan to run up to the Medical Centre, but no one was free." She met his eyes briefly, then looked away again, forcing the words out in a tiny, frightened voice. "Or so they said. But Jyan says that they were sitting there, in a room beyond the reception area, laughing – drinking *ch'a* and laughing – while my baby was dying."

Chen felt himself go cold again; but this time it was the coldness of anger. Of an intense, almost blinding anger. "And no one came?"

She shook her head, her face cracking again. He held her tightly, letting her cry in his arms, his own face wet with tears. "My poor love," he said. "My poor, poor love." But deep inside his anger had hardened into something else – into a cold, clear rage. He could picture them, sitting there, laughing and drinking *ch'a* while his baby daughter was dying. Could see their well-fed, laughing faces and wanted to smash them, to feel their cheek-bones shatter beneath his fist.

And young Jyan . . . How had it been for him, knowing that his mother was in trouble, his baby sister dying, and he impotent to act? How had that felt? Chen groaned. They had had such hopes. Such plans. How could it all have gone so wrong?

He looked about him at the familiar room, the thought

of the dead child an agony, burning in his chest. "No . . ." he said softly, shaking his head. "*Nooooo!*"

He stood, his fists bunched at his sides. "I will go and see Surgeon Fan."

Wang Ti looked up, frightened. "No, Chen. Please. You will solve nothing that way."

He shook his head. "The bastard should have come. It is only two decks down. Three hours . . . Where could he have been for three hours?"

"Chen . . ." She put out a hand, trying to restrain him, but he moved back, away from her.

"No, Wang Ti. Not this time. This time I do it my way."

"You don't understand . . ." she began. "Karr knows everything. He has all the evidence. He was going to meet you . . ."

She fell silent, seeing that he was no longer listening. His face was set, like the face of a statue.

"He killed my daughter," he said softly. "He let her die. And you, Wang Ti . . . you might have died too."

She trembled. It was true. She had almost died, forcing the baby from her – no, *would* have died, had Jyan not thought to contact Karr and bring the big man to her aid.

She let her head fall back. So maybe Chen was right. Maybe, this once, it was right to act – to hit back at those who had harmed them, and damn the consequences. Better that, perhaps, than let it fester deep inside. Better that than have him shamed a second time before his son.

She closed her eyes, pained by the memory of all that had happened to her. It had been awful here without him. Awful beyond belief.

She felt his breath on her cheek, his lips pressed gently to her brow, and shivered.

"I must go," he said quietly, letting his hand rest softly on her flank. "You understand?"

She nodded, holding back the tears, wanting to be brave for him this once. But it was hard, and when he was gone she broke down again, sobbing loudly, uncontrollably, the memory of his touch glowing warmly in the darkness.

★　★　★

The room was cold and brightly lit, white tiles on the walls and floor emphasising the starkness of the place. In the centre of the room was a dissecting table. Beside the table stood the three surgeons who had carried out the post mortem, their heads bowed, waiting.

The corpse on the table was badly burned, the limbs disfigured, the head and upper torso crushed; even so, the body could still be identified as GenSyn. In three separate places the flesh had been peeled back to the bone, revealing the distinctive GenSyn marking – the bright red 'G' forming a not-quite-closed circle with a tiny blue 'S' within.

They had cornered it finally in the caves to the north of the estate. There, Hung Mien-lo and a small group of élite guards had fought it for an hour before a well-aimed grenade had done the trick, silencing the creature's answering fire and bringing the roof of the cave down on top of it. Or so Hung's story went.

Wang Sau-leyan stood there, looking down at the corpse, his eyes taking in everything. Hope warred with cynicism in his face, but when he looked back at his Chancellor, it was with an expression of deep suspicion. "Are you sure this is it, Hung? The face . . ."

The face was almost formless. Was the merest suggestion of a face.

"I am told this is how they make some models, *Chieh Hsia*. A certain number are kept for urgent orders, the facial features added at the last moment. I have checked with GenSyn records and discovered that this particular model was made eight years back. It was stolen from their West Asian organisation – from their plant at Karaganda – nearly five years ago."

Wang looked back at it, then shook his head. "Even so . . ."

"Forgive me, *Chieh Hsia*, but we found some other things in the cave." Hung Mien-lo turned and took a small case from his secretary, then turned back, handing it, opened, to the T'ang. "This was amongst them."

Wang Sau-leyan stared down at the face and nodded. It was torn and dirtied and pitted with tiny holes, but it was recognisable all the same. It was his brother's face. Or, at least, a perfect likeness. He set it down on the chest of the corpse.

"So this is how it did it, eh? With a false face and a cold body."

"Not cold, *Chieh Hsia*. Or not entirely. You see, this model was designed for work in sub-zero temperatures or in the heat of the mines. It has a particularly hard and durable skin that insulates the inner workings of the creature from extremes of heat and cold. That was why it did not register on our cameras. At night they are programmed to respond only to heat patterns, and as this thing did not give off any trace, the cameras were never activated."

Wang nodded, his mouth gone dry. Even so, he wasn't *quite* convinced. "And the traces of skin and blood that it left on the stone?"

Hung lowered his head slightly. "It is our belief, *Chieh Hsia*, that they were put there by the creature. Deliberately, to make us think it really was your brother."

Wang looked down, then gave a small, sour laugh. "I would dearly like to think so, Chancellor Hung, but that simply isn't possible. I have checked with GenSyn. They tell me it is impossible to duplicate individual DNA from scratch."

"From scratch, yes, *Chieh Hsia*. But why should that be the case? All that is needed to duplicate DNA is a single strand of the original. This can even, I am assured, be done from a corpse."

"And that is what you are suggesting? That someone broke into the tomb before this creature broke out from it again? That they took a piece of my brother's body and used it to duplicate his DNA?"

"That is one possibility, *Chieh Hsia*, but there is another. What if someone close to your brother took a sample of his skin or blood before his death? Took it and kept it?"

Wang shook his head. "That's absurd. I know my brother was a weakling and a fool, but even he would not sit still and let a servant take a sample of his blood."

"Again, that is not what I meant, *Chieh Hsia*. What if your brother had a small accident and one of his servants tended to him? And what if that servant kept the materials they used to tend your brother's wound – a piece of blood-ied gauze, perhaps, or a bowl with bloodied water?"

Wang narrowed his eyes. "And you think that's what happened?"

Hung nodded. "That is exactly what happened, *Chieh Hsia*. We have a signed confession."

"A confession? And how was this confession obtained? By your usual means?"

Hung turned, taking the scroll from his secretary, then handed it across.

"Wu Ming!" Wang laughed with disbelief. "And is that all the proof you have – Wu Ming's confession?"

Hung Mien-lo shook his head. "I am afraid not, *Chieh Hsia*. I went back through the household records for details of any small accident to your brother. It seems there were several such incidents over the past five years, but in all but one instance the materials used to tend his wounds were properly incinerated."

"And that single instance where it was not – that involved Wu Ming, I take it?"

"Yes, *Chieh Hsia*. Wu Ming and one other. The traitor, Sun Li Hua."

Wang made a noise of surprise. "This is certain?"

"Absolutely, *Chieh Hsia*. We have a tape of the incident, showing Wu and Sun tending your brother, but no sub-sequent record of the dressings being destroyed."

"Ah . . ." Wang turned, looking down at the corpse again, his fingers reaching out to touch and trace the con-tours of his brother's face. "Then it was my cousin's hand behind all this," he said softly. "This was Li Yuan's doing."

"So it seems, *Chieh Hsia*."

"So it seems . . ." Yet something still nagged at him. He turned back, facing his Chancellor. "How long ago did this happen?"

"Two years ago, *Chieh Hsia*."

"Two years, or almost two years? Be precise, Hung Mien-lo."

"Twenty-two months, to be exact, *Chieh Hsia*."

"A month before his death?"

"That is so, *Chieh Hsia*."

Wang took a deep breath, satisfied. Any earlier and it would have made no sense, for his father would still have been alive, and Li Yuan would have had no motive for his actions. As it was . . .

He smiled. "You have done well, Chancellor Hung. You have more than repaid my trust in you. But there are still two things that remain to be answered. First, how did the creature get into the tomb without the cameras seeing it? Second, where is the body of my dead brother?"

Hung Mien-lo bowed low. "Both questions have troubled me greatly, *Chieh Hsia*, but I think I have the answer."

Straightening up, he drew something from his pocket and held it out, offering it to his T'ang. It was a small, glassy circle, like the lens cap to a camera.

Wang turned it in his hand, then looked back at his Chancellor. "What is this?"

"It is an imager, *Chieh Hsia*. Placed over a camera lens, it fixes the image in the camera's eye and maintains it for a predetermined period. After that time, the imager self-destructs – at a molecular level – dispersing in the form of a gas. While it is there, over the lens, you can walk about quite freely before the camera without fear of it registering your presence, and afterwards it leaves no trace."

"I see. And you think a similar kind of thing – or several of them – were used to mask the cameras about the tomb?"

Hung smiled. "It would explain how the tomb door was opened without the cameras seeing anything."

"And my brother's body?"

"Of that there is no sign, *Chieh Hsia*. However, we did find a trace of ashes in a hollow near a stream to the north of the palace. Halfway between here and the foothills."

"So the creature burned the body?"

Hung gave a slight shrug. "I am not so sure. If he did, then why did we see no sign of it? It takes a great deal of heat to consume a human body and, from the moment the alarms were sounded, every guard in the palace was on alert for anything suspicious. If the creature *had* burned the body, we would have seen it. So no, *Chieh Hsia*, I would guess that the ashes were from something else – some small religious ceremony, perhaps. As for the body, I think it is still out there, hidden somewhere."

Wang considered a moment, then laughed. "Which is where we shall let it rest, neh? Amongst the rocks and streams, like an exiled Minister." Again he laughed, a fuller, richer laughter now, fed by relief and an ancient, unforgiving malice. He turned, looking down at the corpse and the box holding his brother's face. "As for these things, have them burned, Chancellor Hung. Outside, before the palace gates, where all can see."

★ ★ ★

It was quiet in the lobby of the Medical Centre. As Chen entered the nurse behind the desk looked up, smiling, but Chen walked straight by, pushing through the gate in the low barrier, heading for where he knew they kept their records.

Someone called out to him as he passed, but Chen ignored them. There was no time for formalities. He wanted to know right now who had killed his child, and why.

Two men looked up from behind their screens as he entered the records room, surprised to see him there. One made to object, then fell silent as he saw the gun.

"I want details of a child mortality," Chen said, without preamble. "The name is Kao. K.A.O. A week ago it was.

646

A female child. Newborn. I want the registered time of death, the precise time the call-out enquiry was made at this office, and a duty roster for that evening, complete with duty records for all on the roster."

The clerks glanced at each other, not sure what to do, but Chen's fierce bark made them jump. He pointed his gun at the most senior of the two. "Do it. *Now!* Hard print. And don't even think of fucking me about. If I don't get what I want, I'll put a bullet through your chest."

Swallowing nervously, the man bowed his head and began to tap details into his comset.

As the printout began to chatter from the machine, there was a noise outside. Chen turned. Three of the orderlies – big, heavily-built men – had come to see what was happening. From the way they stood there, blocking the way, it was clear they had no intention of letting him leave.

"Get back to work," he said quietly. "This is none of your business."

He looked back. The younger of the clerks had his fingers on the keys of his machine. Chen shook his head. "I wouldn't, if I were you . . ."

The man desisted. A moment later the other machine fell silent.

Chen reached out, taking the printout from the tray. A glance at it confirmed what he had suspected. Jyan had been right. At the time of his daughter's death, no less than four of the medical staff had been free. So why hadn't they answered the emergency call? Or rather, who had instructed them to ignore it?

He would visit Surgeon Fan, the senior consultant of the Centre – the man who should have come at Wang Ti's summons. Would find him and wring a name from him. Then he would kill them. Whoever they were.

Chen turned, facing the orderlies again. "Did you not hear me, *ch'un tzu*? Go back to work. This does not concern you."

He could see how edgy they were at the sight of his gun. Edgy but determined. They thought they could jump him.

647

Well, they could try. But they were mistaken if they thought sheer determination would triumph over him.

He tucked the gun into its holster, then reached down, taking the long, sharp-edged knife from his boot.

"You want to stop me, is that it? Well, let's see you try, eh? Let's see you try."

★ ★ ★

Minutes later he was hammering at the door of Fan Tseng-li's apartment, conscious that a Security alert would have been put out already. He could hear movement inside and the babble of voices. Fearful, panicky voices. He called to them, letting his voice fill out with reassurance.

"Security! Open up! I am Lieutenant Tong and I have been assigned to protect you!"

He saw the door camera swivel round and held his pass card up, his thumb obscuring the name. A moment later the door hissed open and he was ushered inside, the three servants smiling at him gratefully.

The smiles froze as he drew his gun.

"Where is he? Where is the weasel-faced little shit?"

"I don't know who you mean," the oldest of them, an ancient with the number two on his chest began, but Chen cuffed him into silence.

"You know very well who I mean. Fan. I want to know where he is, and I want to know now, not in two minutes time. I'll shoot you first, *lao tzu*, then you, you little fucker."

The elder – Number Two – looked down, holding his tongue, but beside him the youngest of the three began to babble, fear freeing his tongue wonderfully. Chen listened carefully, noting what he said.

"And he's there now?"

The young man nodded.

"Right." He looked past them at the house comset; a large, ornate machine embellished with dragons. "Has anyone spoken to him yet?"

The young man shook his head, ignoring the ancient's glare.

"Good." Chen stepped past them and fired two shots into the machine. "That's to stop you being tempted. But let me warn you. If I find that he has been tipped off, I will come back for you. So be good, neh? Be extra-specially good."

* * *

The House Steward smiled, lowering his head. "If you would wait here, Captain Kao, I shall tell my master . . ."

A straight-arm to the stomach made the man double up, gasping. Chen stepped over him, heading towards the sound of voices, the clink of tumblers.

A servant came towards him, trying to prevent him from entering the dining room. Chen stiff-fingered him in the throat.

He threw the doors open, looking about him, ignoring the startled faces, then roared ferociously as he spotted Surgeon Fan, there on the far side of the table.

Fan Tseng-li stood, staggering back from his chair, his face white, his eyes wide with fear. Others were shouting now, outraged, looking from Chen to Fan, trying to make sense of things. For a moment there was hubbub, then a cold, fearful silence fell.

Chen had drawn his knife.

"*Ai ya!*" Fan cried hoarsely, looking about him anxiously. "Who is this madman?"

"You know fucking well who I am," Chen snarled, coming round the table. "And I know who you are, Fan Tseng-li. You are the evil bastard who let my unborn daughter die."

Fan's face froze in a rictus of fear. "You have it wrong. I was detained. A client of mine . . ."

Fan fell silent. Chen was standing only an arm's length from him now, glaring at him, the look of hatred, of sheer disgust, enough to wither the man.

"I know what kind of insect *you* are, Fan. What I need

to know is who paid you to let my daughter die, my wife suffer." He reached out savagely, gripping Fan's hair, then pulled him down on to his knees, the big knife held to his throat. "Who was it, Fan Tseng-li? Tell me."

There was a murmur of protest from about the table, but Chen ignored it. He was looking down into Fan's face, a murderous hatred shaping his lips into a snarl.

"You had better tell me," he said quietly, tightening his grip on Fan's hair, "and you had best do it now, Fan Tseng-li. Unless you want a second mouth below your chin."

Fan grimaced, then met Chen's eyes. "It was Ts'ui Wei. Ts'ui Wei made me do it."

"Ts'ui Wei?" Chen frowned, trying to place the name. "Did he . . . ?"

He stopped, making the connection. *Ts'ui Wei.* Of course! That was the name of the youth's father. The tall, thin man who had threatened him that time, after he'd had the youth demoted. Chen shuddered. So that was it. That was why his child had died.

He sheathed the knife, then turned, looking about him at the faces gathered round the table. "You heard," he said defiantly. "And now you know what kind of creature your friend, Fan Tseng-li is."

Chen looked back down at Fan, then, with a savage grunt, brought his face down on to his knee.

He let Fan roll to the side, then walked back round the table, seeing how they cowered from him. At the doorway the servants parted before him, making no attempt to hinder him. They had seen what had happened and understood. Some even bowed their heads as Chen passed, showing him respect. Back in the dining-room, however, voices were being raised; angry, indignant voices, calling for something to be done.

* * *

He stood there, in the darkness on the far side of the restaurant, looking across. There were seven of them in all, five of them seated at one of the tables near the pay desk, their figures back-lit, their faces dark. The other two sat at nearby tables; big men, their watchfulness as much as their size telling Chen what they were. The five were huddled close, talking.

"You should go," one of them was saying. "There must be relatives you could stay with for a time, Ts'ui Wei. Until this blows over."

Ts'ui Wei leaned towards him aggressively. "I'm not running from that bastard. He had my son sent down. I'll be fucked if he'll threaten me."

"You do as you feel, Ts'ui Wei, but I've heard that Security have been digging through deck records, putting together a file."

Ts'ui leaned back arrogantly. "So? He can't prove anything. All Surgeon Fan has to do is keep his mouth shut."

The fat man bristled. "Fan Tseng-li is the model of discretion. He, at least, is taking my advice and going away until this is all sorted out."

Ts'ui Wei snorted. "That's typical of that self-serving shit! I should never have listened to your snivelling rubbish. We could have hit him. Hit him hard. And not just a fucking unborn child. We could have hurt him bad. The little girl . . ."

Chen shivered, his anger refined to a burning point. They were not expecting him. That gave him the element of surprise. But there were still the bodyguards. He would have to deal with them first.

Standing there, listening to them scheme and plot, he had felt his anger turn to a deep revulsion. For them, but also for himself – for what had *he* been doing while all this had been happening?

He let out a long, slow breath. No. It could never be the same. For wherever he looked he could see her stumbling towards him like a broken doll, could hear the sound of the detonation . . .

And the child? He closed his eyes, the pain returning, like an iron band tightening about his chest. It was as if he had killed the child. As if he had pressed a tiny button and . . .

Chen stepped from the darkness. One of the hired men looked up at him as he came closer, then looked away, taking him for what he seemed – a night worker stopped for a bowl of *ch'a* before retiring. It was what Chen had hoped for.

Three paces from the man, he acted, swinging his fist round in a broad arc that brought it crashing into the man's face, breaking his nose. As he fell back, Chen turned and span, high-kicking, catching the second man in the chest, even as he was getting up from his chair. At once he followed through, two quick punches felling the man.

Chen turned, facing the men at the table. They had moved back, scattering their chairs. Now they stared at him, wide-eyed with fear.

"Tell me," Chen said quietly, taking a step closer. "My little girl . . . What would you have done, Ts'ui Wei? Tell me what you had planned."

Ashen-faced, Ts'ui Wei tried to back away, but the end wall was directly behind him. He turned his head anxiously, looking for somewhere to run, but his way was blocked on both sides.

Chen lifted the weighted table and threw it aside, then reached down, taking the big hunting knife from his boot.

"I have no stomach for a fight, eh, Ts'ui Wei?" He laughed coldly, all of the hatred and self-disgust he had been feeling suddenly focused in his forearm, making the big knife quiver in the light.

Ts'ui Wei stared at him a moment longer, his mouth working soundlessly, then he fell to his knees, pressing his head to the floor, his body shaking with fear. "Have mercy," he pleaded. "For the gods' sakes, have mercy!"

Chen took a shuddering breath, remembering how Wang Ti had looked, remembering how it had felt, knowing he had not been there for her – and Jyan, poor Jyan

. . . how had it felt for him, knowing he could do nothing? And this . . . this piece of shit . . . wanted *mercy*?

He raised the knife, his whole body tensed, prepared to strike . . .

"Father! No!! *Please* . . ."

He turned, letting the knife fall from his hand. It was Jyan. It was his son, Jyan.

The boy ran across and threw his arms about him, embracing him, holding him so tightly that Chen felt something break in him. He began to sob, the words spilling from him. "Oh, Jyan . . . Jyan . . . I'm so sorry . . . I didn't know . . . I *didn't* know. Was it awful, boy? Was it really awful?"

Jyan clutched his father fiercely, looking up at him, his face wet with tears. "It's all right, Father . . . It's all right now. You're back. You're here now."

He kissed his son's brow, then lifted him up, hugging him tightly. Yes. But it would never be the same.

He turned, looking back into the shadows. Karr was standing there, a troop of his guards behind him. "Are you all right, Kao Chen?"

Chen nodded. "I . . ." He laughed strangely. "I would have killed him."

"Yes," Karr said quietly. "And I would have let you. But Jyan . . . Well, Jyan knew best, neh? After all, you have a life ahead of you, Kao Chen. A good life."

Chen shivered, tightening his grip on his son, then nodded. Karr let his hand rest on Chen's shoulder briefly, then moved past him, taking command of the situation. "All right!" he barked, towering over the frightened men. "Let's get this sorted out right now! You! – all of you! – against the back wall, hands on your heads! You're under arrest, as principles and accessories to the murder of a child, and for conspiring to pervert the course of justice."

★ ★ ★

Karr sat on the stone ledge, staring across at the floodlit shape of the Memorial Stone. It was after nine and the lotus lake was dark. Elsewhere, beneath the lamps that lined the narrow pathways, lovers walked, talking softly, keeping a proper distance between them. Behind Karr, seated in the shadows of the teahouse, Chen sat, his head fallen forward, his story told.

For a moment longer Karr sat there, motionless, and then he sighed, as if waking from a dark and threatening dream. "And that is the truth?"

Chen was silent.

Karr closed his eyes, deeply pained. Of course it was the truth. A tale like that – it was not something one made up about oneself. No. But it was not only Chen he felt sorry for. He had liked the woman greatly. If he had known for a moment . . .

"This is wrong, Kao Chen. Very wrong." Karr was quiet a moment, fingering the dragon pendant about his neck, then he drew it out, looking down at it. He was *Chia ch'eng*, Honorary Assistant to the Royal Household. By right he could claim audience with his T'ang.

He turned, facing Chen across the table. "I will see Li Yuan. I will tell him everything you told me just now."

"You think he does not know?"

Karr nodded. "I am convinced of it. He is a good man. Someone is keeping these things from him. Well then, we must be his eyes and ears, neh? We must let him know what is being done in his name."

Chen turned his head. "And Tolonen? He will have the report of my debriefing by the morning. What if he says you are to do nothing?"

Karr looked down. That was true. He was Tolonen's man, and by rights he should talk to the old man first. But some things were greater than such loyalties.

"Then I must do it now."

★ ★ ★

The wall had changed. Had become a view of Tai Shan, the sacred mountain misted in the early morning light, the great temple at the summit a tiny patch of red against the blue of the sky. Within the room a faint breeze blew, spreading the scent of pine and acacia.

Fat Wong turned from the wall, looking back at his guests, then raised his cup. "Brothers . . ."

There were five men seated around the low table, each the equal of Wong Yi-sun, each the Big Boss of one of the great Triads that ran the lowest levels of City Europe. It had cost him much to get them here tonight, but here they were. All of them. All that mattered.

They stared back at him, cold-eyed, returning his smile with their mouths alone, like alligators.

"I am glad you could all come. I realise what sacrifices you have made to come here at such short notice, but when you have heard what I have to say, I know you will agree that I was right to convene this meeting of the Council."

"Where is Iron Mu?"

Wong turned, facing the old man seated at the table's end. "Forgive me, General Feng, but I will come to that."

The Big Boss of the 14K stared back at him humourlessly. "The Council has seven members, Wong Yi-sun, but I see only six about this table."

"Hear Wong out, Feng Shang-pao," the short, shaven-headed man seated two along from him said, leaning forward to take a cashew from the bowl. "I am sure all your questions will be answered."

Feng sat back, glaring at his interruptor. "We must have laws amongst us, Li Chin. Ways of conducting ourselves."

Li Chin – Li the Lidless – turned his bony head and looked at Feng, his over-large eyes fixing the older man. "I do not dispute it, Feng Shang-pao. But the Wo Shih Wo would like to know what Fat Wong has to say, and unless you let him say it . . ."

Feng looked down, his huge chest rising and falling, then he nodded.

"Good," Wong said. "Then let me explain. This afternoon, I received a letter."

Whiskers Lu, Boss of the Kuei Chuan, leaned forward,

the melted mask of his face turned towards Wong, his one good eye glittering. "A letter, Wong Yi-sun?"

"Yes." Wong took the letter from within his silks and threw it down in front of Lu. "But before you open it, let me say a few words."

Wong drew himself up, his eyes moving from face to face. "We of the *Hung Mun* are proud of our heritage. Rightly so. Since the time of our founding by the five monks of the Fu Chou monastery, we have always settled our disputes amicably. And that is good, neh? After all, it is better to make money than make war." He smiled, then let the smile fade. "This once, however, the threat was too great. Iron Mu sought more than simple profit. He sought to build a power base – a base from which to overthrow this Council. To replace it." He nodded, his face stern. "Let us not hide behind words any longer. Iron Mu sought to destroy us."

Dead Man Yun of the Red Gang cleared his throat. "I hear your words, Wong Yi-sun, but I find them strange. You speak of things we all know, yet you speak of them in the past. Why is this?"

Wong smiled, then turned, going across to the tiny pool. For a moment he stood there, watching the seven golden fish swim lazily in the crystal waters, then, with a quicksilver motion, he scooped one up and turned, holding it up for the others to see. For a moment it flapped in the air, then Wong threw it down on to the dry stone flags.

There was a murmur of understanding from about the table.

"So Iron Mu is dead. But how?" Three Finger Ho asked, eyeing Wong warily.

Wong came closer, a trace of self-satisfaction at the corners of his mouth. "I will tell you how. All thirty-seven decks of the Big Circle heartland were hit simultaneously, thirty minutes back. A force of one hundred and twenty thousand *Hei* went in, with a back-up of fifteen hundred regular guards."

Hei. . . That single word sent a ripple of fear through

the seated men. They had seen the *Hei* in action on their screens, the big GenSyn half-men clearing decks of rioters with a ruthlessness even their most fanatical runners could not match. For a moment they were silent, looking amongst themselves, wondering what this meant, then Li the Lidless leaned across Whiskers Lu and took the letter. He unfolded it and began to read aloud, then stopped, his face filled with a sudden understanding.

This letter from Li Yuan – this brief note of agreement – changed everything. Never before had one of their number received such a favour from Above. Never had the *Hung Mun* worked hand-in-glove with the Seven. Today Fat Wong had gained great face. Had re-established his position as Great Father of the brotherhoods. Li turned his head, looking about him, seeing the look of understanding in every face, then turned back, facing Wong, his head lowered in a gesture of respect.

★ ★ ★

The tapestries were burning. Flames licked the ancient thread, consuming mountain and forest, turning the huntsmen to ashes in the flicker of an eye. The air was dark with smoke, rent with the cries of dying men. *Hei* ran through the choking darkness, their long swords flashing, their deep-set eyes searching out anything that ran or walked or crawled.

The door to Iron Mu's Mansion had been breached ten minutes back, but still a small group of Mu's élite held out. *Hei* swarmed at the final barricade, throwing themselves at the barrier without thought of self-preservation. Facing them, Yao Tzu, Red Pole to the Big Circle, urged his men to one last effort. He was bleeding from wounds to the head and chest, but still he fought on, slashing at whatever appeared above the barricade. For a moment longer the great pile held, then, with a shudder, it began to slide. There was a bellowing, and then the *Hei* broke through. Yao Tzu backed away, his knife gone, three of his men falling in the first charge. As the first of the *Hei* came at him, he leaped forward, screeching shrilly, meeting the brute with a flying kick that shattered the great chestbone of the half-man. Encouraged, his men attacked in a blur of flying feet and fists, but it was not enough. The first wave of *Hei* went down, but then there was the deafening roar of gunfire as the *Hei* commander opened up with a big automatic from the top of the collapsed barricade.

There was a moment's silence, smoke swirled, and then they moved on, into the inner sanctum.

★　★　★

His wives were dead, his three sons missing. From outside he could hear the screams of his men as they died. It would be only moments before they broke into his rooms. Even so, he could not rush this thing.

Iron Mu had washed and prepared himself. Now he sat, his legs folded under him, his robe open, the ritual knife before him on the mat. Behind him his servant waited, the specially-sharpened sword raised, ready for the final stroke.

He leaned forward, taking the knife, then turned it, holding the needle-sharp point towards his naked stomach. His head was strangely clear, his thoughts lucid. It was the merchant, Novacek who had done this. It had to be. No one else had known enough. Even so, it did not matter. He would die well. That was all that was important now.

As he tensed, the door shuddered then fell open, the great locks smashed. Two *Hei* stood there, panting, looking in at him. A moment later a man stepped through, wearing the powder-blue uniform and chest patch of a Colonel. A filter-mask covered his lower face.

Iron Mu met the Colonel's eyes, holding them defiantly. In this, his last moment, he felt no fear, no regret, only a clarity of purpose that was close to the sublime.

Nothing, not even the watching *Hei* could distract him now.

A breath, a second, longer breath, and then . . .

The Colonel's eyes dilated, his jaw tensed, and then he

turned away, letting his *Hei* finish in the room. He shivered, impressed despite himself, feeling a new respect for the man. Iron Mu had died well. Very well. Even so, it could not be known how Iron Mu had died. No. The story would be put out that he had cried and begged for mercy, hiding behind his wives. Because that was what the *T'ing Wei* wanted. And what the *T'ing Wei* wanted, they got.

Yes, but while he lived, Iron Mu's death would live in his memory. And one day, when the *T'ing Wei* were no more perhaps, he would tell his story. Of how one of the great lords of the underworld had died, with dignity, meeting the darkness without fear.

★　★　★

Fat Wong stood by the door, bringing things to a close, thanking his fellow Bosses for coming. And as they left, he made each stoop and kiss the ancient banner.

It should have been enough. Yet when they were gone it was not elation he felt but a sudden sense of hollowness. This victory was not his. Not *really* his. It was like something bought.

He went across and stood there over the tiny pool, staring down into the water, trying to see things clearly. For a moment he was still, as if meditating, then, taking the letter from his pocket, he tore it slowly in half and then in half again, letting it fall. No. He would be beholden to no man, not even a Son of Heaven. He saw it now with opened eyes. Why had Li Yuan agreed to act, if not out of fear? And if that were so . . .

He took a long, deep breath, then, drawing back his sleeve, reached in, plucking the fish from the water until five of the bloated golden creatures lay there on the ledge, flapping helplessly in the hostile air.

His way was clear. He must unite the underworld. Must destroy his brothers one by one, until only he remained. And then, when that was done, he might lift his head again and stare into the light.

He looked down, watching the dying gasps of the fish,

then turned away, smiling. No. His way was clear. He would not rest now until it was his. Until he had it all.

★ ★ ★

Li Yuan stood on the terrace, beneath the bright full circle of the moon, looking out across the palace grounds, conscious of how quiet, how empty the palace seemed at this late hour. No gardeners knelt in the dark earth beneath the trellises of the lower garden, no maids walked the dark and narrow path that led to the palace laundry. He turned, looking towards the stables. There, a single lamp threw its pale amber light across the empty exercise circle.

He shivered and looked up at the moon, staring at that great white stone a while, thinking of what Karr had said.

Standing there in the wavering lamplight, listening to the big man's account, he had been deeply moved. He had not known – had genuinely not known – what was being done at Kibwezi, and, touched by the rawness of the man's appeal, had given his promise to close Kibwezi and review the treatment of convicted terrorists.

He had returned to the reception, distracted by Karr's words, disturbed by the questions they raised. And, as he went amongst his cousins, smiling, offering bland politenesses, it had seemed suddenly a great pretence, a nothingness, like walking in a hall of holograms. The more he smiled and talked, the more he felt the weight of Karr's words bearing down on him.

But now, at last, he could face the matter squarely, beneath the unseeing eye of the moon.

Until this moment he had denied that there was a moral problem with the Wiring Project. Had argued that it was merely a question of attitude. But there was a problem, for – as Tolonen had argued from the first – freedom was no illusion, and even the freedom to rebel ought – no, *needed* – to be preserved somehow, if only for the sake of balance.

Were it simply a matter of philosophy – of *words* – it might have been all right. But it was not. The population problem was real. It could not be simply wished away.

He looked down, staring at his hands – at the great iron ring on the first finger of his right hand. For men such as Kao Chen, a common phrase like "We are our masters' hands" had a far greater literal truth than he had ever imagined. And a far greater significance. For what was a man? Was he a choosing being, forging his own destiny, or was he simply a piece on the board, there to be played by another, greater than himself?

And maybe that was what had troubled him, more than the fate of the woman. That deeper question of choice.

He turned, looking back into his room, seeing Minister Heng's report there on the desk where he had left it.

It was a full report on the "police action" against the Big Circle Triad; a report that differed radically from the *T'ing Wei*'s official account. He sighed, the deep unease he had felt at reading the report returning. The *Hei* riot squads had gone mad down there. More than two hundred thousand had been killed, including many women and children.

Yes, and that was another argument in favour of wiring. If only to prevent such massacres, "necessary" as this one might have been.

He turned back, standing there a moment, the night breeze cool on his face.

The moon was high. He looked up at it, surprised, his perception of it suddenly reversed, such that it seemed to burn like a vast shining hole in the blackness of the sky. A big circle of death. He shivered violently and looked down, noting how its light silvered the gardens like a fall of dust.

Before today he had striven always to do the right thing, to be a good man – the benevolent ruler that Confucius bade him be – but now he saw it clearly. In this there was no right course of action, no pure solution, only degrees of wrongness.

And so he would make the hard choice. He would keep his word to Karr, of course. Kibwezi Station would be closed. As for the other thing, he had no choice. No real choice, anyway. The Wiring Project had to continue, and so it would, elsewhere, hidden from prying eyes. Until the job was done, the system perfected.

He sighed, turning his back on the darkness, returning inside. Yes. Because the time was fast coming when it would be needed.

* * *

Broken glass littered the terrace outside the guardhouse, glistening like frosted leaves in the moonlight. Nearby, the first of the bodies lay like a discarded doll, its face a pulp, the ragged tunic of its uniform soaked with blood. Through the empty window a second body could be seen, slumped forward in a chair, its head twisted at an unusual angle, the unblemished face staring vacantly at a broken screen.

Behind it, on the far side of the room, a door led through. There, on a bed in the rest room, the last of the bodies lay, naked and broken, its eyes bulging from its face, its tongue poking obscenely from between its teeth.

At the end of the unlit corridor, in the still silence of the signal room, the morph stood at the transmitter, its neutered body naked in the half-light. To one side, a hand lay on the desk like a stranded crab, the fingers upturned.

The morph tensed, the severed wrist of its left hand pressed against the input socket, the delicate wires seeking their counterparts, making their connections to the board, then it relaxed, a soft amber light glowing on the eye-level panel in front of it. There was a moment's stillness and then a faint tremor ran through the creature. At the count of twelve it stopped, as abruptly as it had begun. The message had been sent.

It waited, the minutes passing slowly, its stillness unnatural, like the stillness of a machine, and then the answer came.

It shuddered, then broke connection, drawing its wrist back sharply from the panel, a strange sigh, like the sough-ing of the wind through trees, escaping its narrow lips.

Reaching across, it took the hand from where it lay and

lined it up carefully against the wrist, letting the twelve strong plastic latches – six in the hand, six in the wrist – click into place. The hand twitched, the fingers trembling, then was still again.

It turned, looking out through the dark square of the window. Fifty *ch'i* away, at the edge of the concrete apron was a wire fence. Beyond the fence was the forest. For a time it stood there, staring out into the darkness, then it turned, making its way through.

For the past few nights it had dreamed. Dreams of a black wind blowing from beyond; of a dark and silent pressure at the back of it. A dream that was like the rush of knowledge down its spine; that set its nerve ends tingling in a sudden ecstasy. And with the dream had come a vision – a bright, hard vision of a world beneath the surface of this world. Of a world ruled by the game. A game of dark and light. Of suns and moons. Of space and time itself. A game that tore the dark veil from reality, revealing the whiteness of the bone.

On the terrace it paused, considering. From Tao Yuan to Tashkent was six thousand *li*. If it travelled in the dark it could make eighty, maybe a hundred *li* a night for the first ten days or so. Later on, crossing the great desert, it could increase that, travelling in the heat of the day, when no patrols flew. With any luck it would be there in fifty days.

It smiled, recalling DeVore's instructions. In Tashkent it would be met and given new papers. From there it would fly west, first to Odessa, then on to Nantes. From Nantes it would take a ship – one of the big ships that serviced the great floating cities of the Mid-Atlantic. There it would stay a while, biding its time, working for the big ImmVac company of North America, putting down roots inside that organisation, until the call came.

For a moment longer it stood there, like a silvered god, tall, powerful, elegant in the moonlight, then it jumped down, crossing the circle of light quickly, making for the fence and the darkness beyond.

★ ★ ★

DeVore looked up from the communications panel and stared out into the darkness of the Martian night. It was just after two, local time, and the lights of the distant city were low. Beyond them was a wall of darkness.

He stood, yawning, ready for sleep now that the message had come, then turned, looking across at the sleeping man.

Hans Ebert lay on the camp bed, fully clothed, his kit bag on the floor beside him. He had turned up four days back, scared, desperate for help, and had ended here, "rescued" by DeVore from the Governor's cells.

DeVore went across and stood there over the sleeping man, looking down at him. Ebert looked ill, haggard from exhaustion. He had lost a lot of weight and – from the smell of him – had had to rough it in ways he had never experienced before. His body had suffered, but his face was still familiar enough to be recognised anywhere in the system.

Well, maybe that was a problem, and maybe it wasn't. A familiar face might prove advantageous in the days to come. Especially when behind that face was a young prince, burning with ambition and eager for revenge. And that was why – despite the obvious dangers – he had taken Ebert in. Knowing that what was discarded now might prove extremely useful later on.

He bent down, drawing the blanket up over Ebert's chest, then turned away, looking outwards, conscious once more of the guards patrolling the frosted perimeter, the great, blue-white circle of Chung Kuo high above them in the Martian sky.

* * *

Chen crouched there on the mountainside, looking down the valley to where the dark, steep slopes ended in a flat-topped arrowhead of whiteness. It was like a vast wall, a dam two *li* in height, plugging the end of the valley, its surface a faintly opalescent pearl, lit from within. *Ch'eng* it was. City and wall.

The moon was high. Was a perfect circle of whiteness in the velvet dark. Chen stared at it a moment, mesmerised, held by its brilliant, unseeing eye, then looked down, his fingers searching amongst the ashes.

He turned, looking across at Karr, then lifted the shard of broken glass, turning it in his hand, remembering.

"What is this place?" Karr asked, coming closer, his face cloaked in shadow.

Chen stared at him a while, then looked away.

"This is where it began. Here on the mountainside with Kao Jyan. We lit a fire, just there, where you're standing now. And Jyan . . . Jyan brought a bottle and two glasses. I remember watching him."

A faint breeze stirred dust and ash about his feet, carrying the scent of the Wilds.

He stood, then turned, looking north. There, not far from where they stood, the City began, filling the great northern plain of Europe. Earlier, flying over it, they had seen the rebuilt Imperial Solarium, which he had helped bomb a dozen years before. Chen took a long breath, then turned back, looking at the big man.

"Did you bring the razor, as I asked?"

Karr stared at him fixedly a moment, then took the fine blade from his tunic. "What did you want it for?"

Chen met his eyes. "Nothing stupid, I promise you."

Karr hesitated a moment longer, then handed him the razor. Chen stared at it a moment, turning it in the moonlight, then tested it with the edge of his thumb. Satisfied, he crouched again, and, taking his queue in the other hand, cut the strong dark hair close to the roots.

"Kao Chen . . ."

He looked up at the big man, then, saying nothing, continued with the task. Finished, he stood again, offering Karr the blade, his free hand tracing the shape of his skull, feeling the fine stubble there.

Karr took the razor, studying his friend. In the moonlight, Chen's face had the blunt, anonymous look of a thousand generations of Han peasants. The kind of face one saw everywhere below. A simple, nondescript face. Until one met the eyes . . .

"Why are we here, my friend? What are we looking for?"

Chen turned, looking about him, taking in everything: the mountains, the sky, the great City, stretched out like a vast glacier under the brilliant moon. It was the same. Twelve years had done little to change this scene. And yet it was quite different. Was, in the way he saw it, utterly transformed. Back then he had known nothing but the Net. Had looked at this scene with eyes that saw only the surfaces of things. But now he could see right through. Through to the bone itself.

He nodded slowly, understanding now why he had had to come here. Why he had asked Karr to divert the craft south and fly into the foothills of the Alps. Sometimes one had to go back – right back – to understand.

He shivered, surprised by the strength of the returning memory. It was strange how clearly he could see it, even now, after almost thirty years. Yes, he could picture quite vividly the old Master who had trained him to be *kwai*; a tall, willowy old Han with a long, expressionless face and a wispy beard who always wore red. Old Shang, they had called him. Five of them, there had been, from Chi Su, the eldest, a broad-shouldered sixteen-year-old, down to himself, a thin-limbed, ugly little boy of six. An orphan, taken in by Shang.

For the next twelve years Old Shang's apartment had been his home. He had shared the *kang* with two others, his sleeping roll put away at sixth bell and taken out again at midnight. And in between, a long day of work; harder work than he had ever known, before or since. He sighed. It was strange how he had hidden it from himself all these years, as if it had never been. And yet it had formed him, as surely as the tree is formed from the seed. Shang's words, Shang's gestures had become his own. So it was in this world. So it had to be. For without that a man was shapeless, formless, fit only to wallow in the fetid darkness of the Clay.

He turned, meeting Karr's eyes. "He had clever hands. I watched him from where you're standing now. Saw how he looked into his glass, like this, watching the flames flicker and curl like tiny snakes in the darkness of his wine. At the time I didn't understand what it was he saw there. But now I do."

Karr looked down. It was Kao Jyan he was talking about. Kao Jyan, his fellow assassin that night twelve years ago.

"A message came," he offered. "From Tolonen."

Chen was still looking back at him, but it was as if he were suddenly somewhere else, as if, for a brief moment, his eyes saw things that Karr was blind to.

"He confirms that Li Yuan has ordered the closure of Kibwezi."

"Ah . . ." Chen lowered his eyes.

Karr was silent a moment, watching his friend, trying to understand, to empathise with what he was feeling, but for once it was hard. He crouched, one hand sifting the dust. "Your friend, Kao Jyan . . . What *did* he see?"

Chen gave a small laugh, as if surprised that the big man didn't know, then looked away again, smoothing his hand over the naked shape of his skull.

"Change," he said softly, a tiny tremor passing through him. "And flames. Flames dancing in a glass."

END OF BOOK THREE

The White Mountain concludes the first phase of the great "War of the Two Directions", but the history of Chung Kuo – of the long and pitiless struggle between the Seven and their many enemies – enters a wholly new phase in Book Four, *The Stone Within*, as the old order crumbles and the new begins to emerge.

AUTHOR'S NOTE

The transcription of standard Mandarin into European alphabetical form was first achieved in the seventeenth century by the Italian Matteo Ricci, who founded and ran the first Jesuit Mission in China from 1583 until his death in 1610. Since then, several dozen attempts have been made to reduce the original Chinese sounds, represented by some tens of thousands of separate pictograms, into readily understandable phonetics for Western use. For a long time, however, three systems dominated – those used by the three major Western powers vying for influence in the corrupt and crumbling Chinese Empire of the nineteenth century: Great Britain, France and Germany. These systems were the Wade-Giles (Great Britain and America – sometimes known as the Wade system), the Ecole Française de l'Extrême Orient (France) and the Lessing (Germany).

Since 1958, however, the Chinese themselves have sought to create one single phonetic form, based on the German system, which they termed the *hanyu pinyin fang'an* ("Scheme for a Chinese Phonetic Alphabet"), known more commonly as *pinyin*, and in all foreign language books published in China since January 1, 1979 *pinyin* has been used, as well as being taught now in schools along with the standard Chinese characters. For this work, however, I have chosen to use the older and, to my mind, far more elegant transcription system, the Wade-Giles (in modified form). For those now accustomed to the harder forms of *pinyin*, the following may serve as a basic conversion guide, the Wade-Giles first, the *pinyin* after:

p for b	ch' for q
ts' for c	j for r
ch' for ch	t' for t
t for d	hs for x
k for g	ts for z
ch for j	ch for zh

The effect is, I hope, to render the softer, more poetic side of the original Mandarin, ill-served, I feel, by modern *pinyin*.

This usage, incidentally, accords with many of the major reference sources available in the West: the (planned) 16 volumes of Denis Twitchett and Michael Loewe's *The Cambridge History Of China*, Joseph Needham's mammoth multi-volumed *Science and Civilization in China*, John Fairbank and Edwin Reischauer's *China, Tradition & Transformation*, Charles Hucker's *China's Imperial Past*, Jacques Gernet's *A History of Chinese Civilization*, C. P. Fitzgerald's *China: A Short Cultural History*, Laurence Sickman and Alexander Soper's *The Art and Architecture of China*, William Hinton's classic social studies, *Fanshen* and *Shenfan*, and Derk Bodde's *Essays On Chinese Civilization*.

The translations of Li Ho's "On And On For Ever" and "On The Frontier" are by A. C. Graham from his excellent, *Poems Of The Late T'ang*, published by Penguin Books, London, 1965, and are used with their kind permission.

The translation of Li Shangyin's "Fallen Flowers" is by Tao Jie and is taken from *300 T'ang Poems, A New Translation*, published by the Commercial Press, Hong Kong.

The passage quoted from Book One [XI] of Lao Tzu's *Tao Te Ching* is from the D. C. Lau translation, published by Penguin Books, London, 1963, and used with their kind permission. The quotation from Confucius, *The Analects* [Book XII] is once again from a D. C. Lau translation, published by Penguin Books, 1979, and used with their permission.

The passage from Sun Tzu's classic *The Art Of War* is

from the Samuel B. Griffith translation, published by Oxford University Press, 1963.

Six Records Of A Floating Life by Shen Fu – mentioned by Karr in the "Chen Yen" chapter – is a real book, one of the gems of world literature. Published by Penguin, it cannot be recommended enough by this author.

Finally, for those of you interested (like Tuan Ti Fo) to know what it was Lagasek and Gweder were saying to each other in Chapter Five, here is a rough translation of their exchange:

Gweder. Mirror.

Pandr'a bos ef, Lagasek? What be it, Starer?

Travyth, Gweder. Travyth . . . Nothing, Mirror. Nothing . . .

Praga obery why crenna? Bos why yeyn, Lagasek? Why do you shake? Be you cold, Starer?

Yma gweras yn ow ganow, Gweder . . . *gweras* . . . *ha an pyth bos tewl*. There is soil in my mouth, Mirror . . . soil . . . and the well is dark.

Nyns-us pyth, Lagasek. There is no well, Starer.

A-dhywas-lur . . . *A-dhywas-lur*. . . Up from the ground . . . Up from the ground . . .

My bos yn annown . . . *Yn annown!* I am in the world of the dead . . . in the underworld!

Later, Kim says to Tuan Ti Fo, *Yn mes a forth, cothwas*. Out of my way, old man.

As readers of *The Middle Kingdom* will already know, this language is a crude form of ancient Cornish, spoken in the Clay, where Kim originated from.

The game of *wei chi* mentioned throughout this volume is, incidentally, more commonly known by its Japanese name of *Go*, and is not merely the world's oldest game but its most elegant.

February 1991

A GLOSSARY OF MANDARIN TERMS

Most of the Mandarin terms used in the text are explained in context. However, as a few are used more naturally, I've considered it best to provide a brief explanation.

ai ya! – a common expression of surprise or dismay.

ch'a – tea. It might be noted that *ch'a shu*, the art of tea mentioned herein, is an ancient forebear of the Japanese tea ceremony, *chanoyu*.

chen yen – true words; the Chinese equivalent of a mantra.

ch'i – a Chinese foot; approximately 14.4 inches.

ch'i – a term used to denote vital energy, but with connotations of the psyche or spirit of a human being.

chi ch'i – workers; here used specifically to refer to the antlike Ministry of Distribution workers.

chi chu – spider.

chi pao – a one-piece gown, usually sleeveless, worn by women.

Chieh Hsia – term meaning "Your Majesty", derived from the expression "below the steps". It was the formal way of addressing the Emperor, through his Ministers, who stood "below the steps".

chou – the State; here also the name for a card game.

chow mein – this, like chop suey, is neither a Chinese nor a Western dish, but a special meal created by the Chinese in America for the Western palate. A transliteration of *chao mian* (fried noodles), it is a distant relation of the *liang mian huang* served in Süchow.

ch'un tzu – an ancient Chinese term from the Warring States period, describing a certain class of noblemen, controlled by a code of chivalry and morality known as the *li*, or rites. Here the term is roughly, and sometimes ironically, translated as "gentlemen". The *ch'un tzu* is as much an ideal state of behaviour – as specified by Confucius in the *Analects* – as an actual class in Chung Kuo, though a degree of financial independence and a high standard of education are assumed a prerequisite.

chung – a lidded serving bowl for *ch'a*.

erhu – two-stringed bow with snakeskin-covered soundbox.

erh tzu – son.

fen – unit of money; one hundred *fen* make up a *yuan*.

fu jen – "Madam", used here as opposed to *t'ai t'ai* – "Mrs".

fu sang – the "hollow mulberry tree"; according to ancient Chinese cosmology this tree stands where the sun rises and is the dwelling place of rulers. *Sang* (mulberry), however, has the same sound as *sang* (sorrow) in Chinese.

hei – literally "black" – the Chinese pictogram for this represents a man wearing war paint and tattoos. Here it refers to the genetically manufactured (GenSyn) half-men used as riot police to quell uprisings in the lower levels.

hsiao – filial piety. The character for *hsiao* is comprised of two parts, the upper part meaning "old", the lower meaning "son" or "child". This dutiful submission of the young to the old is at the heart of Confucianism and Chinese culture generally.

hsiao chi – an unmarried lady.

hsiao jen – "little man/men". In the *Analects*, Book XIV, Confucius writes: "The gentleman gets through to what is up above; the small man gets through to what is down below." This distinction between "gentleman" (*ch'un tzu*) and "little men" (*hsiao jen*), false even in Confucius's time, is no less a matter of social perspective in Chung Kuo.

hsien – historically an administrative district of variable size. Here the term is used to denote a very specific administrative area: one of ten stacks – each stack composed of thirty decks. Each deck is a hexagonal living unit of ten levels, two *li*, or approximately one kilometre in diameter. A stack can be imagined as one honeycomb in the great hive of the City.

Hung Mao – literally "red-heads", the name the Chinese gave to the Dutch (and later English) seafarers who attempted to trade with China in the seventeenth century. Because of the piratical nature of their endeavours (which often meant plundering Chinese shipping and ports) the name has connotations of piracy.

Hung Mun – the Secret Societies or, more specifically, the Triads.

jou tung wu – literally "meat animal".

Kan Pei! – "good health!" or "cheers!" – a drinking toast.

kang – the Chinese hearth, serving also as oven and, in the cold of winter, as a sleeping platform.

Ko Ming – "revolutionary". The "T'ien Ming" is the Mandate of Heaven, supposedly handed down from Shang Ti, the Supreme Ancestor, to his earthly counterpart, the Emperor (*Huang Ti*). This Mandate could be enjoyed only so long as the Emperor was worthy of it and rebellion against a tyrant – who broke the Mandate through his lack of justice, benevolence and sincerity – was deemed not criminal but a rightful expression of Heaven's anger.

k'ou t'ou – see *liu k'ou*.

Kuan Yin – the Goddess of Mercy. Originally the Buddhist male bodhisattva, Avalokitsevara (translated into Han as "He who listens to the sounds of the world" or *Kuan Yin*). The Chinese mistook the well-developed breasts of the saint for a woman's and, since the ninth century, have worshipped Kuan Yin as such. Effigies of Kuan Yin will show her usually as the eastern Madonna, cradling a child in her arms. She is also sometimes seen as the wife of Kuan Kung, the Chinese God of War.

Kuo Yu – Mandarin, the language spoken in most of Mainland China. Also known as *Kuan hua* and *Pai hua*.

kwai – an abbreviation of *kwai tao*, a "sharp knife" or "fast knife". It can also mean to be sharp or fast (as a knife). An associated meaning is that of a "clod" or "lump of earth". Here it is used to denote a class of fighters from below the Net, whose ability and self-discipline separate them from the usual run of hired knives.

lao jen – "old man" (also *weng*); used normally as a term of respect.

li – a Chinese "mile", approximating half a kilometre or one-third of a mile. Until 1949, when metric measures were adopted in China, the *li* could vary from place to place.

liu k'ou – the seventh stage of respect, according to the "Book of Ceremonies". Two stages above the more familiarly known *k'ou t'ou* (kowtow), it involves kneeling and striking the forehead three times against the floor, rising on to one's feet again, then kneeling and repeating the prostration with three touches of the forehead to the ground. Only the *san kuei chiu k'ou* – involving three prostrations – was more elaborate and was reserved for Heaven and its son, the Emperor (see also *san k'ou*).

mui tsai – rendered in Cantonese as "mooi-jai". Colloquially it means either "little sister" or "slave girl", though generally, as here, the latter. Other Mandarin terms used for the same status are *pei-nu* and *ya tou*. Technically, guardianship of the girl involved is legally signed over in return for money.

nu shi – an unmarried woman; a term equating to "Miss".

pi pai – "hundred pens"; term used for the artificial reality experiments renamed "shells" by Ben Shepherd.

pan chang – supervisor.

pau – a simple long garment worn by men.

p'i p'a – a four-stringed lute used in traditional Chinese music.

Ping Tiao – levelling. To bring down or make flat.

sam fu – an upper garment (part shirt, part jacket) worn originally by both male and females, in imitation of Manchu styles; later on a wide-sleeved, calf-length version was worn by women alone.

san k'ou – the sixth stage of respect, according to the "Book of Ceremonies", it involves striking the forehead three times against the ground before rising from one's knees (in *k'ou t'ou* one strikes the forehead but once). See also *liu k'ou*.

shih – "Master". Here used as a term of respect somewhat equivalent to our use of "Mister". The term was originally used for the lowest level of civil servants, to distinguish them socially from the run-of-the-mill "misters" (*hsian sheng*) below them and the gentlemen (*ch'un tzu*) above.

Ta Ts'in – the Chinese name for the Roman Empire. They also knew Rome as *Li Chien* and as "the Land West of the Sea". The Romans themselves they termed the "Big *Ts'in*" – the *Ts'in* being the name the Chinese gave themselves during the Ts'in dynasty. (265–316 AD).

tai ch'i – the Original, or One, from which the duality of all things (yin and yang) developed, according to Chinese cosmology. We generally associate the *tai ch'i* with the Taoist symbol, that swirling circle of dark and light.

t'ing – an open-sided pavilion in a Chinese garden. Designed as a focal point in a garden, it is said to symbolise man's essential place in the natural order of things.

wei chi – the "surrounding game", known more commonly in the West by its Japanese name of *Go*. It is said that the game was invented by the legendary Chinese Emperor Yao in the year 2350 BC to train the mind of his son, Tan Chu, and teach him to think like an emperor.

yang mei ping – literally "willow-plum sickness"; this Chinese term for syphilis provides an apt description of the male sexual organ in the extreme of this sickness.

yu – literally "fish", but, because of its phonetic equivalence to the word for "abundance," the fish symbolises wealth. Yet there is also a saying that when the fish swim upriver it is a portent of social unrest and rebellion.

yuan – the basic currency of Chung Kuo (and modern-day China). Colloquially (though not here) it can also be termed *kwai* – "piece" or "lump". See also *fen*.

Ywe Lung – literally, the "Moon Dragon", the great wheel of seven dragons that is the symbol of the ruling Seven throughout *Chung Kuo*. "At its centre the snouts of the regal beasts met, forming a roselike hub, huge rubies burning fiercely in each eye. Their lithe, powerful bodies curved outward like the spokes of a giant wheel while at their edge their tails were intertwined to form the rim." [from "The Moon Dragon", Chapter Four of *The Middle Kingdom*]

ACKNOWLEDGMENTS

Thanks must go to the following for their help. To my editors – Nick Sayers, Brian DeFiore, John Pearce, and Alyssa Diamond – for their sheer niceness and (of course) for their continuing enthusiasm, and to Carolyn Caughey, fan-turned-editor, for seeing where to cut the cake.

To Mike Cobley, thanks not merely for encouragement but for Advanced Cheerfulness in the face of Adversity. May both your patience and your talent be rewarded. And to Andy Sawyer, for a thoughtful reading of the text. I hope I can reciprocate one of these days.

To my first-line critic and safety-net, the stalwart Brian Griffin, may I say yet again how much all of this is appreciated. The notes you've done will make a wonderful book some day!

To family and friends – particularly to my girls Susan, Jessica, Amy, and Georgia – go the usual thanks in the face of my at-times monomaniacal neglect. And special thanks this time to everyone I met on my travels to the universities of Leeds, Manchester, Oxford, Cambridge, Southampton, Brighton, Canterbury and Dublin. And, of course, to the Glasgow group. Slainte Mhath!

Thanks, also, to all the musicians out there who (inadvertently) have provided the aural sustenance needed to complete this volume, especially to Tim Smith and the Cardiacs, Peter Hammill, King Swamp, and all the lads at IQ. And to the inimitable Christian Vander. Hamatai!

DAVID WINGROVE

CHUNG KUO BOOK ONE
THE MIDDLE KINGDOM

How many billions lived in the City that filled the great
northern plains of Europe? The two men, crab-scuttling
across the dome that roofed the city, neither knew nor
cared. They thought only of the assassination that was
their task.

Chung Kuo. For three thousand years, the world-
encompassing Empire of the Han had endured. War and
famine long banished, the Council of Seven ruled with
absolute authority. Their boast: that the Great Wheel of
Change itself had ceased to turn.

Yet at that very moment of supreme strength and confidence, Chung Kuo was suddenly vulnerable. A challenge had arisen from men who dreamed of Change –
although Change would mean war and a return to all the
old, half-forgotten savageries of the past.

The Middle Kingdom is the first volume in an epic
future-history, breathtaking in scope and imagination,
patterned with treachery and heroism, betrayal and love,
intrigue and adventure.

HODDER AND STOUGHTON PAPERBACKS

DAVID WINGROVE

CHUNG KUO BOOK TWO
THE BROKEN WHEEL

There had been war – a war which the great world-spanning empire of Chung Kuo had survived. But at a cost.

The Seven – rulers of Chung Kuo – were weak. Weaker than they had ever been. Now, in the teeming lower depths of their great City, the current of change is flowing again, turning the Great Wheel, and one event – a murder, perhaps, or a palace plot – might throw the world into chaos once more.

'Why this epic continues to work so convincingly is because its social forces, and changes, within its China-orientated middle kingdom, are clarified as cleverly as Asimov's *Foundation*, while its characters give all that inexorable change a human dimension. Love, tragedy, joy and a sense of destiny being fulfilled – all human life (and death) is there. Another six volumes to go and I'm not even winded.' *Tom Hutchinson, The Times*

'Extraordinary' *Brian Aldiss*

HODDER AND STOUGHTON PAPERBACKS